BORNE ON RESTLESS WINDS OF LONGING, SHE CRAVED CONSTANCY, CHALLENGE, AND LOVE ...

SEAN—the strong Irishman, he recognized her passionate yearnings, but loved her too much to take what she so naively offered ...

NORMAN—her childhood love, he was dazzled by her rare beauty, disturbed by the voluptuous sensuality she aroused ...

NICHOLAS—the brilliant young student, he learned from her the pain of first love ...

MALCOLM—the reckless rebel, he wanted her, but only on his own terms ...

DAVID—the idealistic rancher, he dreamed of a life with her at his side ...

They would all love Catherine, all desire her. But which of them could hope to hold her, could offer the rich soil of love and friendship in which she could blossom and bloom—a woman, a ...

WILDFLOWER

WILDFLOWER

Jaroldeen Edwards

A DELL BOOK

Published by
Dell Publishing Co., Inc.
1 Dag Hammarskjold Plaza
New York, New York 10017

Dell ® TM 681510, Dell Publishing Co., Inc.

ISBN: 0-440-19374-5

Printed in the United States of America
First printing—July 1982

CHAPTER ONE

The young women looked like butterflies in their bright summer dresses. They fluttered across the dappled lawn, their silk-clad legs and high-heeled slippers flashing in the afternoon sunlight. Branches of poplar trees and Canadian cottonwoods rustled overhead in the warm prairie breeze, and the women's light dresses floated and rippled around their young bodies, pressing against their rounded thighs and firm buttocks. The young women laughed, clutching their skirts, and lifting white-gloved hands to steady their wide-brimmed garden hats against the playful wind. It was a charming familiar scene, but Catherine Summerwell, eldest daughter of one of Calgary's finest families, felt no part of it.

Under the brightly striped caterer's tent, which had been raised on the Mortenson's lawn, Catherine sat in her pink dress and wished the party would end. She hated the dress. The ruffled chiffon was hot and sticky, but her mother and Emily had insisted she wear it because it was fashionable. "Fashionable!" Catherine thought irritably and twisted restlessly in her chair, her pink-sandaled foot tapping impatiently.

She felt a twinge of guilt for wanting the party to be over. After all it was Emily's bridal shower, and she supposed she ought to be enjoying herself.

Two months earlier while Catherine was away at

school, Emily had become engaged to a young man named James Parker. He was head over heels in love with Emily—as were half the men in Calgary. James was an American, but no one in Mount Royal was holding that against him, particularly since he was the descendant of an old New England family, had graduated from an excellent eastern university, and had come to Canada as a young executive with American Petroleum to work in their Calgary offices. James had an excellent tailor, sat a horse well and, in spite of a certain American informality, had charming manners, so it had not been long before he had come to the attention of the leading families in the aristocratic suburb of Mount Royal where he had met and courted Emily Summerwell, Catherine's younger sister.

He had won the approval of Emily's parents and the hearty endorsement of their social circle. Catherine, away at the university, had received letters from friends and family containing such extravagant praise of Emily's fiancé that she had been prepared to dislike him on sight, but upon her return home three days earlier, she had been surprised to find that she liked James very much. He was as handsome, confident, and impressive as she had been told he was, and in her brief acquaintance with him Catherine had sensed also that he was genuine and warm. She knew he would be good for Emily, her exquisite, spoiled, delightful sister, yet Catherine puzzled why she was feeling so apart from what should have been a joyous occasion—a time for celebration. It seemed so easy and natural for her sister Emily to enter the charmed circle.

Catherine could see Emily now, across the lawn. Emily was standing with a cluster of girls under the rose arbor. Her golden hair gleamed in the sunshine and her sweet, high laugh mingled with the sounds of light voices and the clink of china teacups which sprinkled the air.

Helen Mortenson, Emily's best friend, had insisted that she and her mother, Mrs. Mortenson, should have the privilege of giving Emily's bridal shower. As sister of the bride-to-be, Catherine had been invited by Mrs. Mortenson to pour the tea. Dutifully, through the long, warm afternoon, Catherine sat at the wrought-iron table in the party tent overseeing the Mortenson's elaborate Georgian tea service, checking the supply of lemon slices, sugar, and cream, and saying all the proper things to her friends as she remained in regal isolation behind the teapot. She felt bored and matronly and burdened by the formalities that were expected of her.

As the afternoon waned everyone had been served and had wandered off to enjoy the garden, and Catherine had been left alone under the awning of the tent. Etiquette required that she remain at the tea table until she was formally excused by the hostess, Mrs. Mortenson. A fly was buzzing lazily against the hot canvas, and Catherine, sitting in the shadowed tent, looked out at her childhood friends, who were highlighted in the clear sunlight against the green lawn. She had a fleeting perception of herself as a spectator watching a painted slide through a cinescope, or a child looking at a pastel picture through the hole in the end of a sugar crystal egg. With an odd sense of unreality, as though in a twist of time, Catherine recalled how often as a little girl she had played dress-ups with these friends as they had giggled, preened, and paraded in their mothers' silk party dresses and flower-trimmed hats. Today, suddenly, Catherine looked at these same companions and saw they were no longer playing a game. Her friends had become like their mothers. Emily would be first, but the rest of them would soon marry, and the men they married would preside over the city of Calgary. Smoothly, almost imperceptibly, her generation would become the older generation, flowing into society without so much as a ripple, and the wealthy, insular tide of Mount Royal would move on, unchanged. Somehow the thought depressed Catherine, and she shook herself, wanting to be rid of this sudden strange mood.

"Catherine, dear!" Mrs. Mortenson stepped briskly into the tent, her ample figure encased in blue crepe, a long rope of pearls on her spectacular bosom. Long ago Catherine remembered wondering if Mrs. Mortenson wore her pearls to bed, and if so, what they looked like on her nightgown.

"I'm sorry to have kept you chained to this tea table!" Mrs. Mortenson exclaimed. "Honors are seldom pleasant. I suppose that's why people make a thing an honor, otherwise no one would want to do it!"

Catherine smiled. Of all her mother's friends Mrs. Mortenson had always been her favorite. She was solid and real, completely herself, sure of what she believed in and felt a comfortable affinity with her own world. Catherine both admired and envied Mrs. Mortenson. There was never any doubt that Mrs. Mortenson belonged to Mount Royal or that Mount Royal belonged to her. This appropriateness of person and place was nowhere more in evidence than in the Shakespearean garden which Mrs. Mortenson had created and which was the setting for Emily's party.

The story of the garden was something of a legend in the community. More than a decade earlier, Mrs. Mortenson had gone to the regular meeting of the Black Watch Society's Shakespearean Club where Lillian Townsend had presented a lecture on *Macbeth*. That particular morning Mrs. Mortenson could not concentrate on Lillian's remarks, because she was worrying about several flats of primroses which had been delivered to her home just as she left for the meeting. She was afraid they would be withered by the time she got to them. As she worried about the primroses, Lillian's stentorian voice penetrated her thoughts, "The primrose way to the everlasting bonfire . . ." Lillian read from the porter's speech. "Primroses!" Mrs. Mortenson was smitten with the coincidence. "Primroses! Right out of Shakespeare!" The idea burst upon her to make a garden which would contain nothing but flowers mentioned in the writings of Shakespeare. Such a garden would bring together nature, beauty, tradition, and aristocratic intellect—all of which she admired.

With the zeal of a true visionary, Mrs. Mortenson spent years researching Shakespeare's writing and ferreting out every botanical allusion. She spaded flower beds, procured cuttings, imported seeds, and weeded, mulched, planted, and fertilized.

Finally, just before Emily's shower, Mrs. Mortenson put in the last plants—ferns to edge the fencing. She privately admitted to her daughter Helen that it was fern "seeds" which were mentioned in *Henry IV,* but she said, "I shall plant ferns anyway. Ferns from seeds do grow!" She made the arbitrary decision that samphire, which only grows on the chalk cliffs of Dover, was an herb, and therefore she was exempt from planting it. The garden, she pronounced, was finished.

Catherine mentally saluted Mrs. Mortenson's achievement, for she had created a classic English garden with that true mark of aristocratic perception, a refined sense of ordered disorder. This garden represented for Catherine the best and the worst of Mount Royal, her home. This lovely suburb of British insularity—a tiny world buffered against the raw vigor of the booming city of Calgary—was bolstered by tradition and steadfastly turned its eyes away from the vastness and newness of the western Canadian prairies which rolled away on every side to the very edges of the world.

"I'm so glad to see you home again, Catherine," Mrs. Mortenson was saying, her voice warm and gracious. "Congratulations on your outstanding scholastic record. The Governor-General's gold medal! My! We are proud of you."

Catherine's heart expanded with the generosity of Mrs. Mortenson's praise.

"Run along, now, dear, and join the other girls in the garden," Mrs. Mortenson continued. This was the dismissal for which Catherine had been waiting, and she jumped up eagerly. As she stepped forward, the sharp heel of her sandal caught in the soft grass, and she lost her balance. Instinctively, she reached out to steady herself against the table, and a half-filled teacup overturned, spilling its contents the length of her skirt.

"Drat!" Catherine exclaimed, looking down at the spreading brown stain.

"Oh, dear!" Mrs. Mortenson was distressed. "I hope it hasn't ruined your dress."

Catherine looked up with an ironic smile. "Not much of a loss if it has!" she said. "Emily picked this thing out, and it's not exactly my style—if there is such a thing as my style."

"Nonsense!" Mrs. Mortenson said brusquely, reaching for a napkin and gently blotting Catherine's skirt. "Of course you have style, Catherine, dear, a great deal of style. I've known it since you were a little girl. However, . . . perhaps most of your friends . . . are still too young to appreciate it, and you, perhaps, have yet to discover it yourself."

Catherine gave Mrs. Mortenson a sharply inquiring look, but if she expected further elucidation she was disappointed. Mrs. Mortenson silently completed sponging the stain, and then stepped back to look critically at her handiwork.

"It doesn't look too conspicuous," she declared. "Now go and join the party. I must hurry to the house because it's almost time to begin the Ribbon and the Ring Ceremony."

"Hi, Catherine!" A young woman named Jean Hunt waved and broke away from the group. Hurrying across the lawn, she grabbed Catherine's hand and pumped it enthusiastically. "Wow! Father told me you won the gold medal. Top of the class! That's terrific!" The tall, dark girl grinned exuberantly, and her slender face lighted with such warmth and friendliness that Catherine grinned back, delighted to see her.

"Hey, Cath," Jean went on. "Don't you know well-brought-up ladies from Mount Royal don't go around doing things like creaming academic honors at a bona fide university? That's men's work. We're just supposed to go to Miss Roland's finishing school and call it a day!"

Catherine laughed and said, "Jean! How can a girl from Mount Royal who is studying to be a veterinarian make such an allegation? At least I studied liberal arts and humanities, which is a proper province for the female mind."

"Aha!" Jean countered. "You forget! I am not a legitimate, true, dyed-in-the-wool member of this little group." She blithely indicated the shower guests with a sweeping hand. "I belong here only because my father happens to be manager of the bank, and all of this stuff goes with his job. I am not to the manner born, as you were. It's obvious I'm an outsider, since I seem to be the only one at this party who has no idea what this Ring and Ribbon jazz is all about! Is this another of Mrs. M.'s little inventions, like her Shakespearean garden?"

"No," Catherine explained, laughing, "it's an old game. We've played it at wedding showers forever! There's a big wicker basket with colored ribbons hanging over the edge, and inside the basket, on the end of each ribbon, is a party favor. One of the ribbons has a big brass ring tied to it. Each girl chooses a ribbon and pulls it out of the basket, and whoever gets the ribbon with the brass ring will be the next girl to get married." Catherine paused. "I don't think the prediction has ever been accurate, but they keep trying!"

"Can I pick any ribbon I want?" Jean asked.

"No, you pick a ribbon matching a color you are wearing. But there's a slight element of choice if you're wearing more than one color."

"Marvelous," Jean said, with a smile. "As long as there's an element of choice—I think I'll choose not to play."

Catherine laughed and whispered, "I don't think you have that choice!"

"Just my luck!" Jean gave a mock sigh and changed the subject.

"Any chance to come over to your house and see that gold medal? It may be the only chance I'll ever get. It's for sure I'll never earn my own!"

"As a matter of fact you could see it right now." Catherine gave a slightly embarrased laugh. "I brought it in my purse—just in case I'd need it!"

Jean gave a loud laugh, causing several people to turn and look at her with raised eyebrows. "That's what I like about you, Catherine," Jean said in a softer voice. "You're so unpredictable! I'd love to see it!"

"All right," Catherine answered. "Wait here, I'll run up to the house and get my purse."

Catherine walked across the terrace to the back of the Mortenson's house, and opening the terrace door, she stepped inside the cool dining room. She quickly located her purse on the sideboard. In the next room she could hear voices. Emily and Helen were making the last-minute preparations for the game. Catherine heard Emily's sweet, breathless voice.

"Helen, could you do me the biggest favor . . . ?"

"Surely, dear," Helen answered. "Whatever is it?"

Catherine, half-listening, reached for her purse and took out the medal from its velvet box, and as she turned to leave the house, she could hear Emily's voice continuing.

"Look, Helen. This ribbon is just the color of Catherine's dress. Couldn't we take the ring off that yellow ribbon and put it on this pink one?"

Catherine froze, and her fingers tightened around the gold medal.

In an agony of embarrassment she listened as Emily's bright, irrevocable voice rushed on, "Wouldn't it be nice for Catherine to win the ring?" Each word was like a sharp nail in Catherine's mind. "She isn't very popular with boys, Helen, all she has is books and school! I feel so guilty being her younger sister and getting married before her. It would be . . . kind of an achievement . . . if she got the ribbon with the ring on it . . . Don't you think so, Helen?"

Catherine thought she would burst with anger and shame, and, without thinking, she strode through the door into the living room, barely conscious of the guilty, astonished expressions on the faces of her sister and her friend as they looked up, startled by her sudden entrance. Catherine could feel the hot blood pounding in her face, and her lips were trembling. In her hand she clenched the hard circle of her medal. The decorative rim cut into her palm, but she was unaware of the pain.

"Emily . . ." her voice was hoarse with anger. "Emily . . . what are you thinking! How dare you!" Catherine, striving for control, took a deep breath, and the anger rushed out of her, leaving her limp and filled with bitterness.

"Emily, sometimes you are such an ass! How could you think this stupid brass ring could mean anything to me? Is this your idea of some kind of pinnacle of achievement, winning a rigged prize in a silly party game? Nothing I want would ever be tied to a pink ribbon! But perhaps this is about your level of value, since you obviously didn't think a university graduation is even worth attending! Has it ever occurred to you, Emily, there's a whole world out there that doesn't even know Mount Royal exists!"

Catherine's voice was rising, and she saw the surprise and hurt in Emily's eyes, but before Emily could say anything, Catherine snatched up the ribboned basket and continued. "There are people who have never even heard of the Ribbon and the Ring!" The words were flung from her by her fury. "If trinkets are what you want, trinkets you shall get!" She walked over to Emily and dumped the ribbons, the favors, and the basket at her feet, then turned on her heel and left the Mortenson's house, letting herself out the front door and walking quickly to the curb where her Austin convertible was parked. Her face was grim; but the blood still pounded in her flushed cheeks and forehead.

She climbed into the car and only then did she remember the medal in her hand. She put it carefully in the glove compartment and then started the motor and drove down the wide, curving street bordered on either side by the tall maples, green lawns, and stately homes of her childhood.

As the road curved downward into the lower section of Calgary proper, the streets became narrower and the houses closer together. Catherine continued driving slowly, her eyes straight ahead, unseeing, oblivious. With a jolt she realized she was driving through a stop sign without noticing it. Abruptly, she slammed on the brakes, and her car skidded to a screeching halt, barely missing a speeding line of cross traffic. Catherine watched the cars as they roared past, and her hands began to shake. Her body gave a long, involuntary shudder, and she laid her head down on the steering wheel and cried. The sobs racked her body, dry and hard, as though they were wrenched from her. Swallowing the tears, her hands still trembling, she raised her head and carefully drove across the intersection into a quiet side street where she parked her car.

"Stupid!" she whispered, pounding her fist on the steering wheel. "Stupid! Stupid! Stupid! Why did I get so angry?"

Then she smiled crookedly through her tears as she recalled her own words, which, though spoken in anger, had apparently been spoken in truth as well. She hadn't realized how much it had hurt her that Emily and her mother had missed her graduation until she had flung her accusations at Emily in the Mortenson's living room. Did it really hurt so much? Matter so much? And, if so, why? Her father had explained that James's parents had called at the last minute to say they were coming from New York on a business trip and hoped to meet Emily and her parents. Catherine's mother had felt she and Emily could not be absent during their brief visit, since it would be the only time they would meet before the wedding.

Catherine had said she understood, but now she was facing the truth that she hadn't understood. She felt it had been a choice between Emily and herself—a choice between Emily's accomplishments and her own—and her mother had found her less important.

"How is this happening to me?" she wondered, surprised at her pain and unhappiness. "Just three days ago I was something . . . somebody . . ." She thought back a few days to when she sat in the great convocation hall, with the other university graduates, wearing her robe and mortar board. The professors, their hoods a panoply of color—red, gold, purple— against the black of their doctoral robes, sat behind the dais and the vast room was filled with the pageantry, the seriousness, the mystery of the halls of learning.

Her father, in his crimson regent's robe, sat with the council of university regents and smiled down at her, his eyes filled with pride. When she walked up to the platform to receive her gold medal from the university president himself, her father, ill-disposed to any public display of affection, had stood up and walked over to shake her hand. But on a fatherly impulse he kissed her on the cheek instead, to an approving murmur of appreciation from the audience.

As graduation ended the choir sang, "*God give me mountains and God give me strength to climb up,*" and the mighty chords of the anthem vaulted in the hall, complementing the high-flown rhetoric of the words and filling the chapel. Then the president spoke the last glorious words, in the private tongue of academe—the long dead language that forms the private circle, the magic ring of the sweet world of learning. "*Prodite et quaerite quaecumque vera,*" which she translated into English in her mind, "Go forth and seek whatsoever things are true." This was her world, noble and glorious, and she belonged! She had the gold medal to prove it.

She and her father had attended the reception at the university president's home, and as they strolled across the quadrangle to the president's brick mansion on the edge of the river valley which divided the city of Edmonton, her father explained why her mother and

Emily had not come up from Calgary for her graduation.

Her father patted her arm reassuringly. "Your mother and Emily . . . I know they would have come if they could, Catherine."

They stood on the university lawn in the early summer twilight, awed by the portentous silence that had fallen across the campus. The great northern prairie sky was still bright, though the evening was growing cool.

"I love this place," her father murmured, half to himself. "It is solid, enduring. It has gathered the best and brought it into its hallowed halls. Universities are the great conservative institutions. They conserve thought and tradition and language and beauty. But a university is also the great crystal ball, the unfolder of mystery, the bearer of the holy flame, the crucible of tomorrow's thoughts."

"Father," Catherine grinned, "you've been in the courtroom too much lately."

"My prose may be a little purple, I'll admit," her father said, "but if ever there were a moment for purple prose . . ." and laughing, they stood, father and daughter, on the hallowed grounds of their alma mater, and in the pristine summer twilight acknowledged in silence a mutual debt.

For Catherine that was a great moment. It was also the true moment of her farewell to the campus. The next day was a sorting out—a day for going through the ritual motions. She packed up her belongings in the sorority house and said farewells to companions and friends.

Doors were closed one by one, and almost before she realized it, the three years of her freedom were left irretrievably behind. Her father was waiting out by the Packard, patiently reading a paper from his briefcase when Catherine, carrying the last bag, came down the forsythia-lined entrance to her sorority house and stood before him.

"Well," she said, the tears running down her cheeks, "it's over." With understanding, her father did not say much as they drove out of the city of Edmonton, watching the stately brick buildings of the university disappear from view. She settled low in the leather seat and said with a deep sigh, "Oh, the lucky freshmen! They have it all before them."

Clifford Summerwell glanced sideways with tenderness at his daughter and then turned his concentration to driving through the long afternoon. The road was a well-graveled, two-way road, stretching north and south along the flat, unchanging miles of the Alberta prairie. The Summerwells were headed southward, toward Calgary, Mount Royal—home.

Catherine wondered if her father had guessed her real feelings about returning home. She watched him as he drove. His square, firm hands were sure and competent on the wheel of his superbly engineered automobile. He relished the feel of the road, the glorious sense of time and space flashing past, and she understood his intense delight. Driving was her father's time for pondering, and he seemed to draw his whole being into some private communion between man, machine, and the moving scrim of nature. The miles had flown by as they moved farther and farther from . . .

With a start Catherine shook away her reverie. How long had she been sitting here in her parked car? Self-consciously, she glanced around the deserted side street. She felt calmer now and prepared to reconsider the experience in Helen's living room. What was troubling her, Catherine knew, was that after three years of feeling valuable and accepted she now found herself back in a world in which she was regarded exactly as she had been all of her life—clumsy, good-natured, intelligent, well-mannered, reliable—but clearly different, a little unattractive, a little too exuberant and impulsive—and most of all, a bit of an embarrassment. In three years she had changed, but Mount Royal was unchanging and it would not accept her changes. She felt helpless, as though by characterizing her, these people—her family and lifelong friends—trapped her in the image they had of her. She was back—in the mold she had fought to escape.

Feelings of humiliation washed over her again. Her sister and her friend! She had been born to this ordered, impeccable world of Mount Royal as much as Emily and Helen, and yet they were saying she didn't belong—they pitied her! It was ridiculous! It was maddening! It was too much to be borne!

She knew she had behaved rudely in leaving the shower but she didn't care. "They'll probably say 'Isn't that just like Catherine!'" she thought bitterly. A fresh surge of indignation ran through her, and Catherine sat up sharply in her car and started the motor. "I refuse to think about it anymore," she told herself decisively. "I will do my errands and go home."

She crossed the Bow River Bridge that led to the

center of town, and threading through the heavy
traffic, parked her little sports car on Seventh Avenue,
the main thoroughfare of the thriving prairie city.

In the summer of 1937 Calgary was a raw, young
city and in the throes of preparation for its biggest
yearly event—the Stampede. Calgary in the 1930s resembled nothing so much as a farm girl invited to a
debutante ball—all fancied up in a Fifth Avenue
gown, but still wearing a pair of manure-stained work
boots underneath. The city was a study in paradox.
Along Seventh Avenue jewelry stores stood door to
door with tack shops. Small shops selling coveralls and
three-dollar cotton housedresses existed next to sleek,
sophisticated fur salons and thriving book stores. Catherine came to the Hudson's Bay Company, the large department store on Seventh Avenue, which occupied
four sides of an entire block. The huge sidewalk windows fronting the Avenue were filled with the latest
vogue fashions. Shoes from the best bootmakers in Europe and displays of English bone china and crystal
adorned some of the side windows, while others displayed such diverse objects as Hudson's Bay blankets,
coats, guns, animal traps, farm hardware, milk separa-
tors, ice boxes, and straw hats.

The avenue was divided by steel tracks that carried
the old electric streetcars through the city and out to
the farthest suburbs. Packards, Buicks, and Chryslers
rode slowly down the street, passing farm wagons parked
in open lots, and a young cowboy, resplendent in his
new Stampede shirt and hat, rode his horse in a one-
man parade down the main thoroughfare.

Calgary had started much as any other western frontier town. It originated as a little trading post established by Hudson's Bay Company on the Bow River next to an Indian village. The usual raggle-taggle collection of outcasts, trappers, fugitives, and dreamers collected in the early fort. But then the Royal Canadian Mounted Police made the small community one of their western outposts—and as they retired from work, some of the mounties bought or homesteaded nearby land. Soon a core group of dedicated, permanent settlers began to evolve. As the era of trapping ended and civilization encroached on the Alberta plains, more and more of the region's inhabitants turned to farming and settled on the giant prairies surrounding the Bow River. The town which supplied this widening ring of farmers began to develop businesses—banks, feed stores, granaries, feed lots, saloons, bawdy houses, and boardinghouses.

Another historical factor was responsible for the growth of Mount Royal, the beautiful section of Calgary that was Catherine's home. In the late nineteenth century it was the practice of the English aristocracy to send their second sons—as well as sons who disgraced the family name—to the colonies. Since there was still land for the taking in Canada, many aristocratic young Englishmen found their way to the verdant fields of Alberta and the burgeoning community of Calgary. Most of these young men, who came to be known as "remittance men," had an inheritance of annual support from their families, and many of them took their remittance and invested it in the future of Calgary.

These expatriates of the ancient and structured society of England began to recreate their old world on a small bluff overlooking the valley of the Bow River. On this promontory, named Mount Royal, they built spacious formal homes at the start of the century and planted the trees of their remembered youth—oaks, elms, beeches, and willows. They restored the old traditions of four o'clock tea, dressing for dinner, calling cards, and coming-out parties. The Black Watch Society became their club and their hallmark. In a raw new country that boasted no tradition, these men and their families created a tight and comfortable little island. Mount Royal became a microcosm of the England they remembered—structured, elegant, aristocratic, and unbending.

Not everyone who lived in Mount Royal and belonged to the Black Watch Society—named after the Scottish regiment with its magnificent green, blue, and black tartan—was a remittance man or a descendant. Over the years, through marriage, money, or social grace, new families were allowed to join the inner circle. The gracious, restrained society which was Catherine's world influenced all the business and social functions of the city of Calgary.

Walking down the street, Catherine was amazed to observe how strong the American influence had become in recent years due to the discovery of the Alberta oil fields in 1934. American oil interests were avid at the prospect of the rich and easily accessible Canadian oil reserves, and they had rushed into Calgary, buying up leases and oil rights. The city now boasted two new segments in its diverse population, a roistering element of oil rigger and drilling crew members, and a circle of oil-rich American businessmen.

Catherine could see the modern American homes of white stucco and concrete in a section of land south of the city at the far reaches of the city limits. These homes, expensive and elegant, with glass, brick, window walls, and art deco furnishings, hovered on the outskirts of Calgary—so new that there were not yet trees to shield them or soften their cubistic lines. On the road into the city, Catherine had thought that on first impression the American section resembled some futuristic planet.

Despite the passage of years Mount Royal had remained aristocratic and exclusive, inviolate on its own hillside eminence, looking out over the growing city. Catherine smiled as she looked down the streets at the evidence of Calgary's oddly compatible mixture—the old West with its farmers and cattlemen, the English aristocracy, and above all the blatant evidence of rich, black oil wealth and the Americans who brought it. This was Calgary—unique, colorful, and baroque— and Catherine loved it. It was her home, the soil in which her spirit had been conceived, the nourishment of her childhood.

As she walked toward the Hudson's Bay entrance, Catherine paused and looked at her reflection in the store window. "Worse than I thought!" she muttered, making a futile attempt to set her hat straight and to tug her bias-cut skirt into an unwrinkled line.

Then she became conscious of the reflection of another face—someone standing behind her watching over her shoulder. "I'm sorry, my girl, it just won't do!" a deep voice boomed.

With a gasp of excitement she whirled around, and her voice rose with delight. "Norman!" she cried. She threw her arms around the tall young man and gave him a hearty embrace. "Norman! Is it really you?" She pulled back and looked at him, so happy she seemed on the verge of jumping up and down. "Norman!" she cried again. "Your mother said you wouldn't graduate until tomorrow! I didn't expect you home until next week! When did you get here? What are you doing uptown? How long have you been home?" Her voice was breathless and excited. "Imagine! A real lawyer! Just like you always said. It's so wonderful. . . . How did you *get* here?"

The questions spilled out in random order in an exuberant flood, and Norman Pace stood cool and at ease, a gently mocking smile on his handsome face. He did not attempt to interrupt, but waited until Catherine became aware of her own impetuosity and slowed of her own accord. After the last question she paused, and smiling self-consciously, she lowered her voice. Their eyes had met with the practice of old friends, and she had read his message. "I always get carried away, don't I?" she said.

"Not always," he replied, speaking with leisurely elegance, each syllable measured and controlled, "but often." Then he added, in a kinder tone, "It's good to see you, Catherine."

Catherine flushed, and she could feel Norman's eyes taking in every detail of her appearance, her windblown hair, her smudged makeup, and the unflattering dress with the brown tea stain. Norman, as always, looked perfect. He was wearing light flannel slacks and navy blazer, with a soft-collared shirt of dazzling whiteness and a striped tie. His clothes were fitted on his tall, trim frame with meticulous, tailored detail.

To fill the uncomfortable silence which had fallen like a stone between them Catherine asked again, "Why are you home so soon?"

"I didn't stay for graduation," Norman told her calmly. "I felt it was going to be more pomp than circumstance. I left British Columbia yesterday and drove straight through the night."

Yes, she thought to herself, it would be just like Norman to miss his own graduation! He had cultivated his own way of doing things since the days of their childhood, when they had grown up next door to each other.

Norman was two years older than Catherine, but because she had always matched him in physical daring and had been willing to follow his lead, they had become close friends. Norman did not make friends easily. Most of the time he chose to be alone, or only with Catherine, and he had carefully created his individuality. One year when Miss Sinclair's young piano students prepared for the local spring recital, Norman, who was the finest student in the class, refused to learn any of the standard recital pieces. He chose instead a number by Shostakovich, and then, after he had mastered the selection, he informed Miss Sinclair that he did not choose to perform in a recital at all.

He had also refused to ride in the horse shows or to participate in contests because he believed a "true" gentleman should achieve for personal satisfaction— not for competition or public display. Ostentation was not good form, and for Norman, form and style were the essence of life.

Catherine could easily envision him looking at his law school graduation robes and deciding that he would not wear a uniform—even an academic uniform—and so she imagined him neatly folding the robes away, quietly picking up his diploma in the dean's office, and unceremoniously driving through the long hours, home to Calgary.

"Do you have your car uptown, Catherine?" Norman asked, interrupting her thoughts.

"Can I give you a lift?" Happiness at the prospect brightened her smile.

"I left my car at the garage for some repairs. You can save me a ride on the streetcar." Catherine laughed at the disdainful expression on Norman's face as he mentioned the streetcar.

"I need to change the silver pattern in Emily's registry before we can go. My car's across the street," Catherine said.

Norman seemed about to enter the store with her, but then he hesitated, and reaching out his hand, he put it lightly on her arm. "I'll wait for you in the car."

As Norman walked across the street, he felt annoyed with himself. He knew he should have offered to go with Catherine to do her errand, but the truth was he was uncomfortable to be seen with her in public today. Everything about her was wrong—her dress was unbecoming, her nose was shining, and her hair was unruly. She was his dearest and oldest friend, yet her appearance embarrassed him and the ambivalence of his feelings disturbed a basic sense of order within him. Style was important to him, and yet loyalty was important, too, and with Catherine the two were at odds. He never knew how or where Catherine would turn up. There was nothing predictable about her except her unpredictability.

The irony was that Catherine, of everyone he knew, had the surest sense of what was ultimately the finest. He felt she was the only person who understood him, and she was a secret source of strength in his life. But there had been many times when he felt so pained at Catherine's undignified impulses, her exuberant and natural disarray, that he had wanted to reject all ties with her and was ashamed to be thought her friend. He had hoped to outgrow those feelings, but today, even in the first warm emotion of reunion, he had felt a sense of disappointment and dismay at her appearance.

"Catherine," he thought and closed his eyes, leaning back in the leather seat of the Austin. "Catherine," his mind repeated. Somewhere out of the haze of memory he could hear her child's voice calling through the hedge, "Norman! Norman! Come and play!" He could hear her laughter in the hot summer air, and the squeak of the old swing set, as her sturdy body pumped the swing higher and higher until she screamed in fear and delight. "Norman! Come and see!"

Norman's house was always quiet. His mother used to suffer headaches, and she spent the long afternoons of the summer in her darkened room. The servants whispered and in the evening at dinner his mother spoke to him in hushed tones, as though louder sounds might shatter her delicate frame. His home was a place of perfect order and stillness.

His father had died when he was six, leaving him a large trust fund, the Mount Royal home, and the faint memory of a quiet patrician man who spent his afternoons in the study working on a book about Greek architecture.

Years after his father's death, just before Norman left for the university, he had entered his father's study. Everything was as his father had left it when he died—although it was apparent that his mother or the servants periodically dusted and cleaned the room. Gently, methodically, Norman had looked through his father's files. The papers were orderly and extensive, but it soon became apparent to Norman that nowhere was there any original writing of his father's. The files contained notes, research, scale drawings, and photographs—nothing more. Nowhere was there evidence of the beginnings of a book.

As Norman replaced the files, his eye caught a piece of paper sticking out from under the desk pad. Pulling the paper into view, he saw that it was yellowed with age, and blank, except for a few lines written at the top.

"It would not be a sophistry to say that all significant buildings of the Western world have come from the womb of the Acropolis." It was his father's handwriting—just one perfect sentence.

Even as a boy, Norman had known that stillness and order in his life were his enemies. But the stillness never possessed him because Catherine would not let it. She shattered it with her shouting, her laughter, her energetic little body which raced across the lawn, trampled his hedges, and climbed his trees. She teased him, mocked him, provoked him, angered him—and saved him.

* * *

"Norman?" Catherine was standing by the car. "Ready to go?" He opened his eyes and nodded.

They drove through the familiar streets of the city, and as their talk turned to comfortable subjects, Norman felt himself relaxing.

"How was Emily's shower?" he asked.

Catherine frowned and shrugged her shoulders. "All right, I guess," she said. "Parties! How many parties do you suppose we've been to in our lives, Norman?"

Norman laughed. "I don't know," he answered. "Hundreds, probably."

"Tea parties, luncheons," Catherine listed.

"Birthday parties, dinner dances," Norman joined in.

"Receptions, holiday open houses, the opening of the horse show." Catherine grinned.

"The closing of the horse show," Norman continued, "coming-out parties."

"Oh, stop!" Catherine exclaimed. "No more!" Then she sighed. "How many of them do you think were really fun?"

"Fun!" Norman laughed. "They aren't supposed to be fun, Catherine! You miss the whole point. Parties are the training ground where we learn the initiation rites of our society. They aren't supposed to be fun!"

They laughed together and the intimacy of the small car suddenly caused Norman to become aware of Catherine's body next to his. Her full, round breasts had developed early in her teens and had always been a source of discomfort to the teen-aged Norman. In those days he had a vague conception that girls from good families did not have big breasts; they had neat, hard breasts which didn't show. But Catherine bounced and poked out the front of her sweaters in the most disconcerting way.

Now, sitting next to Catherine, he found his eyes being drawn to the rich, womanly curves, which were emphasized by her tight dress. As her hand worked the gear shift, he watched with detached fascination the glimpse of cleavage at her neckline. Incredibly, despite the conflicting emotions of their meeting, he found himself thinking of Catherine sexually for the first time in his life. Their combined sense of daring and their similar intellects had made them friends, but now, in the little Austin, with Catherine chatting cheerfully beside him, he was taken with a physical need for her which caused his mouth to feel dry, and he rubbed his hands slowly on the knees of his flannel slacks.

They drove past the outskirts of the city onto the surrounding prairies where the Stampede grounds stood. There were few houses in this outer area and the large fields were used for pasturing Stampede livestock. It was the time of day when everything moves slowly, and there was a feeling of emptiness in the air, as though the prairie fields were as vacant as the vast blue bowl of the sky.

Suddenly to their right a beautiful Palomino came flying across the empty pasture with a boy in blue coveralls riding bareback. The young horse was running flat out. The boy had lost control of his mount.

"Heavens!" exclaimed Catherine, braking the car. "He's only got a halter on that horse. There's no bit or bridle!"

Without even pausing in its flight, the horse soared over the split rails and landed on the roadway. Gravel sprayed where the hooves struck and the horse seemed to shudder. It continued to run for a few yards, slowly losing pace on the hard gravel road, and then the horse stopped and stood, its fine-boned slender legs trembling, its magnificently molded head and white mane shaking up and down.

Catherine drove the car toward the boy and the horse, but before she reached them, she saw another automobile coming from the opposite direction. It had already stopped, and a man was striding toward the horse. With a start Catherine recognized Mr. Rosenblum.

Mr. Rosenblum was a business partner in her father's law firm. The two men, one a European Jew, the other a Mount Royal Episcopalian, were much alike. They were both short and squarely built, with fine minds and strong hands. Each of them shared a respect for high ideals and people of integrity. They also shared a passion for well-bred livestock and took a mutual joy in the relishing of bloodlines and abundant herds. Mr. Rosenblum spoke with a slight accent, but Catherine had never known what European country was his original home. He never spoke of his past.

As Catherine and Norman got out of the car and hurried toward the trembling horse with the white-faced boy sitting on its back, Catherine could hear Mr. Rosenblum's highly excited tones.

Mr. Rosenblum had seized the horse's halter and was slowly stroking the horse's neck. Gradually his steady, firm hand was having an effect on the frightened animal.

"Boy!" Mr. Rosenblum was saying in an agitated, accented voice. "You should get this horse shot! Shame on you! You have no right to such an animal! Don't you understand what I'm saying? If you want to ride in the city . . . if you ride on the hard pavement . . . you should get this horse shot!" Mr. Rosenblum's voice rose with indignation and his accent became more pronounced as he watched the boy to see if he understood.

The boy's white face seemed to crumple. He slid off the horse's back, and rubbed his eyes fiercely with his dirty hands. Catherine could see that the boy was crying, and Mr. Rosenblum, confused and upset, continued to murmur to the horse and soothe it. Slowly he ran his hand down the slender bone of the horse's foreleg and lifted the foot. He looked at the rough, split hoof and repeated, "Don't you understand? You must get this horse shot!"

Catherine quickly assessed the situation. She didn't know who was in need of the most immediate help—the suffering horse, the frightened boy, or the distressed Mr. Rosenblum. She walked to the boy, gently putting her arm around his quivering shoulders. She knelt beside him so that her face was on his level.

"Are you all right?" she asked quietly.

The boy nodded his head but could not speak. After several indrawn sobs he began, but the words were muffled with crying and the dirty fists with which he was unsuccessfully trying to scrub away his tears. "I didn't hurt Honey, did I? She's going to be all right, ain't she? I never thought she'd take that fence. How's I to know the road was right there? Them cars musta spooked her! But she don't have to die, do she? Her leg ain't broke, nor nothin'. How come I got to get her shot?"

Catherine almost laughed when she realized what the trouble was.

"No, no, I think Honey is going to be all right. I think the gravel hurt her feet is all. She'll be fine as soon as we can calm her down enough to get her back onto that soft pasture. She's fine."

"Then how come that man says I have to shoot her?"

"Not shoot," Catherine said. "Mr. Rosenblum is trying to tell you that you shouldn't ride a horse, and especially not on hard surfaces, unless she has horseshoes. He's telling you that you should get your horse shod. You understand what that means, don't you?"

While Catherine was comforting and calming the young boy, Norman and Mr. Rosenblum checked over the lovely horse. She had obviously been raised with great care. Her golden coat shone like the sun, and her mane and tail were brushed silky. The horse's flanks were sleek and smooth-muscled, and she responded to their firm horseman's touch with the discipline of a gently reared animal.

"This is a fine horse you've got," Norman said.

"Yes," said Mr. Rosenblum, "and you are lucky. She is not hurt. But before you ride her anymore, boy, you must get her shot!"

Relief made the farm boy a little giddy, and he giggled when he heard Mr. Rosenblum say "shot" again.

"Yes, sir, I know I should. But I can't afford shoes for her. On the farm it don't seem to matter. I just ride her in the fields."

Mr. Rosenblum put his hand in his pocket and brought out his wallet. "What's your name, boy?"

"Tom Markham. You ain't goin' to tell my daddy, are you? He may make me and Honey go home and not see the Stampede if he thinks we got into trouble!" The boy's face was full of anxiety and his eyes began to cloud up again.

"No, I'm not going to tell your father. I am going to give you fifty dollars, and I want you to use it to get horseshoes for your pony. Don't use it for anything else. You are not to ride her again until she is shot." With that Mr. Rosenblum extracted a fifty-dollar bill from his wallet and handed it to the boy.

"Well, Catherine," he said, still absently stroking the now quiet horse. "It is good to see you. I planned to call on you to give you my congratulations on your fine achievement. You are a daughter to be proud of, like the great daughters of Israel. Now I must be going. I am late for an appointment." Mr. Rosenblum walked back to his car and Norman accompanied him. Catherine stayed with the boy and the horse.

"Mr. Rosenblum," Norman said, "don't you think it was foolish giving that boy fifty dollars? He's probably never seen that much money in his life. My guess is he'll spend it on himself."

With his hand on the door of his automobile, Mr. Rosenblum turned and looked at Norman.

"Couldn't you see by the look on that boy's face how much he loves his horse?" Mr. Rosenblum asked.

Mr. Rosenblum drove away and Norman stood for a moment looking after him with a quizzical frown on his face, then he turned to look at Catherine.

In the late afternoon Catherine was highlighted in the rays of the setting sun, and the prairie glowed rose

and golden behind her. It struck Norman how different Catherine appeared here in this natural setting, as
though she belonged here and her spirit seemed to
stretch to fit the open sky. Away from the city, away
from the stultifying atmosphere of Mount Royal,
Catherine opened like a flower and took on a natural
radiance. Could this be the same awkward, badly
dressed girl he had seen on the city streets less than an
hour ago? This warm and radiant young woman with
glowing hair, loose and silken, framing her face in the
evening air? Her body, bending toward the boy, was
relaxed and graceful, and her face was sweet with concern and compassion. As she turned to look at Norman, her eyes were caught in the light, and they shone
as green as emeralds.

Norman was shaken by her transformation; it
seemed almost mystical, as though she were a creature
of another world, able to change herself at will. In this
setting, in this moment of caring for the boy, Catherine was revealed to Norman, and reluctantly, almost
like a physical pain, he formed the words in his mind.
"She is beautiful!" He continued to look at her and
the words repeated themselves in his head, this time
with amazed fervor, "She really *is* beautiful!" It was a
poignant realization, unfamiliar and not totally welcome. Norman didn't like the things he counted on in
life to change. Catherine was one of the things upon
which he relied. He had mentally placed her in his life
exactly where he wanted her, but here she was, unpredictable as always, not wanting to stay in her place. He
did not want to think of Catherine as beautiful or desirable, and he tried to shake off this strange, unfamil-

iar view of her, but the image would not fade. She still looked beautiful, even as he stepped up to her and took the reins of the horse. He and Catherine and the boy walked back toward the pasture, and when they had seen the boy and his horse safely on their way, they drove back to Mount Royal. It was dinner time.

Catherine dropped Norman at his door with a cheery wave. "Call me," she said with the casual ease of their long friendship.

"Of course," Norman said quietly, staring at her with a preoccupied frown. She began to drive away, and he shouted after her, "Catherine!"

The shout was so out of character that Catherine stopped the car in confusion and looked at Norman with surprise. He ran up to the side of the convertible, put his hands on the car beside her, and said, "I forgot to tell you—your mother asked if I would be your official escort for the wedding's social events, so we'll be seeing a lot of each other."

Their eyes met squarely, and he knew suddenly that Catherine had known his feelings about her appearance and the reason he had not gone into the store with her.

"You're sure?" she asked, and her laughing eyes teased and challenged him.

"I'm sure," he replied, smiling back at her. Bending over the door of the car, he kissed her on her soft full mouth and then turned with unhurried poise and walked toward the mahogany door of his Tudor home.

CHAPTER TWO

The sun poured through the bay window of the break-fast room as yellow as butter. Bright with morning, the room was fresh and lovely. In the wide window hung lush, pink baskets of flowering impatiens. The buffet against the side wall held baskets of summer fresh fruit, crystal dishes of ripe strawberries, and a silver service steaming with the scent of freshly brewed coffee. Silver-covered dishes held bacon and scrambled eggs, and a Waterford crystal server brimmed with crusty corn muffins, warm from the oven.

At the glass-topped table sat Catherine's mother, Lucy, sipping black coffee from a Beleek china coffee cup. The heirloom china looked translucent in the sunlight, and Catherine noticed that her mother's slim, fine hand seemed almost translucent as well.

As Catherine stood in the doorway savoring the familiar room, and relishing the promise of the bright morning, her mother lifted her head and regarded her daughter with an affectionate smile.

"Come in, my dear Portia," her mother began.

Catherine gave a laughing groan. "Oh, no! Mother, not you, too! I had all the clever classical allusions I could stand at Mrs. Mortenson's yesterday. Next thing I know you'll be planning a Shakespearean garden, too!"

"Don't be extreme, Catherine," her mother said and

smiled. "I was just trying to show you that I am not a complete Philistine. Forgive me my little conceit. You are our Portia, you know," she continued, with a loving look. "You are clever and lovely and an achiever . . . just as Portia was. . . . It is not a bad analogy, now . . . admit it!"

Catherine bent and kissed her mother's cheek, and then sat opposite her at the table, where a place was set with silverware and a glass of orange juice. This morning her mother was at her best, Catherine thought, relaxed, happy, and loving. Catherine wished the morning could last—the two of them sitting alone together in the sun-filled room.

"Thank you, Mother," she said. "I so want you to be proud of me!"

"Of course, I am," her mother said with some surprise. "What mother wouldn't be proud of such fine achievement! Now, drink your juice and tell me about your plans for the day."

"Shall I wait for Father before I begin?"

"Wait for your father?" her mother said, laughing. "Don't you know what a sleep-a-bed you are! It's almost nine o'clock. Hilda fed your father at least two hours ago. He left even before I was up."

Catherine drank her orange juice quickly and then walked over to the sideboard to fill her plate.

"May I fix a plate for you, Mother?" she asked.

"Mercy, no!" Lucy exclaimed. "This coffee is all I dare have! With all these parties and showers and teas— I'll be lucky to come through these wedding festivities without looking like a butterball! There is that awful barrage of pictures to be faced at the end, too."

For a moment Catherine hesitated as she reached for a corn muffin, but then she resolutely picked it up and put it on her plate beside the bacon and eggs. She took one of the small bowls of strawberries in her other hand and carried the food back to the table. Her mother said nothing, but she glanced meaningfully at the filled plate.

"You know, Catherine," Lucy said, in a carefully neutral voice, "you're going to be in those pictures, too."

There was an awkward moment of stillness in the room. Lucy reached over to her husband's chair and picked up the newspaper he had left folded there. She turned to the society column and began to read. Catherine sat in front of the lovely breakfast, but the food was spoiled for her. If she ate, she knew she would feel embarrassed by her mother's unspoken disapproval. If she didn't eat, she would feel like a child whose hand had been slapped—a puppet adult who couldn't even decide when or what to eat.

She glanced at her mother reading the paper and observed again that everything her mother did was graceful. Lucy Summerwell was one of those fortunate women whose body was proportioned and framed in such a way that there was a natural beauty in all her motions. Although in her early forties, she took great care to keep the slender figure of her youth. She gave the impression of being much smaller than she actually was and dressed cleverly to emphasize the daintiness and femininity of her appearance. In speaking of her, friends always used the word "pretty," and if Lucy could have chosen a word to describe herself,

that was the very word she would have chosen—
"pretty." She loved the word! She always talked about
how much she loved to have pretty things around her.

Lucy's hair was a soft, ash blond, and she wore it in
a simple bun with short curly bangs framing her face.
Her features were small and finely cut. Her mouth
and cheeks were a natural bright color, and her deep
blue eyes were framed with fair lashes and brows.
Everything about her was fair and slightly ethereal.
This morning her mother was wearing a peach-colored
satin morning robe with a white ruffle showing at the
neck. Framed in sunlight, she looked as delicate as the
morning dew. "Certainly a different clay than I am
made of," Catherine thought, as she looked at her own
smooth strong arms and small square hands resting on
either side of her plate.

Catherine breathed a sigh and began to eat the
scrambled eggs, which she had allowed to grow cold.
Slowly, methodically, she ate bite after bite, and then
began on the glistening red berries. The food seemed
tasteless to her, and the silence in the room was broken
only by the disapproving rustle of her mother's newspaper and the persistent buzzing of a large fly somewhere over by the window.

Abruptly, her mother put down the newspaper and
reached for the little crystal bell with which she summoned Hilda, the housekeeper.

"Hilda!" she said, as the older woman popped
through the swinging door from the kitchen. "Would
you please bring in a flyswatter and see if you can locate that noisy fellow?"

"Of course, Mrs. Summerwell, right away!" Hilda's
eyes fell on Catherine and her wide, wrinkled face

beamed. "Catherine! It sure does a body good to see you home again. This house just ain't the same when you're away. It's too darn quiet!"

"Thanks, Hilda," Catherine said. "That's a wonderful breakfast you fixed."

"Seems like you and Mr. Summerwell is the only ones that think so," Hilda stated with a meaningful glance toward the full buffet. "It's nice to have someone around who appreciates good cooking."

"We're all glad to have Catherine home," Lucy said firmly. "Now will you please go after that fly?"

"Yes, Mrs. Summerwell, happy to . . ." Hilda ducked back into the kitchen and emerged a moment later with a large swatter in hand. She marched toward the bay window purposefully, the swatter raised in one powerful arm. Her heavy tread shook the room and the silver and crystal jingled on the buffet.

"I feel sorry for that fly!" Catherine remarked, and suddenly her mother was smiling again. Her eyes crinkled with amusement. Hilda grinned as well and continued to stalk the elusive prey.

Suddenly the swatter came down with a mighty slap against the pane. There was a split second of silence while everyone listened for a telltale buzz.

"Did you get him?" asked Catherine.

Hilda was scrutinizing the floor by the fern planter. "I don't know," she replied, "but if I didn't kill him, I sure scared him!"

The three women laughed and Hilda returned to the kitchen. The air was cleared and Catherine's mother turned to her once more.

"Now, you promised to tell me what you have planned for the day. Emily and I are going to a fitting for her bridal gown. If you'd like to come along, we'd love to have you . . ."

"Thanks, Mother, but I don't think so. I thought I might call Jean Hunt and arrange to go to lunch with her. Maybe do a little shopping . . . By the way, Mother, when you are at the dressmaker's, could you please make an appointment for me to get those dresses fitted properly, or I refuse to wear them."

Her mother looked irritated. "I don't know why they don't fit, Catherine. We had them sized to the clothes you left at home."

"I wore those clothes in high school, Mother . . ." Catherine said patiently. "That was four years ago! My figure has changed since then."

"'Hm-m-m. Yes," Lucy said cryptically. "Very well, I'll make an appointment for you tomorrow. You're sure you won't go with us today? I don't know what you see in that Hunt girl! Of course her father's family has some of the best blood in Eastern Canada, but her mother is so . . . American. I mean, they are terribly informal—and so 'horsey.' "

Catherine grinned. "I think you've just explained why I like her, Mother—because I am informal and 'horsey,' too," she said and paused. "I like Jean because she is one of the best friends I've ever had. I mean . . . she makes me feel like she really cares about me as a person. . . ." Catherine groped for the right words to explain, but her mother interrupted.

"Catherine! I really don't have much patience when you talk like that! It makes you sound as though you had a deprived childhood. I don't know anyone alive who has had more friends than you . . . or more opportunities for social experiences. . . ."

"Mother, I didn't mean that as a criticism of my childhood. I was only trying to explain why I like Jean Hunt. Besides, she makes me laugh!"

"Well, all right, dear." Mrs. Summerwell gave a resigned sigh and stood up and walked toward the front hall. "I think I'd better go awaken Emily or she'll be late for her fitting."

"You know," Lucy added, "James and his parents are due to return for the wedding at the end of next week, right after Stampede is over, and then our real whirlwind begins. They have gone to Vancouver—more business—but they'll be back before we know it. There is still so much to do."

"I'll be glad to do anything you and Emily want me to," Catherine said eagerly. "Just ask me, and it's done."

"I know, dear, I know . . ." her mother said absently, her mind already on other things. "We'll talk about it tonight at dinner."

Catherine felt forgotten and dismissed as she sat alone in the empty breakfast room. She thought it odd that even though she had eaten breakfast she felt empty. Hilda burst through the swinging door.

Breaking into a wide smile, Hilda exclaimed, "You still here, Catherine! I thought you went out with your mother." Hilda started clearing the breakfast things, muttering to herself.

"It's just wedding, wedding, wedding around here! You'd think it was the Princess Margaret Rose herself grown up and getting married. Ain't nobody eatin' properly, and the house has got to be spic and span day and night. I tell you, Catherine, it's almost more than a body can take!"

Catherine walked over and threw her arms around the stout woman in a hearty embrace. "Not too much for you, Hilda. Ever since I was little I knew you could do anything! Do you remember the time when you took care of the sparrow I found? It lived when even Daddy said it couldn't be saved. What's a wedding to someone who can save sparrows!"

Hilda blushed and patted Catherine's shoulder. "It sure is fine to have you home, Catherine. Just fine. . . ."

The Louis Quatorze clock in the lobby struck one o'clock as Catherine and Jean Hunt walked into the dining room of the Palliser Hotel. "Welcome home, Miss Summerwell," said the stately, white-haired head waiter. "Shall I give you your father's table?"

"Yes, thank you, that would be very nice." Catherine and Jean followed him to a table in a quiet corner and sat down as he carefully held their seats. "William will be serving you today," he informed them, and handed them ornate menus with heavy gold tassels.

The two young women ordered salads and continued their conversation.

"You know I've always loved animals, Catherine. Never doubted what I wanted to do when I grew up. It took me three years and a lot of pull to get accepted at the Guelth Royal Veterinary College—it's the only one in Canada, you know. All I can say is thank heaven for Daddy's Ontario relatives! When I went back there this year, I discovered I was the only female student!"

"How did the college take it?" asked Catherine.

"Not too well," Jean said. "I think I made both the

professors and the students nervous. Once I was in a study group and we were discussing breeding methods—those discussions can get pretty bawdy. The fellows got so nervous because I was there that they were practically tongue-tied! I finally just said, 'Look, guys, you forget that I'm a woman, and I'll forget you are men . . .' Somehow that didn't go over too well!"

"Anyway," Jean went on, "several of the professors had private talks with me and warned me it was one thing to read about vet work in textbooks, but they doubted any woman could stand it in actual practice."

"Oh," said Catherine, "in other words it's all right for women to perform the bodily functions but not to administer to them—in people or in animals, I guess."

"Yeah, something like that," Jean said. "So they cooked up this great surprise for me on the first day of my Livestock Operations course. 'Today,' announced Dr. Schultz," Jean mimicked a heavy German accent, " 'we are going to show you the method by which sheep castration is normally performed.' At that point every eye in the room turned to me. I didn't feel the least bit squeamish. All I could think of was that I was at last going to get to do something real."

"What happened?" Catherine asked.

"They took us out into the yard where the sheep were penned, and the good doctor gave us a lecture on how slippery the devilish little things were! He went on to inform us that you can't possibly hold the extruded testicles in your hand or they slip back in . . . and then . . ." Jean began to chuckle. "I don't know if I should tell you at lunch, Catherine! It's really awful!"

Catherine was totally intrigued. "Jean, the one

thing about you is that your conversation is never dull! What happened . . . tell me!"

Jean suppressed a giggle. "He held them with his teeth!"

"What?" Catherine gave a small gasp and began to laugh in disbelief. "You're kidding! Tell me you're kidding!"

"No, no! I'm not kidding. It's been done that way for centuries—all over the world!" Jean stopped laughing and wiped the corner of her eye with the napkin. "Of course, I think it was a plot to get me to throw in the towel or the sponge or whatever you throw in at a vet college. But let me tell you, Cath, five people passed out in the course of the morning, and six got sick . . . and I wasn't one of them. I came through with flying colors. After that morning, they figured I had what it takes. If I could do that, they knew I could do anything required of me! I'm going to make it through, Catherine."

Catherine looked at her friend. "I know you'll make it, Jean. You'll be very good at your profession. But what if you go through all this and get married? Won't you feel it was a terrible waste?"

"What are you talking about?" Jean asked, amazed. "I wouldn't marry anyone who wouldn't let me practice my profession. Besides, look at me! Who's going to love a girl who looks like a horse?"

Catherine's face clouded. "Jean, don't say something like that! You are absolutely wonderful looking. The better question would be, who *wouldn't* love you?"

"I don't even talk about it," Jean said. "My looks are so little a part of myself. Unimportant. However, I do see myself clearly. You, Catherine, on the other hand, have the reverse problem."

"What do you mean?" Catherine asked.

"You're the only person I've ever known to whom looks and style are so important, and yet you have absolutely no concept of how you look to other people!"

Catherine felt the old guarded pain and her mouth went dry. She desperately wished that Jean would not say anymore. She had felt so safe in this relationship, judged by Jean's openhearted, exuberant spirit, and yet now she was terrified that Jean was going to confirm everyone else's opinion. Jean saw the fear on Catherine's face.

"Oh, you goose!" she exclaimed. "See! There you are—afraid that if anyone mentions how you look it's going to be bad. Don't you know, Catherine? Sure, your mother and Emily are pretty, and Helen Mortenson is elegant, and Gil Townsend is sophisticated, and Marie Williams has style . . . but you are the only one of the bunch who is beautiful! The only one!"

Catherine's eyes widened in surprise, and then she shook her head and laughed.

"Look, I'm not going to try to convince you, Cath. You have to discover it yourself, I suppose, before it makes any difference. Besides, I don't mean you're gorgeous all the time or anything like that. Sometimes you look awful!" The fresh, flat, breezy inflection of Jean's voice made the statement funny as well as true. "But then," Jean continued, "—and I refuse to discuss the subject anymore, after I have made the following statement—sometimes it all comes together and you are absolutely, completely beautiful." She looked across the table at her friend and squinted her eyes and held up her thumb like an artist.

"Now," she said, affecting the accent again, "eef we could chust hang onto zat . . . zee world vould be at your feet!"

Catherine laughed and picked up the check. "I don't know how good a veterinarian you are, Jean, but you are surely a good friend! Shall we go shopping or drive out to the Stampede Grounds and check out the livestock that's coming in today?"

"Neither," said Jean. "Let's go home and put on our riding togs and go out to the stable. I'm itching to get back in the saddle."

"Capital idea, my dear Miss Hunt!" Catherine and Jean walked out into the sunlight, their slim muscular legs striding in unison.

The next morning Catherine lay in bed listening to the sounds of birds and savoring the morning breeze that blew the yellow-sprigged curtains over the window seat. She had grown up in this room; its patterns were as familiar to her as her face in the mirror. The bed was comfortable, and the pillows deep and fluffy. Hilda must have changed the linens, because the pillowcase had the fresh scent of outdoors, and the sheets were smooth against her bare legs.

Reluctantly, luxuriously, she stretched and climbed out of bed. Tying a robe around her, she headed for the tub. An hour later she came downstairs, wearing a pair of white shorts and a navy blue halter top. Her feet were in old tennis shoes, her long, golden-brown hair was wrapped in a towel. She dreaded what her mother would say when she saw that Catherine had washed out the expensive salon hairsetting she had insisted upon for the shower, but Catherine decided she could not live another day with that tight, kinky hair.

When Catherine entered the breakfast room, the table was cleared and a note was in front of her chair.

Dear Catherine,

Emily wanted to go pick out the gifts for her bridesmaids, and so we have made an early trip to town. We'll stay out for lunch. Don't forget to be at the club by four this afternoon. Swimming and dinner with the Howellses and the Williamses. Your appointment with the dressmaker is today at one.

Love,
Mother

P.S. Hilda's day off, so you'll have to do for yourself. Love.

Even her mother's handwriting was perfect copperplate. Catherine sighed. All alone in the big house, she picked up an apple and sat down at the table, thinking. This morning she could do anything she wanted, but the trouble was she couldn't think of anything to do.

She unwrapped the towel from around her hair and felt the thick wet tangle. Somewhere she had read that brushing hair in the sunlight would bring out red highlights. She ran upstairs and got an old quilt, a book, and a brush. Picking up her half-finished apple, she walked out into the backyard.

The Summerwell's backyard was extensive. It stretched from the terrace through a hedge-divided

flower garden with a wash yard to one side, protected
by a high hedge, and beyond that a secluded untended
section which was screened from view on three sides.
The fourth side looked down from the prominence on
which Mount Royal was situated into the deep Bow
River valley below.

It was in this section of the yard that the girls had
their swings, sandboxes, and jungle gyms when they
were young children. In those days the back edge of the
yard was protected by a high chain-link fence, but the
fence had fallen into disrepair through the years and
her father had removed it. The view was magnificent,
and there was a feeling of seclusion and solitude in
this distant part of the yard. Catherine sat in the sunlight with her bare legs crossed under her, Indian fashion. Propping the book on her knees, she brushed the
radiant fall of her hair. In the hot sun her hair dried
quickly and began to spark and fly under the stroke
of the brush. Her hair fell in natural waves, thick and
shining. As soon as it was dry, Catherine pulled it up
into a loose knot and secured it with hairpins. Glancing at her watch, she saw that it was only ten thirty,
and remembering the swimming party, she looked at
her arms and shoulders.

"I could use a little sun," she thought. In a flash she
jumped up and ran back up to the house. Breathlessly
she rushed into the kitchen and searched through a
corner cupboard until she found what she was looking
for—a bottle of suntan oil. Grabbing another apple,
she hurried back out through the hedges to the back
of the gardens.

Spreading the quilt, she sat down and splashed oil
on her legs, arms, and shoulders. Then she lay down

on her stomach on the quilt. The sun was very warm and she could feel it seeping into her skin. Lazily, she reached behind her to untie her halter at the neck and across the back. She spread her arms out at either side and lay flat against the earth, the lazy hum of insects and the rustle of leaves the only sounds in the summer air. Although she warned herself not to fall asleep, she was soon lulled into a state of semiawareness. The sound of a foot cracking a branch brought her instantly alert.

"Who's there?" she called anxiously.

"Norman." His voice was close. "I was in our back-yard giving Prince some exercise, and I saw you hurrying out your back door. I figured you were headed for our old meeting place, so I walked down to the hole in the hedge. Do you know, it's almost grown over—I could hardly get through."

Norman's voice moved closer. "Don't come through the box hedge!" she cried. "I'm not decent!"

"Don't be ridiculous," Norman's voice replied. "You are always decent."

Catherine realized that he was directly behind her and had probably been standing in the little yard throughout the conversation. Not daring to lift up from the quilt or even to turn her head, she lay rigid. She would have given anything to see Norman's face. On second thought, she decided, she didn't think she could ever look him in the face again.

"If you were a gentleman you would step around the hedge and give me a chance to get my halter tied."

"I am no gentleman. Besides, you got yourself into this situation, and I feel you're equal to the challenge of extricating yourself." Norman's voice was teasing.

She felt her face grow hot with discomfort and anger. "Norman!" she said. Her voice was muffled by the quilt, but she made a great effort at authority. "Get behind that fence!"

He laughed. "I could say that I would go, but how would you know if I had gone or not?"

She changed her tone. The situation was so absurd that she began to laugh, and she knew Norman was just deviling her as he had since they were little children . . . teasing her, mocking her, challenging her, embarrassing her.

"Please, Norman . . ." she cajoled.

"You'll figure out something." Norman's voice was complacent. "I know you will."

Catherine continued to lie flat on the quilt, her mind in a tumult. She knew Norman wasn't going to give in. She knew him too well. What she couldn't suspect was the present tumult in Norman's mind. He had seen Catherine hurrying through the backyard, and since the morning was long and he was bored, he had decided to go meet her in the old play yard, as they had done a thousand times before through the years. When he got to the hole in the hedge at the bottom of his own yard, he was taken aback to see how overgrown the opening was and to observe how the little path to the play yard was almost obliterated by sturdy growth. The vanished path seemed to emphasize the passage of time, the changing years.

He had thought to pop around the wall and surprise Catherine but as he stepped silently into the little yard he was the one who started in surprise. Catherine was lying, seemingly asleep, on a soft-colored quilt.

Her back was bare to the waist, and a glowing mass of hair crowned her head. Her face was turned from him, but his eyes drank in the long white curve of her back, and her full thighs and tapered ankles. He felt like he had come upon a living painting.

His first thought was to steal away before she became aware of his presence, but the sight was so compelling that he stood still and drank it in, not as a voyeur, but with the wonder of a discoverer. As he turned to leave, a twig snapped under his foot, and before he realized it, he had turned the situation into a contest of wills. He could not understand himself, why he refused to do the gentlemanly thing and leave Catherine for a moment. Perhaps it was because a part of him wanted this moment not to end. He wanted her to remain like this while his eyes drank in her lovely flesh. Also, as long as her face was not looking at him, it hardly seemed to him that this was Catherine. This was some glorious woman, fashioned for the pleasure of a man.

"So help me, Norman," Catherine muttered through her teeth, "you'll pay for this. I'm going to step on your feet every time we dance together." She lifted her head up from the quilt and without moving her body bent her arms behind her and tied the back strap of her halter. With that secure she grabbed the two top straps and holding them at her shoulders she rolled over and sat up on the quilt. As soon as she was upright, she pulled the neck straps tight, and bending forward so that her hair would not catch in the bow, she tied the top of the halter. "There!" she said, jumping to her feet. "I've done it! No thanks to you!"

Norman said nothing, but walked over to Catherine and, reaching up, undid the pins in her hair and let the waving mass tumble over her shoulders. He looked at her for a moment. "I don't think you should ever stay in the sun," he said quietly. "Your skin will burn." He was silent again, and Catherine looked at him closely. His eyes had a bemused look.

Norman seemed strange, remote—and their easy familiarity felt strained. "I don't understand you, Catherine," he continued, and his hand reached out and touched the silky waves of her hair. "How is it that yesterday your hair looked like a witch . . . and today . . . it is witchcraft!"

Disturbed, Catherine turned away and made a great show of folding up the quilt. "You mean, today I look like a witch's handicraft!" Her laugh was self-deprecating. "I have to go in and get ready for a fitting at the dressmaker's."

Norman watched as she bent to pick up the book. The full curve of her hips and the swing of her breasts was so natural and earthy that he felt, here in this secluded garden, they were primeval man and woman. His emotions seduced him into feeling that any woman with a body as full and ripe as Catherine's could not possibly be innocent, but somehow, in her very creation, was a special sensuality, a knowledge and preparedness of the body that made experience unnecessary for her to be awakened and aware.

However, Norman knew that a good part of his new perception of Catherine had nothing to do with any change in her. It came from his own experience of the past two years at law school. During his second year his roommate had initiated him into the mysteries of sex by setting up an evening for him with a young waitress who worked at the campus cafe during the daytime and in selected beds at night. Norman continued to date girls from good families and treated them with meticulous respect and courtesy, but the waitress was a different type of girl. A girl to be used and enjoyed. He treated her well, giving her gifts and money when she needed it. Her body was soft and blowsy, but it had awakened and satisfied his needs. Having tired of her, he had stopped seeing the girl in April.

Now he recognized that part of his reaction to Catherine was due to the celibacy of the past few weeks as well as his recent release from the pressures of school. He supposed that his feelings of confusion and heightened sensitivity came from the sudden distortion of a relationship that had been part of his life from early childhood. He and Cath were almost like brother and sister, their minds both quick, alert, and challenging, their perceptions similar, and yet, always in Catherine lurked something unexpected—unpredictable. It was her great charm and also her great failing. She had brought to Norman's life a constant factor of disruption and uncertainty, which both fascinated and disturbed him.

Even now the powerful need he felt for Catherine's body threw his inner sense of order into turmoil. This was Cath, his dear, known childhood friend. She was innocent, the child of strict upbringing, a woman whom he would protect with his life against any dishonor—and yet his own feelings toward her were suddenly filled with passion and an overwhelming desire. When he looked into her sweet, intelligent face, he felt an unreasoning anger that she should so disturb the cool inviolate pattern he had cultivated so carefully in his mind.

"Norman," Catherine was saying, breaking into his troubled thoughts, "I have to go in now." She could not understand why he was acting preoccupied. She was standing in front of him, her ams crowded with the blanket, towel, book, and brush, a puzzled, searching look on her face. The blanket was poorly folded and one corner was trailing down. That was so like her! he thought with exasperation. She could never do anything with precision.

"You're going to trip on that blanket," he said.

She laughed and pulled up the offending corner and awkwardly tucked it under her book. As she moved her arm, the other side of the blanket fell down. "Oh dear!" she said and laughed. "I give up! Gotta go!" and she started jogging across the lawn. Before she went ten steps, her book fell on the grass. "What the heck!" she exclaimed, and throwing down the blanket, she tossed everything into the middle of it and picked it up like a Santa Claus bag, throwing it over her shoulder. Norman stood, shaking his head. "If you'd folded it right in the first place," he called, "you wouldn't have this problem!"

"It's your fault!" she yelled back. "You should have folded it for me."

"Never mind," he answered. "Go get yourself fitted up properly in those dresses, so you will look beautiful, and I'll come pick you up for the swimming party at the club. I'll be here for you at three forty-five, and be on time for once, won't you?"

"Being a lawyer has made you so bossy . . ." Catherine exclaimed, and she ran toward the house, the quilt bouncing on her shoulder. As he watched her go, he recognized the hardest factor in his dilemma. He loved Catherine as a friend. He respected her mind and admired her family. Intellectually, she was all he could ever wish and much to his surprise he found her rich, full body strongly aroused his physical needs. However, the hard truth was that there was another need in his personality which was greater than all of the others, and this was his deep-rooted need for order, restraint, and elegance in his life. In this aspect of his needs Catherine was a continual disappointment. She was casual where he was precise, impetuous where he was controlled, extravagant where he was restrained, and her appearance was flamboyant when he yearned for quiet style.

He knew this was something superficial and absurd in his character and yet it was an indelible part of him. He simply could not marry a woman who did not look right. It would make them both miserable. And yet, the remembered image of Catherine's softly curving back, rosy in the sun, and the inviting roundness of her full hips—even the tender image of her hand, open against the grass—filled his heart with a great yearning.

As he walked along the faint boundary of their old play-worn path, he heard the echoes of their childhood laughter and was filled with a nameless nostalgia. Were those carefree days forever gone? Unless he did something, would the heart of his childhood be lost to him forever, too? He slipped through the old opening in the hedge, and reaching back, deliberately broke away several branches to enlarge the hole. Then on second thought he carefully propped the branches back into the bushes, so the opening was once again obscure.

"I'll tell her tonight at the dinner that I'm going to Red Deer for a few days," he decided. Having made the decision, he walked toward his red setter, Prince, who was sitting in the shade of the lawn swing, and gracefully he stooped, picked up a small branch, and sent it soaring across the lawn. "Fetch!" he commanded the beautiful animal.

CHAPTER THREE

"I'm glad you decided to ride with me in the troop today," Catherine's father said as he met her in the dark upper hallway. The house was shadowy, silent, and they walked together along the thick carpeting to the staircase.

"I'm only doing this for you, Father, not for the glory of the Black Watch Troop—and certainly not for the fun of riding sidesaddle for four hours!" Catherine answered. "Why does the troop still insist that women wear long skirts and ride sidesaddle? That's carrying tradition to the extreme, don't you think?" At the top of the staircase Catherine tugged at the heavy train of her black riding skirt, and then, giving up all hope of grace, gave an exaggerated sigh, pulled the skirt high above her knees, and ran down the stairs. Her shining black riding boots flashed in the dim lights of the entry hall as she bounded down.

When her father joined her at the bottom of the stairs with a disapproving glint in his eye, she was smoothing her skirts and looking prim, but her eyes were dancing with mischief. "Catherine," her father said gravely, "tradition is the mortar of our way of life." Then he smiled. "I would also like to tell you your long riding habit is very becoming to you. I like to see you wearing it."

"You look very dapper yourself, Father," Catherine replied. They stood for a moment in the hall, buttoning their riding gloves and straightening one another's white riding stocks. They buttoned their slim, black jackets and checked the small ornamental spurs on their boots. When all was in readiness, Catherine's father walked to a Chinese chest in the corner of the hall and took out two Black Watch tartan sashes. Each took a sash and, using the wide hall mirror, draped the plaid across the right shoulder and fastened it at the left hip with a golden clasp. Then, Mr. Summerwell carefully lifted out two tissue-wrapped packages and handed one to Catherine.

Inside the tissue was a black Tam o' Shanter with one side caught up in a silver and amethyst thistle pin, a stiff, white brush standing up straight from the thistle. Catherine looked in the mirror and put on her tam at a rakish angle. Then she turned to her father, who looked at her appraisingly, then walked over and removed her hat gently.

"The brush on your hat is a little dilapidated. Can't have the most beautiful girl in the parade looking moth-eaten!" He carefully undid the heavy brooch from his own hat and transferred it to Catherine's. Then, he pinned her brooch to his hat and placed it carefully on his head.

Catherine was touched by his thoughtfulness. "I'll hold my head especially high today," she said. Her father walked over to her, putting both hands on her shoulders and looking into her eyes. "I only want the best for you always . . ." Her father did not often speak affectionately to Catherine, and though her heart sang, she felt shy and awkward. She hung her head, her cheeks flaming with pleasure and self-consciousness.

"Well, now, my girl," her father said in a hearty voice, "let's see if we pass muster."

They stood and looked at themselves in the mirror. Father and daughter—they could as easily have looked at one another as at the mirror, they were so much alike. Clifford Summerwell was not a tall man, and his daughter stood almost shoulder to shoulder with him. She was like a young, feminine replica of her father. Both had fine, well-modeled heads, with strong even features and firm jaws. Their bodies were firm, broad of shoulder, yet balanced and well-proportioned. Even the habitual expressions on their faces were similar: intelligent and pleasant, and each with the same alert, gray-green eyes. Mr. Summerwell in his twill jodphurs, with the black riding jacket and tartan sash, looked trim and compact. Catherine looked lovely in the slim skirt with the full train and the smooth-fitted jacket. Her full curving breasts and hips and her slender waist were nicely emphasized in the line of the clothes, while the white scarf high on her neck framed her face and highlighted the rich coloring of her rose-tinged cheeks and full lips. Soft curls escaped around her face from the loose knot that bound her long hair at the base of her neck. She looked every part of what she was—the cherished daughter of an assured and wealthy family.

As Catherine and her father walked out the door together, the spur of Catherine's boot caught in the hem of her dress, and she hopped down the front walk trying to free herself. "Drat! Sidesaddle!" she muttered, adding the ultimate heresy. "Next year I'm going to ride in a cowboy division on a western saddle!"

Mr. Summerwell, unperturbed, unhooked his daughter's skirt from her spur and draped the train neatly over her arm. "That's how it should be done, my dear," he said, with a tender smile. He took her elbow and, opening the Packard door, helped her into the car. Together they drove to the stables in the predawn light.

The riding club was a scene of chaos and confusion. It was just after five in the morning and the horses were restless and skittery at being roused and saddled so early. Sean Greer, the stablemaster, was everywhere, his calm, deep voice the only element of sanity in the general disorder.

Gillian Townsend, her tall, matronly figure still slender in outline, was ordering the women's troop into position.

"Now, girls," she was trumpeting in her nasal, high-bred voice, "we can't dawdle. The parade doesn't wait for laggards. We must be over to our stations within half an hour. Get those horses calmed down and get yourselves mounted!"

As if to set the example, Gillian prepared to get on her own mount, a large bay gelding named Scipio.

"I say there, Sean Greer, would you come over and give me a leg up?" she called. Sean turned from the horse he was soothing and nodded. Handing the reins to a teen-age boy who was standing nearby he walked over to help Mrs. Townsend.

Mrs. Townsend's black skirt was voluminous, and the stirrup of her tall horse was far from the ground.

Catherine stood watching the proceedings with a smile on her face. The sun had just begun to touch the horizon, and there was enough light in the sky to see the imperious Mrs. Townsend, her reluctant mount, and the frustrated Sean Greer trying to get the former on top of the latter.

"A mounting block." Gillian Townsend was puffing. "A mounting block, that's what we need! No, no, here, Sean! Just give me a leg up!" Mrs. Townsend, grasping her reins and holding the edge of the saddle, would attempt to reach the stirrup, and Scipio— waiting until just the right moment—would turn and move deliberately away from her so that Mrs. Townsend would be sent hopping in a circle, and Sean would follow after, desperately trying to figure out where to grab hold of the ample figure to hand her up onto the horse's back.

Most of the girls were mounted now. The men had gallantly helped them into their awkward side saddles, lifting the lighter girls straight up, and boosting the others—sometimes with the aid of a mounting block or a convenient car bumper. The women were slowly walking their mounts, handling them and calming them. Some of the women were still fussing with their skirts, draping them attractively over their bent knees and across the horses' flanks.

Jean Hunt walked up beside Catherine. Catherine looked surprised. "Are you riding today, Jean?"

"Are you kidding? I'm just helping Sean," said Jean. "Do you think I would submit to that medieval torture?" She pointed to the side saddle on Prosper, Catherine's beautiful chestnut mare.

"You are wise beyond your years," Catherine remarked ruefully. "But I only do it once a year, for the glory of the Watch, and to keep my father company. Besides, being in the parade is thrilling, even on a side saddle."

"Gillian Townsend may never find out," Jean said and laughed as the two watched Mrs. Townsend make another futile attempt at the stirrup.

"You don't know Gillian Townsend," Catherine replied. "I think she rode in the Calgary Stampede Parade before there was even a parade . . . possibly before there was even a Calgary!"

At that moment Mrs. Townsend's voice rose in anguish above the noise and confusion. "Somebody bring me a mounting block at once!" she commanded. Within a minute, four mounting blocks had appeared, and Gillian, choosing the highest, stepped into the stirrup and with a considerable heave from Sean sailed into her saddle like a ship at full mast. With a great gesture of triumph she set the enormous folds of her skirt to rights and cantered over to the women gathered in the riding ring on their mounts.

"Now, girls," she announced, "we are ready to begin."

As dawn filled the sky, the mighty beams of the waking sun sent shafts of gold and rose streaking upward. The members of the troop rode single file along the edge of the roadway in the tall, dewy grass. The bridles on the horses jingled and their hooves made gentle sounds on the soft ground, but the riders were silent, caught in the magical mist of the sunrise, and the hushed expectation of the coming day's events.

This was the day of the great parade. The opening of the annual Stampede that had been a part of their lives, and their parents' lives, from the time it had been a dusty, local one-corral show until now, when it was the greatest stampede on earth, attracting performers and visitors from all over the North American continent. The Western rodeo had its roots in the ancient sports of Rome, the games of Greece, and the playing fields of England, but its modern day form was unique. The events of the rodeo and the skills it tested had sprung from the great prairies of this raw, new land. The rodeo and stampede were wild, raw, and untamed, but in proportion and symbolic inception they embodied the great classical contests—man against nature and man against himself.

That was why this day was so exciting, even to the people bound by the British tradition of Mount Royal—people who still rode English saddles and scorned the horns and heavy stirrups of their western country. They loved the rodeo: the clothes, the animals, the ring, the grandstand, the hard-bitten, single-minded competitors. It appealed to their vision of life as something defined by style, rules, and class. Here was an event in which the people knew who they were. It was life stripped to its most elemental, and therefore, its most exciting components—life and death, triumph and defeat. And the animals! The people of Mount Royal had the aristocrat's true love of animals. They marveled at the cowponies who could turn on a dime and exclaimed over the roping horses who stood straining against the rope until commanded to slacken. They delighted in the deep-chested quarter horses and the mighty, untamed mustangs raging for their freedom.

Each year, like a pageant from the past, citizens of

Mount Royal wended their way to the gathering station where the parade began. There the parade steward directed them to their places and they formed a dignified and beautiful troop. Their presence graced the parade and seemed to deepen the meaning of the Stampede and the festivities.

In spite of Catherine's reluctance to ride sidesaddle, one of the most beautiful sights in the parade was the line of women in the Black Watch Troop, their backs straight and lovely, and the full skirts of their riding habits proclaiming feminity of a day long gone.

Catherine's father rode his dark bay horse beside her as they moved toward the parade grounds. "It's going to be an excellent day for the parade," he commented. "Something about a parade is very uplifting." He paused. "Where's Norman? He always rides in the parade when he's in town."

"Didn't I tell you, Father? He went to Red Deer to visit the Felts. He and Millicent Felt were dating last Christmas, and I guess her family invited him up to their ranch."

"That's an impressive place," her father remarked. "I did some incorporation work for Mr. Felt this year, and I went up there for a few days. Their ranch is absolutely baronial!"

"Yes," Catherine mused, "I can imagine. Millicent is like a baroness herself."

"You don't like her?" her father asked.

"I don't know," Catherine replied. "I couldn't get close enough to her to find out."

"I see," said her father. "When do you expect Norman back? Will he be here in time for his wedding duties?"

"I suppose so." Catherine was uncomfortable with the conversation. "I'm not Norman's keeper, you know. Speaking of Norman and parades," she continued, attempting to lighten the mood. "Do you remember the year he was a Dominion Scout and had to march in the parade instead of riding his horse? He came home afterward and told me that those of us on the horses have no appreciation how hard we make it for the foot soldiers who follow! He said he spent the whole parade with his eyes on the road because he was marching behind the horses of the Royal Canadian Mounted Police! In all my years in the parade I had never thought of that problem!" She reached down and patted Prosper.

Her father laughed heartily. "That must have been quite a trial for your fastidious man!"

"Not my man!" Catherine replied quickly.

The parade ground was in even greater confusion than the earlier scene at the stables. Horses were milling around, high school bands were tuning their instruments, and drum majorettes were twirling their batons. The floats and the dignitaries' cars backed up and pulled forward, nearly running into one another, and the blare of instructions over the loudspeaker intensified the noise. However, almost miraculously, everyone was finally in place, and at the dot of eight, the parade moved slowly out onto the street to begin its long morning route. For its entire length, the parade route was lined with eager spectators. Clowns and hawkers sold balloons, popcorn, and whistles. The air was bright with festive sounds, and the bands played loudly, as the parade's Grand Marshal slowly paced the mighty line.

One of the most exciting sights in the parade was the large Indian contingent. Each year Catherine watched in awe as these silent, mysterious people took their place in the ranks. Each chief seemed determined to outdo the others. Their buckskins were crusted with magnificent beadwork, their feathered headdresses colorful and regal. Catherine thought the chiefs looked more kingly than King George himself. The Indian women in their fringed boots and soft leather dresses were as lovely as fawns. Their necklaces held exquisite silver pieces, turquoise, and beadwork. On their arms they wore bracelets, and most let their black hair hang long around their lovely dark faces. To Catherine the mystery and beauty of the Indian men and women was inspiring.

The parade was longer than Catherine had remembered, and the sun very hot. By mid-morning her leg was cramped in its unnatural position around the horn of the saddle, and her riding habit felt soggy in the heat. She glanced up at Mrs. Townsend leading the women's contingent. "She must be fifty if she's a day," thought Catherine, "and look at her ride! She must have a ramrod under that riding jacket." Mrs. Townsend's back was severely straight, her head was high, and as she rode she looked from side to side with the imperious and impassive stare of a duchess. "I don't know what she's made of," Catherine thought, trying to shift her position on the saddle and causing Prosper to dance nervously out of line. Catherine fought for control; the mare was skitterish on the paved streets with the noise of the crowd and the music of the band. "Whatever Mrs. Townsend has," Catherine thought, as she finally got back into formation under her disapproving stare, "I don't think I've got it."

At the end of the route the participants milled around the parade grounds and then, in desultory groups, returned to their stables or cars. The morning ended with a strange feeling of anticlimax. Catherine was amazed at how tired she was, and after brushing down Prosper and leaving instructions for her feeding, she made her way to the Packard and sat with her eyes closed waiting for her father to emerge from the tack room where he was joking with some of his friends. Before long he came out into the stable yard, and seeing her sitting in the car, walked over and climbed in beside her.

"I think we could both use a nap," he observed, and then voiced the remark with which he had ended every parade day since Catherine could remember. "I think that was the best parade Calgary has ever seen, don't you?"

"Yes, Father," she said, with a private little half-smile, "the very best."

Catherine put off going to the Stampede for several days. One morning near the end of Stampede week she woke up early to find the house in upheaval. There were two days left until the return of Emily's fiancé, James Parker, and his parents. Catherine tried to help with the preparations, but finally in exasperation her mother asked if there wasn't something she needed to do. Catherine laughed. "I can take a hint . . . I'll go off and give Prosper a good run!"

"Yes," her mother answered, with a relieved sigh, "do that, dear."

Catherine ran up and put on her riding clothes. She pulled back her unruly hair and hurried out to her little sports car. The morning passed quickly on her horse, and she would have stayed longer, but she had forgotten to pack a lunch, and in the confusion had also missed breakfast. Shortly after noon she headed for home to get something to eat.

As she drove up in front of the house she thought how much she dreaded reentering the whirlwind of activity inside. She was contemplating heading down to eat at a lunch counter, when she saw Norman walk out the front door of his house and head across her lawn. "Norman!" she called, "when did you get home?"

Norman hurried over to where she was sitting in the convertible. He opened the door and sat down beside her. "Just the girl I'm looking for."

"I'm not hard to find. I'm always here," Catherine responded.

He looked at her beside him. Her face was luminous from the morning's ride, her hair a mass of curls, untidy but lovely. A white tailored blouse was open at her throat showing a teasing glimpse of her abundant breasts, and the jodphurs emphasized her slender waist. She seemed to exude vitality and radiance, and Norman felt magnetized by her presence.

"I'm glad you're here," he said, "because I have two tickets to the Stampede burning a hole in my pocket. For old time's sake let's go together. Let's do all the old things—eat spun sugar candy, watch the broncs, ride the ferris wheel, try the wheel of fortune, and stay until the fireworks after dark."

"Where have you been all my life?" Catherine cried.

"I thought you'd never ask! Let me go and change my clothes."

"Change your clothes! Are you kidding?" he said. "You look great! Move over. I'm driving."

They drove to the Stampede grounds on the outskirts of the city. The parking field was packed with cars. Another large field was filled with buckboards and buggies, and an open corral on one side was crowded with the horses that had brought the wagon families from their farms. About half a mile up the road, Catherine could see the area where the Indians had put up their tepees and tents. The Indians came early, several weeks before the Stampede began, and lived on this quarter section which was reserved for them. During the Stampede they wore their bright costumes and rode their painted ponies, the women carrying their babies on their backs in the traditional way. The smoke from their campfires and the smell of their cooking provided part of the atmosphere of the Stampede.

Norman stopped the Austin and the two young people stepped out and made their way to the ticket gate. Norman glanced at his watch. "The main rodeo events start at two so we can wander around until then. We've got box seats, so we don't have to get to the grandstand early."

Catherine walked through the gate and stood drinking in the noise, the sounds, and the smells of the Stampede. This was a distinctive part of her youth, and the familiarity and nostalgia of the experience always touched her. The Midway area was thick with merrymakers. Children were screaming and laughing on the rides, barkers were enticing people into their shows, and all the bustle was overlaid with the bright, piping calliope music of the carnival. The smells of popcorn and sawdust, hotdogs and spun sugar, animals and people mingled in the hot summer air. From the grandstand, rising in the far background like a modern colosseum, could be heard the muffled cheers of the crowd as they watched the events preceding the afternoon rodeo.

Norman took Catherine's arm. "Ferris wheel first!" He had to shout in order to be heard over the general uproar.

As the ferris wheel swung them high above the Stampede, she felt a thrill and a flip in her stomach. When they reached the top, the operator stopped the wheel. High above the Stampede grounds they rocked in the sunlight. Beneath them, the bright figures of the crowd, the colorful tents of the midway, the rodeo performance ring, even the glittering city of Calgary appeared like miniatures—a vast toyland of charming moving parts.

"Norman!" Catherine turned to him, her face brilliant with happiness. "This is so much fun! I love Stampede week! Don't you?"

Norman shook his head indulgently. "Catherine, that is hyperbole. Don't you think it's a little extreme to say that you 'love' something inanimate? Something as frivolous and as . . . as"—he groped for the word—"earthy as a stampede? I agree it is fun, but to say that one loves it is rather . . ."

"Don't be so pedantic!" Catherine said and laughed. "Anyway, I do love it! It isn't frivolous at all! Men are risking their lives in that ring!" Her voice rose with excitement. "And it isn't inanimate either, it's part of me . . . part of my living experience . . . one of the most real of those parts!" She looked at Norman, who was watching her with a half-mocking smile.

"Okay," she said, subsiding a little, "so I get carried away. Can I help it if I'm enthusiastic?"

Norman's face broke into a wide grin. "Apparently not," he commented dryly, and the ferris wheel began to descend. Catherine looked at him sideways. Her eyes twinkled, and she leaned over to him and whispered emphatically in his ear, "But I really do love it."

They filled up on hot dogs and soda and rode the merry-go-round on the gaudiest horses. Norman threw baseballs at stacked milk bottles and won a Kewpie doll with a sequined necklace and feather dress for Catherine. As two o'clock approached, they walked toward the grandstand, where most of the crowd was drifting.

The rodeo ring was a large fenced ring of bare dirt. It was completely encircled by a dirt race track, and another fence divided the race track from the grandstand.

At one end of the rodeo ring were the chutes and pens where the livestock were held in readiness for the various events.

Norman and Catherine climbed up the grandstand stairs and walked through the bleacher seats toward the center of the stand. They pushed their way to the box seats reserved for them, unconscious of the impression that their expensive clothes and confident manner made upon the people behind them in the bleachers. As they walked to their seats and pulled out their programs they were unaware that they were part of the show, part of the excitement of the city for these farm people who had waited all year for this one glorious week away from the dust and the heat and the grasshoppers. For these few brief days the farmers felt part of the glamour, the excitement, and the drama of the great rodeo. Their lives were often difficult, but at the Stampede they became the spectators, the aristocracy. Here, the wealthy townspeople and the modest farm folk were all part of the same audience—everyone there for the same reasons, watching together, moved by common emotions. It was the rodeo performers who stood alone at this event. They were the extraordinary ones, the champions. Some deep and atavistic instinct within the spectators knew that the real thrill of the rodeo, the bond of the crowd, the compact with the rodeo gladiators was the true and immediate possibility of death. It was the awful, unspoken reality of this penalty that made the rodeo the ultimate spectacle.

Catherine spotted a familiar figure threading through the crowd at the foot of the grandstand. He was heading for the gates that led to the racetrack that encircled the rodeo ring. "Mike!" she shouted. "Mike, over here! Mike Threefeathers! Over here!"

The man turned and looked toward the stands. Catherine stood up and waved her hands wildly. "Over here, Mike!" she called again. As the man waved and began to walk toward Catherine she sat down and explained to Norman, "It's Mike Threefeathers. He's one of Father's law clients. I've known him since I was a little girl."

Norman shook his head with faint disapproval. "He can't be riding in the rodeo today, surely. He must be nearly fifty years old!" Norman picked up one of the programs and began to scan the names listed in today's events.

Mike Threefeathers walked up to the front of the box and shook Catherine's hand. "Well, little Katie, what a nice surprise to see you here. I thought you might have grown out of this stuff."

Catherine laughed with pleasure. Mike Threefeathers was the only person on earth who called her "Katie." When she was a young girl, her father had brought him home for dinner. Catherine could tell her mother was not very pleased to have the dark, quiet man, a half-breed, in her home, but her father had admired and respected him. When he had introduced Mike to eight-year-old Catherine, Mike had put out his hand to shake hers, and said, "How are you, little Katie?" That was the first time she had heard that nickname. Years later she had asked Mike why he called her Katie, and he said, simply, that it was his mother's name.

When Mike was first making a name for himself in the rodeo circuits as a young man, he had come to Catherine's father for help in purchasing a ranch. Mr. Summerwell had bought and managed the property for Mike for several years, until Mike was caught in a series of bad falls. For the last several years Mike had been in the hospital more than on the rodeo trail, and he finally had sold the ranch. After the ranch was gone, he had drifted out of contact with the Summerwell family.

Catherine introduced Norman to Mike, and then she stepped out of the box and walked down to where Mike was standing.

"It's so good to see you," she said warmly. "Are you riding today?"

"Yep," Mike replied. "Bronco-bustin'—what else?"

"Oh, Mike!" Catherine protested, concern and surprise showing on her face.

"I'm right as rain," Mike said. "Never felt better! Thought I'd get myself a stake and then call it my last rodeo."

Catherine looked at the man in front of her. His face was like dark-tanned leather, lined and toughened by the sun. His whole body had a strange, dehydrated look, as though it were made of leather and muscle and bone. He was wearing a finely tailored gabardine western shirt and western-cut pants and at his waist was the heavy silver and gold buckle of a world champion rider. His face was impassive and his body a tight, tough machine. Catherine, soft, gentle, and sweet beside him, could not even imagine the lifetime of courage and daring that had created this man.

"Got to go get into my workin' duds," he commented, and then grinned at her. "You sure turned into a fine hunk of woman, Katie," he said. His face grew serious. "Say hello to your dad. Tell him . . . tell him, I just couldn't talk to him. Tell him . . . hell, he knows . . . just tell him hello." He turned abruptly and walked into the crowd.

"Mike!" Catherine called and ran after him. He turned and gave her an unreadable look. She walked up to him and kissed his cheek. "Good luck today. I'll be cheering for you." She was gone. He moved on through the ragged crowd with the softness of her lips and the sweetness of her perfume gentle in his mind.

She had grown into a lot of woman, full and generous, with a body that was ripe and inviting. Her face, however, was so sweet and innocent that it did not seem to belong to her body—the one giving an invitation which the other did not even understand. Still, Mike could not help but think that such a woman might make him feel warm again. He wondered how long it had been since he had really felt anything—warmth or cold, love or hate. It was as though, as his body toughened, his spirit toughened, too. Mike knew he had become a leather man, lean and juiceless as his saddle. Only one emotion filled him, darkened his mind, and deadened his eye. It was the one thing to which his heart would not be hardened—the constant, compelling fear.

"Mike," the doctor had told him the last time he left the hospital, "there isn't a bone in your body that hasn't been broken, and there isn't a single organ inside of you that hasn't been rearranged. Your insides look like someone's been at them with a Mixmaster. The human body wasn't meant to take the kind of punishment you've given this one, year after year. You're old before your time, Mike, and if you want to live your last years with any kind of mobility, you've got to promise me you'll never sit a bronc again. There's no mending power left in you. I won't answer for the consequences if you ride anymore."

"Yeah, sure, Doc," Mike said, his flat, implacable Indian eyes looking at the man in the white coat. "Do you feel I should quit strongly enough to tell me you won't charge me for yer operation?"

The doctor laughed uncomfortably. "That's a good one, Mike!" he said, and became suddenly brisk.

"Here's your prescription. Make an appointment to see me in three weeks."

Approaching fifty, past the age to compete with the fresh young stars, Mike was now forced to face the ring again, hoping that experience and courage could compensate for lost youth and strength. Whatever happened today, this would be his last chance.

He walked over to the men who were preparing to draw the names of their mounts out of a hat. They made way for the older man with deference, some clapped him on the back. "Good to see you back, Mike." "Always wanted to see you ride." "You draw first" . . . and his hand went into the white Stetson. Mike could not help but notice the slight tremor of his hand as he pulled out the slip with the name of the horse he would ride. "Just this once," he thought to himself, "let me get the break. Let it be Dandy Dan . . . the patsy horse."

Without expression he opened the slip of paper and read the name, then he placed it in his pocket and walked toward his trailer. "Who did you get, Mike?" one of the men called after him.

He turned and looked at them, one hand on his championship belt and the other tipping the brim of his hat. "Painted Lady," he said, and went to change his clothes.

One of the cowboys shook his head. "It sure ain't Mike's day!" he said with an attempt at humor, but the expression in his eyes was solemn. In Mike those young men saw themselves as they could become, and they secretly hoped they would show the same courage, the same unbending, indomitable will in defying the toll of the years.

Catherine and Norman watched the rodeo events with mounting excitement. The first major event was the chuckwagon race. Chuckwagons, with teams four abreast, began in the center of the ring with all the chuck equipment on the ground around the wagon. Four cowboys threw the equipment into the wagon, then the team driver and assistant sprang to their seats, and the other two cowboys, outriders, jumped onto saddled horses. The wagons then made one lap of the inner ring, went out through the gate into the surrounding track, and made four laps of the track. The race was dynamic with the enormous sounds of thundering horses, the roar of wagon wheels, the frantic jangling of harnesses, and the yahooing of the outriders as they urged the teams forward. It was like a chariot race, and the teams were as deadly serious in their competition as any centurions of old. After the excitement of the race, the voice of the announcer heralded the next events—the calf-roping, the bull-dogging, the steer-toss, and the wild-cow milking. It was all exciting, glorious, and fun.

Finally, the great event of the day. The wild broncoriding. Bronc riders were the stars of the rodeo. Their event pitted man against beast and time. Eight seconds the riders must remain on the backs of these violent animals, who could twist and leap and jar and bend and smash any rider alive. The rider had to ride with one hand holding the reins, his other hand high over head, holding his hat, so that it could not touch the animal. During the ride he must continue to goad the horse with his spurs and retain his seat for the full eight seconds. After eight seconds, the rescue riders would come and lift him from the horse.

The announcer introduced the event on the loud-speaker. "First qualifying round, Mark Donner, on Mustard," the voice boomed across the ring. The horses were as well known as the riders. "Mustard," the announcer proclaimed, "a three-year-old roan, who has never been ridden the full eight seconds. Now coming out of chute number three . . . Mark Donner, number thirty-two." Every eye in the audience was glued to chute number three. The gate was pulled and a ton of horse flesh exploded into the ring. The horse was so frantic in its gyrations that it seemed blurred to the eye. The young man riding her held his hat bravely aloft, but in a sudden midair turn the horse unseated him, and grasping for a hold, he fell forward. With a mighty kick of her hind legs, the mustang threw him completely over her head, and then reared up to dash him with her front hooves. The crowd gave a collective gasp of horror, but the young cowboy with lightning reflexes rolled sideways and the horse crashed down on empty ground. Quick as a flash in his awkward high-heeled boots the young man raced for the nearest fence, the horse in hot pursuit. A gasp of relief went up through the stands as Mark Donner leaped to the fence pulling his legs high on the top railing as the horse crashed against it. The hazers came out on their horses and hazed the wild horse down the ring and into the corral. After that dramatic beginning, the remaining bronc riders were announced one after another. Some did not last more than a second. Others came out on horses, such as Dandy Dan, who gave a half-hearted performance and then trotted tamely, without the help of the hazers, straight to the back corrals. Finally, it was time for Mike's ride. The audience picked up a full-throated chant . . . "Mike Threefeathers! Mike Threefeathers!" Catherine's heart sank as she heard the announcer proclaim over the loudspeakers, "Mike Threefeathers riding Painted Lady . . . Ladies and gentlemen, you are about to see one of the great events of the western ring. Two champions pitted against one another! Only one person has ever managed to ride Painted Lady the full eight seconds, and that was Mike Threefeathers, four years ago. Both the horse and the rider are a little older . . . and I expect they are both a little meaner. This is Mike's first return to the rodeo circuit in two years . . . and here he is, coming out of chute one . . . Mike Threefeathers!"

The chute crashed open and for an awful moment the white horse with the gray feather markings stood stock still in the chute, her head pulled back and her eyes showing white. Then suddenly she tore out of the chute, her body up in the air before it even cleared the boards. She landed on straight legs and rose straight up, her body twisting and whipping in the air. The crowd began to count the seconds out loud as the lean, lone figure of Mike Threefeathers held its seat. His hand holding the white hat flew in the air over his head like a defiant flag, and his spurred boots raked the crazed horse. The audience rose from its seats as the horse and the man withstood bone-wrenching punishment, each implacable in their determination, each a mighty contender. Tears were streaming down Catherine's face, and she stood in her box, her hands pounding on the edge as she shouted with the crowd, "Six"—the seconds seemed impossibly long . . . why wouldn't the buzzer ring?—"seven . . ." and finally "eight!" She screamed, but the buzzer still didn't sound, and then, after a long moment, the loud buzz and a mighty roar nearly tore the top off the grandstand. "He did it!" Catherine was laughing and crying at the same time. "Oh, Norman! Did you see that? He did it!"

The rest of the afternoon passed quickly, and as darkness began to descend the ring was hushed and the winners of the qualifying events were announced.

"Let's go back and see Mike," Catherine begged. "I want to congratulate him. Maybe he can watch the fireworks with us in the box."

"No," Norman replied. "I think it's better if we don't ask him."

"Why?" Catherine began to protest, but something in Norman's disapproving frown made her stop and she stared at him with dawning realization. "Oh! You don't want to be seen with him, do you?" she exclaimed indignantly. "Because he's half Indian! That's right, isn't it?"

Norman looked at her coolly. "Catherine, you want to go through life picking up strays! But you don't have any discernment about people or their needs. Mike would not be comfortable sitting here in the box seats with us. He knows that—and I know that! You embarrass people because you don't recognize"—he seemed to be searching for a word and Catherine angrily inserted the words—"class distinctions!"

She stood up, glaring at Norman. "I certainly do not—" she began in an agitated voice.

Norman took her hand and pulled her roughly down beside him. "Catherine, don't make a public spec-

tacle when you are with me." His voice was cold with
warning, and Catherine sat, feeling distressed and
chastised.

"Do you want to stay for the fireworks or shall we
go home now?" Norman asked after a few moments of
strained silence. Catherine felt sick with despair. She
felt she had spoiled everything, and somehow she
could not bear the thought that this day with Norman
should end with him angry and disappointed in her.

"I'm sorry," she said in a soft apologetic voice, feeling a bitter twinge of self-betrayal as she said it.
"Please let's stay and see the fireworks together."

"That's my Cath!" Norman said, turning to smile at
her.

Just then the first great burst of fireworks emblazoned the sky. Catherine lifted her tear-stained face to
watch as the radiant flares formed a flower of light,
and then each individual flame curved out into the
night and began its slow descent until it flickered and
was gone. One after another the brilliant rockets
bloomed in the night and vanished into nothing.

After the spectacle ended, Norman and Catherine
made their way to the car and drove silently back
home. Catherine breathed the cool night air as the
convertible slipped through the sleeping streets. When
they arrived at her house, Norman got out of the car
and opened the door and then escorted Catherine up
the front steps.

"Thank you, Norman," she said hesitantly, still uncertain about his mood and not wanting to say anything to upset him further. "It was a lovely day."

In the darkness Catherine seemed very small, and

Norman found her apprehension endearing. For a moment he felt himself to be the strong, daring, older playmate once again.

Very slowly his fingertips brushed her arms from the wrists to her shoulders. His hands moved smoothly, curving gently against the silken fabric of her blouse and the tender curves of her arms beneath. As his hands caressed her, he sensed the trembling of her body at his touch, and he felt a surge of pleasure.

Lightly, he rested his hands on her shoulders, and then, as she leaned slightly toward him he lifted his hands away with a soft, triumphant laugh.

"Oh, Cath!" he said. "There is no one like you!" He bent and kissed her gently on the forehead.

Catherine turned away from him, confused and agitated, but sensing that for some reason he felt very satisfied with the day. As she entered the house, before she closed the door, she heard him running down the front steps to his car, and she thought she heard him whistling softly to himself.

CHAPTER FOUR

A Mount Royal wedding was an elaborate ritual entailing formal dinners, club parties, teas, showers, dressmaker fittings, meetings with the caterers, luncheons, and endless meticulous detail. When Emily's fiancé, James Parker, and his parents arrived in Calgary at the end of the week, the social pace picked up even more.

When they first met, Clifford and Lucy Summerwell had been relieved to find that the Parkers were not brash and informal—as they feared all Americans were—and the Parkers, Stan and Mary, were relieved to discover that the Summerwells were not stuffy and boring—as Canadians often were. Actually, both sets of parents were much alike, and the wedding festivities took on a special warmth as a result.

Norman served as a willing escort to Catherine, and together they attended the round of parties, if not with much enthusiasm, at least with a great deal more enjoyment than either of them had expected.

Two days before the rehearsal dinner a small, formal supper was held at their club so the Parkers could meet the Summerwells's closest friends. Catherine sat in the club's dining room and watched Emily and James at the head of the table. Mrs. Mortenson was seated next to James and was talking steadily. James was smiling politely, a slightly strained look on his pleasant face. Emily sat next to him. Seated on her right was Mr. Townsend. His patrician features masked a rare comic gift, and Catherine saw Emily laugh at some apparent witticism, but she looked confused. It seemed to Catherine that the two young people looked lost and dutiful in the midst of their parents' friends. They were trying so hard to do everything right.

Catherine turned impulsively to Norman. "When I get married, I refuse to be public property!" she exclaimed.

Norman looked up from the Baked Alaska he was eating. "The meringue's burnt," he commented, and then continued in the same even tone. "What do you mean, 'public property'?"

"Just look at Emily and James. They haven't had two minutes alone since James arrived. If they aren't at a party surrounded by people, they're at home surrounded by family, or else they're off in separate directions running errands for the wedding!"

"What's wrong with that?" Norman asked. "A wedding is a once-in-a-lifetime event. It needs to be surrounded by ritual and tradition and merrymaking. After all, they'll have the rest of their lives alone together!"

"But don't you see? They won't! If they don't have some say in their own lives now, nothing will ever change! They'll get back from their honeymoon, and then they will have to be 'at home,' and all the same people will come calling. Emily is going to be on display—the 'young bride' and James the 'promising young oil executive' . . ."

Norman looked at Catherine, exasperated. "And what would your recommendation be? That people walk downtown and get married by a Justice of the Peace?"

"No . . ." Catherine thought for a moment. "But it seems to me that when you're starting a marriage . . . that's a time when you should be able to think about each other . . . not be so worried about what other people are thinking about you. . . ."

"Catherine, when are you going to understand that there is never a time in life when you can stop caring what other people think?"

"But that's what I mean, Norman! That isn't fair or right! It should be *their* life!"

"It is, you silly," Norman whispered. "And keep your voice down. You don't want anyone to hear you talking this way." He looked at her and smiled in a conciliatory way. "Look, Catherine, believe me. They are going to be fine. Anyone can tell they're right for each other just by looking at them."

"That's what I mean," Catherine whispered urgently in return. "You don't marry people because they 'look right'; you should marry them because they *are* right! I don't think they've been alone enough to know for sure how they feel. It was such a short courtship! But everyone kept telling them they were made for each other."

"It's really not your problem, you know," Norman said gently. "Anyway, they're going to be fine. Anyone can see how happy they are."

Catherine looked again at Emily and James, who were now rising from their seats to go into the dance hall. Emily was smiling at James and he was smiling back at her so lovingly that Catherine felt a twist at her heart. However, Catherine still felt that Emily had a tight, weary look around her eyes, and she wondered what her sister was thinking. She had to admit that the pair looked like a storybook bride and groom—James, so dark and handsome, and Emily, so petite and fair. As they walked toward the dance floor, Catherine turned back to Norman with a teasing smile. "All I know is . . . if any man looked at me the way James just looked at Emily . . . ."

"Okay!" Norman said and laughed. "I give in. Come on, let's dance. If I have to eat one more long dinner of Beef Wellington and creamed lettuce, I am going to atrophy!"

They danced for a while and then made their excuses and Norman took her home. Catherine went to bed, and about midnight she heard her parents come in. An hour or two later she heard Emily going into her room. Much later she roused once more. In the dark she listened, and for a moment thought she heard the sound of crying. She listened, only half-awake, and when she heard nothing else, went back to sleep.

The next morning Catherine rose before anyone else in the house. James and his parents were staying at the Palliser Hotel. Since this was the day before the wedding rehearsal, everyone planned to use the day to clean up last-minute details. No social engagements were scheduled.

Catherine was sitting in the breakfast room with a glass of orange juice. She had on an old white terry cloth bathrobe, and her hair was pulled back in a ribbon. Someone rapped on the bay window and she looked up, startled. It was Norman. He indicated in pantomime that he was coming in through the kitchen door, and a moment later she heard the door open and Hilda's muffled exclamation, "Why, Mr. Norman! You sure take a body by surprise!"

"Good morning, Hilda," Norman replied, and then he came through the swinging door into the breakfast room. "Good morning, fair one," he said, taking in the battered bathrobe and Catherine's bare feet in a single glance.

"If I'd known you were coming for breakfast, I would have dressed," Catherine replied tartly.

"No need," said Norman. "I haven't come for breakfast, I have come to take you away from all this."

"Sounds great! When do we leave?"

"I'm serious. The next two days promise to be grueling, and I thought maybe we could go spend the day at Lake Louise. A little rest and relaxation in the glories of nature should get us ready for the reception line." Norman was to be James's best man.

Catherine paused for a moment, thinking. "I'll have to ask Mother," she said. "They may need me around here today. But if not, I'd love to go with you."

Norman sat down at the glass-top table and picked up the folded newspaper. "I'll have Hilda bring me some toast and juice while I'm waiting," he said. "You go ahead and check with your mother, and if you can go, we'll leave as soon as you come down."

Catherine got up to leave. "By the way," Norman continued, "why don't we stay for dinner at the hotel. You may want to bring some formal clothes."

"I'm so sick of being dressed up," Catherine said. "Can I wear something casual for the day, if I promise to look fancy tonight?"

Norman was already deep in the paper. "M-m-m? Surely . . . ." he murmured.

Knocking softly on her parents' door, Catherine waited for a muffled response and tiptoed into the darkened room. Her parents were both wide awake, and Catherine had the distinct feeling that her father had just returned to his own bed. They both looked at Catherine with identical bland expressions that gave them an oddly guilty look. Catherine felt embarrassed, but she also wanted to laugh.

"Sorry to bother you," she whispered, as though they were still trying to sleep. "Norman wants to take me to Lake Louise for the day. We'd stay at the hotel for dinner and drive home tonight. Do you need me for anything?"

"No, dear," her mother replied. "I'm going to be spending the day with caterers and florists. Emily and James are going to spend the afternoon working at their apartment—I've warned them not to get too tired! You run along with Norman. Don't be too late, though. Remember, tomorrow is the rehearsal, and it will be a long day. Gillian Townsend has done so much work on the rehearsal dinner . . . and the men are planning some kind of bachelor party after that!" her mother rambled on.

"I guess I'll go then." Catherine bent and kissed her mother's cheek and then went over and kissed her father. "How are you holding up?" she asked.

"Fine," he answered. "I can always escape to the office if I need to."

"Please tell Emily I'm sorry not to say good-bye to her. I think she's still sleeping. She got in late last night."

"I know," her mother replied, and her mouth formed a straight, disapproving line. "She's going to have circles under her eyes in the wedding pictures if she isn't careful."

Catherine hurried into her room and threw on a pair of old linen slacks and an old white shirt of her father's. She grabbed the shirttails and tied them around her waist. Then she brushed out her hair and caught up the tresses in a loose, untidy bun. She put on a pair of grubby tennis shoes and rolled up the legs of the slacks. In a small bag she put makeup and evening clothes. Then, grabbing a canvas sling bag, she threw in a towel and her bathing suit and ran downstairs like a child let out for recess. She banged into the breakfast room and put her bags on the floor with an exuberant thump. "I'm ready!" she proclaimed.

Norman looked up from the paper he was just finishing. The paper was as neat and unwrinkled as when he began. He paused for a moment and refolded the newspaper exactly as it had been folded originally. Then he gave Catherine a long look and slowly raised his eyebrows. "You're sure you're ready?" his voice was gently mocking. "You should have kept on the bathrobe."

Catherine looked at Norman. His hair was shining and smooth, his light duck slacks had a knife-sharp press, his dark sports shirt was open at the neck. Impeccable! Even his canvas deck shoes were spotless.

"Oh, Norman," she said and sighed, looking at the

shoes, "don't you even walk on the dirt like other people? How could anyone have clean deck shoes?"

Norman was a wonder to her. She couldn't imagine how any living person could always manage to be so neat and tireless and secure. She felt he must know a magic formula that she had missed. There was something that he and Emily and her mother and her friends knew that had never been told to her! She knew all the right things to say and do and wear, but so often with her everything came out all wrong.

With a shrug of resignation she turned to go back upstairs. "I'll go up and change into something dressier."

"No, of course not. You'll be fine," Norman answered, but his voice lacked conviction.

A flare of anger rose in Catherine, and without considering what she was doing, she remarked, "I thought I was the one you were taking to Lake Louise, not my clothes."

Norman's eyes narrowed with anger, and Catherine knew she had made a dreadful mistake. Just as she knew sometimes she looked all wrong—and was doubly hurt when someone spoke to her about it because she knew it to be true—so Norman was defensive because he knew he was sometimes a snob and was resentful when someone accused him of it. She had offended Norman with her barbed remark.

Norman's voice was cool. "I am taking you. If you still want to go, let's leave."

Without another word, Catherine picked up her luggage and, miserable, followed him through the hall and out the front door. Norman's car, a Buick roadster, was parked in front of her house. In silence they walked to it. He helped her in, closed the door, climbed into the driver's seat and drove through the sun-drenched streets of Calgary, out into the surrounding foothills. By noon they were into the cool mountain roads, past Banff, and on the narrow winding road that led through emerald-green Rockies upward to the jeweled Lake Louise, hidden in the mountain's silence.

The ride had been strained and uncomfortable. As the mountain air bathed their faces through the open windows of the car, and the dramatic vista of the view lifted their spirits. Catherine took a deep breath and braved the subject. "Norman, I'm really sorry about what I said this morning," she began.

Before she could say anymore, Norman turned to her. "I'm sorry, too," he said. "It wasn't anybody's fault. We're both just tired." He smiled at her, but she sensed something measured and appraising in his manner. It reminded her of her mother. She wanted to talk the difference out—wanted him to understand how she felt—but something in his manner told her to leave the subject alone. Throughout the remainder of the day she tried to be her gayest and most interesting. But somehow the day stayed flat, and Norman seemed distant. She felt the outing had turned into a disappointment to him, and he had stopped trying—was simply living it through until he could go home.

They walked around the perimeter of the lake with the great Princess Louise Hotel at the one end. Its long slope of green grass extended to the edge of the lake, and the famous Icelandic poppies of Lake

Louise danced in their vivid colors along the sapphire water's edge.

"This is the most beautiful lake in the world," Catherine said, looking across the lake as it lay in the bowl of the green mountain top, with a brilliant white glacier sparkling on the opposite side. All the colors in the clear mountain air were of an inconceivable brightness, and Catherine drank in the crystal beauty.

"I think I'm going up to the hotel for a swim," Catherine said impulsively. "Do you want to come?"

"I thought we'd go boating," Norman said, "but if you'd rather go swimming . . ."

"No, no!" Catherine replied quickly, feeling she was in the wrong again. "Whatever you'd like to do. I don't care."

"Let's swim," Norman said, after a moment of thought. "That way we'll be at the hotel and can get the early dinner seating. We won't have to be late going home."

"We don't need to stay for dinner, Norman," Catherine said in a small voice.

"Nonsense," Norman replied with false heartiness. "Of course we're staying."

It was late in the afternoon and the pool was almost deserted. A few sunbathers were still lying on the chaise longues trying to catch the last rays of the sun. Norman was already swimming as Catherine walked out of the dressing room, came to the edge of the pool, and tested the water with her foot. He looked up at her as she stood in the late afternoon light. She had piled her hair on top of her head to fit it into her cap, which was dangling from one hand. Her suit was the same color blue as the lake, and it clung to her curved figure. From where he was in the water Norman could not help noticing the looks of the men who were lounging at the poolside. By the expressions in their eyes, he could tell they found Catherine's body as inviting and appealing as he did. And that was what was so remarkable. In clothes, her full bosom and rounded hips were often an embarrassment to him. She sometimes looked matronly and dowdy, but here, when the lines of her body were defined, and the long, slender legs were revealed, she looked like the woman of every man's most private dreams. And yet she never saw that in herself!

He knew this was the thing that drove him mad about her. She was so consistently inconsistent. She demanded to be accepted as she was and felt no requirement to be what he wanted her to be. She went through the years, changing each time he saw her, and yet unchanging in that particular quality. Here she was, in the afternoon light, a goddess!—she who had been a gnome for the whole of the day. He swam to her with short, angry strokes, and she lifted on her firm, small feet and flashed through the air in a perfect dive. Surfacing beside him, her face dripping and merry, she called, "Race you!" In the wild race and the freedom of physical release, they both worked out the tensions of the day. Half an hour later, winded and laughing, they pulled themselves up on the side of the pool. Catherine was gasping for air, and Norman grabbed a towel from the side of the pool and put it around her shoulders since a cool breeze was blowing in across the lake. He began to gently wipe her shoulder dry, patting the towel across her back. The pool was deserted now, as guests had gone in to prepare for the formal dining hour. Slowly Catherine turned and looked at Norman. Her eyes were wide with surprise and longing. With their faces so close he saw the delicate perfection of her skin, its colors like tinted porcelain, her finely modeled nose, the firm, lovely chin, and her eyes, green as glass in the light of the setting sun. Her lips were soft and as richly colored as the poppies.

With infinite care, Norman reached in front of her and took the far edge of the towel in his other hand. Slowly he pulled the edges of the towel across her back and she, gently and naturally, moved toward him as he continued to exert a gentle pressure until she was pressed against him. He could feel the wet imprint of her bathing suit and the full sweet curve of her breast. He dropped the edges of the towel, and as it fell to the ground he put his arms full around her and kissed her parted lips. She seemed like someone mesmerized. She had not uttered a sound—had not resisted him—and yet her arms remained at her sides, as though she were a helpless prisoner, waiting for a command, a direction. He could feel the rise and fall of her breasts against him as her breathing quickened, and he could sense her great swell of feeling.

In his whole life nothing had been so inexpressibly sweet as that kiss. It was as though he were slaking some deep and unknown thirst. What would have happened next he did not know, but a discreet cough in the background caused Catherine to spring apart from him and quickly pick up her towel. The bathhouse attendant made an elaborate show of tending to his broom as he swept past the young couple. "We'd better go dress for dinner," Norman said in a normal voice.

"Yes," Catherine whispered, and then she cleared her throat. "Yes, yes, of course. I'll see you in a while." She hurried into the bathhouse.

Norman had arranged to meet Catherine in the hotel lobby. The Princess Hotel had been built by the Canadian Pacific Railroad, which owned Lake Louise, and it was a work of fanciful art—a glorious fairytale castle in the Rocky Mountains. It was a gathering spot for the great and near great, the wealthy, and the nouveaux riches. The enormous crystal chandelier in the lobby sparkled on a dazzling international crowd.

The bell had rung for the first seating in the dining room, but Norman was not feeling impatient, even though Catherine was keeping him waiting as usual. His mind was still on the wonder of their kiss and the magic of her nearness.

"A penny for your thoughts." Her voice was soft and womanly, and he turned to look at her. Catherine was wearing a draped sea-green dress with stylish wide shoulders and long sleeves. Her neckline was fastened with two diamond clips and her hair was pulled back smoothly and rolled at her neck. She was wearing high-heeled green sandals that showed through a discreet slit at the hemline of the dress. She looked older—sophisticated.

"Perfection," Norman whispered, and tucked her arm in his. They walked toward the dining room, and every eye in the lobby followed the handsome couple.

As they stepped off the deep pile rug onto the polished parquet floor, the heel of Catherine's sandal slipped, and if Norman hadn't been holding her, she would have fallen. "Well," she said, laughing, "that's what I get for trying 'fancy.' I feel like I'm masquerading anyway."

Norman just shook his head and the headwaiter, hiding a little smile, led them to their table. The dinner was not a success. They were both preoccupied by conflicting feelings and thoughts. The security of their old childhood relationship was completely shattered, and as yet they had built nothing to replace it—except for one long, perfect kiss. Neither one was sure, however, just what that kiss meant, and so they ate almost in silence.

They drove home in the clear dark air, with the stars so bright they looked to Catherine as though she could have leaned out the car window and plucked a basketful to take home.

"See you at the rehearsal in the morning," Catherine whispered as Norman took her to the door, and then, impulsively, unexpectedly, she put her hands on his shoulders, and standing on her toes, gave him a shy, hesitant kiss. Hurriedly she opened the door, and he was alone on the steps. For a moment he stood looking at the starry sky. Then he heaved a heavy sigh and walked back to his car.

The house was dark and Catherine took off her shoes and crept up the carpeted stairs. As she passed Emily's room she heard a sound, and she paused. Knocking softly on the door, she waited for an answer.

"Who is it?" came Emily's muffled voice.

"Me, Catherine, may I come in for a minute or are you too tired?" There was no answer, and, disturbed, Catherine opened the door. In the moonlight she could see where Emily was lying on the bed, and she could hear the soft, stifled sounds of her sobs. "What is it, Emily?" Catherine cried, alarmed. "Shall I go get Mother?"

Emily bolted upright in the bed. "No!" she whispered fiercely. "No, oh, please, Catherine, don't tell her! I'll be all right. I'm just being silly." Her sister put her face in her hands and began crying again. Catherine hurried over to the side of the bed and put her arm around Emily's quaking shoulders. "It's all right, Emily, cry it all out, and then we'll talk."

For another minute or so, Emily continued to cry into her handkerchief. Catherine could see she was beginning to calm down a little, and she poured a glass of water for her from the little pitcher on her bedside table. "Now then, can you tell me what's wrong?" she asked.

"I don't think I want to get married." Emily began to cry again, but she struggled to control herself. "I don't think I love James. I don't think I love him at all!"

Catherine felt a desperate feeling of panic. She tried to keep her voice calm. "What do you mean, Emily? Are you sure you don't want me to get Mother?"

"No! No!" Emily grasped Catherine's hand tightly. "No, you mustn't tell her! I couldn't talk to her! I can't tell anyone! It's too awful!"

"What, Emily? What are you talking about? Has something happened?"

Emily began to cry again, and she put her head down onto the pillow. "Look, Em," Catherine said, gently, calling her by their old nickname, "it's just me, Cath, you can tell me anything. I won't tell anyone. I promise." She giggled. "I'll even cross my heart and hope to die!"

Emily lifted a tear-stained face from the pillow, and there was the ghost of a smile on her face. "You never do break promises, Cath, I know that," she said softly. "But, I don't know if I can even talk about it. . . . Oh, Catherine, I don't want to get married. . . . There are so many things I want to do . . . and James . . . what if I have a baby right away. . . . What will I do?"

Catherine sat quietly, her heart felt like stone as an awful suspicion came across her. "Emily," she asked, "has Mother talked to you about . . . you know. . . . about . . . sex?"

Emily kept her eyes down, and her voice was almost inaudible. "She gave me a book and took me to see Dr. Sawyers. He"—her voice dropped even softer—"fitted me for a diaphragm and said he'd answer any questions I had, but I couldn't stand the way he looked at me. . . ." Her voice trailed off. "Everyone's going to know, you know. I mean, they talk about me looking so pretty in my wedding dress, and what a happy future we're going to have . . . and everything like that. But when we leave after the wedding, they're all going to be thinking about what we're doing. They're all going to know. . . . Oh, Catherine, it's so awful! I'm so afraid . . . and James . . ." Emily shuddered.

"What happened?" Catherine asked.

"Today we were at the apartment alone for a couple of hours getting everything ready for when we get back from the . . . the . . ." Emily's voice caught on the word. She stopped and then went on, "the honeymoon. Anyway we were almost finished, and we were sitting on the couch, and James came over and . . ." Emily began to cry again, only this time it was a hopeless, tired kind of crying that was very piteous to Catherine. "Oh! I can't talk about it. . . ."

Catherine patted her shoulder. "It's all right, Emily, you've got to tell someone."

"He came over," Emily continued in a toneless voice, "and you know, we sort of started kissing a little—just nice, happy feelings, and then . . . he changed! I mean he really changed . . . he wasn't gentle or sweet or respectful. . . . He just suddenly touched me . . . I mean . . . Catherine, he really touched me, in private places, and he undid the buttons on my dress, and I said, 'James, what are you doing?' and he said, 'Don't worry, I won't hurt you!' I wanted to scream, but I was afraid someone would hear us. And his voice didn't even sound like James's voice, and he went on telling me how pretty I was and how much he loved me, and how hard it was to wait . . . and I just pushed him away as hard as I could, and he looked at me, and he was sad or angry . . . I couldn't tell which . . . and I told him never to do that again, and he just sat on the couch and said in a really calm voice that I didn't understand this was what marriage was all about—and he loved me, and in two days we were going to be married . . . and I couldn't look at him, Catherine. I don't want to ever see him again. What am I going to do?" Her voice began to shake again, and Catherine forestalled her tears with another question.

"Did James do anything to you . . . I mean, did he try to . . . ?"

"Oh, no! Nothing like that! He told me he loved me too much to do anything to hurt me. It's just that he was so different. So disgusting. He touched me with his . . . his . . . " Emily gave a little shudder, and Catherine felt fear.

"With what?"

"With his tongue!" Emily whispered, and her voice shivered with emotion. "When he kissed me, he touched me with his tongue!" And suddenly Catherine was laughing.

"Emily! Was it really all bad or is part of the reason that you are so disgusted is because you kind of liked it?"

Emily looked up at her sister with an angry glance, and then, as their eyes locked, her face began to soften into a smile. "Well-l-l," she whispered. "At first it was kind of . . ."

"Look, Emily, I don't know a whole lot about marriage and sex, and I imagine Mother thinks she's done her part by giving you that technical book and taking you to Doc Sawyers. But from what I've read in novels I think there's a whole lot more to it than you could find in a manual. If what I've read is right, it can be downright wonderful. Sure, it'll be a new experience for both you and James, but it sounds to me like you are both pretty healthy specimens, with strong instincts, and my hunch is, if you just let James show you the way, you might find it's enjoyable."

"But, he was just like an animal. I mean, panting and pawing . . . I didn't like that!" Emily pouted.

"Em, you've got to understand, you're not going to be a little girl anymore. James loves you, and if you'll let him, he'll make a woman out of you. Let go of some of that . . . you won't get mad if I say the word, will you?"

"No," said Emily.

"Prissiness, Emily," Catherine said. "You don't want to go through life being untouched, a prissy little girl dressed up for a party. I think you're going to love marriage, Emily. Look at Mother! She loves it, and she's still a lady! Besides, you've got enough of Father's common sense in you to do it. I know you can, and I think it's what you need. Don't turn a man away who loves you so much that he almost lost his head over you!"

"M-m-m . . . he did, didn't he?" Emily mused, and she scrunched down under her covers with a smug little smile. "He really did, Catherine." Emily thought for another minute. Then she curled up into a little ball, with her knees close to her chest. She closed her eyes and prepared to go to sleep. "Catherine," she murmured, as Catherine moved toward the door, "I still think it's mean to just tell us about the wedding dresses and the parties. That isn't what a wedding is about at all!"

"I guess," Catherine whispered, and went toward her own room. She paused for a moment out in the hall and said to herself, "I think there's a lot they don't tell us."

* * *

After the confusion of the rehearsal, the wedding party went to the Townsend home for cocktails, before going to the hotel for the rehearsal supper. Cocktails at the Townsends was a rare privilege. The Townsends were the most nobly born family of Mount Royal. Their grandfather had come over as a remittance man but had died as a duke, having inherited the title from his brother who passed away in England.

The old duke, before he died, built one of the finest mansions in the Mount Royal section. The house was now nearly fifty years old and had not been renovated in all that time. The Townsends, living on the interest from an old trust fund, were genteelly poor. Their home was crammed with priceless antiques, paintings, and oriental rugs; their clothes, preserved year after year with gentle brushing and seasonal storage, were made by the finest tailors of England. But the wools were rusty and threadbare, and the velvets and silks worn and fragile. Nonetheless, to every occasion the Townsends imparted a great gentility and style that no amount of money could assure. They lived simply, rarely entertaining, but presiding as the privileged guests at everyone else's parties. They joked about their own eccentricities and frugalities. The Townsend home had been among the last of the homes to get indoor plumbing (and it was rumored that Gillian had sold one of her diamonds to pay for it). They had converted an old water closet into the simplest of bathrooms. By some oversight the room had no window, and the family referred to it with genteel humor as the "Black Hole of Calcutta."

A sister of Mr. Townsend lived with the family and had served for as long as anyone could remember as a sort of household factotum. She was part of their family, and also a quiet, efficient housekeeper, who saw to it that the exquisite family possessions endured even if in somewhat fragile condition. On the rare occasions when guests were invited to the Townsends', it was considered an honor.

After cocktails, the rehearsal guests went to dinner in a private dining room at the Palliser Hotel. Conversation was lively, and Catherine noted that the faces of the other guests were flushed and excited as they joked with the prospective bride and groom. "Emily's right!" Catherine thought to herself. "They're not thinking about how pretty she's going to look in her dress. They're thinking about . . ." She wondered if she dared tell Norman what had happened last night. She wasn't sure that she understood it all herself, and she felt that in the past Norman could have helped her understand. In the old days she could have talked to him easily, but now there was an undercurrent of restraint between them. Although once during the evening, when she was flushed and laughing from the unaccustomed drinking, he had reached under the table and held her hand for a moment. She had turned to him and her eyes widened. He had seemed to blur before her, and then smiled a triumphant, secret smile and had taken his hand away. Now she found herself wishing he would put his hand back. She felt a tingling where his hand had rested and wondered about it. She felt hot and strange.

At the end of the supper, the men rose in a group and excused themselves to continue their party in a private room upstairs. James bent and gave Emily a kiss full on the lips as he was led out of the room.

"Not to be outdone," Norman stated, his voice slightly slurred. He bent and kissed Catherine in a courtly sweep.

"What goes on at these bachelor parties?" asked Catherine, her curiosity inflamed.

"Manhood rites," murmured Norman and left.

The women were driven home in hired limousines. As Catherine and Emily mounted the stairs with their mother, Catherine whispered to Emily, "Are you feeling better?" and Emily turned and gave her a veiled look and shrugged her shoulders.

"What are you girls talking about?" asked Lucy, walking behind them.

"Nothing," said Emily, "just girl talk."

Their mother walked between them and put an arm around each one. "My little girls," she said. Then tears filled her eyes, "After tomorrow nothing will ever be quite the same again."

"Better!" Catherine interjected quickly. "We'll have another man in the family!"

"Yes," Lucy said, "James is a wonderful young man. I know you're going to be very happy, Emily, dear. Now get to sleep, both of you. Tomorrow's the big day."

The day of the wedding dawned fair and clear. Emily looked bright and radiant, with no trace of the tears of the nights before. Catherine, looking at her, prayed that she had given her the right advice. She had said the things she thought would help Emily, but she knew that her own understanding of relationships between men and women was based entirely on novels she had read. Still, when Norman had kissed her the day before, she had experienced a glorious and disturbing sensation, and she sensed that the romantic experience must be as wonderful as the books said.

Like most great occasions which have been eagerly anticipated, the actual wedding day took on an aura of unreality. The hours whirled by in a maze of scenes and events—the cathedral in its solemn hush; the lovely bride in her magnificent train; the photograph session in the garden; the house reception; the wedding party smiling and shaking hands; the sound of the stringed orchestra; the champagne; and the sweet perfume of the flowers. The house looked strange and unfamiliar, with most of the furniture removed and the doors opened wide as if to show off the terrace, the gardens, the lavish caterers' tables, and the great, plentiful baskets of flowers.

When the buffet was served, Emily and James cut the cake and soon after they led the first waltz. The guests joined in dancing, and the evening was filled with joyous celebration.

As the reception drew to a close, Catherine and her mother went upstairs with Emily and helped her dress in her going-away suit. There were kisses and hugs and tears, and James, handsome and flushed, waited for Emily at the bottom of the stairs. The bridesmaids, rosy in their talisman dresses, gathered at the foot of the staircase, and Emily flung her bouquet of orange blossoms and baby's breath. When Helen Mortenson caught it, a shout of hilarity went up! Emily ran down the stairs gaily, and in a cloud of confetti and rice the young couple dashed to the waiting car—which was brightly festooned with streamers and shoes—and drove off into the night.

Catherine's mother came over and gave Catherine a hug, unable to hide the tears in her eyes. "Well, she's gone. And now a part of our lives is gone, too." Catherine understood what her mother was saying, that the childhood years were irrevocably past. Emily, her sister, was now James's wife. She felt a twist of pain, a sudden nostalgia for herself and pity for her mother. With tears in her eyes she nodded and kissed her mother's cheek. The two of them walked down the stairs feeling closer than they had for a long time.

The orchestra was playing, and although the party had thinned, the younger people were still there dancing and talking, and the evening was alive with their merrymaking. Catherine sighed. As maid of honor, she was wearing a yellow dress with a wide ruffled neckline and a very tight waist. Her feet, in high-heeled yellow sandals, ached from standing, and she felt heavy with weariness. The house seemed hot now and stuffy, and the strong fragrance of the orange blossoms cloying. Catherine decided that if she were to make it through the rest of the night, she would have to get some fresh air. She stepped over to the buffet table, took a cool glass of punch, and slipped out the French doors onto the side terrace. The lights from the house did not reach this little section near the kitchen garden, and she stood in the cool dark night, breathing in the breeze from the Bow River valley below.

"Aha! I saw you sneaking out here! Thought you could abandon your duties, did you?" It was Norman, leaning on the doorjamb watching her as she stood in the shadows. "If you intend to play hooky, then I am, too!"

"Your feet can't possibly hurt as much as mine do, Norman. Besides, the last thing they need in there is another girl. We outnumber the men at least three to one. You are a priceless commodity at any party—witty, a good dancer, quite handsome . . ."

"What do you mean . . . quite," Norman demanded. "You know I'm the best-looking man here . . . now, admit it?" He walked toward her with mock menace.

"All right," she said, laughing, putting her hands up as though to fend him off, "I'll admit it. But if you quote me, I'll deny it!"

She shifted mood, and her voice became serious and sweet. "Norman, I want to thank you for being so wonderful to me these past days. You've really . . ." She searched for words.

Norman interrupted. "Don't thank me, Catherine," he said. "Friends don't need to say those words . . ." He walked over to her. A waltz was just beginning, and the sounds of the violins were sweet and faint in their private corner. "Dance with me," he whispered.

Without a word Catherine moved into his arms, and they began a slow and stately circle. They were both good dancers. Catherine instinctively sensed the direction of Norman's lead, and the two moved together almost as fluidly as one. Catherine felt light in Norman's arms. He loved the feeling of her moving to his slightest whim, the subtle rhythms of her body and the smooth swell of her hips. To their quiet spot on the terrace, the music floated as faint as a memory. Slowly Norman stopped dancing, not letting go of Catherine, but holding her against him, scarcely moving, just swaying gently back and forth to the soft music. His arms grew tight around her waist, and he drew her close to his body. She gasped with pleasure and surprise, and when he looked down, her eyes were on his face, trusting and sweet. He could smell her perfume and the gentle heat of her body. Her neckline was wide and where one side had slipped down, he bent and kissed the rounded shoulder bared in the moonlight.

"You're tired," Norman whispered, his voice deep and gentle. "Let's go out in the old garden. We can rest for a few minutes away from all these people."

"Yes," Catherine breathed, and stooping, she slipped off the high-heeled sandals and, holding them in her hand, picked up the full skirts of her dress and walked across the dew-wet lawn. "Oh!" she exclaimed as her stocking foot touched the lawn, "it's cold!" and she began to run. Norman, laughing, ran after her, but he didn't catch her until she had slipped through the high hedge of the play garden and was sitting on the old stone bench by the far wall where the chain fence had been. The view of the city below the hill was magnificent. She sat down on the bench with a great sigh. "You cannot imagine how wonderful it is to get those shoes off and sit down for a minute. But only a minute!" she warned. "I've got to get back."

Norman said nothing, only stood in front of her. His mind was filled with her tonight. He didn't know if it were the excitement of the wedding—the bawdy jokes, the look in James's eyes as he and Emily left for their honeymoon, the drinks, the magic of the sum-

mer's night, the moon, the music, the sweet perfume of
Catherine in his arms—or all of this together. But he
felt as though he were under a spell. Here they were,
he and Catherine together in the quiet secluded garden where they had played as children—but this was
no child before him now! This was a woman. And a
woman he wanted. He looked at her chestnut hair,
spilling forth from the pins that restrained it. Then
his eyes roamed to her lovely throat and the tender,
fragile line that led to the sweet, round swell of her
breast.

Without a word he reached forward and touched
her shining hair, and then slowly he sat down next to
her, his eyes never leaving her face. She sat as still as a
wild thing, frightened, shy, and silent. With hands so
light they scarcely seemed to touch, he traced the outline of her face, the firm sweet chin, and then, cup-
ping her face in his hands, he bent and kissed her. He
continued to kiss her as his hands tenderly caressed the
line of her shoulders. So gentle was his touch that it
seemed the breeze itself was caressing her, and then his
hands reached behind her and softly released her bodice, and the wide-necked dress fell from her shoulders.
Still he did not cease kissing her, touching her eyelids,
her cheeks, her neck, and her full soft mouth with his
light, searching lips.

As her dress loosened he slid his hand down her
shoulder. As he touched her, he felt her lips quiver.
Sweet and dizzy with passion, Catherine moved toward
him. Her lips were opened and her breathing quick
and urgent. Norman's body shook, and he could feel
himself drowning in a wave of such passion that he
almost lost his conscious self.

His arms tightened, and he kissed her with a fierce, demanding kiss. Her response was filled with a flame of passion that matched his own. It was as though he had opened a flood gate, and her open, innocent nature, caught in the wonder of discovery, was yearning toward him, trusting, loving, seeking. Her body was like a magnificent instrument, his to have, to use, to enjoy. She would give it all, he knew—he had only to show her . . . "Catherine," he whispered hoarsely, "so much . . . so much . . ."

He drew back to look into her face. Her eyes had opened wide with astonishment at what she was feeling, and the look on her face was one of trust and love. It was the same look she had had in her eyes when he had climbed the oak tree for her cat when she was seven years old. The look in her eyes when he had rescued her from the class bully. The look she had always worn when he had proposed something outrageous and daring. She had always been willing to go with him. She was always willing to try, even if she were frightened, if he said a thing could be done. It was the look that had made him a man, through all the lonely years of his childhood, it had been this look of warmth and admiration and love that had made him know he was important, that he could do the impossible. He looked into her eyes now, and he knew she was waiting, ready to give him everything that was hers to give, and his body ached to take it. Her body was so impossibly inviting, the body of a Delilah, the body of passion, the body of a woman—ripe and rich. What love could be found there—what love such a body could give!

But above the body—this urgent, womanly body—was Catherine's face. Catherine, his truest friend, his heart's own. Catherine who, even in her giving, would always be herself. Innocent, unrestrained, impetuous, overwhelming—there could be no changing that. The very things that would make loving her an impossible ecstasy would make living with her an impossible reality. And somewhere inside, the part of him he sometimes hated, the part that was calculating and careful, the part that was untouched by feeling—that part of him looked at Catherine before him now, open, trusting, and passionately awakened by his embraces. And as he looked at her leaning toward him, her young face flushed, her body luminous before his eyes, he knew he could not take her. He knew that if he accepted this love here and now, there would be no turning back; and he knew for certain that the decision to love her would ultimately destroy them both. Abruptly he stood up, aware that if he stayed close to her the sweet power of her would overwhelm him. As he stood up she almost fell, and in her surprise, she looked up at him, hurt and uncomprehending at his sudden motion. Her glance fell on her breasts and swiftly she gathered the bodice of her dress and covered herself, looking away from him in confusion and shame. Norman stood staring out over the city and tried to make his voice steady. "I guess all this wedding business went to my head. I'm sorry."

"Sorry!" Catherine's eyes had a hurt and stunned look. "You're sorry!" she repeated. "What's wrong with me, Norman? What did I do wrong? Are you ashamed of me? I don't understand. I've never felt any-

thing like this! I don't know what happened to me.
. . . Norman! Don't say you're sorry! I'm so ashamed.
. . ." She began to cry.

"Catherine," he begged, "don't cry . . . it's all
right. Nothing happened."

"Nothing happened?" Her voice shook. "Norman, I
love you so much. What did I do wrong? Is it wrong
for me to feel these things? What happened? Why did
you stop? Don't you feel it, too? Am I so unappealing
you can't stand to love me?"

He looked at her, all trembling and sorrowful, and
everything in him wanted to reach out to her. The
love was so strong in him that he had to force himself
to remain cool and steady.

"Catherine," he said, struggling to keep his voice
controlled, "you didn't throw yourself at me. Darling,
I practically seduced you! My best friend! Can you
think how awful I feel?"

Catherine was beginning to bring herself under control. She straightened up and took a deep breath, her
voice suddenly calmer. "No," she whispered, "if you
had really wanted to seduce me, you could have.
There's something about me. I'm all wrong. I turned
you away. And I don't even know myself . . . I don't
understand what I'm feeling . . . I only know that I
want . . . I want . . ." Her voice was full of misery.
"Norman, don't make me beg. I want to love you. I
want you to love me, and you can't . . . you won't
. . . you never will. What am I to do?" Her shoulders
sagged and she sat, small and hopeless, before him.

He knelt in front of her and held her chin in his
hand, turning her sad, teary face toward him. He
could remember how she cried even when she was lit-

tle. Her whole face would seem to crumple as though misery broke her serenity into little pieces, and her face would turn red and strained. She had always done everything so completely. "Catherine, I love you more than I will ever love anyone as long as I live. But you know better than anyone else, there is a part of me that doesn't want love, that doesn't want to give up its right to be aloof, superior, untouched by others. You would want all of me. Your love, your passion are too open, too giving, too tender. You would invade me, you would take me over, you would force me out into the roar of life, and I would hate you for it, and you would hate me because I would shut you out. I'd criticize you, too, and try to change you . . . and you don't love yourself enough to be able to take that. Can't you see, we'd destroy one another and all the love that we have? It just wouldn't be enough. Not even all the love you have to give—it's too much—and yet it isn't enough. Can't you see that? It isn't your failure, it's mine. I love you too much to do that to you."

"No, you don't, Norman," she whispered fiercely, "you don't love me enough. All that talk and that noble acceptance of blame. Even my love embarrasses you. I can't even show love like a lady! But Norman," she pleaded, "I could love enough for both of us—I'll change, I promise. I won't try to change you . . . I love you just as you are."

"My darling," Norman said sadly, "I know you believe you'd change—or at least you'd try. But the one thing that I don't want you to do is change. What could you do with that eagerness, that impulsiveness, that pride? It—it's you, Catherine."

"Please, Norman," she was crying softly, her voice infinitely sad. "What can I do with all this feeling . . . it hurts so much . . ."

She had grasped his hands in her fine, firm hands, and he felt the satin warmth of her skin. Slowly, he turned the small, square hand over in his and looked at the palm, like a half-opened flower in his strong dark hand. He bent and kissed the fragrant skin, and then gently released his grip, and stood up. "Catherine, my darling, I didn't want to tell you here, not like this. But I can't let you go on. You'll hate me if I let you say anymore."

He paused and cleared his throat, and looking out across the valley, not meeting her eyes, he said, "Millicent Felt and I are announcing our engagement next week." He wanted to go on and explain to her. He and Millicent had a comfortable platonic relationship. Millicent was independent and undemanding, and he had decided that such a marriage was suitable for him. Before he could say another word, however, Catherine was standing before him, her eyes crackling and her voice full of bitter mockery. "Millicent Felt!" She laughed harshly. "Millicent Felt?" He wondered if she were going to get hysterical, and he wasn't sure he could handle a scene. Then he realized she was laughing, a bitter laughter full of self-mockery and derision, but laughter nonetheless. "Millicent Felt—that namby-pamby stick of a woman, that prim and proper ice cube, that bloodless, pale, untouchable statue! I wish you happiness, Norman, I really do! You are going to need all the good wishes you can get! I just want to know—do you call all your loose women 'darling'? Was I your last fling? I thought you really did love me, Norman, maybe, just a little. But if it's Millicent you want, then I know how wrong I must have been . . ."

She whirled from him, her skirts catching the moonlight, and in a second, she had slipped between the hedge and was gone from his sight. Beside the low stone wall her yellow satin slippers lay on the grass in disarray. Without thinking, Norman picked them up and neatly set them side by side. Then he sat down on the little bench and looked out over the city. For this one blessed moment he felt empty, but he knew in a few minutes he would be filled with loathing and self-hatred. For one last painful moment he allowed himself to remember the sweet passion of her embrace and the gentle surcease of her love, and he knew that all the rest of his life, in the moments of truth just before wakening, he would reach for her in the night. And in the night he would call her name one last sweet time. "My Catherine, my own, my lost darling."

CHAPTER FIVE

For two days after the wedding Catherine stayed in her room. Hilda took trays of food up to her, but they were returned to the kitchen untouched. Numb with misery Catherine sat on the window seat in her old terry cloth robe, her hair uncombed and the yellow bridesmaid dress in a heap on the floor where she had thrown it. She could not stop thinking about the scene in the garden with Norman, her humiliation at his rejection, and her anger at the news of his engagement.

On the third morning her mother came into the room.

"Catherine, dear, I know you're tired after the wedding. We all are. But I'd appreciate it if you would start coming down to meals with the family. Hilda has too much to do to be running up and down stairs for you. Besides, dear, look at you! What if some of your friends should drop in . . . or Norman. You certainly don't want him to see you in that disreputable robe."

Catherine stood up slowly and picked up the yellow dress from the floor. She walked over to her closet and hung up the dress and pushed it into the deepest corner. As she closed the closet door, she turned and faced her mother.

"Don't worry, Mother, Norman won't be dropping in . . ."

"Well, you never know," her mother said briskly. "He was certainly more attentive to you during the wedding week than a formal escort needed to be. I wouldn't be surprised if he were really interested in you, Catherine. If you would just make an effort . . . you know, fix yourself up—make a fuss over him—you still treat him as though he had just dropped over for a game of 'one's up.' You're not getting any younger, dear, and Norman is such a fine man."

As her mother talked, she walked over to Catherine's bed and punctuated her remarks with quick, firm movements as she smoothed the sheets, plumped the pillows, and fixed the bedspread. If she had been looking into Catherine's eyes, she would have seen them fill with pain and anger. Finishing her comments, she gave the bed one last satisfied pat and walked to the door. Her mother called over her shoulder, "I forgot to mention—your trunk came from Edmonton this morning. I'll have the gardener bring it up. I'm going out to do some errands and am having lunch with Gillian Townsend. Remember, we expect you at dinner tonight at seven."

When her mother left, Catherine went over to the bed and surveyed it. The bed was perfectly made—not a wrinkle on its smooth exterior. Angrily she grabbed the spread and pulled it crooked, then she took the pillows and heaved them one by one at the far wall.

There was a soft knock on the door, and the gardener, Mr. Sykes, came in, carrying the heavy trunk which held her college things.

"Thank you, Mr. Sykes," Catherine said, as he put the black-bound trunk on the floor.

"Glad to help, Miss Catherine," he replied, and putting on his soft peaked cap, he walked down the stairs, happy to get back to the yard where he felt much more at ease than in the hushed elegance of the big house.

With a heavy heart Catherine went in to bathe. Norman, her truest friend, the person who knew her better than anyone else, didn't love her—didn't want her. She felt as though life had nothing left to offer her, and she didn't know what to do with herself. It was as though all purpose and joy had fled from her and in their place were only rage and pain and frustration. She could not bear to think about it!

Drying herself with a towel, she put on a pair of slacks and an old work shirt and threw herself into a frenzy of activity. First she opened the trunk and began unpacking it with furious motions, sorting the clothes into piles for cleaning, putting away, or discarding. At the bottom of the trunk were her college papers. She picked them up in armloads and threw them heedlessly into the wastebasket. When the basket was full, she stuffed them into a cardboard box to be thrown away. As she gathered up the last load, one of the papers fell to the ground, and in retrieving it she recognized a poem she had written in Creative Writing.

Professor White, her English professor, was a charismatic teacher with a dark well-trimmed beard and slightly Satanic eyebrows. She had had a crush on him in her sophomore year and had wanted to impress him. This had been the first poem she submitted to him. She remembered working on it for days, polishing and refining. When she had handed it to him, she was convinced he would marvel at her writing ability.

Catherine smiled as she remembered the naive pride she had felt in the poem. "I wonder if it was really any good," she mused, and quickly scanned the lines of the poem to refresh her memory.

HARVEST THE SKY

The prairies reach from the nearest eye
To the farthest touch of the downturned sky,
And the ripened, thread-spun fields of grain
Weave from the wind
In cadent waves
That rise and ebb and rise again
In the long smooth rhythm
Of the endless plain—
A sea of gold.
And over these earthbound fields of treasure,
The blue and limitless arch,
The sky—the star-sown field—
Stays ever constant.
And I, who have watched in wonder
The bounty of the earth's best sheaves,
I, who have seen their mighty measure—
If I could choose it, I,
I would still choose
To harvest the sky.

At the bottom of the page she saw the handwriting of Professor White scrawled across her neatly typed poem. "Good images," the bold masculine writing proclaimed, "but don't you think it's rather extravagant and overdone? Could benefit from wise restraint!" Catherine stared at the words, "extravagant . . .

overdone . . . needs restraint," and a harsh chuckle burst from her lips. "The perfect description of me," she thought.

She stood in the middle of the room and looked at its familiar sights. The ruffled curtains, the frilly bed, the window seat cushions, and the abundant pictures on the walls. Suddenly she rushed over, climbed onto the window seat, and began to yank down the curtains. She tore the bedspread off the bed and began tossing ruffled pillow shams into the hall. Hurrying downstairs she got some old boxes from the basement, and one by one she removed the pictures, the bowls of dried flowers, and the colored bottles. By the end of the morning her bedroom was stripped of every frivolous decorative object. The windows were bare except for the white blinds, and her bed was covered with a simple summer blanket in a white-on-white pattern. The room looked unused and sparse, like an extra bedroom that is used only for unwelcome company.

At six thirty Catherine, ready for dinner in a simple skirt and blouse, came down the stairs carrying the last box of things from her room. Her mother was standing in the dining room arranging flowers for the center of the table. She looked up as Catherine passed in the hall.

"What is that in the box, Catherine? Aren't those the curtains from your room? Where are you taking them?"

"I've decided to change my room, Mother. It looks like a little girl's room—too fussy and . . . and . . . overdone." She said the last word with a peculiar emphasis, and her mother looked at her sharply.

"Catherine," she murmured in a puzzled tone. "I don't understand what you're talking about. You had that room done just the way you wanted it. I told you then it was a bit extreme—with all the color and patterns and ruffles, but you have always said you loved it! If the truth were known, I've grown to love that room, too. And now, just like that!" Her mother snapped her fingers. "You've decided to change it."

"It's because I've changed, Mother. Me! I've changed. I'm not a little girl anymore! People don't stay the same. It's only in Mount Royal that things never change!"

"Catherine, you're not making any sense!"

"Oh, yes, I am, Mother. Yes, I am. I'm a different person than the child who used to live in that fluffy yellow room, but no one will look at me! Nobody cares who I am! I was put in a slot years ago, and it would disrupt people's neat way of looking at things if they let me change." Catherine's voice rose in intensity.

Her mother was genuinely distressed and alarmed at the display of emotion. Unsure of how to handle her daughter, Lucy sighed. "All right, dear, all right. When your father gets home, I'm sure he'll give you permission to redo the room."

Catherine shook her head with resignation. "Oh, Mother," she said softly—bitterly—"Do you really think we're talking about redecorating a room?" She picked up the box of discarded curtains and carried them down to the basement.

The next few days Catherine threw herself into redecorating her room. It was as though she wanted no trace of her past life to show within its four walls. She painted it light beige, and instead of curtains had white shutters installed at the window. The upholstery was removed from the window seat and all the woodwork was painted white. No pictures were hung on the walls, and the dressing table and bureau were bare. On the bedside table was placed a small Maidenhair fern, and that was its only decoration.

When the room was finished, Catherine's parents inspected it. It looked stark and imposing.

"Shows a lot of restraint, don't you think?" she asked them, with a tone of self-mockery.

Mr. and Mrs. Summerwell were by now completely bewildered by Catherine's detached and ironic manner. "Well," her father said with his usual directness, "if you wanted something that would look like a nun's cell, you've got it."

"Clifford!" her mother admonished. "It's very nice," she said, turning to Catherine with a conciliatory smile, "very cool and refreshing for summer. But you know, Catherine, there are different ways of being extreme . . . and this room is so simple, it is only the opposite extreme of what you had."

Catherine looked at her mother, and her eyes widened as she realized the truth of what her mother had said. Suddenly she began to laugh. She was laughing at herself, but her parents couldn't know that. Her laughter acknowledged her own absurdity—but at the same time it was cleansing.

"Mother, you'll never know how right you are! One extreme to the other!" And she began laughing again.

* * *

The day after her room was completed Catherine received a call from Jean Hunt.

"I'm working as an assistant to Sean Greer at the club's stables, and I'd love some company. You haven't been riding in ages. Come on over today, and maybe I can sneak off an hour to go with you," Jean said over the phone.

Catherine put on her riding clothes and hurried to her car. Within the hour she was in the stall with Prosper, grooming the lovely mare. Jean leaned on the stall door watching her.

"You're good with animals," Jean said in a judicial tone, "but you're not great. You don't have that inner passion for them."

"And you do, I suppose?" Catherine asked, brushing Prosper's mane until it shone.

"Yep," said Jean. "But not many people do, you know. You'd be surprised as you watch the people that spend every spare hour here at the stable how few of them really love horses. What they love is the atmosphere of the stables. You know, the smell, the people, the tack room, and the bawdy jokes—all that stuff! Like that Dr. Sawyers and his gang. They hang around here all the time, but it's because it makes them feel like big stuff. Sometimes he gets showing off, and he pulls on his horse's mouth so hard I want to take a riding crop to him!"

"Okay," Catherine said, "now that I know the ones who are in my category . . ."

"No, no," Jean exclaimed, "I didn't mean you were in his category . . . I told you—you are 'good' with horses—and that's pretty high praise coming from me."

"Okay," Catherine challenged, "if 'good' is considered above average, then 'great' must be absolutely terrific! Do you rank anyone but yourself in the category of 'great'?" The teasing between the girls was playful.

"Sean Greer is not only 'great' with horses, Catherine—he is 'exceedingly—great.' I mean, there are no words to describe that man's feeling for these animals. He's wasted at this club with all these dumb snobs, teaching spoiled children and priggish debutantes and ladies who only care if their jodhpurs fit right. I tell you, he's a genius with horses, and no one here really appreciates him. They treat him like some kind of servant. Just because he spent a few years as a cowboy when he first came over from Ireland."

"I'll have to schedule some lessons and get to know this paragon of yours a little better," Catherine remarked. "I've got Prosper ready. Do you have time to go for a ride with me now?"

"Gosh, I can't," Jean groaned. "I told Sean I'd wrap the hunters' legs."

"Okay," Catherine swung up into the saddle. "Then I'm off!"

"Catherine!" Jean cried. "You put on a Western saddle! Your father will kill you! And you can't ride alone—it isn't safe!"

"It's all right, Jean, you don't need to worry—remember, I'm 'good' with horses!" Catherine dug her heels into Prosper's sides and the fine-tuned mare began to canter down the paddock and through the open gate. The last glimpse Jean had of Catherine was the racing horse and rider, galloping across the open fields, mane, hair, and tail flying.

Jean hurried over to Sean Greer's little office at the end of the stables. She knocked hesitantly and went in. Sean was sitting at a battered desk littered with paper work. His face showed concentration and frustration.

"Blast these bloody accounts!" he muttered as Jean walked in. Seeing who it was, he shook his head and grinned. "Pardon my language, Jean. It's just that monthly book work brings out the worst in me! What is it?"

"I'm worried about Catherine Summerwell. She isn't herself. I talked her into coming over for a ride this afternoon, and she wouldn't wait for me. She's gone off by herself, hell-bent-for-leather, if you'll pardon the expression."

"Blast!" Sean exclaimed and hit the table with his clenched fist. "Doesn't she have any sense! Neglects that horse for two weeks and then expects to ride it like that! What is she thinking of? That poor mare— she'll break her wind."

"It wasn't the horse I was worried about, Sean," Jean commented wryly.

"Oh, the girl will be all right. I just hope she has enough sense to give the mare plenty of rest."

Jean left the stables at five. In the late afternoon a group of doctors, lawyers, and bankers from Mount Royal gathered at the riding club. They changed into riding clothes and congregated in the tack room with cocktails. This was the male hour in a male preserve, and the men's language and jokes were coarse and crude. Some of the men brought out their heavy stallions or geldings for a quick round of exercise or a few jumps, but then they turned the cooling-off and rubdowns over to the stable hands and gathered for their evening fraternizing.

Jean didn't like to stay at the stables after the men arrived; there was something in their suggestive looks and lewd comments that made her uncomfortable. They spoiled the clean, wholesome atmosphere of the stables for people like herself who worked with the animals. Men who were the models of gentility when they met her in her father's bank suddenly became forward and offensive in the animal-charged atmosphere of the horse paddocks. They had teased her about her discomfort at first, but eventually they'd come to accept the fact that Jean preferred to avoid them.

The men watched the women riding or walking through the yard in their tight riding clothes, their eyes narrowed in a way that made Jean uneasy. She always felt exposed when she walked away from them, certain that if she turned around quickly she would catch them watching her buttocks and the curves of her body.

Sean, too, avoided the group as much as possible; however, several of them were directors of the riding club, so he had to be careful not to offend them. He did not mind them using the club as their playground so much as he minded their lack of respect for their mounts. The only time he overstepped his place was when he saw someone mistreating a horse, and then he could not restrain himself from speaking out.

So far there had been no serious incidents, but once or twice he had felt an old anger rise in him when he saw a rider give a horse a particularly vicious cut with a riding crop, and it was all he could do not to fling himself at the rider and smash him to the ground.

Sean was an Irishman. His eyes were a clear light blue, and his dark reddish hair set off a face evenly tanned and lined from the sun. It was a square face, with fine, mobile features and a rare but generous smile. His body was lean, but with heavily muscled arms and chest. His legs were powerful machines, knotted and hard as rock. He could grip the most unruly, massive hunter alive and control it with the incredible strength of those viselike legs. Sean had ridden since he was a boy, and from his earliest childhood he had loved horses more than anything else.

With animals he was endlessly patient, but not with people. Twice in his life he had lost his temper and had discovered wells of anger and violence in himself that he had not known existed and which he feared because he had come close to doing great harm. That was why he was always very careful to be quiet and controlled in the presence of club members.

When Jean left the stables that evening, she popped her head into Sean's office one more time. "Catherine Summerwell isn't back from her ride yet, Sean. If she doesn't get back pretty soon, maybe you'd better send someone out looking for her."

"Right," Sean said, his head still buried in the papers. "Don't worry about it."

Nearly an hour passed after Jean left, and Sean got up to stretch his legs. Looking out the window, he saw the men, sitting on barrels and bales of hay, drinking and laughing. If it weren't for their expensive tailor-cut riding habits, he thought, they would look like a bunch of ne'er-do-wells.

Just then his attention was called to a figure racing across the outlying fields in the rosy glow of the sunset. The horse was running fast and hard. As it came closer, he recognized the mare, Prosper, and her rider, Catherine Summerwell.

As the two entered the paddock, he looked at the horse in horror. Her beautiful chest with the Western farthingale across it was foaming, and where the saddle rubbed her flanks, more white lather rose. The mare's flanks were drenched, and she was heaving as Catherine walked her slowly into the center ring and toward her stall.

Sean burst out of his office with the riding crop in his hand.

"You young idiot! You foolish girl! What do you think you've been doing? How dare you ride this mare like that! Look at her, will you? What kind of a creature would do that to a poor animal!" His voice was full of fury. He hit his high riding boots with his crop, but it was apparent to Catherine that he wished he could hit her.

Sean's face was dark and full of fury, and Catherine, trembling, turned and looked at Prosper. For the first time she became aware of what a cruel workout she had given the mare. She saw the lather and the drenched withers and was suddenly filled with shame. When she turned back to Sean, there were tears in her eyes.

"Oh, I'm so sorry! What shall I do?"

"First thing is to get the animal wiped down and then walk her slowly to cool her off. Don't let her drink or eat anything until she has a cooling-down period. You're not turning her over to a stable hand! I'm going to see to it that you stay here until you've undone some of the damage you've caused to this beautiful animal."

"I'll do anything," Catherine said in a subdued tone. Sean grabbed her elbow roughly, and with Prosper's reins in his hand pushed her toward the exercise and cooling-down area. Just then Dr. Sawyers came striding up and with a strong grip on Sean's shoulder, spun him around to face him.

"I say, Greer, what's this I hear you yelling at Miss Summerwell. I think you forget your place, sir." The doctor's face was arrogant and angry.

Catherine exclaimed, "No, no, Dr. Sawyers! It was my fault entirely! He was totally justified. He was trying to help . . . We have to hurry and take care of Prosper, please excuse us. . . ."

The doctor looked dubious, but Catherine's tone was urgent, and so he turned away.

"Very well," he said reluctantly, "if you're sure it's all right, Catherine. But I don't like him taking that tone with one of the members."

Catherine and Sean Greer worked through the evening on the tired horse, and in the darkening twilight they finally turned Prosper, clean and refreshed, into her home stall. Sean was still angry and had spoken hardly a word to Catherine throughout the ordeal. He had gained a grudging admiration for her, however, as he watched how carefully and gently she worked to restore Prosper, and how heartbroken she was at her thoughtlessness.

As they left the stable area, Catherine thanked Sean for his help. He looked down at the young woman. Her face was dim in the twilight, and the mass of her hair, wild and natural, caught the last sparks of light.

"I don't know what private demon you are trying to outrun, Miss Summerwell. If you insist upon working out your summer madness alone on the trails, I concede that's your business. I can't stop you from riding off by yourself, though you know it's dangerous and foolish. But I will tell you this, if you ever misuse another horse like that, you will have to answer to me." His jaw was a hard line, and his eyes pierced hers.

"I never will, I promise you," Catherine whispered. "I am so ashamed! Thank you for helping me."

As Catherine headed to her car, Dr. Sawyers stepped in beside her and walked toward the parking lot. "Are you sure everything's all right, Catherine?" he asked. "That fellow wasn't overstepping himself, was he?" The doctor's eyes were not on Catherine's face as he spoke. She followed his stare and realized that the top button of her blouse had come open. Blushing, she quickly did up the button.

"No, I told you. I was very wrong to have ridden my horse so hard today. He was only helping me to undo the damage I had done."

"Well, he's a cheeky fellow, if you ask me," the doctor went on. His voice changed and took on an odd intimate note that made Catherine uncomfortable. "You shouldn't be spending your time riding horses anyway, Catherine. You could find much more interesting things to do." He weighted the words with veiled meaning.

Catherine felt a sick, excited feeling in the pit of her stomach. She looked into the doctor's face in the early evening light. His eyes were knowing, and his full lips curled in a mocking smile. Slowly and deliberately, he

let his eyes scan her body, and she stood still, shaken
and fascinated by the naked lust on his face.

Neither of them said another word. They parted
and went to their own cars, Catherine wondering if she
had imagined the hungry look in his eyes. That night
she found sleep hard, and by early morning she was in
the car once again, headed for the stables. She prepared Prosper and was on the trails before the stable
hands were fully awake.

Day after day she returned to the stable. She spent
the days riding, and then, in the early evening, visited
with Jean or tended Prosper. The riding was good for
her; it cleared her mind and provided her a private
time where people and the problems they created did
not exist. Sean was right. She was running away from
something. But she never abused Prosper again, and
both she and the horse became fit. Catherine's skin became golden in the sun, and her riding pants threadbare from use.

Catherine, unlike Jean, was attracted as well as repelled by the men's group that hung around the stable
in the evening. At first they treated her with the manners and respect due to her father's daughter, but as
her presence became more frequent the group began to
consider Catherine fair game for flirtation.

Catherine's mother would not allow her to eat in
her riding clothes, and so she ran upstairs to change
before dinner each night. One evening when she entered the dining room there was an uncomfortable silence. Her father was holding a newspaper in his
hand.

He held it out to Catherine. "Did you know anything about this?" he asked, his eyes troubled and loving.

She took the paper. It was opened to the society page. On it was a picture of Norman and Millicent with an announcement of their engagement and wedding plans.

"Yes," Catherine said. "I've known for ages. He told me the night of the wedding."

Her father looked at her with sudden understanding. "Why did you keep it a secret?"

"I didn't keep it a secret!" Catherine burst out. "What does it have to do with me? I mean, Norman's a friend, but that's it! I don't have to talk about what people are doing . . ." She sat down at the table. Her mother and father looked at her with compassion. Unable to bear their gaze, she pushed herself away and stood.

"I'm not hungry. I think I'll go out for a drive."

The next day Catherine rode into the evening. When she returned from her solitary ride, the men were gathered by the jumping ring wagering on some horses who were going through the course. Catherine came over and joined them. It felt good to be surrounded by them. Their easy joviality, their earthy humor, and their obvious admiration for her body made her feel careless and comfortable. She had noticed that the men liked to jostle against her, as if by accident, and often would linger, touching her a moment longer than necessary. Part of her disliked this, but another part reacted with a jolt of pleasure and an odd feeling of power.

One of the jumpers was giving its rider a lot of trouble. "*I* could get that horse to perform!" Catherine said to Dr. Sawyers as they leaned against the high railing of the enclosure.

"I'll wager you a kiss that you can't," he said in his deep, drawling voice.

Catherine blushed and the other men laughed. "I won't take your wager," she said, her head high and her cheeks flaming, "but I will ride the horse."

In a moment she was over the bars and had walked up to speak to the rider. The young man seemed happy to relinquish the saddle, and Catherine was up on the big bay gelding in a flash. The horse was heavy and restive, with powerful legs and a fiery temperament. Catherine looked small astride the English saddle perched on his back.

Sean Greer came over and joined the group of spectators. In the past days he and Catherine had formed a wary friendship. They spoke often, but never of anything personal. Sean felt a nagging sense of concern about the young woman. He did not understand her days of desperate, lonely riding, and he worried about her increasingly casual relationship with the men who hung around the stables. It was as though she took no care for herself, almost seeking to destroy herself, or at least her reputation. There was an innocence about her that made Sean suspect that Catherine had no idea what she might provoke as she stood laughing with the men, her blouse tight across her breasts and her body teasingly inviting in snug riding pants and skin-tight boots.

Tonight he watched her as she concentrated on controlling the restless horse. He saw her legs clench and heard the murmur of her voice as she stroked his neck and tried to gentle him. Her small square hands were firm, and she looked every inch the horsewoman. Sean felt a surge of pride. He had taught her how to love the horses, and she had been a good student. How much she had learned! He became conscious of Dr. Sawyers standing next to him talking to one of the men. Catherine had turned the horse and was now riding away from the group. The horse's smooth flanks gleamed, and Catherine's firm round buttocks and full hips moved in its rhythm.

"Now, gentlemen," said Dr. Sawyers, his eyes drinking in Catherine's figure and his voice redolent with suggestiveness, "that's what I call a wonderful mount!"

All the men laughed at his double entendre and their eyes raked Catherine. Sean felt a surge of anger more violent than he had ever felt in his life. For a moment he thought he would die from fury, or that he would have to kill the man beside him. In a frantic effort for self-control he said nothing, but he gripped the fence railing with his enormous hands, until he could feel the blood vessels break under his fingernails and sweat pour from his brow. He forced himself to concentrate on Catherine as she walked the horse up to the jump. Then slowly, carefully, she rode the horse away from the jump, and suddenly she touched the gelding with the tip of her crop, and he exploded toward the barrier. The powerful sound of hooves pounded across the turf, and then the gelding was soaring over the bars in classic form. Catherine lay flat and smooth on his back. The jump was beautiful, and

Sean's heart flew over the barrier with her. As she turned the horse and rode toward the group of men waiting by the fence, Sean turned on his heel and walked away. He could not bear to be there when the men began to talk to her.

Catherine saw Sean leave, and was sharply disappointed. She had thought he would be proud of her, but apparently he was indifferent to her achievement. The men crowded around her, congratulating her. Dr. Sawyers was especially attentive. He casually put his hand on her leg as she sat on the horse and then he raised his arms to help her dismount. As she jumped from the horse his powerful hands ringed her waist and held onto her a moment too long. Startled, she looked into his eyes, dark with veiled desire. His sardonic smile frightened her. Catherine felt as though he knew he could make her do anything he wished. His sophistication and assurance, his practiced physical charm both attracted and repelled her.

Dr. Sawyers's eyes held her with a strange power and as she turned to accept congratulations from the other men she felt his hand, unseen by the others, gently stroke the curve of her back. Without looking at her again, he removed his hand and walked out of the ring.

She shuddered, and a strange mixture of desire and distaste made her mouth feel dry. "Excuse me, gentlemen, I'm late for dinner," she murmured. Disturbed, she hurried to her car and drove home.

The next day Catherine did not come to the stables until afternoon when the place was almost deserted. Sean, working in the tack room, noticed that Catherine seemed dispirited and tired. She slowly saddled and mounted Prosper but seemed undecided about going out for a ride. As Sean watched her circling the exercise ring, he noticed some movement in the stables on the other side of the club. He saw Dr. Sawyers was saddling a horse.

Something in the doctor's furtive movements bothered Sean. He thought how frequently he had heard the doctor make veiled allusions about Catherine. One afternoon the doctor had joked with another man. "Catherine could find what she was looking for a lot faster if she didn't ride alone. Someday I'll ride with her and give her what she's really looking for." Remembering the doctor's boast, Sean made a quick decision. He walked over and mounted the horse he had saddled earlier for a canceled lesson. Dr. Sawyers came riding past him. "Thought I'd keep Miss Summerwell company today," the doctor said casually as Sean passed.

"I'm sorry, sir," Sean replied, "but she has asked me to go riding with her today. I am showing her some of the new trails, so she won't get lost. You're welcome to come, too, of course."

Anger clouded the doctor's face. "No," he said curtly, "that wasn't what I had in mind."

"Sorry, sir," Sean said and cantered over to Catherine. "Don't say anything," he said to her softly. "Just fall in with me and ride toward the field."

They rode in silence for several hundred yards. Sean, glancing back, was conscious of the watchful dark figure of the doctor on his horse.

Finally Catherine, puzzled and frustrated, could not stand the silence any longer. "What is going on,

Sean?" she asked. "Why are you riding with me? Where are we going? And why the silence?"

Sean gave her a dark, angry look. He had lived his life never letting anyone affect him—never letting himself care for any other person enough that he would not be free to leave whenever he chose. And here was this strange, impulsive unhappy girl—all unpolished and naive—and she affected him like the horses he loved. She was like them. She needed understanding and guidance. She needed caring. Her innocence was no shield for her; it was her greatest enemy.

"You are so foolish!" he exclaimed. "You don't see anything except the things you want to see! Like the first day you rode Prosper into the ground, and you didn't even see you were doing it! Because you just didn't want to know!"

"Why are you riding with me then? If I'm so impossible, why do you even bother?"

Sean gave an exasperated sigh. "I don't want to talk. Let's ride."

They rode through the afternoon, and in a lush green meadow they raced their mounts toward the sparkling river and the green grove of cottonwoods clustered on the bank. When they entered the grove, the warm, humid air closed round them, and the hum of insects and the silence of the woods wrapped them in a spell. They watered the horses and tied them to saplings, and went exploring the river bank.

"Sean," Catherine called, "I found a bush of choke cherries! Come help me pick them!" Sean had been sitting by the river bank tossing stones. He rose reluctantly and walked into the green woods. She was standing by a laden bush, her mouth already red from the cherries she had eaten.

"Have you ever eaten one of these things?" she asked. Then she added in the same kind of tone she had heard the men use at the stable, "They are sweet but they make your mouth pucker."

Sean started in anger and walked over to her. He grabbed her wrists in his powerful hands and began to shake her furiously. "Don't you ever talk that way! Don't you ever speak in that tone of voice or cheapen yourself. Those men are evil, and they are having an evil influence on you, and you don't even care. It's like you are some kind of child playing with dynamite and laughing about it. Do you hear me! You can't tease and play with men and not expect to get badly hurt. Sex isn't a game. Men are not playmates! Love isn't a toy!"

She gasped and raised her hands in front of her face as though she thought he would strike her. "I wasn't playing—I didn't know I was playing," she stammered. "I—I—don't know what I'm doing! It's like some wild thing inside me—I just don't care. I want to stop hurting! I just want to rest—to sleep—to be happy again . . ." Her voice was broken, and the pity of it ran through his heart like a knife. He let go of her wrists and put his arms around her for fear she would fall.

A great burst of feeling flowed between them. It was like a wild joy, a feeling at once of both transcendent happiness and devastating sorrow. He could feel her trembling in his arms and he felt the urgency of her body against his.

Suddenly she threw her arms around him, and in a pleading voice whispered, "Kiss me!" Knowing he would regret it, and yet knowing he could not stop himself, he bent to her and touched her berry-stained lips. He kissed her softly at first like a thirsting bird would drink from a flower and then more and more urgently until he thought his heart would burst with the beauty of it. For the first time in weeks Catherine felt herself escape from her private prison of anger and pain. Sean's strength and warmth, his tenderness and passion, filled her emptied heart and watered the arid misery of her summer.

"Oh Sean, Sean," she whispered, "I love you. I do! I do!"

Nothing else could have stopped Sean. He had been on a great slide moving toward an inevitable conclusion, but the sound of her voice brought him to reality like a harsh, cold wind.

"No, Miss Summerwell," he said, his voice firm and calm. He continued holding her in his arms, but he gently relaxed the pressure. "No, you don't love me. You are just unhappy," he said. "Something or someone has hurt you, and you know that I care. You are my friend, but you don't love me. There can be no love between two such as you and me."

"What do you mean, Sean?" she cried. "Because I'm a club member, and you are the stablemaster? We can't act as a man and a woman?"

"Partly," he answered, "but mostly we cannot love because it was your sorrow that brought us together. To build love on sorrow is to build love that has no foundation, for the love will erase the sorrow, and when the sorrow is gone, the love will go, too."

"But this"—she stroked his cheek with her hand and,

rising, kissed him again on the lips—"was not friendship."

"No," Sean replied. "That was passion, and it was beautiful. But without love, passion is an impostor."

"Then I do not understand a lot of things," Catherine said, and hung her head against his broad chest. She listened to his deep steady breathing. And then looked up at him and smiled, with a touch of mischief. "Are you sure I don't love you?"

His laughter filled the grove, and as the emotions eased, they began to talk. Catherine told him about Norman and he listened gravely. She explained her feelings about Mount Royal and her conviction that she could never fit in or be accepted on her own terms.

"It's yourself you have to find first, Catherine," he said as they rose from the ground where they had been sitting. "You have to find yourself, and love yourself, before you can find someone else to love. It's hard for most men to love a woman who doesn't love herself."

As they walked over to untie the horses, Catherine put her arms around Sean again. "Kiss me one more time—as a friend," she asked. He bent and kissed her, and his arm tightened involuntarily. For a moment he held her very close, and then, slowly and gently he released her.

"I feel I've just been given a beginning," Catherine whispered.

"No more hanging around that doctor and his crowd at the stables," Sean demanded. "Promise!"

"Promise," Catherine said solemnly.

They came out of the grove of trees and mounted their horses. The afternoon was almost over, and their shadows were long in the setting sun. They rode in companionable silence back to the stables. But Sean was troubled because his feelings for Catherine were not as simple as he had told her. He knew he felt great emotion for her, and that such emotion could cause nothing but disaster for both of them if it were ever expressed. He promised himself he would never speak to her on a personal level or be alone with her again. The other thing that was troubling him was that once or twice in the gathering twilight he thought he had caught a glimpse of another rider, far behind them, and he wondered if anyone had observed them together.

"Maybe it would be best if we entered the stable yard separately, Catherine," Sean suggested as they neared the club. Catherine was indignant. She would not consider the subterfuge since she deemed it unnecessary. So, many of the club members saw them ride in together.

As Sean had suspected, Dr. Sawyers had followed them. The doctor remained hidden outside the cottonwood grove during the long period of time Catherine and Sean had spent there. And it only took a few hours for him to spread rumors through the club. By the following morning Catherine's father received an anonymous phone call and two unsigned notes informing him that his daughter was having an affair with the club stablemaster. The notes were signed, "A friend."

Clifford Summerwell closed up his office immediately and hurried home. As soon as he entered the door, he knew that someone had already passed the ugly story on to Lucy. She was sitting in the living room, her face as white as a sheet, tear marks staining her face.

"It isn't true, you know, Clifford," she said as he entered the room. "Catherine would not do such a thing. It is just an ugly, ugly rumor."

"Yes," Clifford said, "it is an ugly rumor. Unfortunately, rumors can hurt as much as the truth sometimes. I am going over to the stable to have a talk with this Sean Greer. Where is Catherine?"

"In her room. She's very upset. I told her we'd talk before dinner."

The scene between Clifford Summerwell and Sean Greer was painful for both men. They were both men of pride and dignity, and they each cared a great deal about Catherine.

As soon as Mr. Summerwell entered the stable offices, Sean rose from his desk and said, looking him straight in the eye, "What they are saying is not true, sir. Catherine and I are not lovers. She is a sweet and innocent young woman."

"I appreciate your telling me that. And I believe you. But as Catherine's father I must ask myself why would a man of reputation and standing such as Dr. Sawyers start such a rumor if he did not have something to base it on?"

"Out of anger and hurt pride," Sean replied.

"What do you mean, sir?" asked Clifford Summerwell.

"It was my impression that Dr. Sawyers had unwholesome designs on your daughter. Yesterday I took the liberty of accompanying her on her afternoon ride. I believe Dr. Sawyers was angry about that."

"Is that all there is to tell?" asked Mr. Summerwell.

Sean took a deep breath. "No," he said. "I have nothing to lose since I have already been released from my job, and I think I want you to know the whole truth. I do love your daughter, but I would never do anything about it."

"What do you mean . . . you love my daughter? How dare you presume . . . ?"

"Because I am a man, and she is a complex and attractive woman. I did not want to love her, and she will never know that I love her. I understand our stations perhaps better than you, Mr. Summerwell. But I will tell you that it was not I who went to her, but she who came to me, in great need. She is filled with sorrow and troubles, and though we did nothing wrong, nonetheless those few hours I spent with her will always be the finest of my life."

Mr. Summerwell looked at the horseman for a long moment and then he reached his hand out and said, "I think I would like to shake your hand. Perhaps you are the only one who has really cared for Catherine. Maybe the rest of us were too busy with the person we thought she should be."

When Catherine was told Sean had been fired from the club and that he had left Calgary without saying good-bye, she begged her father to find him so that they could help him. But her father explained Sean wanted it this way. He did not want Catherine to know where he was, and out of respect for Sean, Catherine must accept that.

Catherine was furious with the Mount Royal Riding Club. "How could they fire a man on the basis of a lie!" she shouted. "How can they treat reputations so callously!"

Finally her father could bear her anger no longer and he spoke to her firmly. "Catherine, Sean knew that he was chancing his job when he went riding with you. He understood that if a breath of scandal were associated with his name no one would trust their children at the club again. Can't you see that you were wrong not to have been more sensitive to his reputation? If you hadn't been so careless with yourself, he wouldn't have been forced to try to protect you. At least try to understand what he did for you, and see if you can't learn something about yourself from this."

Catherine looked at her father with wounded eyes. "I know," she whispered. "I know."

That night Catherine slept fitfully, and she wakened to a sharp sound. Listening, she heard it again. The sound of pebbles striking against her window. She sprang from bed to open the shutters. Down on the moonlit lawn she made out the figure of Norman. He was standing under her window, his hand raised to pitch another stone.

She opened the window. "What are you doing?" she whispered fiercely.

"Come out and talk to me . . . please . . ." he whispered back.

For a moment she thought she would shout no and close the window. But when she saw him standing there, she could not bear not to go to him after all these weeks.

She met him on the lawn in her light cotton nightgown, holding a shawl wrapped around her. He took her arm and pulled her toward the lawn swing. "Do you remember when we were little, and we used to sneak out at night like this and play 'Red Rover'?" he whispered.

"Yes, I remember, Norman," she said with some asperity, "but I'm sure you didn't sneak over here after all these weeks to reminisce about our childhood."

Norman sat down and put his head in his hands. His voice was muffled and miserable. "Catherine, I think I'm going out of my mind. Millicent and I are very happy. She is all I ever wanted in a woman—and we're going to be married in a week . . ."

Catherine stood up. "I didn't come out here to hear about your idyllic life, Norman. Tell it to the newspapers."

He reached up and grabbed her hand. "Catherine, it isn't idyllic . . . that's what I'm trying to say. I thought it was what I wanted—all neat and proper—but there's no fun, no excitement! It's . . . flat. And at the oddest moments I find myself thinking about you. That's the only time I smile . . ."

"Well, I'm glad to know you find me amusing."

"And then I come back from Red Deer, and I hear this dreadful rumor about you and that man from the stables. Catherine, I know it isn't true, but I have to hear it from your own lips. You'd never have anything to do with a man like that—a club employee . . . a . . . cowboy!"

"Norman," Catherine said, and her voice was firm and even. "Norman, he was a man. A man in ways you could never understand. He wasn't afraid to take chances, he wasn't afraid of loving and being loved. He dared to give up everything just for caring about another person. You couldn't even understand a man like that, Norman. He isn't even within your framework of comprehension."

"What are you saying, Catherine? That you were lovers? I know it isn't true. I can't bear to think of you like that! If you did give yourself to him, then why didn't I take you when I could. What did my sacrifice mean? I could have had a memory of love at least."

"Norman, you didn't stop yourself from loving me because of wanting to protect me. You stopped because you wanted to protect yourself. Don't imagine noble motives."

"Catherine, whatever happened, tell me now, in the memory of our old friendship. Did you become Sean Greer's lover?"

Catherine looked at Norman for a long moment in the waning moonlight. This friend who had filled her childhood, this hero who had shaped her dreams, this dream lover who had filled her heart and emptied it in a single blow. She looked at him—vain, selfish, handsome, arrogant, demanding, and brilliant. He had come back to her again, expecting her always to be here, always to be what he wanted, to be his for the asking. The bitter humor of the situation struck her. He needed to believe through the coming years of his marriage that she was still there—the passionate dream, the willing slave, the potential fulfillment of all his private desires—his constant assurance, just as she had been for him through all his growing years. With infinite tenderness she took his face in her hands and kissed him full on the lips, then slowly she stood up and glided toward the house, her soft gown fluttering around her body.

"Catherine," he said desperately, "you must tell me."

She turned to him with an enigmatic smile and said, "When you find out what love is . . . then you will know whether he was my lover or not. Then and only then . . ."

"Catherine!" The word sounded like a groan. She was gone.

CHAPTER SIX

In the following days, in spite of the whirlwind of gossip that refused to die down, Catherine was oddly calm. She did not attend Norman and Millicent's wedding. Instead, she sent the ugliest Dresden vase she could find, knowing that Norman would hate its gaudiness, but Millicent would prize it for its expensiveness. She imagined Norman's frustration every time he would see the vase in his home, but he would never be able to explain to Millicent why he would want to put it away. She was sure Millicent would display it in a conspicuous place. It was a small revenge but it gave Catherine an amused satisfaction.

Catherine's parents were keeping to themselves. They had canceled several social engagements because of the scandal. The Summerwells felt their presence caused a feeling of awkwardness among their friends. The incident was too good a story to be ignored in Mount Royal, especially during the hot, idle weeks of the waning summer; and it was widely circulated and discussed.

Most people in the tight-knit Mount Royal community conceded that Catherine and Sean Greer had been victims of Dr. Sawyers's spite. Nonetheless, it was smugly whispered by many that Catherine had behaved in a most improper manner—riding alone and flaunting herself in front of Dr. Sawyers and the other men. She had been asking for trouble.

The matrons of Mount Royal sat at tea in the hot afternoons and spiced the air with whispered comments about the "known carnal nature of men" and how "one really can't blame a man if he is roused by a wanton woman." The last was said with raised eyebrows and prim lips.

Gilliam Townsend with her usual forthright bluntness said that Dr. Sawyers was a "blackguard" and a "serpent in the midst of innocence," and added, "good riddance to bad rubbish." She also stated in no uncertain terms that Catherine was a fine girl with not a single fault but "flightiness, and Sean Greer is one of nature's noble men and the members of the riding club and the horses will be the worse off without him." After having delivered herself of these opinions, she refused to discuss the matter any further with anyone.

Others were less kind. The rumors continued to be whispered. Teen-aged girls who had taken riding lessons from Sean Greer and half imagined themselves in love with him lulled themselves to sleep with passion-filled fantasies of themselves in the river grove in the embrace of the former riding master. They envied Catherine her experience and embellished it with their own adolescent longings.

Dr. Sawyers, too, had his supporters. Many a young matron attracted to the handsome doctor had accepted his gentle ministrations as he listened to her heartbeat, and while knowing his touch improper, had felt, nonetheless, a dangerous lovely thrill. It seemed to these women now that he had been a fine doctor—a little too forward with the ladies—but perhaps only because he had too warm a heart. They felt it had been forward of Catherine to lure him on. "If she held herself so cheap as to spend her days hanging around the stables, then you can't blame the men for thinking of her in that way!" they whispered.

Mrs. Mortenson felt sorry for Catherine, and remarked to her daughter Helen that she felt it was Catherine's innocence that had led to the whole situation. Helen turned to her mother, eyes wide, and confided, "Oh, Mother, I don't think we really know Catherine at all! Emily says she knows a lot about . . . oh, you know . . . 'those things.' And at Emily's shower she acted so peculiar. . . . I think she must have very powerful passions."

With a slight frown Mrs. Mortenson looked at her prim young daughter who affected such a proper, self-righteous air. Mrs. Mortenson stood up and remarked with some curtness, "For one so young, you seem to have the gift of absolute judgment. Perhaps it is too much to ask that you develop the gifts of loyalty and compassion as well."

Helen looked bewildered. "What do you mean, Mother? I'm not judging! I like Catherine, and I know she wouldn't do anything deliberately—I'm just saying, maybe we don't know her as well as we thought. After all, 'where there's smoke' . . ."

"M-m-m-m"—Mrs. Mortenson shook her head—"there's fire?" She finished the quote. "I believe I have heard that thought expressed before. Catchy phrase—but it doesn't have much to do with the search for truth, I wouldn't imagine."

"Oh, Mother," Helen said, exasperated, "stop talking in riddles. I'm tired of talking about Catherine anyway. One thing's for sure, though. Whatever happened—no decent boy will ever go out with her again, and I doubt if she'll be invited to anymore of the season's parties."

"You have finally said something that I would think is totally accurate, my dear," Mrs. Mortenson conceded. "That would certainly be Mount Royal's way of handling this problem."

Catherine's parents understood exactly what was happening. They knew that people had to talk themselves out. They also knew that when the heat of the summer was over and the fall social season began, the scandal would die down. The Summerwells did not even need to discuss the decision to pass the rest of the summer quietly. They knew they would slowly begin to reenter the social world when the new season began. However, knowing that the scandal would hang over her like a cloud indefinitely, they felt a deep concern for Catherine. Memories were long in Mount Royal, and they were surprised at Catherine's seeming unconcern. She passed her days quietly, writing letters, visiting with Jean Hunt, or reading.

Two weeks passed and one evening Catherine came into the living room after dinner. Her father was reading some legal papers and her mother was stitching a needlepoint cushion. The living room was bright with lamplight, the warm colors of brocade and porcelain against the walls of creamy white. Catherine stood quietly in the archway looking into the room with a tender smile, drinking in the familiar domestic scene.

She cleared her throat and her parents looked up. Through this whole nasty affair they had been sympathetic and supportive. They had not remonstrated or blamed her in any way, and as she looked at them now, composed and concerned, she felt she had never loved them so completely as at this moment when she was preparing to leave them.

"I've made a decision," she said, her voice calm and firm. "I want to tell you about it tonight, but I want you to know it's a firm decision. I am not asking for your advice—this is what I am going to do."

Her father's face clouded and a frown creased her mother's forehead. "Well, I must say your introduction is quite an attention-getter, Catherine," her father remarked dryly.

"It sounds a little ominous, Catherine," her mother said.

"I didn't mean to be dramatic," Catherine said, and took a deep breath.

Clearly and slowly she said, "I have decided to leave Mount Royal."

Her mother gave a little gasp of dismay. "Oh, Catherine!" Lucy exclaimed. "You mustn't leave because of this little trouble. It's all just talk and it will pass over. You belong here."

"No," Catherine replied, "I don't belong here, Mother, and we both know it. I decided long ago that I would need to leave Mount Royal. It isn't this fuss over Sean Greer that's causing me to leave—that's just helped to confirm my decision. I've never really belonged here, Mother. Sometimes I've thought I must be a changeling—or a throwback—I don't know. I only know that I don't fit in here. I'm always doing the wrong thing or saying the wrong thing or looking wrong. I need to go somewhere where I can be myself—not someone trying to fit a pattern."

"But Catherine, dear, we love you. No one is trying to fit you into anything." Her mother's voice was puzzled and grieved.

Cliff Summerwell's voice interrupted. "Listen to what Catherine has to say, Lucy, dear."

Catherine walked over to a gold brocade side chair next to the couch. There was an awkward moment of silence as her parents sat looking at her, and she struggled to find the right words to help them understand.

"You see," Catherine began, "it isn't that I don't love it here—I do. I love both of you, too. It's just that when I'm here I feel—I feel—like I'm a little girl. I always need to worry about pleasing the grownups. Only I never seem to be able to do the right thing, no matter how hard I try. I think the problem is that I'm too old to be a little girl anymore."

Her father nodded, "Yes," and said, "I can understand those feelings. But little girls grow up and become women in Mount Royal all the time."

"Yes, they do, Father," Catherine replied, "but in Mount Royal there are only two ways for a girl to become a woman. One is to get married and the other is to become a spinster. If you wait too long to do the first one, then you automatically become the second. No one will marry me now, not after this Sean Greer scandal. There's nothing left here for me!"

"Oh, dear!" Catherine's mother was crying softly. "You sound as though you hate Mount Royal."

Catherine's voice was anguished. "I don't hate it,

Mother, I love it. I love the order and beauty and tradition. I love the closeness and the elegance. I love the people and the familiar streets. I would give anything to be a part of Mount Royal—but I love it too much to stay and live on the fringes. I understand it too well. I don't want to end up like the Townsends' maiden sister, always puttering around, helping other people's families, bringing little gifts to new babies, and being quiet, eccentric, and extra."

"I don't know what you mean, Catherine." Her mother's voice was tear-strained but indignant. "Everyone likes Anna Townsend! She's certainly not ignored!"

"How long has it been since you've had her to a formal dinner, Mother? Or have you ever—?"

"Well, dear, she wouldn't even want to be invited to a formal dinner. No one likes to make an uneven table. It would be very awkward for her to be the odd number. . . ."

"You see, Mother? I wonder if anyone's ever asked her whether or not she'd mind being asked even if she were the odd number at a table? But no one would ask! We live by these unspoken rules."

"Girls!" Clifford Summerwell broke into the conversation. "I don't think we really want to spend the evening talking about Anna Townsend. It's you, Catherine, with whom we are concerned."

"I'll never have a chance to be anything here but your daughter!" Catherine's voice was agitated. "It's like there's a charmed circle, and a person is either in it or out of it. This place is a throwback to colonial days—you're either a Pukah Sahib or a native—an outcast. Oh, everyone is very polite and kind—that's considered good form—but the circle is closed, and the insiders only connect with insiders. It's like social incest!"

"Catherine!" Lucy gasped and her face was white with outrage. "How dare you say such a word in front of your father and me?"

Catherine flushed scarlet. "I'm so sorry, Mother—Father. . . ." She stammered her apology. "It just came out! You see! That's the way I am. I make mistakes all the time because I get carried away, and I do stupid, impulsive things! But no one gives me room to change or grow. All anyone remembers are the mistakes. People here—your friends, my friends—think this is the whole world. They don't care about anywhere else—not even downtown Calgary. These few charmed streets are the whole world to them, or at least all the world they want to know. Some invisible wall keeps out the untouchables. But if you are like I am—inside the wall but not inside the group—the wall creates a prison, not a haven! Can't you see that? Oh, Daddy!" she turned to her father, imploring him to understand. "Can't you see? I have to leave!"

Her father stood silent, his expression filled with understanding and pain.

Catherine turned to look at him with desperate eyes. "I must go someplace where I can make a contribution, Father, someplace where it will matter whether or not I'm there. I want to feel needed—necessary. I've made some pretty serious mistakes this summer, and I want to begin to understand myself enough to know why I made them."

"I see," her father nodded and continued listening.

"Sean said something to me. He said I needed to learn to love myself before anyone else could love me. Maybe that's why I'm going. To find out if there is somebody in me that I can at least like."

"That all sounds very fancy, Catherine," her father said, his voice quiet and affectionate. "But tell me, dear, there's a part of you that is just plain running away from an unpleasant situation, isn't there?"

Catherine looked up defiantly and met her father's candid eyes. For a moment they looked squarely at one another, then she hung her head slightly. "Yes, I suppose so." She raised her head and continued in a firm voice. "But that doesn't change the fact that I must go. If there's any hope for me, I've got to leave."

"I will lose both my girls in one summer!" Catherine's mother's voice was filled with sorrow and anxiety. "Where will you go? What will you do?"

"That's what I wanted to tell you. I wrote to the Bureau of Indian Affairs, and they have sent me a teaching contract for the Blackfoot Reservation School in Cardston."

"Cardston!" Her mother's voice filled with alarm. "Why, that's in the middle of the prairies. It's nothing but a dusty little farm town, miles from everywhere. You'll be so far away! And Indians! Why would you want to teach Indians? If you really want to leave home and teach, why not get a contract in Edmonton or at one of the private schools here. You could always get a nice apartment . . . or live at home. . . ."

"Mother, please," Catherine said, "this is hard enough. Don't make it any harder. I told you. This is my decision. It's something I want to do, and it's something I've done on my own without using any of our family's influence. In Cardston they don't even know who the Summerwells are. . . . It is me they want . . . Miss Catherine Summerwell, who graduated with high honors, and is young enough and healthy enough and willing enough to take on a one-room school with seventeen Indian children in it!"

"Did knowing Mike Threefeathers have anything to do with this decision?" her father asked.

"I think so," Catherine replied. "I think maybe I'd like to help Indian children have ways of leaving the reservation other than on the back of a rodeo bronco."

"That's a fine thought, Catherine," her father said, his eyes deeply thoughtful, "but it's going to take a lot more than one teacher to change the Indian nation. I'm not trying to discourage you, but I'm not altogether sure education isn't an unkindness until we prepare the white world to accept the Indian people. You might possibly create a generation of Indian children who can't fit into either world—Indian or white. Have you really thought about what you'll be doing?"

"It doesn't matter." Catherine's voice was filled with determination. "The truth is—I really don't care where the contract is or who I'm teaching. I'm not going in order to save the world. I'm just trying to save myself."

Her father sat back on the couch and nodded his head. Something in his face, a look as though he had just finished a successful cross-examination, made her realize he had been asking his questions with a purpose. He was trying to help her understand her own motives for leaving. His clear, logical mind understood her reason even better than she understood it herself.

She was not going on a crusade. She was going on a search.

Something in his face told Catherine he accepted her decision. Her mother was sitting quietly, the needlework still in her hands and her face strained and sad.

"There must be another way, Catherine," she whispered. "Families should stay together. That's the proper thing. We love you and this is your home."

The room was silent and the three sat for a moment sharing the pain and knowledge of their inevitable parting.

Oddly enough, it was Lucy who said the wisest thing. She broke the heavy silence as she rose from the couch and walked over to Catherine. Laying her slim, pale hand gently on Catherine's suntanned cheek, she looked into her daughter's eyes. "Just changing places won't change anything, dear. You always have such impossibly high expectations. You dramatize everything and so you will always be disappointed until you can learn to accept things as they are." She sighed. "I can't imagine how you think Cardston will change you! I don't believe people really change, anyway. I think we just learn to be more comfortable with ourselves."

CHAPTER SEVEN

The train was hot and dusty. After a strained and tearful farewell with her family, Catherine boarded the passenger section in downtown Calgary. On the outskirts of the city, in the heart of the giant stockyards, the train stopped and coupled on a string of cattle cars. The redolent odor of the yards filled the air. By midmorning they moved slowly out of the stockyard station and began a leisurely progress southward through the open prairies of the province of Alberta.

It was not crowded in the car, and so Catherine sat alone on the stiff wicker seat. She regretted having worn her white linen suit, as she saw the skirt wrinkling across her lap, and the pervasive dust from the dry, hot prairies soiling the creases. She looked out the train windows as the hours clicked away and was struck with the enormity of the prairies. Almost two hundred miles away lay the small town of Cardston. To the south, north, and east the fields stretched flat and golden with tall harvest-ready wheat. Nothing broke the line of her vision except in the west where the distant blue ridge of the Rocky Mountains showed itself on the far horizon. Mount Royal seemed like a faraway dream. The air was hot and still and an occasional grain elevator or stock siding was the only evidence of human habitation for miles.

The openness, the sheer expanse of field and sky acted like a fresh, clean wind blowing through Catherine's heart. She felt herself opening up with the hope of a new beginning.

In the late afternoon the conductor came into the car. Catherine was the only passenger left on the train; about an hour earlier, the others had disembarked at McLeod. "Cardston coming up in about twenty minutes, Miss," he said.

Catherine gathered up her belongings from the rack overhead. She had brought only one small suitcase and a shoulder bag. A trunk was to be sent as soon as she had a place to stay. She put on the little straw hat with its navy trim and pulled on her white gloves. Inwardly she was trembling. This was the first time in her life she had been completely on her own.

The train stopped briefly and the conductor helped her onto the platform. Then it started moving again. The train was delivering the rest of the cattle cars to a private siding on a ranch farther down the line. As it rattled off into the distance, Catherine stood on a deserted platform by the small wooden station and looked about her at the small community of Cardston.

Cardston was typical of most Alberta prairie towns. It was built on a river bottom, and since the town was on a low level, it was hardly visible as one approached it from the prairie. The train station was the first building on the road leading into the town. The railroad track and the highway ran from the north, but at the station, the railroad tracks turned west and continued across the prairie. The highway continued south, becoming the main street of Cardston. It was a dusty, two-lane gravel road, and beyond the railroad station it curved downhill into the bowl of the river bottom where the main buildings of the little town stood. The downtown section was one long street lined on either side by wood and brick-front buildings, stores, barbershops, dentist offices, and a small café—all in two treeless, dingy lines sloping downward. The river itself could be seen to the west.

To the right of the station, on a higher level, was the residential area. Catherine could see the tops of trees and snatches of bright green lawn. Directly across from the railroad station, facing the main street, Catherine saw a largish building with a gold-painted sign, "CAMERON HOTEL." Behind the roof of the hotel, about a mile distant, on a prominent rise in the center of the residential section Catherine saw an awesome and breathtaking sight.

Rising like a fantasy from a fabled land was a majestic white granite building with a squared dome, broad columned walls, and long, graceful windows. The building looked like a giant white wedding cake and seemed incongruous in the dusty gray prairie town, which lay so quiet and sleepy in the haze of the late summer afternoon.

"The Mormon temple!" Catherine murmured to herself. She had known the Mormons had built their temple in Cardston, but nothing had prepared her to expect such an impressive structure.

The surrounding scene was so different from anything Catherine had experienced that she was overwhelmed with a sharp stab of nerves and loneliness.

Resolutely she shook off her momentary depression and, picking up her bags, walked across the dusty road to the rundown hotel. The scarred front door led into a small, gloomy lobby. The floor was bare wood, and the furniture consisted of a threadbare couch, an armchair, and a baize-covered poker table haphazardly surrounded by several straight-backed chairs. Two men sat tilted back on wooden chairs in front of the dingy windows, their suitcoats hanging open, their ties loose, and their felt hats pushed back carelessly on their heads.

When Catherine opened the door to enter the lobby, they turned to stare. The clerk watched her approach impassively. When he didn't speak to her, she put her bags on the floor and cleared her throat.

"Excuse me," she said, and was annoyed to hear how nervous her voice sounded. "Excuse me," she repeated in a firmer tone.

"Yeah," said the clerk, who looked as dusty and lifeless as the furniture. "Can I do something for ya?"

"I'm looking for the office of the Indian agent," Catherine explained. "Could you possibly tell me where it would be?"

"Courthouse," said the clerk. Catherine was uncomfortably aware that the two men in the lobby had not taken their eyes off her since she had entered. She could sense them staring at her back, and she wanted to swing around abruptly and confront them, but instead she continued to face the clerk.

"I see," she said. "Is the courthouse far?"

"Nope," replied the clerk.

Catherine felt an edge creeping into her voice. "Could you tell me where it is?"

One of the men behind her spoke up. "Sorry, Miss, it's just that Jed here isn't used to talking to ladies. Maybe I can help you."

She turned with relief. The man who walked over to her was middle-aged, with a face that might have been handsome at one time. Now it had a grayish pallor, and his teeth were tobacco-stained, but still there was an air of expired gentility about him that made Catherine feel better.

"The courthouse is two blocks away. You walk down Main Street here for one long block, then turn right, and walk up the hill toward the temple. The courthouse is a gray granite building on your right. Can't miss it. The Indian agent's office is in the basement."

"Oh, thank you," Catherine said, smiling with relief. "I appreciate your help so much."

"It was nothing, ma'am," said the man. "Not often we see a pretty young thing in these parts. It's always a pleasure to help . . ." He swayed toward her and she caught a whiff of whiskey.

"Well, thank you again," Catherine said, and turned back to the clerk. "May I leave my bags here for the afternoon?" she asked, not wanting to ask for a room in this rundown hotel that reeked of stale tobacco, beer, and Lysol.

"Yeah," said the clerk and walked slowly out from behind the desk and took her bags.

"I'll return for them shortly," Catherine said, nervously torn between the desire to keep them with her and the realization that they were too heavy to carry. She decided she would have to leave them, and trust that the place was more reputable than it looked.

It was a relief to let herself out of the lobby door and back into the fresh air. Catherine would have liked to walk slowly and observe the business establishments, but the afternoon was passing rapidly, and so she hurried down the block, turned right at the corner, and walked up the cross street. Several blocks ahead she could see the temple clearly where it rose on its grassy hill. On her right she saw a substantial square building of gray granite and knew it must be the courthouse.

Catherine entered the lobby and followed the signs leading to the basement offices. The stone-floored corridors were cool, and from open doors floated the comforting sounds of typewriters and voices. Four doors down she saw a door with an opaque glass panel and the gold lettering: AGENT FOR INDIAN AFFAIRS. She knocked on the door, but there was no answer. She knocked again, anxiously. A young woman in a tight red blouse came out of the Records office across the hall.

"Looking for Mr. Raymond?" she asked in a bright voice.

"Yes," Catherine said, her distress showing, "I guess I should have told him I was coming. I assumed someone would be in the office at all times. I'm the new teacher for the reservation school." She hurried on, "My train just arrived and I. . . ."

"Oh, that's too bad," said the girl in a sympathetic tone. "Mr. Raymond left about an hour ago to drive out to the reservation, and it's so late I don't think he'll come back to the office this afternoon."

Catherine's face showed her disappointment, and for an awful moment she felt she might start crying. While she struggled for control, the girl wrinkled her brow in concentration.

"I know!" she exclaimed. "Mr. Brady told me he was going out to the reservation this afternoon, too. If he hasn't left, maybe you could ride out with him and meet Mr. Raymond there!"

"That would be wonderful," Catherine said. "If you're sure it's not too much trouble."

"Not at all," said the girl. "I'll take you over to Mr. Brady's office myself. It's just around the end of the corridor there." The girl pointed and Catherine walked ahead of her down the corridor. As Catherine turned her head to thank the young woman she collided with a man hurrying around the corner. The glass jar he was carrying flew out of his hand and smashed on the floor.

"For Pete's sake," he said roughly, "can't you watch where you're going? What a mess! Well, don't just stand there looking! You could at least help me clean it up."

"I'm so sorry," stammered Catherine. "Of course, I'll be glad to . . . I didn't see you coming. . . ." Her face was scarlet with confusion and embarrassment.

The girl in the red blouse came up to him. "Come on, Mr. Brady, it wasn't her fault! You know that's a blind corner! She's new here besides." The girl's voice took on a tone of familiarity. "Try to be a little nice or she'll go away with a bad impression."

"I'm sorry, Linda, it's just that my wheat is scattered all over this floor, with broken glass mixed into it, and I'm due to leave for the reservation ten minutes ago." He turned and looked at Catherine for the first time. "What did you say your name was?" he asked abruptly.

"I didn't say . . . but it's Catherine Summerwell."

"Well, Catherine Summerwell, I'm sorry if I was rude. Now will you two girls help me clean this mess up?"

Linda smiled at him slyly. "Not unless you promise to do us a favor."

"What's that?" Malcolm Brady asked, pulling an empty envelope out of his briefcase and beginning to pick up kernels of wheat from the floor.

"Promise you'll drive Catherine out to the reservation with you. She's got to see Mr. Raymond, and he left to go out there about an hour ago."

"Aright, aright," Malcolm said impatiently, "but I hope she knows what she's getting into. It's a miserable, hot drive on a day like this."

"Thank you very much, Mr. Brady," Catherine said formally, and then she stooped to help with the job of retrieving the wheat. Linda went for a broom and soon the corridor was clean. Malcolm Brady grabbed Catherine's elbow and with no word of thanks to either of the girls propelled her toward the lobby stairs. "If you're coming with me, you've got to hurry. It's going to be a tight squeeze to make it out there and back before sunset as it is."

He led her to his car, a black Ford coupe with a creased fender and a thick layer of dust. As she sat down on the front seat, dust motes filled the air and made her cough.

"This isn't any palace coach," Malcolm Brady said as he climbed in and started the motor. The car ground into gear and they were off with a jerk.

Catherine had been so upset in the courthouse she

hadn't taken time to look at Mr. Brady, but now as she sat in his car, bumping and rattling down the street out of Cardston and into the fields west of the town, she took a moment to study him.

She judged he must be in his early thirties. He had a lean, tough body, and his face and arms were deeply tanned—the dark, reddish tan of a man who lives and works outdoors. His features were sharp and strong, and when he turned to speak to her, she had the impression of startling blue eyes in the sun-browned face. She had yet to see him smile. He wore an expression of concentrated intensity and impatience, and he spoke in a brusque, deep voice which suited his look.

He was dressed in twill gabardine in a khaki color. His shirt was open at the throat, and his pants were modified jodphurs with high-laced boots. It was a uniform worn by surveyors, archaeologists, and explorers—men who made their living in the fields and untracked lands of the earth. She did not know it at the time, but he was wearing the unofficial uniform of the prairie agriculturist. Catherine thought it a very handsome outfit, and his muscular body wore it well. Beside her on the car seat he had thrown a dusty, wide-brimmed Stetson and his briefcase.

Several minutes passed in total silence, and it occurred to Catherine that Malcolm Brady was not a man who made small talk. It was very possible if she left it up to him that they would drive the entire way to the reservation without conversation.

"What is the purpose of your wheat kernels?" she asked, curious because he had been so protective of them.

"I'm the District Agriculturist," he answered shortly. "Wheat kernels are my business. It just so happened that you spilled some of the finest new hybrid seeds that have ever been developed."

The heat, the long trip, and his rude tone were suddenly too much for Catherine, and she replied with some impatience, "I didn't spill your wheat. You were coming around that corner too fast! Besides, if it's precious, you should carry it in something more practical than a breakable glass jar!"

"Oho!" Malcolm Brady turned and gave her an appreciative look and a sardonic smile. "So the princess has a temper, has she?"

"What are you talking about?" Catherine asked.

"Listen, Miss Summerwell, I know a princess when I see one. The only thing I can't figure is what you're doing in this forsaken place, and why on earth you want to go out to the reservation. You look like you're on your way to Buckingham Palace."

"For your information," Catherine exclaimed heatedly, "I am not a princess, I'm a schoolteacher, and I am on my way to report to Mr. Raymond, so I can prepare my school at the reservation."

The teasing look left Malcolm Brady's face and a frown of genuine concern replaced it. "Why didn't you tell me that in the first place? I could have saved you the trouble of this car ride."

"What do you mean?" Catherine asked, puzzled.

Malcolm Brady gave her a long look out of the corner of his eye. They were driving down a long dirt road. Far in the distance to the west they could see the foothills of the Rockies, and behind them the remote blue mountain peaks like a decorative border on the horizon. On either side of them were expansive fields of wheat and along the dusty, narrow road, mounds of sweet wild clover, filled with the humming of bees. Grasshoppers were thick at the sides of the road, and the windshield was stained with their broken bodies.

"What can you tell me?" she asked again.

"Oh, nothing," Malcolm Brady said flatly. "Mr. Raymond will tell you all you need to know." He thought for a moment, and then in a kinder voice asked, "Why did you want to come here and teach Indian kids anyway? Don't people like you have children, so you could teach your own kind?"

Catherine flared, "There you go again! I think you are being impossibly rude—and I don't know why!"

Malcolm Brady screeched the car to a halt in the middle of the deserted road. The late afternoon sun beat through the windshield and now that the car was stopped the hum of the insects was the only sound on the vast prairie.

"Look out there," Malcolm Brady said. "Do you see that land? It all belonged to the Indians once, as far as the eye could see. Living with that kind of space does something to the soul of man—makes him—untamable. But it does something to women, too—especially women like you, women who have been cared for and pampered and protected. It makes a man free, but it crushes a woman. The silence, the weight of the space, the remoteness of your fellow creatures—I took one look at you in that corridor in your high heels and your white gloves with your untouched face and your innocent eyes, and I didn't know what you were doing here, but I knew for sure you didn't belong. This place will smash you like a 'hopper."

Catherine blazed. "All my life people have been telling me what I could and couldn't do! Where I belonged—where I didn't belong. And I'm sick of it! I belong where I say I belong! And not you, not anybody, is going to tell me what's the proper place for me to be!"

Malcolm Brady reached over and grabbed her hand and pulled off the white glove. He held her hand tightly in his until she winced with pain. "Look at that!" he said. "Just look at it!" He held up her hand next to his own, which was corded, brown, and calloused with labor. "You won't last two weeks," he said with a smile, looking at her tender hand, and then he dropped it. He started the motor again, and Catherine, agitated and angry, glared out the window.

"You don't need calluses to teach children," she said defensively.

"No, but you'll need them to chop wood to keep the fire going in the schoolroom. And you'll need calluses on your soul to sleep alone in the teacherage when the wind's howling up a blizzard, and there isn't a white person within twenty miles."

"You can't scare me, Mr. Brady," Catherine said quietly.

"I suppose not." Malcolm Brady sighed and shrugged his shoulders. "I suppose you're out here trying to prove something. The gift of the great white mother! Don't you understand it isn't gifts these people need. They need to be given back their own life. All you can give them is some sort of substitute. They'll never eat in the drawing rooms of this country.

That's all you can prepare them for, and it isn't good enough . . . it isn't even right! You think you can do so much good—all you do-gooders! You just make things worse and worse. What these people need is the sky and the land—and to be free."

"Maybe that's what I need, too, Mr. Brady," Catherine said softly.

There was a long period of silence, and then Malcolm Brady pointed up the road to a slight rise in the fields. On a windswept, barren piece of land she saw some straggling barbed-wire fences and a few rough wooden dwellings, and rising behind them, a circle of tepees with smoke rising.

"That's the reservation," Malcolm Brady said. "I'll take you up to the schoolhouse and send Mr. Raymond up there to meet with you when I find him. You can probably ride back with him."

He didn't say another word, and she thought he would leave her without any easing of the tension between them. As he pulled up in front of a small, one-room building, barren of paint like all the others, he got out of the car and opened her door. "The schoolhouse—" he said laconically, pointing to the shack. Then just as he turned to leave her, he paused and put an awkward hand on her arm. "Good luck," he said curtly and was gone.

Catherine stood for a moment on the steps of the schoolhouse and stared out across the reservation. In front of some of the government-built huts she saw little children playing on the ground, naked from the waist down. A few mongrel dogs ranged on the sparse grass. There was nothing cultivated, nothing planted, nothing growing except strands of prairie grass, wispy and spindly, and amidst that, the baked, barren earth worn hard by pacing feet and running children, and the ruts of buckboards and grazing horses. There was no color at all except the natural tones of bare wood and bare earth, and arching over all, the impossibly blue prairie sky.

"It's like another kind of prison," Catherine thought with a shudder of apprehension. She walked into the one-room school and drew back instinctively at the stale, urine-laden smell of the air. Hurrying over to the windows, she opened them, brushing away cobwebs and dust. Some animal had apparently made his home in the room; there were droppings on the floor and a nest of old papers in one corner. Broken chairs and overturned desks were heaped in the middle of the room, and the walls were stained and filthy. On the blackboard were written words that she had never heard, but as she read them she understood their meaning, and she felt her face burning.

Angered, she strode across the room and began to rub furiously at the words on the blackboard with her handkerchief. The chalk smeared, but she could still see the outline of the words, and so she scrubbed harder, as though by erasing the offending words she could erase the experiences of the day, and the desolation of this strange place. She was so engrossed in her task that she failed to hear the doorknob turning, and so, when the door crashed open behind her, she turned with a start and gave a small, involuntary scream. Standing in the open doorway was an ancient Indian man. Although it appeared as though he had once been very tall, now he stood bent with age; yet his shoulders were still broad and powerful. He held his massive head with pride as he looked at Catherine with fierce, avenging eyes.

The fury and hatred in his face hit Catherine like a blow, and she stepped backward staring in fear and confusion at the man in the doorway until she found herself pressed against the blackboard. Suddenly, he uttered one word. It was a short word in an Indian dialect, and he seemed to spit it at her—casting it into the room between them like a gauntlet. She did not know the word, but she understood from the sound of it that it was a name—an insulting name—which he was calling her.

"Who—who are you?" Catherine managed to whisper. Her mouth was dry and her voice failed her as she continued to stare at the menacing old chief.

As if in response to her question, the chief entered the room and began to walk toward her. In his hand he carried a gnarled stick upon which he leaned heavily as he walked, and she saw his hands were knobbed and twisted with arthritis. His hair was white and hung to his shoulders, and his face was copper-colored, wrinkled like a dried river bed with deep crevasses. Only his nose, high-bridged and noble, stood in the old man's ravaged face like a fortress against time.

Walking toward Catherine, the man spoke in Indian—a low, steady stream of words that were unintelligible to Catherine except for the venom and animosity audible in every tone and syllable.

Suddenly, with no change in tone or inflection, the old chief began to speak English. Catherine was so terrified that for a moment she did not realize she could distinguish the words and understand what he was saying.

"White women do not belong on the reservation. You come here to teach our children, but you have nothing to give them. All you can give them is more hurt and more pain. You make them realize what they are not, what they cannot be. You cannot teach them what they need to know. You cannot teach them that they are the sons and daughters of the wind, because you do not understand that yourself. You do not love them. You hate them, you despise them. All you can teach them is to despise themselves."

"White women have no place here. You will go now. You will not stay. You are evil! Everything you bring is evil! You must go. I will not let you hurt the little ones."

The old man seemed to be chanting the words. His voice was harsh, deep, and rhythmic, and Catherine felt a stab of terror as he moved closer and closer to her, and her eyes followed the heavy stick as it marked his painful progress across the room. She wondered what she would do if he raised the stick to strike her.

"I should run," she thought, but in the small room she did not see how she could get past him to the door.

"Evil!" the old man said again. "You have come to tempt our sons. You have come to bring your poison . . ."

The old man was directly in front of Catherine now, and he stood before her, his piercing eagle eyes glaring at her, and his hand trembling on the heavy cane. Catherine's heart pounded and her breathing was rapid with fear.

"Chief!" a man's voice called from outside. "Chief! Where are you?"

The sound of the voice broke the spell, and the ancient warrior suddenly shrank down into his rusty old coat and became a shriveled old man. His eyes turned away from Catherine, and she saw an impassive mask settle over his face, until nothing was left of the fierce chieftain but a broken shell.

"Me here!" he grunted in a tired voice.

"Oh! I was looking for you to say good-bye, and I thought I saw you coming this way. Been talking to Miss Summerwell, have you?" The man who had spoken walked into the schoolroom, and although Catherine found herself shaking with relief, she also felt a half-realized sense of regret. Perhaps, if the moment with the old chief had lasted a little longer, he might have revealed some great truth—something real and important might have happened in this quiet room. However, the moment was gone forever, and she did feel gratitude for having been rescued by the man who was now speaking to the old Indian.

"This must be Mr. Raymond, the Indian Agent," she thought, "and if he's going to be my boss, I'd better get a good look at him." Mr. Raymond was a short, stocky man with slightly balding hair and a strained, harassed face. As he talked with the old chief, Catherine watched him, and she noted that he had the kindest eyes she had ever seen. He seemed to look at the chief with a depth of understanding and concern that was far beyond a professional interest, as though he cared about this man as he would his own father or brother. The rest of Mr. Raymond's manner was almost a contradiction of his eyes, however, for he gave the impression of a man who was overburdened, anxious, and intense, and his manner of speaking was rapid and would have been abrupt, were it not for the emotional intensity in his tone. Everything in his exterior bespoke an overworked, impatient man, and every evidence of his personality showed a man who was deeply involved and committed to the people with whom he worked.

Mr. Raymond concluded his farewell to the chief, and the old man turned and walked painfully out of the schoolroom. Catherine could hear his cane as it tapped down the wooden stairs. Standing by the door, Mr. Raymond called after the departing Indian, "I'll be back out to see you at the end of the week, Chief, and I'll bring that medicine we talked about."

Then he turned and addressed Catherine. "And now, young lady," he said in a brisk voice, "what are we to do about you? Why on earth didn't you phone or write to let me know you were coming? There is a letter in the mail to you, probably waiting in Calgary right now—but here you are! Well, there's nothing to be done about it."

"Nothing to be done about it?" Catherine's voice was anxious. "What are you talking about? What letter in the mail, Mr. Raymond? I want to be the best teacher you've ever had work for you, so I thought I'd come down two weeks early to get my school set up properly." She gave a helpless laugh and looked around the shoddy room. "I'm not sure two weeks will be long enough for what needs to be done here. . . ."

"Please," Mr. Raymond interrupted, "please don't go on—you are just going to make things worse. I have to tell you. . . ." He paused to take out a handkerchief and wipe his forehead. Something in his kind eyes told her he was going to have to say something unpleasant, and he was desperately wishing he could avoid the confrontation.

"You see, Miss Summerwell," his voice became crisp and authoritative, "your contract has been canceled."

"Canceled!" Catherine cried. "Why? How can you cancel it? I have it right here!" She began to rummage in her purse.

"No, no," Mr. Raymond said, forestalling her search with a gesture of his hand. "That won't be necessary. I know you have the contract, but it isn't valid, it's of no use. The Provincial Government has canceled it."

"Why?" Catherine's voice was almost a wail. "I don't understand any of this!"

"It has nothing to do with you or your qualifications, I assure you of that," Mr. Raymond said hurriedly. "Please don't feel this is anything personal. If anything, you are overqualified for the job. No, no, it has nothing to do with you."

"Then what is it?" Catherine demanded.

"They've canceled the school, that's all. You see, they've decided not to hold the school on the reservation this year. Many of the students are going off to the boarding school which is run by the Jesuit fathers, so it was thought it would be easier and more effective to bring the few remaining children into Cardston and have them attend regular school. Your contract is canceled because your school no longer exists."

"But what about me?" Catherine asked, stunned. "What am I to do? The school year is almost starting, and here I am, with a contract but no school. What am I to do?"

"You'll just have to go home, I'm afraid, Miss Summerwell. Go home where you belong and find yourself a nice young man and raise some children of your own."

Catherine's eyes blazed, and she walked across the schoolroom to stand in front of Mr. Raymond. Her voice was edged with anger. "I am not a child, Mr. Raymond. I am a woman, and I do not have a home except the home which I plan to make for myself. You and the province of Alberta have promised me a position and a home, and now when I have journeyed here with the full expectation of having both, you inform me I have neither, and expect that I will accept this news passively and like a docile pet return to my kennel. Well, I assure you, I will do no such thing. Because of your contract, it is now too late in the year for me to locate another, and I am going to hold you directly responsible. I expect you to fulfill my contract."

"But Miss Summerwell!" Mr. Raymond exclaimed, his voice sounding even more harassed and his face wearing the bewildered expression of a loving father whose child has just bitten him. "How can I honor your contract to teach in a school when there is no school?"

"That, Mr. Raymond," Catherine replied with some asperity, "is your problem. I suggest that you find a school for me. However, if that proves impossible, then I assure you I will still hold you to the terms of my contract and expect to receive the use of a place to live, and one hundred and twenty dollars a month, since it is you and not I who have made it impossible for me to teach."

Mr. Raymond shook his head and shrugged his shoulders like a man with a problem which is beyond his control. "There is no purpose in our discussing this further here this evening," he said in a tired voice. "This has been a very long day for me, Miss Summerwell. I have been discussing problems of life and death—of survival for the winter with these people—and their needs are so pressing that it is hard for me to understand your feelings about something so trivial as your contract. After all, you obviously come from a family of means, and you do have a home, an education, your health, and a long, lovely life ahead of you. I find it hard to give time and attention to your problem when it could so easily be solved if you would just be reasonable and return to your home."

This was too much for Catherine. The long day of disappointments and unfamiliar experiences seemed to crush her with its weight so that she almost felt like the little girl she had denied being. Tears began to course down her face.

"I can't go home. Don't you understand that? I had to fight to leave, and if I return I'll never be able to leave again. This was my one chance, and you take it away from me as though it doesn't matter—as though I don't matter. Do you think that just because a person has clothes to wear and food to eat that nothing that happens to him is important? Just once I'd like to feel that I count—that it matters what happens to me! I want to be treated like a person—don't you think I at least deserve the same interest and concern that you gave that chief? I counted on this contract!" Her voice broke and it was a moment before she could go on. "I need it very much," she ended and her voice was almost a whisper.

"There, there," Mr. Raymond said, obviously discomfited by her outburst and awkward about what to do with this crying young woman. "Here." He handed her a clean handkerchief from his back pocket, and as she mopped up her eyes, he once again wiped his forehead with the other handkerchief and looked helplessly around the room as though expecting someone or something to extricate him from this difficult situation. When Catherine returned the handkerchief, he began speaking rapidly. "Well, now, then, maybe you're right. We probably do owe you some help. As you said, it's very late in the summer to be looking for a contract, but we may be lucky. Anyway, this is no time to talk about all of this. Let's leave it until tomorrow morning, and then when we're both calm and rested we can talk the thing through."

"All right," Catherine said gratefully. She wouldn't be sent back immediately, and she felt a ray of hope.

"Now, then," Mr. Raymond continued, relieved to see that Catherine was feeling better, "now then. You came out with Malcolm Brady, I know, but he left a few minutes ago and asked if I would drive you back to Cardston, so if you're ready perhaps we should go. It's almost sundown and it gets dark very quickly on the prairies. Where are you staying?"

Catherine flushed. "Well . . ." she said hesitantly, "my bags are at the Cameron Hotel."

"The Cameron!" Mr. Brady's voice sounded shocked. "That is not a proper place for a single young woman. That's a place for drummers and the likes. You couldn't stay there . . . even for one night! Don't you have any friends or relatives here? What did you plan to do with yourself?"

"Well, I thought I would move right into the teacherage," Catherine said in a small voice.

Casting his eyes up to heaven at the foolishness of this young woman who had been thrown into his hands, Mr. Raymond shook his head, and said in an exasperated tone, "Well, we'll just have to find a place for you to board until we can get you situated or sent home. I believe Bishop Watkins will be able to help us."

"Bishop Watkins!" Catherine repeated. "Oh, I'm not a Catholic!"

Mr. Raymond laughed shortly, "Neither is Bishop Watkins. He's a Mormon bishop, and his congregation makes up half the town of Cardston. If there's a home that's willing to take in boarders, he'll know about it, and if he doesn't, his wife Lavinia will!"

"His wife? You mean Mormon bishops marry?"

"Certainly, and they have jobs, too. Bishop Watkins runs the trading post, which is also the town department store. He and his wife, Lavinia, have six children. The youngest is about your age. Ladean is her name, I think."

"Ladean Watkins!" Catherine exclaimed. "I went to university with Ladean Watkins. With a name like that it must be the same person! I knew she came from the southern part of the province, but I didn't know she was a Mormon. We had several education classes together."

With a sigh and a relieved smile, Mr. Raymond guided Catherine out onto the steps of the schoolhouse and pointed toward his car, a battered old Studebaker. "Then that sounds like just the ticket. We'll drive back into town, and I'll take you over to their place. I know we'll be able to work something out."

They walked down the steps and he opened the car door for Catherine. Just before she stepped inside she stood by the car and looked back at the barren one-room school. The sunset behind it was blood-red, and the prairies were already filling up with an inky blackness in the hollows of the fields and the edges of the horizon. The last brilliant edge of the sun showed like an orange sliver behind the distant silhouette of the Rocky Mountains, and the enormity of the empty land, its harsh contrasts, and indifferent majesty over-whelmed her, and in spite of the dusty evening heat she shivered and longed to be inside four walls where there was laughter and kindness.

CHAPTER EIGHT

By the time they returned to Cardston it was dark, and the narrow road leading into town unwound before the car's headlights like a dim gray ribbon. As they entered the outskirts of town, Mr. Raymond asked brusquely if Catherine had eaten anything all day and she mutely shook her head. With an exasperated sigh he pulled into a small diner by the side of the road, and telling Catherine to wait in the car, he hurried inside. In a few moments he returned with a brown paper bag and thrusting it into Catherine's hands said, "Here, you'd better eat something. Heaven knows how long it will be before we get you properly settled for the night."

Catherine opened the sack gratefully and pulled out a ham and cheese sandwich. "Would you like some?" she asked hesitantly.

"No, thank you," Mr. Raymond replied, "I'll eat when I get home. My wife always has something on the stove. You go ahead."

"Thank you," Catherine said, her voice betraying her self-consciousness. She took a reluctant bite of the sandwich and found it surprisingly good. Another look into the bag revealed a carton of milk. Gratefully, she took a long swallow of the cool refreshing milk. As she ate she felt her spirits rising.

Mr. Raymond started the car. "Where are we headed now?" Catherine asked.

"First we'll go to the Cameron Hotel and pick up your bags, and then we'll drive over to Bishop Watkins's to see what accommodations we can find for you. If nothing works out, you'll have to come and stay at my house. My wife's family is visiting so the best we can offer you is a couch."

"Oh, I wouldn't want to put you to all that trouble . . . I mean . . . you've done so much for me already, and I know you're right, I should have phoned or written before I came. I just didn't think. . . ." Catherine felt her cheeks flushing as she stammered her apology.

"Quite right," Mr. Raymond's matter-of-fact voice cut through her distress. "You should have contacted me—would have saved us both a lot of trouble and unhappiness. You young people! You know so much and yet you know so little. . . ." Mr. Raymond sighed again and drove in silence to the hotel.

"You stay here in the car, and I'll get your luggage," he cautioned. "The nightly Cameron poker game will be in full swing, and it's no place for a lady."

Catherine watched as Mr. Raymond opened the battered doors of the hotel, and she was sure she actually saw smoke swirling out of the door into the night, reflected in the single round light bulb that shone weakly over the hotel's entrance.

"The air must be as thick as fog in the lobby!" she thought, trying to see through the dingy windows, but only managing to see a shadowy blur. She felt an involuntary shudder as she thought what would have happened if Mr. Raymond had not insisted in seeing to her accommodations. One thing was certain—a night in that dreary hotel would not have been a pleasant or safe experience.

In a few moments Mr. Raymond returned carrying her bags. He tossed them into the back seat of the car, and then once again they continued through the dark streets of the town. Within seconds they left the main street and turned up a broad street lined with trees and small attractive homes with brightly lit windows. Through the windows Catherine saw people eating, reading, and moving about at household tasks. Their routines looked cozy and warm, and she felt a poignant melancholy as she thought of all the people who had a place to belong. For a moment she felt the forlorn ache of an outsider, looking in.

"I'm keeping you from home," she murmured to Mr. Raymond. "I am so sorry."

"Nonsense," Mr. Raymond growled, "stop apologizing. I'm just doing what's necessary."

They drove up in front of a small, tidy brick house with a wide porch and trim walk, bordered with low hedges. In the shadowed darkness of the evening the windows of the house glowed through white ruffled curtains. To Catherine the place looked charming and welcoming.

"This seems like such an imposition for the Watkinses!" Catherine exclaimed. "I really don't know Ladean very well. It may not even be the same girl . . ."

Mr. Raymond ignored her comments and walked briskly in front of her, mounting the brick porch and knocking emphatically on the door. Catherine stood aside reluctant and shy in the shadows.

The door opened and a robust form filled the

frame. "Ben Raymond!" a man's hearty voice exclaimed. "What brings you to our door at this hour! Come right in!" The man at the door turned and called into the house, "Lavinia! Ladean! It's Ben Raymond. Come and say hello."

"I've brought you a bit of a problem," Mr. Raymond said. "I'm hoping you can help me solve it."

Catherine wasn't at all sure she liked being introduced as a "bit of a problem," but she summoned her social training and stepped out of the shadows, near the door so the light encompassed her.

"This is Miss Catherine Summerwell," Mr. Raymond introduced her.

Catherine extended her hand and Bishop Watkins enclosed it in a huge warm handshake. "Well, now," he said, "this is a pleasure. Won't you come in, Miss Summerwell, so you and Mr. Raymond can tell me what this is all about?"

Before she knew what was happening, Catherine had been ushered into a brightly lit room. It was not an elaborate living room, and its dimensions were small, but it sparkled with cleanliness. The couch, arm chairs, and side chairs were all good quality, chosen with a refined taste, and she noted on the mantel an attractive piece of Royal Doulton. The shelves on either side of the fireplace were filled with books. On the table in front of the couch was a bowl of apples and grapes with the evening newspaper open next to it. On one chair there was some unfinished needlework which had apparently just been set down. The room radiated a sense of well-being and peace.

"Now then, Ben," the Bishop continued, "is this something that we can discuss with the girls present, or shall I ask them to stay in the kitchen with the dishes for a while longer?" Bishop Watkins's manner was so pleasant—warm-hearted and natural—that Catherine found herself relaxing for the first time since Mr. Raymond had informed her she no longer had a teaching contract. There was something reassuring about the presence of this hearty man, and she began to believe a solution to her problems might be found. Unaccountably she sensed she was cared for, and she could hardly wait until Mr. Raymond could explain her problem to the Bishop. She felt confident he would be able to help.

"No! No! Call the womenfolk in, Bishop, by all means," Mr. Raymond exclaimed. "This young lady says she's a friend of Ladean's from university. That's why we thought you might be able to help. It's a long story, but seems the bottom line is this—Miss Summerwell needs a place to stay tonight."

Catherine looked at Mr. Raymond with alarm and her anger began to mount. She opened her mouth to protest that she would not be sent away after only one night! Simply finding her a place to stay was not going to solve Mr. Raymond's fundamental problem of filling her contract. However, Mr. Raymond, seeing her indignation, forestalled her protests by adding, "We also need to find a place for her to stay until we can resolve the issues regarding her employment. Which may"—here he fixed Catherine with an exasperated stare—"take only a few days."

"That seems an easy enough problem to solve," said the Bishop, a smile creasing his sun-browned face. "Ladean is going to be delighted to see Miss Summerwell, and of course she'll stay with us. Now, why don't you two just sit down here and make yourselves comfortable. Have some grapes, and I'll go get Sister Watkins and Ladean, and then you can tell us all about the situation."

Bishop Watkins stepped through a door into a small hallway leading to the rear of the house. Catherine and Mr. Raymond sat in awkward silence. They could hear the rumble of the Bishop's voice, the murmur of women's voices answering, and the clink of dishes. In a moment they heard quick footsteps, and a young woman Catherine's age burst from the hall into the living room, pulling an apron over her head and laughing with welcome.

"Catherine Summerwell!" she exclaimed in a bright happy voice. "I don't believe it! It just seems unreal! I haven't seen you since graduation, and I didn't know you ever came to Cardston! What a wonderful surprise! What are you doing here?!"

Ladean's excitement was contagious, and Catherine rose from her chair, and the two girls stood grinning at each other.

"Oh, Ladean!" Catherine said, and to her chagrin she felt tears rising in her eyes.

"To tell the truth, I'm as surprised to see you as you are to see me! You don't know how glad I am you're here . . . I don't think I've ever been happier to see anyone in my whole life." Both girls began to laugh with the pleasure of seeing one another.

Mrs. Watkins came in a moment later and Catherine was introduced to her by Bishop Watkins.

"This is Sister Watkins, Catherine," he said. "Catherine Summerwell, my dear," he added, turning and smiling at his wife. "She's a friend of Ladean's and apparently has no place to stay."

"Yes, dear, I know. You explained that to me in the kitchen." Lavinia Watkins turned to Catherine. "You do have a place to stay, Catherine, for as long as you like, right here."

Catherine liked Mrs. Watkins at once. She was a motherly woman with a warmly authoritative voice and capable hands. The Bishop and his wife walked over to sit side by side on the couch and Catherine looked at them in the lamplight. They were a handsome couple with iron-gray hair and healthy, ruddy complexions. They were both substantially built, not heavy, but tall and strong-looking, and there was about them a confident sense of well-being and substance. Their faces wore almost identical expressions of kindness, but there was also a touch of something else—a brightness, almost a merriness, as though they looked on the world as a great adventure and found delight in everything.

"Miss Summerwell was contracted to teach at our school on the reservation," Mr. Raymond began. "Last week the Department of Indian Affairs canceled the school, and I sent her a letter informing her the contract was not valid, but before she received the letter, she had already left Calgary to come to Cardston."

"I see," said Bishop Watkins. "So you arrived expecting to be fully employed and in less than one day . . ."

"What a shame!" Ladean exclaimed. "That doesn't seem fair at all!"

Mr. Raymond's face looked harried, and he ran his hand through his thinning hair. "Well, fair or not, that's what happened. And since we didn't know she was coming we certainly had no opportunity to arrange accommodations!" Here he threw Catherine an accusing glare.

"Sounds to me like you're both caught in a situation that's none of your own doing, but you've done the right thing bringing her here, Ben. A real treat for Ladean. She's been feeling kind of lonely with Dan on his mission and all her brothers and sisters married or off working somewhere."

Catherine could see the relief on Mr. Raymond's face as he realized he had fulfilled his responsibility to her—at least for this evening. With alacrity he got up from his chair and bid the Watkinses good night.

As he hurried down the walk, Catherine leaped up and ran to the front door, and opening it, she called anxiously after him, "What time may I see you tomorrow, Mr. Raymond? Shall I come to your office?"

He turned and looked at her standing in the doorway, the yellow lamplight outlining her figure, but her face in shadow. "You are a persistent one!" he exclaimed with a snort of laughter. "Ten o'clock." Then as she turned to close the door, he determined to get the last word. "And don't you be late, young lady!"

Quick as a flash she turned and called, "I won't— I'll be early!" and then she closed the door. Mr. Raymond shook his head ruefully, climbed into his old Studebaker, and rattled off down the street.

*　*　*

Several hours later the last light in the Watkins's home had been turned off and Catherine and Ladean were lying in twin beds in Ladean's feminine pink and white bedroom and talking quietly in the dark.

"I love your family!" Catherine whispered. "I love your house! I'm so thankful for all you've done."

"Yeah," Ladean whispered with an infectious giggle. "Me, too!"

In the first restful slumber of the evening Catherine saw herself in a dream. In the dream she was standing in front of a closed door, aware that behind it was something for her. Like a spectator she could see herself standing, quietly staring at the shut door, and her sleeping heart whispered, "Open it! Open it!" But in the dream Catherine would not move, and then she saw more clearly. The door had no knob on it! It was blank and smooth. Someone would have to open it from the other side.

Suddenly Catherine, in the dream, ran to the door and began to knock frantically. "Please open the door! Open it! Oh, please, please open. . . ." Catherine's hands clenched and she pounded on the unyielding surface—"Please . . . open . . . Let me in!"

Catherine woke with a start! Her pillow was clutched to her breast and she was wet with perspiration. Looking across the room, she could see Ladean sleeping soundly, and with a sigh she replaced her pillow and settled down to sleep again.

"It's all right," she whispered to herself, "everything is going to be all right."

* * *

The next week for Catherine was the best of times and the worst of times. Every day she arrived early to sit in the tiny anteroom of Mr. Raymond's office, and every day he told her the same thing, "The Indian Affairs people will do nothing to help solve your problem." He had telegraphed Edmonton, and they had sent back an adamant note that they accepted no contractual obligation. The Reservation school was closed, and the contract was therefore null and void. Catherine continued to insist that since she had fulfilled her part of the contract, the Bureau of Indian Affairs was responsible to either replace it with another contract or to pay her until she could find one. The impasse was decidedly uncomfortable, and Mr. Raymond began spending long days out on the Reservation away from his office, hoping that he could avoid meeting Catherine. He confided to his wife one evening—after two days of absence from his office—that he didn't feel his strategy would work, and he fully expected that if he tried it a third day, he would see Catherine marching across the Reservation headed straight for him.

"Well, dear," said Mrs. Raymond in a maddeningly calm voice, "it seems to me you have no choice but to get that girl another contract. Why don't you call Ed Solembaugh. He's superintendent of the Southern Alberta Education District. After all, she didn't say you had to get her another Indian contract, she just said another teaching contract. Maybe you'll get lucky, and there'll be an opening somewhere else."

"All right," Mr. Raymond said reluctantly, "but why do I feel like I'm being blackmailed?" He went off muttering something about the most stubborn, persistent, aggravating young woman he'd ever met. . . .

While Catherine hated the days waiting for her contract issue to be resolved, she relished the evenings and afternoons which she spent with Ladean and the Watkins family. Catherine found herself appalled at her ignorance of Mormons, and she was intrigued by the things she was learning about them, both through observation and through conversations with Ladean.

Catherine had always thought Mormons were something like Hutterites—a religious group which lived in colonies and dressed differently from other people. It was a wonder to her, therefore, to see the naturalness of Mormon life. Their homes and their clothes were stylish, and they were enormously interested in politics, newspapers, magazines, and movies.

The second day she was in the Watkins's home she walked in to find Mrs. Watkins seated on the couch reading *Les Misérables.* Her surprise showed on her face and Mrs. Watkins laughed and said, "You must be shocked to see me reading in the afternoon when I should be out picking beans for supper, but our women's church group is discussing this book tomorrow and I have to get it read."

Later when Catherine finally summoned the courage to ask Ladean some direct questions, she mentioned this unusual combination of secular and religious learning.

"Well," Ladean tried to explain, "you see, we really love the world! I mean, we sort of believe that anything in the world that is good or fine is really a part of the Gospel. For us there isn't a line between the

material and nonmaterial. After all, everything was
made by God so it must all be spiritual, right?"

Catherine supposed this explained why the Bishop
and others who ran the church were lay ministers.
They all had jobs of some kind. One evening a young
farmer came to the door. He was still dressed in his
gumboots and work overalls.

"Just brought a load of calves in to be shipped to
the States," she heard him say to Bishop Watkins.
"Thought I'd stop by and check to see if there's anything you want me to do for the meeting on Sunday."

Later on Catherine discovered this young man was
a High Priest, a councellor to the Bishop.

Bishop Watkins himself was one of the well-to-do
men in the community. He owned the Trading Post,
which was the largest store in town. It sold everything—
rather like a small department store. His establishment was situated on the busiest corner of Main Street
where it intersected the street leading up to the temple, and from the side windows of the store one could
see a magnificent view of the gleaming white marble
edifice. One day Catherine stopped in at the Trading
Post to pick up some items for Mrs. Watkins. Bishop
Watkins's office was an open area on the second floor
looking out over the main floor where the hardware
and canned goods were sold. His desk was covered
with accounts and in front of him was a battered old
adding machine with the long white paper tape spilling out and into a heap on the floor. She thought it
was rather symbolic of the man as he sat with the
yards of accounting figures in front of him and the
view of the temple through the window behind him.
Perhaps it was true, as Ladean said, that material

things, if properly used and understood, were just another manifestation of spiritual realities.

Catherine often observed Bishop Watkins talking to the Indians who came into the post. Every time she came downtown she noted there were dissolute Indians standing near the Trading Post doors. They wrapped themselves in blankets and stood silently on the street for hours. Just as mysteriously as they appeared they would vanish. Often she saw old, weathered buckboards, driven by wooden-faced braves and filled with solemn children, papooses, and impassive squaws, rattle through town and out the long, narrow road leading to the reservation.

The Bishop spoke several dialects, and though he seemed to be strong and demanding when he spoke with the Indians in their own tongue, nonetheless he showed them the same serious respect which she had noticed Mr. Raymond showed when he spoke.

She mentioned this to Ladean, and Ladean explained, "Papa has to be strict with the Indians or they'd steal him blind. They're honest with men they admire, but they only admire strong men. Anyway, we think of them as part of the House of Israel and so we care about them a whole lot."

This was too much for Catherine. "The House of Israel? What do you mean?"

"It's a long story," Ladean sighed. "You'd really have to read the whole Book of Mormon to understand . . . but we believe the Indians are the remnant of Israelites who were led over here before the Babylonian captivity. . . . Oh! It sounds so complicated when I try to explain. . . ." She laughed, awkwardly, and then tried to close the subject. "Someday the In-

dians will be a mainstay of the Lord and . . . well . . .
we just feel they're important. Papa could explain it
better." Catherine could tell that Ladean felt helpless
trying to explain ideas to her that were such a natural
part of her family's concepts of life.

This was the one thing about the Mormons which
made Catherine a little uncomfortable. When they
were together in a group they seemed to share so much
common knowledge and experience that it was easier
for them to relate to one another than to an outsider.
Their conversation was dotted with references to
things Catherine knew nothing about—Elders, Doctrine
and Covenants, Relief Society, Visiting Teaching, Mutual Improvement, Degrees of Glory, the Temple Or-
dinance, Sealings, and Missionary Work. Catherine often felt helpless, as though she were in a land where
she did not know the language.

Missionary work was one thing which Ladean was
happy to talk about. Her fiancé, Dan Allred, was on a
mission in New Zealand, and she often read Catherine
excerpts from his letters. When he wrote about the
first time he had eaten raw fish, the two girls laughed
together. He told them about a game he was learning,
which involved throwing and tapping sticks in time to
a musical chant. In the old days the Maori people used
the game to prepare their warriors to have instanta-
neous reflexes in battle. "My partner missed catching
his stick yesterday, and it nearly knocked him cold!"
he wrote.

"When I come home, I will dress in grass skirts
and war paint and dance one of their war-challenge
dances for you. It will bring the house down—

literally!" Dan's letter continued. "I love these people. They have such humble, simple faith and we have baptized many." Just before he finished the letter he wrote, "I can't wait until I get home, Ladean, to show you how they rub noses down here!"

There it was again, this odd interchange of the earthly and the celestial elements of life, and Catherine looked at Ladean's dark, laughing eyes.

"When will he get back?" she asked.

"A mission lasts three years, and he's been gone for one," Ladean answered.

"You mean you're going to wait for two more years before you get married?" Catherine exclaimed. "How can you stand it, if you both know that you're right for each other?"

"I'll be busy teaching and saving money," Ladean replied, rather surprised at Catherine's question, as though what she was doing could hardly be considered extraordinary. "The time will go fast, and after that we have eternity together."

"Eternity?" Catherine asked.

"Yes, we're going to be married in the temple, and that means that we will be married forever." Ladean looked at Catherine with shining eyes. "When you love someone that much, waiting two years doesn't seem so hard."

The temple took on an even greater fascination for Catherine after that. She found herself staring often at the building's strong, graceful lines, the tall, slender windows giving interest to the squared shape, and the beautifully manicured grounds making the building appear to be mounted on an emerald hill.

Everything she saw in the Mormon culture impressed Catherine, but the thing that most surprised her was how natural and comfortable the Watkins family was—and how similar the pattern of their life was to her own. In the Mormon home there was a sense of quiet courtesy and restraint. The house was meticulously clean and orderly, and education, vigor, and service seemed to be greatly valued by each member. Often a married daughter or son would drop in with their little children, and the house would ring with merriment. In the evenings unexpected company would frequently appear, and the Watkinses would get out a card table and play a game similar to bridge called "Rook." Catherine was told that the Church did not countenance face cards, but other games were acceptable.

The family loved to sing, and Mrs. Watkins and Ladean seemed to know all the newest songs. While they worked in the house, they would turn on the radio and sing along with gusto. If members of the family came to visit, someone would burst into a snatch of song, and before long everyone would join in. Their harmony was lovely, their voices rich and joyful.

Catherine had never known such gregarious people. It seemed there was a church party or activity every night, and on weekends everyone—adults and teenagers—went to the church dance. The dance was held in a new building near the main street. The building was called the Stake House, and it had a large hardwood auditorium where the young men played basketball during the week, and the dances were held on the weekend.

The first weekend Catherine declined Ladean's invitation to attend the dance, but the next week she accepted. The dance floor was crowded with parents, university students preparing to return to school, young farm couples, teen-agers, and a fringe of loiterers. No one was permitted to loiter long. An energetic young man approached every eligible boy who was caught lounging and assigned him to a young lady. Ladean saw to it that Catherine did not spend much time sitting, and although Catherine recognized that most of the young men considered it an obligation to dance with her, still they were very nice, and she found herself, surprisingly, having a good time.

She could not help but note, however, that Ladean appeared to be the belle of the ball. Everyone knew her, and with her dark shining hair and quick agile body she was a wonderfully attractive dance partner. Ladean was almost like a queen surrounded by an adoring court, and she seemed to enjoy every moment, radiating youth, joy, and high spirits. Catherine felt a twinge of distress for Dan Allred and wondered how he would feel if he could see his fiancé dancing and laughing with such abandon.

That night as the girls went to bed Catherine asked the question that had been bothering her. "Does Dan feel all right about your going to dances while he's away?"

Ladean's voice was astonished. "Of course he does! He wouldn't have it any other way. If I had to be solemn and suffer for two years, I'd never make it. You can be serious in life and still have fun!"

"I suppose so," Catherine whispered, and then to herself she thought of all the parties she had gone to over the years in Mount Royal. The worst offense in

Mount Royal would have been to have too much fun—
to laugh too heartily—to dance too brightly—to sing or
converse exuberantly. Control and restraint, those
were the passwords of her old social world—but here it
seemed the people valued both enjoyment and purpose. As she slipped into sleep, Catherine mused that
both worlds had their appeal, and yet somehow she
knew she didn't fit either one. Even in the warmth of
the soft bed, she felt a cold chill. Tears sprang to her
eyes. Here it was almost time for school to start! At the
beginning of the week Ladean would begin preparing
her classroom at the local high school in Cardston
where she was going to teach home economics. Yet Mr.
Raymond had still not resolved Catherine's problem.
As far as she knew, he was doing nothing to help her,
and a wave of anger and indignation kept her awake.
"He must do something for me," she whispered
fiercely in her sleep. "I can't go back . . . I won't go
back! What am I going to do?"

CHAPTER NINE

Early Monday morning Catherine was sitting again on the small, straight-backed chair in Mr. Raymond's anteroom where she had sat every workday morning since her arrival in Cardston. When she heard his door opening, she didn't even raise her head, but continued to sit listlessly in the chair, her eyes on her hands folded in her lap. Every line of her body spoke discouragement and defeat.

"Catherine," Mr. Raymond's voice was brisk and impersonal, "will you step into my office, please?"

"He's going to tell me to go home. It's all been for nothing," she thought with despair. School was starting in a few days, and there had been no change at all in the attitude of either Mr. Raymond or the Department of Indian Affairs. Catherine knew if she appealed to her father he could wield his influence and legal knowledge to get a contract for her, but that would be the worst defeat of all. To go to her father to find work would be an open admission that her own abilities and education were not enough to earn her a place.

Catherine sat down opposite Mr. Raymond. The battered maple desk between them was piled high with untidy papers and the office seemed buried in stacks of journals, files, and governmental forms. The small basement window high above his desk gave off pale early morning light, but the lighting would have been inadequate without the plain light fixture directly over his desk. The only object decorating the walls was a picture of the Premier of Alberta, looking very sober and grim. It was a dreary office, but Mr. Raymond was apparently unaware of his surroundings—his total concentration was always devoted to the mounds of work to be done. In the back of his mind he seemed to carry the vision of the endless needs of the people he felt driven to serve.

Through the long days of waiting Catherine had watched this harried man pouring himself into the cause of the Blackfoot tribe. She had heard him speak harshly to the tribal leaders, and understood, as they did, that he spoke not in anger, but in frustration, seeing in their helplessness to change their lot the reflection of his own helplessness. The trait that Catherine most admired about Mr. Raymond was his unwillingness to give up. As enormous as any task might be, and as hopeless the results, nonetheless he appeared each morning vigorous, angry, dedicated, and ready to do battle once again. "And he says I'm stubborn and persistent!" Catherine thought with an ironic twist.

"I think I've got it, Catherine," Mr. Raymond said in a matter-of-fact voice as soon as Catherine was seated.

"Got what?" Catherine asked. She had been so certain she was going to be told to go home that his words made no sense to her.

"Your contract!" he replied impatiently. "Isn't that what you've been dead set on getting, ever since you entered this town? What else would I mean?"

Catherine was still incredulous, and her mind could

hardly absorb the news. "You mean, you really have a teaching contract for me? The Indian Bureau changed its mind? How long have you known? What made them do it? I . . ."

"Now, hold on, Catherine. You never said anything about it having to be an Indian school contract . . . and, if you want my advice, you won't take this contract I'm offering . . . but at least I've filled the obligation you seem to feel I have toward you. I've got a contract here, but it is not for an Indian school." He looked through an untidy stack of papers on his desk and drew out a stapled, printed form. "It's a contract for the Spring Valley School, which is the only school in Southern Alberta at this moment that is available. Ed Solembaugh, the District Supervisor, has been informed of your qualifications and has offered you the position." Mr. Raymond sighed and then a ghost of a smile crossed his face. "No," he continued, "I didn't state that quite correctly. The truth is, if a two-toed sloth walked in the door and said it would sign this contract, Ed would take it! He's desperate. As I said, Catherine, I don't advise you to accept this contract."

"What's wrong with it?" Catherine asked, shaken by conflicting emotions—joy at being told a contract was available, and alarm at Mr. Raymond's attitude.

"Spring Valley is the most godforsaken pittance of a school existing anywhere on this green earth," Mr. Raymond stated in his flat, unequivocal voice. "It stands on a little hill surrounded by hundreds of square miles of prairie and farmland. There's no town at all, just a loosely formed school district that takes in about fifty scattered dry farms."

"You mean the school is all by itself in the middle

of the prairie?" Catherine asked, hoping the answer would contradict that conclusion.

"Exactly," Mr. Raymond replied. "It was built on a piece of land donated by the Ranowskis, their place is the closest one to the school, about two miles down the road. Most of the children come to school by horse or wagon. A few of them are picked up by an old bus—when it runs—and one or two of the parents have trucks, so they drive some of the students."

"How many students are there?" Catherine asked.

"I think Ed said the registration this year was twenty, and they range in grades from first to twelfth. I think you would only have six in the high school age range—the rest are all younger. Most of these children quit school as soon as they're fifteen and the law says they can stop."

"Where will I live, if there isn't a town or anything?"

"There's a teacherage behind the school. Not much of one, I'm afraid, but at least it's snug and convenient. Listen, Catherine, I've grown to admire you through this whole sorry incident, and I'm telling you now, as your friend as well as your advisor—don't even think about taking this job."

"Why not?" Catherine asked.

"For heaven's sake!" Mr. Raymond exploded, and she could see his patience wearing thin. He had spent more time on this troublesome girl than she was worth, and his desk was piled with more important work. "Don't think like a character in a romantic novel. Idealism is the most absurd basis for decision-making in the world! Half of those children you'll be teaching have parents who can't speak a work of English. The parents hate and resent the fact that the government forces them to send their children to school when they could be at home working on the farm. Don't expect anyone is going to feel grateful or admire you for your unselfishness and hard work! You don't have any idea what loneliness you'd feel. How could you possibly survive a Canadian winter in an isolated one-room teacherage? A young attractive girl like you—why do you want to throw your life away like that? Be reasonable, Catherine. Go home where you belong,"

Poor Mr. Raymond didn't know it, but he had chosen just the right phrase to turn Catherine forever from a sensible decision. "Go home where you belong," he had said, and in response she felt her resolve harden into steel. "I don't belong," she wanted to shout, "that's why I have to remain."

In an implacable voice she answered, "I will sign the contract, Mr. Raymond. Please tell me how to contact Mr. Solembaugh, and I will leave for Spring Valley as soon as he can make the arrangements."

"Catherine," Mr. Raymond's dismay and disapproval were mirrored on his face, "you are making a poor decision. I'm sorry I told you about the contract. It was selfish of me."

"It's my decision, Mr. Raymond. You should not feel guilty. You have completely discharged your responsibility to me, and I appreciate it. You will not need to concern yourself with me anymore." She stood up and extended her hand for the papers. "Thank you. I know I have taken much of your time."

Mr. Raymond gave a quick glance at his pocket watch, and the harried frown returned to his face as he thought of the work waiting for him. He looked at

Catherine and opened his mouth as though to try once again to dissuade her, but seeing the conviction on her face, he shrugged his shoulders slightly and handed her the contract. "I give you my best wishes, Catherine, and my prayers. You're going to need both." She walked to the door of his office, and before she closed it, she could see him busily at work on a thick file of papers.

But the day had not yet yielded all of its surprises. In the corridor she saw Malcolm Brady, his arms stacked with files, heading for his offices.

"Mr. Brady?" she said, rather timidly. "Catherine Summerwell. It's nice to see you again."

"Miss Summerwell—Catherine." He smiled his thin, sardonic smile. "What brings you to my corridor again? I thought they closed your school—and I imagined you as long gone back to your palace."

"Not quite, Mr. Brady—er—Malcolm," she replied, her voice tinged with pride and defiance. "My palace for the next year is going to be a one-room schoolhouse in a place called Spring Valley."

Malcolm exploded with a short, mirthless laugh. "You mean they saddled you with that forsaken place? What madness made you say 'yes'?"

"Not madness—necessity," Catherine replied abruptly. "Besides, it should be a worthwhile experience."

"Still the little savior—the woman with a white lamp and a book, eh?" he shook his head sadly. "I can see you will not let me set you straight—you are determined to learn the hard way."

"Well," she said with spirited sarcasm, turning to walk away, "thanks for your good wishes!"

His face clouded for a minute, and he hurried after her and touched her arm gently. "Say!" he said, looking at her intently. "I'm really sorry. I think I was terribly rude right then. I just hate to see you getting into something so—so difficult."

He grinned at her. "Look, if it's really rough, I mean, if you ever need someone—well, Spring Valley is part of my district—call on me!"

Catherine smiled warmly. "Thanks, Malcolm," she said. "You almost sound like you mean that!"

"I do," he said briefly, then he extended his right hand and shook hers briskly. "Good luck, Catherine— and let me tell you, Princess, you've got more guts than I would have believed. You really gave 'em what for, didn't you?" He grinned again and was gone.

That night at dinner the Watkinses had a guest. He was an older man who had grown up with Bishop Watkins. Their parents had come to Canada together from Utah at the turn of the century when all of Southern Alberta was a prairie wilderness and homesteading was still the practice. The parents of these two men had helped found Cardston and several other small towns in the Southern Alberta wilderness. They spoke of memories of those childhood days when the land was so open and untouched it looked like an ocean of grass.

The visitor's name was Carl Nelson, and he farmed a large piece of property out near Glenwood. He had come to town for the day to do some buying at the Trading Post, and Bishop Watkins had invited him for supper.

As the two men spoke of the vastness of the prairies,

Catherine found the courage to share her news. She had been hesitant to tell the Watkinses about the contract for fear they would feel the same way Mr. Raymond had about her accepting the position. There was a moment of silence after her announcement, and then Mr. Nelson spoke.

"Well, there's some fine people out Spring Valley way. A lot of immigrants, but they're hard-working and clean, and they really understand the land. They work their children hard, too, and maybe you can do them some good—teach them as well as their children."

"That's right," Bishop Watkins said, with an encouraging smile. "They haven't assimilated themselves into Canadian society very well. . . . They don't bother to learn the language, and they yank the children out of school as soon as they can. Maybe you can help them to see that they're part of a new country now."

"At least they're so independent the Social Credit gang can't get 'em! And that's to their credit! Not like those hanger-ons around here who sold their votes for twenty-five dollars a month in social scrip." Mr. Nelson's voice was indignant.

"It wasn't quite like that, Carl," the Bishop said calmly. "People were starving. The crops were bad, and with the depression they couldn't even sell what crops they had! I guess the promise of free money sounded too good to pass up." Bishop Watkins's voice was conciliatory.

"I'm telling you, Bishop, if I didn't know how firmly you opposed the Social Creditors, I wouldn't stand here and listen to you talk such tripe," Carl Nelson's voice rose in indignation. "You know, and I know, that people shouldn't try to get something for nothing. Government handouts will turn this whole province into a land of lotus-eaters."

"We can't allow politics to cloud our judgment about other people, Carl. Social Credit won the election and we have to learn to live with it."

"You mean, they bought the election! . . . and I find that hard to live with."

"We can go to battle at the polls, and maybe next time we'll win. If you give people long enough, they can usually see truth from error."

Carl Nelson laughed and pushed back his chair. "It's plain to see why you're the Bishop, and I'm still just an Elder. I'll never be able to countenance anyone with a lily-livered dependence on the government. Mark my words—the day will come when we'll all live to regret letting the government buy our souls."

"Now Carl, I'm as loyal a Conservative as you are, but we still have to live with our Social Credit neighbors, and it's a long time till the next election, so try to be a little gentler in your personal judgments."

"Fortunately, I don't have to be. It's you, not I, who will be a judge in Israel!" Carl stood up and prepared to leave. He and Bishop Watkins shook hands, and after thanking Mrs. Watkins for supper and with a word to Catherine and Ladean, the fiery old man left, his face still thunderous at the thought of the provincial government he opposed so violently.

Bishop Watkins returned to the table shaking his head and smiling affectionately. "There goes a man who is always either hot or cold, the Lord will never sprew him from His mouth! Catherine, if you go to Spring Valley you will be living among people very much like Carl. Those farmers are fiercely independent, and they fear education because the government provides it. They feel education might change their children—take them from them. You have to fight their prejudice and win their loyalty and affection before you will feel welcomed and part of their community. It won't be easy, but I have a feeling, since we've grown to know you, that you relish a challenge. It will be lonely work, though, and you will have to learn the skills of living alone."

For the first time Catherine began to feel encouragement. Here was someone who believed she could do it and someone who felt she might do something of real value. A weight lifted from her spirits and with a radiant smile she looked from Bishop Watkins, to his wife, and Ladean. "I'll learn!" she said, with determination, "I'll learn—and I'll teach!" For the briefest of moments she felt the tight warm circle of the Watkins family open, and she slipped inside, and for that moment she belonged! They smiled at her, pride gleaming in their eyes.

Ladean drove Catherine to Spring Valley three days before school was to begin. They drove on isolated, narrow gravel roads which lay in straight lines across the broad, flat, empty prairie. They traveled about fifty miles from Cardston, although the actual distance to Spring Valley was considerably less if they could have driven a direct route, instead of having to follow roads that intersected at sparse intervals and often backtracked through unmarked fields. As the girls traveled through the early autumn afternoon only the outline of the mountains on the western horizon prevented them from feeling complete disorientation. There were a few farmhouses, clusters of barns and outbuildings, and some lonely grain elevators silhouetted against the sky which indicated a spur of the railroad, but the main impression of the journey was one of awesome immensity and emptiness.

Suddenly Ladean exclaimed, "There's the Ranowskis' house! We're almost there!" Catherine noted briefly a big, white farmhouse with a veranda, and a yard of beaten earth, neat as a painting. Her mind, however, was focusing on the anticipation of seeing her school—the place she would be living for the next year—and two miles further down the road Ladean excitedly pointed to a rise on the opposite side of the road. "Your school's on the other side of that little hill," she said. In another moment the road took them up the hill and from the vantage of the slight rise Catherine caught her first glimpse of Spring Valley School, situated on the far side of the slope. The school was a simple one-room structure with a gable roof and an iron stovepipe sticking up. There were two windows on the side of the building that they faced, and as they turned onto the dirt driveway, Catherine saw that the front of the school supported a sign: SPRING VALLEY SCHOOL DISTRICT. A narrow window flanked either side of the heavy door. Since there were no trees or shrubs, the school stood on bare prairie grass, and the only sign this was a habitation for children was an old swing set, and, next to it, a tall metal pole with hanging chains attached to a rotating ring at the top. This second apparatus she recognized from her own school days was a game called "Giant Stride." She remembered the exhilaration of grasping the bars at the ends of the chains and running around in a circle until the centrifugal force became so great that one was airborne and would swing in a wide circle around the pole until the momentum died. Circling the bottom of this pole, she could see a wide path apparently worn by the children's feet as they ran, pounding as fast as they could go, until the unexpected moment when they would suddenly soar up into the air. The flight, she remembered, was always disappointingly short.

Ladean stopped the car and climbed out. The strong prairie wind caught her dark hair and floated it around her face while her skirts billowed around her legs. "Hey!" Ladean said, looking at the school building. "It's really cute! And just think—it's all yours! Do you want to go in and look at the inside of the school first, or do you want to go around back and see what the teacherage looks like?"

"I don't want to keep you longer than necessary," Catherine answered. "You've got a long drive home. Why don't we go take a peek at the teacherage, and then you can get on your way if you need to."

"Are you kidding?" Ladean responded. "I want to see it all!"

Catherine pulled out the key which Mr. Solembaugh had given her in exchange for her signed contract. Hesitantly, she opened the front door and the two girls looked into the room. On either side were desks, ranged in order from small to large. There was a teacher's table desk and chair at the front of the room, two large blackboards, and a stool. At the back of the room were a black iron stove and a large woodbox. The walls were made into shelves, and the shelves were neatly stocked with books.

Catherine laid down the box of paper, pencils, pens, ink, rulers, and other supplies that had been given to her at the central office before she left Cardston.

"It may not be elegant, but it looks like all the essentials are here," she said in a determined, cheerful voice.

"Wow!" Ladean looked around, her eyes wide with interest. "Don't you feel just like you're in a movie or something? I mean, this is so wonderfully old-fahioned!"

"Yes," Catherine replied with a grin, but remembering Mr. Raymond's warning about romanticizing her life, she added, "I have a hunch when the children appear, it is going to seem very real."

After they examined the school outhouse, they walked down the little path behind the school to the tiny square teacherage of plain clapboard with an off-center front door and window.

Catherine pulled out another key, which opened the door to the teacherage. Inside the single room was impeccably clean, and the thought struck Catherine that someone had anticipated her coming because neither the schoolroom nor the teacherage showed any signs of neglect, dust, or disarray. Her living quarters fairly sparkled with cleanliness. The brightly colored linoleum floor looked freshly waxed and the windows shone. There was a wooden table with two matching chairs, a dry sink with a calico skirt around its base, a narrow bed with a hand-crocheted cover over a dark homemade quilt, and a plump pillow with a snowy white linen cover. In the center of the floor was a small braided rug and, on the wall by the door, two rows of hooks.

"Your closet, madame," Ladean said, pointing to the hooks.

On the little table there sat a pitcher and bowl to be used for washing up and in the pitcher was a handful of Lazy Susans. The bright yellow flowers were like a mysterious welcome.

"Who do you suppose has done all this?" Catherine whispered, staring at the pleasant surprise. Someone had really prepared for her arrival.

"I don't know who it was," Ladean answered, "but I'd surely find out fast. . . . Someone is obviously glad you've come! You can use all the friends you can get out here!" She gestured out the side window, and the two girls stared for a moment at the barren vista that stretched as far as they could see.

"I wouldn't look out that window too often if I were you!" Ladean said and laughed, trying to make a joke of it, but both girls felt a chill at the glimpse of desolation outside the cozy room.

Impulsively, Ladean gave Catherine a quick hug. "You will come and spend Thanksgiving and Christmas with us? Promise! Promise! And any weekends you can come! Oh, we'll have so much to tell each other! And there'll be all the parties! It will be such fun! You'll have so many more adventures to tell me—I shall simply have boring stuff about faculty meetings. Oh, I almost envy you—so many new experiences . . ."

Ladean tried to stave off the moment of leave-taking with her vivid, cheerful voice, but both she and Catherine felt sobered by the coming farewell. They walked together to the car, and as Ladean climbed into the driver's seat, she turned to Catherine with tears in her eyes. "Oh, I do so hate to leave you! You seem so . . ."

Before she could say the word they both dreaded to hear, Catherine forestalled her with a gesture. "Don't say it, Ladean! I'm fine! This is a lovely spot—open and fresh, and someone has already been kind to me. I know I'm going to be happy. How can I ever thank you and your family?"

It was now Ladean's turn and she shook her head. "Don't say it, Catherine! You don't need to, we love you—you are very dear to us. So, it's only good-bye until Thanksgiving! Call if you need anything. I'll remember you in my prayers, and you do the same!"

"You mean you want me to remember you in my prayers," Catherine asked, laughing.

"No," Ladean replied, smiling, "I mean you remember yourself in your prayers—I told you, you're going to need all the help you can get!"

Both girls were smiling bravely as Ladean drove down the short dirt driveway to the main road, and Catherine watched the trail of dust left by her car until it was only a wisp on the far horizon. Looking down the road, she could also see the cluster of buildings that was the Ranowski farm, and she could make out smoke rising from their chimney. A tractor that looked like a tiny toy was moving in their distant field, harrowing the stubble left from the harvest. Except for these faraway signs of human habitation, as she stood on the hill looking as far as her eyes could see, there was nothing but a wide expanse of grass and sky stretching before her.

The sun was high in the sky and the air was swept

clean by the constant wind that rushed down from the mountains and across the vast prairie like an enormous broom. In the silence the word which both she and Ladean had dreaded came into her mind. "Alone." But, oddly enough, instead of desolation she felt a sense of exhilaration. She took a deep breath of the crystal air and shook her hair in the playful wind. Then she whirled around and noticed the Giant Stride, its chains dangling around its pole, jingling as the wind clapped them against one another. On impulse she strode over to the pole and grasped one of the bars. Pulling it out to its farthest extent, she began running around the pole. The other riderless bars swung out on their chains in a circle around her as she ran faster and faster until suddenly she was lifted off her feet and soared in a wide exuberant circle. Slowly, she lost momentum and her feet once again touched the ground. She dropped the bar and jumped out of the way as the chains' thrust carried them around in circular motion once more, and then she watched as the chains wound around the pole like drunken ribbons, clanging in disorderly array, and then fell limp and silent. Catherine's cheeks were flushed and her eyes were sparkling as she walked over to the schoolhouse to prepare for the coming of her students. "It's just possible," she thought to herself, "that being alone has some advantages."

CHAPTER TEN

The first day of school Catherine did not know exactly what to expect. She had worked hard for three days to prepare the schoolroom for the students, organizing textbooks and materials for each grade, planning a tentative seating arrangement, and preparing lesson plans. On the blackboard she had written with colored chalk, "Welcome Back to School. My name is Miss Summerwell," and on each desk she had put paper, pencils, ink, and pens, with two shiny new nibs for each pen—one fine-line and the other wide-tipped. She had written to her father asking him if he would donate a world globe for her classroom, but until the globe arrived she had placed a rolled map of the world over the blackboard which could be released by untying its string. She loved the map; the colors on it were vivid, and she enjoyed seeing the bright pink that signified the British Empire because it dominated the map and gave her a comfortable feeling of belonging to a powerful political entity.

Predictably, she did not sleep well the night before the start of school, and so she rose at dawn. Although it was early in September, the morning air was cold, and she decided to run over to the schoolhouse to start a small fire in the stove to take the chill off so the children would be comfortable their first morning of class. She dressed in a dark blue tailored dress with white cuffs and collar and a black velvet tie. When she glimpsed herself in the mirror over her bed, she had to smile—she truly looked the part of a classic school-marm. With a wry look she grabbed the unruly mass of her hair, brushed it into shining order, and pulled it back into a severe bun. "No one will make the mistake of thinking I am frivolous or too young," she thought.

Starting the fire in the stove proved to be more difficult than she had anticipated. Immediately it was apparent that the wood in the woodpile was cut too large to fit the stove. Since Catherine had never wielded an ax, she found herself wrestling with the awkward tool, trying to chop the wood into smaller pieces. She kept missing the chunk of wood altogether as she swung down with an ax, or else struck it a glancing blow which sent the log spinning off the chopping block. At best, all she seemed able to do was split off jagged splinters and small chunks. The exertion caused her hair to fly out of its pins, and in spite of the cold morning air she was soon panting from the warmth of the unaccustomed effort.

Finally, after almost an hour of inefficient labor, she had a small pile of uneven wood with which to start the fire. She let herself into the school, which was still dim in the early morning light, and she crumpled up papers, put the ragged kindling on top of the paper, and added two good-sized chunks of wood. "There!" she thought, brushing her hair back from her face with a sooty hand. "That should do it." She lit the paper with a match, closed the stove door, and then looked at her blackened hands. "Oh, my goodness!" she exclaimed and flew out the door. The sun by now was rising in the sky, and she knew it must be approaching schooltime. Looking down the road, she could see vehicles moving toward the school. Quickly, she dashed over to the pump and frantically worked the handle. No water came out. "Oh, no!" she groaned, "it needs to be primed!" She headed for the teacherage at a rapid trot, and opening the door, grabbed the wash pitcher, only to discover she had emptied it when she had washed up earlier. In despair she grabbed a damp towel and scrubbed at her hands. She could feel her hair hanging loosely down her back and quickly she smoothed it and pulled it back. As she grabbed hairpins from the table, she saw a wagon stopping by the driveway and several children climbing out, so she hurried from the teacherage and down the pathway toward the school, pinning her hair as she ran.

Before she had left Cardston, in her brief interview with Mr. Solembaugh, she had been given a few words of advice, among which was the suggestion of Mr. Solembaugh that the first day of school would be the most important day of her year. In a solemn voice he had informed her that the impression a teacher made upon the children the first time they saw her was absolutely essential in establishing a relationship of discipline and respect. "Children should not meet the teacher on the playground," Mr. Solembaugh proclaimed. "Their first glimpse of you should be when the bell is rung and the children come in to take their places at their desks. At that time a teacher should be in place behind her own desk, her bearing showing dignity, intelligence, and . . ." here Mr. Solembaugh's voice had swelled with conviction . . . "absolute authority."

Catherine found herself hoping that none of the children would notice her, but she saw them standing shyly in the schoolyard staring at her curiously as she opened the door to the schoolroom and slipped inside. A wave of heat assailed her, and she realized that the little fire she had set in the stove was roaring, and the stove was giving off a blast of heat that seemed incredible from such a small appliance. Catherine recalled something she had heard about stove dampers which controlled the amount of heat and could stifle an existing fire, but since she had no idea where or what dampers were, she could think of no way to slow down the red-hot glow from the iron stove. "It can't go on like this all morning," she reassured herself, "not on two chunks of wood. It will cool down by itself."

She looked at the clock on the wall and realized she must ring the large brass bell in five minutes. She began to rehearse her opening speech to the children, in the meantime glancing nervously out the window at the growing number of children who were standing idly in the schoolyard. Some of the little ones were playing on the swings and a few of the boys had taken a turn or two on the Giant Strides, but most of the students were standing still with lunch boxes in their hands, waiting.

Catherine would have been alarmed that no parents had stopped by to meet her, but Bishop Watkins had warned her that the parents felt school was her business, and they accepted the necessity of getting their children to the classroom, but had little or no interest in what went on there. "You will need to win your way," he had warned her. It amazed Catherine that so many children could appear, seemingly out of nowhere. Not until weeks later did she realize that there were more farms and homesteads within the radius of her view than she realized. The houses were built in riverbottoms or behind small dips in the prairie landscape or behind clumps of cottonwood, so that it was hard to see them unless you knew where to look. Some of the children walked to school, even in the bitterest weather, but most of them came from distances too far to walk. She noticed four saddle horses, hobbled or tied near the school fence, and watched other students arriving in trucks, wagons, and several in a small paneled bus, the paint of which had long since rusted away.

The wall clock began to strike nine o'clock. "Children," she whispered to herself, in a last frantic rehearsal, "I am very happy to welcome you back to school." With a trembling hand she took the brass bell from her desk and walked to the door, opened it, and rang the bell loudly with six vigorous shakes of her hand. Then she hurried back up the aisle between the desks, leaving the door open, and stood valiantly behind her desk waiting for the children to enter.

They came, quietly, apprehensively, solemnly, and stood in an uncertain cluster inside the door. Remembering Mr. Solembaugh's admonition for dignity and authority, Catherine stood primly and looked at them. "Children . . . er . . . students," she amended as she saw several tall, mature adolescents standing behind the smaller children. "I have assigned each of you a desk. The younger ones in the front, the older ones at the larger desks in the back of the room. If you will look at the desks, you will find your names. If any of you cannot find your name, please tell me."

There was a flurry of activity as the students moved from desk to desk, and finally everyone was standing or sitting in place. "Fine," she said, breathing a sigh of relief; at least she had solved the seating problem. "As you can see from the board, my name is Miss Summerwell, and I will be your teacher this year. After we have sung the National Anthem, saluted the flag, and read from the Bible, I will ask each one of you to please stand and introduce yourself to me."

Something was wrong. There was a restless feeling in the classroom. Catherine saw an apple-cheeked youngster in the front row struggling to take off her bulky sweater. The bigger boys in the back of the room were shuffling their feet and glaring at the stove. "It's hot in here!" a child's voice exclaimed. "Yeah! How come the stove's on? It's still summer!"

"Don't apologize! Don't explain!" Catherine repeated the dictum in her mind. Absolute authority—wasn't that what Mr. Solembaugh had explained? If she lost it today, she'd never regain it.

"You!" she said, pointing to the biggest boy in the back of the room. "I'm sorry I don't know your name yet, but could you please open the windows and the door?"

"No, ma'am, I . . ."

Catherine was horrified, her first request and the boy was refusing to obey her. She looked at the young man. He was a good head taller than Catherine, with broad shoulders, a square jaw, and dark intelligent eyes. Suddenly Catherine felt very young and inexperienced and fear made her sharp. "You will do as I ask! What is your name, please?"

"Nicholas Ranowski, ma'am. I can't do it. I can't do what you ask."

"And why not?" she asked, her indignation rising as she felt her control over the class slipping away. She stepped out from behind her desk and walked down the aisle toward Nicholas. As she passed the rosy-cheeked little girl in the front row, the child began giggling. She stared at Catherine and nervous laughter bubbled forth. The little girl clapped her hands over her mouth, but her whole body was shaking with merriment and her blue eyes danced. The boy next to her looked at Catherine and his mouth opened in astonished amusement. Catherine felt her composure slipping, and then she heard a childish voice whisper, "Teacher's got a dirty face." As she stood in the aisle she could feel the children surreptitiously glancing up at her, and then ducking their heads in triumphant amusement.

She looked at Nicholas and her expression must have communicated a look of mute appeal because his firm young man's voice cut through the undercurrent of whispered amusement, and in a respectful and authoritative tone he addressed her. "Miss Summerwell, it was nice of you to fix a fire for us this morning, and we appreciate it. This is a hard stove to operate, but with your permission, I think I can fix the dampers. I can't open the windows because they're insulated, you know—nailed shut, ma'am."

"Thank you, Nicholas," Catherine said, giving him a grateful smile, but keeping her voice disciplined and crisp. "Now children," she continued, "while Nicholas adjusts the temperature, I will ask all of you to re-move your sweaters and jackets." Then some imp in her said the heck with Mr. Solembaugh and dignity, and she added in a merry voice, "And I will remove the soot from my face!"

The class erupted in delightful laughter, and she went back to her desk, took out a handkerchief and compact mirror, and rubbed the soot from her fore-head and cheek. "The first thing I'm going to do is appoint a fire chairman!" she told the class.

"Nicholas! Nicholas!" the class shouted.

"Nicholas it is!" she said. "Now, if you will all stand quietly, we will repeat the pledge of allegiance." She put her hand over her heart and turned to face the Union Jack where it hung from its standard above the blackboard. The classroom was silent, and her heart thrilled as she began the words, "I pledge allegiance . . ." and she heard the chorus of their voices—all twenty of them—following in perfect cadence. "It has begun," she thought proudly, "I am truly a teacher."

By the end of the second week of school Catherine knew most of the children's names and her days had begun to take on a semblance of order. At the begin-ning of each school day she arranged work pages on the desks of the younger students, and while they started these warm-up activities, Catherine would go to the back of the room where the older students sat and give them assignments and explain their study projects. As soon as the older students were involved in their work, she could turn her attention to the younger ones again, teaching math principles to the middle classes and assigning specific work. When everyone was occupied, she could begin the reading lessons with the first graders.

Geography, literature, and general subjects she taught to the classroom as a whole, trying to add sophisticated knowledge to challenge the older students and enough simple facts to interest even the little ones. Whenever the children finished an assignment, they were expected to select a book from the shelves and read until Catherine could give them further direction.

This pattern worked out well, and although there were times when Catherine felt overwhelmed, she could feel the progress she was making. Above all, she delighted in teaching the first graders. When she sat with them in their reading group, they would stand or sit close to her, pushing and pressing their sturdy little bodies around her. They loved the smell of her perfume and her soft hair, and they would touch the fabric of her clothes gently and call her "teacher" with such reverential sweetness that she wanted to sweep them up into her arms because they were so appealing and enchanting.

With the older students she felt less secure in her ability to teach. When she faced the teen-aged students, she felt timorous and inadequate. There were six students of high school age—four girls and two boys, one of whom was Nicholas Ranowski. Nicholas, Dick Wilson, and Julie Lundquist were in the twelfth grade, the three other girls were younger. Catherine had the impression these three girls were simply marking time until they turned fifteen and could leave school. Their interest in school was perfunctory at best. The three seniors, however, were a puzzle to her.

All three had gone against the custom in this community and had continued school after they were of legal age to quit. Nicholas Ranowski was a serious student, and already she sensed an extraordinary intelligence in him, but the other boy, Dick Wilson, was a surly, pimply-faced youth who had yet to complete a single assignment. Julie Lundquist, the senior girl, was a slender young woman, with prominent pointed breasts accentuated by tight sweaters and wide cinched belts. Her hair was as black as midnight and escaped in a mad tangle around her heavily made-up face which wore a continual sullen expression. Julie appeared not only to be indifferent to school, but contemptuous of it. Several times when Catherine had given her an assignment she had discovered Julie reading a movie magazine instead. The third time this happened, Catherine picked up the magazine and put it under her arm. "I will return this to you at the end of the school day, Julie," she said. "In the future I would appreciate it if you would not bring this type of literature to school."

Julie scowled and her face took on a petulant look. She glared at the magazine under Catherine's arm, and then picked up a nail file on her desk and began to file a polished scarlet fingernail.

"Please begin your written assignment now, Julie. If it isn't finished at four o'clock, you will have to stay after school to finish it."

Julie still said nothing. "You are to answer me, 'Yes, Miss Summerwell,' when I speak to you," Catherine said, her face set and composed. Desperately in her mind, however, Catherine was wondering what she would do if the girl refused to finish her work or to obey any requests. She wondered what effect the girl's disobedience might have on the other students, and she dreaded a confrontation. With relief she watched as Julie reluctantly drew a copy book out of her desk and picked up her pencil.

"Yes, Miss Summerwell," she said in a voice that was close enough to insolence to be insulting, and yet not close enough to call for a direct reprimand. Catherine walked away, unnerved by the girl's cool assurance.

Nicholas, in contrast to the others, was an avid student. Every night he carried home armloads of books and his assignments were neatly and rapidly finished, his questions searching and incisive. Catherine sensed in Nicholas a great thirst for learning, and in a way he was the most terrifying to her of the three senior students because she questioned her ability to teach and direct him. Already in some areas she felt his knowledge came close to, or surpassed, her own. She wondered what would happen when he asked her a question for which she could give no answer.

In some strange way she sensed the reason Julie and Dick had continued in school had something to do with Nicholas, but she did not feel that they were friends. The three seldom spoke to one another, and yet Catherine detected an odd undercurrent between them that made her uncomfortable.

Many of the children spoke very little English, but they all had a look of ruddy health, and Catherine saw everywhere the evidence of parental caring, especially in the warm, sturdy clothes the children wore—handknit sweaters, heavy woolen stockings, stout waterproof workshoes, clean shirts and blouses that were freshly starched and ironed—and hair that was brushed and shiny. When the lunch bell rang, out came the children's lunch pails packed with home-made sausages, strudel, thick ham sandwiches on homemade bread, sweet pickles, slices of spicy cakes and raisin tarts. Catherine had never seen such food, and she wondered at the love and effort of the unseen hands which had prepared it. She was curious to see the homes that had created these wholesome, merry children. For the first time in her life she found her-self questioning the absolute value of formal education simple parents. She had to ask herself if it might not who were raised on isolated farms by hardworking, as she saw the strength and stability of these children be as useful and valuable to learn how to make won-derfully flaky strudel, or to card wool and knit the lovely intricate designs of the little boys' sweaters, as it was to learn the succession of the kings of England.

Late Friday afternoon she had seen the children off to their homes and was sitting at her desk marking papers when she heard the school door open. Nicholas Ranowski put his head through the door. "Miss Sum-merwell, may I speak to you for a minute?"

"Of course, Nicholas," she answered. "Come in."

Although the Ranowskis were the most well-to-do of all the local families, Nicholas's appearance gave no suggestion of wealth. He was dressed in the same sturdy simple clothes which the other students wore—heavy, plaid mackinaw jacket, dark work pants, a neatly pressed flannel shirt, and clean, polished work boots. His clothes were appropriate, of good quality, but reflected a life of outdoor labor rather than afflu-ence.

Catherine felt timid toward Nicholas, unsure of how

to assert the proper authority over a young man who towered above her, his broad shoulders and masculine strength so fully developed that it was hard to think of him as a student. His face was intelligent and serious, with dark eyes that seemed to miss nothing, but his mouth had a habitual pleasant look, as though at any moment he might break into a smile. Something in his expression gave the impression of a childlike innocence, but in the strength of his eyes and face she sensed an emerging man of enormous vitality and assurance.

In his manner toward Catherine, Nicholas showed respect and a great eagerness to learn. At recess she had observed him playing with the younger children and had wondered at his patience and sense of fun. He organized games and coaxed the shy youngsters into participation, and his strong arms would swing the little ones high until they laughed with glee. He showed the same gentleness and patience toward the horses the children rode to school. He helped the younger children feed and curry their ponies, and at the end of the day he stayed until they were all saddled and safely on their way before he saddled his own mare and cantered up the road toward his home.

As Nicholas entered the schoolroom, Catherine smiled formally. "What is it you wish to see me about, Nicholas?" she asked.

Nicholas was holding a soft peaked hat in his hands, and she saw his hands clench, as though he found it awkward or difficult to say what he wanted.

She glanced at his face and saw that it was flushed with nervousness. "Mama wanted to know if you could come for dinner tonight?" His voice was hesitant as though he expected to be refused.

"Why, Nicholas . . . " she stammered, taken aback by the invitation because this was the first overture of interest she had received from any of the parents. She had begun to think that she would go the entire year and never see any of the parents' faces. Her face must have shown her confusion because Nicholas dropped his eyes in disappointment.

"I know you're busy, Miss Summerwell, and it's just a plain farm supper, nothing fancy, with all the family, and well, if you can't come, Mama will understand."

"Oh, no!" Catherine exclaimed. "I'd love to come, Nicholas. I'm very anxious to meet your family. It's nice of your mother to ask me. I was just—surprised—that's all. When shall I come? Oh!—and how shall I get there?"

The last thought struck her suddenly as she realized how little forethought she had given to her year at the teacherage. She had provided herself with no transportation at all. Since her groceries were delivered weekly from town, she had felt no need for a car.

Nicholas smiled, and as he smiled he seemed to shrug off his shyness and become more natural. He liked to solve problems, and he had already given this problem some thought.

"Well, ma'am," he said, "I think there are three possible solutions, and you can choose which one you think best. We could walk together and I could lead my horse. "Or," he continued, "we could both ride on my mare. Or, I could go home and saddle up the buckboard and be back for you in about an hour."

Catherine smiled at his careful logic. "What time do you usually eat supper?" she asked.

"Around five," Nicholas replied.

"And it's after four now," Catherine observed, looking at her watch. She thought for a moment. "I think perhaps it would be best if we walked. You go get your horse, and I'll get ready and meet you down by the end of the driveway."

"Yes, Miss Summerwell," Nicholas answered and turned to leave.

As he opened the door Catherine called after him. "Thank you, Nicholas."

He turned and grinned and was gone. Catherine gathered the papers and put them in the top drawer, then went over to the water pitcher by the corner of the room. As she freshened her face and hands, she thought to herself how nice the Ranowskis must be and wondered if they were the ones who cleaned the teacherage and brought the flowers for her arrival. From one of the hooks at the back of the room she took her camel hair coat, pulled her hat, scarf, and gloves out of the pockets, and feeling like a child let out for recess, closed the school door and locked it. She walked down the driveway with long strides toward Nicholas, who was waiting with his horse moving restlessly beside him.

They started out walking. Catherine was dressed in a plaid skirt and cashmere sweater, with scottish brogues on her feet, and so in spite of the chill wind and rocky road, she was comfortable and enjoyed the walk. Nicholas, on the other hand, was having a devil of a time with his mare. The horse, restless and bored from the long day of being hobbled in the schoolyard, was feeling the call of the open road. It was the horse's reflex at the end of the day to carry Nicholas down this stretch of road in a carefree gallop, and the powerful mare was not at all happy about being led by her bridle at such a slow pace. She pranced sideways and tugged on her bridle and nudged Nicholas so hard with her head that she almost knocked him over.

"Come off it, Lady," he said to the horse, and shortened his hold on the rein. "Behave yourself, or Miss Summerwell will fail you in manners."

Catherine laughed, but the horse jerked her head and pulled Nicholas across the roadway.

"Cut it out!" he exclaimed, half-laughing at the antics of the horse, and half-annoyed.

By now Catherine could not stop smiling. The spectacle of the young man trying to be a dignified escort and the unruly horse trying to get her own way was too amusing. "Nicholas," she said, her voice merry with amusement, "when a lady is determined, you'll learn you have to give in! I'm afraid you are going to have to give her a good gallop, or she'll give you no peace. I'm perfectly capable of walking alone, you go ahead and ride Lady, before she pulls away and runs home without you."

By now Nicholas was puffing with the exertion of trying to control the horse and the contest of wills was gaining force. "Are you sure, Miss Summerwell?" he asked, pulling on the reins and then pushing against the mare's shoulder as she began to turn in a circle to avoid his restraints.

"Yes, Nicholas. She deserves a good run after a day of patient waiting."

That was all Nicholas needed, and with quick decision he sprang into Lady's saddle. Horse and rider disappeared down the road in a burst of speed. Catherine had not expected the departure to be quite so abrupt, and she stood for a moment in the center of the road, watching the restless horse thunder away from her, and feeling a strange sense of loss. The loneliness of the prairie struck her, and she began to stroll slowly toward the Ranowskis, surprised at how much pleasure had gone from the walk with the departure of the young man and the horse. The sun was setting lower, and the wind seemed chill. She hunched her face down into the collar of her coat and walked purposefully along the road.

Suddenly she became aware of the sound of hoofbeats, and she looked up in surprise to see Lady and her young rider pounding back up the road toward her. She stopped in astonishment, having assumed they were already at the Ranowski homestead. Without a word Nicholas reached down his work-hardened, young man's arm, and, equally wordlessly, Catherine held onto it and sprang up behind him onto the horse.

"Hold on!" he shouted into the wind, and he wheeled the powerful mare around, and together they galloped pell-mell down the prairie road in the gathering twilight. The air was fresh and vigorous, and Catherine, holding tightly, could feel the tensile strength of Nicholas's body, as though it were made of the finest steel, flexible and strong. He rode the horse with such natural grace that she felt his oneness with the rhythm of the animal, and the steadiness of his hands and knees guiding the mare with expert surety. It was exhilarating and heady, and Catherine heard herself laughing into the wind, and heard Nicholas's answering exultant laughter—horse, wind, air, twilight, and youth. They were not student and teacher, but two people feeling the natural delight of being healthy, young, and alive.

When they came to the entrance of the Ranowskis' farm, Nicholas reined in the horse and sedately turned down the long drive leading to his large, square, two-storied home. A neat post and barbed-wire fence lined the driveway, and Catherine noted again the beaten earth of the front yard which was neatly swept in the European fashion. Breathlessly, she dismounted, and so did Nicholas. They still did not speak, and she turned to him, the exultant smile fading on her lips, but her eyes still sparkling. "Thank you for the ride," she said, trying to sound formal. Looking at him she felt he was more in command of the situation than she.

He replied with simple dignity, "You're welcome."

She could not meet his eyes, but instead raised a hand to her hair. "I must look a mess!" she murmured.

Again he looked at her, his eyes serious and direct. "No, Miss Summerwell," he said. "I'll go put Lady in the barn and meet you on the front porch."

"Fine, Nicholas," she answered, and walked up the driveway.

The Ranowskis were like no other family Catherine had ever known. The parents came from Bohemian Europe, and though they had learned English and insisted their children learn and adopt the ways of their new country, something of the robust, earthy spirit of the old country lingered in every corner of their lives.

The farmhouse in which they lived was one of big, square, sturdy rooms which needed no architectural frills. The walls were spotless white, and the floors were covered with shining linoleums in vivid, gaudy patterns. The front room was for guests and the family rarely used it. In this room was a heavy stuffed chesterfield couch and matching chair, with lace antimacassars on the back and arms. There was one picture, an inexpensive reproduction of a scene depicting the European Alps in electric blues and greens, which hung over the couch. There was also a vase filled with paper flowers. The room was spotless and unlived-in. The staircase leading up to the bedrooms was in this room, and on the other side of the stairs was the dining room, which was formally furnished with a heavy oak round table on a carved pedestal base and twelve dark oak chairs. A sideboard held hand-painted dishes and crystal from Europe.

However, it was in the huge kitchen that the house came to life. The kitchen ran the width of the house in the back. It was painted white, and in the center of the room was a long harvest table which could easily seat twenty people. On each side of the table were benches, and at the ends were hand-wrought wooden chairs with curved backs and deep, comfortable seats. A black cook stove dominated the room and the capacious woodbox at its side was filled with well-seasoned split logs, golden in the evening lamplight. The stove was covered with steaming pots and the kitchen was fragrant with delicious smells. Fresh baked bread was stacked on a work table under the windows at the side of the room, and a pie cupboard by the back door was filled with a dozen pies of delicious variety. Off the kitchen was the milk pantry, containing the milk separator and the pans with cream rising. A large wooden butter bowl was filled with creamy butter, into which a wooden paddle was stuck. The stone floor was lined with pickle crocks and the kitchen rafters were strung with cheeses, sausages on strings, a ham and sheaves of onions drying.

Nicholas's mother had met Catherine at the door, as Nicholas had gone to find his father. The first minutes of the visit had been extremely tense and uncomfortable for Catherine and Mrs. Ranowski as they sat formally in the barren front room. After a few painful attempts at conversation, Mrs. Ranowski jumped up and said she thought something was burning in the kitchen.

Catherine asked if she could help. At first Mrs. Ranowski refused the offer, but then natural social instinct caused her to accept. Sensing Catherine's feeling of awkwardness, Mrs. Ranowski brought her into the kitchen, and as soon as Catherine saw the homey room, she felt herself relaxing.

"Mrs. Ranowski!" she exclaimed. "This is the most wonderful room I've ever seen!"

"Oh," said Mrs. Ranowski with a deprecating shrug, her strong mid-European accent coloring the words, "it is just a woman's room. Come! I want you to meet my daughters-in-law, Anna and Kristina."

Catherine turned to see two women dressed exactly like Mrs. Ranowski in voluminous gingham dresses, with crisp white aprons tied around them and matching scarves on their heads covering their hair like babushkas.

The two younger women had faces similar to Mrs. Ranowski's also. All three women had high cheekbones, rosy full cheeks with dark, wide eyes, and full mobile mouths. Their faces were strong and filled with laughter and contentment, and although the women's hands were worn and reddened, they moved quickly and unceasingly at their tasks—and their tongues were as quick as their hands. They laughed and murmured and chatted as they moved about the kitchen, each one knowing exactly what her duties were, and each one performing them expertly and without wasted motion.

As Catherine sliced the bread, she saw the three women produce a supper table of almost magical proportions. The work was done so efficiently and rapidly Catherine almost felt she was witnessing magic.

The long kitchen table was covered with a snowy white cloth, and Mrs. Ranowski apologized to Catherine. "I'm sorry we are not eating in the dining room, but Mr. Ranowski stayed in the field so long he didn't get the fire going, and it is too chilly in there." Catherine thought to herself how glad she was that Mr. Ranowski had been late. She could not imagine anything more charming than eating at the table in this wonderful room.

The women set ten places with white ironstone plates, ruby glass tumblers, and heavy cutlery. White napkins of thick cotton were placed by each setting, and the table was decked with butter dishes, pickled beets, mustard pickles, gherkins, four jars of home-made jam, and a crock of honey. The mound of fresh bread which Catherine had sliced was placed in the center, and then bowls of creamy mashed potatoes, a large plate of thick sliced sausage meats and cheese, a vat of homemade cottage cheese, and bowls of cooked carrots and green beans were added. Finally, the oven door was opened and out came a ham, roasted to perfection, its skin crackling brown, with a thick, sugary glaze basting its sides.

When the ham was in place, one of the women stepped to the back door and called to the men who could be heard laughing and talking in the wash yard by the back door. The noise rose in volume as she opened the door, and Catherine could hear the hearty laughter of men, and suddenly, a great whoop and a shout and the crack of a towel being flipped. Mrs. Ranowski walked to the back vestibule and called out the door, "Steven! None of that! You want the new schoolteacher to think you are bad?" There was a sudden stillness, and then the men began to file in the door, shyly, their hair slicked down and wet from the washing-up, their faces and hands clean, but their work overalls still dusty from the field.

There were six men altogether, and they seemed to fill the kitchen, large as it was. All of the Ranowski men, beginning with the father, were tall and broad-shouldered, their hands large and powerful and their bodies forged by hard, honest labor. They all had dark hair and eyes, and high cheekbones and mobile lips like their mother. It was a Slavic face, more pronounced in the mother than in the sons. The father's face was narrower and his nose was high arched and prominent. His face was more northern European, and his influence in the boy's heredity refined and enhanced the faces of his sons. Catherine thought these five young men were an excellent example of the blessing of fine breeding. Each was handsome and intelligent and emanated the glow of health.

"Derek—Anna's husband," Mr. Ranowski intro-

duced each one of her five sons as they entered the
room, and they nodded or awkwardly shook Catherine's hand. "John—Kristina's husband; Rueben, who
has just been engaged: and this is Steven, who needs a
wife." The whole family roared at what was apparently
a family joke, and Steven boldly took Catherine's hand
and grinned at her as he shook it. "Every family needs
a black sheep," he said with a wicked grin, and then
added, "Welcome to Spring Valley. Some of my best
years were spent in your school, but I must say we
never had a teacher that looked like you! Nicholas always has the luck!"

Mrs. Ranowski shook her head in exasperation.
"Steven! You must not talk to the teacher like that!
Now sit down and be good!" The kitchen was warm
with laughter, and as Catherine was introduced to Mr.
Ranowski and escorted to her place on his right hand at
the table, she noted the husband and wives exchange
hearty kisses, and saw them clasp hands warmly as
they sat side by side at the table. Nicholas took his
place at the other end of the table next to his mother,
and the family was silent. Everyone bowed their heads
as Mr. Ranowski took his place, and a sweet stillness
filled the room. Then his deep voice intoned the
words of prayer in a beautiful, guttural language that
was unfamiliar to Catherine. When the words were finished, there was a murmured "Amen" from around the
table, and then the hearty, lusty sound of the men's
voices as they reached for the plates of food. Mr. Ranowski carved the ham and piled thick, rich slices on
Catherine's plate.

Catherine had thought that an army would be unable to eat the food which had been placed on the ta-

ble, but she watched in wonder as the men devoured plateful after plateful, and the bowls emptied.

Catherine noted also that although her plate was served with the men's, the other women waited until all the men were eating before they filled their own plates. Throughout the meal the younger women were up and down replenishing milk glasses and serving dishes before they were asked. It wasn't until much later that Nicholas told her it was very modern and daring for their family to eat together. Most of the local farmers still retained the European custom of having the men eat alone while the women served them, and then the women eat what was left. Mr. Ranowski, however, thought the food tasted sweeter when the women were at the table with the men.

Mr. Ranowski was a quiet man. He ate his food slowly, with obvious enjoyment, and as he ate his eyes drank in the length of the table. His face was scored with deep, weather-beaten wrinkles, and his eyes were fixed in a permanent squint which gave his face the appearance of a constant smile. The laughter wrinkles around his eyes were like rays of merriment and those eyes themselves showed obvious delight in the sight of his family. As he quietly watched them eating, joking, and arguing, his face registered a sublime contentment, like that of a king watching over his treasure house with replete satisfaction.

Once in a while he would look at Catherine sitting beside him and smile. "Eat!" he would say. "It is hard work teaching school. My Katherine is the best cook in Canada. Maybe in Europe, too. Eat!" Then he would turn back to his pleasant contemplation of the abundant table and his robust family.

Apparently there had been some disagreement in the fields that day, and Steven and Derek began to discuss it. "You know that field needs a year of fallow!" Steven declared. "I tell you, another year of crop on it, and the soil will be so depleted we'll cut the yield in half!"

"No," Derek said, his voice slow and more considered than Steven's. "I think if we rotate to another type of crop, we can use it one more year and then run it fallow."

"Rye grass, maybe," Steven said, "but nothing else!"

"Rye is not a moneymaker," Reuben injected.

"Rye grass is not a worthwhile crop—no money and no use," Derek added.

"Ever since you married you've been in a hurry to get rich," Steven said heatedly. "You can't spoil the land for the rest of us just because you want to go your own way!"

"Steven!" Mr. Ranowski's voice cut through the argument like steel. "You will not argue family matters in front of a guest. You will apologize to Miss Summerwell at once."

Catherine blushed. "No apology is necessary. I—"

"Yes," Mr. Ranowski said, "it is necessary. Steven, immediately!"

Steven looked at his father and Catherine half expected to see defiance, but instead the young man looked honestly contrite, and in a respectful voice replied. "I am sorry, Papa. Miss Summerwell, sometimes I forget my manners, we have so few guests." Then he turned back to Derek, and with an irrepressible grin he added, "But I'm still right!"

A flash of anger showed in Mr. Ranowski's eyes,

and then Derek began to laugh. "You are impossible, Steven!" he declared. "This is the tenth day of this argument! Will you never give up?" The family began to laugh and the talk veered to other things. Someone asked Catherine about the school, and she told them some amusing stories about the younger students.

Before she knew it, the table was being cleared and the dessert course set out: bowls of home-preserved peaches, a steaming rice pudding, a fruitcake bursting with nuts and raisins, and a decanter of sweet wine. Catherine had thought she was too full to eat another morsel, but she found herself tasting the desserts, seduced by their sweet richness. Mr. Ranowski insisted that she finish with a glass of the sweet wine, and so she ended the meal in utter repletion. The wine went to her head and made the colors, the light, the warmth, and the faces around the table melt together in a lovely harmony.

All too soon the table emptied. The husbands and wives went upstairs to their rooms, and Steven and Reuben excused themselves to prepare for their dates. They were going to drop Catherine off at the school in the buckboard on their way to pick up their girls.

After the kitchen was clean, Mr. and Mrs. Ranowski took Catherine back into the living room to visit with her until it was time to leave. Nicholas made a move to join them, but Mrs. Ranowski forestalled him.

"Nicholas, why don't you go out and hitch up the wagon, so it will be ready to leave when Reuben and Steven come down?"

"All right, Mama," he replied and went out into the night.

When they were seated, Mr. Ranowski began. "We

wanted to talk to you, Miss Summerwell, about Nicholas."

"Yes," Catherine said, somewhat puzzled. "What is it?"

"You see," Mr. Ranowski began, "we are simple people. We came from Europe with nothing. My wife was the daughter of a peasant, and I was the son of a traveling teacher. We brought nothing to this land but our wish to work, and we have given much to this earth—it has given much back to us. We are very grateful. It is a good life, and we would wish nothing better than this for our sons. Always we have thought they would be farmers, and I have planned and homesteaded my land in such a way that someday they will each have their own portion. My boys are good boys and good farmers—and good Canadians. We have tried to learn the ways of this new land, and though much of it is strange, we want our children to be at home here. That is why we donated the school—so our children could learn and be modern."

"We, Katherine and I, have little schooling, and so when our children went to school for twelve long years, we thought they were very educated, very modern. But Nicholas, he is different. The others went to school for obedience. He goes because it is in his blood. He is a good farmer, but it is books that give him joy, not the land. So now he tells us that he wishes even more schooling. He wants to leave Spring Valley and go to the university. He has great dreams, and if that is what will make him happy, we want it for him, too. What we must ask you, Miss Summerwell, is will it be possible? Or is he going to be hurt?"

Mrs. Ranowski eagerly joined the conversation. "He

has only been taught in this small little school. It is a fine education for a farmer, but when he goes to the university, will they laugh at him? Has he learned enough even to be accepted at the university? Is he smart enough to go where there are real scholars?"

Mr. Ranowski nodded his head at his wife's questions. "Will he be hurt is what we want to know."

Catherine's mind was whirling. "University!" She had never thought such a thing. Had never dreamed that she would be expected to prepare someone to take the Provincial Departmental exams—the difficult comprehensive examinations which must be taken and passed before anyone could enter the University of Alberta. She knew that Nicholas was a bright student, but she also knew that the education offered to him in a one-room school could not possibly compare to the preparation given to students at large high schools throughout the province. He would be competing with every other student in the province when he took the examinations.

Mr. Ranowski sensed her hesitation. "Do you think this is a possible thing which Nicholas wants?" he asked again, anxiously.

Catherine knew she must weigh her answer carefully, and she prayed she would say the right thing. "I know that Nicholas is a good student, intelligent and able, Mr. Ranowski, but I won't pretend to you that it would not be a drawback to have attended such a small school. Before I could tell you whether it would be possible for Nicholas to go to the university, I would need to spend some time testing him to see just how wide his learning experience has been. I really can't tell you any more until I have given him those tests. Perhaps then we could talk again."

She knew she was being cruel, telling them the truth and confirming their fears, but she felt that was better than raising false hopes. However, her impression of Nicholas caused her to reiterate the possibility that he might qualify. "He is a very intelligent young man, and there is a real chance that it may be done—if he has enough background to build on, and if he's willing to work hard for the entire year, he could possibly take the exams and do well."

"That is all we wanted to know," Mr. Ranowski said with great dignity. "We will trust our boy to you."

"Oh no!" Catherine wanted to cry out. "I'm not qualified to prepare him. This is the first year I have taught, and I have so much to learn." But she looked into the Ranowskis' faces, and they were beaming with such trust that she could not disillusion them any further. She determined that she would send for the preliminary test tomorrow, and after Nicholas had taken them, she would see what kind of a task had been given to her.

She sat between Reuben and Steven on the seat of the buckboard as they drove through the night. Their big bodies were bulky in wool jackets, and she felt warm and safe. The glow of the bright, scented kitchen seemed to linger in her mind. Steven was in a bright mood and teased her about her silence and her solemnity. "You look like a little girl playing at being a teacher!" he told her.

"Well!" she retorted, "I'm glad you weren't one of

my students. You probably spent your time dipping the girls' pigtails in the inkwell!"

"No," he replied with a frank laugh, "I was never interested in the little girls—only in the teacher!"

Reuben turned and gave Steven a disapproving look, then he said to Catherine, "Sometimes Steven forgets himself trying to be funny. I apologize for him."

"Miss Summerwell is going to think that all my family does is go around apologizing for me!" Steven said, laughing as they drove up the driveway past the school to the little teacherage that looked desolate and cold huddled on its barren hill.

"*Br-r-r,*" said Steven, looking at the dark little house. "Are you sure you want to go in there alone? Maybe I should come in with you and start the fire?"

"No, thank you," Catherine said, "I've already made you late. I'll be fine. Thank you for a wonderful evening."

Reuben sat on the buckboard and touched the peak of his hat in good-bye. He looked impatient to be gone, so Steven waited until Catherine had opened her door and then he, too, touched the brim of his cap and said good-bye, hopping back onto the wagon. Reuben slapped the reins on the horses' backs and she heard him say, "Next week we get the car and Derek has to drive this rig." The horses trotted off and Catherine closed the door. By the time she had her kerosene lantern lit and the fire going in the stove, it was still only eight o'clock, and the prospect of the long, lonely evening spread before her. With a sigh she sat down in one of the straight-backed chairs. The room was still chilly, and in the flickering light it seemed empty and cheerless. Suddenly she felt a wave of loneliness, and the memory of the Ranowski kitchen with its warmth and laughter rose in her mind. The contrast with her existence in this tiny empty room struck her with poignancy, and she drew in a long painful breath.

"What must it feel like to be part of something so vibrant, so useful, so loving?" she wondered. The room of the teacherage only echoed back with bleak shadows, and she shivered and hugged her arms around herself in the chill. Suddenly she could feel herself once more upon Lady's back, riding reckless and carefree, her arms tight around the strong, warm back of Nicholas. In memory she could feel his muscles against her breasts, his powerful arms as they raised her and lifted her to the horse, and she closed her eyes for a sweet moment, letting the memory flood out the loneliness. Then she shook herself with self-disgust and rose up quickly. She stoked the fire and, moving to the shelves at the foot of her bed, she took out a book which her father had included when he sent the globe for the classroom. The book was new, with a shining cover and crisp, fresh pages. She removed her clothes and pulled a white flannel nightgown over her head. On her feet she put woolen night socks, and throwing a shawl over her shoulders, she climbed into bed. For two hours she tried to concentrate on the book, but the pages passed before her eyes, and she had no memory of what she had read. Finally, with a sigh, she put the book down and climbed out of bed. The room was warmer, and she walked over to the table, pulled some paper out of the little drawer, and opened her fountain pen.

"Province of Alberta, Department of Education,"

she wrote. "Dear Sir: Will you please send me copies of last year's Departmental Exams, as well as any preparatory examination material which you have available to evaluate potential candidates for qualification to write the Department Examinations in April of this school year. Thank you." She ended the letter with her signature and then added, "Teacher, Spring Valley School, Southern Alberta School District #54."

She put the letter in an envelope and addressed it, and then with a strange feeling of excitement, as though she had just begun a great adventure, she put the letter in her coat pocket, and pulling on her boots and coat over her night clothes, she walked out into the night, down the path past the outhouse and the school, and then down the incline of the driveway to the road. At the entrance to the schoolyard there was an old, battered mailbox. She opened the box and placed the envelope inside, and then pushed up the red flag. As she climbed back up the driveway to the school, she turned and stood in the night air and looked out across the prairies. She looked small and lone beside the school building with the black roll of the fields stretching around her like the dark breast of an endless sea, and above her the stars in a black sky, cold, unblinking, and eternal.

CHAPTER ELEVEN

The examination packet for Nicholas arrived in the mail on a Saturday morning the week before Canadian Thanksgiving, which was October the eleventh. Catherine took the envelope out of the mailbox, feeling an odd mixture of excitement and apprehension as she realized the challenge lying in her hands. It was a cold, brisk October morning, with a fresh wind blowing across the prairies, and Catherine decided to walk the two miles to the Ranowski homestead to make arrangements for Nicholas to take his preliminary examination. She was anxious to go to the Ranowskis' for another reason, too. She needed to use their telephone. In the early autumn, when Ladean had said good-bye to her, they had agreed that Catherine would come to Cardston to spend Thanksgiving with the Watkins family. However, with the demands of school, plus the concern of preparing Nicholas for his tests, Catherine now felt she should remain in Spring Valley for the October Thanksgiving weekend.

Thanksgiving, in Canada, was a strange holiday anyway. The celebration was held a month earlier than the American Thanksgiving, and it had no historic tradition other than the Canadians' desire to thank the Lord for the bounties of the earth. Although Catherine acknowledged this was an admirable concept, nonetheless it was difficult to teach to her school children. In desperation, trying to give the holiday some special significance, she had gone so far as to tell her students about the American pilgrims and explained that eventually some of those pilgrims' descendants became Canadians, when the Loyalists moved from New England into Canada during the American Revolution.

The children, however, remained unimpressed about the concept of Thanksgiving; in fact, they were much more excited about the prospect of Halloween, which would follow shortly. Jack-o'-lanterns and costumes had a more direct impact on their minds than a day to thank the Lord for a harvest for which many of them had almost broken their backs. Harvest to these farm children was the memory of working in the blazing sun with blisters on their hands, prickles down their shirt necks, and grasshoppers flying in their faces. To some of them harvest was also the memory of their father's silent, somber face as he returned with the harvest trucks, emptied of their grain, and a check in his hand which was barely enough to cover the expenses of the combine and the harvesting crew.

Catherine feared it would be difficult to drum up much enthusiasm for the Thanksgiving at Spring Valley. Her fears were confirmed when she asked the class if they would each like to share a thought about why they were thankful. Eddie Kozinski, a merry, blue-eyed ten year old, raised his hand with a mischievous grin to announce that he was thankful for Thanksgiving because there was no school on that day. Everyone laughed. Then Pers Larson, a sturdy little boy with straight blond hair and apple cheeks, said he was thankful because he could eat all the turkey he wanted. Brita Asplund said she was thankful because as soon as Thanksgiving was over, Halloween would come and she was going to be a witch. Catherine gave a rueful shrug as she remembered their comments and decided that without pilgrims and Indians to talk about, Canadian Thanksgiving was meaningless to them.

Anyway, the holiday wasn't important enough to interrupt her work to go to Cardston. She had determined that she would telephone Ladean and make arrangements to come see her during the Christmas break.

When Catherine entered the Ranowski driveway, she saw Anne and Kristina, the two sisters-in-law, out in the chicken yard, feeding the fowl. She walked over to them and could hear them chattering to each other, their bright voices matching the clucking of the hens. The wind was flapping their aprons briskly around their skirts, and their cheeks and noses were pink in the cold air. Catherine could feel her own cheeks tingling from her vigorous walk. With delight the young women greeted her.

"What is it you have come to see, Miss Catherine?"

"How nice you are here!"

"How pretty you look in that hat!"

Their happy voices intermingled with warmth and enthusiasm. Laughing at their good humor, Catherine answered their greetings and then asked, "Are Mr. and Mrs. Ranowski home? And Nicholas? I have something I need to discuss with them."

"Ya, sure," said Anna, "you take Miss Catherine into the parlor, Kristina, and I'll go get them for you."

She was off across the farmyard, her heavy skirt whipping around her strong legs.

Catherine soon found herself seated in the front room with a thick mug of strong black coffee in her hands, and Kristina bustled around setting the lace antimacassars straight and flicking specks of imaginary dust with her white apron.

"It's terrible! We never use this room! It gets very messy!"

It was all Catherine could do to keep from laughing out loud to think that anyone should believe a fleck of dirt would dare enter this spotless domain.

Nicholas burst into the parlor. He had hurriedly pulled his cap from his head, and his hands looked cold and red as though he had been doing some hard work with bare hands in the frigid air. His face was tight with anxiety. "Is anything wrong, Miss Summerwell?" he asked.

"No, no, Nicholas, I didn't mean to alarm you. The examination materials came in this morning's post, and I thought perhaps we should talk with your parents and get started on your studies as soon as possible. After you've taken these tests, we'll have a fairly good idea if there is a possibility of your taking the Provincials this year."

Sometimes Nicholas seemed young, but at other times he surprised Catherine with his maturity and dignity. It was so now. He looked at her steadily for a moment. "I want that very much," he said with assurance.

Nicholas's parents were in complete accord. They told Catherine that anything she could do to help Nicholas would give them great joy. They agreed to give him all the free time that would be necessary for him to do the work required by her.

The testing date was set for the day after Thanksgiving.

After the arrangements were made, Catherine asked if she could use the Ranowskis' telephone. Then she lifted the receiver. There was a long wait before the operator answered.

"Could you please connect me with a Cardston number?" Catherine asked. "Number thirty-six . . . three, six. Thank you."

The operator asked a question and Catherine answered. "Yes, yes, I'm calling from the Ranowskis' phone in Spring Valley. Could you let me know the charges for the call, please? . . . Eighty-five cents? Thank you very much. Oh. For three minutes? Yes, thank you."

She waited while the operator made the connection. Twice she heard the line broken and a voice exclaiming, "It's busy!"—then the click of the party-line receiver being hung up.

At last she heard Ladean's voice. "Hello! Hello!" Ladean shouted into the phone. The connection was faint and full of static. "Is that you, Catherine?"

"Yes!" Catherine shouted back. "It's wonderful to hear your voice!"

"We could probably hear each other better if we went outside and shouted into the wind," Ladean exclaimed.

"The connection isn't very good," Catherine conceded.

"What?" Ladean asked. "I can't hear you!"

"The connection isn't very good." Catherine raised her voice.

"That's better!" Ladean boomed back. "When are you coming?"

"I'm sorry, Ladean, I appreciate the invitation very much, but I'm not going to be able to come for Thanksgiving. Something's come up. I have a student who's starting to prepare for the Provincials, and . . ."

"What?" Ladean's voice was blurry. "I can hardly hear you. You're not coming . . . I heard that . . . but not the reason . . ."

"I'll write you a letter," Catherine called. "I'm sorry . . . I'll miss seeing you."

"We'll miss seeing you, too, Catherine." Ladean's voice was cracking with the strain. "Will we see you at Christmas?"

"Yes!" Catherine shouted. "Wild horses wouldn't keep me away."

"Okay," Ladean yelled, "barring wild horses, or blizzards, we'll count on you for Christmas. Write to me and tell me everything."

"You're a wonderful friend!" Catherine shouted, her voice shaking with emotion.

"You, too," Ladean called back. "Take care and remember your prayers!"

Catherine heard the phone click down, and then she heard another distinct click. Someone on the party line had been interested in what the teacher had to say to her friend in Cardston. Catherine smiled to herself as she thought how few secrets were kept in this remote community.

Catherine spent Thanksgiving day with the Ranowskis and enjoyed the abundant food and the pleasant family gathering.

Nicholas and Steven drove her home at the end of the day. She warned Nicholas to get a good night's sleep and gave him his instructions.

"Eight o'clock in the morning. Sharp. Meet me in the schoolhouse and we will begin the examinations. There are four exams, and each one takes two hours, so you will be busy for the full day. You should bring a good lunch with you. Now try not to worry tonight. Just relax and sleep. That will be your best possible preparation."

Even to herself the words sounded ridiculous, but she felt it was the kind of thing a teacher should say. Steven laughed. "For the amount of sleep Nicholas is going to get tonight, you might as well take him in and begin the exams right now!"

Nicholas laughed at his brother's remark, and then once again, with that strange assurance which always caught Catherine off guard, he stated, "Never fear, I shall sleep."

Later, as she prepared for bed, Catherine thought about Nicholas and his last remark. She had sensed, even in the few weeks she had known this young student, that there was something exceptional about him. It was as though he had taken all the best qualities from his mother and father—from the vast and powerful land on which he lived, from the steady and serene sky under which he had grown, and from his strong and loving family—and had added a peculiar inner strength that was all his own. He was quiet, but not shy or inarticulate; he was a voracious and retentive reader; he was mature beyond his years, yet innocent and direct; and although in stature and development he was a grown man, still he accepted graciously the roles of student and son. The thread that ran through his character like a strand of gold was his rare and avid intelligence. He absorbed learning and understanding at an incredible speed and seemingly could not be satisfied. It was this reaching intellect which both frightened and fascinated Catherine. As a teacher she rejoiced in the challenge of training and developing a mind of such dimensions, but as a young woman, inexperienced in scholastic skills, she quailed at the responsibility. "Oh, well," she thought as sleep overtook her, "tomorrow will tell the tale. Perhaps he will be so far from the mark that the Provincials will be impossible for him this year. Then I won't have to worry. His parents can send him away to another school or something."

At eight o'clock sharp the next morning the school door opened, and Nicholas walked in. Catherine was seated behind her desk. Her hair was pulled back, and she was wearing a dark, tailored dress. The first examination was on the desk at the back of the room where Nicholas customarily sat during school. Beside the booklet were three freshly sharpened pencils and an eraser.

"The exam will begin when I set this alarm clock, Nicholas," she told him. "If you have any questions, please ask them now, as no talking is permitted during the examination period."

"No, Miss Summerwell, no questions," Nicholas said and smiled at her, and there was a confident sparkle in his eye. He looked rested and refreshed, and she felt a surge of confidence spring into her heart.

"Very well, Nicholas. Good luck. You may begin now." She pulled out the pin of the alarm clock which was set for two hours. Nicholas opened the examination booklet, picked up a pencil, and began to read. The room seemed enormous to Catherine as a great volume of silence stretched around her and Nicholas. The only sound was the soft ticking of her desk clock. It seemed they were the only two people in the world.

The day passed slowly. After each two-hour period, Nicholas brought his completed booklet to Catherine's desk. He would take a brief rest, get a drink of water, and go out to stretch his legs for a moment. The next test would then begin.

Catherine gave Nicholas an hour for lunch. She went to the teacherage by herself to have a cheese sandwich and a cup of tea, and when she came back to the schoolhouse, Nicholas was sitting on the bench in front of the school, his half-eaten lunch on the bench beside him. He was sitting very still, with his head buried in his hands.

"Nicholas," Catherine said softly, "it's time to begin again."

He stood up quickly and reentered the schoolroom, and she could see the first signs of strain in his face. As she handed him the last booklet she looked at his hand and noticed that the fingers that held his pencil were stained and blackened. His hair was rumpled from running his fingers through it, and there were tight lines around his eyes and mouth.

"Nicholas, perhaps it is too much to take all four exams in one day. When you take the departmental exams in the spring, they give you two days. Would you prefer to wait and take this final test tomorrow?" she asked.

With a deep breath Nicholas drew himself up to his full height. "No, thank you, Miss Summerwell. It is important that we find out where I stand, and how far I have to go before I can succeed. The sooner we begin, the better."

She looked at him with pride. "Very well. Here is the last booklet—and for the last time today. Good luck. You may start . . . now."

As the early twilight began to deepen across the fields outside the school windows, the alarm rang for the fourth and last time, and Nicholas wearily closed the final booklet. For a brief second, he closed his eyes and pushed himself tiredly against the back of his desk chair. Catherine left her seat and came to the back of the room. With a gentle hand she picked up the booklet.

"You've done well, Nicholas. I will spend tomorrow grading these booklets with the official key, and if you would come to the school Sunday afternoon, we may discuss the results."

"What time, ma'am?"

"Two o'clock."

"Thank you, Miss Summerwell." His voice was tired. He took his hat off the hook by the door and went out into the early darkness. Catherine gathered up the booklets and, holding them tightly against her breast, stood for a moment in the silent, shadowy schoolroom. Then she turned, and letting herself out the double doors, she locked the bar and hurried down the path toward the teacherage. There was a sinking feeling inside of her, because she knew that once she took out the official key and began marking Nicholas's tests, the die would be cast, and his future, one way or another, would be in her hands.

On Sunday afternoon Catherine was standing by the window in the schoolroom when Nicholas drove up the frozen road in the Ranowskis' old pickup truck. When he came into the schoolroom, Catherine asked, "Are your parents with you?"

"No, ma'am," Nicholas replied.

"Oh," she said, surprised, "I thought I saw someone else in the truck with you."

"It's Julie Lundquist. We've been out for a drive, and I was taking her home." Nicholas's face flushed with embarrassment.

Catherine felt an unreasoning flash of irritation. How could he have spent the most important day of his life with that shallow, flashy young woman, she wondered. The girl waiting out in the car seemed to trivialize the whole affair. She thought of the long day and night she had spent working over his examination material, while he had apparently been enjoying himself without a care in the world.

"Well," Catherine said coldly, "if you'd like to come over to my desk, I'll go over the examination results with you. Why didn't your parents come?"

Nicholas looked at her calmly, but he seemed puzzled by her abrupt manner—and by the question.

"They won't be involved in this situation anymore, Miss Summerwell. They feel it's your concern now. They have a lot of confidence in you and when they promised to give me free time for extra study, and asked you to help me, they felt they had done all they could." He explained this to her carefully, as though she were a child, and he was explaining something that everyone would know.

Catherine realized again how little she understood these people. The Ranowskis had made a considerable concession in giving Nicholas the opportunity to prepare himself to go to the university. The other brothers would probably need to handle many of his chores, and the father was prepared to buy him whatever extra books and materials were needed out of the family's common funds. But they saw the work of teaching and studying as the job of the schoolteacher and Nicholas. The family would not be involved in any way. Each person in the Ranowski family did the job assigned to him without fuss, and without praise, and Catherine, their schoolteacher, was expected to do the same thing.

"I see, Nicholas," she said.

For a moment Catherine groped for words to begin what she had to say, and she felt the tension in Nicholas as his eyes searched her face.

"In some areas you were brilliant," she began. "Your answers were well-written and your logic and perceptions were excellent. Those sections where you have had training, you answered with great accuracy. It is obvious you have an extraordinary memory and a fine ability to express yourself."

She had expected her words to relax her young student, but instead of being pleased she noted that he had become more alert and tense, and she realized that he knew she was only making preliminary remarks, preparing him for the truth. With a rush of compassion she dropped the objective mask of the schoolteacher and spoke to him directly and sympathetically.

"The only examination that you passed with adequate marks was the English test, and even there I had to allow for errors in syntax and grammar. In the technical subjects there were significant areas where you have had no exposure to formal learning, and those gaps in your knowledge cost you passing grades, even though the areas in which you had studied were outstanding. Your schooling simply has not been comprehensive enough to cover the breadth of these examinations."

Nicholas still had not spoken. She had expected his spirit to be broken by what she had told him, but she was surprised to see him still watching her with expectation. He seemed to be waiting for her final conclusions. She took a deep breath.

"It comes down to this. You will need to accomplish in five months much of what most students take four years to learn. You have a smattering of knowledge, and in the next few months you must try to fill in all the gaps. You certainly have the intelligence and ability to learn everything you need to know, but whether anyone can possibly learn it within such a tight time frame, I just don't know." Catherine paused and, without thinking, gave a sigh.

Nicholas smiled for the first time. "That is what I wanted to hear. If you can tell me what it is I must learn, then I promise you I can learn it."

"Oh, Nicholas!" Catherine exclaimed, anxiously. "I—I—Maybe you need someone else! Someone with more experience . . . more background in the sciences

. . . a larger library . . ." Her fingers drummed on the examination booklets stacked before her in indecision, and her brow furrowed as she thought of the enormity of the task before them.

"I don't think you understand what you would be taking on," she insisted. "It would mean giving up everything else. You would need to study day and night—and even then, with no assurance of success. Wouldn't it be better to take another year. Maybe go into one of the towns . . ."

"Do you think another school would take me, as old as I am, and create a special program for my needs? Would an experienced teacher be willing to try such a thing? I don't think so, Miss Summerwell. I believe you can do it. I believe if you are willing to try, we can do it together." Nicholas's voice was filled with conviction, and his enthusiasm was contagious.

Catherine sat silently for a moment, and they looked into one another's eyes steadily, each trying to gauge the depth of determination in the other.

"All right," Catherine said with sudden resolution, "I'll do it. *We'll* do it!"

"Yahoo!" Nicholas shouted, leaping up from his chair and throwing his cap high in the air. Instantly, he was contrite and turned to Catherine. "I'm sorry, Miss Summerwell—I just couldn't help it."

"Very well, Nicholas," Catherine said, trying to sound severe. "That may be the last moment of freedom you have for the rest of the year."

"Now," she continued dryly, "I think perhaps you should go outside and drive Julie home. She is probably half-frozen. Then I would like you to return, and I will give you your first group of assignments."

"Thank you, Miss Summerwell." Nicholas grabbed her hand and shook it vigorously. "You won't regret this, I promise you!"

A moment after he left the schoolhouse, she heard the truck start up with a roar and a bang. She could hear it rattling away from the school with a burst of speed. Hurrying to the window, she saw the old vehicle disappearing down the long, empty road, bumping along at an incredible pace. "I hope he makes it back in one piece," she thought ironically, "or this experiment will be finished before it's begun."

In the weeks that followed Nicholas and Catherine established a routine. During school Nicholas was given advance assignments, but he did not interrupt her work with the other students during school hours. However, early each morning and after school each day, Catherine gave extra lessons to Nicholas, and on Saturdays she spent four to five hours tutoring him. Every week she handed him the books he was to read, and a list of reports, experiments, and mathematics assignments.

Late afternoons, in the early darkness of winter, became the most productive time. Nicholas remained at his desk, reading, studying, or writing, while Catherine worked at her desk preparing lesson plans for the next day or marking papers. Whenever a question arose, Nicholas would interrupt Catherine's work, and she would answer the question or help him find reference material to supply the information.

It was an excellent arrangement and enabled Catherine to fulfill her other duties as well as continue the intensive help she was giving Nicholas. The amazing thing to Catherine was how rapidly he learned. She seldom had to repeat a lesson, and his reading retention was extraordinary. Often he asked questions that were beyond her ability to answer, and these she wrote down carefully to send to others for clarification.

Her father expressed an interest through his letters in what she was doing, and gradually it became possible for her to send all requests for supplementary help to him. He seemed to enjoy hunting down the book or individual who could give her resource help.

Everything seemed to be going well until Catherine's peace of mind was shattered by outbursts from two of her students. The first confrontation was from an unexpected source.

By early December, the days were very short. The children came to school in darkness, and the kerosene lamps in the school were lit most of the day. The little black stove devoured wood, glowing red-hot from morning till evening, but even then, the cold seemed to seep through the doors and windows, and the children clustered around the stove at every opportunity.

Chopping wood was the job of the older school boys; Catherine rotated the task each week. It came time for Dick Wilson to fill the woodbox; he was the other senior boy who occupied the last row of desks with Julie and Nicholas. Catherine noted with dismay when she came into the schoolroom early Monday morning that the wood had not been chopped or placed beside the stove as was customary.

In the time she had been at Spring Valley, Catherine had mastered the arts of wood chopping and fire building, and so she quickly prepared the wood herself and filled the box. When the children arrived, the fire was roaring. Dick Wilson was late for school, and Catherine fixed him with a stern look. "Dick," she said, "I would like to speak with you at recess."

As recess was announced, the children piled on their heavy woolen outerwear and raced outside into the light snow cover. She could hear them laughing and calling in the cold, crystal air as they slid down the hill on flattened cardboard boxes.

"Dick," Catherine said, "did you forget this was your week to prepare the woodbox? The children must not come into a cold school, and I do not have time to start the fire in the mornings. You let everybody down today."

"Yeah," Dick responded sullenly, "why don't you just get Nicky-boy to do it for you? After all, you do so much for him. It seems a teacher's pet should have to do something in return."

Catherine's face colored at the insolence, and she looked at the big, gawky boy in front of her. His face was pimpled, and his hair hung down over his eyes. There was a belligerent expression on his face that baffled Catherine.

"That's nonsense, Dick," she replied, "and you know it. Everyone takes their turn at keeping the woodbox filled. It's your turn and I won't have you neglecting your responsibility. As for the extra time I spend with Nicholas Ranowski, I would be more than happy to spend extra time with you as well. I wish you would be willing to put in extra work. As of now you are failing in nearly every subject. Why don't you come in for extra tutoring after school?"

"Huh!" Dick snorted. "Are you kidding? I've had all the school I can take."

"Well, then, Dick," Catherine answered, genuinely curious, "if you dislike school so much, why do you continue to come when you don't have to?"

"Them Ranowskis!" Dick exploded, and his eyes sparked with bitterness. "They think they're so high and mighty! They ain't nothin' but dumb, hunky immigrants, and the only reason they's so rich is because their ma went and had all those baby boys. Their pa works 'em like slaves, and so of course they get rich and then try to go lording it over all of us true Canadians, like they was better than us! Them foreigners grab up all the best land and then expect us to work the grubby stuff that's left!"

Catherine was appalled at the venom in Dick's voice. "But what has this to do with your being in school?" she asked.

"My pa says if them Ranowskis can afford to let their son keep goin' to school, then he ain't goin' to let no Ranowski be better than a Wilson. We'll show 'em we're just as good as they think they are!" Dick said with a snarl. "So as long as Nicky-boy goes to school—I go, too!"

"But Dick," Catherine said, trying to keep her voice calm and reasonable, "just sitting at a desk doesn't mean you're going to school. If you want to gain what school has to offer, you have to try to learn—you have to study and listen."

"Look, Miss Summerwell, it ain't my idea to be here. It's my pa's, and he don't know nothin' about what goes on at school, 'ceptin' what I tell him. It beats the hell out of bein' home and havin' to do chores. And you can't kick me out, 'cause the law says

I can come as long as I want to. As long as Nick gets a free ride—so do I."

Catherine stared at the sullen boy for a moment. "I think I shall have a talk with your father," she declared.

"Wouldn't do you no good. He don't think much of you anyway, Miss Summerwell. Besides, I could always tell him that the reason you don't like me is because you spend so much 'private time' with Nicky-boy." There was a suggestive leer on Dick's face. "Like I said—all he knows about school is what I tell him."

In her whole life Catherine had never been faced with such amoral viciousness. She almost recoiled from the sight of the sneering boy and his crude attempt at blackmail. Fortunately, her temper came to her rescue and she faced Dick with blazing eyes.

"Young man, I will tell you this once and once only. You are right, I cannot force you to do your schoolwork, and I cannot force you to leave school—unless you commit an offense that justifies expulsion. However, as long as you are in this classroom you will behave properly. You will speak to me politely, and you will perform your class duties—or you will spend the rest of the year on the bench outside the school door. Do I make myself clear! Perhaps it is true that your father only knows what you tell him about school. If your attitude does not change, I intend to rectify that circumstance, and I will go see him and make it very clear what goes on in this classroom. I will discuss your total lack of cooperation, your failing grades, and your disrespectful behavior! And, since blackmail is a two-edged sword, I will also mention to him that you have discovered attendance at school is an ideal way in which to avoid work. I imagine your father would be most interested in that unique concept.

"And now I will give you the remaining ten minutes of recess to refill the woodbox, and before you leave this evening, I expect you to fill it again for the following morning. Do you understand?"

Dick Wilson was obviously surprised at Catherine's outburst and apparently cowed by her vigorous authority. It was probably the result of years of living with an authoritarian father. Reluctantly, and with great resentment, he moved to the door, and as recess ended, the children came trooping in, Dick following with a ragged armload of badly cut logs, which he dumped roughly in the woodbox.

Catherine felt no sense of triumph—only an odd feeling that Dick Wilson was a looming threat to the peace of her classroom.

The second upsetting confrontation came a few days later, and it seriously changed her relationship with Nicholas. One afternoon a light snow began falling. It was early dusk. Catherine was marking spelling quizzes, and Nicholas was sitting in his desk completing an essay on Tolstoy, Dostoevski, and Chekhov. In the silence both Catherine and Nicholas felt a tense awareness of each other, as though the air were charged. Suddenly Nicholas gave an exclamation of disgust and threw his essay book across the room. He leaped to his feet and began pacing back and forth like a caged animal.

"I can't stand it!" he exclaimed. "I am so sick of those gloomy Russians! I am sick of this cramped desk! I am sick of reading and writing and not enough sleep and never talking to anyone. I'm sick of watching my brothers do my chores and never complaining. I'm sick of having no friends."

The room crackled with his tension and frustration.

He turned to Catherine. "Christmas is less than two weeks away—and I don't even know it! I don't even know what time of year it is—what time of day it is. I haven't been able to run or laugh or talk or work since October! This isn't human!" He looked at Catherine, who was sitting, unmoved, at her desk. He strode up and leaned across it, his hands clenched as they gripped the table edge.

"How do you stand it!" he shouted. "Day after day at that desk. Always in command. Cool and calm. Is it that you are not human? Have you become like the blackboard and the books and your own desk—some inanimate part of this room! I finish one assignment and you hand me another. Like I am a machine! Never a word of encouragement. Never a 'this was well done, Nicholas!' or 'you're making real progress.' No! A pile of new books and pages of problems—that's all you have for me. It isn't worth it! I'm sick of reading about life. I've got to live some of it, too. Maybe reading is enough for you, but I can't stay in this silent room another minute. I have to have something more . . ." His eyes were like fire.

"Nicholas," Catherine's voice was calm, but her heart was beating uncontrollably with compassion and anxiety for the suffering young man in front of her and with pain for the things he had said about her. "Of course it's difficult. I told you from the first it would be. You've got to hold on. You can't slow down or get discouraged now. It's only until the first of April, and then it's all over! I haven't told you how you're doing because I can't judge yet. I do know this—you can't stop! There is something in you that reaches out to know, to understand—you can't deny that part of you. Already you have gone beyond me in so many ways, and you must go to the university where you can study with teachers whose minds will match yours. There is nothing you can't accomplish, if you'll just hold on!" She stopped, then added quietly, "Of course, the choice is yours." She bowed her head, and her shoulders sagged slightly. Catherine felt immeasurably weary. She placed her pencil carefully on the pile of corrected spelling papers.

"That will be all for today, Nicholas. I will know your answer, if you come in the morning for your assignments."

Nicholas stood staring at her, his face tight with disappointment and anger. "Is that all you have to say? You won't even talk to me . . ." His voice broke.

"No, Nicholas," Catherine said, standing and gathering up her coat and hood. "I think perhaps too much has been said already." With painful control she walked down the aisle between the vacant desks and out the front door of the school. His words rang in her mind. "Are you not human? A part of this room?" She wanted to cry or scream, but she kept walking down the path.

Nicholas arrived early the next morning and handed in the completed essay on the Russian authors. Silently, Catherine gave him his new assignments, and he took them. He continued to work in the same grueling schedule, but something had gone out of their relationship. Nothing was ever said about Nicholas's outburst, but from then on there was a strain between them, as though he now worked because she required it of him.

She also noted that Julie Lindquist had pulled her desk closer to Nick's, and once or twice during school she saw Julie's hand resting on his arm, her pert face grinning at him. They would whisper together, and she would hear their muffled laughter. At recess time the two of them walked down by the fence, and she could see Julie standing close to Nicholas, almost pressing against him as they talked, her saucy eyes teasing. Sometimes after school Nick would take his homework assignments and walk out with the other students. "I'll work at home today," he would say briefly. "I don't have any questions on this material." Twice on such occasions Catherine saw him walking down the road with Julie. One afternoon she glanced out the window and saw them both riding on Lady's back, cantering across the field. Julie's face was next to Nicholas's, and she was laughing with total abandon. With a twinge Catherine turned from the window. "She's so cheap," she thought. "She isn't worth his little finger—and he's too young to see he only likes her because she's pretty."

The uneasy tension between her and Nicholas continued, and at Christmastime it was almost a relief for Catherine to give Nicholas his assignments for the two weeks of holiday and leave for Cardston.

CHAPTER TWELVE

Catherine was driven to the Watkins' home by a young farmer and his wife who were going to Cardston for Christmas. She was greeted like a long-lost member of the family, and the days of holiday flew by as she and Ladean talked and exchanged stories like schoolgirls. Long into the night they would discuss their experiences as teachers, the problems of the students, and their feelings about themselves.

"It's strange," Catherine said one night as they lay in the darkened room, each one warm and cozy in her bed, with the first pleasant drowsiness of sleep. "It seems that I went from childhood to adulthood in one huge step. I mean, everybody in Spring Valley thinks of me as . . . old and mature . . . but there's a part of me that wanted to do it more gradually. I don't think I've quite caught up with myself."

"I know what you mean," Ladean murmured in a sleepy voice. "They want to keep you a child for so long. 'No, you can't do that!' 'Finish your plate,' 'Make your bed,' 'Be in by ten.' And then suddenly one day it's 'That's your decision,' 'You're an adult now,' 'It's your problem!' Even worse, people start asking your opinion and expecting an expert answer. Sometimes I want to yell, 'Hey! Wait a minute . . . shouldn't there be something in between?' "

The girls laughed together and then Catherine yawned. "Oh well, as long as no one knows it's a masquerade, I guess we can go on fooling them," she said. "Someday maybe I'll start feeling like 'Miss Summerwell.' In the meantime, I'll just go on playing the part."

Through the fog of sleep she heard Ladean's voice. "I'll bet you're a terrific teacher, no matter what you say."

It was wonderful having a friend with whom to share her concerns and feelings, but one day Catherine was struck with a pang of guilt. She had not even thought of Spring Valley or her school children for two days! Suddenly the image of Nicholas rose in her mind, and she remembered the day she had witnessed his outburst in the classroom. She thought of how much these past days with Ladean had meant to her, and the contrast between this warm companionship and her bleak, lonely existence in Spring Valley gave her a painful awareness of the emotions Nicholas had been trying to express. It wasn't that Nicholas wanted to quit or that the work was too hard. It was his awful isolation he was rebelling against. He had lost the ability to communicate with his family about his studies, none of his friends had any interest in his work, and the loneliness of the ivory tower she had built for him was smothering his usual thirst for knowledge. It was a vivid realization, and she knew that if she were to help Nicholas through the next months, she would have to become his link to the world of people and conversation. She would have to find a way to be his friend as well as his teacher.

The next day she told Ladean she needed to leave a few days earlier than expected. The Watkinses helped arrange her ride to Spring Valley, and on the way back to school she stopped at the Ranowskis to leave a message for Nicholas to come see her.

Early the next morning Nicholas was sitting at her desk. His face was cold, and he looked guarded and unresponsive.

"Nicholas," she began, "what I am going to say is hard for me to express. I know these past weeks have been difficult for you—for both of us. I just wanted to tell you that I think I know how you feel, and I have thought that perhaps it would help both of us if we added discussion periods to your tutoring. What I had in mind was that two afternoons a week instead of writing your assignment we will read and discuss the material together."

He did not reply.

"Does the idea appeal to you?" She didn't know what she expected—whether he would reject the overture completely or be enthusiastic about it.

"I think," he said quietly, carefully, "I would like that very much." Then he smiled at her for the first time in weeks. "Miss Summerwell," he added.

It took awhile, but gradually the strain between them eased, and in the month that followed Catherine was gratified to see Nick's enthusiasm for learning rekindled. It became difficult to draw their discussion periods to a close, and one afternoon, after a particularly intense and searching discussion about Plato and the utopian societies, Catherine had to admit to herself that Nicholas had contributed better ideas and concepts than she had. "I knew the pupil would outrace the reacher," she mused to herself, "but I did not imagine so soon."

She began looking forward to their conversations. His brilliant mind and growing assurance amazed her. They grew to know one another's thoughts, and there was a sweet intimacy to their winter afternoons in the quiet schoolhouse.

A new stack of books arrived for Nicholas from Catherine's father on a late day in January. She took the package into the teacherage and cut the twine. As she lifted each heavy text, reading the titles and flipping through the smooth, freshly printed pages, she smiled to herself and thought how amazed her father would be if he could see how quickly Nicholas would read through the material and understand it. Even the massive chemistry text would not daunt his spirits. "He's going to do it!" she whispered to herself. "I feel it in my bones! He's going to do it!"

CHAPTER THIRTEEN

On a cold morning in February Catherine walked up the snow-lined path between the teacherage and the schoolhouse. The snow was several feet thick, tired, and crusty-looking. It was old snow, trampled by the children's feet and smeared by the horses and wagons. She entered the dark schoolroom with a sigh, lit the kerosene lamp, and started the stove.

The children arrived and began to take their seats. "Pa says it's a chinook arch for sure!" "Can't tell 'til it's brighter outside!" "Nope! My pa says chinook, and he ain't never been wrong."

Catherine listened to the children's excited conversation. "What are you talking about?" she asked.

"Chinook arch!" Eddie told her. "Pa says he can see one over the Rockies this morning for sure."

"What does that mean?" Catherine asked.

"It means there won't be no snow by noon!" shouted Pers.

"Oh, nonsense!" exclaimed Catherine. "I know chinooks are warm winds, but they surely could not melt all this snow in a few hours. That is what we refer to as a 'folk myth.'"

"Well, you can call it what you want, Miss Summerwell," Eddie replied, "but by noon we're going to be knee deep in mud, my pa said."

Shortly after the reading lessons began, the schoolhouse was shaken by the first gust of wind. The wind grew stronger. Not a harsh, roaring wind, but a steady incessant whir outside the windows. Within minutes Catherine detected an unfamiliar sound. She stopped reading aloud in order to listen. It was the steady dripping of water from the roof. Looking out the window, she could see the enormous icicles that had hung from the eaves for weeks. Water was dripping from them, and every few moments one of the smaller icicles would crash to the ground.

The children were restless, and as the sound of the wind mounted, it became harder to hold their attention. At recess time she was relieved to tell them to get their coats and go outside to play, but when she opened the door to let them outside, she was astonished at the sight which greeted her. The air was mild as spring, and water from the rapidly melting snow was pouring down the schoolyard hill. The road leading up to the school was muddy and slick, and patches of bare ground were already visible on the playground. The melting snow looked terrible—patchy and dirty—and Catherine could tell that if the warm wind continued, it would only be a matter of time before the roads were so muddy as to be impassable.

"Children," she said, "I think we had better have a half day today. Any of you who need to wait for your parents, stay in the schoolhouse. The rest of you had better start walking home while the ground is still frozen, or you will be caught in the mud."

Within an hour all of the children had been picked up by anxious parents, and at noon Catherine stood in front of the school, looking in astonishment at the rivulets of water racing down the schoolyard, which was already almost bare of snow. The wind continued, warm, strong, and dry. Nicholas was the last to leave.

"Don't worry about the mud, Miss Summerwell. This wind will keep up all day, and by evening it will have soaked up most of the water. Tomorrow the roads will be fine."

Catherine laughed. "This morning I wouldn't have believed you! But I do now!"

It was true. By late afternoon the powerful wind had dried the lane and the road so that they were passable. Catherine decided she would need to prepare for school the next day, and so she pulled a stack of copy books toward her on the little table in the teacherage to begin her work. Just then, there was a knock on the door. She opened it to find Steven Ranowski leaning against the door jamb, his hat pushed back on his head and a wicked grin on his face.

"Hi, teacher!" he said. "Long time no see."

"Steven!" she exclaimed. "What are you doing here?"

"Just thought I'd pay you a visit, since you seem to have been avoiding the Ranowski household lately."

"Well, if I am," Catherine said, laughing, "it's a Ranowski's fault. Tutoring Nicholas takes up most of my spare time."

"Well now, that's what I've come to see you about," Steven answered, with a twinkle in his eye. "Do you mind if I step in for a moment?"

"Oh, of course not," Catherine replied. "Here." She pulled up one of the straight-backed chairs and sat down in the other one. "What is it?"

"I was just wondering, if you have all that time for one of the Ranowski boys—maybe you could spare a little extra for another one. I wondered if you'd like to go to a movie with me this Saturday?"

Catherine was so astonished at the invitation that for a moment she was speechless. "Why, Steven!" she exclaimed. "I don't know what to say."

"Well then, just say 'yes,' and I'll be on my way."

"Oh, I don't know," Catherine stammered. "I . . . I . . . don't think so, Steven. I don't think I should. Thanks for asking me anyway."

"Why not?" Steven asked, his voice impatient. "There's no law that says teachers aren't human. They can have a little fun!"

"No written law maybe," Catherine answered, "but people do talk. It's a bit like living in a fishbowl . . . and . . ."

"And my reputation wouldn't do you any good. Is that it?" Steven asked with a sardonic grin.

Catherine could not meet his eyes. "Maybe another time, Steven. I'm just not prepared to make a decision right now. I . . ."

"For Pete's sake!" Steven burst out impatiently. "I'm not asking you to marry me or anything. Just a simple date. Only a schoolteacher could make a dilemma out of that!"

The disgust in his voice stung her, and tears sprang to Catherine's eyes. "I'm not a schoolteacher—not yet!" she exclaimed. "That's why I have to be so careful to do everything right. . . . Oh, you wouldn't understand!"

"Wanna bet!" said Steven and he got up and went over to her. Taking her chin in his hand, he tilted her face up so that she had to look at him. "Why do you think I came over here tonight? I couldn't help thinking about you. To me, you look like a little girl playing dress up. I thought about you all alone in this tiny box of a house with that crazy chinook howling outside, and the water dripping and the awful restless feeling this wind brings, and I thought no one should have to be alone on a night like this. You're trying so hard to be brave and independent! Don't you think it shows—the little girl part—all around the edges?"

She reached up and took his hand, and tears continued to tremble on her lashes.

"Am I really so transparent?" she asked tremulously.

"Naw," Steven answered, "only to someone who understands girls. And that's me!" He laughed, and his humor was so contagious that she found herself laughing, too.

"You see!" he said. "You need to see more of me. I might even make you remember you're a woman first and a teacher second."

With that he pulled on her hand, and she fell against him. With lighthearted ease he bent and kissed her soft lips, open with astonishment. Her reaction was so sudden it took both of them by surprise. Without thinking, she slapped him across the face.

Her face turned crimson and so did Steven's. "Oh," she cried, "I'm so sorry. I didn't mean to—but you shouldn't have done that."

"No," said Steven, surprise and anger in his eyes, "I can see that!"

She sat down at the table and buried her face in her hands. "I'm sorry."

"Catherine"—Steven's voice was deep with hurt—

"I'm sorry, too. It's just that you looked so vulnerable. I only meant it in fun. Maybe you've forgotten what fun is! Or maybe I'm the wrong Ranowski!"

Her head jerked up and she looked at him with blazing, tear-filled eyes. "What do you mean by that?" she asked in a fierce whisper.

Steven looked stricken and came over to stand beside her. "I didn't mean it, Catherine. I was mad, so I sounded off! But maybe there's a grain of truth in what I said! No one needs to tell me how extraordinary Nicholas is. I'm his brother—we all know how easy it is to admire him . . . to like him . . . to love him. You should watch yourself, Catherine."

"That's ridiculous!" Catherine gasped. "I'm his teacher. I'm older . . ."

"And think of him, too, Catherine. He's young and impressionable—and you don't know yourself at all. You don't even see yourself—how desirable you are . . . how . . ." Steven foundered for words and realized that every word he was saying was only inflicting more hurt.

"Forgive me!" he stammered. "I shouldn't have come! I've really made a mess of things. It's just that I wouldn't want to see either one of you get hurt."

"Steven," Catherine said, drawing herself up with dignity. "You don't understand. It isn't only that Nicholas is going to be ready to take the Provincial examinations. It's much, much more than that. I haven't told anybody this—not even Nicholas—and you must promise never to breathe a word of it to him. I think there is a real possibility that he will not only pass the exams but that he will win the highest award. I think he has the potential of passing with high distinction in all four categories! Do you realize no one has ever done that! Can you imagine what this could mean to all the little rural schools throughout the province? If a student could come out of a small one-room school and win all the prizes, it would be so wonderful! I think he can do it, Steven! I really do! That's why I'm working him so hard, why we're spending so much time. That's what is at stake. It's only ideas we see when we're together, Steven! Nothing more! How could you spoil it by imagining—by suggesting—Oh, that's hateful!"

Her eyes were glowing and the soft lamplight highlighted the shining ripples of her hair. The color of her skin was like a banked fire, and her breast rose and fell with her agitated breathing. Steven stood staring at her—at the emotional vitality she radiated, and it was all he could do to restrain himself from grasping her in his arms again, and kissing her until her walls of reserve and restraint came tumbling down. Instead, he shook his head and moved toward the door. "Yes, of course," he said softly as he prepared to let himself out. "Ideas. Nothing more." He looked once more at her lovely face, radiant in the light, and went out, closing the door softly behind him. Standing outside in the darkness with the chinook wind pushing against him, he looked at the door of the teacherage and whispered with tender concern, "Ah, Catherine! There are none so blind as those who will not see. Poor Catherine! Poor Nick!"

* * *

February passed into March, and the tutoring moved at incredible speed. Chemistry and trigonometry were the two hardest subjects for Catherine to teach, but fortunately Nicholas showed an affinity for both and often understood the concepts without Catherine needing to explain them. By mid-March she knew there was no question that Nicholas was prepared to pass the examinations, and now all of her efforts were focused on her secret goal—to give him the opportunity to take the highest prizes. With only a few weeks left she increased the work load, and she also increased the amount of time she spent with Nicholas, teaching and instructing him. Lately she had noticed he often took the initiative in their discussions, and more and more she felt she was no longer the teacher, but a listening ear, a mind off of which he could bounce the vigorous ideas of his creative intellect.

Often after these sessions Catherine felt drained and exhausted, but Nicholas seemed to gain vitality from her, and left exhilarated and filled with energy. One afternoon the sky became dark earlier than usual and Catherine used the darkness as an excuse to cut short their lesson. She felt unaccountably weary as she looked at Nicholas. His face had matured during the year. His jaw was firmer, and there were fine lines around his eyes which gave him an older, almost distinguished look. But he still had his youthful grin. His shoulders were broader, and she thought he had grown a little taller—at least he looked it to her. For an odd moment she felt he had thrived on this long, difficult battle, but it had aged her.

"Why don't we call it a day, Nicholas?" she suggested. "I still have a lot of papers to grade, and I find myself very tired."

Nicholas looked at her carefully. "It is getting dark," he conceded, "but it's not late. I think we must be in for a big snow." He looked at her again. "You don't look very well. Maybe you should come home with me, Miss Summerwell. If there's a big blizzard, you could be snowed in that little teacherage."

"Now, Nicholas! Don't worry about me! I'll be snug and warm. You just hurry on home. Finish your assignments, and we'll continue our discussion tomorrow."

"Let me chop some wood for you first," Nicholas insisted. "I'll leave it by your door before I go."

"Oh, all right. Thank you very much. I'll see you tomorrow then." Catherine gathered up her school books and went back to the teacherage. The sky was heavy and gloomy, and a cold wind had begun to blow. She looked at the small pile of logs beside her stove and decided it would last her until the next day. "I'll bring Nicholas's logs inside first thing in the morning," she decided.

She didn't feel hungry, so she fixed a fire in the stove to warm up the room, boiled some water, and fixed herself a mug of hot tea. Holding the steaming cup in her hands, she climbed into her bed with a heavy shawl pulled around her shoulders. Nothing seemed to warm her, though, so reluctantly she got out of bed again and put more wood on the fire. She looked with concern at the diminishing pile, but decided again she had enough wood to last until morning. Shivering violently, she hurried back into bed. It was only after she lay down that she realized she had a fever. With a great effort she got up once more and took two aspirins. Then she stoked the fire, set the damper, and fell back into bed.

Exhaustion and illness overcame her, and as the blizzard rose in force outside the little frame house, she slept, oblivious to the deep folds of snow which the laden sky and the howling wind were laying across the frozen earth and around the walls of her teacherage.

She woke in a silent room. Bright sun streamed through narrow lines at the tops of her windows but the rest of the window was dark. The room was bitter cold. Her fever was broken, but she still felt weak and tired. "Drat!" she thought, not wanting to move out of the warm cocoon of her covers. "I'm going to have to get up and build a fire." Sowly, she slid her legs out of the warm spot in the center of the sheets. The rest of the bed sheet was icy cold. Reluctantly, she swung her legs out of the covers and wiggled her feet into her slippers, then grasping her shawl around her shoulders, she hurried over to the stove. With the last of the wood, she soon had a fire blazing. The room was still very chilly, and she stared for a moment at the darkened windows. Then, with a gasp she realized the windows were packed with snow. With swift terror she looked at the empty woodbox. "Oh, no!" she prayed, fear clutching her heart. "Please . . . No!" She ran to the door and tried to open it. The door would not budge. Next she ran to the windows, and frantically tried to open them. They were frozen shut. For a panicky moment she thought of smashing the windows with a chair, but as she assessed the depth of the snow, she knew she would not be able to crawl out of the window, and if she broke the window she would freeze.

The fire was emitting heat, so she pulled up the chair to sit beside it. "I will get warm, and I will think of a way out of this," she told herself, fighting off the feelings of panic and claustrophobia that threatened to overwhelm her. "Someone will think of me! They'll know I'm here. Someone will come! I know they will!" she began whispering to herself. "I can burn the furniture. Why didn't I bring in the wood last night? The roads must be terrible! But the storm's stopped, and someone must be out with the plows. I mustn't panic! It may be hours before anyone comes. I'll have to think what to do!" She gave a frightened little sob and buried her head in her hands for a moment. The room was warm, but she began to shiver again, whether from the return of her fever or from fear, she wasn't sure. Her head ached fiercely, and she pulled the shawl around her shoulders more tightly and rocked back and forth on the little chair. "I'm all right!" she told herself. "There's plenty of food, and if I'm careful, I can keep the heat going." She looked around the room to assess what she could burn. There were several school books as well as the table and chairs that could be used for fuel.

The room was dim, with only the light from the slim opening between the top of the snow and the top of the window showing. It suddenly occurred to Catherine that she was faced with another problem. The stove used oxygen to burn, and with the windows and doors packed with snow, there was no replenishing source of air. The thought of suffocating terrified her, and she ran to the door and frantically pushed against it. "Oh, please! Please!" she sobbed. "Won't somebody come?" Hysterically, she beat her fists against the door, crying until she was exhausted. Her illness caused her to tremble with weakness, and the room began to spin. The stove was cooling, but her strength was spent, and slowly she made her way back to the bed. Using the last of her energy, she pushed her bed over by the stove, and shaking with fever and exhaustion, she climbed under the covers.

For a while she must have slept, and when she woke again the room was freezing. Even under the heavy blankets she felt the bitter chill. She felt weak, and she knew that she had to get up to start the fire again. Her aching body protested, but she forced herself up, and taking one of the books, tore the pages out and placed them in the stove. When she lit the paper, it burned with rapid brilliance, but gave off little heat. In despair she realized she would need to break up one of the chairs to burn for wood. She picked up the chair and raised it over her head while her fever-racked muscles protested. Just as she prepared to dash the chair to the floor she heard the scraping sound of a shovel, muffled and rhythmic.

She stood absolutely still and listened, trembling, afraid to believe it.

Again, unmistakably, she heard the sound, and a rough thumping—impatient, powerful.

"Who is it?" she shouted. "Can you get through? I'm here! I'm here!"

She began crying with relief and weakness. She slumped down on the chair and sat facing the door, watching and listening in relief and anticipation. The noise continued louder and louder, until finally she heard a voice. "Miss Summerwell, are you all right?" It was Nicholas's voice—muffled and breathless.

"Yes! Yes!" she screamed, laughing and crying. "Yes! I'm all right! Please hurry. It's so cold! My fire is out!"

"I'm coming!" he shouted back. "A few more feet, and I'll be able to get in."

She could hear the shovel banging against the door frame. Her head was ringing and she was shivering terribly, but the excitement of being rescued filled her mind, and she was scarcely aware of anything else. She had not realized how frightened she had been until she experienced this overwhelming joy and thankfulness at the prospect of release.

"Nicholas!" she cried, hardly able to bear the waiting. "Will it be much longer? It's so cold!"

"Now!" he called, and she heard the heavy shovel hit the door with several loud thumps. Then the handle turned, and slowly, pushing against the residue of snow, Nicholas pulled the door open. The door squeaked and protested against the barrier of snow, but light poured in through the opening, and soon it was big enough for Nicholas to enter.

Catherine was standing by the door with tears streaming down her pale face. Her lips were blue with cold, but her eyes were burning with fever. When she saw Nicholas, her knees buckled. In one quick stride he was beside her and caught her before she fell. "Nicholas!" she whispered. "How did you get through?"

"I started early this morning"—his voice was desperate with worry—"I knew you would be snowed in. I knew you would need me . . . but the roads were terrible. It took all morning to get here. Are you all right? What's wrong?"

He was holding her against him, and she felt so weak and ill that she could not move. "I was so frightened!" she cried. "It was so cold . . . and my head aches so . . . and I thought no one would come!"

He touched her hair and her forehead, and his arm tightened around her. "Didn't you know I'd come? Didn't you know I'd think of you all night? I would have come then, if I could. Don't you know I think about you always? I would do anything for you." He whispered these last words, and she felt the strength of his arms as they held her fast and secure. Where her body pressed against him, she now felt a warmth that made her glow from within. She wanted to move even closer, to immerse her entire body in that warmth, and to destroy the bitter cold and the fear. So she continued to stay in his embrace, weakly leaning against him and scarcely hearing his words or understanding their meaning—only knowing that she was safe and warm.

He laid his cheek against hers and felt the dry heat of her fever. He also felt the trembling of her muscles and the weakness of her body as she leaned against him, and though he would have given his life to continue to stand there holding her, he knew that he must get her into bed and warm up the room, or she might develop pneumonia. Gently he lifted her and carried her to the bed. He tucked her under the thick covers and then hurried outside. With the shovel he uncovered the stack of wood he had left by her door the night before. Within minutes a roaring fire was heating the room. Next he prepared some strong tea, and rummaging in her cupboard, found the aspirin. He boiled more water and filled a hot water bottle. As soon as the room became warm, she fell asleep. He sat silently by her bed watching her face as she slept. Her long chestnut hair was undone and covered the pillow. In sleep the stern expression she wore when she was teaching softened, and the pleasant sweetness of her face made her look very young. Under the covers he saw the swell of her breasts as they rose and fell in quick rhythm. Twice she groaned and called out in her sleep. She moved restlessly as though in pain, and he saw her lick her lips, dry and chapped with the fever. With infinite tenderness he lifted her head and coaxed her to drink. She drank without opening her eyes, or gaining full consciousness, and then fell again into troubled, fever-ridden slumber.

Nicholas knew that if she didn't show signs of improvement he would need to go for help. But for these few hours he sat beside her, watching her, caring for her, and he would have fought anyone who attempted to take away the privilege.

Finally, just as he was beginning to despair, she gave a deep sigh in her sleep. Fine beads of perspiration had gathered on her forehead and upper lip. The aspirin had taken effect. As tenderly as a mother with a sick child, he found a soft flannel cloth and wiped the dampness from her face. He felt her forehead and relief flooded his spirit as he realized the fever was broken. Within a few minutes Catherine, still asleep, began to push away the covers. The room was as hot as an oven because he had kept the stove going steadily. She pulled off her shawl and twisted restlessly in the bed, and then her eyes flew open, and for the first time she seemed aware of her surroundings.

"Nicholas!" she exclaimed. "Then it wasn't a dream! You really are here!" She sat up in bed. "What . . . ?"

"It's all right," Nicholas reassured her and came over and gently pushed her against the pillows. "You've been sick. I think the fever's broken now, but you still need to rest."

"How long?"

"Not long. Only a few hours."

"Oh," she slumped back, relieved. "And you've stayed with me the whole time? How can I thank you? I'm sorry to have been so much bother. Not much of a teacher today, I'm afraid." She tried to make her voice light, but it suddenly caught and a tear slid out of her eye. "What would I have done if you hadn't come!"

Nicholas knelt by the bed and held her hand in his. His face was next to hers and he searched her eyes. "You knew I'd come!" he said. "You must have known!"

"Well," she said weakly, attempting to turn the conversation. "I knew you were a dedicated student, but I didn't know you'd go to all this trouble for a lesson."

He did not smile, and his eyes continued to scan her face as though he could never see enough. "You know it wasn't the lessons that brought me. It was you. I—I—love you, Miss Summerwell. I can't help it. I do."

"Oh, no, Nicholas!" she cried. "No! Don't say such a thing!" She reached out her hand and laid it on his lips. "Nicholas, don't say another word. These things must not be said. Not now. Not ever. You do not love me."

He bent his head and kissed the palm of her hand as it lay against his lips, and then he reached up and took her hand in his strong, warm hands. With the maturity and dignity which she had noted in him so often, he replied simply, "Yes. I do."

She pulled her hand away from him and turned away with weary misery. "Nicholas, you don't know what you're saying. If any breath of this were to leave this room, it would destroy us both. Student and teacher is a privileged relationship. It cannot—it must not—be touched by scandal. I am your teacher, and perhaps you are confusing gratitude or admiration or proximity for love. You are too young . . . you don't know what love is. I am too old . . . I am your teacher." She whispered the last word vehemently. "Such a love could only bring disgrace. Your whole future is waiting for you. Don't ever speak of this again. You must promise me!"

Nicholas reached up and brushed the hair from her forehead. "I will speak of it. It is the truth. I don't care what people say. We can leave this place and go somewhere where we are no longer student and teacher but man and woman. I love you. Do you know what it is like to spend day after day with you in that deserted schoolroom, to be within a hand's grasp of your presence, to smell your sweet perfume, to watch your body as you bend and move, to hear your voice . . . your smooth skin . . . your beautiful hair, all pinned up and proper . . . Sometimes I have felt I would go mad! And I know you have felt it, too. Sometimes I feel you reaching out to me in the silence, like an electric current between us. You can't lie and tell me you don't feel it! I know you do! I know you do!" He put his arms around her and pulled her toward him. "You love me, too."

With the last of her strength she pushed him away and sat up. "No, Nicholas," she shook her head and spoke in a cold, unemotional voice. "I do not love you." She clenched her hands under the covers until the nails bit into the palms, but she kept her voice controlled. With a pain like part of her heart being torn from her breast, she said the words that would send him from her forever. "I do not love you. I am your teacher, and I have helped you because you showed great promise. It is your future I love—the possibility that a student of mine can conquer and achieve . . . can be the best! That is what I love—the promise of your success. Don't you see, Nicholas, your potential is endless. That's what I love—as a teacher and only as a teacher—your future, Nicholas. That's what we had together . . . nothing more."

He stood up and stared at her, his eyes searching her face. If she had cracked even a little, if she had shown a sign of warmth or affection or distress, he would have pitted his will against her. He would have taken her in his arms and kissed her and held her until she admitted to him and to herself that she loved him. Catherine knew that if ever in her life she was to do something for someone else, now was the time. There was no hope at all for their love. Everything to lose and nothing to be gained. "He will hate me," she thought, "but he will still have his future, bright and shining with promise, and once he has entered that world he he will forget about me. He may even come to a time when he will understand and forgive me."

With iron control she kept her face as stern as a mask. His brow furrowed in disbelief. "You really mean it, don't you?" he murmured. "You really mean it! I was just a thing to you—a puppet!" His voice gained in volume as his realization of what she had said grew, and bitterness and hurt flooded his heart. "See Nicholas learn! See Nicholas perform! See Nicholas make me a success! I was never anything to you as a person . . . only a student, passing through to a great future. Someone you could point to with pride to prove you were a teacher. Well, it was my misfortune to think that under the teacher there was a person. And I was dumb enough to fall in love with that person. I see now how wrong I was! There's nothing under there. Nothing at all!"

"Nicholas"—her voice was filled with pain—"please try to understand."

"My problem is I understand too well, teacher. You've taught me excellently how to discern subtleties. Only this isn't a book—we're real people . . . I'm a real person! And when you prick me I bleed real blood! Real feelings! But I gather teachers don't know anything about that. Students are their product, not their friends . . . not their . . ." His voice was harsh, and her headache returned. She put her hands up to the side of her face and pressed. "Not their lovers."

"I'm sorry," she whispered. "Keep on. Take the exams. Things will look different then." The room began to spin, and she had trouble hearing what he was saying. His voice came from somewhere far off.

"Never!" she thought she heard him say. "Never, never, never, never . . ." The word kept reverberating in her mind, and she wanted to ask him if he meant that he would never forget or that he would never take the exams, but somehow she couldn't form the words.

* * *

Much later Catherine woke. The fever had broken again, but this time she could tell it was not because of the aspirin. She felt clear-headed and stronger, and she knew she was recovering. The room was dark again, but a shadowy figure was sitting on the chair beside her bed next to the stove.

"Nicholas," she whispered.

The man turned to her. "No, Catherine, it's me— Steven. I came over late in the afternoon to see what was keeping Nicholas. He told me how sick you were, and I told him I'd watch you while he went to get Mama."

"Is your mother here?" Catherine asked, raising on an elbow and looking around.

"No," Steven said, "I don't think they could get through. The wind's come up again, and the snow is starting to drift. We came on snowshoes. Mama can't do that."

Catherine began to cry, slowly, miserably. "I'm so much trouble!" she wept. "You—Nicholas—your whole family have been so good to me. Nicholas saved my life and I—I—" She couldn't say anymore, but sobs racked her body.

"Hey!" Steven said. He came over and sat on the side of her bed and patted her awkwardly. "Hey, cut that out! You're stuck with me, so you might as well make the best of it. Come on! If you feel well enough, we could play a game of cards, and the snowstorm wouldn't be a total waste!"

She laughed and pulled herself up to a sitting position. "Steven, you are good medicine." He looked at her in the darkened room which was only lit by the glowing stove. Outside the wind was howling.

"This is probably going to destroy your reputation, Miss Summerwell, but there is no way I can leave here tonight."

Suddenly she was anxious. "Are you sure Nicholas made it home safely?"

"Why is it," Steven asked, "just when our conversations get interesting they seem to turn to Nicholas? Yes," he replied patiently, "I am sure he got home all right. I gave him my snowshoes."

"Thanks for coming, Steven. I didn't want to sound ungrateful. I was just worried. The wind is so strong."

"He left hours ago . . . long before the wind started up again. As a matter of fact he left the minute I came. I hate to say it, but he acted like he couldn't wait to get out of here. You were half out of your head with fever . . . and he seemed . . . just plain out of his head." Steven remained on the edge of the bed. He was smiling but his eyes were serious. "Do you want to talk to me about it?"

"Could I please have a drink of water and a brush?" Catherine asked. Her emotions were in such turmoil she didn't dare speak to Steven. Quietly, he did as she asked, and after she had drunk the water and brushed her hair, she leaned back on the pillows, her heart heavy with sorrow.

Steven took his place on the chair in front of the fire, and for several minutes they sat in silence. She began talking softly, and Steven listened without looking at her, as though he knew she had to speak impersonally. "You warned me," she said, "you warned me, and I wouldn't believe you." She paused. "He said he loves me. It isn't true, I know it isn't true. But he thinks it's true—and he believed I loved him, too."

"And do you?" Steven asked, so softly she could hardly hear.

"I don't know," she answered. "Even if I did, though, he could never know it. His whole future is out there. It mustn't be jeopardized."

It was hard for her to continue. "The thing I don't know is . . . did I really make this happen? Is there a part of me that wanted it to happen? What did I do to make him love me . . . or think I loved him? What have I done? Was it what I wore? What I said? Did I want this to happen?" Her voice rose hysterically.

Steven turned to her and, putting his hands on her shoulders, shook her gently. "Don't talk that way! Don't blame yourself. It wasn't you—it was the situation. I knew this was going to happen. You see, boys on farms grow up very fast. You can't be around animals all the time and not . . . oh, you know . . . it's everywhere. Besides, we work hard all week, and girls don't stay pretty too long on the prairies . . . you sort of have to get 'em while they're young."

Her face turned red and Catherine turned away from him. "No!" Steven said sharply. "That's your whole problem. You don't want to know . . . you don't want to face reality. But if you're going to be a teacher, you've got to know these things."

With an effort she turned back to listen. "But you see," he continued, "Nicholas was different. I mean, he had all the desires and the needs . . . maybe even more, because of all those books he read . . . but he also had a sense of himself that wouldn't let him cheapen himself. He couldn't simply grab like the rest of us, so he was innocent and idealistic in some ways. But he's a man—a man with strong needs."

"But I'm his teacher," Catherine whispered. "How can this have anything to do with me?"

Steven gave a painful half-laugh. "Teacher! What do you think you look like to farm boys who've never seen a girl whose hands aren't rough, or smelled a girl who didn't smell of milk or baking bread. Everything about you—you are like a page out of a magazine, a breath of another world that most of us thought only existed on a movie screen."

"But I'm not!" Catherine protested. "I'm a very ordinary person! What are you talking about!"

"Catherine! Why can't you see yourself as others see you, and not in comparison with some imaginary perfection you've dreamed up. I'm trying to tell you—it isn't anything you do. It's you. You make men want to love you."

Catherine shuddered with fear and self-disgust. "That isn't love . . . that isn't me!"

Steven took his hands away and shrugged his shoulders. "I'm not good with words. I'm trying to say you don't need to feel guilty. It's Nicholas's problem. Unless, of course, he's right and you do love him, too."

"I don't know," she whispered. "I don't know anything anymore. Maybe I'm that despicable! Maybe I wanted him to love me . . . maybe I love him. But none of that matters now, Steven! The only important thing is that none of this gets in the way of his writing the examinations. No matter what he feels about me. He must take the exams! You've got to help him! He has to hang on until April. Can you do it? Can you see him through? He won't accept my help now."

Steven thought for a long moment. "I don't know. I'll try, but I just don't know what he'll do! He's hurt and he's angry. I don't know . . ."

There was stillness in the little room as they each thought about Nicholas, and then Steven stood up. "I'm going to fix you something hot to eat, and then I think you should try to sleep again. By morning the roads will be clear, and you should be better."

"Where will you sleep?" she asked with genuine concern.

"I'll fix up something on the floor here by the stove," he said cheerfully. "Now let's get you taken care of."

In the middle of the night she woke for a moment. She could hear Steven's breathing in the dark room and she was comforted. "Steven?" she whispered.

"Yes," he answered softly, promptly.

She knew he was lying awake on his pallet on the floor. "Will you hold my hand?" she asked shyly. In a moment she felt his strong, hard hand groping for hers, and it engulfed her small warm hand in a tender grip. She felt a sense of ease and peace and promptly fell asleep again. Through the long, sleepless night Steven held her hand in his and his body ached to hold her in his arms.

Early the next morning Catherine woke to the jingle of harness. Steven opened the door to the Ranowski family, who had made their way to the school in the old sleigh. Mrs. Ranowski bustled in and soon had all the men shooed outside, shoveling snow and chopping wood.

"Next time there's a blizzard on hand, Miss Summerwell, you must come home with us," Mrs. Ranowski was saying. "From what Nicholas and Steven tell me, you've had a close call. Snowed in, and sick as well! We're fortunate the boys made it through."

"Is Nicholas with you this morning?" Catherine asked. "I'd like to thank him again."

"No," said Mrs. Ranowski cheerily. "He stayed home to do some chores for Papa. Probably wants to get right back to his studyin'. Could you tell me how he's doing, Miss Summerwell? Do you think he's going to pass the examinations?"

"Oh, yes!" Catherine exclaimed. "He's going to do very well indeed, Mrs. Ranowski. All his work and your sacrifices are going to pay off. He should make you very proud. He will be a great man someday." Catherine's voice broke, and she struggled for control. "I'm glad to have had a little part in helping him achieve that future."

"Well, now! That's something a mother loves to hear. Papa and I have always said—just so long as our boys are happy. That's the only success we care about for them." Mrs. Ranowski hummed tunelessly as she straightened up the room and cared for Catherine. When everything was as shining and spotless as her own home, she called out the door, "All right boys, let's be on the way home." She turned back to Catherine. "I'm sure you'll be fine now, Miss Summerwell. Someone will be by to check on you this evening. Shall we send word that school will be canceled for a few days until you feel better?"

"Perhaps tomorrow I won't teach. I'm sure by the

next day I'll be ready—thanks to you and your family, Mrs. Ranowski. I don't know how to tell you. . . ."

"Now, now"—Mrs. Ranowski was embarrassed— "don't say thank you. You have done so much for our Nicholas, it is little enough we have done for you."

In two days she was back in the schoolroom, pale and weak, but strong enough to resume class. Nicholas sat in his usual place, but he was like a wooden man. He did not speak to her. He did not ask for special assignments or complete the extra work that was given in class. All day, as she worked with the other students, she was conscious of his implacable presence.

In the days that followed his interest in Julie Lundquist became intense. He spent every spare moment with her, and the two young people were inseparable in the schoolyard. They left school together every afternoon. Catherine could only imagine what happened in the long hours after school. Julie seemed to feel Nicholas's attention was a victory, and she became insolent and flippant toward Catherine. Nicholas no longer came for extra tutoring.

Several times Catherine tried to approach Nicholas and ask him to come for a private interview, but he continued to avoid her assiduously. His work became careless, and he refused to read. It was as though in refuting her he refuted everything she represented. The short weeks until the time of the examinations sped by, and Catherine felt a sense of panic.

The blizzard had been winter's last breath. Before Catherine knew it, a chinook had devoured the snow, and within weeks, the days grew longer and the barren prairie began to show the early April promise of spring.

One evening Catherine was sitting up late correcting papers. Her eyes were tired and she stopped to rub them. Suddenly there was a pounding on the door. Startled, she hurried over and opened it. Steven rushed into her room. "Is he here?" he rasped, without preamble.

"Who? What?" Catherine exclaimed.

"Nicholas! Have you seen him?"

"Not since school. What's wrong?"

"Oh, that young fool! I hoped against hope it wasn't true. I thought maybe he would at least have talked to you. How could he be so dumb? You say he's so intelligent? I say he is stupid! Throwing away his life on a bag of . . ."

Catherine was almost frantic. "What are you talking about? Explain it to me, for pity's sake."

"He's run off with that young slut, Julie Lundquist. Knowing him, he probably has some noble notion about marrying her. He could have had her for a string of dime-store pearls!"

Catherine gasped in pain. "No! The exams are only ten days off!"

"I know that, and you know that!" Steven said roughly. "Apparently Nicholas has forgotten."

She slumped down in her chair. "It's my fault!"

"It's not your fault! If it's anyone's fault, it's that hot little hussy and her conniving mother. That Lundquist woman's had her hat set for a Ranowski boy ever since Julie put on silk stockings."

"It sounds like you speak from experience," Catherine observed caustically.

"Listen, I'm no craddle robber—even though she tried hard enough! When I wouldn't fall, Julie went after Nicholas, and he was so dumb he couldn't even see what she is. Well, he's done it good and proper now."

"Is there anything we can do?" Catherine asked desperately. Her heart felt like a piece of cold lead.

"No. We don't even know where they've gone. He left a dumb note saying they were going off together. We'll have to wait until they come back. Let me tell you, there's no shining future for a boy tied to that little slut."

"Oh, Steven, don't say it!" Catherine cried. "There must be something we can do."

"Nothing," Steven said dully and headed for the door. "So much for all the sacrifice and sorrow . . . what an ending!" His voice was bitter with disappointment.

"If it was his choice," Catherine began.

Steven whirled around and shouted at her. "It wasn't his choice. Stop talking like an ignorant woman. He didn't choose. He didn't know what he was doing! He was desperate for love, and Julie saw that and used it . . . used him!"

Catherine sat miserably at the desk. "Is love that important?"

"Maybe it is!" Steven said bitterly. "Maybe it is. You could have given him something. Some little piece of hope. But no, not you! Not Miss Pureheart! I'm not your judge. I guess none of us can help what we do or what we feel. I wish with all my heart that neither one of us had ever loved you!" He threw open the door and stormed out into the night.

Catherine went to see Julie's mother, Mrs. Lundquist, the next day. As she walked up the Lundquists' yard littered with rusty cans and farm implements, she thought what a contrast between this unpainted, ill-kept home and the white and tidy affluence of the Ranowskis'. Mrs. Lunquist came to the torn screen door. She was a fat, untidy woman with stringy hair and a dirty housedress. When she smiled, she showed gaps where teeth were missing, and her breath was stale and strong.

The room which Catherine entered was filthy. The sofa was worn, with batting coming out of a hole in the arm. Movie magazines and newspapers were stacked in untidy piles around the floor and ashtrays, overflowing with butts of cigarettes and cigars, were scattered on the end tables.

Catherine had heard the rumor that Mrs. Lundquist did not support herself and Julie by working the farm—rather, she worked the farmhands. It was well known that during harvest season a continual poker game was held by Mrs. Lundquist, and roving farmhands could find temporary lodging—and other accommodations—in the Lundquist home. Looking at the slovenly room, Catherine felt a wave of pity for Julie, growing up in such a depressing and unwholesome environment.

"Maybe she's no better than she deserves to be," Catherine thought.

"I've come about Julie and Nicholas," Catherine told Mrs. Lundquist. "Have you heard from them?"

Mrs. Lundquist's face leered at her. "From what I hear, you're more interested in hearing about Nicholas than Julie. Well, it won't do you no good now, Miss Summerwell. He don't care about you and those fool exams anymore. He's got my Julie—and she's got him. As soon as he can get his share of his pa's money, they'll be off for California and my Julie will be the star she deserves to be."

"What!" said Catherine, desperately wanting to disbelieve what she was hearing. "What are you talking about?"

"I'm talking about my Julie." The woman pointed to the stacks of magazines. "She's prettier than any of them starlets. All she needed was the money and someone to protect her, and now she's got that."

"But Nicholas has to take the exams. Don't you understand . . . he isn't an ordinary student. He's brilliant. He can't be wasted. Surely Julie will understand if she loves him."

It was then Mrs. Lundquist began to laugh. Her laughter was so ugly and derisive that Catherine felt unclean just listening to it. Without a word she turned and walked down the sagging steps and hurried back to the road. What had she done to Nicholas? How had she ever left him vulnerable to this terrible influence! There were so few days left until the exams, and Nicholas had ignored his studies for so long, she wondered if he would remember anything. Would he be able to pass now, even if by some miracle he still wrote the examinations?

The days passed in slow agony. Then one night, three days before the exams were to be taken, Steven Ranowski came to see her again. She was sitting in the schoolroom, and he walked between the desks, a weary smile on his face. "That was my place," he remarked, pointing to the desk where Dick Wilson sat. He bent and looked under the seat. "Yep! There are my initials carved on the bottom."

She smiled in return, and he pulled up a chair and sat by her desk. "It always seems to be Nicholas that we talk about. He's come home, and he's going to go to Cardston and take the exams."

Joy lit her eyes. "Steven! That's wonderful! Can you tell me what happened?"

"Well, seems married life wasn't all it was cracked up to be. I guess it didn't take your young genius very long to figure out he'd been had. They came home a week ago, and we could tell they were miserable. All over the house you could hear her yelling at him from their room."

"Anyway, Pa went up and had a long talk with her one day while Nick was out working. Seems she didn't want Nick or us at all—only the money! When Pa explained Nick wouldn't have any money for years and years, she kind of went off her head. Kept talking about Hollywood, and how she couldn't wait until she was old enough to go, and what dumb hunkies we were. So Pa gave her enough money to get to Hollywood, and to live on for a year, and she was gone before Nick got back from the fields. Pa is going to have the marriage annulled. He had a long talk with Nick, and tomorrow they're off for Cardston and the exams. Do you think Nick's got a chance in Hades to pass?"

"I don't know," Catherine said wearily. "I just don't know."

"One more thing," Steven said sadly. "I don't know how to tell you this. Ma and Pa know about you and Nicholas. They don't blame you, but they find it hard to understand. In their culture a teacher is like a nun, so they can't understand how it happened. I think it will be hard for them to feel as kindly toward you for a while. I'm sorry, Catherine, I'm truly sorry."

"It's all right, Steven," she said. "I understand."

Suddenly Steven stood up and came over to her, taking both of her hands in his. "I think it will be hard for me to ever stop feeling for you. Even if there was nothing in it for us, Catherine, I'm still glad I knew you."

"You're talking in the past!" she said, alarmed.

"I know you, Catherine—you're going to leave us as soon as this year is over. Aren't you?"

"Yes," she whispered, "yes. I couldn't stay. I wish with all my heart things could have been different."

Steven gave a short laugh. "I wish I didn't have to be my brother's keeper. It was always Nicholas between us. I knew that."

"I came here to be a teacher," she said.

"Yes. So you did. Well, I think we have all learned a great deal, don't you?" His voice was tender, and ironic.

"I hope so," she replied. "I really hope so, Steven."

Nicholas did not come back for the final weeks of school after he took the exams. Julie Lundquist had gone to Hollywood, and Dick Wilson hung around, unable to decide which was worse—going to school or staying home to help with chores. The prairies came alive as planting season approached. Tractors harrowed the wide fields, and trucks and cars bumped past on the school road. The children began to get restless and bored with their books as the weather improved. Some days Catherine couldn't blame them; looking at the blue skies of early May, and the freshening wind in the greening pastures, she too felt the tug of nature.

School ended officially the third week of May. It was a beautiful day, and the children squirmed in their seats, anxious for the final bell. Catherine gave a prepared speech about what she hoped they had accomplished in the past year, and then from an overflowing heart, told them she would miss them.

The children looked at her, and for a moment she felt their affection. But she knew that as the summer approached they would forget her. A school year, once finished, quickly became a memory. Catherine knew there was nothing lasting for her here.

The parents came to the door to pick up the children. In broken English they thanked her and led their children home for the labors of the farmer's season. Eddie Kozinski came running back with a handful of crocuses, and impulsively he hugged her. "You were a real good teacher!" he exclaimed, blushing beet red, and then ran down the hill.

For the next hour she remained in the schoolroom, cleaning out desks, putting the books in order, wiping down blackboards, and emptying her own desk.

Nicholas had once asked her, "Are you just an inanimate part of this room?" But to her, right now, the room did not seem inanimate. It was alive with memories—the voices of the children, the cold days of winter, and the hot stove, the laughter, the quiet afternoons with Nicholas. She paused, and putting down the books she was holding, she walked back to his desk.

"Nicholas," she whispered aloud to herself. And

then, miraculously, the door opened, and there he was—looking unchanged, a little thinner perhaps, but strong and assured.

"Nicholas!" Her voice was warm with delight and astonishment. "I'm so glad to see you!"

He looked at her steadily. "I'm glad to see you, too. I was hoping you would still be here in the school-house. I wanted to see you here where all the happy memories are—not in the teacherage."

She nodded, and an awkward silence stretched between them.

"I . . ." they both said at once. "No," Catherine said, "you say what you want to first."

"I took the exams," he said. "I wanted to be sure you knew that."

"How were they?"

"Hard, but I think I did well. I wanted to thank you."

"When the results come out in June, could you write and let me know how you do?" she asked hesitantly. "It would mean a great deal to me. Just send the letter to Bishop Watkins in Cardston. He'll know how to reach me."

"Yes," Nicholas answered. "Yes, I'll do that."

Impulsively, she turned to him. "You're going to love the university, Nicholas," she exclaimed. "It will be like a whole world opening up to you. It's the most wonderful experience. I wish I could go back and do it all over again with you!"

Nicholas watched her, and again she felt that strange reversal of roles, as though he were the older one. "I wish you could, too," he said. "Maybe then things would be different."

She looked at him for a moment—his face infinitely dear and familiar—and she tried not to let herself examine her emotions. There are some things it is better never to know, she thought. "Yes, Nicholas," she answered, "perhaps things would have been different—but we can never know."

"I know," Nicholas said simply.

She felt awkward, suddenly, as though school being over had changed their relationship, too, and there was a strangeness—a distance—between them.

"Thank you for coming to see me, Nicholas. I have felt so . . ." She didn't want to pursue the thought, and so she said, "It was a great kindness not to let me leave without talking to you. I feel better about going now."

"May I help you pack?" he asked, looking at the stack of books.

"No, Nicholas, I think we have said the things that needed to be said. Your parents . . . I think you should probably be going home now."

"No," he answered decisively, "everything that needs to be said has not been said. I want you to know that I understand what you did. I understand why you did it. I will never forget you. No matter where I go, no matter who I meet for the rest of my life, I will know that once I knew a true teacher, who was a woman as well."

CHAPTER FOURTEEN

Cardston was unchanged. The broad dusty streets, the white, shining temple, the neat houses, and the treeless length of Main Street with the Cameron Hotel topping the hill at the northern end of the street and the long sidewalk sloping down for several blocks until it dwindled into the shrubs and cottonwoods lining the banks of the winding creek below.

The Watkins family, in their sweet, domestic serenity, seemed unchanged, too. There was almost a sense of homecoming for Catherine as she entered their family life once more. But as Catherine returned to Cardston from her year of teaching at Spring Valley, she knew that she had changed—irrevocably—and she knew it would take her months of thinking and evaluation before she would understand what those changes were and how they would affect her future. For the present, however, she wished she could stop worrying. She yearned for a period of quiet time in which to heal the wounds left by Spring Valley. Her unresolved feelings for both Nicholas and Steven burdened her heart and mind. She felt guilt for having somehow failed both of these men who had loved her. Had she loved them in return—and if so, how? Each, surely in a different way. She questioned if she were capable of being a teacher. She viewed the professon idealistically and believed strongly that relationships with students should be as sacrosanct and free from harm as those of a physician with his patient. She had not been able to maintain her professional distance—had not developed that unique ability to be involved without personally involving her own emotions or those of her student. Moreover, she might have jeopardized Nicholas's future. Her mind recoiled from the thought! It made her feel unworthy of continuing in her chosen career.

She was hurt, too, by having lost the esteem of the Ranowski family. She had grown to love and admire the Ranowski parents—and knowing they felt she had failed only emphasized the feelings of failure in Catherine herself.

During good moments, however, Catherine found herself looking back with pride and affection to the happy times at Spring Valley. How nice to think back to that first day at school—which seemed a hundred years ago—when she had nearly roasted her students! Her heart swelled as she remembered evenings in the Ranowski home—their warmth, the abundance of their table, the fun and the hard work in their life-style—and some defiant part of her nature asserted that while she may have unintentionally hurt Nicholas, she had also helped him to achieve his dream. More and more she hoped that he would pass the exams! If Nicholas were to make it into the university, then she felt she could accept all her other failures and shortcomings.

Ladean had changed, too; Catherine noted subtle differences in her friend. There was a restlessness in Ladean—a tension that showed itself in a too-bright smile. Her cheerfulness seemed forced, her laugh too quick. Catherine thought perhaps the year had held surprises for both of them, and she knew that as the summer passed, they would gradually share their experiences with one another. In these first few days of being together again, however, the young women began to reestablish the pattern of their friendship.

"I guess I'll teach summer session at the high school," Ladean told Catherine when asked about her plans. "What are you going to do?"

"I'm not sure," Catherine said slowly. "I report to Mr. Solembaugh on Thursday, and I'll have to tell him I'm not going to accept the contract for Spring Valley for the coming year. I don't know what will happen. Maybe he'll tell me I'll never work again!"

"Boy!" exclaimed Ladean with a short laugh. "You don't sound like the same girl who sat on Mr. Raymond's desk until he saw that she got a teaching job.

"Listen, Catherine," Ladean's eyes sparkled with enthusiasm. "I happen to know that the English teacher at Cardston High is transferring up to Lethbridge, and I don't think they've got anyone to fill her contract. They're probably sending out feelers through the system, but you're right here! And you certainly have the qualifications! Why don't you speak to Mr. Solembaugh about it and see if there's a chance. Wouldn't it be wonderful? We'd be teaching together! Oh! Catherine, it would mean so much to me!"

Hope sprang in Catherine's heart. Always before her, like a specter, hung the fear that she would be forced to return to Calgary in jobless defeat. The teaching position at the high school sounded ideal, and Catherine felt a quick surge of excitement at the thought.

"I'll ask," she said hesitantly, "but . . . well . . . it all depends on Mr. Solembaugh."

"And you, Catherine!" Ladean said earnestly. "It depends on you, too. I know you! When you're determined, you always get what you want! Oh, please, please want it that much!"

"You're wrong, Ladean," Catherine replied with a ghost of a smile. "I very seldom get what I really, really want. But it would be wonderful."

The girls were sitting on the porch steps in front of the Watkins home, and they leaned back against the stairs, each lost in her own private thoughts.

Thursday morning Catherine prepared for the meeting with Mr. Solembaugh. She had bought herself a smart new suit especially for the interview. It was a light gray flannel with a narrow skirt and fitted top with a slight peplum. The collar and cuffs were a crisp white, and she topped it off with a little gray hat with a charming feather worn tilted on one side of her head. With white gloves and shining black pumps to complete the outfit, Catherine knew she looked trim, tailored, and professional. She had rolled her hair in the current style and just before leaving the Watkins's home, checked one final time to make sure the seams in her silk stockings were ruler straight.

At the door of the courthouse she paused to stare at the granite building. It was one of those impressively official buildings which seem perfectly suited to their function. Catherine smoothed down her skirt, took a deep breath, and marched purposefully up the wide stone stairs toward the heavy brass doors. As she reached the door it swung open abruptly, nearly knocking her off balance. Before she could recover her composure, Malcolm Brady came striding out. The door sprang closed behind him, and he dashed down the steps.

"Malcolm!" she called to him. "Malcolm Brady!"

Hearing her, he swung around impatiently at the bottom of the stairs to face the caller. When he saw it was Catherine, the irritated look left his face and he smiled. In three bounds he remounted the stairs and grasped her hands. "Catherine!" he exclaimed. "I didn't know you were in town! Oh! The Devil! I'm meeting my supervisor over at the experimental station, and I'm deucedly late! I can't talk! Will you meet me for lunch?" His voice was rushed.

"Where?" Catherine asked.

"The coffee shop! It's just around the corner. About a block up from the Trading Post. See you there at one?"

Not waiting for an answer he cleared the steps, leaping down several at a time, and in a minute she heard the roar of his old car as it left the parking area. She smiled, shook her head, and entered the building.

The beginning of her interview with Mr. Solembaugh was stiff and awkward. She had no idea what he had heard about her teaching, and she dreaded having to explain to him why she did not wish to return to Spring Valley.

After the initial pleasantries, Mr. Solembaugh looked at her searchingly. "I have heard fine things about your teaching, Miss Summerwell. Your attendance records were excellent—a good indication of student interest. I was also astonished to hear that one of your seniors had taken the Provincial Departmental exams this year and that you undertook the task of preparing him yourself. It strikes me as a rather ambitious undertaking for a first-year teacher."

Catherine was nervous. She wondered what else Mr. Solembaugh had heard about her relationship with Nicholas or if it were only her tutoring of Nicholas which made him doubt her judgment.

"He is a brilliant student," she said quietly. "I didn't do anything but direct him. He taught himself."

"Do you honestly think he has a chance of passing?" Mr. Solembaugh asked incredulously, looking at her intently. "Or do you think you simply exposed him to an unpleasant experiment in which he could not possibly succeed? The curriculum at Spring Valley is hardly designed for this kind of achievement, and I find it impossible to imagine that anyone could overcome in a few months the educational deprivation of many years."

Catherine thought with despair how confidently she could have answered Mr. Solembaugh if the incident of the snowstorm, and Nicholas's hasty marriage with Julie, had never occurred. But they had! And now she sat across from Mr. Solembaugh realizing that if she overstated Nick's potential, and he failed the exams, she would be made to look like a fool. However, her old, impulsive nature impelled her on.

"But Nicholas Ranowski is an exception! He is really an extraordinary student, and I believe he will not only pass the examinations but do so with honors—possibly even with distinction!"

Mr. Solembaugh frowned, as though he did not like to have his judgment questioned, and Catherine experienced a sinking feeling. "I've done it now!" she thought.

"Well," Mr. Solembaugh said primly, "we shall know very soon, shan't we? The results should be coming within the month. And now, Miss Summerwell, it is my rather unpleasant duty to inform you of a change in the school district. It has for some years been contemplated that we should phase out all rural schools in favor of consolidated schools in more populous areas. This year the Spring Valley School is included in the consolidation program. We will be closing the school as of this summer. So I am sorry to inform you that your contract will not be available for the coming school year."

A wave of relief went through Catherine. She would not have to back out of her contract after all. She would not have to explain to Mr. Solembaugh any of the reasons why she did not wish to return to Spring Valley. And better still—she could tell he felt uncomfortable and guilty because he thought he had fired her! Now's the time! Catherine thought.

"Mr. Solembaugh," she said solemnly, "what am I to do?"

The school superintendent looked uncomfortable. He cleared his throat and tapped his fountain pen on the desk in front of him. "Mr. Raymond and I assumed that after one year at Spring Valley you would probably desire to return to Calgary and your own home."

"My home is where my work is, Mr. Solembaugh. I am not a child."

"Yes, yes, of course," Mr. Solembaugh rumbled.

"Perhaps I could look through the school district and see if there are any contracts which might be suitable . . ."

"What I would really like, if it were possible, Mr. Solembaugh, would be to find a contract right here in Cardston," she said sweetly. "Are there any contracts open at all?"

Taken aback, Mr. Solembaugh looked at the young woman in front of him. There was a great feminine determination about her that made him decidedly uneasy. "There's only one opening this year. It's at the high school for an English literature teacher. I don't think . . ."

"But that's perfect, Mr. Solembaugh!" Catherine exclaimed. "English is my major. I am fully credited in secondary education and an English literature graduate. I am also the winner of the Governor-General's gold medal in that field. If you would care to review my résumé, you will find this is the job for which I am best qualified."

"I know that your training is in this field, Miss Summerwell. However, this is a most challenging position, and I plan to have it filled by someone with significant experience."

"But I have experience!" Catherine exclaimed indignantly. "I have taught twelve grades for a year . . . and that should be equivalent to twelve years of experience! You yourself said good things about my teaching. And I'm right here, ready to begin! Summer school starts in two weeks. How could you find someone better qualified than I in so short a time?"

Mr. Solembaugh had a glazed look in his eyes, as

though he could hardly absorb the enthusiastic and vigorous rush of Catherine's arguments.

"Well . . ." he hesitated, not knowing how to answer.

"Please, Mr. Solembaugh. Won't you at least give me a chance?" she pleaded.

"Miss Summerwell," he said sternly, bringing her pleas to an abrupt halt. "I do not award contracts because people want them. I award them because people are capable of fulfilling them. I honestly do not feel you are ready to assume this position at the high school. However, to show that I am a fair man, I will give you the contract, conditionally."

"Oh, thank you! Thank you!" Catherine burst out, but he cut her thanks short.

"Don't thank me until you hear my conditions. I will allow you to teach—on probation—at the high school during the summer session. During that time I will have supervisors observe your teaching ability. If their reports are positive, I will consider giving you the contract for the following school year upon one final provision."

"That sounds fair," said Catherine. "What is the final provision?"

"That young Nicholas Ranowski passes the Departmental Examinations." Mr. Solembaugh looked at Catherine with a crafty and satisfied smile. Catherine stared at him in astonished silence.

"You see, Miss Summerwell, I feel that nothing shows the success of a true teacher half so well as her students. If you were able to take a young man who has received his education in a deprived one-room school, and make it possible for him to pass the provincial examinations—competing with every other twelfth grade student in the Province of Alberta—why, it seems to me you will have proved that you are a teacher! However, if the young man fails the exam, it would seem to me that by exposing him to a humiliating experience—by misjudging the situation so badly that you thought you could accomplish the impossible—you will have shown that you are inexperienced and much too impulsive to accept a contract of responsibility such as the one at the Cardston High School."

Catherine listened to the school superintendent's sententious voice and her stomach knotted with apprehension. Maybe he was right. Maybe the fact that she had encouraged Nicholas was only a sign of her own arrogance and inexperience. She thought from the tone in Mr. Solembaugh's voice that nothing would give him greater pleasure than to have both her and Nicholas fail—because it would prove his judgment to be right. At this thought a spark of anger began to glow steadily and hotly in her being.

Her jaw firmed and her eyes sparked. "Mr. Solembaugh," she said, "you've got a deal! I will teach English during the summer session, and I promise you, I'll be the best literature teacher I know how to be! As for Nicholas Ranowski—I don't mind a bit that my future depends on how well he does in the examinations! I will look forward to seeing you when the results are posted. I hope you'll be ready to sign my contract!"

She stood up, drawing on her white gloves. "Thank you very much. I know you won't regret it."

Mr. Solembaugh stood, and there was a look of puzzlement in his eyes, as though he didn't quite know how he had lost control of the interview. "I hope I don't!" he said fervently. "I certainly hope I don't regret it! Good day, Miss Summerwell."

As she left the courthouse Catherine was exhilarated at the possibilities of earning the teaching contract at the high school, and yet frightened at the conditions imposed by Mr. Solembaugh. Ironically, she thought, her future now depended upon Nicholas, when for so long she had lived with the feeling that his future was dependent upon her. "Well, Nicholas!" she thought, "it looks like our fates are entwined for a while longer. We shall each sink or swim on the result of our year's work together."

"You're different," Malcolm said without preamble as they sat across from one another in the painted wooden booth at the coffee shop.

"How?" she asked, surprised at his comment and curious about what it was he saw changed in her.

"Oh, I don't know!" he shrugged. "You seem more genuine, I suppose. Some of that glossy Mount Royal veneer has been rubbed off. Maybe you even got bruised a little!"

She smiled and he looked at her more closely. "That part's good," he added, "but there's another part." He stared at her for another moment. "I detect a squaring around the jaw, frown lines between the brows, and a firming of the mouth! Great Scot! This woman might turn into a teacher—a veritable classroom ogre—if someone doesn't rescue her from such a fate!"

"Malcolm!" she exclaimed, amused in spite of herself, but irritated, too. "That's not very funny!"

Malcolm's strong, sun-browned face looked grim, and he watched her with his clear blue eyes. "I didn't mean it to be. You know, you have to watch the exercise of authority! It has corrupted many a better woman than you. Nowhere is authority so absolute as in the classroom. Every teacher has the potential of becoming a despot."

"And what happens to corrupted agriculturists?" Catherine asked tartly. "Do they become dictators of the wheat fields?"

"No!" said Malcolm. "They attempt to impose the laws of genetic breeding on civilization as a whole. A district agriculturist run rampant is a terrible sight!"

Catherine blushed. "For heaven's sake, Catherine!" he said. "A year of real living and you still can't face the word 'breeding'; maybe there's more Mount Royal blood left in you than I thought!"

"Let's change the subject," Catherine suggested, "okay? What are you going to be doing this summer?"

"That's a nice, safe subject," Malcolm teased her. "You don't need to worry that I'll make your life difficult," he went on, "unless you're planning to be in Edmonton for the next year."

"What do you mean?"

"I'm off for a year's special assignment in the department's offices in Edmonton. I'm doing some research in cattle diseases and so I've been given a sabbatical."

Catherine was unprepared for the disappointment she felt and she realized she had come to count on Malcolm Brady being in Cardston. Theirs was certainly not a close or comfortable relationship, and yet she somehow felt he was her friend, and she knew she could depend on him.

Her voice tender with regret, Catherine exclaimed, "I'm sorry you're going! I'll miss you!"

Malcolm looked at her keenly and said in a surprisingly gentle voice, "I really believe you mean that!"

"I do!" she assured him. "I'm going to be teaching here in Cardston this summer, and then, if all goes well, there's a chance I may be teaching here for the school year, too."

"If that's what you want," Malcolm said, "I really hope it happens for you, Catherine. If it does, I'll be back by next spring, and maybe you'll still be here! I'd like that!"

They spent the rest of the lunchtime discussing the special project on which Malcolm was working. The conversation they shared made Catherine realize that although his manner was sometimes cynical, Malcolm was an inwardly sensitive and compassionate young man. His interest in animals was keen and genuine, and he took great pride in his work. His impatience for ignorance and his contempt for incompetence surfaced frequently, however, and she thought he would not be an easy man to work with—or to get close to.

After the lunch they parted on the sidewalk in front of the cafe. "I'm leaving tonight," he said, "driving up. Thought I'd miss the heat of the day that way."

"Hey!" he said, with a sudden thought. "You wouldn't like to ride up with me as far as Calgary, would you? You could spend a few days with your folks and . . ."

"No!" she said, too quickly—too vehemently. "I—

I—" she faltered, realizing how abrupt her refusal sounded. "It isn't that I wouldn't enjoy the trip, I just have so much to do to get ready for school, you know. . . ." Her explanation sounded lame, even to herself.

He gave her a sardonic smile. "Yeah!" he said knowingly, "still not ready to face them, huh? I thought by now you would have worked out whatever ghosts you're carrying around in your system. Looks like Mount Royal casts a long shadow." He shook his head and then bent quickly and kissed her on the cheek. "That should hold you until I get back." He started to walk away, putting on his wide-brimmed Stetson, but then thought better of it and took the hat off again, turning to face her. "You know, Catherine, sooner or later everyone has to go home!"

"I know that!" she responded. Her smile was full of gay bravado. "But you have to know where home is before you can go!"

"Touché!" he responded in the same bantering tone. Then, with a flourish he saluted her with his Western hat, and, settling it firmly on his head, he turned from her and walked briskly up Main Street.

Catherine and Ladean began their duties at summer school. The days were hot and the classrooms were only half-filled with reluctant students who were trying to make up credits or whose parents had insisted they "do something worthwhile with their summer." Facing such indifferent teen-agers proved a challenge, and the two young teachers soon discovered there was a significant difference between the start of summer school and the pleasant excitement at the beginning of a full fall term.

In order to capture the attention and enthusiasm of her students, Catherine found herself putting in countless extra hours trying to develop projects, visual aids, and lesson plans that would spark their interest. She was teaching two courses. One, a comprehensive poetry class, and the other, Shakespeare. On several afternoons she found herself coming back home and collapsing on the porch swing. "I can't do this one more day!" she would groan. Ladean, sitting beside her, would begin swinging gently, and the springs would squeak rhythmically. "Me, too," Ladean would say. "So what are you going to do tomorrow?"

Then they would both giggle. Usually Mrs. Watkins had a pitcher of lemonade waiting for them, and often she would join the two girls and the three of them would visit together.

As the heat of the summer increased and the hot dusty air of the prairies glowed golden in the blazing sun, the flies, bees, and 'hoppers made a constant humming. It became harder and harder to face the square, solid brick school with its high-ceilinged classrooms and tall windows. Even though the windows were kept open to catch the rustle of the constant prairie wind, it only seemed to blow in heat, dust, and flies.

Catherine noticed that Ladean was becoming more irritable with each passing day. She scarcely spoke at dinner time, and replied sharply to the most innocuous comments made by her parents. One evening at supper her mother asked what news Dan had sent in his last letter from Australia. Ladean jumped up from the table, upset and angry. "Nothing! No news! Just the usual. I don't want to talk about it! If you want to know what he's doing, why don't you write to him?" Ladean paused, obviously embarrassed at her outburst, but did not apologize. "I'm going for a walk!" she said.

It was after dark when Ladean entered the bedroom. Catherine was already in bed, her weary feet and body anxious for sleep, but her concern for Ladean keeping her awake.

"Do you want to talk?" she asked Ladean, in the dark room.

"No!" Ladean said shortly, and Catherine could hear Ladean's bed creak as she climbed into it. "I just want to sleep."

"Another time?" Catherine asked.

There was silence in the dark for a long moment, and then Ladean's voice said softly, "Maybe."

Added to the difficulty of teaching was the pressure of the visiting supervisor on Catherine. Without notice during any classroom period, the door would open and the supervisor would enter her class and sit in one of the back desks. Silent and alert, he would remain for a time, and then, just as abruptly, he would get up and leave. From the bland expression on his face, Catherine could tell nothing of what he was thinking or how well she was doing. Another worry, as the month passed, was that the time for the announcement of Nicholas's examination results was almost due. Catherine tried not to think about it. She wanted to concentrate on the job at hand.

One day while the class was reading *Midsummer*

Night's Dream Catherine got a brilliant idea. "Let's not read this play!" she exclaimed to the class. "Let's produce it! We'll do a summer theater production. I know the teacher of the home economics class. She can help with costumes and scenery. We can put on the play for the last day of school! What do you say?"

The class was eager for an activity that would relieve it of studying, and they greeted the idea with enthusiasm. As each student assumed a part, a sense of vitality began to develop in the classroom. Each day the pupils argued interpretations of the various speeches, and as Catherine explained to them the theatrical methods of the Old Globe Theatre, they began to warm to thoughts of production and scenery and became determined to recreate the dynamic Elizabethan fervor for drama. Gradually, the project became the purview of the students, and Catherine became an advisor and provider of facts and suggestions. Her pupils threw themselves into the activity with all their youthful energy.

When the supervisor happened upon them one day, the students were rehearsing the scene of the guild players in the woods. The class was determined to create the best possible comedy in the farcical sequence. The young man who was playing the part of Bottom had a natural flair, and each student in the class was eagerly contributing his or her thoughts and suggestions. During the rehearsal, Catherine interjected questions about the process of comedy. "Why," she asked the class, "is it so funny when one of the players becomes a 'wall,' and then another player talks to the wall? What element of humor do you see there?"

"Absurdity!" one student called out.

"What do you mean by absurdity?" Catherine asked, and the class was at it, eagerly defining and analyzing the sources of humor. It was a noisy class—not at all traditional—but the air crackled with ideas. Catherine noticed uneasily that the supervisor stayed for the whole class period. She still could tell nothing of his reaction to her methods.

It was on a humid morning a week later that Catherine was called out of her classroom by a messenger from the office. She walked down the corridors of the school, her heart beating madly, wondering what could be wrong. As she entered the office, she saw Mr. Solembaugh standing by the door of the principal's room. He turned and saw her. "Oh, yes, Miss Summerwell. Sorry to interrupt your class, but I have some news I thought you should know."

Catherine's heart sunk! What news could bring her out of her classroom? And why did Mr. Solembaugh look so serious!

"Just come into the principal's office with me. He has stepped out for a minute."

Listlessly, she followed him into the office. No matter how hard she worked it seemed things never went right! She was convinced she would be informed her summer work was considered unsatisfactory, and she would be told to look for a contract in another district . . . or else to "go home."

"Well, Miss Summerwell!" Mr. Solembaugh began in a hearty tone. "The results from the Provincials have arrived!"

Her eyes opened wide with astonishment and excitement. "They've come! The results are here! Do you know how Nicholas did?"

"Yes, yes, my dear. Now please calm yourself," Mr. Solembaugh looked at her gravely. "It was certainly not as you anticipated."

Catherine's heart plummeted. Nicholas must have failed! She had gambled both of their futures, and they were both losers. Her head dropped and she could not look the school superintendent in the eye.

"No, no," the superintendent continued, not noticing her discouragement. "I told you . . . if you had been more experienced . . . any experienced teacher would have know immediately that she was working with a genius—a true genius. There is no question! This boy should have been brought to the attention of the finest educators in the district. An experienced teacher would have known just how extraordinary this student was! You should have come to us as soon as you suspected! But then I can't complain, I suppose, because even though you elected to handle this yourself, due to your lack of judgment, nonetheless, all's well that ends well . . . to quote the man whom you are teaching this summer."

Catherine was confused and distressed by the rambling discourse of Mr. Solembaugh. Her mind clung to one word and one word only—"Genius!" He had referred to Nicholas as a genius! But why?

"Mr. Solembaugh, how did Nicholas do on the examinations?" she asked in an agony of suspense, desperate to hear his answer.

"Oh, of course!" Mr. Solembaugh laughed heartily, "You don't know! And here I am rambling along! He placed highest in the province in three of the examinations. This has only been accomplished one other time in all the years of departmentals. He placed in the top ten in the other exam. His record stands as the highest ever achieved." Mr. Solembaugh continued to speak, but Catherine was oblivious to what he was saying. Over and over to herself she was repeating, "You did it, Nicholas! You did it! And now it's all yours . . . that wonderful future! I don't have to feel guilt or sorrow anymore, because I made it possible. You did it, but I made it possible!" She felt light-headed and almost giddy with relief and joy.

Suddenly, she became aware that Mr. Solembaugh was still speaking to her.

". . . A little unorthodox, but the supervisor says he feels the children are learning Shakespeare. We accept some latitude in summer school which, I must warn you now, we would not do during the regular school year. Nonetheless . . ."

"Are you trying to tell me," Catherine whispered incredulously, "that you are offering me the contract for next year?"

"Haven't you been listening to me, young woman? That is exactly what I've been saying. Here is the contract. If the terms are satisfactory, you may sign it right now."

"I don't even need to read it!" Catherine exclaimed. "I'm going to sign it before you have a chance to change your mind." She jumped up and picked up a pen which was lying on the desk. With a dramatic flourish she signed her name.

"There!" she said, with a radiant smile, handing the legal contract back to him. "You're stuck with me for another year at least!"

The school superintendent took the paper from her, and a fatherly look of exasperation and concern crossed his face. "You are a very impulsive young woman! Someday it is going to get you into a great deal of trouble."

When Catherine announced the news at the supper table to the Watkins family, they beamed at her, and their congratulations were filled with affection and joy.

When the round of good wishes was over, Catherine looked seriously at the loved faces surrounding her and made another announcement. "There is no way I can thank you for all you have done for me. You have made me feel welcome in your home—in your family. But now that I am assured of a position, I know the time has come when I should look for a place of my own. I can't continue to impose on your generosity. Tomorrow I will start looking for a place, and hopefully you'll be rid of me soon. Although you'll never be rid of me because, of course, we'll still see each other often. . . ." She felt the beginning of tears, and so she stopped speaking.

Tears were sparkling in Mrs. Watkins's eyes and Bishop Watkins had a sad expression on his face that touched her deeply. "You know you can stay here, Catherine dear," Mrs. Watkins said.

"I know," Catherine replied. "You are so good to me. But it's best if I go."

"I understand," said Bishop Watkins. "We will miss you, though, Catherine."

Ladean did not say a word. Catherine was hurt by her silence, but she did not try to probe.

On a side street across from the luxurious grounds behind the temple Catherine found a little house. A young couple lived in the front part of the house, which was neatly kept, although the paint was worn on the plain clapboard front. The house was divided by a back hall and entry to which some former owner had added a small apartment. It had two rooms and a bath. The main room was a combined kitchen and living area, and there was a small separate bedroom. The rooms were cheerful and pleasant, with bright windows that looked out over a pretty vegetable and flower garden. The apartment had its own entrance, and the hallway at the back of the other house served to buffer any sounds between the two living areas. The place seemed ideal to Catherine, and she signed a lease with the young owners.

The next afternoon after school she asked Ladean to come over and look at her new home. Ladean seemed reluctant to come, but Catherine persuaded her, and the two young women walked the few blocks to the house. After Catherine had shown Ladean through the rooms—with scarcely a comment from Ladean—the two girls sat down on either side of the little eating table in the kitchen area.

"Say something!" Catherine demanded. "Tell me what you think!"

To her surprise Ladean burst into tears.

"What's the matter, Ladean? What is it?" Catherine was dismayed. "What have I done?"

The next thing she knew Ladean was laughing through her tears and wiping her eyes. "Oh, you silly thing!" Ladean said. "It isn't you. It's me! I'm so jealous I could die! What I would give to be moving into a place where I could be on my own! And now I won't have you at home to make life bearable! I don't know what I'm going to do! I don't know how I'm going to make it through!"

Catherine was astounded. "But I thought you loved living at home. I mean, your parents are fantastic! Why would you want to leave?"

"Oh, you are such a goose, Catherine! For someone so smart, you say such dumb things sometimes. Don't you think if I ever went to your home as a guest I would be saying exactly the same thing to you? 'Why do you want to leave, Catherine? Your parents are so fantastic!' " she mimicked Catherine's tone, and they both laughed.

"You're right!" Catherine said, "I guess there comes a time . . . But if you feel that way, your folks would understand. Why don't you move in with me! The rent is very reasonable, and divided two ways, we could both save! Think about it, Ladean! It could be such fun!"

Ladean's eyes lighted. "Maybe I will!" she said. "That's a wonderful idea!"

The two girls began planning and dreaming, and the afternoon passed in a whirl of talk. Ladean announced her decision to her parents in Catherine's presence. They said very little but the next few days the girls were in such a flurry of activity in preparation for the move that Catherine failed to notice how quiet the Watkinses were. The following Saturday Catherine packed the last of her things and took them over to the apartment. "I will start scrubbing out the tub and cleaning the oven!" she called to Ladean as she left. "You bring your stuff over as soon as you can, and we'll get to work painting the bedroom. I'll come back this evening to say a proper good-bye to your parents."

A few hours later the door of the apartment opened. Catherine's hair was tied up in a scarf, and her hands were covered with rubber gloves. She was black up to her elbows with oven grease. "About time!" she called as Ladean entered. "I was beginning to think you'd deserted me."

Ladean did not smile. She stood by the door and her face could not conceal her misery.

"I am deserting you," she said simply. "I can't move in with you."

Catherine could not believe what she was hearing. "Not move in? You mean you've changed your mind? I . . ."

"No!" Ladean said vehemently. "I don't want to talk about it or discuss it! That's all my parents have done for days is talk to me! Please just listen to me, Catherine. I'm not moving in with you, and the reasons are too complicated to explain! I feel like I'm in a box. An awful box, and there's no way out! Mother and Daddy are so reasonable—everything they say is so reasonable and so true—so why do I feel like I'm going to suffocate? Why do I want to scream? I should be the happiest person in the world. I'm engaged to a boy I love, my parents are kind and loving, I have a wonderful home. It's all wonderful! Why am I so miserable?"

"But Ladean . . ." Catherine interrupted.

"Don't!" Ladean exclaimed. "Don't try to reason with me or help me understand myself. I do! But it doesn't help!" She took a deep breath and continued in a more controlled tone. "Mother and Daddy are right. I would be squandering my money to pay for rent and food if I moved here—when I can get it free at home. I have to save for my wedding next spring when Dan gets home. He still has two years of college to finish, and we'll need the money. And like they say, it wouldn't look good for me to be living with someone who isn't a member of the Church."

Catherine reeled back as though she had been struck.

"Oh, Catherine! I didn't mean to hurt you! You are a wonderful person, and nothing you do would be a bad influence on me! Mother and Daddy know that! But it would cause talk in the town. It's such a small town, you see, and the Bishop's family lives in a fishbowl, and well, people would say I was leaving the church or getting too uppity for it or something like that!"

Here it was again, all around her. Catherine had been fooling herself! She was an outsider here, more of an outsider than she had ever imagined! She knew that the courtesy and love she had been given were all genuine, but she also saw now that she was clearly different. There existed a deep, quiet inward circle in Cardston to which she was not admitted—an undefined circle where people knew and understood one another because of deeply shared ideas and beliefs. It didn't need to be spoken or expressed, it simply existed—like the magic inner circle of Mount Royal or the family circle of the Ranowskis. She was only a visitor—cared for, accepted, admired—but not really a part of it.

Catherine tried to ignore her pain, because she could tell Ladean was suffering even more than she was.

"Three years!" Ladean cried. "Three years of wait-

ing for Dan! And only two of them gone! Living on
memories and letters! And his letters have changed.
He's changing! All he talks about now is the work—
the glory of serving the Lord—and here am I, changing, too! Only not for the better!" she laughed bitterly. "I'm getting old, Catherine! I can see the first
hints of wrinkles, and I pulled out a gray hair yesterday. Do you ever look at those twelfth grade girls
we're teaching! They look so fresh and new . . . and
they think we're old. Old! What if he comes back, and
I look old to him? What if he sees one of those fresh
young girls and—Oh, Catherine! What if he doesn't
love me! Three years wasted! I'll be too old to start
out again! I don't want to be an old maid!" Ladean
put her face in her hands and then wiped her eyes impatiently.

"Do you know how long it's been since I had any
fun? Months and months! It's like I'm living on ice,
and all my happy emotions are on ice, too, and sometimes I think they may never thaw out! I went to a
dance last weekend, and the wildest boy in town asked
me to go out to his car with him. And I almost went!
Here I am! A righteous, upstanding Mormon girl! A
schoolteacher! Engaged to a missionary! And I almost
went! As a matter of fact I would have gone, if someone hadn't cut in on us."

"What am I turning into, Catherine? Remember
when we talked about people wanting us to grow up?
Well, my folks want me to be so grown up that waiting another year won't bother me, but they still want
me to be enough of a little girl that I can continue to
live at home! Catherine, I'm scared! I don't know if I

can do it. Maybe next time when someone asks me to his car, I won't be stopped!"

Out of her own pain and hurt Catherine tried to answer Ladean. "I don't understand your church, not really, Ladean. I don't suppose I really deserve to understand it since I've never bothered to study it. But 'eternity' is what you said . . ."

"Eternity?" Ladean asked, not comprehending.

"Yes," Catherine said, "isn't that what you told me? You and Dan loved each other so much that you would be married for eternity. It seems to me, if Dan loved you that much before he left, he won't change in three years—at least, not change in how he feels about you! You're beautiful, Ladean. You'll always be beautiful! Why do you think boys still want you to go to the car with them? Nothing's changed . . . except you get prettier. You've got to hang onto the thought of eternity. It's the only way this next year will seem possible! But it is possible, Ladean! Even the hardest, longest years pass. I found that out at Spring Valley. If you can make it through the summer, you'll make it through the year.

"Tell you what!" Catherine went on, and it took all of her courage to extend the invitation, she was so afraid of a rebuff after what Ladean had said about her being a non-Mormon. "Maybe you could come up to Calgary with me when summer school's over and spend a week. That would give you something to look forward to."

Ladean's eyes lit up and her face broke into a delighted smile. "I'd love it, Catherine! Maybe that's what I need—to get away for a little while! How wonderful of you to ask! I'd love to come!"

Catherine was still unsure. "Are you positive your parents won't object?" she asked hesitantly.

"Of course not . . . why?" Ladean looked at Catherine and realized how hurt she was. "Oh, Catherine!" Tears sprang to Ladean's eyes. "Forgive me! Please forgive me and forget what I said. I didn't know what I was saying! I was so upset! Please, please . . . we love you. Mother, Daddy, me . . . we all love you!"

Catherine got up and hugged Ladean. "It's forgiven," she said warmly, but there was a sad note in her voice, and Ladean looked at her with sweet sorrow in her eyes and said knowingly, "Forgiven—but not forgotten. I would give my soul to take back what I said!"

Then Catherine laughed and the tension between them cleared. "No, you wouldn't, Ladean! You Mormons are very careful with your souls!"

CHAPTER FIFTEEN

There was a thin silver crust of moon in the black velvet of the prairie night, and the stars hung so low and bright above the schoolyard that Catherine stopped walking and looked up in awe.

"Ladean," she whispered, "do you think if we climbed to the top of the temple we could reach up and touch a star?"

Ladean laughed. "The thought of climbing up the temple is a little sacrilegious. But"—she paused and sighed in wonder at the beauty of the night sky—"on a night like this the whole world seems like a temple."

"Well said!" Catherine agreed.

The two young teachers were the last to leave the school building, and the hour was late. It was the night of the performance of *Midsummer Night's Dream*. The school auditorium had been packed with parents and friends, and the community as a whole had supported the project, partly because it had been a long summer and everyone was a trifle bored so that anything new or different was automatically appealing.

Catherine had been astonished by the turnout and worried that the performance of her students would not merit such enthusiasm. However, her fears had been ungrounded. The students turned in very creditable performances, and one or two of them were even

quite remarkable. The scenery and costumes which
Ladean had coordinated, designed, and created in her
home economics classes were delightful and imagina-
tive, and the audience had enjoyed the evening thoroughly.

It was with a sense of regret and a nagging feeling of
loss that they had packed away the scenery, said good
night to the young actors and stage hands, and finally
turned off the house lights to stand on the empty stage
in the empty school building.

"It was absolutely"—Ladean searched for a word to
express her feelings about the evening, but no single
word seemed big enough so she compensated by saying
the word with emotion and force—"wonderful!"

Catherine looked at her on the dim stage. "Yes, it
was, wasn't it? I still can't believe it! I hated summer
school so much at first. I simply couldn't wait until it
would be over, and then I came up with this half-
baked scheme to put on one of the plays, and the idea
sort of grew. I never dreamed it would end so . . ."
She, too, searched for a word and, giving up, used Ladean's word again . . ."wonderfully!"

"Wonderful acting! Wonderful audience!" Ladean
went on.

"Wonderful costumes! Wonderful scenery!" Catherine interjected.

"Wonderful directing!" Ladean bowed to Catherine. By now they were so tired they were giddy, and
they walked off the stage giggling.

"Wonderful school!" Catherine said as they walked
down the hall.

"Wonderful principal's office!" Ladean said as they
walked past the offices.

"Wonderful Mr. Solembaugh!" Catherine added, nodding formally at the plaque with the list of school officials written on it.

"Wonderful doors which we will not see for four whole weeks!" Ladean said as they reached the front entrance.

The two girls had walked out into the night, and its quiet beauty rendered them speechless for a moment. After they had commented on the stars, they began walking slowly, savoring the majestic night and the immensity of its solitude.

As they left the schoolyard and began walking toward Catherine's apartment, Ladean turned to Catherine and said in a sweet, strong voice, "Wonderful friends!"

"Well said!" came Catherine's voice, happy and assured.

The girls had said good-bye to the Watkins parents after the performance. They planned to spend the night at Catherine's apartment, and early the next morning, driving the Watkins's car, they were traveling up to Calgary for a visit with the Summerwells.

Ladean was excited about the trip. She had never been to Calgary, except for a brief stop on her way to Edmonton and the university. She had asked Catherine a hundred questions and was puzzled by Catherine's seeming reluctance to talk about her home. "You'll see it all for yourself when we get there, Ladean," she said. "I can't really describe to you what it's like. You'll have to see it for yourself!"

But even Catherine's diffidence about her home did not cool Ladean's enthusiasm. If anything, it fanned her curiosity, and she was eager to be on her way.

As the hour of departure drew closer, Catherine, on the other hand, felt an increasing sense of apprehension. She wondered if the scandal of her abrupt departure was still alive, and if it was, how it might have changed the way her friends and family would react to her visit. She found herself thinking about Norman, and her heart was filled with dread at the thought of encountering him. Try as she might, she could not decide how she would feel. Would she feel the same love? The same desire and need for him? Would she remember the years of friendship and be able to view him as her oldest and dearest companion? No! She was sure she could never think of him simply as her childhood friend again! And yet, could all those years be forgotten? They were as much a part of her as the breakfasts with her father or the mornings at riding lessons or the evenings of play with Emily. Whether she liked it or not, Norman was woven into her memories of home, and whatever happened, a return to Mount Royal would always, on some level of her consciousness, mean a return to Norman.

She thought she had forgotten him and had put him out of her life forever. But, as the trip to Calgary came closer, she knew that she had only been fooling herself. She wondered, too, if her relationship with her parents would be different. Would they be glad to see her or was their life more comfortable now that she was gone?

For the first time in over a year she began worrying about her appearance. Her hair had grown long, and she anxiously tried several styles, trying to find one that did not make her look like a schoolmarm. She bought a fashion magazine and noted that all the stylish women were wearing their hair bobbed or tightly waved against their heads with a few strands loose on the forehead to soften the effect. "Everyone in Mount Royal will be looking stylish!" she thought. "But if I cut my hair, I'll have to fuss with rollers and curlers when I'm teaching in the fall." In spite of the old-fashioned look, she decided to leave her hair long and simply bundle it up with pins.

She wished she could stop worrying about how she looked, but the thought of her mother's face when she entered the house haunted her dreams. If she didn't find a smart-looking outfit somewhere, and get her hair into some kind of order, she could imagine the look of dismay and exasperation that would greet her!

At the woman's dress store in Cardston she found a good-looking linen dress in a golden beige and bought spectator pumps and white gloves and a big-brimmed neutral straw hat to match.

When she surveyed herself in the mirror, she thought the effect was all right, although the dress pulled a little across her full bust, and she thought how much smarter it would look if she were thin as a stick, or small boned and tiny like Ladean.

She was uncomfortable thinking about Mount Royal, worrying about measuring up to all the old standards again. She didn't like it. That's why she didn't want to talk too much about her home with Ladean—it stirred up too many memories, too many traces of thought and feeling which she thought she had removed forever from her life.

As the girls walked home through the summer night, Catherine faced the fact that the trip was at hand, and by tomorrow evening, for good or ill, she would be seated at the table of her childhood home. Inside all her mixed feelings, there was a part of Catherine which wanted very much to go home, yearned to see her parents, to love them, and to know they loved her. Underlying the reluctance and fear, Catherine felt a lifting of eagerness and joy at the thought, "Tomorrow I will be home."

Things went badly from the first minute they arrived. Ladean was overwhelmed when she was greeted by Hilda in her maid's uniform, and her discomfort increased as she entered the impressive foyer of the Summerwell's Mount Royal home. Catherine sensed Ladean's astonished awe, but she was so concerned with her own emotions that she was unable to attend to Ladean's sudden shyness.

Mr. and Mrs. Summerwell were overjoyed to see Catherine, and they extended a warm and gracious welcome to Ladean, but a feeling of awkwardness persisted through dinner and the evening's conversation was forced. The two young women retired early, weary from their long drive. Ladean had been put in Emily's old room, and Catherine was in her own bedroom. The girls didn't have the opportunity to visit alone before going to sleep, and so the discomfort Ladean felt at the homecoming in this awesome household persisted through the night.

Catherine lay in her old bed looking at her room. Her parents had left it untouched. The white walls and bare, shuttered windows were not the familiar fluffy, cluttered decor of her years of childhood, but were instead a bitter reminder of her last troubled summer when she had impulsively redecorated her bedroom.

But as the visit continued, the strain lessened. Catherine and Ladean spent long, fun days with Jean Hunt at the club. The three girls got along famously! They also went to see two movies together and spent one day riding, but Ladean was not a good horsewoman, and the club was so full of painful memories for Catherine, they did not go again.

Old friends called, and there was the usual round of afternoon teas and formal dinners. It was these events which proved a source of continuing awkwardness and discomfort for both the girls. Catherine was painfully aware that although Ladean was considered a "princess" in Cardston, her homemade clothes and natural, straightforward manner made her seem gauche in Mount Royal. With impeccable manners, the people of Mount Royal were sublimely gracious to anyone who was an outsider or who did not seem to fit in, so everyone was extremely courteous to Ladean. Too much so. Ladean was bright, and she knew she was being treated like someone deserving pity and special attention—like a poor relative. Ladean's reaction to this was to become stiff and formal. And Catherine felt helpless because she knew it would only compound the problem if she became oversolicitous, too.

Emily was expecting a baby and she was so caught up in the experience that Catherine's visits with her sister consisted of Catherine listening to a monologue about her sister's house, obstetrician, and James. She felt she could not penetrate Emily's self-absorption and this saddened her.

Another element that surprised and disturbed Catherine was the feeling she had of intruding on the privacy of her parents. Since she and Emily had left home, her parents had developed a new relationship with one another—a private, loving relationship. Though it seemed absurd, Catherine almost felt as though she were intruding on a honeymoon. Sometimes she felt it was with effort that her parents tore themselves away from their private shared world to include her in a conversation or a meal.

They were loving to her and obviously delighted to have her at home, and yet she had the nagging feeling they would be relieved when the house was their own again.

Early in the visit Catherine's mother, Lucy, made it a point to tell Catherine that Norman and Millicent were not in Calgary. They had gone to Europe for a month and would not return until after Catherine's visit. "What a shame!" Lucy said. "You and Norman were such good friends, it would be so nice if you could know Millicent better."

Catherine said nothing, but she felt a rush of relief, followed instantly by a shock of disappointment as she realized she would not be seeing Norman—at least not this summer.

The events of the last evening of their visit in Mount Royal changed the perceptions Catherine and Ladean would take with them when they returned to Cardston.

Mrs. Summerwell had planned a dinner party and summer dance for their going-away. "It will not be a grand affair," she told Catherine, "just the 'old' crowd." Catherine understood, without her mother

telling her, that the "old" crowd referred to those
friends who had stayed close to the family during the
months of scandal over the incident with Dr. Sawyers
and the riding master, Sean Greer. After the scandal
had died down, Catherine's mother had never reestab-
lished her broken friendships with those whom she
felt had failed to prove their loyalty.

The afternoon before the party, Catherine was
hurrying down the hall toward the bathroom to sham-
poo her hair. She was not wearing slippers—a liberty
for which her mother would have soundly corrected
her in the past, but which she had now mellowed
enough to ignore—and so Catherine's feet made no
sound on the soft carpeting. As she passed Emily's
room she heard the squeak of bedsprings. Looking in,
she saw Ladean, lying in bed, the covers pulled up to
her chin.

"What are you doing napping?" Catherine called
through the bedroom door. "Unless you get cracking
you won't be ready for the big event!"

"I'm not coming," Ladean said in a small voice.
"I'm not feeling well."

"What!" Catherine exclaimed, instantly concerned.
"What's wrong? Shall we call the doctor?"

"No! No!" Ladean answered quickly and she
flushed crimson. "I'll be all right in the morning. I
just need a little rest, that's all."

Catherine looked at her carefully, then she sat down
on the edge of the bed. "Okay, Ladean," she said,
"what's really bothering you? You are about as sick as
I am! It's the party, isn't it! Surely you can stand one
more! I know they're an awful bore and . . ."

"No!" declared Ladean. "No! They're not boring!

I love the parties! It's me! I'm all wrong. If I have to go to one more party and look at all those girls in their beautiful clothes while I'm wearing a white blouse and a dirndl skirt, I think I'll die!"

Catherine threw back her head and began to laugh. "Oh, Ladean!" she gasped between laughter. "If you only knew how well I understand!"

Ladean sat up indignantly. "You don't understand!" she insisted. "How could you understand? You have clothes that are nicer and more expensive than any of them! You don't know what it feels like to be so . . . dowdy!"

Catherine stopped laughing and looked at Ladean soberly. "It isn't just the clothes, you silly! It's also how a person looks in them! The best clothes in the world can't make a person look right if you're not. Oh, you wouldn't understand!" she cut off abruptly. "Besides, you don't need to. Look at you! If you had even one-third their money to spend on clothes, you could knock their eyes out! Say! That gives me an idea!"

Jumping up from the bed, Catherine ran over to Emily's closet and threw open the double doors. The closet was still hung with dozens of dresses, suits, and coats, which Emily had not considered suitable for a married woman.

"Here!" Catherine said, throwing out several evening dresses. "Let's try these on. You're about the same size as Emily. Some of these dresses were never worn. Emily bought them for a trip to London, and then she got engaged and never went."

"Oh, Catherine!" Ladean exclaimed, her eyes shining. "Are you sure this will be all right?"

"Of course!" Catherine told her. "Mother is going to feel terrible that she didn't think of it herself."

The girls spent the rest of the afternoon choosing the clothes Ladean would wear, and planning their hair and makeup.

When the front doorbell announced the arrival of the first guests, Catherine gave Ladean one last appraising glance. Ladean was wearing a pale green chiffon dress which hung smoothly over a dainty satin slip. Her hair was brushed into a shining pageboy, with a jade and gold clip highlighting its dark mass, and her soft bangs touching the smooth arch of her eyebrows. Her black eyes and milk-white skin were enhanced with a touch of mascara and dark pink rouge. At her ears and neck she wore matched pearls.

"I feel like Cinderella!" Ladean whispered nervously at the top of the stairs.

"Just don't forget you've already found your Prince Charming!" Catherine reminded her. "Now go down there and wow them!"

The two walked down the stairs together. Catherine felt a thrill of pride as she saw her friends' faces register astonishment at Ladean's transformation. Particularly the young men in the crowd. In a matter of minutes Ladean was surrounded by an enthusiastic group of admirers. For the first time in their visit, Catherine saw Ladean acting like herself—naturally and at ease. Her Mount Royal friends were obviously charmed and treated Ladean as one of their own. Seeing Ladean having such a marvelous time, Catherine felt the evening a great success, and she felt a warm gratitude to her mother for having arranged the party.

Catherine herself was wearing a flattering silk jersey dress with slender straps, and a skirt that fitted over her hips and then swirled out in fluid fullness. The dress was topped with a lovely long-sleeved white jacket. She wore her hair rolled, with a deep wave on one side. Knowing that Ladean was having a wonderful time made Catherine more relaxed, and her conversations with old friends brought forth happy memories. It was a radiant evening, and she was shining with happiness. After dinner there was dancing on the terrace. Catherine smiled as she saw the boys line up around Ladean. Ladean's eyes were sparkling and she was reigning with her usual gaiety and élan.

Catherine was standing on the sidelines talking to Mrs. Townsend when her father came up to ask her to dance. "Catherine, my dear?" he said formally, extending his hand. They danced with a smooth grace that was pleasing to behold. "You are still the best dancer in Mount Royal," her father said, smiling at her affectionately. "You, too," she replied, smiling back at him.

Impulsively, she added, "It's been wonderful being home, Father."

He looked at her wisely, and his smile faded a little. "Yes," he said, "but I think perhaps you feel it is more wonderful now that you are close to leaving again."

"Oh, no!" she began to protest.

"Catherine, dear"—he shook his head knowingly at her—"this is your father speaking. I probably know you better than anyone in the world. I know this hasn't been an easy time for you. You've been feeling rather lost, I think."

Catherine found it hard to meet his eyes. "Maybe . . ." she conceded reluctantly.

"No 'maybe' about it," her father replied firmly. "You've been acting as gingerly as a cat. Catherine, this is your home! Don't you understand? It doesn't matter where you go, or what you do with your life . . . this will always be your home!"

Catherine was embarrassed by her father's acute perception of her feelings, and she wished he would change the subject. Instead, he stopped dancing and looked at her. "Catherine, let's go into my study and visit for a few moments. There are some things I think should be said before you leave tomorrow morning."

Catherine followed her father into the study. They sat across from one another on the leather chairs that flanked a low table. When they were settled there was an awkward pause, and then her father began to speak.

"You've changed, Catherine, and as far as I can tell, it's all for the good. You seem more sure of yourself, quieter, and more controlled. But the price of growing up isn't throwing away the past, it's learning to live with it. You've succeeded in convincing me that you need to create a life of your own, but that still doesn't mean you have to destroy the part of your life which will always exist here—in this home—with us."

Catherine was moved by what her father was saying, and she knew it was true.

"I know. But I'm not sure I'm strong enough yet," she whispered. "I'm finding it hard to live in one world—let alone two!"

"We're so proud of you!" he said. "We're proud of your work—that young Ranowski boy—what an achievement! We're proud of your new contract in the high school! We like your friend, Ladean."

"So does everyone else!" Catherine said, laughing. "Did you see the line waiting to dance with her?"

"Yes, Catherine, I did," said her father quietly. "There'd be a line for you, too, Catherine, if you'd let it form."

Catherine's face went scarlet, and as always, when people started talking about personal things, she wished the conversation would end.

"Don't you know how beautiful you are, Catherine?" her father asked, exasperated. "There are some burdens from the past which you go on carrying around with you like Marley's ghost. And you don't need to, Catherine! They are false perceptions—childish perceptions—which it is time for you to outgrow! One of them is this foolish idea that you are not pretty!"

"Oh, Father!" Catherine cried, distressed, but halflaughing. "How can you know! The fact that you think I'm pretty is one of the false perceptions you carry around!"

"I don't think you're pretty! You aren't pretty—you're beautiful!"

Her father looked at her angrily, his jaw hardening. "You really don't know! You have no idea! You see 'pretty' as one thing and one thing only—but if you could only see yourself! There are times when you are so filled with radiance and magic . . . there is something about you that is so extraordinary. You can be almost too beautiful. You are tonight, for example. You beauty is so intense, so brilliant. It takes a strong man not to be frightened by it, Catherine. Someday there will be such a man, and he will have the courage to reach for you, like a man reaches for

the magnificent jewel in the eye of an idol. He will
have the courage to break through all the absurd pro-
tections and barriers you have built around yourself.
He will need to see beyond those, to the tender needs
inside of you. He's out there somewhere, Catherine,
and when he reaches for you, he will need to have the
courage to win."

"Father!" Catherine's cheeks were flaming and her
hands trembled with self-conscious anxiety. "Please!
Don't! You are making me very uncomfortable. I don't
like to talk about myself!"

"I know," her father said with a sigh. He waited for
a moment and then continued. "Very well, I will now
talk about the other thing which I wanted to say to
you. It's about your mother. I love your mother very
much, Catherine. That doesn't mean I don't see her
clearly, and I know sometimes her values tend to be a
little . . . shallow. She puts great stock in appearances, and I think you have resented that. But the
truth is, Catherine, you underestimate her. I think the
time has come in your life when you should try to understand her—learn to love her a little better. I think
it would help you in understanding yourself. You see,
the funny thing is, you and I have always thought we
were alike, and your mother and Emily were alike.
But I have noticed in these past weeks that in some
ways you are very like your mother. Sometimes you
even look like her!"

"Now, Father!" Catherine smiled ironically. "Don't
go too far!"

"You do!" said her father. "There is a serenity and
strength that shows itself in both of you by a certain
tilt of the head, a line of the cheek. Your gestures

. . . your eyes . . . nonetheless, I think I should tell you that after you left, your mother went through a very difficult time here. There were a lot of unpleasant rumors, snubs, and awkward social moments. She never uttered a word of complaint or self-pity. Her one concern was you—and her loyalty and dignity would have made you proud! If you could have seen her weathering that storm, you might have understood how much she loves you!

"There's no way to recreate the past, Catherine, but there is no law which says you are doomed to keep reliving it in your future. The time has come to put away the old hurts and resentments. I have a hunch that you and your mother are both survivors. Whatever life has to offer you, you will both surmount and triumph over it. That's not a bad legacy for her to have given you! Will you try a little harder?"

There were tears in Catherine's eyes. She knew that everything her father was saying was true, but she also knew she would need to sort out and discard years of feelings and half-absorbed experiences before she could overcome her childhood perceptions of her mother. "I'll try, Father. I really will," she promised. "I do love her, you know. I love both of you!"

"I know," her father said. "I think the day may come when you will be able to love yourself fully, too, Catherine."

He stood up and Catherine faced him. "You go back to the party," she said. "I think I'll need to powder my nose first." He smiled and kissed her cheek. "See you in a minute," he said.

She watched him go. It felt as though a weight had

rolled from her, and she tried to discover what it was within her which had been resolved.

"Mother won him!" she thought, "but I won, too! Because it was never really a contest!" She thought how funny it was. Somewhere in her mind she supposed she had always been competing with her mother, hoping that by winning her father's attention she would somehow prove she was better. "And that wasn't what I wanted at all! I wanted a father—and that's what I've got! And now," she thought with a strange feeling of relief, "maybe I can have a mother, too." It felt to her like something had settled into its proper place.

The next day Ladean and Catherine left Mount Royal. They drove through the streets of Calgary. Catherine announced with amazement, "I missed the Stampede this year for the first time in my life! And I didn't even think about it!" The city fell away behind them, and the open road stretched into the distance. "It's splendid to go home and know it is still there!" she said to Ladean. "But it also feels marvelous to be free!"

The girls returned to Cardston and devoted themselves to their classroom preparations. Ladean reminisced about the visit in Calgary frequently, and with constant retelling her memory of the vacation became more and more rosy, until she remembered only the glamor, the happy times, and the excitement. The trip had helped curb Ladean's restlessness, and she settled down contentedly to wait until spring when her fiancé would return from his mission.

For Catherine the year began differently. The more

settled and happy Ladean became, the more restless and discontented Catherine felt. As the year progressed, the girls could feel their lives diverging slowly, like two rivers which have run together and now must divide to pursue their own courses.

CHAPTER SIXTEEN

It would be hard to say exactly when the change began. Perhaps it had been as early as Ladean's chance remark about her being a non-Mormon. Perhaps it had begun when Catherine returned from visiting her family in Calgary and was more conscious than before of the differences between Cardston and her childhood home. It may have been the simple fact that as Catherine was maturing and changing, she became aware of a desire to find something permanent and meaningful in her life. Whatever the causes, the school year progressed, and Catherine could feel a sense of distance developing between herself and the people around her—Ladean, her fellow teachers—and Cardston.

She started to notice small things that had escaped her attention before. She noticed the tendency of the high school faculty to divide themselves into Mormons and non-Mormons at lunchtime. She supposed it was a natural thing, since the Mormon group did not drink tea or coffee, and they often had some church matter to discuss. But once Catherine became aware of it she began to feel awkward about eating lunch with Ladean, and gradually she joined the other group.

Since Cardston was more than 90 percent Mormon, having been settled by a group of Mormon homesteaders a generation earlier, the social life of the community revolved around the church. The roots of these people extended deep into a past of persecution and faith, and most of their parents and grandparents had braved the hardship of the western migration to Utah, and the subsequent migration to the virgin prairie of Southern Alberta at the turn of the century. These people were the children of pioneers, and their shared heritage and faith wove them into a vigorous, hardworking, fun-loving, religious community. It was this strong tradition that made Catherine admire the Mormons, but which also made her feel apart from the closeness of their society. In stores, restaurants, banks, and at the school she sometimes felt she must have "non-Mormon" emblazoned on her forehead, for there was a subtle and unwitting difference in the way people spoke to her and related to her. She would enter a store and a clerk and customer would be chatting familiarly about a mutual friend or an experience at the church. When the clerk turned to Catherine, the smile on her face would remain, but it would become impersonal and professional. Catherine came to feel awkward and strange in a community which she had hoped to adopt as her home. She did not realize that the Mormons were puzzled about how to treat her, and anxious not to impose their beliefs or way of life on her. So her dissatisfaction grew, and Catherine felt more isolated as the months passed.

She remained close to Ladean and the Watkins family, but even there she was becoming acutely aware of the parts of their lives to which she had no access. It wasn't that the Watkinses did not want to include her; it was just that their lives were so rich and satisfying they were unaware that the web of comfort and familiarity which they wove about one another might serve to make a close friend feel excluded.

The gulf was exemplified for Catherine when she dropped in on the Watkins house one day in early April. Mrs. Watkins was visiting with another church member, a friend from her ward in Cardston, when Catherine arrived.

"We won't be a moment, Catherine, dear," Mrs. Watkins said. "Do sit down and talk with us."

The other woman was describing a recent visit to Great Salt Lake. "It was a wonderful conference! President Grant spoke so beautifully and I think everyone and their half-cousin was there! Land sakes! After the meeting, would you believe we saw Helen and Dave right in front of the sea gull monument? Can you imagine! All those thousands of people and there they were, just as big as life!"

Mrs. Watkins was knitting. "It sounds like a fine time. The Bishop wanted to go down, but there's been trouble at the Reservation, and he's the only one who knows the Indian dialects so he had to stay and do some mediating."

"Vi and Clawson send their love," the woman continued. "They've got a nice little house over on Fifth East. They can see Tabernacle Square just down the way. I asked if they missed Canada, and they said, 'Sometimes, but it surely feels good to be in Zion.' "

"Humph!" snorted Mrs. Watkins, putting down her knitting with a thump. "That shows how much they know. Zion's just as much here as it is there!"

"That's what I told them. I said, you don't have to live in Utah to be part of the Kingdom."

Catherine sat listening to the conversation with the

uncomfortable sense of having been dropped into a foreign land. With sorrow she wondered how she could feel suddenly superfluous in a home where she had at one time almost been part of the family. It puzzled her. She knew the Watkinses had not changed—she had become sensitized to a situation that had always been there, but which she had screened out of her consciousness because she wanted so desperately to belong.

Leaving the Watkins home that day, Catherine returned to her apartment. She felt as isolated as she had in her teacherage at Spring Valley.

A few days later when Mr. Solembaugh called her into his office in early April and offered to renew her contract for the following year, he was surprised to see her face register no reaction.

"I thought you'd be delighted, Catherine!" he remarked, disappointed by her quiet demeanor. "After all, this past year was considered a probationary year, and I don't mind telling you, you have passed with flying colors! The contract is yours, I'm sure, for as long as you want it!"

Catherine took the papers quietly. "I think perhaps I'll take the forms home with me, Mr. Solembaugh, and sign them there. Will it be all right if I make my decision and return the contract by the end of the week?"

"Of course," Mr. Solembaugh replied, astonished at her cool response. "There's no hurry. That will be fine." He paused, then asked, "Is there anything wrong? Any way I could help?"

"No," Catherine said, slowly. "I'm not sure, exactly, what I want to do next year. I need a little time to think."

Catherine was surprised herself at the lack of enthusiasm she felt when Mr. Solembaugh handed her the contracts, and she walked home slowly, knowing she was facing a difficult decision.

The school year was almost over. It was April, and soon the buds and flower blossoms would burst forth from the grip of winter. The prairies would be humming with activity, and the children would run from the corridors of the schools into the sunny fields.

"A teacher's season is as brief and ephemeral as a grasshopper's," she mused. "Or . . ." she continued, quoting to herself, " 'like the snowflake on the river—a moment there—then gone for 'iver'." She remembered how she and Norman had derided that terrible rhyme, but at this moment she felt the sentiment had a touch of immortality—even if the poetry was awful.

Unexpectedly, thinking of Norman made her feel even more depressed. She reflected how long it had been since someone had known her as thoroughly as Norman did—someone to whom she could talk in a sort of verbal shorthand because of shared experiences and common background. Had she made a mistake by leaving all she had known and attempting to start life anew?

She entered her small apartment and shivered in the chill of the early spring evening. The room was gloomy, but she did not turn on the lights. Instead, with a sigh, she sat down in one of the wooden chairs facing the back window and looked out at the darkening sky. The back garden looked barren and unkempt. The snows of winter had melted and the dead foliage of last summer lay brown and wet, flattened against the mud by the spring thaw. It was a dreary scene and it matched Catherine's mood.

Change was all around her. Within two weeks Ladean would be married and because she was being married in the Mormon temple, Catherine could not attend the wedding. However, she was invited to the reception in the church recreation hall on the evening of the wedding day. Somehow Catherine felt the marriage symbolized the ending of her close ties with Ladean. Apart from Ladean and the Watkins family she had not made close friends in Cardston, and she reflected with grim satisfaction that nobody would miss her if she decided not to return next year. "If this is building a life"—she chided herself—"it is a pretty tenuous sort of business!"

She looked at the contract papers lying on the table and remembered a year earlier that she had been convinced all it would take to make her happy would be a major teaching contract, won on her own merits, with the respect of her fellow professionals. Now she had reached that goal, and she felt no glow of satisfaction—only a cold, empty feeling that seemed to affirm the hollowness of the victory she had won. Would she go on year after year, she asked herself, teaching children until they all seemed to look alike and lecturing on the same classics until she knew them by rote and living on the fringes of this close-knit society in which she would eventually become the eccentric "Miss Summerwell"? Everyone in town would come to know who she was—the odd, old maid teacher, a familiar fixture, but always an outsider.

It seemed a forlorn prospect indeed. "If I went back to Calgary now," she thought, "I wouldn't go back as a failure. There would be old friends, a familiar way of life"—she closed her eyes and smiled ruefully—"and there I could be little Sarah's old maid aunt and listen to Emily tell me about the social life of the young matrons and how hard it is to be a mother! I'd watch Mother and Father try to pretend they don't feel sorry for me, and I would get prim and odd and very, very proper."

"Oh!" Catherine groaned out loud. "What shall I do? Where shall I go?" She put her arms on the table and buried her face in them. Her shoulders shook with stifled sobs as the loneliness and pain of the past years swept over her. The room grew dark behind her, and the cold wind of the prairies found the cracks under the door and around the windows. She stopped crying, but she did not move from her position. The room grew chill and night filled the corners.

The next morning, stiff and weary, Catherine dressed for school. As she brushed her hair, she looked into the mirror on her bureau. "All right, you!" she said, looking her puffy-eyed reflection straight in the eye. "That's enough self-pity for the decade! If you're going to be silly . . . I think it's back to Calgary with you! It won't be so bad—certainly the lesser of two evils!"

She walked slowly to school, mulling over the decision to return to Calgary. By the time she faced her first-period class, she felt certain she was taking the right step. She decided to write her father on the weekend and ask him to see if he could secure a position for her to teach in one of the Calgary schools. She decided she would return the contract to Mr. Solembaugh, unsigned, and tell him she had changed her plans. But she wondered why she didn't feel better once the decision was made. There was no lightening of her mood, and she found herself walking home with a deep feeling of hopelessness and defeat. Trying to lift her spirits, she reassured herself, "I'll feel better as soon as I'm back with old friends—in a more familiar place."

As Catherine rounded the corner of the street leading to her house, she slowed her walk in surprise. In front of her small clapboard cottage was a parked car. It was a car she had not seen before, and she knew it was not from Cardston—a foreign sports car in silver and black, sleek, low-slung with shining spoked wheels and rich leather upholstery. Even though the day was cool, the top of the car was down and the dashboard gleamed in the light of the afternoon sun. Dreading to have her worst fear confirmed, and yet compelled by long-buried longing, Catherine hurried toward the house.

She came to her door and could see the lights on inside and smell the woodsmoke. Whoever was waiting for her had made a fire to warm up the room and had been waiting for some time. Hesitantly, as though she thought the knob were hot, she reached for the door, and with a bold thrust she opened it and stepped over the threshold.

Her guest was sitting with his back to the door, leafing through a magazine, and he did not turn around when she entered. He simply stopped riffling the pages and sat as still as stone. "Hello, Catherine," he said, his voice deep and assured. So like him! she thought furiously, to sit there confidently, waiting for her to come from behind to face him. Emotions overwhelmed her—joy, anger, fear, curiosity. Her heart thumped wildly, and she thought she could not take a step without falling. A part of her, as stubborn and independent as he, made her want to stay where she was, to force him to turn to look at her. For a brief moment, therefore, there was silence in the room, and the two of them were absolutely still, frozen in their positions. He won, though, as he always did, because she could not bear the tension any longer, and quickly she walked around him to the other chair and turned to face him.

"Norman," she whispered, and sat down quickly, as though her legs could no longer hold her.

"Norman," she said again, her voice strained with unspoken feelings. Her eyes traced his face hungrily, searching for his reassurance, his strength, his very thoughts. He had not changed at all, she thought, except perhaps, he was handsomer than she remembered. He was looking at her, too, with an affectionately ironic smile in his eyes. Unhurried and controlled, he crossed his legs. Leaning back slightly in his chair, with one hand in his jacket pocket, he contemplated her as though she were a familiar painting or a cherished possession that he was evaluating after a long absence. His appraising eyes measured her and she remained transfixed and silent.

"Well, Catherine," he said finally, "in all the years I've known you I believe this is the first time I've seen you speechless! I think I miss the old enthusiasm."

The soft taunting tone roused her, and she looked at him sharply. "Maybe I've grown a little more discriminating—my enthusiasms are harder to come by these days, Norman." Her voice was more cutting than she had expected, and she flushed.

"Oh-ho!" Norman said and laughed. "So the mouse has developed sharp teeth!"

"What brings you to Cardston?" Catherine asked in a carefully neutral tone, refusing to let him bait her anymore. "Is Millicent with you?"

"I drove down on a sudden impulse this morning," Norman replied. "Since you used to be the expert on impulsiveness, perhaps you can understand my behavior. I'm not sure I do myself."

She laughed, and the tension was relieved. "Nobody understands impulse. If it were rational, it wouldn't be impulsive."

"That was certainly a philosophical observation," he said, still smiling and watching her—waiting for something, some relaxation of her guarded manner, some look in her eye or tone of voice. But she was determined not to betray herself by giving him a glimpse of what she was feeling.

Guardedly, she observed him, and wondered with perverse pain how he could be sitting in this room, which she regarded as home. This was a place of refuge and comfort to her—but now, seeing him elegant, suave, and impeccably groomed, sitting at her table, the room suddenly looked cheap and shabby. The tilt of his head, the set of his shoulders in his camel hair jacket, his dazzling white shirt and dark tie—even the knife-sharp crease in his trousers—everything about him bespoke all the sophistication of her heritage, which she had failed to achieve.

"Norman," she said, in exasperation, "you drove all the way from Calgary, and you don't even have a wrinkle in your trousers! Nothing seems to touch you!

Not heat, not wind, not dust, not weariness—not even time!" She shook her head and then sighed deeply, and all the fight went out of her.

She glanced at her own dusty shoes and reached up a tired hand to smooth a strand of hair that was brushing against her forehead. In his careful gaze she was suddenly conscious of her appearance. "I must look a mess," she murmured in an abject tone.

That seemed to be the signal he had been waiting for. He leaped up from his chair and came over to her. Seeing her before him, her defiance broken, he felt his old dominance established.

"Catherine!" he whispered, his voice compelling and passionate. "I must talk to you! I've come all this way to see you. We must talk. Please!"

He reached down and took her hands and raised her, unresistingly, to stand before him. "There's so much I want to say. I need . . ."

He was looking deeply into her eyes as he spoke, and he said, as though to himself, almost whispering, "You haven't changed. I know you haven't. Your eyes . . . those eyes . . . so trusting, so true."

She stood silently before him not wanting to think and only wanting to absorb the idea that he was with her; after the years of desiring and needing him, he was here, with her—and she didn't want to think beyond this moment in time.

Restlessly, he let go of her hands and began to pace in the small room. "Catherine, let's go somewhere where we can talk. I can't think in this dreary little room. Please, go get your coat—fix yourself up. We'll go somewhere. I've been waiting all afternoon, and if I don't get out of here, I'm going to go mad with claustrophobia!"

Catherine's head snapped up and her eyes blazed. "This dreary little room happens to be my home, Norman. If you want to talk to me, I can't think of a better place in which to do it!"

"No, no!" he had the grace to be embarrassed by his blunder and rushed to apologize. "I didn't mean that the way it sounded. It's just that I don't think well indoors. Please come with me."

She felt the familiar power of his charm, and as if by instinct, she responded to him as she had years ago.

"All right," she said, defeated, "I'll go freshen up," and she walked slowly into her bedroom. She could hear him walking restlessly in the other room. He opened the stove and stirred the fire with a poker, then added another log. Then he was silent.

In the privacy of her bedroom, Catherine slowly undid her dress and pulled the pins out of her hair. Listlessly she sat on the side of her bed and brushed the waving cascade of golden-brown hair. Without bothering to reknot it, she bent to slip off the worn oxfords in which she had walked home, then she sat holding one of the shoes in her lap, staring at it as though she could find some revelation in the dark, practical leather. She knew she should be hurrying—Norman hated to be kept waiting. In her mind was the faded memory of his boyhood voice impatiently calling through the hedge, "Hurry up! Hurry up!" She had always hurried for him, but she sat now in the dim room, in her simple white slip, her hair wild about her shoulders, her feet bare, and she could not force her-

self to move to get ready. In all of her confusion, somewhere deep within her she knew that if she got up
now, dressed herself in her best clothes, walked out
where Norman was waiting, and entered his car, she
would be making a decision from which she could not
turn back. And she feared the consequence of that decision as though it were a deep and yawning pit that
would suck her into darkness and ruin. Her thoughts
were not distinct or clear, only filled with the sense of
impending disaster and the overwhelming desire to
run recklessly toward it. Fear, caution, and weariness
held her silent on the bed, unable to move.

"Catherine!" he called through the closed door.
"What's taking you so long! We're not going to a
dance . . ." His voice was impatient and autocratic.
"Do you want me to choose what you should wear?"
He walked toward the door of her bedroom. She could
hear his feet on the wood floor.

"No," she called hastily. "No! I think I'm too tired
to go anywhere, Norman. Perhaps we should . . ."
She didn't get to finish the sentence. He opened the
door of her bedroom and stood outlined in the light
from the other room. Instinctively, she crossed her
hands over her breasts in the meager slip and gasped
in surprise at his intrusion. Silently, he stood in the
door, one hand on the knob, the other stretched out
resting on the door frame. His body blocked the light,
and though she could not see his face, she knew that
the light from the living room spotlighted her as she
sat on the bed.

"By the stars!" he murmured in a hoarse voice.
"You are beautiful, Catherine."

She shuddered at the sound of his voice and felt warmth surge through her, but fear shook her also, and she shrank from the confrontation of their feelings.

"I'm not beautiful!" she retorted, her voice shaky but strong. "I'm undressed! There's a difference!"

With slow deliberation he closed the door behind him. "Norman!" she exclaimed, her voice rising in alarm, as the light disappeared, and they were together in the dim room. "What are you doing? What if someone found us here? I could never teach again! Please, Norman, go out of the room and I'll get dressed. I'll go for a ride with you, anywhere you want—only go!" Her voice was filled with desperation. "Please, Norman!" She watched him walk toward her, and he sat down carefully on the side of the bed several feet from her. The bedsprings creaked, and he turned and faced her in the gloom. He made no move to touch her or to speak.

"Please, Norman," she whispered, almost in tears. "Please."

He still made no move, but sat looking at her in the shadowy room. "It's all right, Catherine," his voice was soft and gentle. "Don't be frightened or worried. I'm with you, you don't have to worry ever again. I won't hurt you—I won't do anything that would hurt you. I only want to talk, and this is best. We'll talk quietly, here in this room. I won't touch you, I promise. Only don't make me leave, Catherine. I only want to look at you here, like this."

Her breath was coming in little gasps like sobs, and she was trembling.

"Sh-h-h-h, little Catherine," his voice soothed her,

"sh-h-h, it's all right. How can it matter? We are like one person anyway. We always have been. Surely you've known that someday we would have to be together. There is a great unfinished piece in each of us that has to have the other. We had to see each other. This meeting was as inevitable as the turning of the earth. You must have known that. I know you have known it, just as I have—because I know you, Catherine. I know how you feel and think—and what you need. I know you better than anyone. How can this be wrong? Our being together? It's the only right thing that has happened to either of us in a long, long time."

She was crying now, softly, her hair hanging so that it screened her face from his view. With an impatient hand she wiped the tears from her face. Norman smiled in the darkness and reached into his breast pocket and pulled out a handkerchief.

"Here," he said, "you never could remember to bring your handkerchief."

Without looking up she reached for the handkerchief and blew her nose, but she still didn't look at him. "What do you want, Norman? What is the purpose of your coming here?" As she spoke her confidence rose, and her voice took on a spark of challenge. "I don't see that it was right or inevitable that we should be together again at all. It seems the last time we were together any . . . relationship . . . which we had was terminated! If it wasn't terminated then, it surely was when you married Millicent!" As she spoke Millicent's name Catherine flung her head up, in defiance. She faced Norman with blazing eyes. "That seemed pretty definitive to me!"

"Catherine," he said, his voice as careful as though he were reasoning with a child. "I made a mistake, a terrible mistake. I was young, and I suppose I was blinded by Millicent's style—and her money—but there was never anything there . . . no feeling . . . nothing like what we had."

Catherine's voice was hard. "And just what was it we had, Norman?" she asked bitterly. "Love? Friendship? What would you call it? What emotion was it that made you show me all the wonderful things I couldn't have? What sweet relationship was it that made you open up my heart and then turn away? My best friend? What best friend gives pain? My lover? What lover would show the world of delight to someone and then close the door forever? It seems to me that what we had wasn't worth very much to either one of us, Norman."

Her voice was ragged with hurt and stored anger, and Norman listened without answering. When she had finished, he said nothing. Reaching over to her, he took the shoe from her unresisting hand and placed it neatly on the floor beside her other shoe. Slowly, he moved until he was sitting beside her, taking her limp, cold hand in his.

She did not try to withdraw it because she was too distraught to be aware of what was happening. Softly, disarmingly, he began to talk.

"That's all passed, Catherine, my darling. Passed, and it should be forgiven and forgotten. We can't go on for our whole lives being punished for the mistake of one foolish summer. My marriage is a sham, a mockery. Millicent and I are like two polite strangers.

We don't even share the same room, let alone the same bed."

"Don't!" Catherine exclaimed. "I don't want to hear these things. Don't tell me this, Norman."

Gently, he began to stroke her bare arm, his hands as light as a feather. She shivered, but still she could not pull herself away. It was as though he had hypnotized her, and she felt her powers of self-determination melting away. He was exerting the old fascination and power which he had always had over her.

"You have to know, Catherine, so that you will understand how much I need you. You will never know how many nights I have lain awake thinking of you—how you looked the night of Emily's wedding—your hair, your skin, the touch of your lips. It was like a cruel torture, and I would wake from my dreams to find you fading from me. I thought I would go mad!

"I've tried to forget you. That's why Millicent and I went on our trip to Europe last summer. I thought maybe if I left Mount Royal where everything reminded me of you, maybe Millie and I would have a chance. But it didn't make any difference. There was nothing—just cool, frigid politeness and my dreams of you. I've fought it for two years, and today I couldn't fight it anymore. I got in the car and drove to you. Every mile of the way, as I came closer to you, I knew it was right. This is where I belong! I was never more sure than when I walked into this bedroom tonight and saw you."

His hand was on her shoulder, and he tenderly gathered her flowing hair and cupped the back of her head in his hand. Slowly, patiently, he drew her toward him. His head dropped as his lips touched hers as softly as a whisper, then again more urgently, and then he pressed his warm, strong lips against hers with masterful desire. Catherine did not respond, but she did not pull away either. Her mind was in turmoil and her emotions were whirling so violently that she felt almost blank with confusion. He kissed her again, and the delicious power of his kiss penetrated her distress, and she felt herself falling into a dark void.

"No!" she whispered, pushing against him weakly, and turning her face from his kiss. "No! Norman, please! This isn't right!"

"You're cold, my darling," he said, and pulled her against him, his strong warm hands stroking her arms and shoulders. His face was pressed in her fragrant hair, and he murmured, "Don't try to think it through, Catherine! A love like ours defies the rules of logic and society. It spans the breaches of time and convention. This is meant to be, Catherine. You and me together. Your body was made for this—for love and for passion—for the night and the delights of the one man who can love you as I can."

"But your marriage—" she protested.

"Hang my marriage!" Norman said. "It has nothing to do with you and me. I'd divorce Millie in a minute if her father's lawyers wouldn't make me pay through the nose! There is no way she'll ever let me go—but that doesn't need to matter to you and me. You don't want to live in Mount Royal anyway. You've made that perfectly clear. There's no reason why you need to live this far away, though. We could find you a place in High River or Nanton. You'd be close enough

to visit—I could come and see you. We'd be close
enough to go off together. Millie doesn't care where I
go, or how long I'm gone. She never asks questions.
You can lead a private life—no one would need to
know what you did on your own time. Don't you see,
Catherine? It's a perfect arrangement! We can be together as much as we like! I'd take care of you for the
rest of your life. I love you so much, Catherine. I know
I could make you happy! I know it! Let me show
you!"

He turned her face toward him and kissed her
again, and lightly his hand traced the outline of her
body. "Beautiful!" he murmured. "Beautiful!" He
bent his head and kissed the base of her neck then he
kissed her shoulders.

Catherine's heart was pounding in her breast, and
her breathing was shallow and rapid. "Norman!" she
said with a moan. "Let me think. Let me understand
what you're saying."

He kissed her again. "This is what I'm saying," he
murmured, and slowly he began to lower her body
onto the bed. Suddenly Catherine was stiff. A great
surge of alarm ran through her body and propelled
her upward. In a single powerful move, she was standing beside the bed. Her motion was so sudden that
Norman remained sitting, off-balance and discomfit-
ted. "What's the matter, Catherine?" he asked, his
voice ragged with astonished irritation.

"You are the matter, Norman!" she replied, her
voice shaking with fury. "Did you honestly think you
could come to me after two years with nothing
changed? Did you think I had been sitting here, wait-

ing for you to enter the door—ready and willing to do whatever you wanted? I don't believe you love me or know me at all. I used to think so. I used to think you were my dearest friend, and I loved you with all my heart. I loved you so much I would have died for you. There was a time when I would have given you everything I have to give and never looked back, but you wouldn't take my gift. You were too afraid, too protective of your bright future—not mine—yours! Well, you only get that chance once, Norman. Never again!

"What was it you had in mind? That I would come and be your mistress? You say you love me, and you come promising me a lifetime of living in shadows and corners! No risk at all to you and your neat Mount Royal marriage. One day when you see someone younger and prettier and less difficult, it would be easy to say good-bye to understanding old Catherine. You honestly believe that, don't you? All the time I thought you cared about me—protected me—and all the time it was really only yourself you cared about! You only wanted me because I wanted you so much it made you feel important!

"Oh, Norman! I think I'm seeing you for the first time—and I can't stand what I'm seeing! You are a hollow man! All those lovely manners, those perfect clothes, your wonderful body—and there's nothing inside. All form—no substance. You have all the decorations—but they forgot to put in a heart."

Catherine was staring at Norman as he continued to sit on the bed. He watched her as she spoke, her words tumbling over each other and her voice vibrant with emotional timbre. Her color was high and she had forgotten she was only wearing a slip. As she threw her accusations at him her breast rose and fell in distraught gasps. Norman's face was composed, and as Catherine came to the end of her speech, he smiled at her with his old ironic look. "I thought you had changed—cooled down a little. I see I was wrong," he said and chuckled.

"What kind of a man are you?" she asked in a fierce whisper. "You come in here and try to seduce me—to destroy whatever life I may have built as though it were nothing—and then turn it into a joke when I refuse! Do you really think so little of me?"

"No, Catherine," Norman said, standing up with a sigh. "I do not think so little of you. I think too much of you. I told you, I think of you all the time. You are like a thorn in my mind, and I want desperately to be rid of it."

"I don't think you remember me because of what we were to each other," Catherine said. "I think I trouble you because you didn't have me. I'm your one lost conquest and that rubs against you. I'm your unfinished business."

"Perhaps that's true," Norman said. "I live my life as I want. Since I was very young I have had a plan—a pattern—and I have molded and fitted my life until it conforms to that pattern perfectly. You were the one thing that never fit, and yet I couldn't give you up—not when we were little, and not now. You wouldn't fit into any category—you wouldn't discipline yourself to any style. Always you were yourself—impulsive, inconsistent, exciting, awkward, hurt, shy. I couldn't stand to be with you, but I couldn't stand to be away from you either. Maybe it was because only with you I really felt alive. And now you're gone, and I feel like

I'm turning into a piece of my own furniture. Everything is so right and smooth, but the one part of me that still hurts is the part that misses you. I thought—I hoped—perhaps if you could come and be part of my life once more I could turn back. I think I could change, Catherine," his voice was deep with conviction, "if you'd come with me . . . maybe . . ."

Catherine walked over to him and put her hand gently on his lips. "Don't say anymore, Norman, or I will cry. You lost your way a long time ago. You've stepped through the mirror and there's no turning back. Not for either of us. We've made our choices. You stayed in Mount Royal and fit the mold, and I left and became the permanent outsider. Our tragedy is that we both knew too much and understood too little. But there's no changing it now, don't you see? We're not children anymore, we can't write our own rules, and besides we are both doing what we chose to do. That won't change."

"Oh, Catherine!" he groaned. He reached for her and kissed her one more time. Her lips were hot and dry, and there was the salty taste of tears. "Paradise was so close!"

"Paradise or purgatory," Catherine whispered back. "We'll never know which!"

His hand traced the line of her arm, and he smiled into her face. "You haven't changed," he said, "and I do love you—as much as I can love."

"I know, Norman," she answered, with a pain-filled smile. "It just isn't enough. Not for either one of us."

Without another word he went to the door of the bedroom and opened it. Walking into the lighted living room, he picked up his hat and coat and headed for the outside door. Catherine grabbed a wrapper from the back of the bedroom door and hurried after him into the other room.

"You're going?" she asked.

"I think so," he answered. "We've said all there is to say. Maybe too much. I don't think we will meet again, Catherine. This has all the earmarks of a grand finale."

She laughed, and their eyes locked in a smile that was almost an embrace. "Between us, there are no farewells," she said, "only doors that have closed on the rooms of the past."

"Nice simile," Norman said approvingly. "I must remember that!"

"And me?" Catherine asked in a small voice. "Just once in a while."

"And you," Norman said, and for the first time the look of the suave sophisticate dropped from his face, and she saw the Norman of her youth, arrogant and unsure, ruthless and tender, loved and loving. "Yes, dearest Catherine, may heaven help me, I think I must remember you, too."

With that he turned, opened the outer door, and was gone in an instant. For a moment Catherine stood rooted to the floor, numbed by the sudden devastation of his departure. It took all her power to restrain herself from rushing after him and begging him to come back—to stay with her and talk to her—to be her friend or her lover or her life. But instead she forced herself to walk slowly to the stove. Opening it, she stood by the heat as though she were chilled to the bone, and slowly, methodically, she rubbed her hands to warm them by the fire, willing herself not to hear the sound of his powerful engine as it roared into gear and the scrape of the gravel as he turned in the middle of the road and drove off into the night.

CHAPTER SEVENTEEN

The next morning, after a wakeful night, Catherine rose and dressed automatically. She took the contract out of her briefcase and sat in the living room, staring at the legal paragraphs. Slowly, she took out her fountain pen, and turning to the bottom page, she signed her name. There would be no returning to Calgary—no new beginnings—no comfortable flight to the nesting place after all. Last night she had realized that she had said no to Norman once, but she would be unable to say it again. Had he walked back into her room five minutes after he left, she would have gone with him. Her will to resist was gone, but the practical side of her knew that to go with Norman on his terms would be the end of everything worthwhile in her life, and so she had to turn her face resolutely away from the past and from Calgary. She was too tired to go somewhere new, and so she signed the contract to remain where she was in Cardston, uncomfortable and strange, but at least self-sustaining and independent.

Although it was Saturday, she decided to take the contract down to the courthouse and give it to the secretary at the Department of Education offices. Pulling her hair into a tight twist, she jammed on an old felt cloche, threw on her coat, and walked briskly down the street. The morning wind was raw with the promise of rain, and the sidewalk was muddy underfoot.

But the cold, bracing air was stimulating, and she felt her spirits rise as she tramped through the empty morning streets.

The courthouse was almost deserted. Several of the offices were closed on Saturdays, but the Education offices stayed open until noon. She walked into the anteroom where the secretary sat pecking away at her typewriter in a desultory fashion. The building had a vacant feeling, quiet and echoing.

"Is Mr. Solembaugh in today?" she asked the receptionist.

"No, he isn't coming in this morning. I think he's over at the high school," replied the young woman. "May I help you, Miss Summerwell?"

"Yes, please. I have brought in my signed contract for next year. I wonder if you could give it to Mr. Solembaugh and tell him thanks for me."

"Yes, of course. I'll put it on his desk. He'll get it first thing Monday morning."

"Thank you very much," Catherine said, and handed over the manila envelope with the signed papers. A year of my life, she thought, and it passes between us like an invitation to lunch.

Catherine continued to stare at the envelope on the secretary's desk.

"Is there anything else?" asked the secretary. Her voice was still courteous, but she was obviously anxious to get back to her work.

"No! No!" said Catherine, still torn by the finality of her move, and almost wishing to snatch the envelope back. "No, that's all." She turned slowly, and walked out of the office.

In the corridor a sudden wave of nausea struck her,

and the floor began to tilt at a crazy angle. Catherine felt like she was going to faint, and she put her hand on the wall to steady herself. Her head was spinning.

"Here now, what's wrong?" A man's voice came dimly, as though from a distance, and she felt a strong arm reach out to support her. Then everything went black.

The first thing she was aware of was a bright light. It hurt her eyes and she wanted to turn away, so she twisted her head back and forth. Something was stinging her nose and eyes and she shuddered.

"She's coming around," said the man's voice, and a woman answered, "What a scare! She was acting kind of funny in the office. I wonder if she's sick!"

"I'm not sick," Catherine said, but her voice sounded funny—mumbled and thick. "I'm not sick!" she repeated, making an effort to speak more carefully.

"Catherine," the man's voice said, "are you all right?"

"Yes!" she said, trying to focus on the faces above her, but the light hurt her eyes. "Yes. What happened? Did I faint?"

"You certainly did! It was a beaut!" It was Malcolm Brady's voice, and now her head was clearing and she could see his face.

"Malcolm!" she exclaimed, her voice still blurry, but warm with surprise. "How? Where? Am I seeing things?"

"No. It's me all right. My first morning back! This is quite a reception. You faint at the sound of my voice!"

Her head was completely clear now, and she saw

that she had been moved into the Education office.
The secretary was standing above her holding some
smelling salts, and Malcolm was sitting beside her on
the couch where she was lying, rubbing her wrists.

"Are you feeling better?" he asked. "Do you have
any spots in front of your eyes? Or double vision?"

"No," she answered, "I'm feeling a little weak, but
my head is completely clear. I think I should have
eaten breakfast before I started out on my walk."

"Yes," said Malcolm, "that's probably all it is, but I
think you should go see the doctor anyway, just to be
sure."

"I'm really sorry to have caused you so much trouble," she said. "This is so embarrassing. I've never
done anything like this in my life!"

"Well, if you're sure you're feeling better, why don't
you let me take you home. You probably should spend
the rest of the day in bed," Malcolm said.

They walked out to his car together. He supported
her on his arm, and she found that she felt surprisingly weak and was glad for his strength.

"Malcolm! It's so wonderful to have you back! I've
really missed you!" she said warmly. "Thank you for
helping me this morning."

"My return is less than glorious!" Malcolm said,
with his usual sardonic tone. "It seems I'm not cut out
for office work. I cut short my project in Edmonton.
That bureaucratic mess gave me a pain! So I asked to
be assigned back to my field office a few months
early. I'm back in time to help with the spring calving
and the seeding."

She could sense the bitterness in his tone, and she
guessed the year had been a disappointment to him.

She searched for something to say that might help. She knew he would reject anything that smacked of sympathy, so she kept her voice matter of fact. "Hard year?" she asked.

"You can say that again!" he answered, and turned to her with a crooked smile. "Looking at you, right now, I'd say you haven't had one of the best years on record either."

She smiled back at him. "You can say that again!" She mimicked his voice, and they both laughed.

She rolled down the window in his car, and as they drove through the streets she leaned her head back on the car seat and drew in gulps of the cold, clean air.

"You're going to freeze my tail off!" he shouted at her over the noise of the old car and the roaring air, "but if it makes you feel better, go ahead!"

The cold air whipped color into her cheeks, and she felt herself growing stronger.

"I'm feeling much better, Malcolm, really I am!" she called back.

"You're looking better!" he boomed, glancing over at her as she sat by the window, her face buffeted by the cold air. They arrived at her house, and he came around and opened the door for her. "Shall I come in with you?" he asked.

"No, I'll be fine. I think I just need to eat something, and then I'll rest for the remainder of the day," she replied.

He took her to the door and, with a last admonition to call the doctor, left her. As he was closing the door, he called out, "I'll phone you this evening to check and see how you are."

The following week she went to the doctor for a

checkup. As she was buttoning her blouse, the doctor came back into the examining room with her test results. He was a general practitioner with an office full of crying babies and pregnant women.

"Your tests are all fine, Miss Summerwell. I don't think there could be any physical cause for your fainting spell. You appear to be a little tired and run-down, which is probably normal after a year of teaching active high schoolers, but it seems to me a more reasonable explanation is that you are living under some kind of a strain. I have no idea what that strain might be, but I can tell you that our emotional and spiritual needs are as real as our physical needs, and they won't be denied. You wouldn't expect your body to do without food and rest and exercise, and continue to function, would you? Well, you can't expect it to continue to function without relaxation and happiness either. I think what I would prescribe for you, Miss Summerwell, is more leisure. Do you have a hobby? A sport? Or some kind of recreational outlet? Go to the movies once in a while!—or dancing! I think you need to do something to feed the young woman inside of the schoolteacher. You're too tense, and I believe this fainting spell was your body's way of telling you that if you continue to live so intensely, you're going to have to pay the piper."

"You think I should take up stamp collecting?" Catherine asked with a wry smile.

"Fun is what I'm suggesting, Miss Summerwell," the doctor said crisply. "You need to relax! The way in which you do it is up to you, but you are wound as tight as a watch spring. Seems funny to me—here you are young, unencumbered, free as a bird. And you're fainting from tension, while I have a young woman out there just your age who's expecting her third baby in three years, tied down in a little box of a house with diapers and crying children, and she's as relaxed and happy as a child herself. There's no explaining it!"

"I guess not," Catherine said stiffly. "I appreciate your advice."

"Then take it!" Dr. Young said brusquely, putting his rimless glasses back on, and tucking her chart under his arm as he headed for the door of the examining room. "I don't want to see you in here again—next time it could be more serious."

Catherine nodded and tried to smile as he left. "Fun!" she said to herself scornfully. "And just how does one go about it? Maybe he should have given me a prescription, and I could have gone to the drugstore—'A bottle of fun, please, and don't spare the balloons!'" She got up from the examining table slowly and gathered up her coat and purse. When she left the doctor's office, she was surprised to see Ladean in the waiting room.

"Ladean! What are you doing here?" she exclaimed.

"Waiting for you," said Ladean with a smile. "When you said you were having a checkup this afternoon, I thought it might help to have a friend afterwards, just in case you heard something ominous. Why don't we go down to the coffee shop and have a cup of hot chocolate? You can tell me all the gory details."

Catherine smiled at Ladean over the table in the booth at the coffee shop. "This was really nice of you, Ladean. Especially when you're so busy getting ready for the wedding."

"The truth is I was uptown anyway, trying on my wedding dress, so I just popped up to Doc Young's office when I was through, hoping you'd be there. We haven't had a good visit in ages, and I've really missed our time together."

Catherine managed a smile. "I guess we're going to have to get used to that. You'll be going out to Dan's farm for the summer, and then up to Edmonton for the school year. We're still friends, of course—we will be—but . . ."

"I know," Ladean said and sighed. "I've looked forward to being married for so long, and now that it's so close, it kind of scares me! So many things are changing. But not our friendship, Catherine. Nothing will change that."

They drank their hot chocolate, each thinking gravely about the wedding and what it would mean to them. "You'll love the reception, Catherine," Ladean said brightly, trying to lighten the mood. "Everyone's coming! It's going to be loads of fun!"

"Fun!" Catherine gave a short laugh. "Your reception may be what the doctor ordered!"

"What?" asked Ladean, puzzled. Catherine told her about her doctor's visit. "Oh, Catherine! He's right—I know he is. You've been so serious all year, and you've worked so hard! Promise me you'll dance and laugh and have a wonderful time at my wedding, or I'll never forgive you!" Ladean exclaimed.

"The problem with fun, Ladean, is that it is very hard to have alone. Now do you happen to have someone at your wedding who is willing to commit his evening to filling your prescription for me?"

Ladean's pretty face assumed a thoughtful frown.

"Dale Vernon—no, he's such a stick! Ray Bradshaw—no, he's going with that dumb Susan Henry! Um-m-m. . . ."

"You begin to see the problem," Catherine remarked, then added, "Am I the only person you've invited who isn't a member of your church?"

"Just about," Ladean admitted. "Father's invited a few couples who are business acquaintances, and—oh! I heard Malcolm Brady is back in town, and I think Father invited him last week. I doubt if he'll come, though. He never comes to 'churchy' things, as he calls them!"

"Hm-m-m," Catherine mused, "I wonder—"

Dan Allred arrived home from New Zealand the following week. He was a tall, handsome young man with brown hair and serious blue eyes. In his luggage he carried a large and improbable collection of Polynesian artifacts, and his conversation centered almost exclusively on the Maori people whom he had learned to love and admire. His voice was enthusiastic and fluent with vitality, and Ladean sat beside him beaming with happiness. Catherine liked Dan the minute she met him, and it was obvious that he adored Ladean. Ladean had never looked prettier, as though happiness had lighted a candle inside of her which highlighted her face and eyes; but, for Catherine, the social trappings were all too reminiscent of Emily's wedding.

Too many people, too many parties, and the prospective bride and groom surrounded by well-meaning adults and friends. Watching them, Catherine wondered how they could stand the lack of privacy. After three years she would have thought they would have yearned for quiet time together, to explore the changes in one another. She was haunted by the memory of Emily's unhappiness on the eve of her wedding, and wondered if Ladean and Dan were being given a chance to prepare themselves to be alone together as husband and wife. However, she had to admit, she had never seen two people who looked happier, and the circle of their joy seemed to seal her out more firmly than before. Now she realized that the brief time she and Ladean had shared over hot chocolate in the coffee shop might well have been the last private conversation of their friendship, and the thought saddened her. In Ladean's happiness she saw the reflection of her own loneliness and emptiness. The two women were like mirror images—the one moving into fullness, the other into a void.

Two days before the wedding, Catherine was walking home from town carrying a dress box with her new outfit for Ladean's reception. She felt foolish and extravagant purchasing a new dress for an event at which she was sure she would feel insignificant; nonetheless, she had decided to do Ladean's farewell in style, and so she bought a filmy mauve-colored dress that looked like spring, with a spray of violets to wear in her hair. Walking up Temple Hill, she noted the buds beginning to swell on the cottonwood trees and the new spring grass beginning to green the lawns. The air was cool, but it held a promise of warmth, and the breeze seemed almost gentle. The walk was doing her good, and so she slowed down to a stroll, feeling no hurry to get home to her quiet apartment.

A car pulled up beside her. Turning, she recognized Malcolm Brady at the wheel. He leaned over and rolled down the window on the passenger side of the car.

"Hey!" he called. "Give you a ride somewhere?"

"Hello, Malcolm. How's the calving and the seeding going?"

"Fine! How's the passing out going?"

"Oh, that was a onetime event," she responded. "I did go to see the doctor as you recommended, and he pronounced me healthy as a horse! His only advice was that I learn how to have fun, which didn't seem too professional to me." She laughed. "Thanks for the offer of a ride." She climbed into the car. "I accept."

"You're changing, Miss Summerwell," Malcolm Brady observed. "Maybe you're coming down off that marble pedestal and realizing you're just one of the crowd after all."

"I don't know what you mean," Catherine said indignantly.

"I think you're finding out that no one can exist solely on ideals and hard work—it makes for mighty tough living. As a matter of fact, you're almost human these days, but I don't think you find it comfortable yet." Malcolm looked at her with a quizzical smile.

"I don't find this conversation comfortable!" she protested.

"Okay, okay! So I'll change the subject! What are you carrying in the big white box? Nothing to eat, I'll warrant. I'm starving."

"In answer to your question—no, it is not something to eat. It's my dress for Ladean Watkins's wedding reception. Are you going? She said you were invited," Catherine said.

"Well-l-l," Malcolm answered, looking at her with a

wicked grin, "I wasn't planning to go since those glad-some church events leave me cold, but now that I hear you, another true-blue gentile, are planning to go, maybe I'll change my mind. As a matter of fact, if you'll invite me for supper, I'll even take you"

Catherine was taken aback by his self-confident assumption that she would go with him, but his affrontery amused rather than insulted her. "What makes you think I'd be seen in public with you?" she asked, her eyes alight with raillery.

He laughed. "Pardon me, Miss Summerwell. Let me rephrase my request. Would you do me the honor of attending Ladean Watkins's wedding reception with me—and would you also be kind enough to offer to feed a starving man?"

Catherine laughed and shook her head. "Really, Malcolm! You are incredible! I'd love to offer to feed a starving man, but you know as well as I do that a schoolteacher in this town has to live her life like a nun. If word got around that you had supper in my apartment—alone with me—my reputation wouldn't be worth a bent nickel. I'd love to have you to dinner sometime, but I'd have to have other guests as well—otherwise, it has to be in public."

"Maybe you haven't come down off that pedestal as far as I thought," Malcolm remarked. "Lady, I think the time has come for me to take you in hand. You live your whole life for the approval of other people. Don't you know a life isn't worth living unless you live it for yourself?"

"That may be—but I can't afford to lose my contract," she began.

"Oh, forget it!" he cut her off. "I won't insist on

eating at your table. Let's drive out to the diner and eat together. What do you say to that? It wouldn't hurt your reputation, would it?"

She flushed. "Please try to understand, Malcolm."

"Fine," said Malcolm, "don't talk about it anymore. Let's start out all over again! We'll go have dinner, and then I'll drive you home at a nice proper time, and on Saturday night I will pick you up, all properly dressed in my one blue suit, and will escort you, very properly, to the church for the reception. Will that meet your approval?"

"Yes, I'd like that, Malcolm," she said in a small voice.

Suddenly, he was laughing. "Boy!" he said. "I sure know how to pick 'em!" He continued laughing, and suddenly she joined in, laughing harder than she had in years. He pulled the car to the side of the road and the two of them bent double, speechless with silly, exhilarated laughter. Catherine laughed till the tears ran down her cheeks, and he looked at her laughing and could not contain his own amusement. Finally, she pulled out a handkerchief, and gasping for breath, she wiped her eyes. He continued to chuckle, and Catherine found it was several minutes before she could speak without giggling. "Malcolm!" she said. "You are a breath of fresh air."

"Yeah!" he answered, still smiling. "So are you!"

The evening of Ladean's reception Malcolm picked Catherine up to drive her to the church. He whistled when Catherine came to the door, and she smiled, self-consciously holding out the skirt of her dress. "You like it?" she asked shyly.

"It's a knockout," he said, but his voice was curiously flat, and she had the feeling that he was indifferent to women's clothes. She felt nervous and the fact they were going on a date seemed to change her relationship with him. He was unlike anyone she had ever known—unpredictable and enigmatic. She sensed he only played by rules when he chose to do so, and that made her apprehensive. She had never known anyone who did not act in accordance to the unwritten rules and standards of her own codes. But here was a man who held the world in low esteem, who cared passionately about some things and not a fig for others, and the only standard for his choices was his own quixotic desire. When they were acquaintances, she had thought him amusing, but as a date she was unsure how to react.

They drove down the street toward the Mormon stake building where Ladean's reception was to be held. The street north of the temple was clogged with traffic. Cars, buckboards, trucks, and pedestrians jammed the area. They were all heading in the same direction.

"The whole town must be going to the wedding!" Catherine gasped.

"The whole town?" Malcolm remarked sardonically. "The whole southern end of the province is more like it!"

Light spilled out of the recreation hall, along with the sound of a small dance orchestra. People were laughing and talking, moving up and down the outside stairs. The reception was lovely. Ladean, Dan, and their families stood in a line in the Relief Society room with flowers banked beside them. Guests waited on line to greet the bride and groom and their parents, and Catherine, observing, noted the love and courtesy which was shown each. The humblest farmer in rusty trousers and broken shoes was greeted, kissed, his hand shaken with as much enthusiasm as the wealthier townspeople who were friends of long standing.

Malcolm Brady was well-known and well-liked. "Nice to see you, Mr. Brady!" "Welcome back, Malcolm!" "Coming out to my place next Thursday? I've got a problem with my soil." Husbands and wives called to him, or came to shake his hand, and he seemed completely at ease.

The parents of Catherine's students approached her shyly. "John's surely enjoyed your class, Miss Summerwell!" "I came to your play last summer. That was a real treat! Are you going to do one this summer?" She smiled and shook hands, glancing from time to time at Ladean, who was radiant with happiness. The Watkins family was radiant, too—brothers, sisters, and parents seemed to shine with happiness. As Catherine stood in line waiting to congratulate the bride and groom she overheard Mrs. Watkins whisper to her husband. "The last one, Father. Married in the temple! We have made it through!" And Bishop Watkins beamed a look of such boundless affection on his wife that Catherine felt she should turn her head rather than witness such a private and overwhelming emotion.

When she reached Ladean and Dan, Ladean threw her arms around Catherine in an enthusiastic embrace. "Oh, Catherine!" she whispered. "It was so glorious! Eternity won't be long enough! The ceremony was beautiful!"

Tears came to Catherine's eyes. "I'm so happy for you, Ladean!"

Dan hugged her, too, a little stiffly, as though he weren't used to that sort of thing. His smile was warm and boyish, but there was a manly strength in his face and an upright lift to his head. "Thank you, Catherine, for being such a good friend to Ladean while I was gone. It's too bad we can't rub noses. That's how the Maoris show affection, and I want you to know we will both always consider you with great affection." Catherine, looking at him, wondered at the depth and serenity he showed. Here was a man who had traveled halfway around the world and lived for three years in a unique culture. She wondered if anyone would ever know the things he had experienced and suffered, and yet still he had returned filled with a buoyant love for life and for other people. In him she sensed a young man whose purposes were built upon a foundation as secure as a rock. Ladean would never need to fear leaning on him, or casting her lot with his, because Catherine felt he was one of those rare men who would never fail. A man to be depended upon—a man who was strong because he was not afraid to care.

"I will treasure your friendship," Catherine murmured.

Malcolm had followed her through the line and behaved courteously, but as they left the Relief Society room, he grabbed her elbow. "If I have to make anymore small talk, I'm going to say something we'll both regret, so let's get out there and dance!"

He was a good dancer, and the orchestra, made up of local church members, played smoothly. Catherine was having a wonderful time. The music was good, and everyone seemed warm and friendly, making a real effort to reach out to her and Malcolm. The refreshments were on a long table at one end of the dance hall: party sandwiches, cakes, and a sparkling, nonalcoholic fruit punch. Malcolm made a wry face as he tasted the punch. "I'm not sure if my body is ready for this!" he said, drinking the glass in a single gulp and going back for a refill.

At first while they were dancing Catherine tried to make conversation, but then Malcolm pulled her close and whispered in her ear, "I once left a girl standing in the middle of the dance floor because she talked all the time. If you're going to dance—dance. Don't talk!"

"I won't say a word!" Catherine whispered and put her hand over her mouth.

He laughed shortly and whirled her around. They danced through the evening, except for one or two brief stops at the refreshment table, and a short program at intermission, when the bride and groom came in to cut the cake, and guests offered some amusing toasts with the fruit punch. A girls' chorus sang some charming old English love songs. The atmosphere was all homey and warm, and feelings of genuine affection were palpable. Husbands and wives danced together, grown sons and daughters greeted their parents with delight, friends reached out to friends. Catherine realized she had never seen so many manifestations of love—it poured forth, touching and infusing everyone. Between the married couples it seemed most obvious. The wedding seemed to serve to remind them of their own precious ties, and in their joy at Ladean's marriage they seemed to reflect the joy of their own.

As the evening whirled on, time seemed to stop, and Catherine felt herself smiling, dancing, light as a feather, in the midst of a rainbow of happy faces.

"They're leaving," Malcolm observed, stopping suddenly on the dance floor and turning to the large double doors leading into the hall. Ladean and Dan were standing by the doors dressed in their traveling clothes. Everyone surged forward, throwing rice and confetti. "The bouquet!" someone called. "Throw the bouquet!" Ladean seemed to search the crowd in front of her, and then her eyes caught Catherine's. With a mighty heave she tossed the flowers in a high arc, like a basketball, straight toward Catherine. Just as Catherine thought she would have to catch it, a teen-ager standing in front of her jumped high and intercepted the beribboned nosegay. A happy throng gathered around the girl, laughing and teasing, and Dan and Ladean dashed for the door.

After the bride and groom left, a sweet mellowness seemed to settle on the party. The Bishop and Mrs. Watkins came out to dance. They spoke to Catherine with affectionate reproof, "We never see enough of you anymore, Catherine dear," Mrs. Watkins said. "Now that Ladean's gone, you should move into her room. We're going to be so lonely without her!" There were tears in Mrs. Watkins's eyes but her face shone with happiness.

Someone dimmed the lights and a slow waltz began. Malcolm took her in his arms, and they started to twirl slowly onto the floor. During the evening Catherine had understood why he had told her not to talk and dance at the same time. There was something about dancing without speaking which made it an experience both sensual and absorbing. She had never enjoyed dancing so much as she had this night. The music was soothing and Malcolm's body moved with sure grace. Catherine was tempted to close her eyes and give herself fully to the experience, but she felt it would look foolish and so she kept her eyes open, and her dancing stiffly proper.

Malcolm pulled against her, but she maintained the acceptable distance between them. He looked into her eyes with a knowing half-smile and then shrugged his shoulder wryly and looked away, absorbed once more in the dance.

It was during this dance that Catherine's mood had changed. Everywhere her eyes turned married couples were dancing. Old couples, middle-aged couples, young couples, and they all appeared to be wrapped in secure folds of love. Where she was raised, conjugal affection was a social habit, a ritual which was enacted in accordance with strict norms of etiquette. Marriages were, by and large, convenient arrangements of equals, and the few marriages where genuine affection or sexual attraction existed were considered a little shocking, particularly if those feelings were apparent in public social activities. Yet here, these Mormon couples seemed to have discovered some marvelous secret. They were complete in one another, and she wondered what magic it was which could create so many relationships of seemingly disparate individuals, yielding such security and joy. What was it they knew? Was it so simple a thing as how to love? And how did one find it? She didn't know, but it was obvious that it had filled this hall during the hours of the wedding reception, and as families began to drift home, she could see more evidence of their affection for one another.

Sons kissed their aging mothers farewell, fathers held their daughters and shook hands with sons-in-law, gripping their hands between both of their own in a token of esteem. Husbands and wives walked to their cars holding hands, or arms, with practiced tenderness.

As the waltz ended, Malcolm took her arm. "Shall we go?"

"Yes," Catherine said weakly. "I'll get my wrap."

Driving home in the car she was quiet. Malcolm looked at her inquiringly a couple of times and then turned his attention to his driving, saying nothing. As they reached her apartment, he shut off the motor but made no attempt to get out of the car. She gathered up her purse and gloves, ready to leave, but he turned to face her, pulling one knee up on the car seat, so that he was sitting sideways. Though he put his arm across the back of the seat, he did not attempt to touch her.

"Okay, what's up?" he asked.

"What do you mean?" she asked, tired and dispirited.

"Look, you started this evening out like a lighted rocket, and I'm bringing you home like you'd been to your grandmother's funeral. What is it? I'm not much of a conversationalist, I'll admit—but I'm a darn good dancer!" He laughed mirthlessly and took out a cigarette. "Mind if I smoke? All that clean living has gotten to me!"

Catherine sighed and looked out the window. "I don't know what's the matter with me, Malcolm. I had a wonderful time. You're a great dancer, and people were nice—Ladean is happy—you liked my dress. What could be the matter?"

"That's what I want to know!" said Malcolm. "And you'd better figure it out fast, I've got a tough day ahead of me tomorrow."

"It's not your problem!" Catherine said, angered by his abruptness. "I'll go in now." She started to open the door.

He reached over to pull the door closed again, and for a moment he kept his hand on her door handle, so that she was pinned down, his one arm behind her and the other reaching across her. His face was very close to hers, and she could smell his tobacco. "I'll give you ten minutes," he said, "so talk!" Then he smiled at her, his eyes veiled with private amusement, and settled back in his position by the steering wheel, still looking at her.

"I—I—" She didn't want to talk to him, and his rudeness made her angry, but he was so outrageous and straightforward that she found herself amused and disarmed as well. "I can't simply analyze my feelings on cue!" She shook her head. "You don't really care anyway; you only want to be reassured that I wasn't bored with you! As soon as you find out that I thought you were charming and irresistible—and my problem is something else altogether—you'll be off in a flash, to leave me in my misery."

"Maybe," he said, "but aren't you curious why you're feeling this way. I personally think it's because your friend is married, and you're feeling very let down and left out."

"Yes," Catherine conceded, "I know that's part of it, but it's more than that. Didn't you feel it at all, Malcolm? It's as though all those people there tonight knew something—a fabulous secret—like they had found the Holy Grail, and they all knew where it was, and we're still wandering in the woods, lost and looking. How can they all be so happy?"

"Well, they aren't all happy! And even the happy ones aren't happy all the time. Besides, what do you mean by happiness?" Malcolm answered with calm logic.

"Oh, I don't know! It's just—they all seemed to have a place to belong—a place they fitted! There was so much love. Didn't you sense it? All those husbands and wives who seem to have found a secret formula?"

"If I didn't know better, I'd swear someone had spiked your punch!" Malcom jeered. "You are, without doubt, the most foolish, blind, innocent woman I have ever known. Sure there's lots of good marriages here. Family is a way of life for these people, and they work hard at it. They've survived a lot of persecution and suffering, and they're intelligent, dedicated people. The one thing they have learned for sure is that you can survive a lot of things if you have loving and caring people around you. They cultivate those feelings! It isn't easy! No magic formula! It takes self-control and training and patience and a hundred other things. They're just like other people and some of their marriages are better than others. The thing is they keep working at it, because they believe in it so much. Tonight you saw them at their best and the Watkinses are the best of their best! It's a different world for them, Catherine. Everything they do is based on a philosophy of life that stretches farther than you could imagine. Sometimes"—his voice was quiet and he looked out into the night—"sometimes I envy them, and I'm almost tempted to try to . . ." He snapped out of the contemplative mood. "Don't go idealizing what you saw! It isn't for you, anyway!"

"What do you mean, Malcolm, it isn't for me?"

"Look, Catherine, like it or not, you're part of the real world. It's a world where people get hurt, and where people don't care about each other. It's a tough world, but it's a place where you can be free. You can do what you want, be what you want, think what you want—and act like you want! Your problem is that you refuse to step into either world. You stand on the fringes like a frightened child, and you're afraid to explore. What have all your prim, silly conventions done for you? That apartment of yours is going to become a sealed box, if you don't do something! You stand and look at other people's worlds and idealize them. You think they are what you see—you blind yourself to realities. It's time you began to explore your own world!"

"What world?" she asked.

"Well . . . my world." Malcolm replied, and ground out his cigarette in the ashtray by his door. "This world." His arm reached down against her shoulder and pulled her abruptly toward him, and he kissed her lips. His mouth was hard and uncompromising against hers, and he continued to kiss her until she gasped for breath and struggled against him. He released her as abruptly as he had embraced her. "Do you dare?" he mocked. "Do you have the courage to give it a try?" Then he laughed out loud as he looked at her. "You should see yourself. You look like a rabbit caught in the headlights!"

She was staring at him, her eyes wide with confusion, her hair falling out of its pins and tumbling to her shoulders. Her evening wrap had slipped from her arms, and she felt awkward and ridiculous. "I think I should go in now," she said.

He reached over and caught her arm in his powerful grip. "No!" he said. "You're not going to run away from this or put me off with your party manners. I want you to listen. You're going to dry up and turn into an old maid schoolteacher if you keep on the way you're going. Keep your dignity, you'll lose everything else! I'm offering you a chance to taste life, Catherine. Don't you want to have some fun, to laugh, to throw convention to the winds—to make some friends who don't expect you to always be toeing the line?"

He watched her carefully, and then let out a great shout of laughter. "Look, I'm not propositioning you, if that's what you think! I'm just asking if you want to go out with me—if you're willing to go to the places I go, with the people I like. I want to show you a part of living you don't even know exists! What do you say? Will you give it a try?" He moved over closer to her, and his voice was softer, gentler. "Someday you might even dissolve some of that shell and find a soft, warm woman inside."

He didn't touch her again, but his eyes slowly searched her face, his lids half-closed and a taunting smile on his lips.

Stung by his words she rose to the challenge. "I know more about life than you imagine! Yes, I'm willing to explore your world. You may not have so much to teach me as you think!"

"Brave words!" he replied. "Very well, next Friday night?"

"Fine!" she flung back at him. "I'll be ready!"

He made no move to get out and open her door for her, and when she realized he was waiting for her to leave, she gave him an indignant look and opened the car door herself. Gathering up her things, she threw him a puzzled look.

"Aren't you going to the door with me?"

"Catherine," he said, "you may as well know right from the start. I'm not Lord Fauntleroy, and this isn't the high school prom. You're an adult, and so am I— those are my only rules. Don't think that anything between us is going to lead to a garden path. I'm not that kind of a man. Are you sure you still want to go out with me?"

She sat by the open car door with one foot on the running board, her head raised proudly and defiantly, and she looked him square in the eye. "You don't frighten me!" she answered. "I've never looked for garden paths anyway."

With that she jumped from the car and hurried down the walk to the door of her apartment. In the darkness she fumbled for her key. She sensed that Malcolm Brady was watching from his car with amusement, and that only made her more clumsy. She dropped her handbag and knelt down in the dim moonlight to pick up the spilled items. From the darkness of the car she thought she heard a chuckle. Finding the key at that moment, she stood up and held it aloft, facing the car. "Curse you, Malcolm Brady!" she called, brandishing the key. She heard him laugh, and as she put the key in the door, he started the motor

and drove off. Shaking her head in exasperation, she
entered the apartment. "He is impossible!" she expos-
tulated and threw her gloves on the table. "Impossible! Why did I ever say I'd go out with him!" She
paced back and forth angrily. "He is the rudest, most
contemptuous"—then suddenly she was laughing—
"most unexpected, ridiculous, posturing . . ." She
continued to think up adjectives as she went out on
the sidewalk to retrieve her handbag.

CHAPTER EIGHTEEN

It was the hottest summer season in the memory of Southern Alberta. The heat began in late May. Oppressive and brilliant, the sun beat down from the early morning sky and stayed late into the evening. The prairie wind blowing from the slopes of the Rockies failed to bring its usual cooling air but blew dry and sere instead. The fields were sown with wheat, and as the tender seedlings began to break through the black rich earth, the farmers stared at the azure, cloudless sky, and the constant sun, and squinted into the distance toward the mountains, scanning the western horizon for the hint of a cloud that might promise rain or a break in the shimmering heat. But none came. The irrigated farms were safe, and the irrigation ditches and canals ran daily, bringing water to the sprouting fields, but the dry farms were scorched and brown, and the tension in the town crackled as worried farmers stood in the Trading Post in anxious silence or entered into serious discussions about the problems of weather and 'hoppers. Disaster loomed, but it was beyond the control of man, and so a strange kind of helpless lightheartedness infected the townspeople.

The Cameron Hotel was crowded day and night with merrymakers. The ice cream parlor was jammed with teen-agers and youth. Women sought the stores and wandered up and down the aisles aimlessly, fingering the merchandise and carrying on bright, meaningless conversations, while their husbands loitered in the feed store, the hardware store, or the Trading Post. There was a breathless sense of waiting, and watching, and without realizing it, everyone had taken to watching the sky. While engaged in conversation, someone would inevitably forget what was being said, and involuntarily look upward, scanning the empty blue. The concern was habitual and hopeless, and the sky remained the same, minute by minute, day by day, as the watchers watched and the sun moved slowly through the stations of the long summer day, unshaded, unwinking, uncaring, while the prairie earth writhed and cracked and dried in the heat.

At night few could sleep. Lights were extinguished, but porches and lawns were alive with people escaping the stuffy sleepless rooms. They sat in the dark in creaking rocking chairs, or squeaking porch swings, and the night was full of whispered conversations, yearning for the moments of blessed coolness when the night breeze stirred the air.

For Catherine the heat and restlessness outdoors underscored the restlessness within her. She knew she could not return to Calgary for the summer. The thought of meeting Norman was too painful to bear. Her sense of betrayal was still fresh and cruel, and she was consumed with self-disgust that she had ever believed him to be the noble and desirable person she had created in her mind. She wondered if anyone was what he seemed. As the summer progressed she became more and more embittered. Within her grew the conviction that people were basically selfish. She told herself that if she hoped to find anything of pleasure in life, she would need to seize it, as others did, without thought for rules or the needs of others. She hated these thoughts, but she felt the entire foundation of her world had crumbled under her feet. In finding that Norman, her idol, had betrayed her so deeply, she wondered if she could trust anyone or anything as much as she could trust herself.

Malcolm approved of her changing views, and he encouraged her to see the selfishness of others. "That's how you get ahead, you know," he would say. "You've got to decide what you want and go after it. If you wait for someone to give it to you, you'll wait forever!"

True to his word, Malcolm was showing her a world she had never known before. It was a world made up of cowboys, young unmarried ranchers, shop girls, bank clerks, government workers, and a few nurses and teachers like herself. The crowd was hard-drinking, fun-loving, reckless, and bright. They drove their cars across the prairie roads at breakneck speeds and raced in caravans from town to town. They knew every cafe, hotel bar, and dance hall in Southern Alberta.

As the summer began, the attention of the crowd focused on Waterton, which was a ninety-minute drive straight west from Cardston, dead into the heart of the foothills and on into the fastness of the Rocky Mountain chain. The village of Waterton was bustling with tourists, and the crystal blue lakes which dotted the mountain roads and passes were sprinkled with rowboats and fishermen. Tents and cabins dotted the mountain slopes.

The town itself was made up of rustic cabins, dusty and dingy from the long disuse of winter. The mountain roads were covered with a thin layer of gravel and tar whose pungent aroma mingled with the overpowering scent of pine needles in the valley. Waterton Lake was filled with icy water, fed constantly by streams flowing from the glaciers of the surrounding mountains. On a bluff overlooking the large lake was a magnificent hotel named the Prince of Wales, because Prince Edward himself had once visited it. It was an English-style, half-timbered building standing in eminence at the head of the lake. The clientele of the hotel was mostly weathy Americans and eastern Canadians.

On the main street in Waterton a small movie theater showed a nightly film as well as a Saturday matinee. Nearby was an indoor heated public swimming pool, with chlorine-strong water, and a high wooden roof from which the shouts of children echoed and reverberated as though the children were swimming in an open tin drum.

On the street beside the lake was an old wooden dance hall. It was this dance hall and the liquor store next to it which attracted young people from miles around every weekend. The dance floor was crowded and dirty, the bands were loud and the air was blue with tobacco and thick with wild laughter. It was exactly the kind of place Catherine would have strenuously avoided, and yet, with Malcolm Brady she found herself enjoying the free-wheeling atmosphere. She danced on the packed floor with all kinds of men—young, middle-aged, sober, humorous, amorous, polite, forward—and she learned to handle them and found herself, oddly enough, having fun.

One night when the air was particularly stuffy she found Malcolm standing by the door, a beer in his hand. "Malcolm," she gasped, "I've got to get out of here to breathe!"

"Me, too," he agreed. They squeezed through the crowded doorway and began walking toward the lake. Within moments the lights of the dance hall faded, and the sounds of laughter and music became faint. They walked down to the rocky shore and wandered down the beach away from the town. The sky was sparkling with stars, and the velvet mountain darkness wrapped them in silence. Gradually, the scent of pine was overwhelming, and the infinite silence of the night was broken only by the lapping of the water against the shingle and the squeak of tethered canoes rubbing against one another in the gentle waves. Catherine stood, looking out over the lake. On the bluff, high above the water, shone the bright lights of the Prince of Wales Hotel in the distance. It looked like something from a fairy tale, remote and fanciful. She thought she could hear the faint sound of music coming from the hotel, and on the hotel terrace overlooking the lake she distinguished moving figures.

Malcolm followed her glance, and looked at her meaningfully. "Lo, how the mighty are fallen," he said.

"What!" she exclaimed, shaken from her reverie.

"You," said Malcolm. "That's where you belong. Up there! Those are your kind." He came and put his arm around her, turning her face toward the elegant hotel. "See how high it is! None of us down here in the smoky, noisy valley would even dare touch it! Oh, it isn't that we couldn't afford it. Any one of us could go up there and pay for a dinner and an evening of dancing. Nah! It isn't the money—it's something else. The minute we walked in they'd know we didn't belong! They would sense it, or smell it—I don't know how— but they'd know! You, on the other hand, you can come down here and dance in our crowded, noisy hall and pretend you're one of the gang—but we know you don't belong here. Right now you could go up there, and they'd know you belonged. You will always belong up there. Darned if I could tell you why, Princess, but that's your world."

"No!" she exclaimed vehemently, tearing herself away from him and turning to face him fiercely. "It isn't, it isn't! I don't belong. The moment I entered they'd know I didn't belong—I never did! I was just a changeling."

His smile was slow and challenging. "Bet?" he asked.

"Bet!" she agreed, her jaw set.

"Okay, we're going up there, and I'll prove you're wrong!" He grabbed her elbow and started propelling her toward the road where his car was parked.

"What are you talking about?" she screamed. "I can't go up there, I'm not dressed properly. We don't have enough money. We don't have a reservation!"

He stopped walking and stared at her. "Okay! Maybe they'll kick us out—then you'll win the bet! Are you too afraid to try?"

"Not on your life!" she asserted, gathering up her impulsive courage. "A bet's a bet. It's just that I've never been thrown out of a place before."

They drove up the winding road toward the hotel. "What are we betting for?" she asked, a little timidly.

"If we're going to bet, we should know what the stakes are."

"Hm-m-m, good question," Malcolm said. "How about—how about the person who loses has to do one thing—anything—which the other person asks."

"Oh, no!" Catherine exclaimed. "That's too open-ended! It has to be more specific!"

"Okay," Malcolm conceded airily, "you think of something! We're almost there."

"Oh, all right! You're going to lose the bet anyway!" Catherine exclaimed. "And I can think of a dozen things I'd like you to do for me—starting with weeding my garden."

"All right then," Malcolm said, "here we go!" They had driven up to the parking lot of the hotel, and as they drove past the doorman, Catherine saw the look of astonishment on the man's face as the beatup Ford pulled into an open space.

"I don't think this will take long," she said wryly to Malcolm. With a flourish he restrained her from opening her door, and sprang out on his own side, and hurrying around, he opened her door and assisted her out of the car. "When in Rome . . ." he said, taking her hand courteously and tucking it inside his bent elbow. They walked confidently toward the imposing entrance. The doorman, still looking distrustful, opened the door for them. "Good evening, madam, sir," he said, his tone formal but his eyes skeptical. Catherine smiled at him. "Thank you," she said graciously, as she passed through the door. The doorman looked at her and smiled. Touching the brim of his peaked hat, he saluted her.

"First test passed," Malcolm said jauntily, out of the corner of his mouth.

"It doesn't mean a thing," said Catherine. "Wait until we try to get into the dining room. It's the dinner captain who will throw us out!"

They walked through the lobby with its spectacular view of the lake and mountains. The lobby had a five-story-high ceilings with hallwaylike balconies on all the room levels facing inward into the lobby. Looking upward, they could see guests entering and leaving their rooms, and strolling down the inside stairs toward the public rooms below. To their right the dining room glittered with crystal chandeliers, and well-dressed handsome couples moved in and out of the doors. The terrace outside the windows was dotted with couples and families, dancing to the soft music or standing on the parapets enjoying the night air.

"It's lovely," breathed Catherine.

"Quite a contrast to the public hall!" Malcolm murmured. "Are you ready for the real test?"

"I guess so," she answered, "but this is really going to be embarrassing—are you sure you want to go through with it?"

"I tell you—" Malcolm asserted, "I bet you—they will never throw you out of a place like this! Me, they'd throw out in a minute!"

Together they walked to the doors of the dining room. Catherine's hand was trembling, but she put on her most confident smile and held her head high. This was, after all, just a dining room captain, and she had handled them all of her life.

"Good evening," Malcolm said, in a grand imitation

of the doorman's style. He began to sweep past the captain, but the man blocked the door.

"Good evening, sir," the man's voice was cold and commanding. "If you will excuse me, do you have reservations for the late seating?"

Malcolm looked at her blankly, and she rushed in to fill the gap. "No. However, if you have a table, perhaps we could enjoy a late supper. What do you think, dear?" She smiled at Malcolm serenely.

"I don't think so." He smiled back at her and surreptitiously squeezed her arm. He had no intention of paying a fortune for their experiment. "Let's just go in and dance for a while."

"All right dear," she said sweetly. Again they stepped forward to enter the room, but the captain remained in their path. "I'm sorry, but you understand dancing privileges are for guests only . . . ." he began, his voice polite, but steely.

"Of course," said Malcolm, "but Miss Summerwell happened to be in town for the evening, and she heard some of her friends were at the hotel. She was hoping to see them."

The captain looked skeptically at Malcolm and then turned to Catherine. She found the old social confidence coming back to her naturally, and she looked the captain in the eye with an expression of self-assured superiority. "We, of course, would not go in if it is against the policy of the hotel," she said, and the tone of her voice implied that the hotel was so poorly appointed it was hardly worth entering anyway.

The captain shifted his eyes uneasily. "Unless of course you were expected . . ." he began.

"Oh, no!" Catherine went on coolly. "We were not expected. Malcolm, shall me . . ."

At that moment a couple walked out of the dining room, and as the captain moved aside to let them out, the young woman let out an exclamation. "Catherine!" she called. "Catherine Summerwell! What are you doing here?" The girl was a friend of Helen Mortenson's from Toronto, who had come to spend a summer in Mount Royal the year the girls graduated from high school. "I haven't seen you in years! Oh, this is my husband, Jamie Traskell!"

After the quick introduction, Catherine and Helen's friend chatted and gossiped for a few minutes. "We're just going up to our room," said the girl, with a silvery laugh. "We're still on our honeymoon—"

Her husband, Jamie, laughed, too. "You are a shameless woman, Beth!" he told her. "What will Miss Summerwell think!"

"That I'm happily married!" Beth retorted, with a saucy grin. She gave Catherine a quick hug. "Do say hello to everyone in Mount Royal for me! Awfully nice to see you—and to meet you, Mr. Brady." The young couple walked to the stairs and were quickly out of sight.

When Catherine and Malcolm turned back to the dining room entrance the captain was standing to one side and smiling. "Please go in and enjoy yourselves." His voice was obsequious. "It is a lovely evening."

Malcolm bent close to her ear and whispered, "I won!"

Suddenly, it wasn't funny to Catherine anymore. She turned to the dining room captain. "Thank you very much, but I think I am too tired. Malcolm, would you mind taking me home?"

He sensed her change of mood and together they left the dazzling lobby. Moments later they were winding their way back down the dark mountain road to the village below. "I don't feel like going back to the dance hall, Malcolm," she said. "Do we have to drive any other passengers back to Cardston tonight or could we drive back now?"

"I'll drive you back to Cardston," he said calmly, "but I won our bet, and so you have to pay up—now!"

"Now!" she exclaimed, alarmed. "What are you talking about? I'm too tired to do anything right now. I want to go home."

"Oh, no, you don't!" His voice was determined. "A bet's a bet! You can't renege!"

In the close, dark car she felt claustrophobic and apprehensive. "All right! If you're going to be ridiculous!" she said haughtily, "what do you want me to do?"

He pulled the car into the deserted parking lot behind the wooden building that housed the swimming pool. When he turned off the motor and doused the lights, the silence and darkness were oppressive. Catherine squeezed over against her door.

He chuckled in the darkness and slid across the seat toward her, his voice soft and taunting. With one finger he reached up and touched her ear, tracing the rim slowly. "Poor little Catherine," he said softly, mockingly. "It looks like you're trapped. You've made a promise and you have to keep it. I'm prepared to collect."

"You can't be serious!" she gasped, feeling a weight

of fear on her chest so tight she could hardly breathe. "Malcolm, you don't think . . ."

"I think I'm going to collect my dues right now. The wager was that you would do whatever I asked. One thing. Well, right now—tonight, I want you to"— his voice remained husky and intimate, and he leaned over and whispered in her ear—"go swimming with me."

"Go swimming! Is that what you're asking?" Catherine exploded with relief and surprise. "Go swimming! At this hour! You are crazy, Malcolm Brady! Stark, staring insane!" She was laughing. "Besides, the lake will be like ice—it would be dangerous. I don't have a suit . . ."

"Not in the lake—in this lovely heated pool," Malcolm said.

"But the pool's closed! We can't go swimming at midnight."

"We're going to break in and swim by ourselves."

"Maybe you are!" Catherine retorted. "I've done enough daring things for one night."

"Very well, then," Malcolm said, moving even closer to her on the seat. "If you refuse to do this one thing, then I will have to choose another." There was no mistaking the tone in his voice, and Catherine realized he meant what he was saying.

"But I really don't have a swimsuit, Malcolm."

"No problem! They rent suits at this fine establishment, and we'll be able to pick one up at the counter."

They crept up to the darkened building. "Anything this dilapidated has got to be easy to get into!" Malcolm insisted. The doors were locked tight, but Malcolm patiently worked his way around the building, trying every window. In a few moments she heard him whistle, and running to the side of the building, she saw an opened window with a hand beckoning her. The window was fairly high, but Malcolm was standing on a bench inside, and he reached down and pulled her in.

They were in the boys' dressing room. As they made their way through the darkness, she knocked over a towel stand and the noise reverberated through the building, echoing and reechoing. They crouched for a long minute, listening to see if they had roused anyone. But only silence returned. "Wait here," Malcolm whispered when they got out into the pool room. The water shimmered in the moonlight through the windows, and a light steam rose from the heat. In less than a minute he was back and thrust a black wool suit into her hands. "Hope it's the right size," he whispered.

She tiptoed into the girls' dressing room and took off her clothes, pulling on the suit. It was a one-piece suit, cut like a leotard with straps, and it was too big. She folded her clothes into a neat bundle and walked hesitantly into the room with the pool. Malcolm was already in the water. Somehow he had lowered himself silently, because the slightest splashing would have been amplified in the empty domed room. She slipped down the ladder into the deep end and swam a single stroke. The splashing sound was terrifying, so she quickly changed to an underwater breast stroke. Malcolm was swimming silently, too. They met in the middle of the pool and swam a full silent arc. In synchronized movement, they glided through the water, back to the deep end. Under the diving board, they grasped the

edge and rested. "It's scary," she whispered. "What if
we get caught?"

"We haven't stolen anything or hurt anything,"
Malcolm said. "What can they do to us?"

"Breaking and entering is still a crime," she whispered.

"Okay, one more length, and we'll get out. Where's
your sense of adventure?" he responded. Slowly, they
pushed off, and silently, side by side began to move
through the water. An odd, hollow stillness surrounded them. The water was so close to their body
temperature that they almost felt they were floating,
disembodied. The slow motion and the strange emptiness of the pool area lent the scene a quality of mysti-
cism, and the fear of being caught only added to the
unreal strangeness of the mood. As they came to the
shallow end, Catherine put her feet down to walk to
the ladder, but it was too deep. She had miscalculated,
and the water closed over her head. Malcolm, taller
than she, was standing, and he reached out his hand to
pull her forward to a more shallow spot. As his hand
touched hers under the water she clung to it, and he
lifted her toward him. Laughing, she came up out of
the water, her hair streaming in her face.

"Sh-h-h!" he said. "You're the one who doesn't want
to get caught."

They stood still in the water, listening, hearing only
the water dripping from her hair and shoulders. Convinced that all was silent, they began to breathe easier.
Malcolm stopped listening, but he did not let go of
her. Instead, he reached under the water and put his
two hands on her waist. Pulling her off her feet in the

buoyant water, he lifted her up and kissed her. Then, he let go of her body, and as she floated back down into the water he lifted his legs so that he floated with her, and their warm wet bodies moved together. His legs came around hers in a powerful embrace, and his hands began to caress her arms and back in the warm, gentle water.

With the agility of a seal she twisted herself and freed her legs. With a powerful, quick motion she began a strong swimming stroke that shot her away from him out into the center of the pool. The splashing echoed back as loud as a waterfall.

"No!" she called, and her voice came back *no, no, no,* as it echoed off the roof. "I already did your one thing. The bet's off! Squared! It's time to get out of here and go home!" Every word she said echoed back to him. She could not see his face, and all she could hear was the awful sound of her own voice, loud and imperative, in the dark pool house. She was treading water, wondering what he would do.

Without a word he moved to the nearest ladder and climbed out. She swam to the far ladder, and finding her clothes in the dark, quickly slipped off the wet suit and put on her things as best she could over her damp body. Barefooted, she walked over to the boys' dressing room and tapped on the door. "Are you ready, Malcolm?" she whispered. There was no answer and a wave of panic hit her. What if he had left her here alone? She knew she couldn't manage the window by herself, and she had left her purse in his car. How would she get back to Cardston? She would be found here in the morning. Disgraced. For the first time in weeks she thought about her teaching contract and how a scandal would affect her career.

She thought she had become free, daring, adventurous—even a little bohemian. Now she felt her recklessness was some mysterious self-destructive need. Her way of saying, "I don't care!"

Tears of fright came to her eyes, and as she started to leave the dressing room to start exploring other avenues of escape the door opened, and Malcolm's hand reached out for her. "Come on, let's get out of here," he said. She sobbed with relief. He didn't say anything more but took her over to the window, hoisted her over the sill, and lowered her to the ground on the other side. With an agile jump he was on the ground beside her, and they pushed through the bushes behind the building and into the car. He put the key in the ignition, but before he turned it he suddenly said, "Sh-h-h," grabbed her head, and pushed it down. She heard a car drive onto the gravel of the parking lot. A beam of light shot over their heads. She heard feet crunching and a door rattling, and after what seemed an eternity the car drove away.

They remained crouched in the seat for a few more moments. Then Malcolm said, "I think it's safe now. That was our local constable making his rounds."

"Oh, Malcolm," she exclaimed. "If we'd been in there five more minutes . . ." Her voice was filled with apprehension.

Malcolm chuckled. "Yes, if we'd been in there five more minutes, who knows what might have happened."

* * *

After that wild night Catherine did some thinking about what she was doing with her life. Her relationship with Malcolm was a puzzle to her. He was not any of the things she had always imagined in a man. He was not gentlemanly. His idea of a good time was wild excitement and his friends were chosen carelessly. He was arrogant and self-confident. Not only did he make no attempt to hide his faults, he wore them like badges of accomplishment. He teased her and mocked her and made fun of everything she valued. With clear eyes she could look at him and at the madness of the summer together and know she was headed for nothing but trouble and regret. But it was the very excitement of him that held her. Some impulsive, wild part of her wanted to confront, risk, experience—and he was irresistible in his reckless, hell-bent way. Wisdom told her she should stop seeing him, terminate the relationship while she could still walk away relatively untouched by the contradictions of his life, but he exerted a compelling fascination for her. Besides, she felt at times that he really cared for her and understood her better than she did. Somewhere in her heart she felt he was not entirely the man he pretended to be. She had seen him caring for sick animals, had experienced his sorrow as he left a dry farm where a man sat helplessly watching his life withering away in the hot sun of the wheat fields. She knew Malcolm was hating this summer, hating the awful destruction of the white-hot days and the voracious grasshoppers in the dry and dying fields, while he stood helplessly by. She understood that there was a part of Malcolm that acknowledged the dissipation and waste in his own life, and the lives of his friends, but he used it as an escape.

The drinking, dancing, wild rides, and midnight escapades helped him to forget and got him through the days. He believed in nothing but himself, and when the earth dried up and showed him he could be defeated, he turned from that defeat in a kind of glorious defiance against all the rules of God and man. She, too, had known defeat, and maybe that was their true bond. They were both shouting in the wind, living for the minute—the hour—and the devil take what was left.

She could not stop seeing him anymore than she could stop the endless days of summer or the despair that was settling on the drought-stricken prairie town like the fine dust that sifted through the windows and doors and coated everything.

After the night in the swimming pool, Malcolm did not try to touch her again, but he still took her everywhere with him. They traveled the long roads of Alberta, usually with three or four other young people in the car, singing songs and telling jokes while the men drank beer and smoked. Some of the girls smoked, too. They saw small rodeos in little towns and stayed afterward to dance or eat. The men invented ridiculous contests, like throwing a penny so that it would stay on the molding of a cafe door, and the girls would gather around and cheer. The wagers would be paid with gusto, and another contest would be invented.

One evening after a local rodeo, the cowboys rounded up horses and the group went riding. They rode western saddles, and Catherine felt free and excited to be on a horse once more. Her mare was spirited and muscular, a tough little cow pony, with strong legs. She handled the animal well, and one of the cowboys came over to her. "Where'd you learn to sit a horse like that, Miss Summerwell?" he asked with open admiration.

"I was raised on a horse," Catherine answered.

"I'd be honored if you'd ride with me tonight," the young man asked.

"Happy to," Catherine answered, and the two of them set off across the prairie, their horses galloping across the open field.

It was exhilarating and they rode for over an hour, outdistancing the rest of the group until they were alone on the moon-bright plain. In the warm summer night Catherine could have gone on forever, but when they realized the rest of the party was nowhere to be seen, they turned their horses reluctantly and went back to rejoin the rest of the group. Malcolm was sarcastic when they returned. "Enjoying a bit of the local color?" he asked, looking meaningfully at the young cowboy, but addressing Catherine.

"You were welcome to come along—anyone who could keep up was welcome to come!" she replied spiritedly.

Malcolm pretended to wince at her cutting reply. "Whoa!" he exclaimed. "Maybe you're learning more from me than I thought!"

He reined in his horse and wheeled away from her. In a few moments she saw him talking to a young woman from Magrath. The girl worked in a doctor's office, and she had a sharp, pretty face and wore cheap, tight clothes.

After they put the horses away the group went into town to a small restaurant for a dinner of hamburgers and onions. The men had a flask of whiskey in one of the cars, and as the night progressed several of them became rowdy and flushed. One or two of the girls went outside and came back with a telltale brightness in their eyes and color flaming their faces. The girl who had been with Malcolm earlier had gone outside to have a drink on a dare from one of the young men. When she came in, she was giggling and her walk was a little unstable.

It was the first time Catherine had seen a woman drunk, and she watched with fascination. One of the men had a guitar, and when he began playing a western tune, the girl began to sing. It was a sad song about a horse that no one could ride, and the tune and the words were touching. The girl's voice was slurred, but she had a lovely voice, musical and sweet, and a general feeling of appreciation settled over the group. Suddenly the music picked up, and the young woman begin to sing "Oh, My Darlin', Clementine." "Sing along, everybody!" she shouted, and the guitar player began to sing with her. She walked over to Malcolm and sat on his lap, throwing her arms around his neck and pressing his face against her swelling bosom. "Sing!" she importuned him, and then bent back until she almost fell off his lap.

He reached out, laughing, and grabbed her, and holding her on his lap, he joined in with hearty gusto. "You are lost and gone forever, dreadful sorry— Clementine."

By now everyone was singing, and one of the other girls jumped up on a table and pretended she was leading an orchestra. "Next!" cried the girl on Malcolm's lap. "What shall we sing next?"

"By the Light of the Silvery Moon!" someone called, and the girl on the table began to sway to the music. She was a short girl with shapely legs and a tiny waist. As the music continued, she proceeded to do an imitation of a musical comedy star, dancing on the tabletop, kicking up her legs and shaking her shoulders provocatively. The men whistled and applauded, and her face flushed with the attention. The girl seemed almost mesmerized by the applause, standing alone on the tabletop in the sleazy cafe, dreaming it was a stage. She was spellbinding. One of the young ranchers, a big, quiet, hard-working man, had been drinking. He watched the girl dancing, and suddenly, without warning, he stood up, staggered over to the table, and pulled her down. He was so tall and strong that her feet did not touch the floor, and he walked over to the far corner of the room to a dim booth, carrying her. The group laughed and shouted catcalls. "That's the way you get to own a ranch!" "Just take what you want, right, Jake?" The rancher ignored them and pushed the girl into the booth and slid in beside her.

Catherine saw him kiss the girl harshly, and she wondered why no one said anything or tried to stop him. "Do you think she needs help?" she asked the young cowboy who was sitting beside her.

He snorted. "Are you kidding! She's been trying to snag him for a year now. If you tried to interfere, she'd probably scratch your eyes out!"

"What do you mean?" Catherine whispered.

"Wal-l-l," drawled the cowboy, "there ain't too much for a woman around here except gettin' married—and there ain't too much to marry except poor dumb cowboys and dirt farmers. So's if you're lucky enough to get a fellow like Jake there, who owns a fair piece of land and a good herd of cattle, well, you've come a far piece in a short time. Only thing is Jake knows there's plenty girls out there dyin' to get him, and he's a little tight with his belongin's, so he's been mighty careful. He'll spring for a good time but not much else. Reckon the only way he's going to get caught is if some girl catches him, good and proper, and can prove it. You know what I mean?" The cowboy had been drinking, too, and it had loosened his tongue.

Catherine knew exactly what he meant, and she looked back at the young rancher and the young woman in the corner of the cafe. Something told her that what the cowboy had said was right—the girl was trying her hardest to seduce the rancher, and from what Catherine could see she was doing a good job of it.

She glanced over at Malcolm to see what he was thinking. The other girl was still sitting on his lap, laughing and singing, and around them the others were humming, eating, and flirting. The room was filled with cigarette smoke. Five men were playing cards at one table, with girls watching over their shoulders. Suddenly, the girl on Malcolm's lap bent down and kissed him full on the lips, then her head slumped. "I think I'm going to be sick," she groaned. Malcolm jumped up and assisted her out the door. In a few moments they returned. The girl's face was white and Malcolm was supporting her weight.

"Hey! Dave, didn't you bring Mabel?" he called to a bank clerk who was playing in the poker game.

"Yeah," the man replied.

"Well, I think it's time you took her home. She's about ready to pass out," Malcolm said.

The group began to move toward the door. The fun had worn off the evening, and they were tired. Heads were aching from the drink and the smoke.

By the time Malcolm and Catherine drove into Cardston the dawn was already staining the eastern sky pink. Catherine had a bitter taste in her mouth from the coffee grounds, and her skin felt scorched and bruised as though all the nerves in her body were lying exposed. It was almost painful to sit against the rough car seat, and the bumping of the car across the roads was jarring. When Malcolm drove up to her house, she was out of the door almost before the car had stopped.

"Catherine," he said, "if it makes any difference, I'm sorry. That girl didn't mean a thing. Besides, we're not tied to each other!"

"There's nothing to be sorry for," Catherine said. "Good night, Malcolm."

"Good day, you mean," he said, looking up at the sky, bitterly. "And it looks like another scorcher!" He drove away, and she walked listlessly into the house.

Malcolm didn't call for two weeks. During that time Catherine worked on her garden, sewed some new clothes for the coming school year, wrote long letters to her family and friends, and walked every afternoon to the creek and back.

The days passed with agonizing slowness, and she found herself regretting her decision not to teach summer school. When the regular year had ended, she had felt burned out and tired. She had decided she needed the summer to read and refresh herself before starting to teach again, but now she thought it had been a foolish decision, and the weight of the summer days hung heavily upon her. She tried not to think about Malcolm. If his intention had been to show her a side of life she had never seen, he had certainly succeeded in doing that, but she felt certain his uncharacteristic attraction for her was over. She remembered their last evening together with feelings of disgust and shame— and pity, too, for those young people, self-destructive and undirected. She had observed the meaninglessness in their lives and had pitied them; but if she looked at herself objectively, she knew that she was somewhat like them.

She had left Mount Royal disgraced. She had loved and lost the wrong man. Her childhood friends had found meaning and security in their lives, but she was left alone. And now, in the emptiness of her little apartment she knew that she could not bear to think this was to be her life—this little room and the classroom. It wasn't enough! At least the company of Malcolm's friends had filled the hours and created an illusion of belonging, and of gaiety and warmth.

With all her heart Catherine longed to outgrow her need for Malcolm. She refused to become like the girl dancing on the table, so desperate for affection that she would grab at lust and call it love.

One night she wakened and her bedroom was stifling hot. She went out into the living room to open the windows. A small rustle of breeze stirred the curtains as she poured a glass of water and sat at the table sipping it. Weariness pressed down on her, weariness and hopelessness, and she felt the perspiration running between her breasts and thighs. With an impatient gesture she undid her nightgown and walked over to stand by the window. The breeze began to cool her, and impulsively, she pulled off the gown and stood in the breeze unclothed, gasping for the cooling air. As she turned slowly in the breeze she saw herself outlined by the moonlight in the full-length mirror that hung on the back of her door. In the darkness her ripe breasts, slender waist, and rounded hips reminded her of a woman in a painting. She lifted her hair from her neck, and the lift of her arms gave her body a classical, graceful line. "In the dark, without clothes, I am beautiful," she thought sadly, wistfully, "and no one will ever know. No one will ever see me like this—or care. It doesn't matter! All of this for waste—all this love—this body—wasted! And it will get old and wither, and no one will ever know." She stared at her unexplored body, which she herself so seldom saw, and mourned it as though it were a lost friend.

When Malcolm called, she did not hang up as she had originally planned. His voice was tense and angry. "I've got to get out of this burg, or I'm going to do something rash!" he said without preamble. "Another week of this heat, and there won't be enough crops left to feed the grasshoppers. It's like living at a wake! Will you go up to Waterton with me for the dance tonight?"

"Yes," she heard herself saying.

"Pick you up in an hour," he said and hung up.

Catherine walked out to the car when he honked. She was wearing a thin white silk blouse and a linen skirt with sandals on her bare feet. "Is it just my imagination, or does it seem even hotter than usual this afternoon?" she asked.

The sky was not its usual clear blue, and over the distant mountains clouds were forming. "The weatherman at the courthouse says the humidity has picked up. He thinks it might even rain one of these days. About a month too late is all." Malcolm's voice was harsh and impatient. "What are we in business for? Why do I study all my life to help men bring in better crops, when a stupid thing like the weather can twist you like a piece of chaff! What good is it?"

He drove at a reckless speed down the straight dusty road out of the town into the surrounding countryside. On every side the signs of drought were visible. The wheat was sparse and brown in the fields. Herds of cattle foraged listlessly in dusty pastures, and the irrigation ditches ran half-filled with sluggish muddy water. As they neared the foothills, the road began to climb and twist and the breeze became cooler and more brisk. At the hills the grass along the road began to green, and a few wild flowers grew on the slopes.

The road climbed higher and the hills became more precipitous, winding perilously along the sides of slopes, past valleys and small lakes, until they reached the altitude where trees began to grow. Pines lined the roads as they twisted upward through the jagged, thrusting mountains, cutting through a pass made by a chain of lakes, and finally dropping into the mountain-surrounded town of Waterton. It was early evening, but it was already growing dark, and looking up past the enormous, brooding peaks that shadowed the town, Catherine saw that the sky was darkening with heavy clouds.

"It really may rain," she said to Malcolm, trying to lighten his mood.

"Don't hold your breath!" was his short reply. "Besides, rain in the mountains is a far cry from rain on the prairie."

The evening was a failure. Malcolm danced roughly, carelessly, and he refused to talk. She danced with a few others who cut in on them, but when she returned to Malcolm his face was like a thundercloud. "What do you want to do?" she asked him. "I don't think either one of us is having any fun. Why don't we just go home and call it a good try."

Without a word Malcolm turned and walked toward the door. She almost had to run after him to keep up with his angry strides. When they were in the car, he wrenched it into gear and sped out of the village. Without slackening his speed, he roared down the winding mountain roads. Twice he forced oncoming cars to turn off the road as he sped by them, and Catherine became frantic with fear.

Malcolm!" she screamed. "What are you doing! Stop! You're driving like a maniac. You can't drive this fast on these roads! Stop!" By now she was crying. "Please, please, please, stop! You'll kill us! Please, Malcolm! Please!"

He ignored her pleas and continued to careen around the dark curves, his tires screeching and his headlights sweeping the night. She had hidden her face in her hands and was sobbing. The sound of her sobbing must have penetrated his fury because gradually he slowed the car. Finally, at a small intersection he turned off the road and drove the car slowly to the brow of a hill overlooking a small lake. With a deep sigh he stopped the car and pulled on the emergency brake.

He put his hands on the top of the steering wheel and leaned his head against them. "I'm really sorry to have frightened you, Catherine. It was like something in me had to come out! I needed to shake my fist at the gods or something like that, I guess.

"No," he continued sadly, turning to look at her, "I think maybe I needed to shake my fist at you. I needed to say to you, 'Who needs you, Catherine Summerwell?' I don't need anybody and certainly not a high-bred, mixed-up, tightly wound schoolteacher. So why can't I ignore you. Go my own way? Why do I have to keep coming back again and again? What is it that brings me back to you?"

"It's all the kindness and affection we have between us," Catherine said with gentle sarcasm.

"Don't," he said, and put his finger on her lips. "Don't! I taught you to talk like that—but not tonight!" His voice was filled with genuine anguish.

"I think it's because I want you," he said, his voice controlled and analytical. "I think I've wanted to make love to you from the first moment when you bumped into me in the hall and spilled all of my wheat seeds. All that desire pent up for so long, it's bound to make a man do strange things." He laughed mirthlessly.

"Catherine," his voice was like a groan, "I can't sit next to you anymore and not reach out—I have to touch you. Do you understand what I'm saying? I'm not a marrying man. I told you from the start. I'm not a man you can count on or trust—I don't believe in traditions or ties or old debts. So if we have anything, all I can promise is that it will be for now—and no more. But I also must tell you that unless you give me what I need, I am going to have to find it somewhere else. I'm human, Catherine, and this crazy game we've been playing all summer has to stop. One way or another, this is the end right here, right now."

All Catherine heard were the words "the end." She knew he meant it. He was a hard and proud man— self-reliant, arrogant, and unbending. This was an ultimatum, and she understood his terms exactly. If she told him no, he would turn the car around and drive her back to Cardston, but he would never call again. She thought about the rest of the summer stretching before her, the white endless days—the years stretching ahead, one exactly like the other. She thought about her virgin body withering under the stiff, dark clothes of an old maid schoolteacher.

"What did it matter anyway? Who would know? Who would care?" she thought bitterly.

"All right," she said.

"What do you mean by 'all right'?" Malcolm asked.

"I mean, do with me as you will—or whatever women say in these circumstances."

He didn't laugh. Seriously, he asked, "Are you sure, Catherine, because if you are, there's no turning back. I won't be stopped."

"Yes," she said quietly, staring straight ahead through the windshield at the starless night and the black lake.

Without another word, he pulled her toward him

and kissed her. She submitted to his embrace without resistance, and his lips hungrily roamed her eyes, her cheeks, and her lips with soft, searching kisses. Then he gathered her against him with fierce strength and kissed her lips hard and long. She remained in his arms, her own arms quiet at her sides, her lips soft but unresponding, and all the time he was kissing her, her mind would not stop. It was as though she had left her body on its own and was watching dispassionately as it was held and loved by this hard, complex man.

"So this is how it's to be," she thought, "in the front seat of an old car with a man I don't love. How little I'm worth, if I could give myself away, just to put off being alone for another day—another week—another year. I thought I was so much better than those other girls, but I might just as well have drunk the wine and danced on the tabletops.

"What a joke, I imagined I was valuable—that I needed to be sought after and won—and here I am, giving myself to a man who has never done a thing to please me or try to win me! Even now—no promises— no future! He doesn't even want me to remember to-night if it means I would be tied to him!"

He was kissing her again, and his hands were rough on her body. His breathing was heavy and he struggled to get out from under the steering wheel. She moved over closer to the door, and he moved to the center of the seat where his arms were freer.

A gust of wind shook the car, and her head jerked up. The trees by the lake were whipping in the wind, like dark shadows. He continued to hold her with one arm, but with the other hand he stroked her silk blouse, and then slowly began to undo the buttons on her blouse. It took all her will to keep from pushing his hands away, so she continued to stare out the windshield, pretending a calm she did not feel, like the rigid indifference she assumed in the doctor's office when he listened to her heart. She felt Malcolm's hands on her breast, and without wanting to do so, she glanced down and saw her blouse open and the curve of her breasts outlined above the line of her bra.

Malcolm moved his head back slightly and rested his hands on her shoulders, his eyes resting on her. "You are beautiful. More beautiful than I imagined!" he muttered, and his voice was almost angry.

Another gust of wind shook the car, and she began to cry. Not sobs, just a thin stream of hopeless tears that coursed down her face. He raised his hand to her cheeks and wiped the tears away with the palms of his hands. A sudden gust of rain hit the windshield, and she winced at the sound. "I'm sorry," she whispered. "It's raining."

"So it is," he said, and his voice sounded weary and sad. She made no move to button her blouse, and he took his hands away from her shoulders and sat back, turning in his seat so that he could look at her, but not touching her.

"I guess it wasn't your body I wanted after all," he said, his voice thick with bitterness. "Not like this anyway! A man can hardly make love to a corpse. Let me tell you, Catherine, you have found the perfect way to kill desire. Nondefense is the perfect defense. I guess you're stronger than I am, after all. You win! Or maybe you lose! I don't know, because I don't know what it is you want!"

She was still crying. "I don't know either, Malcolm.

I don't know either. But I guess it isn't this. Couldn't we . . ."

"No!" Malcolm replied vehemently, "don't try to go building this into something it isn't. I can go buy what I want if I need to or find it in any receptionist office or dime store in the territory. I go alone, Catherine. I always have and I always will. Although, heaven help me, if there were ever a woman who could have changed my mind, it would have been you. But you're too much for me! Too complicated, too strong. I'd wear out against you!"

He looked at her one more time, and his hand, very tenderly, traced the pulsating line of her breast. "What a waste! What a terrible, terrible waste!" he said, echoing her own thought.

She bent and buttoned her blouse, and he slid under the steering wheel. In silence they drove through the rain-drenched night. The hot, heavy air was made cool and fresh, and the summer rain poured down upon the mountains and the hills and the dry thirsting prairies. The rain ran in rivulets through the yearning fields and on into the emptied ditches and ponds. Roots that were half-dead reached down and drank, and the animals, sleeping in the fields, breathed deeply and felt their hot tired hooves mire into the mud. Farmers turned to their wives in cooling bedrooms, wakened to the prayed-for sound of rain pounding on the roof, and they held the women in their arms and celebrated the seeds of new life being planted.

Catherine felt the bitter restlessness wash from Malcolm as they drove through the rainy night. A crash of lightning illuminated his face, and she saw he was smiling, watching the rushing rivulets on the side of the road like a starving man glimpsing provisions. All around her in the night was the sense of awakening life and vitality. She alone, in the abundant rain, felt herself shrinking, drying up inside.

"It's a funny thing," she said, as they drove. "I lost one man because I was too eager, too passionate and vibrant. And now I've lost you because I was too unresponsive. I think there must be something basically wrong with me."

"No, Catherine," Malcolm said, "you haven't found yourself, that's all. You have to reach out for what you want. You can't wait for others to fill you up. Maybe, when you know what it is you're looking for—then you'll know how to get it!"

"I have lost you, haven't I, Malcolm?" she said later as they drove up in front of her house.

"Yes," he said, and his voice was heavy with sadness. "But then we never really had each other. There's nothing for us, Catherine. We are bent on different ways, and all we can give each other is a lot of hurt. We'll see each other around town, of course, but I don't think we should go out together again."

"Can't we be . . ." she began, but he cut her off roughly.

"Friends!" His voice was harsh. "Don't be a child, Catherine! It isn't like that in real life. No! We can't be friends." He reached over in front of her and opened the door so she could get out. She stepped down from the car and the rain, gentler now, sprinkled her hair and face. But she was indifferent to it as she waited, holding the car door open, feeling it couldn't end like this so finally and abruptly.

He pulled the door away from her to close it, but then he opened it again and looked at her standing lonely in the rain.

"Not friends, Catherine. But if you ever need me . . . I'll be there—for old times' sake." He paused. "You're quite a girl!" he said, and with that he slammed the door and drove off into the wet night. She walked alone down the path to her quiet, empty rooms.

CHAPTER NINETEEN

A year passed. As each week and month was added to the next, Catherine's days gradually became so similar as to be almost indistinguishable. She taught her required courses with rigorous and meticulous care, and her classroom presence held the attention of her students. But somewhere along the way she had lost the fire and enthusiasm of her first years of teaching, and now she deliberately kept a professional distance between herself and her students. In the early months of her teaching career she had researched, organized, and created fresh approaches to each of her subjects, but now she found that keeping up with the daily demands of the students and school administration left her little time or energy for further study or deviation from her meticulous lesson plans. The students spoke of her as a good teacher. Their whispered evaluation was that you learned a lot in her class, but it was "kind of boring." "Besides," they would add, "she's really strict."

The monotony of her routine struck her as she pulled out lectures that she had given before, or heard students asking the same questions that she had answered for their older brothers and sisters a year or two earlier.

In the morning she walked to school, and in the afternoon she retraced the same route back to her apart-

ment. She spent evenings grading papers, writing report cards, and completing the countless types of
paperwork required of teachers. Then she ate a simple
supper and would go for a short walk or read a book
until bedtime.

Catherine had made a few friends among the other
unmarried faculty members, and occasionally they
would get together for a game of bridge or to see a
movie. On the weekends, however, the other teachers
usually went home to farms or towns in the surrounding area, and Catherine would spend the weekend
cleaning house, gardening, or shopping.

Ladean and Dan came home for Christmas, and
Catherine spent the holiday week with the Watkins
family. It was a joyous time of togetherness, but after
Ladean and Dan returned to Edmonton, the winter
set in, long, dark, and dreary.

The following summer Catherine arranged to take a
walking tour of the British Isles. She was anxious to
do research in the Northern Lakes area to see if she
could add some life to her teachings of Sir Walter
Scott and the Romantic Poets. She saw some magnificent performances of Shakespeare, and she and the
other English teachers on the tour found the countryside magnificent. However, the tensions in Europe
were severe, and the English people, viewing the resur-
gent power of a Germany that they believed defeated
in 1918, were angry and disturbed. The future hung
like a dark cloud on the horizon in England.

Catherine prepared to return to the wide vistas of
the Canadian prairies with relief. The tour group
parted with tears and promises that they would write
and keep in touch, but Catherine knew that summer

friendships had a way of evaporating in the first chill of the winter. The teachers scattered to their various schools, and at the end of August Catherine returned to Cardston and her small apartment.

As she entered the room she was struck with its bleakness and cramped space. It alarmed her that she had lived in this room for over two years and had become oblivious to its inadequacy. "I am not living," she said to herself, "I am merely going through the motions."

That evening, after she had unpacked, she got out her notebooks with the lesson plans for her courses in the coming year. By chance, the first book she opened was Shakespeare. When she riffled the pages, a loose sheet fell out of the book, and as she stooped to pick it up, she saw that it was a yellowed program from the summer performance of *Midsummer Night's Dream*. She read over the names of the actors and conjured up in her mind the memory of that warm summer night with the audience packed with townspeople laughing and applauding.

"Where had it all gone?" she wondered. "Why don't I reach out for it anymore? Have I become so afraid to try, to expose myself to failure or ridicule or caring or pain? I've done to my life what I did to my bedroom all those summers ago. I've taken out everything that gave it any warmth or light or gaiety, and I am living inside a bleak, white cell. One extreme to the other. Too much or too little."

The next morning as she was washing out her travel clothes and arranging her fall wardrobe, there was a knock on the door.

"Come in," she called from behind the ironing board.

"Coming!" called a happy voice, and the door was flung open.

"Ladean! I didn't know you were in town. How marvelous to see you!" Catherine left the ironing board and threw her arms around her friend. "You look great! Where's Dan? How long are you going to be in town?"

"Oh, Catherine! It's so good to have you back! We've been here most of the month, and I'm really cross at that old walking tour for keeping you away so long!"

"Please stay and visit," Catherine begged. "I've been feeling sorry for myself this morning—alone and blue, you know—and not at all happy about facing the prospect of those school rooms for another year."

"Well, Dan and I are about to change all of that! You need to get out of this room and have a fling before work begins! Start by having dinner with us tonight! Okay?"

Catherine hesitated for a moment. "You're sure I wouldn't be imposing?"

"Oh, Catherine!" Ladean exploded. "How could you say such a thing? We've only got three weeks before we have to return to the university. Another year and Dan will graduate! I can't wait!"

"Is it hard?" Catherine asked sympathetically. "Your letters are always so cheerful . . ."

"Yes, that's the written record, but sometimes . . ." Ladean paused, and her face fell. "I lost a baby this year."

"Oh, I'm sorry!" Catherine said.

"I didn't write you about it," Ladean continued. "It was only a miscarriage—but I had to stop working, and, well, time passes very slowly when you are home alone all day. Dan's so wrapped up in his studies." She visibly brightened. "Things will be better next year! Dan's got a fine job offer from a cattle broker in Calgary when he graduates. Once we get away from Edmonton and the university . . ."

"What's wrong with the university?" Catherine was surprised and concerned by Ladean's revelations.

"Nothing's wrong with the university, if you're a student. But I'm neither fish nor fowl. All those cute coeds walking around in their darling clothes, while I have to save every penny! I feel so old when I go on the campus! I look at those kids walking around, and I want to shout at them, 'Hey, don't look at me like I'm nothing! Three years ago I was prancing around these halls just like you, into every activity, flirting with the boys!' What happened to that girl, Catherine? I can't find her anymore—she's turned into a former schoolteacher, a little wife who meets her husband in his lab. The university is like a living memory for me, and it's filled with the shadows of the person I was— who doesn't exist anymore!"

Catherine, listening, didn't know what to say. How could it be that Ladean, who seemed to have everything, felt lost and lonely. Maybe it was true what Malcolm said of her—she only saw people as she wanted to see them. Idealistically. She didn't really know or understand them at all.

"But you and Dan—" she struggled to ask. "You're all right, aren't you? I mean, doesn't he understand how you feel? Nothing's changed between you, has it?"

Ladean was quiet for a moment. "No, we haven't changed. We still love each other, and I love being Dan's wife more than anything in the world! That's worth everything! But no, I don't believe he knows how I feel—how could he? He loves school—to him it's classes and learning. It's his world! When I see him there, he's part of it and I'm the one left out! He doesn't even know he's part of anything. He's so unaware of his environment—it would be like trying to explain water to a fish. He wouldn't know what I was talking about!"

Catherine gave a short involuntary laugh and began to fold up her ironing board. "I thought, if you found someone to love you—and you loved him back—that was enough! You'd be set for life!"

Ladean looked at Catherine thoughtfully. "I know. It's the 'Happy Ever After' syndrome. It's true, though, in a funny way. This is going to sound dumb, but it is enough—even though it isn't enough."

"You're right," Catherine said, "that was dumb!"

The two friends laughed, and then Ladean pondered with a frown. "What I mean," she tried again, "what I mean is that love isn't the whole answer, but it makes a secure foundation on which to build the rest."

"Well, a foundation's a far cry from a completed structure," Catherine observed. "I guess you're right, though, it's hard to build anything without one."

"Oh, Catherine," Ladean said and flushed. "I didn't mean to say anything to hurt you. There are other foundations . . ."

"No," Catherine replied calmly. "You haven't hurt me! Truly you haven't, Ladean. As a matter of fact, it helps a lot to know I'm not the only one with problems. If that offer for dinner's still good, I'll go get my hat and we can walk over to your house together."

The next three weeks whirled by. Dan seemed to appreciate the influence Catherine had on Ladean, and the two young women chatted eagerly, while Dan listened and made occasional comments with his engaging smile. Once, as they were walking home from a movie, he remarked, "I haven't seen Ladean so happy all year, Catherine. You are like a tonic for her!"

"She's a tonic for me!" Catherine replied. "And so are you, Dan! I haven't had this much fun in ages!"

"Friendship is the next best invention, right after Motherhood and Apple Pie," Ladean pronounced.

"Right!" said Dan, and linked arms with both of the girls. "And I say here's to friendship—may it last forever!"

Catherine basked in the warmth of their affection, and her days were filled with merriment and laughter. She had almost forgotten the impending days of school, the dusty files of lesson plans, and the gray winter days looming around the corner.

September was golden, and the harvested wheat flowed into the bins in great abundance. Fattened calves grazed in the early autumn pastures, and root cellars were filled with carrots, onions, potatoes, beets, and the provender of winter. Mrs. Watkins was busy canning fruit, and she enlisted Catherine and Ladean's help while Dan went to the Allred farm to help bring in the harvest.

The women canned pears and peaches. The juice in the bottles looked like liquid amber. They pickled beets, cauliflower, and cucumbers. They filled the stoneware pickle crocks with vinegar, spices, and alum, and the rich scent of the pickles filled the basement. They canned tomatoes, with bay leaf and onion, and put up jars of apricot jam with the apricot pits cracked and roasted so they tasted like almonds in the jam. They put up raspberry preserves and apple-sauce—bottles of corn, peas, beans, pear butter, and chili sauce. On the dark basement shelves the colors of the fruit gleamed in the clear shining bottles, and as the bounty mounted on the shelves, Catherine thought no miser could be more proud of hordes of gold than were these women as the work of their hands caused the storeroom to groan with plenty.

Late one evening Ladean, Catherine, and Mrs. Watkins were in the kitchen. They had finished the last batch of cherries and were wiping the bottles with a damp cloth to remove any outer spills before they tightened the caps.

"That's the last of it!" said Mrs. Watkins. "Winter can come; I'm ready for it!"

Catherine felt a clutch at her heart. It was true, winter was on its way. Ladean and Dan would be leaving in a few days, and her school would start the following week. She looked around the warm, cheery kitchen, at Ladean and her mother, and the bright lamplight. The window was open, and the cool evening air was blowing the curtains.

"I guess I'd better be getting home," Catherine said tentatively. "It's getting late and I have a preliminary faculty meeting tomorrow morning."

"Oh, Cath!" Ladean cried. "Can't you stay a minute or two longer? Dan should be in from the farm any minute. Maybe we can go get an ice cream cone or something."

"Well, maybe," Catherine said, her spirits lifting a little. "I can wait a little longer."

They sat chatting in the kitchen, and in a few minutes they heard the front door open. "Dan!" exclaimed Ladean, with a happy lilt in her voice. She ran out of the room. Mrs. Watkins and Catherine were left in the kitchen. With her hands up to the elbows in suds at the sink, Mrs. Watkins was washing the last of the canning utensils. "You go on, Catherine! Have that ice cream cone with the young folks and then get on to bed if you've got a meeting tomorrow. You've put in a hard day."

"All right, Mrs. Watkins! I guess I will go. I've really had a wonderful time. Who would think that canning could be so much fun?"

"Many hands make light work!" Mrs. Watkins said with a motherly smile. She came over with her sudsy hands and gave Catherine a kiss on the cheek. "Thanks for helping. Now get on with you!"

"Good night," Catherine smiled, and walked out of the kitchen, down the little hall into the living room. Without thinking she stepped into the living room without announcing her presence. Dan and Ladean were on the couch. Dan's arms were holding Ladean on his lap, and he was kissing her with such intense passion that Catherine gasped with surprised embarrassment! At the sound, Ladean and Dan sprang apart guiltily, and their faces were infused with color.

"Are—are you ready to go?" Ladean asked, blushing and awkward.

"Oh!" Catherine said. "I'm sorry, I didn't—" She collected herself. "I was coming to tell you that I think I'm too tired for ice cream. I'll just run on home!"

"No! No!" Dan said, his voice unsteady. "We'd love to have you come!"

"Thanks, Dan—Ladean, but I have that meeting in the morning—I'll see you tomorrow probably. 'Night!" Catherine hurried to the front door quickly, and walked rapidly outside.

"How could I have been so stupid?" she berated herself. "I must have looked so foolish! The original third wheel! They must be starved for privacy, and I've accepted every invitation to be with them!"

Entirely by chance she had caught a glimpse of their private world, and she realized now how precious and enclosed it must be. It wounded her that she had, albeit unwittingly, intruded upon that world. She wondered how many times she had been with them when they had privately yearned to be alone, and she had been there like a pebble in the way of a closing door.

The next morning she got out a dark cotton dress with shirt waist collar and cuffs, and brushed her hair in crisp, punishing strokes, pulling it back into a tight, smooth twist. She put on sensible square-heeled oxfords and when she looked at her makeup on the dresser, she suddenly thought, "Why bother!" With a quick swipe of her hand, she whisked the jars and tubes into the top drawer.

Tailored, neat, and plain, Miss Summerwell entered the faculty meeting and took her place. Former teachers greeted her, and she was introduced to the new members of the staff. A few inquired about her summer, and then Mr. Solembaugh began the long meeting, explaining policy, answering questions, and presenting the school year calendar.

A heavy black fly was buzzing in the bottom of the window next to Catherine. Outside the window the sky was blue as turquoise and the cottonwood trees were golden yellow along the neat streets of the town. The temple glistened white and lovely in its nest of blue spruces at the top of the hill. "Like a painted ship upon a painted sea," she quoted to herself. The colors were vivid and bright.

When she got home from the meeting, Ladean was waiting in the garden behind her apartment. "I thought you'd be getting back about now,". Ladean said cheerfully. "It's such a lovely day, do you want to go for a little walk?"

"Fine," said Catherine, quietly.

They walked for a few moments in stiff silence, then Ladean spoke, awkwardly, shyly, "I'm sorry about last night. I hope you didn't feel embarrassed. It's just that, well, it was kind of a special—I mean—"

Catherine was uncomfortable with the stammered apology. "For Pete's sake don't apologize! You have a perfect right to kiss your husband. I just felt ridiculous walking in on you like that. I should have . . ."

"You shouldn't have done anything!" Ladean interrupted, her voice firm. "We don't normally go around doing that sort of thing in living rooms, but it was an important day for us! Dan says I can tell you. I went to the doctor yesterday, and he told me that I'm going to have a baby. This time it's really going to happen. I can tell—I'm going to carry this baby—and have it!"

Ladean's eyes were glowing. "We were so happy, Catherine . . . and I want you to be happy for us, too!"

"That's wonderful!" Catherine's eyes were shining with loving tears. "I couldn't be happier, Ladean. I know it's what you've wanted."

Ladean turned and faced her with shining eyes. "So now you must promise that you will celebrate with us Saturday night. We want you to have dinner with us and then go to the church dance. Please say you'll come, Catherine. It will be our last party before we go back to Edmonton. Please!"

Catherine smiled at Ladean's friendly urging. "I don't think so, Ladean," she said hesitantly. "I have so much to get ready for school, and you and Dan won't want to have to worry about me . . ."

Ladean grasped her hand. "You are so silly. We want to worry about you! It's our last chance! Don't say no, Catherine, it would leave us with such sad feelings."

It was impossible to resist Ladean's warm pleas, and Catherine shook her head in resignation. "Very well, if you want me. But dances are not my cup of tea—if you'll pardon the allusion!" The friends started laughing, because Ladean, as a devout Mormon, had never had a cup of tea.

"You'll have a splendid time, I promise you!" Ladean declared as they walked back to Catherine's house.

Turning to face her friend, Catherine gave her a mock glare. "If you dare to line up dances for me, and twist your friends' arms to be 'nice' to me, I'll never—never—never go to one of your dances again as long as I live! I promise you!"

"With someone as pretty as you, who needs to line up dances?" Ladean asked. With an impish grin, she turned and sashayed down the path. Catherine stood by the door of her apartment and waved good-bye to Ladean, who stopped at the gate and waved back. "See you!" she called.

On Saturday night the air was golden with the autumn haze and the smell of burning leaves. Not wanting to go to the dance, Catherine had avoided getting ready until the hour before Dan and Ladean were to pick her up. She bathed and brushed out her hair, and then stood in front of her closet trying to decide what to wear. All the clothes in her closet were unsuitable for a dance. They were tailored and dark and mustylooking—an uncomfortably accurate reflection of her life. In sudden defiance she reached under her bed to pull out her heavy leather valise. In it she had placed all her old party dresses and the outgrown clothes that she had brought with her from Calgary when she first came to Cardston. Most of the dresses were unsuitable and out of style. She ransacked the case, pulling out silks, chiffons, linens, dotted swiss, and smiling as the bright-colored light fabrics reminded her of her past. Parties, dances, teas, social afternoons, bridge parties— how long had it been since she had needed to dress for any such occasions?

In the bottom of the suitcase, she found what she was looking for. It was a dress she had bought for the fall prom during her last year of college. Made of burgundy taffeta, the dress was low cut, with capped sleeves, and a simply made bodice and draped skirt. She wasn't sure the dress would still fit, but as she lifted it from its tissue wrappings, and heard the crisp rustle of the lovely fabric, she felt an excitement and anticipation she had not known for a long time.

With care she touched her face with rouge and powder. Her eyes were sparkling, and her long dark lashes needed no mascara. She gathered up her mass of wavy hair and pinned it in a loose chignon, with curling tendrils falling on her forehead and cheeks. Then with her heart thumping, she lifted the whispering skirt over her head and wiggled carefully into the dress. It settled on her shoulders and around her breast with graceful ease. She twisted to do up the side zipper and then tugged at the bodice to be sure it was straight. The dress fitted to perfection, although it was lower than she had remembered, and she worried about the expanse of creamy breast that it revealed.

Stepping into the living room, she paused to look at herself in the full-length mirror. What she saw amazed her. In the dim light of the outer room she looked mysterious and unfamiliar. The shadows around her blended with the dark red of the dress and her shoulders and arms gleamed white. It was a woman who gazed back at her from the mirror, a woman proud and sensual and lovely.

"Well!" she thought to herself, embarrassed at her moment of pride, "It's obvious that the dimmer the lighting—the better I look!" Impatiently, she snapped on the lights and, carefully avoiding looking at herself in the mirror again, she pulled out her box of jewelry to see if she could find something to fill in the bare neckline. She found an old rhinestone necklace in an elaborate imperial pattern, but she knew it was too ostentatious. Finally, she settled on a double strand of pearls. Just as she was screwing on the pearl drop earrings that matched the necklace, there was a knock on the door. "Come in," she called, "it's open."

Dan and Ladean came in, and with them a blast of crisp autumn air.

"Wow!" Dan said when he saw her.

"Yes!" Ladean echoed. "Wow! You look absolutely smashing, Catherine! You're going to knock them dead!"

Ladean was wearing a black satin evening gown with long black sleeves and a sheered bodice. With her black hair the dress was stunning. She had made the dress, copied from a Vogue pattern, just before Dan had returned from his mission. In her hair was a black feather fastened with a rhinestone clip.

"Wow, yourself!" Catherine replied.

"It's clear I am going to have the two best-looking women at the dance," Dan declared, and the girls laughed, feeling young and excited. "Well, let's get going. We don't want to waste a perfectly good orchestra," he said.

As the three of them walked toward the car Ladean talked excitedly to Catherine. "Everyone's going to be here tonight. They're coming from miles around. The harvest is in, and winter's on the way, and this is sort of the last big bash! All the college students leave on Monday—and I know you're going to have fun. Do I really look all right? This dress is so form-fitting! I told Dan I thought I was poking out already, and he told me that was wishful thinking! What do you think, Catherine? Will anybody know? Will they be able to tell?"

Catherine burst out laughing. "No, you goose! You are as thin as a stick! You're just hoping people will guess because you can't stand to keep a secret! The only way people will know you're having a baby is if you tell them!"

"Oh, pshaw!" Ladean pretended to pout. "I was hoping I could start the rumor!"

Dan laughed. "Never fear, honey, they'll know soon enough!"

"Dan's going to give it away himself," Catherine teased, "if he doesn't stop looking like the Cheshire cat!"

They arrived at the chuch hall and joined the crowd of young people surging into the door. The dance floor was packed, and couples swayed shoulder to shoulder, back to back with other couples. The three friends threaded their way to a far corner where a group of young married couples were filling out dance cards. Several of the young husbands signed Catherine for a dance, and for the first half of the evening she passed the time pleasantly, dancing with friends of Ladean and Dan. Toward intermission she was dancing a waltz with a pleasant-looking young pharmacist. He had graduated from the university the year before Catherine, and they were busily comparing notes about mutual friends and professors they had known when Catherine glanced over his shoulder and noticed several of the young wives, clustered in the corner, glancing her way and whispering. The pharmacist's wife was frowning, and irritation and disapproval were evident in every line of her face.

Catherine met the wife's eye, and there was such resentment in the look that Catherine flushed and turned her head quickly away. She was suddenly conscious of her low-cut dress, the vivid rustling skirt, her exotic hairstyle, and she felt conspicuous and ridiculous. "What must they be thinking about me?" she wondered. "What are they saying?" She was suddenly intensely aware of the people around her, and she wondered if it were just her imagination or if they were all looking at her covertly, whispering, speculating. "What is Miss Summerwell doing? Trying to act like a young girl? Immodestly dressed! Who does she think she is?"

She felt the young pharmacist's hand on her waist. Was it grasping her a little more tightly than was proper? She looked into his eyes. He was still talking to her, yet she noticed that he was not looking at her face but taking little darting looks at her bosom as he held her against him. Her head spun in confusion, and she thought that all evening she must have unconsciously been inviting this kind of interest. There was no excuse—she had known the dress was too tight, too low, too flamboyant, and she had worn it anyway. Now she felt the horrible desire to hide. She wanted nothing more than to be back in her own private, dark rooms. Or was she simply imagining all of this? Maybe nobody had even noticed her—or cared.

The confusion of her feelings blurred her mind, and she looked around helplessly, wishing the waltz would end. "I think I'm feeling a little faint, Mr. Harker," she said. "Perhaps I should go out and get a bit of fresh air."

"Why, of course." The serious young pharmacist was instantly concerned. "Are you all right? Shall I go with you?"

"No! No!" she exclaimed, alarmed. That would be dreadful! What would people say if he disappeared outside with her. "No! I'll be back in a few moments! Please just leave me here and return to your wife. No reason for concern at all." She slipped away from him into the crowd by the side of the dance floor and escaped into one of the halls. The building was large, and she was disoriented. Dan had taken her coat, and she couldn't remember where the coat room was. Hurrying along the corridor, she found a small exit door and impulsively she opened it and slipped outside.

She found herself at the side of the building, on a short flight of concrete steps that led to some high shrubs bordering the property. The darkness was a stark contrast to the lighted hall, and there were no windows to shed light onto the area. Only the tiny bulb above the door cast a glow on the steps. The evening was colder than she remembered, and she shivered, but she could not bring herself to go back inside, so she walked forward and sat down on the top step, wrapping her arms around herself to keep warm.

It was then she became aware of the smell of tobacco and a small glow over by the hedges. Someone was smoking in the deserted section of the dark churchyard.

She felt like a schoolteacher at recess, but she knew she had to say something. In her most authoritative voice she began, "I'm sorry, but you do know this is a Mormon church, don't you? There is no smoking on these premises."

A rich, masculine laugh came through the darkness.

"Caught!" said a deep voice, and she heard the sound of a pipe being knocked on a shoe. Then footsteps walked toward her where she sat on the step. She did not want to meet this audacious man, whoever he was, and if it would not have been undignified, she would have stood up and hurried back through the door before he reached her. Instead, she remained seated on the step trying to look calm and self-confident.

The man who appeared in the pale light from the door was of medium height. He had a muscular build, with broad shoulders, and he appeared to loom above her. She still could not see his face very clearly, but she could see he was wearing gray flannel slacks and a tweed jacket with leather patches on the elbows.

"You're shivering," were his first words to her. Then he added in a blunt, matter-of-fact voice, "That's not much of a dress to be wearing on a chilly night like this."

"Well!" she answered, her irritation aroused by his presumption. "It looks like neither one of us was too well prepared for this occasion. I'm overdressed and you are underdressed!"

He was silent for a moment thinking through her remark. "Oh!" he said, without a trace of self-consciousness. "You mean my tweed jacket in the midst of all those Sunday blue suits and pinstripes! At least they're not wearing dinner jackets. Wouldn't make any difference if they were—this is all I have anyway!"

"I'm sorry," Catherine muttered, ashamed of having made such a personal remark. "I shouldn't have said that!"

"Not at all!" The man laughed again. "Look, I didn't mean I didn't like your dress or think it was appropriate. I only meant it isn't warm enough for outdoors. Look! Let's start over again, shall we? But first, may I offer you my jacket?"

By now Catherine was almost blue with cold, and the chill wind was causing her teeth to chatter. For some reason she did not want to leave, and so reluctantly she replied, "If you're sure you'll be warm enough—I wouldn't want to bother you or impose . . ."

"Done!" said the man, and unbuttoning his jacket, he whisked it over her shoulders. It was made of Harris tweed, a harsh, scratchy, manly fabric, and as it settled over her shoulders, she caught the mingled scent of pipe tobacco and aftershave lotion and the indefinable scent of the man himself. She found herself breathing in the delicious odor and her senses reeled with pleasure.

"Now," he continued, "why don't we get off to a better beginning? I'm David Reid." He held out his hand and she shook it formally.

"I'm Catherine Summerwell. How do you do?"

They continued to sit side by side on the stair, and there was an awkward pause. He chuckled. "This isn't a much better start, is it? I'm afraid I'm not very good at social conversation."

"I am," Catherine answered, "but it's boring, so I've gotten out of the habit."

He turned to look at her with curious amusement, and she now could see him more clearly. His face was deeply tanned, and his eyes were dark. Although his features were even, his face had a rugged quality, and judging from the firm set of his jaw, she thought he must do work that was physically challenging. His hair was dark brown and rather longer than was fashionable, and yet he had an appearance of ease and quality that made her feel he was comfortable with himself.

"Yes," he said, regarding her with gentle humor, "I believe you would know all about social conversation. However, since I don't, may I ask a direct question?"

"By all means," Catherine replied. "Since I don't need to answer it if I don't want to."

"Fair enough," he said. "What I want to know is what you are doing at this affair?"

"What do you mean?" she asked, taken aback.

"Well, it seems to me you don't belong here much more than I do. If you did, you certainly wouldn't be sitting out on the side stairs all alone, shivering."

"I don't see that that's any of your business . . ." Catherine began haughtily.

"Of course it's none of my business," he replied, unperturbed by her indignation. "I'm curious, that's all."

Then Catherine found herself laughing. "I'll tell you if you'll tell me why you're here."

"I'm a rancher," he answered. "I live up in the foothills past Lundbreck—almost up to the Crowsnest Pass area. I got all my harvest in and thought I'd come down to civilization for some fun before the winter sets in. Some friends asked me to the dance. I thought I might get to meet some pretty girls." He paused and looked at her quietly. She thought he was going to say more, but instead he kept looking at her, and a slow, generous smile crossed his face.

"I'm a schoolteacher," Catherine said. "I guess my reasons are about the same as yours—only I was hoping I might meet some handsome fellows!" She looked up at him with a teasing, challenging light in her eyes.

"There's a lot of them in there, I suppose," he said.

"A lot of pretty girls, too, I suppose," she answered.

"M-m-m," he assented, and felt for his jacket pocket.

"Oh! I forgot I'm wearing your jacket!" Catherine exclaimed. "Are you getting cold, do you want it back?"

"No," he answered, "I was reaching for my pipe out of habit. I keep forgetting I can't smoke around here! Hey, look!" he said abruptly, "I've got an idea!" He looked at her and hesitated. "I mean, I was thinking, if you aren't planning to go back to the dance, maybe I could take you home or something. I'm not having much of a time, to tell the truth. All those strangers, and it's so crowded! I suddenly feel very old when I look at those college students on their way back to school."

Catherine didn't say anything for a minute, and he stood up. "I guess you're anxious to get in and dance some more," he remarked politely. "I'm probably keeping you."

"No," Catherine said, carefully, cautiously. "I think I'd like to go home now. It's just—we've only met, and I don't know if it would be proper to leave with you—"

He laughed heartily, his head thrown back. "I forgot! You know all about proper things! I told you—I don't. Well, it was nice meeting you, Miss Summerwell."

He walked toward the door and opened it for her. She jumped up from the step. "I'll do it!" she exclaimed with impulsive resolution. "Let me go tell my friends I'm leaving. Do you know where the coats are? I'll meet you there."

She handed him his jacket and hurried off down the hall before he could say another word. She squeezed her way through the noisy crowd in the dance hall, pausing briefly a couple of times to exchange greetings with acquaintances and former students. Still she felt conscious of her revealing dress, and she hurried to find Ladean and Dan. "Ladean," she called breathlessly, spotting her friend by the punch table. "I've been looking for you."

"You've been looking for me!" Ladean exclaimed. "We've been looking everywhere for you! Ted Harker said you went out for air, and we couldn't find you anyplace! Are you all right?"

"Fine!" said Catherine. "Fine! But I think I'm going to go home now, Ladean. I've had a very nice time. Thank you for inviting me. It's only a few blocks, and the walk will do me good. I'll call you tomorrow!"

Ladean was shocked. "You can't walk home alone tonight," she whispered fiercely. "There's all kinds of people in town for the dance. You can't be out on the streets by yourself! It wouldn't be safe!" Ladean's eyes were round with alarm.

"Don't be silly, Ladean"—Catherine scoffed—"I'll call you tomorrow." She started to leave, but Ladean caught her hand. "Don't you dare go! I'm going to call Dan. If you insist on going home now, he'll have to come and escort you! I won't let you go alone!"

"I won't be alone!" Catherine blurted out, sorry the minute she had said it.

"Not alone!" Ladean was consumed with curiosity. "You found someone. Who is it? I'm not surprised, in that dress! Is it Milton Warner?"

"It isn't anyone you would know," Catherine said. "He's waiting for me and I have to go."

Ladean clung to her hand. "Who is it? Tell me! Tell me! You can't leave me here to die of curiosity!"

"His name is David Reid," Catherine said impatiently. "I'll tell you about it later. I've got to . . ."

"How did you meet him?" Ladean persisted.

"At the dance," Catherine said.

"You aren't serious!" Ladean's voice rose in alarm, and two people turned to stare at the two girls. "Sh-h-h!" Catherine exclaimed. "Don't make a fuss, Ladean!"

"Someone you've just met!" Ladean said in a fierce whisper. "You're going to leave and spend the rest of the evening with a man you don't know anything about! Catherine, what are you thinking of? You could be attacked!" Her voice sank in a horrified whisper, "Raped!"

It was too much for Catherine. She started laughing. "You've been reading too many novels lately!" she said and giggled. "Nothing's going to happen. He's a very nice man. Besides, men don't rape schoolteachers." She whispered the last into Ladean's ear, and Ladean started giggling, too. Then her face grew very serious.

"Catherine, sometimes you are so impulsive! It scares me! Someday you're going to do some impulsive thing, and it will ruin your whole life!"

Catherine shrugged her shoulders. "Or maybe save it! Who knows! Thanks again, Ladean." She slipped off, through the crowd, and into the hallway. Around the corner she found the room where the coats were kept, but the room was empty as was the hallway. Awkwardly, she stood in the doorway looking up and down the vacant corridor. David Reid was nowhere to be seen, and she could not believe the disappointment that engulfed her. How could she care so much about being stood up by a man with whom she had only exchanged a few sentences? She waited a few more minutes and then dejectedly found her coat and put it on. A handful of stragglers were by the main door, drifting in and out of the hall, and she moved out of the building with some young people and walked down the broad front steps heading for the sidewalk.

Behind her, she heard a voice call. "Miss Summerwell? Catherine? Is that you?"

She turned, and he was standing by the front door, waving to her. "Wait up a minute!" He ran down the stairs and came up to her. "I thought we had an agreement! Wasn't I going to get to take you home?"

"Yes," she said, keeping her voice cool. "I thought we were supposed to meet at the coat room, and . . ."

"I know!" he said, "But I waited there so long I thought there must have been some mistake. I went in the dance to look for you, and when I came out, I thought I saw you leaving. I'm glad I caught you! May I still take you home?"

"Yes," she said, smiling, "I'm sorry I kept you waiting. My friends wanted to talk!"

"They probably told you not to go with a man you didn't know!" he said, his eyes crinkling with merriment. "They're right, you know, you shouldn't."

"I know," she assented.

"Okay. As long as you know, let's go."

They walked out into the cool night. As they left the lighted building, silence descended, and the stars brightened in the huge black sky. They walked side by side, not touching. She did not attempt to put her arm through his, but their steps were in rhythm, and they were each very conscious of one another's close presence.

"David," she said, and it seemed the most natural question in the world. "Tell me about yourself."

CHAPTER TWENTY

David called for her the next morning at ten. They planned to spend the day together, and she had packed a picnic lunch. She was wearing a heather-colored wool skirt with a white turtleneck sweater and an old rose-colored cashmere cardigan her mother had given her. For a moment she was tempted to put on pumps since they made her legs look better, but she decided, instead, to wear the sensible walking shoes she had bought in Britain. She brushed her hair out into natural waves and tied it back with a silk scarf.

While she waited for David, she thought over the things she had learned about him the night before. Mostly he had talked about his cattle. With boyish enthusiasm he described the dream of his lifetime, which was to own his own ranch in the foothills and to breed a line of cattle that could withstand the bitter winters. His goal was to create a strain of Herefords that could weather the harsh Canadian mountain storms, much as the shaggy, tough cattle of the Hebrides, but which would still yield prime beef and grow to a healthy marketable size. His herd was growing, and this would be his third breeding year. Last year's calf crop had proved to be durable, sturdy, and beefy, and he had great hopes for the calving in the coming year.

"They know me, Catherine!" he had exclaimed happily, speaking of his herd. "I go into the hills and call them, and they appear out of the valleys and crevices and come to me like pets. In all honesty, I must tell you it isn't my personality they like. I carry salt in my pocket, and they know it! They come and lick it out of my hands! They're beautiful, I tell you! As the Scotsman who sold me the bull says, 'They're fine, bonny beasties.' "

She could have listened all night. He was so alive and intense when he spoke of his ranch and his herd. Pride and challenge shone in his eyes, and his voice was deep and vibrant.

"How wonderful, David!" she exclaimed, her face lit with admiration and interest. "I would love to see them!"

"And so you shall one day!" he declared. "The whole world will see them! They will be on the cover of every cattle magazine from here to Australia! How does this sound? The 'Reid Breed.' " He laughed with self-mocking delight, and she joined in.

Then her voice grew soft and serious. "I believe it will happen," she said.

For their picnic, they drove out along the creek road south of town, until they came to a coulee area with high, grass-covered bluffs, leading down to the banks of the creek. The trees along the creek were decked with the remaining autumn leaves of gold and brown, and the afternoon sun was pleasant. They clambered up and down the bluffs and found a batch of wild service berries in a hollow. They picked the sweet, mealy berries and stained their mouths and hands with the juice as they ate them.

The water sparkled down below, and when they

were hungry, they walked down to the creek to spread their blanket on the banks. Catherine pulled out the sandwiches, fruit, and cake, and they ate to repletion. The afternoon breeze snapped with the crackle of the turning season, but the sun continued warm, and the water rippled, dark and shining beside them. David put his hands behind his head and leaned back on the blanket. "That was very nice, Catherine. Thank you," he said. Then, without another word he closed his eyes, and in a moment his breathing became deep and regular, and she knew he was asleep. As quietly as possible she cleared up the remains of the picnic, and then pulled out a book that she had tucked into the basket. For a few minutes she pretended to read, but giving up the pretense, she leaned against a rock and watched him as he slept. In sleep he looked younger, but even in sleep his face held an alert vitality. He was a man of tensile strength, strung like a poised bow or a blooded stallion at the gate—ready and fit, but holding his power with self-control and intelligent restraint. She felt there were depths in him she could not even imagine, and he fascinated and attracted her, and yet he frightened her, too, because she knew that here was a real man. He was a man a woman could only win—she could never demand or beg or trap him. If he ever gave his heart, it would be earned, and even then he would have to give it—it could not be taken.

He woke quickly, his eyes instantly alert, though he did not move, only looked around until he saw her. Still not moving, he smiled up at her. "Catherine," he said, "forgive me. You fed me too well."

In one smooth powerful motion he was on his feet. "Up and at it! What shall we do now?" He walked

over to her and took her hands and pulled her up to
her feet. He was stronger than he had realized, and she
came up off-balance and fell against him. For a moment she leaned against his chest, feeling his hardness
against her softness, and then they sprang apart as
though they had been burned, and he flushed.

"Sorry!" he muttered, and moved away quickly to
gather up the blanket and basket.

Self-consciously, they began walking back to the car,
careful to keep their distance. To relieve the strain
Catherine asked a question.

"What were you doing before you bought your
ranch?"

"More of my life story?" he asked quizzically. "I
would have thought you had heard all you wanted to
know last night."

"Please tell me!" she begged.

He told her about his years at the university. His
father had been a farmer with a big dry farm near
Medicine Hat. For several years the harvest had been
meager, and all the family's money was spent on saving
the land. When it came time for David to go to university, his father had informed him he would have to
support himself.

"It wasn't glamorous or exciting!" he warned her.
"It took time, that's all. I took six years to graduate,
instead of three. I felt like an old man my senior year.
I worked on farms and oil rigs and worked on road
crews—anywhere I could earn enough to put aside a
little for the next year."

He told her that after he had graduated he had
found a good job as a bank loan officer, specializing
in loan evaluations for cattle herds. He had lived for

several years in one room, cooking on a hot plate, never going out, having no friends, because he did not want to incur the expense of entertaining. Except for the barest living expenses, he had put everything he earned into savings, and with each year came closer to his dream of buying a ranch and starting his herd.

"Almost three years ago I was reading the *Lethbridge Herald*, and there it was! The place I had always imagined—a ranch for sale in the foothills with a small home, outbuildings, and deep pastures. There were only a few acres under cultivation, and the rest of the land was natural grazing property. Ten percent of the land was owned outright, and the other 90 percent was in a ninety-nine-year lease to the government. The only problem was I wasn't ready to buy. I had enough money to swing the down payment for the ranch, but it would leave me with nothing left over to buy stock or the purebred bull I would need."

"What did you do?" Catherine asked, fascinated by the story of his long struggle and his single-minded dedication.

"I gambled," he said.

"What!" she cried. "After all those years of doing without—the sacrifice—how could you dare to gamble it all away! Wouldn't it have been wiser to have waited a few more years?"

"Wiser? Yes. But I was sick of waiting. Sick of living for tomorrow, and my chance was there—right within my grasp—so close I couldn't turn it away."

"But you didn't really gamble!" she exclaimed, disbelieving. "I mean, not with cards or dice, did you?"

He laughed. "No, I kept my gambling perfectly respectable. I figured cattle were what I knew, and so cattle had to be the way out. I bought a herd at auction and gambled they'd bring a profit in the Chicago market."

"You mean," she asked incredulously, "that in one shot you hazarded all of your savings? What if the market had gone down? You could have been ruined!"

"I would have started over again," he said simply. "However, it's all history, anyway, because the market went up, and I sold my speculative herd for a nice profit. I bought the ranch and the beginning of my herd."

She sensed the pride in his quiet words, and her eyes were shining with admiration. "I'm glad the market went up," she said.

He laughed. "It isn't much of a ranch, you know! The market didn't go up that much! I live in a log house the old Englishman built for himself, and I haven't anything left over for improvement. It's still a very tight existence, but the cattle like it." He grinned at her.

On Monday she started school. "I have some business to attend to," he told her, "but may I spend the evening with you? We'll do whatever you like."

She felt as lighthearted as a girl, but when she entered the school, the gloomy halls and the smell of chalk and musty gym lockers dimmed her mood. In class the students were restless and excited. They were much more interested in seeing one another, and comparing the classes and teachers they had been assigned, than in beginning the classroom routine. Ever since her experience at Spring Valley, Catherine had been careful to keep an emotional distance between herself and her students, and so she stood in front of her class, formal and stiff, explaining the outline of the year's course. Even to herself the words sounded dull and monotonous. With a jolt of surprise she realized she was not thinking about what she was saying at all! Her mind was on the picnic the day before—the breeze and the rippling water and David's sleeping face.

After school she collected the papers and class records quickly, and hurried down the corridor. As she rushed past the administrative offices Mr. Solembaugh came out of the door and saw her. "Oh, Catherine!" he said heartily. "Just the person I came to see! Could you step in here for a moment, please?"

"Well, I'm in a hurry, Mr. Solembaugh. Is it important, or could it wait?"

He frowned and looked severe. "It is important and I'd like to speak to you now, if possible."

"Of course," she said, resigned, and walked into the office. When they were seated, he cleared his throat. "Catherine," he said, "I have a difficult situation developing here, and I don't quite know how to solve it. You see, we are closing two more rural schools this term, and we have teachers in those schools who have tenure. One of them, Miss Stapleton, has full credentials as an English teacher—and we are under an obligation to see that her contract is fulfilled."

"Yes, Mr. Solembaugh," Catherine said, somewhat impatiently, "I would think you do have that obligation."

"The thing is, Catherine, that all of our English teachers have tenure—except you." Suddenly Catherine's scalp prickled with alarm and she sat up straight.

"What are you saying!" she exclaimed. "You can't fire me just because I don't have tenure! I have a year's contract and you must . . ."

"Now, now! Catherine! You are always jumping to conclusions! I am not talking of firing you. What we wanted to suggest to you is that maybe you would be willing to function in an administrative role for this one year, and then next year, when the teacher adjustments again take place, we are certain we could find you another teaching position, if you wished it."

Catherine was boiling with indignation. "An administrative position! You mean a secretary! What would I be, some kind of glorified office girl? Maybe the roving substitute teacher! Why don't you find another place for this Miss Stapleton?"

Mr. Solembaugh shook his head with exaggerated patience. "Catherine! Catherine! You have to understand that this woman has been teaching for twenty years. She is not qualified to do anything else! We couldn't insult her . . ."

"You couldn't insult her, but you can insult me! Is that it, Mr. Solembaugh?"

"Please, Catherine, let's talk about this like adults!"

Catherine stood up, her head held high and her eyes bright with anger. "I do not choose to talk about it. Not as an adult or in any other way, Mr. Solembaugh!" She walked to the door and opened it. "I am late for an appointment, if you will excuse me!" Her eyes were cold, but her cheeks were blazing with angry color.

"You're upset," Mr. Solembaugh said placatingly. "There's no hurry. We can talk about this in a day or two. I'm sorry this has happened, but the Provincial

Department made the decision last week because of enrollment changes. Please promise me you'll think about it?"

Catherine said nothing. She refused to meet his eyes and marched out of the building, enraged, confused, and worried about this sudden development. She walked with angry strides past the temple square and down the street toward her house. Her coat was open, flapping around her wildly, her hair flying loose in the wind. She gripped her schoolbooks in front of her tightly, so lost in thought that she almost walked past David's car. He was sitting in the vehicle next to the curb waiting for her.

"Hey, Catherine!" he called out the window when he saw her striding down the street. "Catherine!" he called again and jumped out of the car. She did not seem to see him or hear him, and her face was tight with concentration. "Catherine!" he shouted again and put his hand out to her.

"Oh!" She seemed startled and turned toward him. "David!" she cried, "I didn't see you! I'm so glad you're here! Can we get in your car and drive somewhere—fast?"

"Of course," he said, puzzled. He asked no questions but helped her into the car and started the motor. He drove out into the prairies, and as they hummed along the deserted road she stared out of the window, pondering her inner thoughts. Finally, she exploded. "How dare he!"

David pulled the car off on the shoulder of the road, and in a stream of anger and hurt she told him what had happened.

"If I'm not a teacher—I'm nothing!" she exploded,

as she concluded the story, and then the tears came. At first they were tears of rage, wild and hot, but slowly they changed, and huddled in the car seat, her hands over her face and her shoulders shaking mutely, she began crying with hopelessness and sorrow.

David said nothing. He made no move to touch her, and yet she sensed the sympathy and understanding in his silence. When the storm of tears began to subside, he got out of the car and quietly opened her door. "Why don't we walk for a while?" he said. They walked out onto the open prairie, and as the twilight began to gather, she felt her spirits lifting.

"He didn't fire you, you know," David said, after they had tramped for a time in silence. "He's trying to solve a difficult situation as fairly as he knows how. You could always think of the year as a sabbatical."

She picked up a stone and chucked it across the field. "I suppose," she said quietly. "It's just that it all seems so pointless. No great cause! Nothing important to do! I'm so unessential—so perfectly interchangeable. It's like a game of musical teachers—and we're the chairs not the players!"

He laughed at her analogy. "You make it sound like the end of the world. Don't you know that a person isn't what they do—they are what they are inside? Believe me, you are not an interchangeable sort at all. I've never met anyone quite like you!"

"Thanks!" she said, and smiled, touched by his compliment.

A while later, as they walked back to the car, he asked her, "What do you think you'll do?"

She answered with a shrug, "I don't know. I honestly don't know!"

She went through the next few days at school thinking of nothing but the evening when she and David would be together. He told her that his business was going to keep him in town for the rest of the week. The next night when they went out to dinner, he told her about the old Englishman who had owned the ranch before him.

"He was a dried up bit of a man, with an aristocratic voice and gentle eyes. With isolation he had grown as shy and quiet as his animals, but nonetheless there was an aristocratic gentility about him, which all the years of living alone, lost in the foothills, hadn't faded away. He'd lived there by himself since coming from England as a young man, and his only companions were books and an old half-breed who helped him build his house and worked the place for him.

"He was so English that he built the house in a hollow, where there were tall currant bushes and some birch and spruce trees. It gave him the illusions of the trees of his homeland. Only an Englishman would have built in a valley when there were tall hills around, begging to be used. Well, he soon saw his folly. The melting snow collected in his hollow, and in the spring the ground was wet like a sponge, and an underground spring caused the house to settle.

"The main room, which he had originally planned as a combined dining room and formal sitting room, began to sink into the ground. By then, however, he had discovered that he had no need for formal rooms anymore, and already he had confined his life to the large kitchen room and the small bedroom off to one side. Fortunately, those rooms were built on solid ground. Every year the formal room sinks more, until now the floor slants at a downward angle, and the windowsills are close to the ground.

"The rest of the house somehow manages to stay firmly intact. Over the years he used the sinking living room for a receptacle for his books, and when I went up to buy the property from him, he showed me the room. Unfurnished, bright with sunlight from the windows, a sharply sloping floor, and the whole room stacked with books! All around the edges of the room, books—piled about three feet deep. They were in stacks in the center of the room and leaning against one another. At one time he got ambitious and constructed a few bookshelves at the far end of the room. Those shelves were crammed to overflowing. I asked him how he was ever going to remove all those books when he left. 'I'm not!' he said, 'I've already read most of them, and the ones I haven't read, I'm not interested in!'

"In a later conversation he told me that he had bought out the town library in Crowsnest Pass when it closed for lack of funds and lack of use. I guess the coal miners thought the saloon was more interesting than the library. He carted out the books in wagons, and through the years he had been slowly reading his way through the entire library."

Catherine could have listened to David forever. It seemed they had so much to say to one another. They laughed at the same things and reacted to one another with a mutual intensity and interest that she had never experienced before. One evening as they said good night, she impulsively exclaimed, "I love talking to you, David! I feel like we never run out of things to say!"

"Yes," said David. "I feel that, too. Good night, Catherine. Tomorrow?"

"Yes," she whispered happily.

The next day was Friday, and as Catherine left the school, she looked at the closed door of the administrative offices and realized with a shock that her whole future was hanging in balance, and she hadn't even made a move to resolve her problem. "Monday will be time enough," she thought grimly, "after David's gone." She felt a sick, hollow grinding in the pit of her stomach—two more days and he would be gone! She hurried down the street, not wanting to waste one moment with him.

David was waiting for her, his face tired-looking and serious. "Is anything wrong, David?" she asked.

"Nothing to trouble you," David answered shortly. "What shall we do tonight?" He seemed determined to avoid any further questioning. They went to a movie and afterward he drove her home. For the first time in their relationship she felt the shadow of fear. "He's getting bored with me," she thought. "I must look so unglamorous, dragging home from work every night. He could be enjoying himself with someone younger and prettier. He probably feels like he's stuck with me!" The thoughts wounded her, and she turned to him, wanting reassurance that he cared for her, but he was silent, staring out the windshield deep in thought.

"Won't you tell me what's the matter, David?" she asked softly. "I've unloaded all my troubles on you. Maybe it would help to tell me about yours."

He was obviously reluctant, but he spoke without looking at her. "I haven't succeeded in doing what I came here to do, and I have to go back to the ranch right away. The man who is taking care of the cattle has to leave the first of the week."

"What did you come here to do?" she asked.

"I was looking for someone . . . to go back to the ranch with me." He hit his hand on the steering wheel in disgust. "It was probably a crazy idea anyway!"

"What idea?" she asked, bewildered. "What are you talking about? A hired man?"

"Sort of." David sighed and looked at her. "I told you I used all my money to get this thing started, and I'm hardly making enough to keep going. I sell a little hay, a litter or two of pigs, and any calves that aren't true bred, but that doesn't bring in a whole lot—there isn't much left over for anything. I really can't afford to hire a winter hand—there isn't enough to keep him busy around the place anyway. So the last two winters I've gone it alone, and"—he paused and looked at her bleakly—"you can't imagine how lonely it gets in those foothills once you are snowed in! No one can get through off the main roads for weeks at a time, and the neighbors are few and scattered. It . . ." He paused and she could sense it was painful for him to go on.

"It must be hard," she whispered, wanting to encourage him, but not wanting him to stop until he had told her what he was trying to say.

"I fear I'm going to become like the Englishman. A strange shadow person. This probably sounds funny, but there were days last winter when I'd go up into the hills and shout in the snowy fields just to hear the echo and know I still had a voice! Isn't it an irony? I've got everything I've ever wanted! I wouldn't leave it for anything—but I think I will go mad if I spend another winter snowed in up there alone."

"Oh, David!" she said softly, her voice like gossamer in the air.

"It's the stillness," he went on, almost talking to himself. "I thought maybe I could find someone—you know, a drifter or an out-of-work cowboy who'd be willing to spend the winter up there—do a few chores, that sort of thing—for no wages but a roof over his head. They're all too smart, they know what the white stillness is—and nobody wants to have any part of it."

"Maybe if you keep trying," Catherine said.

"No, I can't. I gave myself a week. Now I've got to get back to the place and my animals. Winter will be on us in a matter of weeks, and I've got a lot to do to get ready. No. There's nothing for it but to go through another winter." He shook himself and grinned at her crookedly and made a determined effort to lighten his voice. "It won't be so bad! I've started reading my way through the library," he said and laughed, but his laugh had a bitter edge to it.

Catherine felt his pain, and she sat so still she was hardly breathing. What could she say? What could she do? In that moment she knew she loved him and that she would do anything for him. Impulsively, knowing she was risking everything, she turned to him.

"David!" she cried. "Do I understand you? You really want someone as a companion—not really a hired hand to do heavy work but just someone to talk to—to provide human contact—someone to be there?"

"I guess that describes it!" David said. "That's a little more poetic than I would have made it, but basically that's what I'm looking for, I suppose!"

She took a deep breath and screwed up her courage. "How about me?" she asked brightly. "Would I do?"

"What!" David's voice exploded. "What do you mean! Look, Catherine, it isn't like you to make jokes in bad taste . . ." He was indignant. "You make me feel ridiculous."

How could she convince him without being too eager and turning him away as she had with Norman?

"Oh, no!" she pleaded and placed a hand on his arm. "Oh, no, David, I wouldn't joke about something like this. I understand, really I do! But don't you understand, in my own way, I have the same problem. If I lose my teaching job, I lose human contact. My apartment may not be in the snowy foothills, but sometimes it's as empty and remote as though it were! David, can't you see? I know you don't love me or anything like that . . . but we get along so well, and we enjoy each other's company. I could go as your companion. It could work out—I know it could!"

"Catherine!" He looked at her with confusion. "Catherine, you're talking nonsense! You don't know what you're saying!"

"Yes, I do!" she insisted. "It's the first time I've wanted something in so long. Please, David! I wouldn't be any trouble. I could even help around the ranch. I'm good with animals."

"You're serious, aren't you?" he said incredulously, after a long pause. "You really mean this!"

"Yes," she said, forcing herself to speak with calm conviction, her voice controlled and reasonable. "I think it could work out for both of us! We're friends, David, and surely that is something precious. A beginning . . ." She stopped speaking and sat dejected. She

had done it again! Impulsively, stupidly, she had destroyed her relationship with this man she had grown
to love. What must he think of her? That she was an
immoral woman? Or a mad woman? Or just silly and
irresponsible? She cringed from her own absurdity and
wished she could run away from the car. She didn't
want to hear what he would say next. But she sat in
horrified silence waiting for him to denounce her or
ridicule her or humor her.

David was struggling with confusing emotions. He
could not believe what Catherine had said! The surprise of her words had hit him like a thunderbolt. He
saw her as a beautiful, intelligent, aristocratic woman.
She reminded him of the wealthy coeds at college who
had never noticed him or spoken to him. He was the
quiet, hard-working farm boy from Medicine Hat, and
they were the sorority girls in their rich clothes and
their privileged circles. At university he would never
have presumed to date one of those girls, and the only
reason he had presumed to date Catherine this past
week was because of the unusual circumstance of their
meeting.

During their days together he had felt himself
drawn to her with an overwhelming attraction, and
though she was pleasant and sweet to him, he couldn't
get over the conviction that she considered him a nice
fellow who would be leaving soon, and so she had
treated him with courtesy and warmth. He could not
imagine that she would be attracted to him, a poor
rancher, struggling in poverty with an ambitious and
absurd dream. How could she find anything noble in
something as earthy as cattle-breeding? No, he had
imagined her interest in him as platonic and tempo-

rary. Yet, here she was offering to go with him to his ranch. Offering herself as though it were the most natural thing on earth that they should be together! Nothing had prepared him for such an idea.

He couldn't imagine that Catherine's suggestion was based on any feeling for him, although he himself had spent the week wanting to touch her, watching her full, rich body as she walked and moved and spoke to him, and yearning to hold her. Something in her manner, though, some coolness and self-containment, had made him feel that if he touched her, she would resist his advances. He was a reticent man, and she was like a woman sheathed in delicate glass. He feared to touch her for fear his clumsiness would shatter her and fill her with contempt and derision for his presumption.

He looked at her. Nothing had changed. She was sitting, quiet, still, far away from him on the car seat. There was nothing provocative or suggestive in her manner. He thought, "Her emotions are not involved. This is a pragmatic decision she has made, and if I am to handle this correctly, I must not let her see that my emotions are involved, or she will turn away." It was then he admitted to himself that the strongest emotion he was feeling was joy. He loved her—wanted her on any terms—and she was offering herself. Not, certainly, in love, but at least she had said she would come and be with him—his companion—his friend.

"She must be more desperate than I had imagined," he thought to himself. "She must be unhappy beyond anything she has told me. Perhaps she needs me!"

"Catherine," he said, his voice deep and candid. "You know what you're saying. We would be alone together in my home. Snowed in. The world would know we were together. What you are suggesting—it would destroy your reputation. You could never teach again!"

"I don't care!" She felt her heart lurch with sudden hope. "We wouldn't need to tell people. Nobody will care where I go! I could tell people I have a job for the winter. You said it was isolated! We're good companions, aren't we, David?" she asked defiantly. "Wouldn't you rather spend the winter with a friend than someone you might not even like?"

At that he laughed. "What a ridiculous question! I'm not talking about what I'd like! I'm talking about reality, about convention! What you're suggesting— even if we felt right about it—wouldn't do. The consequences are too great."

Catherine clenched her fists and turned to him, her eyes blazing. "I am sick of convention! I am sick of doing things because other people think it is what I ought to do! Or the world thinks it's proper! David! We are two strong, independent adults, and we are beholden to no one. We like one another, and we both have a need of being together this winter! If it weren't for the fact that you are a man and I'm a woman you wouldn't hesitate—but that one fact alone doesn't change things . . ."

David grabbed her clenched fist in his strong hand and opened it gently. "Catherine, Catherine!" he said firmly. "It changes everything, and you know it! The scandal would destroy you. I couldn't do that to you. You're right on every other count. It is a perfect solution. A wonderful solution. But it's impossible!"

"I've got to go somewhere, David," Catherine whispered. "If you won't take me, then I'll have to go somewhere alone. What a pity! Why should we both have to be alone?" Her voice was wretched, and she started to open the door.

"Don't!" His voice tore at her heart, and she thought she could not turn to face him. She had risked everything and lost. "At least," she comforted herself, "I didn't tell him that I love him. He couldn't reject my heart because I didn't offer that—even though it is already his."

"Don't go!" he repeated, and his hand on her shoulder restrained her. "It is a pity," he said quietly. "Are you determined to go away?"

"Yes," she said.

"If you break your contract here, you won't get a job anywhere else."

"I know," she said softly.

"There's one way it could work," he said carefully. "Now don't get upset when I suggest it. Think about it calmly. You and I know this is an arrangement of convenience, and I will not violate any terms you wish to impose. However, for the benefit of the world, I think, if you come with me, we must be married. Would you be willing to marry me? I promise you I will not require anything of you which you do not wish to give—after the year is over, you may seek an annulment. Under those terms your idea just might work for both of us. What do you say?"

She turned slowly and looked at him. With an effort he kept his face calm and unemotional. "This is a business contract," he told himself. "Don't frighten her by letting her see what you are feeling."

Her heart was pounding in her breast, and she yearned to throw her arms around him, to kiss him, to declare her joy, but she saw the harsh lines of his face and the cool appraising look in his eyes, and she kept herself in close control.

"Yes, of course, that would make it work! A marriage of convenience with neither one of us bound by anything—and next spring you can go your way as free as a bird!" Her heart twisted. How could she ever let him go? "Surely by the spring I will win him!" she reassured herself. "Through the long months of winter we will find our way to one another. I will make him love me!"

The following day David arranged for a marriage license while Catherine went to Mr. Solembaugh and resigned her contract. "I'm getting married," she told him. He looked at her in disbelief. "This isn't much notice," he said coldly. "I had thought we were friends, Catherine. You've mentioned nothing about marriage plans, and suddenly . . ."

"He's a rancher from up Lundbrek. I . . . we . . . haven't known each other for long, but he needs to return to his ranch, and I'm going with him. We're being married tomorrow afternoon in the courthouse offices."

"Are you sure you know what you're doing?" Mr. Solembaugh looked disapproving and concerned. "Don't you think you should wait awhile . . . get to know him better. . . ."

"I know him enough, Mr. Solembaugh. I really do. Thanks for what you've done for me. I'm sorry you feel I'm leaving you with bad grace."

"It's that impulsiveness of yours!" Mr. Solembaugh

shook his head, and she felt he was washing his hands
of her. "I knew it would get you in difficulty! You
know you will never obtain another teaching contract
in Alberta with this unofficial resignation on your record, don't you?"

"Yes," said Catherine calmly.

"Well then," Mr. Solembaugh said, shaking her
hand briskly, "I have done all I can do. You are so
strong-headed and stubborn, there is no more point in
my talking with you!"

"No," Catherine said, her head high and her eyes
snapping. "There isn't. Good-bye, Mr. Solembaugh."

The following afternoon Catherine Summerwell and
David Reid were pronounced man and wife in a three-
minute ceremony in the office of the court clerk.
David had bought her a narrow gold band, and when
he put it on her finger, the justice said to David, "You
may kiss the bride." He bent and kissed her gently on
the cheek. "There you are, Mrs. Reid," he said awkwardly. They both felt self-conscious. He was wearing
his tweed jacket and a woven tie. She was wearing her
gray wool suit with the white trim. The room was
chilly, and their witnesses were the maintenance man
and the justice's secretary.

Catherine had phoned Bishop Watkins and told
him what she was planning to do. Both he and Mrs.
Watkins had come over to her apartment and talked
to her for an hour. They were alarmed at her attitude
and disapproving of her decision. When David came,
she had introduced him to them, and they were impressed with his demeanor, but they again stated their

concern about the marriage. Catherine sensed that David was embarrassed by their anxiety.

"They're right, you know," he said to her after they had left. "It isn't too late. You can still back out!"

"No!" she said vehemently. "They're not right! No one else can decide what is right for us!"

After the wedding David led her to the car. Her things were already packed and loaded in the trunk and back seat. She was taking all of her belongings except her party clothes. Those she had packed up and left to be shipped home to Calgary. She had sent a telegram to her parents, telling them about her marriage, and giving them her new address. They would be hurt when they realized she had been married without their presence or blessing. But after she had written them a few letters telling them about David and the ranch and how happy she was, she thought they would be relieved and grateful that she had finally found a place of her own. If they had known the truth—that she had made a bargain with a man who did not love her and that she was gambling her whole future on the hope that she could win his love—they would have been heartbroken. Catherine was determined that they would never know.

From the beginning of the trip Catherine sensed the relationship with David was changed. Their conversation in the car was awkward and formal and the pleasant ease of their former relationship seemed lost. "What is the matter with us?" Catherine wondered miserably.

"David," she said after an uncomfortable period of strained silence, "you know this wedding band doesn't change anything. I—I won't wear it, if you don't want me to!" She wanted to reassure him that she was not going to make any unfair claims upon him. She was not going to demand to be treated as a wife. With all her heart she wanted to put him at ease, to establish their old, comfortable warmth. But rather than accomplishing that, her remarks seemed to make him more remote, more silent.

David listened to her comment about the wedding ring, and his heart sank. He wondered if she was trying to tell him that he had no right to think of her as his wife. Was she telling him, in her clear, cool way, that the bargain stood and that they must live together as companions? Suddenly David began to see the enormity of his decision. She was sitting not two feet away from him. The sweet scent of her perfume filled his nostrils; her warm, rushing voice filled the car as she exclaimed over the beauties of the landscape, her silk-shod legs crossed and uncrossed in the corner of his vision, and the swishing of soft womanly fabrics murmured of the secret places of her inviting body. He thought he would not be able to stand the hours of driving home—and if this was unendurable, what about the nights with just the two of them together in the remote cabin? How was he going to live with her and not declare his feelings? And if he did, would he shatter the bargain—and would she view him as contemptible?

His dilemma was an agony, and he could not trust himself to speak. Gradually, she stopped speaking also, and they drove through the afternoon, sealed in their own unhappy thoughts.

Late in the afternoon they drove off the highway,

which was threading through the high foothills, onto a secondary road. They followed the road, in its deserted splendor, for about twenty miles and then turned onto another road—hardly more than a one-car track—which twisted deeper and deeper into the solitary majesty of the high reaching hills. They drove for about ten miles and passed one small home with some straggling outbuildings. The foothills rose dramatically behind the house, and the splendor of the gigantic Rockies rose like a jagged background behind the rolling hills.

"That's the Bartlett place," David said, speaking for the first time in many miles. "They're our only neighbors. About six miles by road, but, as the crow flies over that hill there"—he pointed to a large hill rising behind the Bartlett house—"our place is only two miles away."

"Oh!" she said softly, afraid to say more because of his strange, brooding mood. Shortly afterward, they drove between two sloping hills and came into a deep valley area. She could see a mountain stream rushing down the hillsides and pockets of autumn-bright shrubs and trees clustered in the fields of deep, browning grass. They came to a cattle gate across the road, with barbed-wire fencing stretched on either side. "This is my boundary line," he said simply, but his head lifted with a tilt of unconscious pride.

"It's beautiful," she gasped. "I can see why you love it, David! It's so lovely—magnificent, wild, and untamed—but rich and—oh! It's absolutely beautiful!"

He smiled at her for the first time on the journey. "I'm warning you! The part that Mother Nature did may be beautiful but don't be disappointed when you see the man-made part! I told you! The buildings aren't much!"

They drove further, and then dipped down into a valley filled with trees and bushes. Through the trees she could see a wide roof with a gentle slope, and as the car entered among the trees, they pulled up in front of a low-lying cottage built of heavy logs. There was something charming and European in the cottage. Catherine was reminded of the rustic hunting lodges in the Alps, and she was sure that the old Englishman had intended the comparison.

"It's charming, David," she cried. "Really! It's delightful! You had me prepared for a shack!"

She waited for him to open the door for her, and he watched her face carefully as they entered the main room. This was the room which the owner had intended to be used as the kitchen, but his concept of home had been formed in a country mansion on the English moors, and so the room was of noble proportions. On one wall under chamber windows were cupboards, a dry sink, and a sink with a pump, and on the back wall a huge black coal range with a wide oven. A table and chairs were situated within the ell formed by the cupboards and stove. In the far wall was a wide stone fireplace, its stone chimney reaching to the ceiling. On either side of the chimney were old couches, with Indian blankets thrown over them to hide the worn upholstery, and in front of the fireplace was a shaggy sheepskin rug, carded and brushed into a thick white cloud. The room was tidy and clean, but it had an unlived-in feeling. She shivered in the cool darkness of the room. Evening was descending and the mountains were blocking the rays of the setting sun.

"You're cold!" he exclaimed. "Let me set a fire!"

"No!" she said. "I'll do that! I know you're anxious to see your herd. Where do you suppose your hired man is?"

"He left this morning," David replied. "Yesterday was the last day he could stay. That's why I had to get home!"

"Let me help you then!" she said. "You must have all kinds of stock chores to do before dark!"

He brought in the luggage, and there was a moment of awkwardness. "You take the bedroom," he said to her. "I'll bunk out here." He took her bags into the small bedroom, and wordlessly, she took them. With a great effort of will, he left without touching her. He couldn't even tell her how welcome she was because he could not trust his voice. Closing the door behind him, he leaned against it for a moment and heard the rustle of her movements as she opened the case and began to undress. Then with an angry jerk he threw his own bag on the couch and pulled out his work clothes.

Within a few minutes she came out of the door. "Ready!" she called too brightly. She was wearing heavy cords and a flannel shirt. "You wouldn't happen to have any extra work boots, would you?" she asked. He laughed as he recognized his old shirt. She grabbed the long tails and tied them at her waist. "I hope you don't mind. I didn't have anything suitable for feeding stock."

She looked so serious and funny he wanted to throw his arms around her and whirl her around, but he stilled the eagerness in his heart. "Fine!" was all he said.

She turned away, feeling she had made a fool of herself. "What right do I have to wear his shirt?" she thought. "I won't make any such presumptions again!"

He took a lantern and gave her a pair of his old gum boots. "These should do," he said. "On Saturday next we can drive down and pick you up a pair of proper boots. You'll need them."

In the gathering twilight he showed her the outbuildings—his stable with the two plow horses and his riding horse, the milk barn with its two milk cows and the calf which was almost a yearling. He took her to the pigpen and showed her the huge old sow with her broodling pigs. "She gave birth too late in the season," he said, worried, "and she's as mean as a wild boar. Don't get near her, Catherine. She could slice you up for bacon!"

Next he showed her the chicken house, and she gathered eggs while he prepared the hot mash for the pigs. "I'll take care of the horses, if you want to milk the cows," she offered. He seemed reluctant and she laughed. "I've been taking care of horses all my life— you can trust me."

The horses had been in their stalls all day long, and she sensed their restlessness. Their stalls led out to an enclosed paddock, and she opened the doors and shooed them out into the exercise area. The horses whinneyed and shook their manes and pranced up to the fence, rubbing their necks against one another and trotting from side to side. She smiled at their antics and then looked at their stalls. They were filthy. "Where's a shovel?" she called to David, who was milking, the ping of the streams of milk loud against the empty bucket.

"Over here!" he called back. She got the shovel and began to clean out the stalls. The warm familiar scent of horse manure made her feel at home. She scraped the stalls clean and then brought armloads of fresh hay to pad them. The time had come to get the horses back into the stalls, but when she went into the paddock she realized that wasn't going to be easy. The horses were prancing and playing, reveling in their newfound freedom. She realized the hired man had probably neglected to exercise them, and they were feeling wild and half-broken.

She approached the saddle horse first. Talking quietly, she walked slowly toward the animal. He eyed her suspiciously and stamped his front feet and shook his head. Catherine did not know that David had come up behind her silently and was watching from the paddock fence. Her voice was soft and compelling. "Whoa, boy!" she said, clicking her tongue. "Whoa, boy, slow, slow . . ." The horse shook his head, still restless, but standing still. Without alarming him, she reached her hand forward slowly and grasped his halter. "Now, boy," she said, not pulling, just patting his head and stroking his neck until he gentled, "time for bed." As docile as a kitten, the horse followed her into the fresh, clean stall. The other horses came willingly when they saw their companion already bedded.

As she closed the third stall, David clapped. "Well done!" he called. "You have made a conquest!" She laughed happily at his compliment and walked toward him.

"I'll climb the fence," she said, and quickly pulled herself up to the top rail and swung her leg over. David, watching below, looked at the clean lines of her body, silhouetted against the fading light, and thought to himself, "You have made two conquests!"

She jumped down on the ground beside him, her face catching the last rosy rays of the dying sun. "All done?" she asked.

"Yes," he said shortly. "Thank you for your help!" He wanted to kiss her so desperately that he had to turn away.

She had hoped that working together would break down the strange barrier that was rising between them, but it only seemed to have made things worse! Puzzled and heartsick, she followed him into the house.

CHAPTER TWENTY-ONE

The days passed slowly, and the tension in the house became almost unbearable. Catherine became convinced that David regretted bringing her with him. She was certain he felt he had been tricked into marrying her before he was ready to make such a commitment.

David, on the other hand, was fighting desperately to keep his passion for Catherine under control. Every kind act she did, every attractive gesture or generous word was like a sword in his heart. His physical need for her was overwhelming, and yet he was honorbound not to show it. He could not demonstrate his love without touching her, or taking her in his arms, and he knew he was too human to be able to do so without breaking the floodgates of his control and being compelled to make love to her. He thought if that happened before she was ready, she would leave him forever, and he knew it was better to live in this state of daily pain than to suffer the void of having her leave him.

Some evenings when she sat by the fire with the firelight playing on the glory of her hair, and her face soft and dreaming, he would have to get up and leave the room, tramping out into the night or hurrying into the book-filled room to choose another volume to divert his mind. To Catherine these abrupt departures, after inexplicable silence, served as a condemnation of her. "He is sorry I am here. As a friend, he could care for me; but as a wife, I am a burden."

One evening she was arranging her bedroom, and she opened the bottom drawers of the bureau. In the bottom drawer were some lovely old nightgowns. They were made of fine white flannel and were embroidered with little white flowers around the neck. Without thinking, in sudden anger, she pulled one of the gowns out of the dresser, and tearing off her clothes, she put on the gown. It settled around her naked body like a soft cloud. She threw open the door of the bedroom. David was sitting on the couch, and the sound of the door crashing against the wall startled him. She walked into the room, the gown billowing around her body. She was hurt as only a woman who feels rejected can feel when faced with the suspicion of another woman.

"Where did this come from?" she demanded. "Left by one of your former companions, I presume! Or was it left by the hired man? Did you have company on the long winter nights last year, too?"

His voice, in response, was cold. "Those are all interesting possibilities, but the truth of the matter is the old Englishman left them, and I have no idea where he got them. Perhaps they were something he kept for sentimental reasons. Maybe he wore them himself. I don't know!"

She was fascinated, and her anger faded as abruptly as it came. She forgot she was wearing nothing but the nightgown. Walking over to the couch, she sat down by David. "He left them! They're lovely—and expensive. I wonder if he was engaged once—or even married! Maybe he lost his young wife, and he kept her gowns for a memory. Oh! Isn't it romantic, David?" She sat close to him, and he could almost feel the warmth of her skin. Her soft waving hair cascaded over her shoulders. Under the fine fabric he could see the outline of her soft breasts and the curve of her hips. For a moment his eyes drank in her beauty, and his hand moved toward her. "It would be so easy," he thought, "to take her now . . . to carry her . . ." He looked into her clear, trusting eyes, and self-disgust filled him.

"I haven't given it much thought," he said to her, and stood up abruptly. Her eyes were wounded. Ashamed, she looked down at herself in the revealing gown.

"He can't even stand to look at me," she thought. With a silent sob she ran to her bedroom and closed the door. David paced in the other room, his hands trembling with pain and desire.

David's cattle roamed in the foothills. They were bred for the weather and the open fields. They were canny foragers and knew where to find the best fodder in the lush meadows and pastures. Even as the onslaught of autumn dried the grass and froze the ground, the cattle still fed well. David had established feeding stations where he brought supplementary grain and mash. His herd was small, but the animals were sleek and fat with thick, gleaming coats and sturdy placid white faces. Catherine thought Herefords to be the most beautiful cattle on the face of the earth, and she was never happier than when she and David tramped through the fields to find the cattle in their hidden valleys and shelters, or when David would stand in the low meadows with salt in his hands calling to them, and the cattle would appear, as if by magic, following their private paths over the hills to lick his hands.

There were happy moments, and sometimes in the open air, when their spirits were high, Catherine and David could forget the strain between them and laugh and talk with the open good nature of their early times together. But once inside the house, locked in one another's presence, the barriers of their misunderstanding would resurface, and they would peer at one another from behind their own suffering and pride.

One night David went out carrying hot, heavy pails of mash to feed the pigs. Catherine had finished her chores and was preparing a batch of fresh bread for supper. As she was lifting the white, puffy dough into the long bread pans, and placing it on the oven rack, suddenly from the farmyard came the raucous squealing of the sow. This was a sound she had grown to hate. The heavy ferocious animal had cruel, small eyes, and it would lie on the ground in its freezing wallow, while its shoats gluttonously pulled at its swollen teats. To Catherine it seemed like the fierce sow fed the piglets with resentment, but her mean nature would not let anyone else near them. Catherine knew the deceptive lassitude of the huge sow could change in a twinkling if anything came near her, and with savage swiftness she would attack with tusks and hooves.

The sow had not stopped squealing. Usually when she was fed, she squealed as the mash was poured into the trough and then stopped while she snarled up the food. Suddenly, Catherine heard another sound. Holding the bread dough in her hands, she ran for the door. David was calling for help. The sow continued squealing in rage, and Catherine ran to the pigpen to see what had happened. Apparently the sow had been savaging one of her piglets. David was holding the bloody little body of the piglet in his hands, and he was lying in the wallow behind the trough where he was jammed between the trough and the fence. The sow could not attack his body or head, but she had sliced a gash in his leg. If David tried to raise his head or move, the huge pig would lunge at him.

Catherine stood by the fence, not knowing what to do. "You've got to distract her." David's voice was calm and it cut through her panic. "I could get up and climb over the fence, if you could get her to stop watching me for a few seconds."

Without thinking, Catherine opened the gate and entered the pigpen. "No!" David shouted. "Stay out of here where you're safe!" She ignored him.

"Run, David!" she called, as the sow turned and saw her. With a grunt of rage, the sow wheeled and bore down on the new victim. "Run!" Catherine called to David. "I won't leave until you're safe!"

David pulled himself up, vaulted the fence, and then ran to the open gate to yank Catherine out of the pen. He knew he was going to be too late! The sow was almost on top of her! Realizing David was safe, Catherine started to leave, but she was terrified to turn her back on the charging animal, for fear it would overrun her. She stood for a fateful moment of indecision, and the enraged sow lowered its tusks to slash her. Without thinking, Catherine took the heavy wad of dough out of the bread pan, which she still held in her hands. Desperately, she threw it in the pig's face. The sticky dough blinded the crazed animal, and the sow stopped abruptly and shook her head ferociously. Some of the dough oozed into her mouth, and the pig quieted. With total absorption, the wild, savage animal stood stock-still in the middle of the pen and began eating the bread dough as it dripped down her snout.

Catherine wheeled and ran from the pen. David secured the bolt with a furious thrust. His face was white with shock and pain. "You're safe!" he said, with incredulous relief. "You saved my life! Catherine, how can I ever repay you? What if you hadn't been here?"

The horror of the thought washed over her. What if she hadn't been here? David, her beloved David, would have been killed horribly. No matter what happened, she thought to herself, I will be able to remember this. Even if he doesn't love me, I was able to give him his life.

Tenderly, she washed his leg and cleansed the terrible gash. "We should go see a doctor," she said. "This needs stitches, or it will almost certainly be infected." But he refused to leave the ranch, and so she poured iodine into the open wound, while he gritted his teeth with the pain.

Daily she washed and dressed the cut and meticulously cleansed away the dying, proud flesh. Strong new tissue gradually began to form, and Catherine knew he would recover. For David her tender nursing was a bitter joy. The touch of her hands, the sweet,

caring sound of her voice nearly drove him wild with
need for her, and yet she always seemed to remain cool
and distant. She never gave him an indication by word
or touch that she felt any more for him than the noncommittal friendship they had agreed upon. Now he
owed her his life, and he felt doubly bound to honor
his vow not to demand more than she was ready to
give. His iron control became stronger. "When we
come together," he told himself, "it must be because
she gives herself to me completely, because she wants
me as her husband, her lover—not because I have demanded it or because I am stronger. If I take her body
now, without first winning her love, I may never win
it."

CHAPTER TWENTY-TWO

On a cold, gray day in November they went for a walk into the foothills. He walked in front of her, his powerful legs striding across the rough, frozen ground confidently in his heavy boots. She followed, trying to match his stride with her own quick steps, but her lighter boots made the going harder, and she found herself stumbling over the frozen clumps of pasture grass in the lower fields and skirting patches of iron-cold brambles, which he had walked through without hesitation. In her anxiety to keep up she found herself half-running. Her breath came in little gasps as the cold wind from the mountains filled her lungs and caused her cheeks to redden with cold and exertion.

As they cleared the lower pastures, they followed a faint cattle trail, which wound its way up the hill, and the hike became a little easier. Catherine walked close behind now, noting with pleasure the muscles of David's legs as they moved against his jeans, and the strength of his broad shoulders in his dark woolen jacket. In spite of the cold, she felt a warmth glowing inside her. Just to be here with him, to be part of this vast, majestic world that was his, was all she asked. It didn't matter if he didn't speak to her, didn't walk beside her or touch her; it was enough to be with him.

David ascended the crest of the hill and stood looking at the panorama before him. His dark, handsome face was unreadable, but his eyes drank in the scene as though he could never see enough. It seemed to her that his eyes were hungry—hungry for the sight of his land, for the sight of his herd, and for the sight of the magnificent mountains towering on the horizon.

Catherine mounted the hill beside him and, following the direction of his eyes, looked down into the valley and spotted a small group of his cattle. Their coats were thick and rough in preparation for winter, and undaunted by the chill of the wind, they foraged contentedly in the frozen grass. Beyond the cattle ran a turbulent stream of water so cold it looked black as it rushed from its faraway mountain fastness, down through the ranging foothills.

Past the valley and the stream she could see the folded foothills, each row rising higher and darker than the other, and then on the far western horizon in incredible majesty rose the craggy peaks of the Rocky Mountains, their summits already deeply blanketed with snow and their slopes almost hidden in a white covering. Only a few blue stands of the tallest pines and spruce still raised their heads above the encroaching snows of winter.

The sky above them was the color of steel, and heavy clouds bulged with their load, like huge tarps laden with winter's burden. "Soon it will snow," David said, his face lifted to the sky, judging the wind with his acute sense of the outdoors. "After the first big snow we won't get down to the main road again until spring."

Catherine lifted her eyes and searched his face, trying to determine what he was thinking. Was he thinking with regret that it was too late to send her away? Was he angry? Or sorry? His face betrayed nothing—it remained impassive, strong, and indifferent. "I'm not sorry," she thought, defiantly. "I'm glad. Now I'll have time to make it right. And I'll do it! I know I will!" Her heart leaped with hope, and she turned her face from him for fear he would read the joy in it. Eagerly, Catherine began to scramble down the hill heading toward the valley and the stream below.

In a moment David caught up with her, and they jogged down the brown frozen slope, barren of vegetation except for the frost-covered grass. Only the white and blue of the distant mountains relieved the landscape. As far as the eye could see, everything else was earth-colored and lifeless, waiting the onslaught of winter.

Near the bottom of the hill Catherine stumbled, and David instinctively put out his hand to catch her. She clung to the strength of his warm, muscular hand until they reached the bottom of the hill, and then he withdrew it and thrust his hands into the pockets of his jacket. They continued to tramp across the frozen floor of the valley side by side and soon came close to the boisterous brook. They could now see that the spray from the water had frozen the bare tangle of branches along the streambed. Ice was forming along the banks of the stream, and the rushing, gurgling sounds of the water were like a last defiant attempt to resist the freeze.

Looking upstream, Catherine gave a sudden gasp of pleasure and ran toward a thatch of gray, leafless branches intertwined in a hedge along the side of the brook. In the midst of the dead branches she had caught sight of a cascade of glorious color. A spray of bright red and yellow berries flowed over the gray wood in profusion. The flamelike hues of the berries were incredible against the sullen pewter winter landscape.

"Bitterroot!" she exclaimed, turning to him, her eyes sparkling with discovery. "It's magnificent!"

David walked up to her and looked at the brilliant berries on the flowing vines. Then he smiled one of his rare smiles. "Bitterroot," he repeated. "The Englishman who owned this place brought it with him." Touched by her girlish delight, he added a quiet, unguarded comment, "It's my favorite plant."

As soon as he had said it, he regretted the impulse, feeling that he had sounded ridiculous, but she seized upon his remark as though it were a gift, and for a moment it seemed to her they were like they had been at first—without barriers between them, just two people sharing their thoughts and caring. "Why?" she asked, desperately wanting him to answer, not wanting this moment to end.

David hesitated a moment before replying. He refused to make himself a fool, and he was afraid she might think it absurd that he should find beauty in something so wild and natural as this common plant. But maybe if he could answer her question, he might somehow be able to make her see what he couldn't say to her directly. Maybe she would be able to sense how much he needed her—why he lived in fear of losing her.

Perhaps, he thought, he could make her see beyond

the toil, the isolation, and the wildness to understand that he wasn't a man who thought of nothing but the cattle and feed and shoveling manure, but that he lived with a vision of which she had become the most essential part. She was its very core. He began hesitantly. "It's because the bitterroot is beautiful when no other plant is beautiful—when the earth desperately needs beauty." He paused, and it took a great effort of will for him to add the next sentence. "I need beauty." His deep voice shook, and he turned his face toward the mountains as he spoke so she could not look at him.

She was wearing an old sheepskin coat grabbed from a hook by the door and her thick, unruly hair was blowing untamed in the winter wind. "Beauty!" she thought miserably, and she dredged up in her mind the beautiful ones—Emily, dainty and pink as china; Millicent, cool and stately; Ladean, dimpled and slender with her dark cloud of hair.

Without noting that she had turned away from him, he continued, carefully, trying to choose his words, finding it hard to cut through the wall of masculine pride and restraint he had built. "You see, bitterroot grows all summer long in the full green bushes, and it isn't even noticed. But when the first blast of winter comes, the plants that like it easy quit trying, give up their greenery, and play dead. In the worst cold these crazy little vines burst out in all this ridiculous color! It's as though hardship brings out the best in them. Out of difficulty and bitterness they create beauty." David turned and stared at the profusion of colorful berries gracing the dead gray branches. The berries were the only spot of color in the landscape. "Maybe," he said softly, almost to himself, "all true beauty must come from bitter roots."

Did she understand what he was trying to say, he wondered. Could Catherine grasp what he was trying to tell her—that from their own difficult beginning they could bring forth beauty. He willed her to understand—to feel how he needed her beauty and her warmth. Her face was as still as marble, but her eyes were puzzled. He saw with heartstick need the glorious color of her skin in the brisk air, her hair in its magnificent disarray with red gold highlights as radiant as the berries of the bitterroot, her strong lovely features, proud and impervious, and her generous body as straight and desirable as that of a young Amazon. How could he possibly know that to herself she did not seem beautiful when to him she was the most beautiful and compelling woman on the earth? How could he understand that for Catherine the meaning of beauty was cast in the genteel, delicate molds of the drawing rooms of Mount Royal—and, to her, it seemed forever unattainable. She felt he had required of her the one thing she could never give—beauty.

He turned and he strode back across the valley toward the hill. She waited for a long moment before following after him. She had not understood his last words—the code of his heart trying to speak to hers.

"Perhaps"—the echo of his voice borne on the harsh winter wind whispered out to the prairies—"all true beauty must come from bitter roots."

* * *

The next day the sky was still lowering. David got up early in the morning. "I think it's certain we will have snow soon. I should go down and provision up. We may be locked in here for who knows how long!"

"I'll stay and keep an eye on things," she said. "You go on down to the village."

After David left she sat for a long time thinking. He didn't love her, of that she was sure, and yet every day she was with him she grew to love him more, but it seemed hopeless.

"How can I bear it much longer?" she thought, in tears. "When he returns, I will tell him the truth— that I love him and I want him to love me as a wife. Maybe he will turn away from me, but I must risk it! I cannot go on this way any longer!" She felt better for having made the decision. Briskly, she stood up and began her cleaning chores.

A knock at the door startled her. She thought David must have returned unexpectedly, but why would he knock? She hurried to the door. "David?" she said, opening it. A man whom she had never seen was standing on the doorstep. The wind was blowing cold and chill through the door, and she could see a battered old pickup truck in the road by the barn.

"How do," said the man. He was a thick old man, with straggly gray hair and bad teeth. His overalls were grease-stained, and his hands were dirty.

"My name is Sam Bartlett, I live down the road apiece. Been meaning to come welcome you, Mrs. Reid—me and the missus—but the missus has been kind of poorly these past weeks."

"How do you do, Mr. Bartlett," Catherine said. She was nervous about the man, but he was so elderly and ineffectual she didn't feel she had much to fear. "Is there something I can do for you, or is this just a neighborly visit?"

Mr. Bartlett looked uncomfortable, and he stood on the doorstep, twisting his hat in his hands. He looked away from her and squinted up at the sky. "Snow on the way," he observed sagely, smacking his lips and sucking on his teeth. "When it hits, we're goin' to be in for it, for sure."

"Yes," Catherine agreed, "so David says."

"Mr. Reid," Mr. Bartlett said, relieved to be able to talk about something with authority. "Now there's a man who knows what he's talking about! That man is sure one fine catch, Mrs. Reid. Hard-working and educated at the university, too!"

"Yes," Catherine said. There was another awkward silence. Catherine hesitated to invite the man in. David had not told her much about their neighbors except that Mr. Bartlett managed a living by working at ranches in the area during the summer and running a few scrawny range cows. His property had actually been his wife's when he married her—inherited from her father, who had never worked it—and they apparently had lived in grinding poverty and labor without ever appreciating the grandeur that surrounded them.

"It's about the missus," Mr. Bartlett said, looking up at the sky again, as though he could not meet her eyes. "She's got something ailing her bad, and I thought maybe, well, you being a woman and all—maybe you wouldn't mind coming over and having a look at her. Maybe you could tell me what to do."

"Mr. Bartlett!" Catherine exclaimed, taken aback by the request. "I'm not a trained person—I mean, I know nothing about medicine. If your wife is ill, shouldn't you get her down to the hospital before the snows come?"

"She won't go!" Mr. Bartlett whined. "I told her that's what we should do, but she's got some fool notion she'll die there and never get back up home if she leaves. That's why I thought maybe a woman could talk to her. I was thinking if she knew there was going to be another woman up here with her, it might make her feel easier about things."

Something in his voice struck a chord of sympathy in Catherine's heart. He was such a pathetic excuse for a man, and yet as he spoke of his wife she heard the rusty tones of love in his voice, and she knew that whatever else this odd pair might be they were, somewhere deep inside, tied with a bond more precious than anything she owned. She could tell what an agony it was for this awkward, unlearned man to come begging at her door.

"All right!" she declared. "I'll come with you. But don't get your hopes up. I don't imagine there's much I can do to help!" Quickly, she grabbed an old jacket by the door and walked out to join him in the yard. Together they got into his vehicle and bounced down the road.

When they arrived at the Bartlett home, Catherine was appalled at the neglect she saw everywhere. What had once been fine outbuildings were now unpainted ruins, falling in disrepair. Rusted, abandoned machinery dotted the yard, and chickens pecked in the overgrown, dried weeds. The ground was frozen underfoot, but Catherine thought it must be very muddy and ill-kept in the summer. The house they entered was made of logs with a stone foundation. On the outside the sturdy home looked indestructible. But as Mr. Bartlett opened the door, a musty, sickly sweet odor assailed Catherine's nostrils so strongly that she almost turned away. The room they entered was dark, but Catherine could tell it was the kitchen and all-purpose room. As her eyes became accustomed to the gloom, she saw a room littered with unwashed dishes and filth. The floor was unswept, and piles of dirty linens were pushed in the corners. Blinds, torn and dusty, were pulled down over the windows, and the curtains were ragged and filthy. In the corner of the room was a couch. The room was freezing cold, heated only by one small branch burning in the stone fireplace. A pile of worn blankets on the couch in the corner moved, and a dim figure raised itself.

"That you, Sam?" asked a reedy, querulous voice.

"I brought someone to see you, Lil," Mr. Bartlett said, his voice coaxing and anxious. "It's Miz Reid. Thought maybe she could help you decide what to do."

"It's a pleasure to meet you, Miz Reid," said the voice. "I'm sorry Sam troubled you. Ain't nothing wrong with me that a little rest won't cure." The woman lay down again. "Sorry the place is such a mess!" she whispered, and Catherine thought she heard the sound of weeping. Walking over by the couch, she bent and looked at the woman. The woman's face was as white and gaunt as a skeleton's. Her hair was pulled back off her forehead, and her eyes were closed and sunken. At first Catherine thought she was very, very old, but then she looked closer, and something told her the woman was probably only in her middle years. Why did her skin look so dry and old, she wondered?

"What seems to be wrong with your wife, Mr. Bartlett?" she asked. "I mean, what are her symptoms?"

"Well, seems like she can't keep anything on her stomach. She's been throwing up everything for days, and she just keeps getting weaker and weaker."

Catherine didn't know much about medicine, but she had been sick with the flu when she was a little girl, and she had dehydrated. She could still remember the dry stretched feeling of her skin, and suddenly she knew that Mrs. Bartlett needed help.

"Sam—er, Mr. Bartlett. Do you have any tea?" she asked, taking charge.

"Yes, ma'am!"

"Well, hurry and boil some water, and get a good cup of strong tea made! We have to get your wife to take some fluids. I think she is dehydrated."

Mr. Bartlett bumbled around, while Catherine sat beside the woman's bed watching her. Before long he came over with a steaming cup of weak tea. Carefully, Catherine began spooning the liquid into Mrs. Bartlett's mouth. The first spoonfuls dribbled down her cheeks. "Please, Mrs. Bartlett," Catherine whispered, "you've got to try to take some of this. You need it."

Slowly the woman accepted one spoonful and then another. As the soothing liquid worked its way to her dry throat the woman's thirst returned. Catherine helped her sit up on the couch, and she began to sip from the cup.

After Mrs. Bartlett had finished the cup, Catherine thought her color looked better. Mrs. Bartlett sank back on the pillows. "I think perhaps if I gave her a sponge bath it would help," she told Mr. Bartlett. "Could you build a large, warm fire, and then find me towels and soap?"

It took a good hour before the room was warm enough for the project. Catherine could not find any clean towels, and so she had improvised with some folded blankets and a torn sheet. Mr. Bartlett was embarrassed by the women's activities in the room, and when he saw Catherine preparing to bathe his wife, he muttered something about "chores to do" and disappeared outside.

Catherine bathed Mrs. Bartlett, and then fixed her another cup of tea. The woman retained the liquid and Catherine was relieved. "So far, so good!" she said to Mrs. Bartlett, and the woman smiled and sank back, prepared to sleep again.

Catherine went into the bedrooms and found some clean sheets in the closet. She came back into the main room and stripped the bedding off the couch. The fire was glowing cheerfully, and the room was warm and comfortable. Helping Mrs. Bartlett to sit, Catherine remade the couch with clean linen, and then tucked her in. "You sleep for a while now," Catherine said. "When you wake up, maybe you could take some broth, and we can talk." Mrs. Bartlett nodded her head and sank into a refreshing sleep. Her color was clearly improved, and she seemed stronger.

With a sigh, Catherine looked around the dirty room. "Where did that man go?" she wondered crossly.

"I don't care if his wife is sick. There's no excuse for living like this!"

She went over to the windows and raised the blinds, letting the gray light of the cloudy day flood the room. Then she found the copper wash kettle and put it on the stove to boil, and stripped the curtains from the windows and gathered up the dirty clothes around the room. The whites she threw into the boiling water on the stove. The colored clothes she took into the back room to wait for the second wash.

Next she stacked the dirty dishes in the sink, and using extra water from the washtub, put the dishes to soak while she began scrubbing. With strong lye soap she scrubbed down the room. Walls, windowsills, tables, chairs, and finally—after a thorough sweeping—the floor. Immediately, the room looked brighter, and it took on the smell of boiling wash, lye, and fresh-scrubbed wood. Catherine dried the last of the dishes and wrung out the whites. "I'll hang them outside," she thought. "I know they will freeze, but it will make them smell fresh." She pulled on her old jacket and carried the clothes out in a basket. Soon the wet things were flapping on the line in the cold mountain air. Catherine glanced at the sky and saw it was growing late. "I'll need Mr. Bartlett to take me home soon," she thought.

"Home!" she repeated sadly in her mind. "It isn't my home yet!" Still, she yearned for her return to David's house.

When she entered the room, Mrs. Bartlett's eyes followed her as she crossed over to the couch. "You shouldn't have done so much! I don't know how to thank you! It's a terrible thing, lying here thinking you're going to die."

"You aren't going to die, Mrs. Bartlett," Catherine reassured her, "but I think you'd get better a lot faster if you'd let your husband take you to the hospital. You've probably just gotten run down, and they'll fix you up in no time. I want you to get well so I can have a neighbor. I'll need someone to gossip with, and we can trade recipes and talk about women things. Won't you try to get well, Mrs. Bartlett?" Catherine's voice was soothing and convincing. "Sam needs you," Catherine whispered. "You've got to get well for him."

Mrs. Bartlett smiled and closed her eyes for a minute. "Sam," she murmured, and her voice was warm with love. "Mrs. Reid, if you think it's best, I'll let Sam take me first thing tomorrow, but promise me you won't leave me until I go. I've got this terrible fear of dying in the night. Will you promise me you'll stay? Don't leave, and I'll do whatever you say."

"But, Mrs. Bartlett, my husband won't know where I am!"

"Sam will tell him, Mrs. Reid." Mrs. Bartlett's eyes were full of tears. "He could drive over there right now and tell him. Please stay."

Catherine looked at the emaciated woman, and the story of wretched, lonely days was written in her desperate eyes and her work-worn hands. "All right, I'll stay, if Sam will go over and tell David."

Catherine went out into the yard and found Mr. Bartlett. He was milking a scrawny cow in the tumbledown barn, but he left immediately to take the message. She watched his truck go and felt a twinge of pain. Even to be away from David for one night seemed like a punishment.

As dark was falling she heard Mr. Bartlett's truck returning. When he came into the room, she was feeding his wife some soup. "What did David say?" she asked.

"Nothing," replied Mr. Bartlett. "He wasn't there. I waited around for a while, but it looks like he ain't comin', and it was gettin' late, so I left a note and came back home."

"Oh," Catherine said, disturbed that David had not returned. "He must have had trouble getting everything he needed."

"Yep," Mr. Bartlett conceded, "winter shopping takes a lot of time."

The evening passed quickly, as Catherine cared for the sick woman. She tended the fire and cleared up the supper dishes. Mr. Bartlett dozed in one of the chairs. Around midnight he got up. "I think I'll go in and sleep, Mrs. Reid," he said. "If I got to drive into town tomorrow, I'll need my rest."

"Fine," said Catherine, groggy with weariness herself. "I'll stay and keep watch." The long night stretched on. Once or twice Mrs. Bartlett cried out in her sleep, and Catherine went to her. "I'm here, Mrs. Bartlett, just as I promised," she murmured, and the older woman, soothed, fell back to sleep.

When she heard the rooster crowing, Catherine woke in the cold, gray light of dawn. The fire had burned low, and the room was chilly. She got up and added some logs and the movement wakened the other woman. "Now?" said Mrs. Bartlett. "Is it time to go?"

"Almost," Catherine told her. "Don't be afraid, everything will be fine." Catherine helped Mr. Bartlett gather some of his wife's things into an old leather suitcase. Mrs. Bartlett was weak, but her eyes were clear, and she smiled at Catherine. "I'll be back before the deep snow," she said. "That's a promise! We'll have those neighborly visits one day soon. Thank you for all you've done!"

Mr. Bartlett wanted to drive Catherine home, but the road was rough and the extra twelve miles of driving would have been hard for his frail wife. "No!" Catherine insisted. "It's only two miles if I go over the hill. I'll be home in less than an hour. You get on to that hospital!" The pickup truck rattled out of sight and Catherine spent a few moments gathering in the wash.

For the third successive day the sky was threatening and leaden, and the wind was chill. Catherine realized she was bone-tired, and the thought of going home spurred her on. "Just two miles of hiking, and I will climb into my own bed and rest!" she told herself. Throwing on the old sheepskin jacket, she set off up the hill. The climb was steeper than she had realized and her limbs protested at the strain of the activity. She pulled her jacket around herself more tightly, wishing that she'd had the foresight to bring a scarf. The cold morning wind whipped her hair around her face and her fingers were numb. "No scarf and no gloves!" She couldn't believe she had been so careless. "Oh, well, it's not far," she thought. Her legs were aching with weariness, and the hill seemed endless.

Just as she mounted the crest of the hill, a gust of wind blew against her, carrying a blast of cold sleet that dampened her hair and legs. She shivered in the cold and began to walk faster trying to warm her aching cold feet. Raising her chin out of the protective collar of her coat, she looked around. The hill she had just climbed led into a shallow valley, and beyond it was a taller one. She recognized the second hill and knew that her home lay beyond it, snuggled in the next valley.

There remained a long hard distance to be traveled. She jammed her freezing hands into her pockets and burrowed her face into the collar of her coat. The light sleet continued to fall, and her hair became soaking wet, with rivulets of water running off her head and down into the neck of the jacket. It seemed nothing kept her warm now, and she plodded on, putting one foot in front of the other, concentrating on nothing but the next step. The rhythm of her steps was hypnotic, and suddenly she felt as though she were floating in the air above herself, looking at a foolish, wet woman, plodding through the cold foothills, stumbling and staggering and moving on.

"Why?" she asked herself. "Why bother! If David really cared he would have come for you when he saw the note. He would have come over to the Bartletts no matter how late he came home. He would have come searching for you. No one knows where you are and no one cares!" She continued to struggle up the hill, shivering so violently that she lost sense of time or direction. Tears were coursing down her cheeks and the bitter cold seemed to be inside her now, chasing away all her warmth. She could feel the cold sinking into her, and the small warm core inside her body shrank away from the freezing chill. Twice she stumbled and picked herself up.

Near the brow of the hill the terrain became steeper, and as Catherine tried to lift her foot, the cold seemed insurmountable. The chill gnawed her insides. She stood looking stupidly at her foot, willing it to lift, but it would not move. Then slowly, like a snowflake drifting down, she sagged to the ground. "David," she whispered with her last strength.

David had come home long after dark the night before. His car had broken down, and the delay in his return worried him. When he drove up, the house was dark. He assumed that Catherine had gone to bed. "Catherine!" he had called. "I'm home!" There was no answer and he went to her bedroom door and knocked. "Catherine, I'm back," he called. There was still no answer. Assuming she was asleep, he prepared himself for bed, and exhausted from the long and frustrating day, he fell into a sound, unbroken sleep. Early the next morning he woke. The sky was light, but there was no stirring in Catherine's room. He fixed himself breakfast, noisily clanging pans in the hopes of waking her. Finally, he could stand it no longer and he knocked on her door. "Catherine!" he called. There was still no response. With a sudden rush of apprehension he threw open the bedroom door and in horror saw the untouched bed. His mind went blank—he could not imagine where she had gone. The only thought in his head was that she had left him. His worst fear had come true. "Gone!" the word was like a death knoll in his head. Only for a minute—then reason prevailed.

"She didn't have a car!" he remembered. "No one

comes up here—except Bartlett! Maybe he'll know something!" He rushed to the front door and that was when he saw the note on the table by the entrance.

"Mrs. R. is taking care of my wife, who's sick. Home in the morning." It was signed "S. Bartlett."

Weak with relief, David threw on his coat and jumped in the car. As quickly as he could, he navigated the bumpy road to the Bartlett place. When he arrived, he ran up to the front door. No answer greeted his loud knocking, and finally he pushed open the door. The room was cleaner than he had ever seen it. On the table was a stack of neatly folded laundry, and a fire was flickering low in the fireplace. He looked around the farmyard and discovered that the Bartletts' truck was gone. "How could they be driving Catherine home, if I didn't pass them on the road?" David wondered. He was puzzled. The Bartletts were gone, Catherine was gone. They had not driven her home, and yet where would they have taken her?

A sick feeling washed over him. "She's left!" he thought again. "She saw what the isolation and hardship did to Mrs. Bartlett, and she made up her mind." He sat on a chair and buried his face in his hands.

But his mind wouldn't stop working. It continued to worry about the puzzle of her absence. "Would she really leave like that?" he asked himself. "Without saying good-bye or confronting me?" Everything he knew about Catherine told him she was too honest and courageous to run away from anything. He remembered standing in the pigsty facing the charging sow. He thought of her quick, capable hands tending his wounded leg. He heard her voice singing in the mornings, and her quiet laughter when she was happy.

"Where is she?" he asked himself. Then he tried to imagine how she must have acted the day before. Bartlett would have come to the door. She was probably a little frightened and puzzled by the man. Then, when he asked for her help, she would have made a quick impulsive decision. If she were neeeded she would go!

Looking around the room, he could imagine her disgust and distaste at the shocking state of the Bartlett home. He could see her scolding Mr. Bartlett into helping and then her quick, forthright attack on the dirt. She had swept and scrubbed and cleaned and rid the place of filth. Her energy and determination were boundless. He could also envision Catherine caring for the sick woman. Ministering to her needs, despite the fact that she had no medical training. "Of course! That's it!" he thought. "She would have persuaded them to go to the hospital! That's where they are! I'll drive down to town and pick her up." He was certain he had solved the puzzle, but as he left the house something nagged at him, and he paused to think what had struck him as wrong.

If Mrs. Bartlett was sick enough to be in the hospital, David knew Catherine would be determined to get her there as early as possible. By first light she would have had her on her way. Then why had Catherine stopped to take in and fold the laundry? And the fire was still burning on the hearth. Surely she would not have delayed the trip to the hospital for such mundane things! Then it struck him. "The reason I didn't pass the Bartletts bringing Catherine home is because she sent them on to the hospital without her. She must have decided to walk home the back way!"

The idea was so logical that suddenly he was absolutely convinced he was right! He flung himself out the door and started up the hill. His powerful strides pulled him forward with speed, and he topped the first hill rapidly. The sleet was heavy, but he was wearing several layers of clothes, and he had pulled a heavy cap out of his pocket and put on his gloves.

His visibility was hampered by the heavy sleet, and David slid down the far side of the hill. The second rise was steeper and the going was tough on the frozen slippery ground. Anxiety propelled him forward. "She must have gotten home before the storm began," he told himself, as though by saying it he could make it true. In a protected hollow, he bent to pick up an object lying on the ground. It was one of the combs from her hair. Spurred on by this proof of his logic, he continued up the last steep incline.

He almost passed by Catherine without seeing her. She lay unconscious, and the sleet had covered her so that she looked like a small mound on the hill. It was her hair that drew David's eye. The wind that whipped across the top of the bluff caught the tendrils of her long hair. The motion caught the corner of David's eye, and with a cry he rushed to her. "Catherine!" he called. "Catherine!" But her face was the color of the sleet, and there was no response. He picked her up in his arms and, slipping and sliding, he traversed the far side of the hill and entered the shelter of trees around their home.

He pushed the door open with his foot and carried her in and placed her by the fireplace. Working as fast as he could, he grabbed every blanket and rug in the

house and piled the rugs under her and the blankets
on top of her. With rapid motions he built a fire in
the stone fireplace and heaped on dry logs and kindling until the wood blazed. Then he turned back to
Catherine. She was still lying lifeless. Her hand felt
like cold marble in his own. Without hesitation, he
pulled back the covers and began to strip the wet
clothing from her body. He pulled off his own clothes,
too, and pressing his body close to hers, he pulled the
heavy blankets over the two of them. With his own
body he began to massage her, but under his rhythmically moving arms and legs she remained cold and perfectly still. He rubbed and rubbed her body slowly,
until finally, she began to warm a little. The room
became as hot as a furnace, and he reached over to
throw more logs into the blaze, then went back to rubbing and holding her. "Catherine!" he kept calling,
knowing it was imperative to make her conscious.
"Catherine! Help me!" he called to her. "Catherine!"
His voice was demanding and loving. "Catherine! I
know you can hear me! Wake up! Help me! Catherine! I need you! Catherine! Catherine!"

She was somewhere far off in a cold, cold land
where everything seemed white. She was white, the air
was white, the snow was white, and she was frozen into
the snow; she was part of the snow and the sky, and
she was heavy, so heavy! She couldn't move and she
didn't want to move. It would hurt too much. She
wanted the snow, the cold, the nothingness. But something wouldn't let her alone. Something kept disturbing her, pulling at her in the white nothingness. It was
far, far away; she couldn't see it or hear it. It was like
a little flickering light, a pinpoint of warmth, and it

flickered and beckoned. She knew if she went to it, it would hurt, and she would have to leave the white nothingness. But the flickering wouldn't go away—it urged her, lured her, and distracted her. She was irritated. Go away, she wanted to say, go away! But it continued to flicker, and she felt it coming nearer her, and suddenly it was inside her, a feather of warmth, but it made the whiteness seem suddenly cold, and she began to shiver and wished the warmth would go away and leave her in peace. The cold only felt cold when the warmth was there, deep inside of her. But the small flame wouldn't go away, and she began to shiver again.

Then she heard it. From a great distance across the snow, someone was calling her. "I won't go!" she thought, "I won't!" But the voice came to her and would not be denied. "Catherine!" it said, "Catherine! Come here, I need you!" No, she wouldn't go to her father. He didn't need her. Nobody needed her—only the snow, the pure white snow. "Catherine!" The voice was sharp, and she turned her head angrily. "That must be Norman," she thought. "I won't go to him, not ever! He can call forever if he likes!" She felt irritable and frightened. The voice wouldn't go away, and the warm flickering was getting stronger. She was shaking with cold and pain. "Leave me alone!" she mumbled. "Let me sleep. The snow. I want to go back to the snow!"

"Catherine!" The voice was inside her head. "Catherine! Please try to wake up. You've got to help me! Catherine, try harder!"

"No," she mumbled. "Why should I try? It doesn't matter anyway! The cold is better! It's easier!"

"Catherine!" The shivering shook her violently, and she shuddered away from the voice and the warmth. "Sleep!" she mumbled. "Sleep!"

Suddenly rough hands grabbed her and shook her. "No!" the voice shouted. "I won't let you sleep. You're going to wake up and live, Catherine! Wake up! Catherine, I love you. I need you. Don't leave me! I need you!" Someone was lying on her. The weight was heavy but pleasant, and suddenly the flickering warmth took root inside of her. She opened her eyes, and the fireplace danced in the darkness. Without thinking, she pushed against the weight on top of her, and it moved. "Catherine!" David raised his head and looked into her eyes. "Catherine! You're awake!" Drowsily, she nodded. "How did I get here?" she murmured. "How did I get home?"

"Home!" he said, laughing. "Yes, darling, you are home, and I'm going to keep you here forever." He embraced her and felt the body warmth coming back into her flesh. Holding her as gently as a child, he began to rub her arms and legs. The room continued to glow with heat, and gradually her terrible shivering subsided. Between the blankets their bodies met and the glowing heat of his own melted into hers. As the morning passed he worked on her, and gradually he felt her grow supple and warm beneath his hands. Exhausted, the two of them slept.

He wakened first, and feeling her alive and whole, he reluctantly slid out from the covers and put on his robe. Quietly, he sat by the bedroll to keep the fire roaring. As she slept he studied her face—the smooth, tender forehead, the delicate arched eyebrows, the long-lashed eyes, and the sculptured lips. There was not a single feature that was not more precious to him than his own life.

He made a decision as he watched her sleeping, and once the decision was made he felt a sense of peace. In the afternoon he drifted off to sleep on the couch, and when he woke, Catherine was also awake, her eyes clear and alert. She had not moved under the heavy blankets, but was looking at him, sleeping, and the look on her face was unfathomable. He did not move either, and for a moment they simply gazed at one another, each trying to read the other's expression—to test the feelings and thoughts that hung in the silent room. The long moment lengthened, and the silence drew out like a thread, broken only by the crackling of the blazing logs in the fireplace.

Catherine spoke first. "You found me!" she whispered.

"Yes," David answered and sat up on the couch.

"And—and—" she hesitated. "You brought me here and . . . undressed me?"

"Yes," he answered again simply.

"I had a dream—" Catherine's voice was unreadable, soft and direct. "Were you— Did I dream it or were you . . . with . . . me in this bed?"

"Yes," David answered again, and stood up and walked over to the rustic mantel. He stood by the fire, his face turned away from her.

Under the covers, Catherine's hands lay beside her naked body. She could feel the weight of the covers on her bare breasts, and the blankets, harsh against the tender skin of her thighs. Naked! And he had lain with her! The memory of her dream floated in her mind, and she had to know. "Did anything happen between us?" Her voice trembled with emotion, and she dropped her gaze in shy confusion.

"Nothing happened between us," he said, in a quiet voice. "I saved your life—nothing more. And now I guess we're even, Catherine. Isn't that what the Chinese proverb says—'A life for a life.' Well, you saved my life, and so I was bound to honor your wishes—but now I have saved your life, and I am not bound anymore."

"What are you saying?" she cried. "I don't understand what you mean!"

"Catherine," he said, and laid his hand on her shoulder. She stilled under his touch and turned to look at him again.

"Catherine," he said, his voice firm. "This is a foolish bargain we have made. I have wanted to tell you for weeks, but since you saved my life, I felt I couldn't renege on your wishes. Today, however, watching you as you slept, I have known that it is only cruelty to both of us to keep up this sham!" His words frightened her. What was he trying to say?

"There was no sham," she answered him quickly. "I knew exactly what the terms were when I came to the ranch. There has been no deception."

"Catherine." His voice shook with passion. In all the weeks they had been together she had not spoken a harsh word. She had been efficient and helpful, though remote. In all that time hadn't she once needed him as he needed and wanted her? He had to know, and he could no longer deny his right to know.

He looked at her lying before him, her eyes intent, her self-possession unbroken, and he shook with frustration and desperate need.

"This whole relationship is impossible!" he exploded. "We are man and wife! I know I promised you, if you came—if we married—I would never impose upon you the imperatives of our marriage contract, and I have kept my word! But I am a man, Catherine! A man of flesh and blood, with all the needs and passions of a man—and there is no way that I can continue to live with you and not have you."

She gasped at his words, and her eyes widened as a thrill of answering passion shook her.

David looked into her eyes, and she saw in his face the resolute decision of a man who would no longer be denied. The pent-up emotions of weeks of self-control flooded his mind and body, and he grasped the edge of her blankets and tore them away, revealing her body, huddled in shyness and modesty, the long alabaster curve of her back pristine before his eyes. He touched her shoulder and with a startled cry she turned over, her arms instinctively covering herself.

"David!" she whispered, her voice tremulous. "David!" She reached for the edge of the blanket, but he pulled it away from her and stood looming above her. With a single gesture he untied his robe and threw it on the couch and looked down upon her, his face dark with passion and unreadable thoughts.

It was the first time she had seen a naked man, and as she saw his magnificent body towering above her, she was shaken with an emotion more powerful than any she had ever known. Her own flesh cried out to him—to be covered by him—and to be held, to be loved. She wanted to reach out and embrace his strong legs, to stand next to him and press her body close to his mighty chest, to feel the strength of his muscular arms around her. But she did not know if it was love or lust she read in David's face. If she moved toward him and let him know of her own passionate love, would he turn from her? She lay on the bed of rugs and blankets with the firelight dancing on her rosy skin and her tangled mass of hair, and she held herself completely still.

He did not move either, but his eyes drank in her beauty. He looked at her until he thought he would burst with desire and passion, and then, when he could bear it no more, with a sound more like a groan than her name, he said the single word, "Catherine!" and knelt to lift her in his arms. With savage desire he kissed her body, and his hands sought to waken her with fierce urgency. He touched her and his hands filled with her scent and the warm richness of her satin skin.

Finally, he took her swiftly with hard passionate strokes. Within her his whole being was filled with an ecstasy he had never thought possible. But a bittersweet pain cut his heart in two as he saw her beneath him, her dear eyes dark and wondering. He released her with a moan and rolled over beside her, his face expressionless and his eyes fixed on the ceiling. "Whatever comes of it," he thought, "it is done."

Catherine was trembling. She had not imagined such glory! Could it be wrong or unwomanly to feel the things she was feeling? Was she an unnatural woman that she should feel such joy, such need and desire? Her body was filled with a languid sweetness that made her limbs flame with warmth. If only she could talk to David, ask him what she was feeling. Tell him. But she shrank in shyness from the thought. What would he think if she spoke to him of her need for love? He, who had never spoken to her of love. Surely, she thought, he must feel something for me. He could not have held me, could not have taken me with such power, if I meant nothing to him. She waited for him to speak, trembling with hope.

David lay beside her. He knew that his need for her love and high regard was as great as his need for her body. She would, he knew, submit her body to him, again and again if he insisted, but it was the woman inside he yearned for—and that, she would not submit by force. There was no way of taking her heart.

Beside him she was silent, and he could only try to imagine what she must be feeling. His pride rose.

"I'm sorry, Catherine," he said. "I didn't mean it to happen this way." He slowly pulled the covers up over her and got to his feet, putting on his robe. She was silent; and when he looked at her, he saw tears had sprung to her eyes.

"I'm sorry if I hurt you," he said softly. He walked over and threw another log on the fire. "If you like, I'll sleep in the bedroom tonight. You'll need the fire. But I'll keep it going—you don't need to worry about anything." He went to the bedroom door, and Catherine seemed to come out of her daze. She sat up in the blankets, clutching the top covers to her breast. Her eyes were glowing and her hair was silhouetted in the fire. He thought, as she stared at him, that she had never seemed more beautiful.

"David," she whispered, "don't go to the bedroom."

Then she held out her arms to him and the blankets dropped to her waist. "Come back to bed with me, I'm cold." She was smiling faintly, a sensual, languid smile, and David felt an enormous strength surge through him. In two strides he crossed the distance between them, and bending down, he picked her up in his arms, wrapped her in the loose blankets, and held her in a powerful embrace. He covered her face and hair with passionate, triumphant kisses. Then he made love to her again, slowly, languorously in the darkened room with the firelight glowing. Afterward they slept in each others' arms through the long, sweet night.

The next morning Catherine awakened and stretched luxuriously. The fire was still crackling, and the room was warm but the mattress beside her was empty. She smiled to herself as she thought of David and their night together.

Wrapping a blanket around herself, she walked barefoot to the window and looked out through the trees to the barnyard. The sun was shining brightly and there was no trace of yesterday's storm. A brisk wind shook the bare trees.

She could see David carrying milk pails into the barn, and she wanted to call to him, to run to him, to see his face. Could he possibly feel as gloriously happy as she? she wondered. Humming under her breath, she began to straighten up the room. She put a kettle on the stove to heat water for breakfast. When David came in, she wanted everything to be perfect.

After she folded away the blankets and pillows, she ran into the bedroom to dress. She threw on a dark skirt, a white pullover sweater, and moccasins. When she brushed her hair, she looked carefully at herself in the mirror, wondering whether the transformation she was feeling could show in her face. Then Catherine hurried back into the kitchen to stir up some buttermilk biscuits. The room was soon fragrant with the scent of her baking.

As David worked at his outdoor chores, he knew that he had never been happier, and yet his very happiness filled him with apprehension. Catherine was still a mystery to him, and for the first time in his memory he realized that his destiny and the realization of his lifelong dreams no longer resided in his hands alone. It now rested in the unknown heart of this puzzling woman whom he loved!

He was ready to give her everything he had—his land, his cattle, his home, his dreams, his very life— and yet, for the first time, these things seemed like a paltry gift. All these things, which to him seemed so fine and satisfying . . . how did they seem to a woman like Catherine? Would this harsh existence, the earthiness and isolation of life on the ranch eventually destroy her? He hadn't thought about that before he had known the full measure of his love for her. He found himself wishing for wealth so that he could give her everything she deserved, the things to which she had been accustomed.

It occurred to him that she still had not said she loved him—at least, not in words. He had to know! He found himself wanting to hear her say it. He wanted to hurry to her, to listen to her voice, to hold her. As he turned to go back to the house a sleek black car roared up the mountain road and turned into his barnyard.

He watched in astonishment as a tall young woman dressed in a magnificent sable coat and matching hat climbed out of the driver's seat. "My good man!" she called to David as he stood speechless in his denim work clothes, holding the milk bucket in his hand. "Could you please tell me where I might find the Reid Ranch?"

"This is it," David said. He knew by her tone of voice that she had taken him for a hired hand, and normally that would have amused him, but something in the sudden appearance of the expensive car and its wealthy occupants rang a warning bell in David's mind and he felt resentful of their intrusion.

A man wearing a British-tailored topcoat, who looked to be in his forties, stepped out of the car. The man was handsome and aristocratic and he glanced around the muddy barnyard with its simple buildings with an impassive expression that enraged David because it seemed to be both condescending and disparaging.

"I guess this must be the place, Jean," the man said, and to David, his uninflected voice was like a direct insult. He felt anger rising. Who were these people, and what right did they have to come onto his property and judge it as though they were the lords of the land visiting the peasants?

"I suppose so, dear," the woman replied, but her voice sounded dubious as she looked around at the unprepossessing yard with the rustic cabin that stood bare and unprotected now that the trees had lost their leaves. "You don't suppose . . ." she said, staring at the house. Then she turned back to David. "Excuse me. We are looking for Mrs. David Reid. I am an old friend of hers." She pointed to the cabin. "Is this the main house?" Her voice was courteous but her face registered disbelief.

"Yes," David said, his eyes blazing, but his tone remaining civil, "it is."

"Oh!" The woman made an effort to smile. "Well, it's charming." She turned to her husband, and her voice rose with an effort to sound excited. "Isn't it, Gordon? It's absolutely charming! And the mountains . . . Why! they are magnificent!"

The woman's false enthusiasm angered David more than her husband's cool appraisal, and he wanted, with all his heart, to order these pretentious people off his land. Before he could say anything, however, the woman began picking her way carefully through the thick mud of the driveway toward the flagstones that led to the cabin. He looked at her polished calfskin high heels, and he knew that one pair of shoes like that would cost as much as he earned on an entire load of hay.

The man gave David a look which seemed to say, "Women! What can you do with them?" and with a slightly sardonic nod of the head, he turned to follow his wife. David said nothing. He could think of no graceful way to tell them who he was, and he was still so enraged at their intrusion and superiority that he made no effort to be civil.

He turned back to the barn to let the horses out into the corral. Leaning on the fence and watching the animals frisking and leaping, he began to feel better. Nothing was more beautiful than a running horse, and the brisk mountain wind seemed to blow his anger away. Moments later he heard Catherine's excited voice calling him. "David! David!" and he knew he would have to go to meet her friends formally. Of all days, why did her former life need to intrude on this day, the first real day of their life together?

There was a moment of awkwardness as Catherine introduced David to Jean Hunt and her husband Gordon Beaumont. The Beaumonts were obviously embarrassed at having mistaken David for hired help, and David did nothing to ease their discomfort.

Suddenly Jean laughed, and the natural candor of her personality shone through. She held out her hand to David and shook his hand with warmth. "Sorry!" she said, with refreshing directness. "We thought you were a cowhand. But what do you expect when you're out in the barn? I was a stablehand myself once anyway, and I don't see anything to apologize for in that occupation."

David could not help but laugh, even though he still felt resentful of these friends of Catherine's. "Well, in point of fact," he answered, "I am the cowhand, and the hired hand, as well as the owner. Our winter crew consists of Catherine and myself."

Jean Beaumont raised her eyebrows but did not comment. Instead, she turned and gave Catherine a long look.

David looked at Catherine, too, and he could not help but note the contrast. Catherine's long hair was brushed out and hung in natural waves, her plain sweater and skirt made her look young, and her face without makeup was rosy from outdoor work. Her hands were roughened from labor and red from washing and scrubbing, and her bare feet were thrust into worn moccasins.

Next to her, Jean sat in a sleek tailored suit, her hair bobbed and set, her makeup flawless and her silk-clad legs gracefully crossed. As she pulled off her gloves her hands were white, with manicured and polished nails.

"Whatever you are doing, Catherine," Jean said brightly, "it seems to be agreeing with you. I've never seen you looking so happy."

Catherine blushed and got up hurriedly to make tea for the visitors. David took Gordon out to look at his breeding stock. He was reluctant to discuss the things he was struggling to accomplish with this wealthy, confident man. He assumed that such a man would know nothing of the thrill of risk and achievement. Gordon asked intelligent questions and praised the herd, but he sensed David's hostility, and so he suggested they return to the house.

"Must be on our way," Gordon said. "Beastly drive ahead of us! Hope to make Calgary by nightfall." Jean's husband spoke with an English accent. "I say, old man," he continued, and put his arm on David's sleeve so that David stopped walking and turned to face him on the path. "Before we go in to the girls, I thought perhaps I should warn you why we're here. The girls were awfully keen about one another—grew up together—best friends and all that sort of thing, you know. I met Jean two years ago at the horse show in Toronto. Married her on the spot and took her off to England. Poor girl hasn't been home since. When I told her I had to come over to western Canada to make a tour of the family holdings, she insisted she must come along with me. She's been a wonderful sport about it. Hasn't minded roughing it at all. Anyway, we've just finished our business in British Columbia, and we're on our way back for a few days in Calgary and then back to England. Jean has it in her mind that nothing will do but that she captures you and Catherine and carries you back to Calgary with us for these last few days of her stay. What do you say, old man? I'm sure she's already asked Catherine."

The thought of spending several days in the company of the Beaumonts was unthinkable. David refused to even consider the possibility. "No, thank you," he said brusquely. "I cannot possibly leave the ranch."

"Then what about Catherine?" Gordon persisted. He adored Jean, and ever since their marriage he had been unwilling to deny her anything her heart desired. "Surely you could spare her for a few days. Besides, it would do her good! She could see her family, visit old friends, buy some new clothes, get her hair fixed—all the things these pretty little creatures love most!"

David stared at the older man. His smooth intelligent face and his clear eyes bespoke indulgence and old wealth. Was this man right? Was this really what women longed for? Was Catherine secretly desiring to escape, to be with this kind of people . . . people that she had grown up with, who lived in ease and extravagance? Suddenly, he was disgusted, with himself and with the Beaumonts, for the privileged life-style and the air of worldliness they represented. He stared up at the rugged peaks of the mountains rising against the blue sky, with the low-lying foothills in the foreground, and he thought of his cattle roaming free and strong among the hills.

"Catherine may do whatever she wants," he replied shortly. "She is a free agent."

"Yes, old fellow. Give the pretty little things whatever they want, spoil them a little! Makes for a happy life, I say!"

An uncomfortable pause followed as both Gordon and David recognized the irony in his remark. Then Gordon turned to David and said in a hearty voice, "You know, I've been enormously impressed with what you have shown me today. I've got a lot of investments here in Canada that aren't nearly as promising as what you are doing. You wouldn't possibly be interested in taking on a limited partnership, would you? You know, someone like me who could provide you with a little working capital. Could speed things up a bit. Say five thousand cash, for a 10 percent interest. No strings at all, of course, just a gentleman's agreement. I'm sure it could give you a boost—buy some stock, spruce up the place a bit, buy a few luxuries for yourself . . ."

David knew Gordon's offer was well-intentioned, but it struck him as an insult, and he was infuriated. "I do not need your charity," he said, his heart like a stone.

"I was not offering it," Gordon responded with dignity. "I was making a sound business proposition."

"Well, hang your proposition!" David said angrily and threw open the door into the house.

When the men entered the kitchen, it was apparent the women had been talking about the proposed trip to Calgary. Catherine's eyes were glowing, and she ran up to David.

"Oh, David, did Gordon tell you! Is it possible? Could we go home for a few days?"

David flinched at her use of the word "home" in reference to Calgary. "I can't," he said curtly. "You may do whatever you like."

Catherine looked at him with puzzled eyes. "Well," she said softly, "of course you're right, I guess we couldn't leave the animals." She turned to Jean with a forced smile. "You'll explain to my mother and father, won't you, Jean? There really isn't any way we can break away."

Jean's face showed her disappointment. "Oh, surely, Catherine! Just for a few days! David! You must tell her to come!" In her agitation, Jean became thoughtless. "Surely you can't expect her to stay," and her eyes swept the room with a look of pity, "for the whole winter without one bright spot to remember!"

David's face suffused with anger at Jean's implied insult. His jaw hardened in fury and his voice was like steel. "I told you, I don't care what Catherine does," he repeated, and turned on his heel and left the room.

Catherine ran outside after him. "David! David!" she called, running behind him, breathless and shivering in the cold mountain air, until he stopped and faced her. "What's the matter?"

"David, please!" she pleaded. "Jean didn't mean anything. It's just that . . . she told Mother and Father I would be coming home with her. We haven't seen each other for ages. It wouldn't be for long, David, but if you really don't want me to go . . ." She looked into his eyes and with every yearning of her heart she wanted him to say, "Stay, Catherine. Stay, because I need you and love you."

But the anger and hurt of the morning filled David's mind and his stubborn pride held him rigid. "I told you. Do whatever you want," he answered.

Catherine, as proud and stubborn as he, felt her anger flame at his curt words. "All right!" she shouted at him, impulsively, furiously. "You insult my friends! You humiliate me! If you don't care what I do, then I will go!" Without another word, fearing that he would see the tears brimming in her eyes, she turned and sped down the path back to the house.

Half an hour later she came out to find him. He was keeping busy oiling the harnesses in the barn. Her manner was stiff and calm.

"I'm packed and I guess I will be leaving now," she said quietly.

"Fine," he answered, his voice controlled. "Shall I come carry your bags out for you?"

"No, thank you. Gordon has already put them in the trunk." They stood there uncomfortably for a moment, and in the silence they could hear the restless movement of the animals in their stalls, and the cows munching in the feeder.

"I guess this is good-bye for a while, then," Catherine said softly, trying to smile.

"I suppose so," David replied. "Will you let me know your plans?"

"Yes, oh, yes!" she replied, too brightly, too eagerly. Then one last time she whispered pleadingly, "David, if you don't want me to go . . ."

He interrupted her with a quick, negative gesture of his hand. "Let's not start that again! You've made your decision. When you come back, well, we'll know . . ."

Suddenly, her head snapped up, and she looked at him with blazing eyes. "We'll know?" she exclaimed. "What do you mean we'll know!"

They faced each other, two strong, proud, stubborn people matched in their strength, each wanting the other to give in and each unable to bend. David stared at her proud face, the challenge of her will like a gauntlet thrown between them, and he reached out and grabbed her shoulders in his sun-bronzed hands, and pulling her against him, he bent and kissed her lips, pressing against them fiercely until he felt them open. She pushed against him, angry and strong, until the strength of his kiss flared her passion. Abruptly, he released her, and she stepped back, her lips bruised and scarlet, her eyes flashing.

"Perhaps," he said, matching her challenging eyes, "when you come back, we will both know better who we are and what we want." She could not meet his penetrating gaze, and running from him, she left the barn. In a few moments he heard the sound of the engine as the powerful car roared out of the driveway. In the silence that followed he walked slowly out of the barn, and for a long time he stood looking up at the empty blue sky and the wispy trail of white clouds dusting the heavens with the future promise of ice and snow.

CHAPTER TWENTY-THREE

Returning to Calgary, Catherine felt as though her past was waiting for her, unchanged. Delighted to see her, her parents plied her with questions about David and the ranch and wondered when they might meet him.

Catherine replied to their questions vaguely, and her parents sensed that something was wrong. But with the trained diffidence of polite, civilized people they refrained from asking direct questions and waited for Catherine to tell them about her marriage when she was ready to do so.

Within a few days her parents stopped inquiring about David and limited their conversation to news of recent events in Calgary. By mutual and unspoken agreement, the subject of Catherine's marriage was mentioned only in passing.

Grateful for her parents' restraint, Catherine set about filling her days. She and Jean spent most of the week together. When the day came for Jean to return to England, they cried; they knew it would be years before they saw one another again. Jean, with great tact, had never mentioned David or the scene at the ranch, but as she hugged Catherine good-bye she whispered in her ear, "You've got yourself a real man, Catherine! I like him. I really do! But living with him will never be easy." Catherine grinned. How like Jean! Straightforward to the end.

Under her mother's tutelage Catherine started to take an interest in needlepoint, and she began to embroider a group of chair covers for the ranch cottage.

"You do have chairs, don't you?" her mother asked. "I'm sure the ranch is rustic, but charming, and the wonder of needlepoint is that it is so durable! It never wears out, and would do well, even in a rugged environment!"

"There are two windsor chairs," Catherine conceded, wincing at the memory of the big old kitchen with its shabby, comfortable furniture and the tall stone fireplace. She selected wools of rich earth tones and began needlepointing a flame stitch design for the chairs. In her heart she wondered if the chairs would ever be covered with the cushions, but it was oddly comforting and domestic to sit in the living room of her childhood home and work the lovely pattern with the rhythmic weave of the needlepoint stitch.

Her parents lived a quiet life, but were still active in club activities, and were frequently invited to dinners. They tried to include Catherine in their social activities, but she declined their entreaties to join them, and soon they decided she really preferred to remain at home, and they stopped prodding her.

Her parents took her to the movies and dinner, and several old friends called for lunch or an afternoon of shopping. The days passed swiftly and still Catherine hesitated about returning to the ranch. David had not written and in some angry, proud stubborn corner of her mind she did not want to return until he asked her.

One afternoon she went for a long walk and noted with anxiety the signs of winter on the distant mountains. There was a frosty wind and she bundled up in her fur coat. The cold air exhilarated her, and she was grateful for the time alone. Though she tried to concentrate on other things, her thoughts inevitably turned to David. Were his cattle prepared for the blast of winter? Was he lonely? Did he miss her? The awesome faraway mountains kept his secrets.

Emily and her husband, James, and their two-year-old daughter, Sarah, came over for Sunday afternoon dinner. Catherine was disturbed to see that Emily constantly nagged at her husband, and that James accepted her whining with resignation. Emily's pretty face had changed. She wore a continual pout, and her face was marked with tiny frown lines of discontent. Sarah was a pretty child who resembled her mother, and everyone spoiled her shamelessly. Fortunately, Sarah had her father's mild, sunny disposition, and so she accepted the adoration of the grownups with a sweet even temper.

"You have no idea, Catherine!" Emily exclaimed in her high, quick voice, as they sat together in the living room after dinner one Sunday, watching Sarah play dolls by the fireside. "Between the hospital volunteer league and the debutante ball which I must chairman for the Black Watch Society this year, I haven't a minute for myself! Running a home, entertaining, and trying to take care of Sarah—she's a handful I can tell you! You have no idea how difficult it is to be a mother! If I had known, I would have told James that I wouldn't consider having a child until I was much older!"

Catherine was watching Sarah hold her doll. The little girl's face was rapt with concentration as she examined the buttons and frills on the doll's dress, and then put her arms around the toy and gave it a hug. "Sarah seems to think being a mother is quite wonderful!" Catherine observed with a smile, nodding her head in the direction of the little girl, who was holding the doll tenderly in her arms.

"Let me tell you!" Emily exclaimed, piqued by Catherine's implied criticism. "I'm a good mother! Anyone will tell you I am—but being a mother is a great deal different than playing with dolls. For one thing, dolls do not dirty their diapers. You can't imagine how hard it is to toilet train a two-year-old!"

Without being told, Catherine understood why Emily was trying to impress her with how busy she was. In an indirect way she was trying to apologize to Catherine for not spending more time with her, and for not including her in more of the social activities of her set.

"Then there's all the entertaining we're expected to do! How I envy you, Catherine! You are having such a nice, peaceful rest here. I'm sure that's what you've needed—to gather up strength to go back to that ranch! Is it really rustic? Does David actually expect you to help with the chores? It must be awful!"

Unlike her parents, Catherine's sister, Emily, had shown no reticence about the subject of Catherine's marriage. Her curiosity knew no limits, and she could not refrain from asking prying, searching questions whenever they talked. Catherine answered the questions with noncommittal monosyllables which served only to fan Emily's curiosity further.

Emily had spoken to her mother about it in private. "I know something's wrong, Mother. Catherine is so secretive! She hardly knew the man at all and went up into the wilderness with him. Something awful might have happened! Don't you think we have the right to know? Everyone is wondering and talking about it!"

Catherine's mother looked at her young daughter sternly. "When Catherine is ready to tell us, she will. In the meantime she is home, and we will do the most we can to see that she is happy."

Emily was irritated that her mother did not side with her about insisting Catherine tell them everything.

"You have it so easy, Catherine!" Emily repeated. "Marriage to a young executive is certainly a different thing than marriage to a rancher. We are having twenty people to dinner this Friday, and James's salary is too small for a caterer, so I have to make do with my own maid—and Hilda when Mother will lend her to me!" Emily sighed, and then she flushed at the thought of what she had just said. "Oh, Catherine! It's only a business dinner! Nothing you would enjoy! I'd invite you, but I know you'd be bored. Besides, you came home to rest, and getting into this terrible social whirl is not restful at all!"

"It's all right, Emily," Catherine said, smiling. "I understand." Catherine picked up her needlepoint. "It's always hard to set a table for a single guest. It makes the seating pattern uneven."

Emily looked at her sister sharply, as though she suspected she was being mocked but wasn't quite sure. Catherine smiled at her reassuringly. Just then James came into the room. He was still good-looking, but his hair was beginning to thin, and he was developing a small middle-aged paunch, even though he was only in his early thirties.

"James, where have you been?" Emily demanded. "You know if we get home late, Sarah's schedule is off!"

"I was talking to your father, honey!" James replied placatingly. "We can leave right away, and Sarah will be in bed within half an hour."

"Of course, you don't care!" Emily went on. "You don't have to get up with her in the night when she fusses! You know how important it is that we don't upset her schedule!"

"Yes, dear, I'm sorry, we lost track of the time." James went over and picked up Sarah. He gave her a hug and a kiss and she laughed and squeezed him around the neck. The father and daughter laughed.

"I don't think you should be so demonstrative with her in public!" Emily protested. "It doesn't look proper for a father and daughter to act that way!"

"Nonsense!" James said pleasantly. "This isn't public, Emily, dear! Now don't fret, we'll be home right away." He stooped and picked up Sarah's doll and headed toward the door. As he reached Catherine, sitting on the sofa, he stopped. "It's been nice being with you, Catherine. You know, I think you get prettier every time I see you." It was an ingenuous compliment, and she knew James meant it. He hadn't thought her very attractive when they had first met years ago, and it astonished him now to see how beautiful she had become.

"I say, Catherine," he said impulsively, "we're having a few of the crowd over for dinner this Friday. Why don't you join us? You'd know lots of them— Helen Mortenson Donleavy will be there, and some others. What do you say? We'd love to have you come! Wouldn't we, honey?" he asked Emily, turning to her enthusiastically as he developed the thought.

"Well, er—" Emily was flushing, whether with anger or embarrassment, Catherine wasn't sure.

"Thank you, James," Catherine said, smiling, touched by his open-hearted invitation. "But I think perhaps I'd rather spend a quiet evening at home. I'm still just relaxing. Maybe another time if I'm still here. Please ask me again."

Well," he said reluctantly, "if you're sure we can't change your mind. Good-bye. We'll see you next Sunday, I hope."

Emily came over and gave her a quick perfunctory kiss on the cheek. "See you next Sunday!" she echoed and hurried out of the room.

In the hall she heard Emily hissing at James, "You never should ask someone to dinner without consulting me! I am so humiliated!"

"I'm sorry, dear," James replied, "I thought it was a good idea. I still do—"

"Oh!" Emily's voice exploded in exasperation. "What do you know! You don't have to worry about all the details. You think a party just happens out of thin air!"

Catherine shook her head and wondered what it was that had soured the relationship between James and Emily. Emily wore her discontent like a badge of martyrdom, and Catherine could not help comparing the barren relationship of Emily's marriage with the warmth and love that bound Ladean and Dan together. It seemed to her an irony that Emily and James, who had material comfort and security and all the outward trappings of success, were so discontent, while Ladean and Dan, living frugally and facing a future of hard work and independence, let nothing threaten the bonds of respect and love that held them together.

"I suppose Malcolm was right when he told me there is no magic formula for marriage. Two people have to be willing to declare their love and give it without reservation—and then work very hard," she thought. What did I do wrong? The question haunted her day and night. No matter how much she might try to avoid it, her thoughts always veered back to David.

Almost three weeks had passed since Catherine had come to Calgary with the Beaumonts. Jean and her husband had long since returned to England, and still Catherine had received no word from David. Finally she grew desperate, and decided that no matter how her pride might suffer, she had to return to the ranch to face him. As she wrestled with her decision, she received a letter from David that promised to lengthen their separation indefinitely.

> *Dear Catherine,*
> *The first snows fell shortly after you left and the roads were impassable for a while. Conditions have improved, and I was able to plow out and get down to the post office.*
> *I have received a letter from a rancher in Wyoming who has been interested in my herd. He*

has invited me to Cheyenne to attend the annual meetings of the American Breeders Association, and afterward I will spend some time on his ranch studying his methods.

I can't really afford the time or the money to go, but this is a wonderful and necessary beginning for international recognition of my breed and I must take the opportunity.

Sam Bartlett is going to watch the ranch for me, and I've hired a young hand to stay in the house and do the daily chores while I'm gone.

I am sure you are having a fine time in Calgary and will welcome another month with your family.

I will let you know when I return.

David

She put down the letter slowly. Did he really need to go or was he avoiding her? she wondered. Tears filled her eyes. "What a star-crossed pair we seem to be!" she thought with a sorrowful, ironic sigh.

December was beautiful. Two weeks before Christmas the clouds had dumped huge drifts of fluffy snow. As Catherine did her last-minute gift shopping along Seventh Avenue, she enjoyed being among the throngs of merry shoppers and admiring the festive shop decorations. The snow made everything look fresh and new, and the windows blazed with the treasures of a merry year. The depression was over, and even though the news from Europe was worrisome, people had money in their pockets and felt optimistic about the future.

It felt wonderful to Catherine to be back in the city of her youth. She loved the familiar streets, and occasionally she would recognize the face of a school friend or family acquaintance, and they would stop to exchange season's greetings. Catherine felt a warm sense of belonging. As she glanced in the windows of the Hudson's Bay Company she remembered the summer when she had graduated and had met Norman on this spot. It seemed so long ago, and the awkward, ill-dressed girl she had been was like a dim memory. Catherine paused and looked at her reflection in the window. She had cut her hair to her shoulders and was wearing it in a soft pageboy. Her fur coat and matching hat were beautifully cut and hung gracefully on her slender body, and her scarf was tied in a fashionable bow at her neck. Even Catherine admitted she looked chic and sophisticated. "I wonder if my life would have been different if I had looked like this when Norman saw me that summer day, all those years ago?" she wondered, looking at her image appreciatively. "But he couldn't see beyond the unfinished girl I was then."

In her buoyant mood, Catherine accepted her family's urging to attend the Christmas buffet at the club. Her midnight blue satin dress with high neckline, long sleeves, and bias cut clung to her body nicely, emphasizing her lovely curves. On her wrist she wore an antique bracelet which had belonged to her grandmother. It was a heavy design of emerald cut brilliants, with clustered earrings to match. Her hair shone, and she wore it in a simple flattering pageboy style.

This was the first formal social occasion Catherine had attended since her return home, and she was nervous about how she would be received. When she entered the club, heads turned to see who was coming in, and recognizing Catherine with her parents, people paused in their conversations, astonished. An uncomfortable hush fell over the gathered guests. Then Mrs. Townsend turned to see what had caused the awkwardness, and catching sight of Catherine, she moved toward her regally.

"Catherine!" she boomed in her aristocratic voice, her perfect tones projecting so that the entire room could hear her greeting. "Our dear, dear Catherine! Home at last! How we have missed you!" And there, in full sight of the club membership, Mrs. Townsend put her arms around Catherine and embraced her in an uncharacteristic display of affection. The crowd broke forth in excited conversation and surged forward to greet and exclaim over the lost sheep.

Over and over again Catherine answered the same questions. "When will we get to meet your husband, Catherine?"

"He's in Wyoming right now."

"How long will you be staying?"

"Probably longer than I expected."

The conversations almost always included some amazed exclamation, "You are really looking wonderful, Catherine!" Or, even more bluntly, "My! You certainly have changed!" Once or twice it was just a simple, direct compliment. "You are really lovely" or "beautiful," and Catherine felt that most of the speakers really wanted to say something like "I never thought you'd turn out like this" or, "The Ugly Duckling has become—well, if not a swan—then at least a pretty duck!"

In spite of all the attention, Catherine was enjoying herself. After dinner there was dancing, and Catherine enjoyed the holiday spirit and the pleasant formal atmosphere. She danced with old friends and new acquaintances, but long before the evening was over she began to feel tired. The smoke and the noise and the heat of the dance floor began to bother her. Feeling slightly nauseous and weak, she went to find her mother. "I think I'll go into the lounge and sit down for a minute," she said. "I'd be happy to leave whenever you and Daddy want."

"Catherine!" her mother whispered. "Are you all right? You look a little pale."

"I'm fine!" Catherine answered. "Just too much party. I'm used to quiet living."

She walked out into the dim light of the lounge. A group of couples in the lounge were enjoying a late evening drink, and with a jolt, Catherine realized that Norman and Millicent were among them. She turned quickly to leave, but one of the men caught sight of her. "Catherine?" he asked, walking over to where she stood. "Catherine Summerwell? I don't believe it! Do you remember me? Fred Barstow. We were in mounted troop together in eighth grade!"

She laughed. "Yes, Fred. I remember!" She looked at him. He had been a round innocent-faced youngster with a gift for mischief.

"I even had a crush on you for a while," she added, "because you were the only one who could jump the full handicap course. And besides, you could make me laugh."

"Well, I'll tell you, Catherine," Fred said, looking at her with frank appreciation, "if you'd looked like this in eighth grade, I would have had a crush on you, too!"

She laughed again, and he took her elbow. "Come over here and have a drink with the late-night crowd. We just got in from an evening at the theater, and we're fortifying ourselves before joining the older crowd." He propelled her forward, and before she knew it she was in the center of the circle, being greeted by old acquaintances and introduced to new ones. As Fred introduced her to the group he came to Norman and Millicent. "Of course, Norm and Millie you already know."

"Yes," she said, her face tight. "How are you, Millicent? Norman? It's nice to see you."

"We heard you were home," Millicent said stiffly. "I've been meaning to come over to call, but we are closing up the house for the winter, and I've been so busy."

"Closing up the house?" Catherine asked.

"Yes," Millicent replied. "We can't stand another of these Canadian winters. We're motoring down to California. We'll be there until spring."

"Oh," Catherine replied, smiling. "How nice for you."

Norman had said nothing. The group were obviously good friends, and the conversation surged on, with much good-humored raillery and gossip. Catherine listened and answered questions, but all the while she was surreptitiously observing Norman. She was seeing him in his own habitat for the first time in years. He was dressed in a perfectly tailored dinner jacket, his black tie hand-knotted, and the front of his shirt as white as snow. Sometime since she had last seen him he had started wearing a ring on his little finger, and now he was also sporting a silver cigarette holder.

Watching him, she observed the odd, finicky gestures that had become an unconscious part of his manner. He held his head high as though he were looking down from a great height. The affectation amused her, rather like the posturing of John Barrymore in the movie when he always contrived to be photographed in rigid profile; even when he bent to kiss a girl, he managed to keep the profile in perfect alignment. Norman was aware of her watching him, and his nervous gestures became more pronounced. Several times he flicked imaginary ashes from his spotless lapels, adjusted the crisp white cuffs with their onyx cuff links, and when he sat down, lifted the crease of his trousers, and carefully pulled the trouser leg to just the right angle so that it would not wrinkle. Witnessing his pompous eccentricities she wondered how she ever could have thought he was a man to be desired or relied upon. Feeling as though a weight were lifted from her heart, Catherine knew she was finally free of him.

Her thoughts flew to David tramping in his jeans and work boots across the hills, shoveling feed to his cattle, the harsh mountain wind blowing his hair, his face ruddy, his hands hard and cracked from physical toil. In her mind David seemed like a giant, a god, compared to this fragile dandy who sat across from her in his impeccably tailored clothes with his cold autocratic face and meticulous hands.

Catherine was still feeling unsteady and she couldn't keep her mind on the frivolous conversation of the group. She was so preoccupied with her own thoughts that when Norman moved over to sit beside her, he had to speak twice before she answered.

She turned to him, startled to see him on the chair next to her. "Norman! I'm sorry! I was thinking."

"Yes," he said, ironically, "so I observed. It's good to see you again, Catherine. You are looking very lovely." His eyes held hers and he repeated with deeper emphasis, ". . . very lovely."

"Thank you, Norman," she answered formally. "You are looking well, too. So is Millicent. Where is she, by the way?" Catherine looked around wondering where Norman's wife had gone. Ever since Catherine had arrived, Millie had stayed close to Norman's side, but now she was nowhere to be seen.

"She went to powder her nose, I suspect," he said indifferently. He turned to Catherine and lowered his voice. "I've wanted to come to see you desperately, but Millie has been watching me like a cat ever since you arrived home. I think she suspects us."

Catherine looked at Norman with wonder, and suddenly she burst out laughing. She was so amused by his furtive whisper, by his obvious fear of his wife's temper, by his blind presumption that she was waiting for him with bated breath! "Oh, Norman!" she whispered back to him, wiping the tears of laughter from her eyes. "Grow up!"

Norman sat back as though she had slapped him and looked at her imperiously. "What do you mean by that, Catherine! It's the kind of absurd thing you would say—you always did like to shock people!"

"I didn't mean to shock you, Norman. It's just that I can't believe you are still living in the past. What could Millie suspect about 'us'? There is no 'us'! Sometime, a long time ago, a funny, awkward little girl had a great affection for a boyhood hero. But heroes grow up and become real people, and so do awkward little girls, and what they were ceases to exist—except in memory. Norman, we're free of each other. We don't even know each other anymore."

Norman's face went white, and he stared at her for a long moment. "Yes," he said finally, "the butterfly."

She frowned in puzzlement. "Now you're the one who's talking strangely."

"It's the transformation," he said, with a wry half-smile, "the butterfly was always there in the cocoon, and I couldn't see it. You've emerged, and I should have known, but I didn't. And now, I can't come near you because you have wings, and I don't."

"Norman," she said, smiling, "are you a little drunk?"

He tipped his glass at her in a slight salute. "Just a little," he said carefully. "Perhaps not enough." He saw Millicent bearing down on them from the other side of the room, and he stood up hastily. Before he left, he turned so that Millicent could not see his face, and he gave Catherine a smile of profound sadness. "Good-bye, Catherine, my darling." He turned, and with elegant style, made his way over to the bar.

After the evening at the club party, Catherine continued feeling poorly. The Christmas season came closer. Friends came to call, and little Sarah brought joy to everyone as she filled the days with happy expectation. But Catherine often awoke feeling weak, and on several occasions the prospect of the morning meal seemed intolerable, and she would stop eating breakfast in mid-course and rush from the room, sick.

When time failed to make her better, she decided she should see a doctor. And so, without telling her parents, she made an appointment with a new doctor in town whom she did not know.

The doctor was a young man, spruce and trim in his starched white coat, and extremely earnest. He took her history carefully, and gave her a full physical examination. After the examination ended and she had dressed, the nurse showed her into his office. The doctor was sitting behind a huge, impressive mahogany desk, but Catherine privately thought he looked like a little boy playing doctor at his father's office.

"Well, Mrs. Reid," he said in a hearty voice, "you are in excellent physical condition."

"But . . ." she prompted.

"No 'buts,'" he said. "You are in excellent health, and I would think you will come through this pregnancy without any difficulties whatsoever."

The room reeled, and Catherine's face went white, and she slumped in her chair. The doctor leaped up from his desk. "Miss Hanzlick," he cried, "bring some water and some smelling salts!"

Her fainting spell was brief, and Catherine opened her eyes to see the young doctor kneeling on the chair in front of her and calling her name. "Mrs. Reid! Mrs. Reid!"

"Oh," she gasped. "I'm sorry!"

"That's perfectly all right," the doctor reassured her. "It's my fault. I had no idea the news of your pregnancy would come as a surprise to you. I assumed—I thought—I didn't see how you could not know. I merely thought you were coming to me for a checkup."

"No!" she whispered weakly. "I didn't know!"

The doctor and his nurse asked if she wanted to lie down on the couch, but she refused, and continued sitting in the chair, feeling stronger, and clear-headed. "When will the baby be born?" she asked, knowing that she could have figured out the date precisely since there was no question about the day when the baby had been conceived.

"You are a little over two months pregnant," he told her. "You'll continue to feel some nausea and tiredness for another month or so, and then you will probably begin to feel much better, and a month later you should begin to feel the baby moving. I'm going to give you some vitamin pills to take and a prescribed diet. We'll want you to come see us once a month. But, as I told you before, you are in excellent health, and I believe you will have a very easy, normal pregnancy."

"Thank you, Doctor," Catherine said, her face still white, but she was in complete control. "I will make another appointment when I leave."

She got up to go. "Are you sure you feel strong enough?" the doctor asked, concerned. "Apparently you've had quite a surprise! I'm sorry I broke it to you so abruptly."

"No, no," she waved him off with her hand. "It wasn't your fault. I should have known. Thank you again."

Catherine drove home very slowly. When she arrived, her mother was in the dining room polishing the silver. "Catherine!" she called. "Where have you been? Would you like a cup of tea?"

"Not now, Mother," Catherine called back in a lifeless voice. "I'm a bit tired; I think I'll go upstairs and lie down."

When she got to her room, Catherine closed the door and lay down on her bed, staring at the ceiling. Slowly her hands sought her abdomen, and she rubbed the smooth, firm, tautly stretched muscles. Inside, growing in comfort, was the offspring of David's seed, the union of that one glorious night, the living memory of all she had hoped for and dreamed.

"David's baby!" she thought, and hot tears scalded her cheeks. "We should be together!" she thought. "Why won't he come for me? Oh, I want him so much, so much!" She turned over, and clutching her pillow, cried herself to sleep.

One morning at breakfast, she picked at her food, and her mother eyed her anxiously. "Are you still feeling unwell, Catherine?" she asked. Catherine smiled a shade too brightly. "I'm fine, Mother, not very hungry, that's all." Catherine excused herself from the table and ran upstairs to her room. Closing her door she ran into her bathroom and threw up. When she came out of the bathroom, wiping her face with a cool towel, her mother was sitting on her bed, waiting for her.

Lucy Summerwell patted the bed beside her and smiled at her daughter. "Come and sit here, Catherine," she said. "I think it's time we had a mother and daughter talk."

Catherine smiled wryly. "I guess so," she said. "I guess after twenty-seven years it's about time."

Lucy was not put off by her daughter's remark. "You were not an easy daughter to talk to, Catherine," she said. "Perhaps you still are not—but I want to try anyway."

Catherine sat down beside her mother and was silent. Her mother cleared her throat a little nervously, and Catherine suddenly noted with surprise that her mother looked older and rather frail. She had always thought of her mother's beauty as indestructible, but now she could see how human and fragile she actually was.

"Catherine, dear," her mother began, "I think I know what is the matter. You're—you're—" Lucy blushed, and it was obviously difficult for her to say what she wanted to say. "You're going to have a baby, aren't you?"

Catherine realized what an effort it had cost her mother to be straightforward about such a personal subject, and her heart reached out to her.

"Yes, Mother," she said gently, "I am."

"And are you happy, dear?" her mother asked, anxiously.

"Yes, Mother, I'm very happy!" Catherine replied with conviction. "I want this baby more than I have ever wanted anything in my whole life."

"Have you told David?" her mother inquired tentatively.

"No, no I haven't."

"Oh, dear!" Lucy said. "Poor man! Such a happy time, and he doesn't even know it. You must write and tell him. He's missing so much!"

"If he doesn't know it, Mother, then he can't be missing it, can he?" Catherine said with some asperity, not wanting to talk about David. The subject seemed to bring his presence painfully close.

"But he must be missing you, Catherine," her mother said in an even voice. "What a pity that you came to visit right when he had to leave for the States. He's coming home soon, though, and I'm glad for both of you. We love having you here, but I can't help but think of that poor man alone . . ."

Catherine was upset. "I don't want to talk about it, Mother," she said abruptly. Her mother had obviously developed an affection for David, sight unseen, and her sympathies clearly lay in that direction.

"I know, dear," her mother went on, "you miss him, too, and it must be painful for you to talk about him. I'm happy about the baby, though. Catherine, you know, I have learned one thing in my life, and I want to share it with you. Babies are wonderful! You love them and teach them, and they fill up your days. But they leave you, Catherine. Before you know it, they are gone! Children cannot be the foundation of your life!" Catherine's memory jogged at the word "foundation," and she remembered Ladean telling her that Dan was the foundation of her being.

Her mother continued. "You mustn't let this baby substitute for what you and David are together. Always put the best of yourself into your marriage—that is the only thing that lasts. Oh, I know, men can be difficult and uncaring and selfish, and sometimes you wonder if it's worth it. But Catherine, dear," Lucy turned to Catherine with a radiant smile, and Catherine had the feeling that in her whole life this was the first time her mother had talked to her honestly, without pretense of any kind. "Marriage is worth whatever you need to give—it really is worth it!" Tears came to Catherine's eyes, as she understood for one brief moment her mother's own vulnerability, and glimpsed the personal strength and determination that Lucy had called upon to create an enduring marriage to the ambitious, complex man she had married.

Lucy's words echoed in Catherine's mind, "It's worth it—whatever you have to give—it is worth it!"

Her mother's hands fluttered and she looked away with a self-conscious laugh. "Well, we can't sit here talking all day. Perhaps you should rest, dear, we must take good care of you." She smiled. "Of 'both' of you," she corrected.

Catherine was tired, and she allowed her mother to tuck her in for a nap. As Lucy Summerwell pulled up the blanket over Catherine, she looked down at her face and smiled with a profound sweetness. "You weren't an easy child, Catherine, you know," she said softly, "but you always brought so much joy into the house! You have never given us anything but joy." Her mother slipped out of the room and quietly closed the door. In the silence Catherine's tears flowed. "Joy!" she thought. "How could Mother say such a thing? I have brought them nothing but sorrow!" Still her mother's voice had rung with conviction, and Catherine felt her heart opening and responding to the love in her mother's tone.

* * *

The week before Christmas a thick chinook arch formed over the distant mountains. Sweeping off the warm Japanese current in the Pacific Ocean huge winds blew at breakneck speed across British Columbia until they hit the forbidding wall of the Rockies. On the western slope they dropped a thick veil of moisture, and then, over the mountains the massive air current slid down the snow-covered eastern slopes at reckless speed, gathering force as the hot, dry air rolled across the flat expanse of prairie lying at the foot of the mountains. The winds were warm, and the air dry as tinder. The hot wind blew across the snow-covered foothills and prairie, melting the snows and sucking up the moisture. It was a freak storm, and the wind blew day after day. Temperatures soared, and the snow vanished from the earth. Soon the mud was dried up, too. People began to worry.

"It's bad when it gets this warm so early," her mother said, looking at the lovely peach trees in the backyard. "Those buds will open if this continues another week, and then they'll winter-kill when the freeze starts again."

The constant wind made people restless. The earth lay in ominous suspense, waiting for the winds to stop and the bitter cold of winter to come blasting forth once more.

One afternoon Catherine went out for a walk, but the wind was blowing so strongly she felt gritty and irritable and so she returned home to have a bath and rest until dinner. After bathing she got on the scale. Though she had not gained any weight, as she looked down at her naked body she could see the unmistakable swell of a growing child. Her heart leaped, and she thought, with eagerness, that she could not contain her secret much longer.

David got out of his car slowly. He had not expected the Summerwell's house to be so grand and its elaborate eminence troubled him. He took a firm grip on his bag, however, and walked briskly to the front door. Without hesitation he rang the doorbell, and waiting for an answer, he turned and surveyed the neighborhood. The houses were all large and pretentious, with landscaped yards and an aura of comfort. He had known that Catherine came from a privileged background, but until now, he had had no idea of the wealth.

The door was opened by a stocky woman in a maid's uniform with an open, homely face. "You must be Hilda!" David exclaimed. "You look just as nice as Catherine said you were!"

Hilda's eyes opened in surprise and she surveyed the handsome, sunburned man in the doorway with his wide shoulders and work-toughened hands. She grinned in delight and her face broke into a hundred wrinkles. "You must be Mr. David. Land sakes! I've never been so happy to see a body in my life!"

Hilda threw her powerful arms around him and gave him a thorough hug. "That Catherine's been moping around here for weeks like a shadow of a person. It's about time you came to claim her!"

David laughed. He was still standing on the front step. "Would you mind if I come in?" he asked.

With a sheepish shrug, she stepped aside. "Of course! I'll tell Mrs. Summerwell you're here!" She started to walk away and then turned around and smiled at him again. "You sure are a fine-looking man, Mr. David. I can see why Catherine married you."

David stood awkwardly in the foyer. He felt uncomfortable amidst the parquet floor, the rich carpeting on the stairway, the brass and crystal lamps. This was another world! It was Catherine's world, and he had presumed to ask her to leave it forever. A sickening feeling of hopelessness descended on him, and he wished he had never come.

Mrs. Summerwell hurried into the hall. "David!" she exclaimed, coming forward to meet him, with elegant grace. "Why didn't you let us know you were coming? We could have met you at the train. It is such a pleasure to finally have the opportunity to become acquainted with Catherine's husband. Do come in!"

David was unprepared for the warmth of her greeting. Catherine's mother was a small, pretty woman with none of the dramatic intensity and power of Catherine's beauty, but something about her made him think there was more strength under her delicate exterior than one would imagine.

"Thank you, Mrs. Summerwell," he said stiffly. "I'm sorry I couldn't send word. I didn't know I was coming myself until yesterday, and I just drove my car down."

"Please sit down, David." Mrs. Summerwell indicated the couch opposite her, and he sat awkwardly on the edge of the seat.

"Well, we are happy to see you," Mrs. Summerwell said pleasantly and picked up her needlepoint. "Of course, Catherine is not expecting you. She's lying down sleeping. Perhaps we could visit for a few minutes before I send Hilda up to waken her."

"How is Catherine?" he asked. His heart lifted as he said her name, as though talking about her made her closer, more real.

"Wonderful!" Mrs. Summerwell's eyes were shining. "She is feeling much, much better. But then one usually does about this time!"

David was puzzled by her words.

"Has she been ill?" he asked, alarmed.

"Oh, dear!" Lucy Summerwell's eyes were round with alarm. "She hasn't written you yet? Oh, my! I am usually so discreet, but I assumed that was why you had returned! Please forgive me, David. I had no right to break the news!"

"Is she ill?" He was truly distressed now, and his agitation was so apparent that Lucy was touched by his concern. Lucy laughed. "You must pretend you don't know if I tell you! Catherine is the one who should, but I have alarmed you, and I feel so badly—" Mrs. Summerwell blushed. "You are going to have a baby, David," she whispered. "Isn't it wonderful!"

David felt as though an electric shock had passed through his body. Yesterday he had struggled down off the mountain in the mud and melting snow to try to bring Catherine home. And now he had been told that she was bearing his child. A wild unreasoning joy surged through him. He knew he had to make things right between them. Somehow he must bridge the gap!

"Mrs. Summerwell," he said quietly, "do you think I could see Catherine now?"

"Yes, of course, David! How thoughtless of me to

keep you both waiting! You must have missed one another so much! I'll run up and get her myself."

Mrs. Summerwell hurried up the stairs and knocked softly on Catherine's door. "Catherine," she called softly, "are you awake?"

"Yes, Mother," Catherine's voice answered. "I was just going to get up."

Mrs. Summerwell entered the room, her eyes shining. "Oh, Catherine, I have the most wonderful surprise for you downstairs in the living room. Please get up and put on your nicest dress and come down!"

"What is it?" Catherine asked curiously.

"You'll never guess!" her mother smiled, bristling with secretiveness, and suddenly Catherine's heart chilled.

"It isn't David, Mother?" she whispered. "Not David!"

"Yes, dear!" exclaimed her mother joyfully. "David is really here. He's downstairs waiting for you. What a nice young man, Catherine. I really like him. We had such a good visit—"

Catherine's face went white. "I'm not coming down yet, Mother. I can't," she whispered. "I don't know what to say."

Her mother turned to her, astonished. "What are you saying, Catherine? Of course you are going down immediately."

"No, I'm not, Mother. I'm not ready." Catherine's jaw set in a stubborn line.

Her mother turned on her and cold determination showed in her eyes.

"In my home I will not tolerate that kind of self-indulgence, Catherine," she said authoritatively. "I do not care how you feel, or what is wrong between you and that young man, but I will not have you keep him waiting any longer. You are to dress yourself and come downstairs. I do not care what you say or how you say it, but you must face him."

Catherine was shaken by her mother's firmness and she struggled to control her conflicting emotions. "Very well, Mother," she said, "I will be right down."

Lucy stared at her daughter with bewilderment. "Catherine. I don't understand you. That is a fine young man down there. Darling, in every marriage there is one who gives more than the other. There is no disgrace in being the one that gives. How can a marriage hope to work when neither one is willing to sacrifice anything? If it were me, I would be willing to do a great deal to keep such a man as David Reid." She walked to the door, and as she reached it, turned to look at Catherine once more. "Sometimes you have to be willing to give away a piece of yourself, Catherine. It's the price that must be paid for the things we really want."

With expectant heart and trembling hands Catherine dressed. How would she look to him? she wondered. Would he be happy to see her? She slipped on a wool wrap dress in a soft rose-colored tone that highlighted the nervous brightness in her cheeks. She put on a single strand of pearls and brushed out her hair. She wondered if he would like her new hairstyle, and then she put down the brush and gave a short laugh. He wasn't coming to see how she looked, he was coming to resolve the future of their marriage.

Carefully, slowly, she walked down the stairs. From

the top of the staircase she could see through the open
archway into the living room, and her heart beat faster
as she caught a glimpse of David sitting alone. He was
perched on the couch, his arms resting on his knees
and his shoulders bent forward. His head was hanging down as though he were looking at his hands
clasped in front of him. Catherine could not see his
face, but everything in his posture bespoke weariness.
It took all her self-control to stop from running down
the stairs and throwing her arms around him, but instead she moved gracefully, and stepped into the living
room with deliberate grace.

"Hello, David," she said softly and his head snapped
up and he jumped to his feet.

"Hello, Catherine," he replied. She thought he
should have looked out of place in her formal elegant
home, but there was about him such a sense of self-
awareness and dignity that she believed he would look
natural in the most aristocratic surroundings. He was,
she thought, his own man. She could imagine the discomfort he was feeling as he tried to reconcile the
Catherine he knew with the privileged trappings of
her background.

"I met your mother," he said. "She's a lovely
woman."

"Yes," Catherine said. "Please sit down, it makes me
feel awkward having you standing."

They sat down facing one another from opposite
sides of the coffee table. "You're looking well, Catherine," David said. "How have you been?"

"Well," she replied. "And you?"

"Fine," he answered. There was a stiff pause. "Mrs.
Bartlett is fine, too. She came home from the hospital

just before the heavy snow. She asked me to thank you for all you did."

"I'm glad to hear that," Catherine said. Another pause.

"I came back from Wyoming yesterday. This Chinook had opened the roads, so I left my things at the ranch and came down to . . ." He stopped midsentence.

He wanted to finish the sentence, to say " . . . to take you home with me," but, as he looked at her exquisite house he wondered if a ranch could ever be home to her, and he paused uncomfortably.

"Yes, David?" she said, waiting for him to continue. They sat looking at one another.

"Why didn't you write to tell me about the baby?" David burst out, his voice harsh with emotion. "How could you keep a thing like that from me? Don't you think I have a right to know about my baby?"

"Your baby!" Catherine flashed back. "You have made precious little investment in it!" She immediately regretted her sharp words and would have given her life to take them back. David, stung, turned and picked up his coat and suitcase.

"I can't talk with you here, Catherine," he said wearily. "Not in these surroundings. I am not a drawing room man. Standing here, I feel like I am fighting your past. We have things that must be said to one another, but they must be said when we can see each other more clearly on neutral ground. I am staying at the York Hotel. I'll be there until tomorrow morning, and then I must get back to the ranch. It's up to you, Catherine. If you want to talk to me, I'll be waiting."

He left quickly without saying good-bye. She heard

the front door close softly. Wearily she mounted the stairs, and entered her room, where she sat on the window seat by the bay window and gazed out over the backyard until night fell. Hilda brought up a tray for her supper. Although Hilda said nothing to her, Catherine noticed that Hilda's mouth was set in a firm line of disgust and her eyes were accusing.

"Looks like David made another conquest," Catherine thought to herself.

Very late that night there was a rap on her door. It was her father. "May I come in, Catherine?" he asked formally.

"Of course, Daddy," she replied.

He walked into the dark room. "Shall I turn on a light?" he asked.

"Whatever you want," Catherine replied indifferently.

He didn't switch on the light, but he came over and sat beside her on the window seat in the moonlight.

"I met David this evening," he said. "We spent several hours together. I was very impressed with him, Catherine. I do not know what is wrong between you two, Catherine, but I think the time has come for you to set it right."

Catherine began to cry then—steady, hopeless, silent tears. Her father's eyes were sympathetic. As he stood up he said, in a weary voice, "I never thought I would say this to you. But I think perhaps we spoiled you, my daughter. I love you, and I feel sorry for you, but I think perhaps you need to forget who you have been and realize who you are now."

Her father walked out of the room and closed the door, and Catherine was left alone. For the rest of the night she huddled on the window seat, wrapped in an old comforter. Her eyes were dry, and her mind was filled with thoughts and memories. Early in the morning, before anyone was awake, she dressed, and, sitting at her old desk, she wrote a brief note. As quietly as possible she crept down the carpeted stairs, propped the note on the breakfast table, and then, carrying her suitcase, she took the keys to her mother's car from the ring by the kitchen door.

In the soft predawn light she drove through the streets of Calgary to the entrance of the York Hotel. At the desk she inquired for David Reid's room, but just as she walked to the elevator bank in the deserted lobby a motion caught her eye at the foot of the stairs. Turning, she saw David walking briskly toward the outer doors, suitcase in hand. "David!" she called. "David!" He turned and saw her. "David!" she exclaimed joyfully and ran toward him. Her foot slipped on the marble floor, and she almost fell. He threw his things down and in an instant was beside her, his arms reaching around her. "Are you all right? Are you all right!?" He held her, his face tight with fear and love. He kissed her hair and her face. "Oh, my darling, are you hurt?" She raised her hand gently and touched his cheek.

"No, David! I am not hurt! I have never felt so well in all my life!"

He picked her up and carried her over to the couch, much to the astonishment of the bellman and the desk clerk who were the only two people in the vast lobby. "I almost missed you!" she whispered. "Oh, David, I have been such a fool! It has taken me all these weeks and an entire night of thinking to realize that you must care for me—at least a little!" And then, remembering her mother's words, she forced herself to say what was in her heart.

"And, oh, David, I love you so much! It doesn't matter if you love me or not—I will love you enough for both of us!" She looked at him exultantly, proudly, defying him to challenge her determination.

His reaction baffled her because he threw back his head and began to laugh a laughter so joyous it was like a shout of triumph. "Oh, Catherine! Oh, Catherine!" he exclaimed. He took her in his arms and kissed her as she had never been kissed before. It was a kiss of love—full-bodied and passionate, but tender and possessive as well. As he kissed her she felt herself melting into him—into his life, into his thoughts, into the center of his being.

When they broke apart, he held her and looked into her eyes. "How could we have wasted these months! A whole season of our life together, and we have wasted it! Such proud, careless fools we are!" His voice was mocking and gentle. "To think what we might have had—such days! Such nights! And we wasted all that time, stepping so neatly because we didn't dare to take a chance on our own happiness!"

"But now, we have all the years ahead of us, David," she said, her eyes shining.

"Yes!" he exclaimed. "But years won't be enough—there will never be enough time with you—even one second wasted is too much—"

Catherine smiled a secret, reflective smile and her eyes seemed far away.

"What is it?" David asked.

"I was just thinking of something a friend of mine told me—'When there is love, eternity is not long enough.'"

Catherine had said good-bye to her parents in her note. She had also told them the car would be at the York Hotel. She and David drove back to the mountains in his car. The chinook had stopped blowing, and the temperature was dropping below freezing again as they approached their home. It was early evening and the full moon cast a silver glow on the bare winter hills. A cloud drifted across the face of the moon, and David squinted up at it. "We'll have snow within a day or two," he said. "We may be snowed in for weeks." The words rang with warmth and happiness. They climbed out of the car and stood on their property.

Catherine looked at the little ranch huddled in the dark hollow below the massive peaks of the mountains. Bitter cold wind whistled between the crags and crevices and the night was empty of life, except for the two of them standing beside their car. They walked a few paces, and David put his arm around her. "Don't get cold," he said protectively and she felt his masculine strength. With feminine prescience she knew there would be times when she would be cold—and alone—and unhappy. And she knew there would be nights when isolation and hard work and the pressures of living with this ambitious man would erode her happiness and cause her to struggle against him and his dreams. She and David had not found a life for themselves yet—that would come to them one day after another through striving, loving, searching, sacrificing for each other. But she also knew it was all there waiting for her, stretched out in the endless night like a harvest of stars. And most important, what they had found was one another—their foundation, their love, and a beginning.

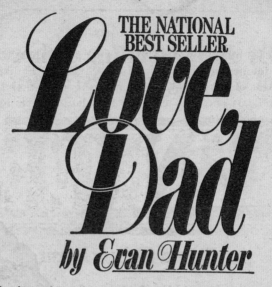

THE NATIONAL BEST SELLER
Love, Dad
by *Evan Hunter*

A deeply moving novel about a father and daughter reaching out to each other as changing times and changing values drive them apart. It is so moving, so true, so close to home—that it hurts. For we all have been there.

"Gripping. Moving. Enormously readable. A fine and sensitive novel that deals with an important aspect of the sixties."—Howard Fast, bestselling author of *The Immigrants*

A Dell Book $3.95   (14998-3)

Dell Bestsellers

The KITCHEN MARRIAGE

Books by Gina Welborn and Becca Whitham

The Montana Brides Series

Come Fly With Me (eBook novella)

The Promise Bride

To Catch a Bride (eBook novella)

The Kitchen Marriage

The KITCHEN MARRIAGE

Gina Welborn
and
Becca Whitham

ZEBRA BOOKS
KENSINGTON PUBLISHING CORP.
http://www.kensingtonbooks.com

ZEBRA BOOKS are published by

Kensington Publishing Corp.
119 West 40th Street
New York, NY 10018

All Kensington titles, imprints, and distributed lines are available at special quantity discounts for bulk purchases for sales promotion, premiums, fund-raising, educational, or institutional use.

Special book excerpts or customized printings can also be created to fit specific needs. For details, write or phone the office of the Kensington Sales Manager: Attn.: Sales Department. Kensington Publishing Corp., 119 West 40th Street, New York, NY 10018. Phone: 1-800-221-2647.

Zebra and the Z logo Reg. U.S. Pat. & TM Off.
BOUQUET Reg. U.S. Pat. & TM Off.

First Printing: October 2018
ISBN-13: 978-1-4201-4399-7
ISBN-10: 1-4201-4399-9

eISBN-13: 978-1-4201-4400-0
eISBN-10: 1-4201-4400-6

10 9 8 7 6 5 4 3 2 1

Printed in the United States of America

Mothers are a force to be reckoned with. Mothers teach, counsel, and guide. They impart wisdom. They comfort. They reflect the heart of God. We are blessed to have mothers who, to this day, still use their compassion, joy, wounds, wisdom, and skills for the good of others.

This story is for our mothers for leaving a legacy of peace, patience, kindness, and goodness, of faithfulness, and of hope. Oh, and for teaching us how to cook.
Our families are most appreciative.

ACKNOWLEDGMENTS

In addition to the same people who helped us with *The Promise Bride*—our agents, Dr. Ellen Baumler of the Montana Historical Society, everyone at Kensington Publishing, and our families—we also want to thank:

Stephanie Miller who offered Becca, whom she'd only "met" via Facebook, her air-conditioned home and a Wi-Fi connection when Becca's power went out a week before this story was due.

Valir Physical Therapy and Ferrara Chiropractic for helping Gina recover from the damage she did to her arm and shoulder after falling out of a bed. (It was a really, really small bed.)

Author's Note

Today's average American has heard of William Shakespeare. His works have been performed on countless stages, read in countless classrooms, and spawned countless movies and TV shows, including *Clueless, 10 Things I Hate About You, Lion King, Warm Bodies, House of Cards*, and *Sons of Anarchy*. Let's not fail to mention the Broadway hit *Something Rotten!* which my (Gina's) husband took our family to see in Tulsa, OK, while *The Kitchen Marriage* was being written. Until the early 1700s, the prolific English bard was unknown in France. French playwrights eschewed corpses, bad language, violence, sex, and subplots. In their opinions, his plays had "too many characters, too much variety of speech and action, were morally ambiguous, and (worst of all) were written in blank verse" ("French Hissing," *The Economist*, 31 Mar. 2005). Those Shakespearean plays that did reach the French stage were gutted and sanitized of their "lusty Shakespearean vitality—and meaning." (Harriss, Joseph A., "The Shocking Monsieur Shakespeare," *The American Spectator*, 23 May 2014). You can learn more about Shakespeare in France in John Pemble's book, *Shakespeare Goes to Paris and Conquered France*.

Throughout our story, we have interspersed real people, places, and events to interact with our characters. One of the real people is Joseph Hendry, whom we introduced in *The Promise Bride*. We alluded to his death in the epilogue of that story, then elaborated on it more in this story. Per *The*

Livingston Enterprise newspaper, Joseph Hendry died of typhoid fever on December 13, 1887, at the age of twenty-eight. According to the news article, he was "fearless as a Roman gladiator" and was "not afraid of death, but sought to live to continue his manly work." The writer of the obituary then says: "Death has silenced his pen and his work is done; but his memory will never die in the hearts of those who knew him and his fame will be known in history for all time to come. In this we know his life will be everlasting."

We brought him into our story to honor him. We hope he will forgive us for exaggerating the cause of his death.

. . . a fact that all women who ever answered a matrimonial advertisement, or ever intend to answer one, should remember: No man who has the ability or means to support a wife in comfort needs to advertise for one.

—CHICAGO DAILY TRIBUNE, 28 December 1884

What strange creatures brothers are!

—JANE AUSTEN

Courtship consists in a number of quiet attentions, not so pointed as to alarm, nor so vague as not to be understood.

—LAURENCE STERNE

Certainly, a good cook will manage to make an agreeable dish of a material a bad one would reject as unpresentable. The most skillful agriculture is not always found in the richest districts.

—MRS. TOOGOOD, *Treasury of French Cookery*

So let's not get tired of doing what is good. At just the right time we will reap a harvest of blessing if we don't give up. Therefore, whenever we have the opportunity, we should do good to everyone—especially to those in the family of faith.

—GALATIANS 6:9–10 (NLT)

Prologue

Helena, Montana
July 4, 1887

Jakob Gunderson lifted his chin to acknowledge friends as he marched, pie plate in hand, across the lawn in search of a solitary tree. Normally, he loved everything about the Independence Day church picnic: spending hours chatting with friends, the band playing military marches, the children bouncing inside potato sacks racing against one another toward a red streamer, and the patriotic banners draping tables burdened with food. Oh, how he loved ice cream and fruit pies! But this year, nothing he loved could cut the bitter taste in his mouth.

He sat down and leaned against a pine tree, the bark's ridges gouging into his back.

"Are you over here pouting?" Yancey Palmer strolled up to him, her dress the same color as the vanilla ice cream mounded on her tin pie plate. "Because if you are, I'd like to join you."

Jakob scooted over despite his grumpy mood. "Hale ignoring you again?"

Yancey sighed. She plopped down on the grass beside

him. "One of these days, Mr. Hale Adams is going to regret how much time he wasted ignoring me." She spooned a bite of ice cream but didn't eat while staring across the church lawn to where Hale stood. "Do you see how the Watsons are giving me the stink eye?"

"Never mind them." Jakob focused on eating his second helping of ice cream and pie while she picked at her dessert. Despite both the sheriff's office and the city marshal's office confirming Joseph Hendry's salacious article, Jakob still struggled with believing his friend, Finn Collins, had worked with Madame Lestraude, one of Helena's richest brothel owners, to lure mail-order brides out West and sell them into prostitution. Word on the street put Yancey on Lestraude's payroll because she had stood in as a proxy bride for Finn's first victim, Emilia Stanek Collins. If that was true, Mac— the county sheriff and Emilia's betrothed—had to be on Madame Lestraude's payroll, because he was her son.

Jakob would stake his life on *that* not being true.

The only thing that made sense was Finn alone working for Lestraude. Emilia, Yancey, and Mac were unwitting victims. However, Hendry's article had stirred up a hornet's nest in the community. Helena's citizens weren't sure who they could trust. Finn had been a faithful church member and helped dozens of local area ranchers recover after the blizzards of '86. Finding out he'd lied to everyone—even his closest friend, Mac—made people distrust their neighbors and certainly anyone with a connection to Finn.

It would be a while yet before the Watsons and people like them stopped glaring. Jakob looked their way and smiled, which was how he'd handled all the censuring glances and questions over the past month. Soon enough, a new scandal would swing attention somewhere else. In the meantime, let them talk. That wasn't what was bothering him.

Jakob peeked over at the source of his sour mood. Emilia stood beside Mac. They were well suited, but Jakob had hoped to pursue the lovely Emilia for himself not so long ago. He wasn't bothered so much by Emilia's disinterest in him as he was in the general female population of Helena. There were plenty of girls willing to fall in love with him, but they all saw him as Isaak Gunderson's irresponsible twin brother. Jakob refocused on his ice cream. It'd be nice to find someone who would see him as his own man.

"Mail order worked out pretty well for Mac and Emilia. Maybe I should give it a go."

He didn't realize he'd spoken aloud until Yancey sat up straight and twisted around so fast her spoon fell off her still-full tin plate. "In Luanne's last letter, she mentioned a lady in her church is—are you ready for this?—a matchmaker."

Jakob didn't know whether to laugh or take her seriously. He opted for the latter. "How does her business work?"

"Luanne didn't say. I could telegram her tomorrow and ask."

"Let me know what she says."

"Are you really interested?"

He nodded. Emilia was proof a man could meet a girl through mail correspondence who was kind, intelligent, and pretty.

Yancey's smile faded. "Maybe I'll answer an advertisement myself."

Her woebegone tone of voice told him what she was thinking before he even asked. "Is this about Hale?"

"Unfortunately, it always rolls back around to him." She fiddled with the fabric of her skirt for a long moment. "Why doesn't he like me? Everyone likes me."

"Joseph Hendry certainly does." Jakob shifted his gaze to where the reporter stood holding a tin plate and looking their way. "Might be time to give another man a chance to see what a gem you are."

"Maybe you're right." She placed her hand over his fingers

and squeezed them tight. "Sometimes I wish I could fall in love with you."

They'd tried once. A few years ago. Before they both realized they were much better suited to a type of brother-sister relationship.

Jakob tilted his head and gave Yancey his most charming grin—the exact one she always teased could make grown women swoon. "But what will my mail-order bride have to say about that?"

Chapter One

Manhattan Island, New York
Wednesday, February 29, 1888

Her future rested upon one flawless meal.

Zoe de Fleur maintained a leisurely pace as she walked home from Central Park. Remains of last week's snow were still nestled in rooftop crevices and frost blanketed the grass. Birds chirped, on the hunt for food. Smells of roasting chestnuts. White plumes of smoke rose from newly stoked hearths. An icy breeze nipped at her likely reddened cheeks, reminding her that winter—and February—enjoyed an extra day this year.

The perfect leap year day for the perfect dinner.

She exhaled, creating a puff of cloud. How could she capture the morning's beauty in food? Not for tonight. She had no time to experiment. But for Easter. Meringue certainly.

And what else?

She strolled along the marble wall that encircled Mrs. Gilfoyle-Crane's Fifth Avenue mansion, pondering future dessert ideas. While construction of new mansions could be seen up and down the avenue, this five-story white marble home on the corner had been for the last decade considered "almost too splendid for comfort."

Or so Zoe had been told.

Although she had spent her childhood and youth living in numerous European castles, the Crane house surpassed them all, in her estimation, because of its spacious and modern kitchen.

Meringue, marzipan flowers, and . . . cake.

But what kind?

"Hey, Miss de Fleur, you want a paper?" Up ahead, Nico—and his red-tipped nose—stood on the street corner with his daily stock of newspapers in his cart . . . and with that flat beige derby of his cocked jauntily to the side fitting his devil-may-care attitude.

"Not today," Zoe said as she always did. As she stopped next to him, she eyed the bandage on the fourteen-year-old's right hand. His knuckles were swollen. His face, though, bespoke no bruises, nor did he stand in pain as he had after last week's beating. "How are you zis morning?"

He grinned. "All to the merry, I say."

"Nico," she said, stretching out the vowels in his name to convey her displeasure.

"What?" came with a big cloud of breath.

"You know I dislike . . ." She paused, trying to think of the right words in English. Façade faces? Emotion masks? "Fake cheer. Be honest with me about"—she pointed to the bandage—"zat."

His smile fell. He fisted his bandaged hand. "I fought back, all right. You told me I had to stand up for myself."

That she had.

Her advice had also come with encouragement to be the bigger man and walk away from the argument before it became physical. Or, even better, start a conversation to bring harmony, to understand the other person's feelings. Become friends. Not fight back. Never fight back, because fighting brought pain. Brought scars. Not all of which were physical.

"When I was a child"—she unwrapped the woolen scarf about her neck—"my papa said embarrassing a bully with words can be as effective as responding with fisticuffs. I did what he told me, and I was horrified because of how my words made ze other girl cry." She draped the scarf around Nico's neck. "How did hitting zat boy make you feel?"

"Strong."

Zoe clasped her gloved hands together. "Were his feelings hurt?"

Nico shrugged. "Don't care. I wanted him to stop pestering me." He shoved his hands in the pockets of his brown corduroy coat. "I'm not ever going to see him again anyway. I'm never going back to the orphanage. With all I've saved, I can buy a train ticket to California and . . ."

Zoe nodded as he rambled on and on about his grand plans to start over out West. Open a saloon. Become a blacksmith or a trapper. Maybe even dig for gold. Or marry some rich old lady about to die. The poor boy had hopes and dreams enough for a score of orphans. If only half the stories he told about life in the orphanage were true, she would hate living there. In the last three years of Nico trying to sell her a paper, he had vowed at least twice a month that he would never return to the orphanage. And yet he had.

As he would today, too.

"Find me after you have sold your stock," she said, interrupting Nico's description of his future house and its six floors.

His blue eyes widened. "Can I taste what you're cooking for tonight?"

"Some."

"With wine?"

"No," she said, and then smiled and patted his shoulder. "Come to ze kitchen around eleven. I will make you hot cocoa, but you must be gone before Chef Henri arrives or he will have both our heads." She swiped her hand across her throat.

Nico's upper lip curled, enough of an action to clarify to Zoe what he thought of the renowned and current president of the *Société Culinaire Philanthropique*, who had an exclusive contract to cater any and all of Mrs. Gilfoyle-Crane's parties. Unlike Papa and Chef Henri, Zoe could never become a member of the Société because she was female, a rule Mrs. Gilfoyle-Crane called "a medieval practice." It bothered her greatly that Zoe could not claim the respectful title of chef, despite her French blood, despite following European tradition and apprenticing over a decade under her father's tutelage, and despite taking over Papa's job as chef for the Gilfoyle-Crane household.

If anyone should be offended, Zoe should be. And she was not. Changing the Société rules was tantamount to changing her sex. Impossible. Complaining would accomplish nothing.

Mrs. Gilfoyle-Crane paid Zoe a salary equal to what Papa had earned, even though, at twenty-two, she had less than two years' experience managing a kitchen on her own.

At that thought, Zoe smiled. "Life is good here."

"For you it is." Nico's brow furrowed as he studied her. "Why are you always so happy?"

"I have much to be zankful for. God is good to me." She tugged his derby down over his red-tipped ears. "Be not late for lunch."

"You're swell, Miss de Fleur."

"Zis is true."

He laughed. "Don't let Chef On-ree convince you otherwise."

Zoe waved as she walked away. She turned down the alley behind the homes lining Fifth Avenue. As the BEZEE'S

FLOWERS delivery wagon waited in front of the steps leading to the Crane house basement, which was only a little below street level, similar to the other nearby brownstones, the hired florist and her workers unloaded the profusion of flowers.

Zoe breathed in the fragrant air. Tonight's dinner guests would enjoy an ethereal and fragrant floral feast.

While the florist issued orders to her workers, Zoe silently slipped past them. She hurried down the five steps to the servants' entrance. Electric sconces brightened the narrow hall that, even in the full light of day, received no outside sun.

She stepped into the kitchen.

Mrs. Horton was adding a tea set to a tray. Nothing but crumbs remained of the breakfast scones, coddled eggs, and ham Zoe had prepared for those on staff.

"Good morning," she said, removing her gloves. She shrugged off her hat and winter cloak, then hung them on a wall peg. "Is zere anything I can do to help?"

To Zoe's relief, Mrs. Horton shook her head. "You have enough to do before Chef Henri and his crew arrives," she said with a fair amount of pity in her tone. She finished preparing a tea service. "The Nephew has requested his morning tea."

Zoe sighed. Mrs. Gilfoyle-Crane's oldest nephew had a name—Manchester Gilfoyle IV—but, in private, the rest of the staff simply called him the Nephew. If Zoe were Mr. Gilfoyle, she would feel crushed to know she was so disliked. Of course, if she were Mr. Gilfoyle, she would be a more considerate person.

Mrs. Horton picked up the service tray. "I'll be back to check on you later."

"Zank you." As Mrs. Horton left the kitchen, Zoe claimed her freshly washed white apron from the peg next to her coat.

She looped the apron over her head, then wrapped it around her serviceable gray work dress. From the apron pocket, she withdrew a white kerchief, folded it into a triangle, and draped it over her curly black hair, knotting the ends at the base of her neck. Her uniform failed to testify to her skills. But if she were to wear Papa's double-breasted chef's coat and *toque blanche* . . .

Chef Henri, in affront, would banish her from the kitchen.

She breathed deeply and slowly, as she always did to focus her mind on work. Tonight could not fail. She owed it to Mrs. Gilfoyle-Crane.

After a quick cleaning of the remains from breakfast, Zoe sat at her office desk in the small room connected to the kitchen. In the center of her desk was the dinner menu Chef Henri had created with Mrs. Gilfoyle-Crane's approval. Embossed gold font on Egyptian linen parchment. The writing was in French, even though the hostess could barely speak the language.

Zoe sighed. Oh, the irony.

Four dishes in the twelve-course meal were Zoe's creations. Not to Chef Henri's pleasure. He had conceded to Mrs. Gilfoyle-Crane's request, although his outrageous fee would remain the same.

Chef Henri was greedy and arrogant and—

Worth none of Zoe's thoughts.

She opened the notebook Chef Henri's assistant, Chef Gerard—who constantly boasted he used to be a *pâtissier* in a shop near the Palais-Royal in Paris—had given her a month ago. He had listed what *she* needed to purchase, what *she* needed to have prepared ahead of their arrival, and what *she* needed to do during the four-hour meal to aid them as they cooked. Though detailed, his list was inefficient. Nor did it allot her time to prepare her four dishes. Why would anyone consider doing something in a way so obviously cumbersome and impractical?

Zoe grabbed her fountain pen. A few adjustments were

necessary for a better flow for all. Content with the changes, she put down her pen. "Tonight will be a success," she muttered.

And then she went to work.

That evening

"You are a genius in the kitchen" came a husky voice, soft enough for Zoe to hear over the yelling and cooking noise from Chef Henri and his assistants.

She looked left and flinched in shock at how close the footman, Robert, stood to her. As she continued to whisk the egg whites, while holding the bowl at the perfect fifteen-degree angle, she took a step back to put more space between them. That she was an excellent chef was true. A genius? That had been her father.

Now was not the time to disagree with Robert's praise.

Every second of this evening mattered. Every second increased her taut nerves. She hated cooking in the same kitchen as Chef Henri, whose every look in her direction was icy and critical. Because he refused to allow the windows open, the kitchen temperature neared unbearable. He was quicksand to all the joy, pleasure, and beauty she usually experienced while cooking.

As long as he and his assistants continued to ignore her, she could endure the heat.

Zoe smiled at Robert, then nodded toward the platters of hors d'oeuvres to begin the dinner's third course. To achieve a successful twelve-course dinner in four hours in *service à la russe*, courses must be brought to the table in sequence. At the precise time.

Precise.

Or else.

Robert leaned against the counter as if he had all the time in the world. "While I was clearing the oyster platters, the talk was about the vinaigrette you'd made. The banker you asked me to observe wholeheartedly agreed."

Zoe's curiosity perked up. "Oh. What was said about ze soups?"

He shrugged. "What does it matter? You didn't make any."

"I wish to know."

"No one seemed overly impressed with any of them."

Not surprising. None of Chef Henri's soups had ever impressed her. If Papa were alive, elephant consommé would never have been put on the menu.

Zoe moistened her dry lips, then glanced down at the upside-down watch pinned to her apron's bib. One minute left to whisk the eggs and then she—

"Girl, where are the truffles?" Chef Henri bellowed in French, and Zoe flinched. He never spoke to her while catering a dinner. Nor had he said a word to her when Papa introduced them four years before.

Because Chef Henri behaved as if he was entitled to respect—but mostly because there was no person she disliked more—Zoe responded in English. "On ze supply shelf." *Where all is organized alphabetically.* Despite the ache in her arm, Zoe kept whisking the eggs into a stiff froth. "Go," she ordered Robert. To convey urgency, she motioned with her eyes to Mr. Peterson, the ever-punctual butler, who carried the third-course wine selection.

That was all it took to prod Robert into action. He grabbed two platters of hors d'oeuvres.

Zoe checked the time. Almost finished whisking.

"Find them for me!"

She jerked her attention to the center of the kitchen, where Chef Henri stood at the chopping block counter, preparing the filling for the roasted fowls. She waited for one of Chef Henri's assistants to aid him. Doing so was their job. At this point of the evening, her only responsibility was her three remaining dishes.

No one moved to help.

Zoe stopped whisking. She peeked at her watch and then at Chef Henri's glaring face and then to the bowl of perfectly stiffened egg whites she held. Now was the exact moment to add them to the cooled coffee mixture. Chef Henri was closer to the larder than she was. In three steps he could grab the truffles from—

He punctuated his "Now!" with fists pounding the chopping block. "Or you will never work in this city again!"

Every assistant stared at Zoe.

If she helped, her soufflé would be ruined. If she disobeyed—

It is better to give an artist what he wants than to argue with him. Papa's admonishment echoed louder in her mind than any of the kitchen sounds.

Thus she set down the bowl of stiffened whites and went in search of truffles.

Sometime after midnight

Zoe dropped the scrubbing brush and covered her mouth with the back of her hand, shielding anyone from seeing her yawn. Not that anyone would. For the last hour, Chef Henri's assistants, in their bundled coats and scarves, sat outside on the benches under the basement windows, looking up to the street level, smoking, and sharing the remaining food and several bottles of wine from the dinner. They had no more concern for the evening temperature than they did for helping her clean the kitchen's disarray. At least the two footmen had helped with removing the trash.

She gripped the kettle in the sink and closed her eyes, taking a moment to rest. The dishwater was lukewarm. Once she finished washing the last of Mrs. Gilfoyle-Crane's copper kettle, she needed to . . . needed to . . . to—

Her chin hit her chest. Zoe gasped and jolted awake. She stretched her eyes open, slapping her cheeks with her wet palms and shaking her head until the drowsiness passed. Now was not the time to fall asleep. She withdrew the last copper kettle from the dishwater, rinsed it, and then grabbed the drying towel.

The kitchen door opened.

"Miss de Fleur?" came Mr. Peterson's reserved voice. "Your presence is requested in the drawing room."

Zoe looked to where the impeccably dressed butler stood next to the kitchen's propped open door. How did he manage not to look tired? Like her, he had been awake since before dawn.

Leaving the kettle on the counter next to the plethora of washed dishes, she followed Mr. Peterson out of the kitchen.

They climbed the stairs to the main floor on ground level, then made their way down the marble hallway to the front of the house. Light from the crystal chandelier shone brightly in the drawing room. Mrs. Gilfoyle-Crane sat in a chair by the crackling hearth. Brilliantly arrayed in diamonds and a pale oyster gown from the House of Worth, she looked as beautiful and pristine as she had when the dinner had begun—six hours ago!

Chef Henri sat on the gold velvet settee in front of the heavily draped double windows.

Zoe stepped into the room.

Chef Henri stood.

Zoe found her place on the Persian rug's center medallion.

Mrs. Gilfoyle-Crane motioned for Chef Henri to leave the room.

He dipped his head in acknowledgment. As he passed Zoe, the corner of his mouth indented.

"I expected better from you," Mrs. Gilfoyle-Crane announced the moment they were alone.

Zoe blinked, confident she had not heard correctly.

"Chef Henri explained everything, specifically your interaction with the footmen." Mrs. Gilfoyle-Crane sighed.

That one breath conveyed all Zoe needed to know.

Disappointment.

"Did my cooking meet your expectations?" Zoe asked, and hoped her tone did not sound desperate and insecure.

"Of course it did"—Mrs. Gilfoyle-Crane shifted on the chair—"and that is why it devastates me to have to ask you to leave."

Leave?

Zoe stared in shock.

Mrs. Gilfoyle-Crane strode to the hearth. Her gaze focused on the crackling flames, her hands clasped tight. "Your unimposing nature causes you to be overlooked and overpowered by others. Your father knew this . . . and believed you had the skills to be one of the finest chefs in the country. Before he died, he asked me to help you rise to your potential." She regarded Zoe. "That is why I have put up the collateral you need to secure a loan for your own restaurant. I know your cooking rivals Chef Henri's."

"You zink too highly of me."

"And you think too poorly of yourself." Said in a manner more firm and decisive than anything Zoe had ever heard her employer speak. "You need someone to believe in you so you can learn to believe in yourself."

Zoe studied her clenched hands.

"Tonight wasn't a failure." Mrs. Gilfoyle-Crane's words drew Zoe's attention. "Your dishes impressed Mr. Soutter. You will go to the bank at two o'clock tomorrow afternoon to sign the loan papers and discuss available locations for you to rent. Mr. Soutter is expecting you."

Managing a restaurant was beyond her expertise. Papa had never worked in a restaurant either; he had only served as a private chef. To those of noble blood. To those of nouveau-riche blood.

And yet Zoe nodded at Mrs. Gilfoyle-Crane's command.

"You may stay here through the end of the week. I have done all I can to help you build your reputation. However, I cannot continue to employ a household cook who fraternizes with the men in my service when she should be focused on her work." Mrs. Gilfoyle-Crane gave a sad shake of her head. "I'm sorry, Zoe. I know you did nothing of the sort, but Chef Henri will say otherwise."

Zoe regarded the crackling fire, mesmerized by how it flickered and moved on its own. Nothing forced it. Yet it stayed confined to the hearth even when it had the power to consume this room, this home. It stayed because it had no mind of its own. It stayed because it was as subjugated as Chef Henri's assistants.

She looked at Mrs. Gilfoyle-Crane. "When I was at ze critical point of my soufflé, if I had explained zat to Chef Henri, would he have asked someone else to help him?"

Mrs. Gilfoyle-Crane was quiet for a moment. "I am quite aware of his attitude toward women chefs. Despite his medieval and misogynistic views—and I am disgusted at the position in which he has put me—I must behave as if I believe his word over yours."

Tears blurred Zoe's vision.

"Please tell me you understand why I must do this," Mrs. Gilfoyle-Crane said.

Zoe nodded.

Mrs. Gilfoyle-Crane's reputation in society would be impugned by standing beside a lowly female's word over that of the esteemed president of the Société Culinaire. She needed Chef Henri catering her dinners more than she needed Zoe to be her household cook.

"Why does he hate me?" Zoe asked. "I am insignificant to him."

"As I would be, were it not for Mr. Crane's bank account. Men like Chef Henri—" Mrs. Gilfoyle-Crane waved at nothing. "Enough about him. I see greatness in you, Zoe de Fleur, but you need someone to push you out of your complacency."

"You do zis for my own good?" Zoe could not help but ask.

"Yes, dear girl, I do." Mrs. Gilfoyle-Crane walked to Zoe. "You will become a great chef once you learn to stand firm for what you know is right. Don't let any man limit your success."

"I shall never forget all you have done for me . . . and for Papa," Zoe managed to say despite the tightness in her throat. "I will make you proud."

Mrs. Gilfoyle-Crane smiled. "You already have. I'll be here for you if you need me. Now go conquer the world."

Chapter Two

Zoe trailed her gloved fingers along the marble wall surrounding Crane house. She strolled with no need to hurry. In three days, she had to leave the only home she had known since emigrating with Papa to America. But she was also free of the incessant competition between Mrs. Gilfoyle-Crane and her sister, *the* Mrs. Marsden—the designation hers—to prove which one of them hosted the best dinner parties. Why did it matter?

A party should never be a means to affirm status in society or lead siblings into a verbal battle.

A party should be about spending time with loved ones.

Into Zoe's mind popped the memory of Papa sitting at a table with her, enjoying the tea and pastries she had prepared. Vision blurring, she stopped walking. Tears slid down her cheeks. She sniffed and wiped them away in time to see a rock skipped across the sidewalk. It landed exactly where her next step should be. She looked up.

Ahead on the corner was Nico, waving and grinning broadly.

Zoe trudged forward.

He had not been on the corner when she left the mansion to walk to Central Park. He seemed more interested in her than in waving papers at the carriages, hackneys, and wagons moving as slowly down the street as she was.

"How was the dinner party?" he called out.

As she neared Nico, she eyed the space between him and the marble wall. She could easily slide past him and turn down the alley, but before she reached the servants' entrance, he would have caught up to her. Such an action of hers would only incite his curiosity. As much as she wished to avoid him—avoid everyone—the wisest thing would be to behave as usual.

Which was why she stopped at the corner and said, "Ze dinner was a success."

"I knew it would be." He tipped up his cap and frowned. "You don't look well. I've never seen your face so blotchy. You sick?"

"Ze night was long and my sleep fitful." Of the five hours she had lain in bed, she may have slept an hour. She glanced inside his cart. Four papers comprised what was left of his stack.

"You want a paper?" he asked.

Zoe hesitated. If she had a newspaper, she could ask Mrs. Horton to help her find a boardinghouse or an apartment in the classifieds.

She nodded. "Wait here. I will go find a nickel."

He gave her a sheepish look. "Uh, you wouldn't have any leftover dinner, would you?"

"Zere is some." She tried to smile, but her heart ached too much to put on a mask of false cheer. "Why do you ask?"

"How about a trade?" He looked hopeful. "A paper for lunch."

On the tip of her tongue was *When did you eat last?* She suspected his last meal had been the one she had served him yesterday.

Instead, she said, "Come with me."

She turned down the alley. Once they reached the basement stairs, Nico stored his cart beside the Crane house's servants' entrance. He grabbed a paper, then opened the door. She led him down the hallway to the kitchen. After their coats and hats were hung on the wall pegs, she pulled on her apron and wrapped the kerchief around her head. Mrs. Horton, whom she expected to see in the kitchen when she returned from her walk, was nowhere to be seen. The dear woman must be managing the housecleaning . . . or meeting with Mrs. Gilfoyle-Crane. A new household cook would need to be hired. If Mrs. Horton failed to find one, she would be responsible for the cooking until one was employed.

Which did not have to be. Zoe could stay and cook.

Tears again blurred her vision.

Blinking them away, Zoe pointed to the table in the far corner of the kitchen. "Sit."

Nico obeyed.

Zoe then focused on her work. She warmed the oven, collected a pot of stew from the icebox to feed her fellow servants, set it on the cookstove for it to reheat, grabbed a dinner plate, and then descended to the cellar to study the contents. The remains of last night's banquet would be enough for Nico. She filled his plate with salted petit fours and a few dry and glazed ones, leaving what was on the platter for the rest of the staff to enjoy with their stew.

She eyed the shelves. The cellar needed restocking after last night's dinner. She should go after her meeting at the bank and—

Her chest tightened, her pulse raced, her heart pounded, and she suddenly felt moisture on her forehead. The ceiling had no leak. Could it be . . . ? She touched her face. Why was she perspiring? She shivered. The cellar was nippy, even more so in the winter. It was so cold down here that fine hairs on her arm verily stood tall. Verily? A panicked bubble of laughter slipped across her lips. Why did she laugh? She had nothing to laugh about. And yet another panicked bubble of laughter slipped out.

Unsure of what was happening to her, she grabbed a half-filled bottle of milk, pulled the string to turn off the light, and then hurried up the steps to the kitchen. She closed the cellar door. Leaning against it, she drew in a deep, calming breath. The strange panic that had washed over her began to lift.

"You all right?" Nico asked.

Zoe nodded. She walked to the table. "Please say grace," she said, setting the heaping plate of food and the milk bottle in front of him. She waited until he bowed his head before she closed her eyes.

"Come, Lord Jesus, be our Guest, and let these gifts to us be blessed. Amen."

"Amen," she echoed. Leaving him to eat, she stepped to the worktable in the center of the kitchen. She lifted the fine cloth covering the rolls she had prepared before leaving for her walk to the park. Perfect. She slid them into the oven to bake.

After making herself a cup of café au lait, she sat across from Nico.

He frowned. "Aren't you going to eat?"

She shook her head. Truth was, she had no appetite.

Where was Mrs. Horton?

Zoe glanced at the kitchen door, then at the watch pinned to her apron bodice. The time for the housekeeper to prepare Mr. Gilfoyle's breakfast tray had passed. Zoe had little time to spare to wait around to help her. In an hour and four minutes, she must leave for the bank. She must change clothes. She must—

Her lungs tightened, restricting air, and her heart pounded like horses racing down a track. What was this happening to her?

Hearing a noise from the hallway, Zoe glanced again to the kitchen door. She waited.

It stayed closed.

"You worried about someone finding me here?" Nico asked.

"No. Everyone knows I feed you from time to time."

"Then why do you keep looking at the door?"

"Mrs. Horton should be arriving soon with Mr. Gilfoyle's meal request."

"Ah, the Nephew." Nico returned his attention to his food. "I've seen him come and go with that odd dog of his."

Zoe lifted the teacup to her lips. As she sipped the warm café au lait, the kitchen door was flung open.

"Miss Difflers, I—"

She froze.

Manchester Gilfoyle IV, in a three-piece gray suit, stepped into her kitchen, clenching his black derby in one hand and the leash of his three-legged dog in the other . . . and looking decidedly annoyed. The door closed. His dog lay down and released a low-pitched "awrrr-oomph."

Mr. Gilfoyle's mouth pressed together in an angry line. "You have a guest," he said, glaring at Zoe.

"Nico sells papers on ze corner. Your aunt encourages her staff to show kindness to all." She looked from Mr. Gilfoyle to Nico, then back to him. According to the staff, Mr. Gilfoyle called all servants "you there." He had called her Miss Difflers this time. Better than when he called her Miss de Flowers. She set her teacup on its saucer. "Is zere something you need?"

He quirked a brow. "My aunt told me what transpired. I've heard the servants laud your kindness, so I am surprised you would attempt to sabotage such a great chef."

The sabotaging had been Chef Henri's. She would never!

Mr. Gilfoyle tapped his derby against his thigh. "Before

you leave my aunt's employment on Saturday, you will prepare me a five-course meal which will include poulet à la crème and mille-feuille."

"Why?" Nico put in. "She doesn't work for you."

Mr. Gilfoyle's blue-eyed gaze narrowed upon Nico, and Zoe had the distinct impression he was weighing and measuring the boy and his impertinent comment.

"Who are you?" he asked.

Nico's chin lifted. "I'm Miss de Fleur's friend. Close friend. Almost a brother."

His answer was enough—or possibly more—than Mr. Gilfoyle sincerely wished to know, because he turned his annoyed attention to Zoe. "Inform Mrs. Wharton to deliver the food at two-fifteen Saturday afternoon. Not a minute later."

"You mean Mrs. Hor—"

"Shh." Zoe hushed Nico before he impolitely corrected his—their—superior. She considered Mr. Gilfoyle but then paused, taking time to choose her words. "It has been an honor to cook for you."

He stared at her blankly before blinking and saying, "Of course." After he gave a minuscule tug on the leash, his dog rolled onto its feet. The pair left the kitchen.

"I don't know what all the fuss is about," Nico said. "The man is a bad egg."

Zoe ignored the insult.

Nico gulped the last of the milk. He set the bottle on the table. "I take it Mrs. Gilfoyle-Crane sacked you because of Chef On-ree?"

Zoe nodded, then pulled the newspaper in front of her.

"I don't mean no offense," Nico said in a most caring tone, "but can you read any of that?"

"*New York Times*. March 1, 1888." She pointed at a paragraph. "Zis, no."

"You speak pretty decent."

"I understand English when I hear it, most of ze time, but words written—" She shrugged. "English has too many conundrums, too many exceptions, too many inconsistencies with pronunciations. Why is *trough* pronounced *troff*, *rough* pronounced *ruff*, *bough* pronounced *bow* to rhyme with *cow*, and *through* pronounced *throo*? All too confusing."

"Like reading Shakespeare."

"I have never read his work," Zoe said with pride. "Before leaving France for America, Papa took me to a performance of *Romeo and Juliet*. Adulation for ze play confounds me. It was a pleasant story with an expected ending."

Nico's eyes widened. "You expected *that* ending?"

She nodded. "A romance always ends with a happily ever after."

"You must have seen a different play than I did."

"I wish I had not seen it at all."

"Sometimes I think you're strange." Nico grabbed the paper. "So, what are you looking for?"

"I need work and zen a place to live."

His brow furrowed as he studied her. "Why stay in the city? If I were you, I would start over somewhere new, where people appreciated my cooking. I'd also want to cook for someone who doesn't believe the worst of me when he hears criticism like the Nephew did."

Zoe opened her mouth, but the back of her throat tightened and closed, hindering her from speaking. Leave the city? Start over somewhere new?

At that thought, the tightness in her throat abated.

If she found employment in a private residence as a household cook, she would oversee the kitchen her way. She could make a home there. Perhaps she would marry the butler or gardener. They could live in a little cottage beside the grand house and start a family. She would no longer have to have a job. She would no longer have to work. She could be a wife and a mother. Everything could be perfect again.

If she started over somewhere new.

If.

When.

When?

Needing a moment to ponder this new possibility, she sipped her lukewarm café au lait. She liked to try new things. She liked to experience new things. She had loved the anticipation she felt each time she and Papa moved from one castle in France to another. When Papa suggested they move to America, she happily agreed to another exciting adventure . . . because they were together. She now had no one to journey to the unknown with. No one.

Could she do this on her own?

If Papa were here, he would say she should never leave the future to chance, and instead do all she could do today to make her future better. That was how he had lived.

"Carpe diem," she whispered.

"Here's something!" Nico slapped the folded newspaper on the table, then turned it to face her. He pointed at an eight-line advertisement. "'Finest kitchen west of the Mississippi seeks trained chef. Only women need apply.'"

Zoe studied the words. The only words she recognized were *fine* and *dining,* which must also mean *kitchen* in the English language. As for the Mississippi River, she thought it divided the country in half, but she was unsure. That the river was not next to New York she knew with confidence.

She looked at Nico. "Where is zis kitchen located?"

"Denver, Colorado."

"Colorado is in ze middle of ze United States, yes?"

He nodded.

"Zat is too far to travel."

"No. It's barely over the Mississippi." He leaned forward. "I heard Denver is called the New York of the West. It's an exciting town, Miss de Fleur. Here in New York, you are one of dozens of French chefs. Denver—well, I doubt they have more than one. If that. Move there and you'll reach stardom."

"Stardom?"

"You'd be a celebrity."

"Ah." Zoe moistened her bottom lip as she considered being a cook in Denver. Any job would be temporary until she fell in love and married. "Is zis kitchen in a hotel?"

"Does that matter?"

"I have never worked in a restaurant, but I know zey are loud, smoke-filled, and busy." She leaned forward and lowered her voice. "I fear I will abhor it."

Nico turned the paper and read the advertisement. His brow furrowed. "I'm pretty sure this is a private residence. It also says chefs will be required to demonstrate their skills. That shouldn't be a problem. You're the best chef in all of New York." His lips parted, and he hesitated a moment before saying, "I could go with you, if you'd like. Help read things. I don't suppose you can write English, either."

She shook her head.

"You really need me to go with you."

Having him along would be convenient.

Zoe beheld the spacious kitchen and sighed. This was no longer her home. If she left now for Denver, Colorado, she could miss the meeting at the bank. She would spare herself the discomfort of explaining to Mr. Soutter why she did not wish to take out a loan or even open a restaurant. If she left now, she could avoid Mrs. Gilfoyle-Crane and her vocal disappointment that Zoe had refused a loan. If she left now, she would not have to cook a meal for a man who was too full of himself to learn another person's name.

She wanted to create delicious food for people who appreciated her skills.

And she could.

In Denver.

Where she would meet the man of her dreams.

She smiled at Nico. "We shall go West."

Capitol Hill, Denver, Colorado
Tuesday, March 6

Zoe rested her gloved hands atop the blue-beaded reticule in the lap of her blue-striped dress as she waited for Mrs. Archer to return to the parlor. The woman's two-story wood-framed home paled in size to the Crane house, but the ornate carved mantel and the wall paneling looked to be made of mahogany, Zoe's favorite wood. Sunshine streamed through the windows framed with yellow silk curtains. The room smelled of roses. Likely from the four arrangements about the room.

She breathed deeply.

Her future home would have fresh flowers. Brought home by her husband.

She loved the house's dollhouse-style architecture. She loved the porch that wrapped around the front and sides. She loved that the house had been painted the same shade of yellow as the parlor curtains, while the spindles and fish-scale shingles under the eaves were a vivid peacock blue. Most of all, she loved how the parquet de Versailles in the hallway flowed beautifully into the parlor. Were she to ever own a home, she would choose warm wooden floors over cold marble flooring like in the Crane house, which was exquisite to look at yet required constant washing.

Nico bumped his arm against hers. "Why are you smiling?"

"Zis could be my new home."

His mouth indented in one corner. "Could be." He patted her arm. "Thanks for inviting me to come with you to Denver. This is a new opportunity for both of us."

Zoe nodded, yet felt as if his words held an additional meaning. What could it be? He had offered to join her, had he not? Or had she done the inviting? She could not recall.

What mattered was that he had been gracious in helping her purchase tickets for her travel in a ladies' Pullman car, while he happily traveled in third class. He even found them a lovely hotel next to the cable line. He had secured directions to Mrs. Archer's home. Even though Zoe disliked his insistence at the depot and to every conductor on the journey that they were siblings, Nico had been a true friend.

"Ah, here we are," Mrs. Archer said cheerfully, sailing into the room with a thick folder in her hand, her lime-green taffeta skirt rustling. "I apologize for making you wait. You are the first prospect to arrive in person." She sat in a chair opposite Zoe and Nico. "This isn't how I usually do this. Everyone else has sent a letter, per the dictates of the advertisement . . . but because you're such a beautiful young woman, well-mannered and well-spoken, I'll adjust." Her brown-eyed gaze lowered to the coffee table's bare surface, her smile dying and her brow furrowing. "Antonia didn't bring refreshments?"

Zoe exchanged a glance with Nico.

He shrugged.

She looked at Mrs. Archer. "No one has seen to us."

Mrs. Archer glanced at the grandfather clock in the corner, farthest from the crackling fire in the hearth. "She may have left already to visit Luanne, so I shan't complain about her absentmindedness. In the last nine months, Luanne has taught my daughter more about behaving as a lady should than I've been able to accomplish in twenty-four years. Antonia even joined the Ladies' Aid Society at church. I know she only did so because Luanne had. I choose to see this as Antonia finally moving past her grief over her father's unexpected passing. He died eighteen months ago."

Zoe smiled to be polite.

Mrs. Archer rested the file on her lap. "Mrs. Luanne Bennett is a few years older than Mr. Gunderson—"

Mr. Gunderson?

"—but their families are close." Mrs. Archer took a breath. "Luanne highly endorsed him. If you wish to interview her, I know she will agree. She confirmed everything in his letters, as well as those letters from his three references—a judge, a reverend, and a prominent widow. My standard practice when an unfamiliar man secures my services is to seek out additional references. My clients, except Mr. Gunderson, live here in Denver."

Clients? Had Mrs. Gilfoyle-Crane been this detailed prior to hiring Papa? Zoe could not remember. Unsure if Mrs. Archer expected a response, Zoe continued to smile

And Mrs. Archer continued to talk. "I subject them to intense interviews to ensure their motivations are sincere. Jakob Gunderson is"—she gazed heavenward for a long moment—"let's say he is less affluent than my regular clients, not that he is poor by any stretch of the imagination. His family owns an exclusive resale shop in Helena and is working toward opening a second store, which Mr. Gunderson will manage. Of course, I don't know why a man of his ilk isn't already married." She sighed.

Zoe shifted in the chair, trying to make sense of the woman's treatise on her client, Mr. Jakob Gunderson. Could he be the one who wished to hire a chef? "Madame Archer, where is Helena?"

"In the Montana Territory," Mrs. Archer answered.

Zoe looked to Nico.

"The state above Colorado is Wyoming," he said with devastating calm, "and Montana Territory is far north of here. It's uncivilized. You don't want to go."

Upon the first opportunity, Zoe was going to buy a map of America.

Mrs. Archer's confused gaze shifted from Nico to Zoe.

"My dear Miss de Fleur, Montana sounds farther away than it is. Helena is quite civilized. Over ten thousand people live there." Mrs. Archer opened the file. "Let me find you Jakob Gunderson's photograph. Once you see it and read his letters, you will understand my willingness to help him find a bride."

"A bride?" Zoe interjected. "I wish to apply for ze chef's position. Ze one posted in ze *New York Times*. Zat is you, yes?"

Mrs. Archer blinked a few times. Her gaze then shifted to Nico.

Zoe turned on the settee to face Nico, who sat there with a strange, smug grin. "Is zere something you failed to tell me?"

"I lied, Zoe, about the newspaper ad. It wasn't for a chef. It was for"—he shrugged—"a mail-order bride. Tell Mrs. Archer you aren't interested and we can leave."

Men ordered brides to be delivered by the mail? She had never heard of such a thing.

Zoe opened her reticule. She withdrew the folded advertisement she had clipped out of the newspaper, then offered it to Mrs. Archer. "Will you read zis to me?"

Mrs. Archer took it from her. "'WANTED: Correspondence with a refined lady aged eighteen to twenty-three with a view to matrimony. The Montana Territory gentleman, aged twenty-two, conducts business in the city, enjoys an active routine, including the theater and fine dining, and faithful church attendance. Send inquiries and references to the Archer Matrimonial Co., Denver, Colorado.'"

Zoe looked at Mrs. Archer in confusion. "Zere is no 'finest kitchen west of ze Mississippi?'"

She shook her head.

"No chef wanted?"

She shook her head again. "Miss de Fleur, I would be remiss if I didn't ask if you can read English."

Zoe opened her mouth to confess her limitation.

"I made it up," Nico blurted out. "It was all I could think

of to convince you to leave New York. Besides, you didn't want to stay there and open a restaurant anyway."

Zoe stared at him, stunned. "I fail to understand why you would lie about such a zing."

"I had to." A shadow fell across his features, literally from a cloud, perhaps, blocking the sun, and yet he looked weary and repentant. "Grand Central Depot refused to sell me a ticket. Said children had to travel with an adult. I was desperate, Zoe. Life will be so much easier for me if you keep pretending to be my sister. Please, please believe me when I say I did this for your own good."

"And yours," Mrs. Archer murmured.

He raised his chin. "Zoe, you said it yourself—carpe diem. You have to admit we've had fun. We're a good team."

Zoe moistened her bottom lip. What fun it had been, meeting Nico at Grand Central Depot, and then starting West in hope of a grand future. It had been the first time she had felt eager expectation since Papa's death.

Carpe diem.

She *had* seized the day and loved every minute of it.

Her sketchbook contained drawings of the ladies who had traveled all or part of the trip to Denver, of a ferry boat on the Mississippi, and of bison in Kansas. She had seen the most glorious sunsets and sunrises over the plains. The farther they traveled from New York, the greater space between towns and homes and any sign of civilization amid the rolling hills and expansive grasslands. And the Rocky Mountains—

Oh, to explore them as she and Papa had explored the Alps and Pyrenees and Vosges.

After all the serenity she had seen—*felt* while traveling West—she refused to return to New York. Maybe this was how God was answering her prayers. Ever since Papa died, she had been alone. Until this trip. It would be nice to have a family of her own, where Nico could live as her brother.

She wanted a husband. And children. And a pet dog . . . and a bird that talked.

But to marry a man who ordered a bride like one ordered a dress from a catalog? To marry a stranger?

She waited for her lungs to tighten, for her pulse to race, for the panic to strike her as it had at the Crane house when she thought of going to the bank to secure a loan.

She felt no panic. She felt—

Intrigued.

"I wish to see Mr. Gunderson's photograph."

Mrs. Archer placed the advertisement in the file, then withdrew a photograph. She gave it to Zoe, who immediately sighed with pleasure. With his light hair and strong jaw, Mr. Gunderson was a handsome man. Had he or his parents emigrated from Scandinavia?

"Zis man is impressive."

"Indeed he is," Mrs. Archer put in.

Nico bumped against her shoulder. "He doesn't look that impressive to me."

"His eyes are happy," Zoe noted. Just like Papa's had been.

Mrs. Archer smiled. "Interesting description, and fitting. Jakob Gunderson's references all described him as a happy man. Would you like me to read his letters?"

Zoe hesitated, her cheeks warming with embarrassment. She was unable to correspond with him without dictating her letter to someone else. "Is writing to him my only option?"

Nico stared gap-mouthed at her. "I can't believe you're considering this."

Zoe ignored him.

Mrs. Archer did as well. "Written correspondence is usually the first stage in courtship. Seeing that you appear refined, intelligent, and have an interest in cooking, I believe we can move on to the second stage, whereby the potential bride—that would be you—moves to the client's hometown, where he secures reputable boarding for sixty days, during which the two of you engage in a proper courtship. I would need to telegraph Mr. Gunderson first to see if this change is acceptable to him."

This seemed reasonable.

"What if your client is a bad egg?" Nico asked.

"That, young man, is a fair question." Mrs. Archer looked at the grandfather clock, then at Zoe. "If at any time the potential bride, whom I shall refer to as you, feels pressured or threatened or realizes my client has not been forthright, you may return to Denver using the train ticket I will give you. I will then help you secure reputable employment. However, do know I have several other clients, men of great means, with whom you would be suitable. One of whom speaks French."

Nico pressed his lips into a peevish expression. "This all sounds fishy."

Zoe nipped at her bottom lip. Maybe she should be warier, like Nico.

Mrs. Archer laid Mr. Gunderson's file on the table between them. "I am an honest businesswoman. If necessary, I can supply references, including ones from the city marshal and the regional judge."

"I'd like to read them," Nico answered, "*if* we were taking your offer seriously. But we aren't." He stood. "Come on, Zoe. I saw several chef openings in the newspaper."

Zoe stayed seated.

"I'm serious." Nico's voice rose. "If you do this, I won't help you. There's no future for us in Montana."

Zoe studied Mrs. Archer. Nothing about the older woman seemed dishonest. But then, neither had Zoe suspected Nico had been anything but honest. He had lied repeatedly and too easily. Although she never would have left New York were it not for Nico. This *was* a new opportunity for them both.

Jakob Gunderson might become a wonderful husband.

She should give him a chance. If his courtship failed, she

could return to Denver. She had options. Best of all, this was her choice. Not Mrs. Gilfoyle-Crane's. Not Nico's. Hers. To seize what she truly wanted—a husband, a home, a family for her to love, feed, and cherish.

She studied the photograph of Jakob Gunderson and his happy eyes. "Mrs. Archer, I would like zis man to court me."

Chapter Three

Helena, Montana
Friday, March 9, 1888

Isaak Gunderson bounced his fingertips against his thigh while he waited in the wedding reception line to congratulate his employee, Emilia, and her new husband. What was taking so long?

He tilted his head to the side. Emilia and Mac were nodding and smiling at Mrs. Simpson, a widow, who was holding up the line with a long discourse. Seeing her reminded Isaak to check on Mrs. Johnston, one of the widows in his church. He pulled a notebook and pencil from inside his coat pocket and added the task to his ongoing list. Perhaps he should have given up chairing the Widows and Orphans Committee when he decided to run for mayor of Helena, but the heavy campaigning wouldn't kick off until May, and he didn't want the church committee to return to its haphazard and inefficient ways.

A quiet, "About time," came from the man ahead of Isaak in the reception line.

It took considerable effort not to reprimand the older gentleman for allowing a rude comment to pass his lips in the presence of ladies, but Isaak held his tongue as he took a small step forward. To answer rudeness with rudeness did no good.

Isaak tucked the notebook and pencil back inside his coat while glancing around the basement reception hall. His eyes snagged on Madame Lestraude standing near—but not against—a wall. Even though she was the groom's mother, she didn't belong here. Given the wide circle of open space around her, the other wedding guests agreed.

Everyone except Emilia's father, who stood chatting with the brothel owner who'd nearly succeeded in selling both of his daughters into prostitution. Mr. Stanek clearly ascribed to Emilia's philosophy of showing forgiveness in the same measure as Christ meted out. Isaak honored them for their charity, but wasn't sure he could be as forbearing given the same circumstances.

The line moved again.

He stepped forward to greet the bride. Emilia McCall glowed in a gown of creamy satin and lace.

"Mrs. McCall." Isaak lifted her hand with his right hand and bowed over it per custom, but he laid his left hand over the top and gave it an extra squeeze. "It was a beautiful ceremony. I wish you and Mac every happiness."

Tears filled her caramel-colored eyes. "Thank you, Mr. Gunderson. And thank you for everything you've done to make this day possible."

"It was nothing." He took another step and greeted her husband. "You're a lucky man."

Mac's smile was filled with awed pride, and his handshake was stronger than usual. "I'm well aware."

Isaak wanted to say more, but his throat constricted with sudden emotion. Even though Mac was four and a half years older, he and Isaak had forged a tight bond over the past year. In fact, lately it felt like Mac was more a brother than Jakob was. Isaak squeezed Mac's hand tighter in lieu of words. Based on the way Mac sobered and tightened his grip in return, he understood all the things Isaak wanted to say but couldn't.

"I'll take good care of her." Mac let go of Isaak's hand and smiled at his bride.

Emilia turned her gaze to her husband, and the look of love that passed between them twisted Isaak's heart with unmistakable envy. He didn't want to be married. Not yet anyway. He was only twenty-two with a long list of things he needed to accomplish before taking a bride, but the rationale didn't loosen the knot in his chest.

Isaak moved away from the formal reception line to where Luci Stanek was waiting for him. Like her sister, Luci was petite. Unlike her sister, she looked older than her years in a cotton print dress with a pink silk sash and small bustle in the back. Emilia had chosen it to make Luci feel fancy without being too sophisticated for a thirteen-year-old, and because it could be worn to parties at the Truetts' or to church sometimes. Quite a practical choice.

Luci threw her arms around his waist. "Hi, Mr. Gunderson."

He patted her back, then pulled away. "I hear you will be staying with the Truetts while your sister is on her honeymoon."

Luci nodded, her brown curls bouncing against her shoulders. "But not until next week. Roch is staying for a few more days before reporting to Fort Missoula. He and Da are going to ride there together, so I get to stay with Melrose until Da gets back." Luci's gaze traveled across the reception hall. "It's a nice turnout, isn't it?" She twisted her neck to look to her far right. "Even the mayor, the city marshal, and that other judge—the one that made Emilia and Roch stay in jail last year—are here." There was a tiny hitch in her voice.

Was she still affected by what her sister's first husband—a man she'd never met—had almost done? Or by Edgar Dunfree's near molestation of her? Both men were dead, and the scandal had died when a more sensational news item monopolized the front page: the murder of Joseph Hendry who had been a reporter for the *Daily Independent*.

Isaak patted the girl's back again to offer some consolation. He was about to ask if there was anything he could do to help, but Melrose Truett bounded up to Luci, pulling her arm and whispering in her ear about whatever thirteen-year-old girls found fascinating.

He turned his attention to greeting friends and acquaintances, all of whom were eager to hear what he planned to do if he won the mayoral election in November. Mr. Palmer wanted less horse dung on Helena Avenue by making all the streetcars steam powered; Mr. Watson wanted part of the proceeds from the annual Harvest Festival to go to the school district; Mr. Truett wanted to get rid of the steam-powered streetcar already running because it belched smoke and was so loud it spooked horses; Mr. Cannon wanted stricter punishment for counterfeiters; Mrs. Danbury wanted to know when the red-light district was going to be shut down for good. After about ten minutes of informal campaigning, Isaak went in search of his brother.

Jakob was near the back of the reception hall, pulling coins and penny candy from behind the ears of a small crowd of boys.

Desiring a moment alone with his brother, Isaak turned the boys' attention to the wedding cake and they all scampered off. "Seems like yesterday we were that young."

Jakob offered Isaak a piece of candy. "And Ma and Pa always made us wait until everyone else was served."

"I was thinking the same thing." Isaak placed the candy in his mouth, tucking it between his teeth and cheek. "How are things going down at the new store?"

Jakob reached in his coat pocket and withdrew a second piece of candy for himself. "Great. In fact, things are going so well, I'm taking tomorrow morning off."

Isaak crushed the candy between his teeth. This lack of focus on Jakob's part was exactly why he couldn't be trusted to make sure the new store opened on time. Isaak swallowed the shards of sweet. "I don't recall you saying anything about needing to be gone before now."

Jakob looked out over the crowded hall. "It came up a bit ago."

"A bit as in an hour or a week ago?"

"Does it matter?" Jakob's tone was clipped.

Isaak's temper heated. "It does when it affects the schedule for the grand opening of The Import Company." He dislodged a stray piece of candy from behind his molar with his tongue while telling himself to remain calm. "You're barely keeping to the schedule as it is. How can you afford to take a whole morning off?"

Jakob started walking, tipping his head to indicate that Isaak should follow. Once they reached a more secluded corner of the church reception hall, Jakob stopped.

"This thing . . ." He paused and, for a flickering moment, looked nothing like his usual confident self. "It might not end up being anything."

Isaak took a slow, deep breath. "When you"—*begged*—"asked to be in charge of The Import Company's build and grand opening, you promised to follow it through to the end. This past week you've spent more time with Roch Stanek than at the store, which set your work crew back by three days. Last week, you held things up for two whole days because you couldn't decide on stain colors. And now you want more time off? I can't keep covering for you, Jake. You have no idea how much work I have to accomplish in one day. I can't afford to keep checking up on you to make sure things remain on schedule at The Import Company, too."

The tips of Jakob's ears turned red. "First of all, it's not your job to check up on me. Second, by your own admission, I'm still on schedule. And third, I don't need your permission to take the morning off to meet someone." His gaze shifted away.

Isaak turned to see who his brother was looking at.

Emilia.

What did the bride have to do with meeting someone on a Saturday morning?

Isaak tensed. No! It couldn't be, could it?

They'd talked about this. Months ago. After the Independence Day picnic when Jakob had asked what Isaak thought about a correspondence courtship. It was a nonsensical idea, which they'd both agreed on; at least Isaak *thought* they'd agreed on it because the topic never came up again.

Until this morning at breakfast.

Isaak looked back at Jakob. "I wondered where all your talk about how lucky Mac was that Emilia answered that mail-order advertisement was leading. You've ordered yourself a bride, too. Haven't you?"

"And what if I did?" Jakob patted his own chest "Why can't I have my chance at love?"

"Because what happens if"—Isaak lowered his voice to keep the rest of the wedding guests from overhearing—"she turns out to be like one of those women who are out for money? The newspapers have been full of warnings for years."

Jakob smirked as though Isaak was the lunatic here. "I've been in contact with a matchmaker in Denver."

Was that supposed to make it better? Whether a bride-finding service was called mail-order or matchmaking didn't change the basic fact that they were all scams. "How much did you have to pay this so-called Cupid?"

Jakob pressed his lips together in a tight line.

Isaak shook his head. "That much, huh? What if this woman shows up and she's entirely unsuitable?" And she would be. In cases such as these, either the bride or groom turned out to be dishonorable—sometimes both. For proof, Jakob need only look to Emilia's near-disastrous proxy marriage to a man who intended to sell her and her sister into prostitution, or to Mrs. Wiley, their housekeeper—who'd lied about her four children to a groom who'd lied about his *prosperous* farm.

Typical Jakob—never considering the ramifications when it contradicted what he wanted to do.

Isaak raked his fingers through his hair. "You'd better not expect me to clean up after you."

"And you'd better not pull your big-brother act and mess this up for me."

"There won't be any need because tomorrow morning, when you meet this mail-order bride of yours, she'll be closer to fifty than twenty. She'll also be dragging along a relative she's never mentioned who happens to need a little money to get back on his feet."

Jakob studied the floor. After a long moment, he raised his head and spoke in a composed voice. "In which case my contract states I can put her on the train, send her back to the matchmaker in Denver, and receive a full refund."

The rationale did nothing for Isaak's temper. He glanced around the reception hall to give himself a moment to calm down. Hale Adams was looking their way with a censorious frown on his face.

Isaak turned back to his brother. "We will continue this discussion at home."

"No, we won't." Jakob tugged on the lapels of his suit coat. "I love you, Iz. You're my favorite brother, but I'm a full-grown man who can make decisions on my own."

"The wrong ones."

Jakob looked Isaak in the eye. "In your opinion."

"If you think I'm wrong, why did you hide this correspondence courtship?"

"I don't necessarily think you're wrong, I just don't think you're necessarily right either."

"What does that mean?"

Jakob opened his lips, closed them again, and huffed. "I haven't told you about any of my correspondence courtships because, after every one of them failed, I would have heard an *I told you so*."

There'd been more women before this one?

Isaak stepped closer. "You think this next one will be any different?"

"Right there's the difference between you and me. I *hope* it will be different. You prepare for the worst." Jakob gripped the side of Isaak's arm. "I know you always look at things to see what could go wrong so you can avoid mistakes, but that isn't always good. It closes a man off to countless possibilities. Sometimes you need to jump into something and see what happens."

The convoluted logic stopped Isaak's next argument in his throat. If Jakob believed his own nonsense, there was no reasoning with him.

Jakob released his grip. "I'm going to Ming's Opera House tonight with Yancey, Carline, and Geddes. Don't wait up for me." With that, he turned on his heel and rejoined the wedding guests.

Isaak watched his brother's progress through the crowd as he joined his friends. Both Yancey and Carline lit up the moment Jakob appeared. Of all the many reasons this mail-order or matchmaking or whatever he wanted to call it scheme was a bad idea, at least one of them should have penetrated Jakob's thick skull. And why was he in such a hurry to get married? They were only twenty-two.

This better not be another of Jakob's it'll-be-fun ideas. Courtship was a serious business. A man didn't go into it unless he was prepared to marry.

At least he *shouldn't*.

Hale walked across the hall to where Isaak stood. "In light of the fact we are celebrating a joyous event, I should be polite by not mentioning that I wasn't the only one who noticed the disagreement between you and Jakob."

Isaak grimaced. "Think I lost any votes?"

Hale pushed his wire-rimmed glasses up on his nose with one finger. "Voters have short-term memories. Anything I can do to help?"

"Actually, you might." Isaak paused for a moment to frame his question. "Have you ever run across a matchmaking service that offers a refund for a bride who doesn't turn out to be as advertised?"

Hale's eyes narrowed. "Indeed I have."

Something in his tone of voice made Isaak look closely at the man he considered an older brother and had always admired for his unflappable good sense. "You already know about Jakob and the Denver matchmaker, don't you?"

Hale's expression didn't change.

"You should have talked him out of such foolishness."

"Not my place. Not yours either, in point of fact."

Isaak groaned. Had the whole world gone mad?

He strolled through the reception, keeping a look out for important people he'd need to greet. He lifted his chin to acknowledge J. P. Fisk, the man who'd sponsored his membership to the exclusive Montana Club in downtown Helena. He'd worked hard to carve out a place beside the millionaires, elected officials, and powerful men of the territory. Sometimes his conscience said he'd gone too far, but every compromise of his integrity was for a greater purpose. A man couldn't wield power and influence for the people he served—and for those he loved—if he wasn't in a position of authority.

Regrets over things like Finn Collin's unintended death

and inciting wrath against Joseph Hendry until he was also eliminated were useless at this stage of the game. His only option was to keep moving forward with his plans.

He checked his pocket watch. Fifteen minutes before he needed to leave for his meeting about the November election and the Gunderson problem. Bribery was out. With Hendry dead, so was any chance of putting a nosy reporter on the hunt for a skeleton in the closet.

But something needed to be done. Isaak Gunderson was too good as a candidate . . . and too likely to win with the Honorable Jonas Forsythe backing him. However, there was trouble brewing between the twins. Two men fighting over a woman always ended badly.

How might he use that to his advantage?

Chapter Four

His photograph failed to capture his true appearance.

For a long moment, and since fellow passengers continued to stroll past, Zoe took her leisure in staring at Mr. Gunderson's impressive profile. His blond hair, from what she could see under his black hat, looked neatly trimmed. He was as tall as Mrs. Luanne Bennett had described, taller than anyone else on the platform, and stocky, although not corpulent based on how closely fit his black suit was.

He stood on the train platform a car's length away from Zoe, both hands clenching a bouquet of yellow roses as he scrutinized the train windows.

Likely looking for a woman who fit an "eminently suitable" description.

Zoe chuckled under her breath. The vagueness of Mrs. Archer's words continued to amuse her. The telegram Mrs. Archer had shared yesterday during tea with Zoe, her daughter Antonia, and Mrs. Luanne Bennett had been brief.

UNEXPECTED ARRIVAL OF EMINENTLY
SUITABLE WOMAN IN DENVER STOP ADVISE
YOU MEET IN PERSON IMMEDIATELY STOP
WIRE FUNDS FOR TRAIN TICKET BY FRIDAY
IF YOU APPROVE STOP

The three ladies had insisted that Mr. Gunderson's wiring of the funds within hours of the telegram being sent boded well for Zoe. She wanted to be hopeful. Mrs. Bennett had repeatedly raved about him, calling him her little brother because of how close their families were. While Mr. Gunderson and his brother were not the richest of the rich in Helena, their stepfather had made a significant amount over the years. Thus Jakob and Isaak Gunderson were, in Mrs. Bennett's estimation, two of the most eligible bachelors in town.

Good, respectful, considerate, God-fearing men.

Zoe moistened her lips in nervous anticipation.

Mrs. Archer's follow-up telegram conveyed Zoe's full name and when to expect her arrival in Helena. Nico had called her decision rash. She preferred to think of it as adventurous.

Mr. Gunderson tugged on the bottom of his blue brocade vest, then pulled on his suit coat lapels one at a time.

Zoe drew in a breath, took a step forward, and stopped.

He turned.

His gaze met hers, and Zoe smiled, hoping she looked eminently suitable to be his future bride. To increase the likelihood, she had worn her midnight blue traveling dress with an underskirt in brown and cream stripes and a matching straw hat adorned with feathers. She had also ruthlessly tamed her black curly hair into a modest bun at the nape of her neck.

His mouth gaped.

Zoe took his response as affirmation that he was pleased with what he saw.

She weaved through the crowd and extended her gloved hand. "Mr. Gunderson, I am Zoe de Fleur."

He shook her hand, his blue eyes focused on her. "I never expected you to be this pretty."

Zoe felt her face warm. "Zank you. I am most happy to—" Her words died as a youth darted around a cluster of men. Nico? She leaned to the right to get a better look, but no dark-haired youths were in view on the platform.

"Is something wrong?"

Zoe looked up at Mr. Gunderson, his brow furrowed with concern. "No, no. My eyes tricked me into zinking I saw a friend from home."

He thrust the yellow roses at her. "Welcome to Helena."

She raised the bouquet to her nose and inhaled the sweet fragrance. "Zey are exquisite."

"Just like you."

A throat cleared.

Mr. Gunderson's gaze shifted to the conductor. That moment looking away from her was all it took for Mr. Gunderson's composure to steady, his shoulders to straighten, and his awkwardness to leave him. He smiled at her. And Zoe's breath caught. He truly was a strikingly handsome man.

He took her gloved hand and drew it over his arm. "We need to leave."

Zoe noted the number of glances their way as Mr. Gunderson escorted her toward the luggage porter, where a crowd of people waited to claim the trunks, cases, and hatboxes being unloaded from the train. While they waited their turn, Zoe looked for Nico . . . or at least the youth resembling him.

People moved.

Mr. Gunderson stepped forward.

". . . suggested I borrow a surrey," he was saying, with no realization she had been distracted, "so we don't have to walk to the boardinghouse I've secured for you. Once we drop off your things, we can go to lunch. Or you can take

some time to refresh yourself after your journey and we can
share a meal this evening."

"Will zis make trouble with your family?"

"Trouble?" He snorted a laugh. "Oh, Miss de Fleur, the last
thing you should fret about is my family. Someday they're
all going to thank me for bringing you to Helena. I'm glad
you're here. So glad." Mr. Gunderson inched forward again as
the crowd around the luggage porter thinned. "I've already
made reservations for both lunch and supper at a new restaurant. It has the best food in town."

Zoe felt dazed. "You made reservations for both lunch
and supper?"

"I wasn't sure which meal you would prefer to have." He
gave her a sheepish grin. "I didn't want to take a chance on
inferior food on your first day in town."

His words warmed her heart.

"Next!"

The luggage porter's shout jolted Zoe out of her admiration of Mr. Gunderson. She handed the bouquet back to him,
then dug inside her reticule for the baggage tickets.

The porter took her claim tickets. He called out the
numbers to the men inside the luggage compartment.

Mr. Gunderson returned the bouquet to Zoe.

She stood patiently while he hefted, loaded, and strapped
down each of her wood-and-leather trunks into the surrey.
Her four hatboxes were added last. With the same ease he
had used to load her luggage, he lifted her into the surrey,
spacious enough to seat four adults comfortably, and then
walked to the other side.

"It's warm for March," he said, climbing in. He pointed
to the floorboards. "There's a quilt under the bench if you
get cold. Good thing for us the breeze is from the south."

"I will let you know if I am cold."

As his eyes—a lovely robin's egg blue with specks of

brown near the center—focused on hers, the seconds stretched into minutes. The silence deepened.

Zoe moistened her bottom lip, unsure whether she was expected to speak.

His lips twitched. "I'm glad you're here."

"You have already told me zis."

"I hope you're not tired of hearing it, 'cause I'm not tired of saying it." He flicked the reins and the surrey started into motion, his action relieving her of having to utter a response.

Zoe clasped her hands together in her lap, smiling to herself. She liked his ability to make her feel comfortable, as if they had known each other for years, not minutes.

Truth was, she liked every bit of Jakob Gunderson.

As they made their way up the hill, heading toward the cluster of buildings southwest of the train depot, Mr. Gunderson shared the history of Helena. The dirt-hardened roads here were hilly and crooked, reminding her more of the roads in France than in New York. The buildings were shorter, less grand. But the air carried a sweetness not found in New York or Paris. Or even Denver. The pedestrian and horse-drawn traffic on the road increased, and Mr. Gunderson slowed the surrey's pace as he continued to speak.

Based on his numbers, with over ten thousand residents, Helena had a fraction of the populace of Denver, but his beloved town had plenty of entertainments and the modern conveniences Zoe had grown accustomed to in New York City—the streetcar line, telephone service, and electric lighting.

"I love ze theater," she said when he paused to take a breath.

"I do, too, but I should warn you, if a building in Helena is called a theater, it's likely not the type for a lady of good breeding. Ming's Opera House always provides wholesome entertainment. The Helena Orchestra is performing all this week. I'll buy us tickets." The hopefulness in his voice—joy, wonder, and anticipation—drew her attention away from the scenery.

Zoe studied his chiseled profile. How was it he was not already married? "I would like to attend ze opera with you."

As they approached a two-story, triangular-shaped building on their right, she noticed the business's name was painted in black near the flat roof. They stopped at the Y-shaped intersection, where the road they were on merged with two others. A group of Indians crossed in front of them, walking west. Each man wore blankets wrapped about him. The women carried baskets strapped to their back. The group entered the building, the same words painted in black also etched into the shop's wide front window.

Zoe recognized THE and CO., which could be pronounced *Ko* or *So*, depending on whether the C was soft or hard. Before she could sound out the middle word, Mr. Gunderson flicked the reins. The surrey sprang to life again.

"This October will be our third annual Harvest Festival," Mr. Gunderson said, glancing at her. "Have you ever ridden in a hot-air balloon?"

Zoe admired the blue sky sprinkled with random puffy clouds. To fly a mile or more above the ground . . .

She shuddered.

He chuckled. "I'll take that as a *no*." He lifted his brows and grinned mischievously. "Would you ever ride in one?"

"I would if I felt safe," she admitted.

"Challenge accepted. Trust me, it'll be fun." His gaze returned to the road, and before Zoe could respond to his comment, he spoke again. "Mrs. Archer's telegram said you *arrived* in Denver, not that you were from there. Where is home for you?"

"Paris."

His eyes widened. "As in Paris, France?"

"I was born zere." She clenched her hands together and

rested them on her lap. "For ze last four years I lived in New York City."

"The farthest I've ever traveled from where I was born was Denver. I never—" He broke off, his expression no longer seeming happy.

"What is it, Mr. Gunderson?"

"Please call me Jakob," he said absently, his attention on driving the surrey. "Mr. Gunderson is my brother."

After four years of living in America, where people were laxer in etiquette, she still could not use his Christian name after so short an acquaintance. Calling him—any male—by his first name implied a certain familiarity.

She turned on the seat to face him. "I am most interested to meet your twin," she said, because it was the truth, but also because she hoped changing the subject would improve his spirits.

"Isaak and I aren't identical, so you don't have to worry about not being able to tell us apart."

"You are much blessed to have a sibling." She paused for a moment before adding, "My papa passed away a year ago. We traveled many places and saw many wonderful sights."

He rested a hand atop her still-clenched ones. "I'm sorry for your loss."

"Zank you."

He clicked his tongue twice, then pulled on the right rein, directing the horse to pull the surrey into the alley behind a two-story wooden building in dire need of a whitewashing. He halted the surrey, tied off the reins, and shifted on the bench to face her. "I'm glad you're—"

Zoe held up a hand, silencing him. "I am glad I am here, too."

He chuckled. "Welcome to Deal's Boardinghouse. It's the finest one in Helena . . . and farthest from the parts of town a woman like you needs to avoid."

A stately man stepped into the alley. "Jakob! I see you

have our newest guest." The man smiled at Zoe. "Miss de
Fleur, I am Alfred Deal. My wife and I are honored to have
you stay with us."

A raggedly dressed boy younger than Nico pumped his
arms up and down as he came running down the alley. He had
sunken cheeks and a pinched expression in his brown eyes.

Mr. Gunderson jumped from the surrey to block the boy's
path. "Slow down, buddy!"

The boy scrambled to stop. He slipped and fell back onto
the cobblestones. "Sorry, sir. I didn't mean nothin' by it."

Mr. Gunderson helped the boy to his feet. "What's your
name?"

"Timothy Sundin the Third"—he peeped at Zoe, then at
Mr. Deal, then back at Mr. Gunderson—"but most folks just
call me Timmy."

"Well, Mr. Timothy Sundin the Third, because you're
here and I could use some help, how'd you like to earn yourself a dollar?"

The boy's eyes widened. "A whole dollar?"

Mr. Gunderson nodded. "And if you do a good job of it,
I'll hire you to help over at that new brick building going up
on Lawrence Street."

"That's your building?"

"It sure is."

"Whoa! It's grand!"

Mr. Gunderson grinned in obvious pleasure over the boy's
words. He grabbed two of the four hatboxes off the floor-
board between the front and second surrey benches and
handed them to Mr. Deal. He then grabbed the other two and
offered them to the boy, who took them.

"Follow Mr. Deal," Mr. Gunderson said before walking
to Zoe's side of the surrey.

The boy gave Mr. Deal a nervous look. His gaze lowered.
"Uh, sure, sir."

Mr. Deal motioned for the boy to enter the boardinghouse first.

Mr. Gunderson waited to speak until the boy and Mr. Deal were inside. "Helena has some sundry elements I wish I could shield you from, but I can't. You'd be shocked to know what some children—girls, in particular—are conscripted into for the sake of a measly dollar. That boy is likely the child of a prostitute. I hope you don't mind that I asked him to carry your hatboxes inside."

Zoe studied his face. "Your photograph did not tell ze whole story of you."

"My photograph?"

"I saw ze happiness in your eyes, but ze photograph failed to capture your kindness. And I do not mind zat he is helping. Zis is a wonderful zing you have done."

He grinned. And she grinned, too.

After a long, comfortable moment, he helped her out of the surrey.

The next half hour was taken up with carting luggage up to Zoe's room on the ladies' side of the second floor and meeting Mr. and Mrs. Deal and their niece, Janet, the only other female residing in the boardinghouse. The Deals dutifully shared how, for being a frontier town, Helena had theaters, restaurants, hotels, and a variety of shops, which they vowed Zoe was sure to enjoy.

She fingered the key to her room as she listened to the Deals yet watched Mr. Gunderson kneel in front of little Timmy Sundin, the pair speaking too softly for her to overhear.

Mrs. Deal touched Zoe's arm. "Please, Miss de Fleur, have a seat in the dining room. I'll bring you some tea and cake."

Tea would be nice. So would cake. Breakfast had been hours ago. As much as she would also enjoy a nap, her heart's strongest desire was getting to know Jakob Gunderson. The question of why he had yet to marry lingered in the back of her mind. If he was hiding something, she wanted to find out before her heart grew too attached.

She smiled at the older woman. "Zank you, but Mr. Gunderson is taking me to lunch." And . . . because he had reservations, maybe supper, too.

Four hours later
The Resale Company

Isaak checked the clock in his office. Two-thirty in the afternoon. Was Jakob back to work? He'd promised to only take the morning. Assuming the train was on time, he'd picked up the woman over four hours ago.

Plenty of time to realize he'd made a terrible mistake and buy the woman a ticket straight back to Denver.

Knock, knock, knock.

"Isaak?" Carline Pope, who was filling in for Emilia McCall while she was on her honeymoon, opened the door to his office without waiting for an invitation to enter. "Mr. O'Leary is here to see you. He says it's important."

"Send him in." Isaak sat straight in the ladder-back chair. What had Jakob done—or, *not* done—to prod the foreman of the work crew up at The Import Co. into running here for help?

Carline disappeared, and O'Leary took her place in the doorway.

He held his cap in both hands, wringing the brown tweed like it was a piece of laundry. "I'm sorry to bother you, Mr. Gunderson, but the men are ready to hang windows, only we don't got any."

"Where's Jakob?"

O'Leary twisted his cap tighter.

"You haven't seen him all day, have you?"

"Not since nine this morning, sir. After we had our crew meeting, he said he was gonna meet someone at the train station and then go to lunch."

Isaak's jaw muscles tightened. "Did he say where?"

"No, sir, but Moses said he saw him at the Grand Hotel around noon."

Isaak stood. "I'll go get him."

"What do you want me and the men to do in the meantime?"

"Whatever you can so we meet the May 4 grand opening."

O'Leary's eyes flitted to the floor.

"Is all construction at a standstill until the windows go in?"

"No, sir. We can still work on the upper floors."

Isaak's fingers curled as he imagined wrapping them around his brother's thick neck. "Do what you can."

"Yes, sir. Thank you, sir." O'Leary didn't turn to leave.

"Was there something else?"

"Yeah. A lad by the name of Timmy showed up an hour ago. Said your brother hired him to clean up wood shavings and the like. You know anything about that?"

"No, but it sounds like Jakob." Isaak took his coat off the back of his chair. "Is the boy working hard?"

O'Leary nodded.

At least Jakob had done one good thing today. "Then let him stay on."

"Very well, sir." The foreman nodded again, then turned and left the office.

Isaak followed, slipping his arms into the sleeves of his coat as he hurried to the hat rack and retrieved his black bowler. He walked into the retail portion of The Resale Co. Carline was behind the counter ringing up some books and a pile of tapered candles for Mrs. Snowe. Isaak greeted the woman and chatted with her about her husband's carpentry designs for The Import Co. while her items were wrapped.

He walked her to the door, turned around, and told Carline he'd be back in an hour.

"You're leaving me?" Panic laced her question.

"You can manage." He checked his inside coat pocket to be sure his notebook and pencil were inside. "If anything comes up that you aren't comfortable handling, write it down."

She twisted her hands in the skirt of her blue calico dress. "What if I suspect someone of giving me counterfeit money?"

Carline and Yancey Palmer were best friends. Yancey's fiancé, Joseph Hendry, had been killed right after returning from Dawson County, where he was investigating counterfeiting. Everyone knew Hendry was killed by angry brothel owners because his inflammatory articles stirred up sentiment against the red-light district, resulting in raids and more stringent laws against prostitution, but Yancey and Carline connected his death to the counterfeiting. No amount of rational argument could dislodge the association.

"If you suspect something, put a little star or dot by the name when you record their purchase in the ledger. Then put the money in a separate place, and I'll deal with it when I get back."

Carline regarded him solemnly.

He smiled. "You'll be fine. You know what's on the shelves better than you think you do."

A bit of wariness faded from her blue eyes. "I've shopped here often enough." She glanced down at the ledger, then back at Isaak. "All right. As long as you aren't too worried about counterfeit money, I suppose I'll be fine until you get back."

"I'm certain you will." He put on his hat and walked into the sunshine.

He held himself to a steady pace while walking the five blocks to the Grand Hotel. Despite how irritated he was with his brother, he managed to greet people with a smile and chat with them. A few white clouds hovered above, the kind in which he and Jakob used to find shapes. They'd lie in the grass and point to the various clouds, trying to outdo each other by coming up with more and more outlandish like-nesses. Isaak stopped and put a hand up to hold his hat in place while picking out a sideways pear and a soup pot with a whiff of steam escaping the top. Funny how it only took a second for him to find the shapes even after years of not playing the cloud game—one he didn't have time to play anymore. Unfortunate, but a fact of life.

He dropped his hand and started walking again. At Jackson and Sixth, the sight of Hale's law office reminded Isaak that he needed to reschedule their dinner at the Montana Club, but he didn't have enough time to stop now. The Grand Hotel was the next building, and he could see his brother through the window. Half curtains blocked his lunch companion except for a tall brown hat trimmed with feathers.

How could a woman who was desperate enough to become a mail-order bride afford such a stylish hat?

Isaak yanked his attention away from the window and schooled his features before nodding at the man holding the door open for him.

"Good afternoon, Mr. Gunderson."

"Afternoon, Abe. How's the family?"

"Can't complain, sir. Can't complain."

Isaak dug a dollar coin from his pocket and tipped the man. With six mouths to feed, he needed it. "Give your lovely wife my best."

"I will, Mr. Gunderson." Abe touched the brim of his red cap and opened the door an inch wider.

Isaak stepped into the hotel lobby. He crossed to the restaurant and told the *maître d'hôtel* he wasn't there to

eat but to talk to his brother, looking to where Jakob sat
for emphasis.

Jakob was laughing at something, his face filled with . . .
what? More than the polite disinterest Isaak expected—no,
hoped—to see.

Confound it all, his brother was taken with the woman!
Her dark blue dress, with a gold-and-brown-stripe underskirt
was made of silk. A potted tree hid her figure, but as best
Isaak could tell, she was slender. None of which fit his
mental picture of a distressed or otherwise unacceptable
female who would be hopeless enough to become a mail-
order bride. She turned her head toward the window, and
Jakob stared at her with a silly grin on his face.

Jakob looked up, his expression melting into irritation
when he saw Isaak.

Isaak answered Jakob's scowl with one of his own.

Jakob shook his head and looked pointedly at his companion.

Isaak jerked his head toward the lobby.

Another shake of Jakob's head.

Knowing Jakob wouldn't want his precious mail-order
bride to overhear their upcoming conversation, Isaak
stepped through the archway separating the lobby from the
dining area.

Jakob jolted to his feet and appeared to excuse himself
from the table. His entire demeanor turned sour as soon as
he was out of his companion's view.

Isaak stepped back, squared his shoulders, and braced for
their confrontation.

Chapter Five

Zoe waited until Mr. Gunderson was beyond the table before turning her head just enough to watch him stroll toward the potted plants framing the arched entrance that led to the restaurant lobby.

Goodness, the man was impressive!

Mr. Gunderson's laughter reminded her of Papa's—deep-chested and ending in a snort. When she spoke, his gaze never veered from hers, his lips curving in a you-fascinate-me smile. She considered mimicking his smile. She wanted to, but she had never been good with flirting. This man she wished to flirt with. And yet her mind had thought of nothing coquettish.

She was clearly more like Papa than *Maman*.

Zoe sighed.

She turned back to the table, her gaze catching on the coffee cup next to Mr. Gunderson's half-eaten chocolate cake. Coffee with breakfast she understood. But during a dinner meal? Mrs. Gilfoyle-Crane had insisted upon coffee after the solids had been removed from the table because she favored the way the bitter brew paired with sweets. Zoe agreed. She also knew coffee was a less costly alternative to liquor or wine for aiding digestion.

For someone who drank four cups of coffee with his meal—if this was normal behavior for him and not merely nerves—Mr. Gunderson should have sallow skin in addition to intestinal issues; his tanned complexion could disguise sallowness. It was no wonder he had to leave the meal in search of a washroom.

Poor man.

Embarrassed for him, Zoe focused on her dessert, which, upon her first bite, was as disappointing as the main dish. The flavor of the chicken fricassee would have been improved if the chef had added some thin-sliced, cold-boiled ham during the stewing. She picked up her spoon, uncertain whether she wanted another bite. The crème brûlée was too eggy. The pâtissier should have layered in another half cup of whipping crème. A pity, for the brûlée was perfect.

She tapped her spoon against the toasted sugar, cracking off another piece. Her spoon hovered over the ramekin. If she slid the spoon under the sugar, she could avoid the lackluster custard. She ought to eat it; Mr. Gunderson was paying for the meal. She should. Especially because she had managed to endure only half the main dish.

To her relief, at that moment Mr. Gunderson slid back into his seat, grinning. "It's an unseasonably warm day. Let's go for a walk. It'll be fun."

"Zis is true, but what about ze surrey?"

"I'll fetch it later."

He was gazing at her with an unnerving intensity. The sun streaming through the restaurant windows brightened the heavenly blue of his eyes.

Zoe laid down her spoon. "I would enjoy a walk." She considered asking, *Where to?* but how much more fun it was to be surprised.

While Mr. Gunderson paid the bill, Zoe sought out the washroom. He was waiting for her in the hotel lobby, holding the bouquet of roses, her leather gloves, and her winter cloak. He draped the cloak over her shoulders, then gave her a moment to pull on her gloves before handing her the bouquet.

She had not felt so treasured since Papa passed away. But this was different. Jakob Gunderson was not her father.

A voice cleared.

She turned to the sound.

The doorman held open the door. "Hey, Jakob, would you tell my brother to come by here after work?"

Mr. Gunderson patted the side of the man's shoulder. "Will do, Abe. Give your wife my love."

The doorman chuckled. "And give her a reason to regret marrying me? Not on your life." He looked at Zoe. "Ma'am, we appreciate you visiting the finest hotel in Helena. We hope you'll come back again soon."

"Zank you." And then she stepped outside.

Mr. Gunderson motioned to the right. "This way."

A pair of horse-drawn wagons drove past. Several men on horses rode by, too.

Zoe partially listened as Mr. Gunderson acknowledged fellow pedestrians and talked about the businesses they passed. How pleasant not to be the one required to carry the conversation. She also enjoyed sensing how much he loved this town and the people in it. Yet he was still unmarried. Why? The question had nagged at her during the drive from the boardinghouse and throughout the meal. It still nagged.

As they passed another business, which had old barrels filled with soil on either side of the entrance, Zoe brushed her fingers over the green shoots peeking through the rich brown dirt. In another month, flowers and greenery would brighten this main thoroughfare through town.

While buildings lined both sides of the street, to the north-west, white-topped, rugged mountains peppered the view.

The largest—Mount Helena.

Of all the letters and references Mrs. Archer had read to Zoe, the one from the reverend had been the most descriptive of God's created majesty surrounding Helena. She had been wary of his narrative. She now agreed with the words he had chosen. Nothing obstructed the vast blue skyline. On Manhattan Island, the best view of the sky came when standing on the Crane house rooftop, Papa's favorite place to watch the sunrise. Yet even there, the sky was partially obstructed by the taller buildings blocks away.

A streetcar bell sounded as it stopped at the upcoming intersection. Zoe smiled with optimism about creating a future here as she watched passengers climb off before others climbed on, including a mother with her three identically dressed, stair-step little girls.

"In the next few years," Mr. Gunderson boasted, "the streetcar line will extend beyond this one line direct to the train depot. There will be tracks through neighborhoods."

Zoe looked up at Mr. Gunderson and listened as he spoke. She had never expected to feel such an instant compatibility with a stranger.

He enjoyed hiking in the mountains. She did, too. He enjoyed sunsets. She did, too. He enjoyed helping those less fortunate, attending worship services, and spending time with friends and family. She did, too! Her favorite story was of how his stepfather had agreed to raise twin babies as his own, even though they would bear their real father's last name. A lot could be understood about a man in how he spoke about his parents. Jakob Gunderson clearly treasured his.

By the time they reached the intersection, the streetcar had moved on. They crossed the street, the sound of hammers against wood growing louder as they walked.

"Here it is!" Mr. Gunderson said. "The Import Company."

They stood there, looking at a grand three-story, red-brick building with stone accents under the window frames and around the double-doored entrance. Zoe admired how THE IMPORT COMPANY had been carved into stone over the third-floor windows in between the brickwork.

When a person was looking for a business—

She gasped. "Oh! Zis is your building. You wrote about it in your second letter."

He smiled with pride, as if presenting her with his greatest treasure.

"I like it," she said. "When will ze construction finish?"

"We've had an unexpected delay on the windowpanes, so they won't go in until next week. The interior work will be finished by the middle of April. That leaves us two weeks to arrange displays and price the goods before the May 4 grand opening."

Six arched window openings on each of the second and third floors. Two wide ones on the ground level. She leaned to the right and counted the side window openings. Eight . . . no, ten.

"Is your papa's other business in a building zis grand?"

"No. The Resale Company could fit inside this one's first floor," he said in a curious voice, as if he had never realized the difference in the buildings' sizes. "The plan is to rent the second floor as office space."

"And ze third floor?"

"Storage."

When he said no more, she looked up at him. "That whole floor only for storage?"

He swallowed, his Adam's apple shifting in his throat. "There's also an apartment for me and my future family." He motioned to the building. "Shall we?"

"Certainly."

Five minutes later, they stood in the center of what would be The Import Company. Sunshine streamed through the window openings and cast elongated rectangles on the unstained floorboards. Hammering sounded on the upper floors.

Zoe eyed the handful of different tin tiles adhered to the ceiling. She favored the one on the far left with the *fleur-de-lis*.

Mr. Gunderson touched her arm, and she met his gaze. "Stay here. I need to check on today's progress, and I don't want you on our makeshift staircase."

"I am content to admire ze view."

As soon as he disappeared through a doorway in the back wall, Zoe strolled around the wide, open space—empty save for sawdust, six support pillars, and her. Everything about Helena smelled earthy and new. She imagined the register near the front and display racks abounding with merchandise. If she were arranging the store, she would segregate the merchandise by the regions where they were made, so that when customers moved around the store, they would feel as if they were traveling the world in eighty steps instead of in eighty days. And she would sell scented candles and oils.

How nice it would be to have cookbooks of recipes from different cultures.

A whistle drew her gaze to the doorless entrance.

Nico?

Zoe stared, unable to believe he was there. After her first meeting with Mrs. Archer, Nico had broken Zoe's heart when he refused to support her decision to allow Mr. Gunderson to court her. She had believed Nico to be her friend. But a true friend would never desert her as he had. Once they had returned to her hotel, he had thanked her for helping him reach Denver and wished her well. She had not seen him since.

But she *had* seen him. Earlier, at the train depot.

Nico motioned her to walk his way.

Zoe hurried over. "Why are you here?"

"You need my help."

She gave him a look to convey exactly what she felt about his claim.

"You do," he insisted. His brow furrowed. He looked

tense . . . and a bit worried. "That man you came here with isn't what he seems."

"How did you come by zis belief?"

"I just know."

Zoe released a weary breath. Nico had also insisted courting a stranger was a bad idea. If he had returned to Mrs. Archer's house yesterday morning as Zoe had, he would have listened to the matchmaker read the reverend's reference letter. Mr. Gunderson and his brother were pillars of society, their parents some of the earliest settlers of Helena. Mrs. Luanne Bennett, a charming woman four years older than Zoe, had also confirmed everything written in Mr. Gunderson's letters and in those written by his other references.

Amid all these truths, there was one lie: Nico's, about the advertisement.

She had no cause to trust him again.

Except . . .

None of Mr. Gunderson's family had sent a letter of reference. She understood his parents because they were still away on their tour of the country. But why not his twin? Mr. Gunderson had said little about his brother during the meal. Perhaps his family was not as perfect and loving as he claimed.

Nico was here because he was concerned and worried about her. He had lied because he had no other way to escape New York. He needed her help, needed her to be his friend. Not to forgive him would make her an unkind and ungrateful person. The most gracious and wise thing she could do was give a listening ear to his concerns.

Zoe gave his shoulder a little squeeze. "I am pleased to see you."

He enveloped her in a hug. "I'm sorry, Zoe, for getting angry and leaving you." He choked up. "I love you. You're the only family I've got."

She rested her chin atop his head. He was the closest she

had to family, too, but she had signed a contract agreeing to a two-month courtship. She had to—no, she *wanted to*—give Mr. Gunderson a fair chance to woo her.

She drew back. "Go to Deal's Boardinghouse and I will pay for you a room."

"Thanks, but I found somewhere to stay." The moment her brow rose, he added, "It's reputable. Trust me. I met someone at the depot who gave me a job making deliveries."

That was Nico—ever resourceful. During the train ride to Denver, he had convinced the conductor to hire him to work in the passenger cars, selling sandwiches, cigars, and newspapers.

She gripped the lapels of his coat and tugged until it rested properly on his shoulders. "Zen come to ze boardinghouse in ze morning at eight. I will buy you breakfast and tell you all I have learned about Mr. Gunderson. You will see he is a good man."

Nico grimaced. "You'd better have a plan for what you're going to do if this courtship doesn't turn out like you're dreaming it will. 'Cause I know it won't. He's not the man for you."

Zoe held her response. Now was not the time to try to convince Nico to be optimistic.

"See ya tomorrow." He gave her a quick hug, then dashed away.

Minutes passed before the hammering stopped.

She glanced around the empty store. Mr. Gunderson was still upstairs. On the second floor? Or was he examining the work on the third floor, his future living quarters? To have her own home would be another dream come true.

But if things did not go as she hoped—

Zoe nipped her bottom lip. That grand lady who had sat next to her on the train from Butte to Helena had mentioned a new luxury hotel and hot springs resort "unlike any other in the world" set to open in a year. The exclusive Broadwater was exactly the kind of place that would desire the services of a French chef. Or she could apply to work in the Grand Hotel restaurant, for they could use someone with her skills. In a town of ten thousand people, Jakob Gunderson could not be the only decent bachelor interested in marriage.

Tomorrow she would explain to Nico the number of other paths her future could take, if she chose to leave the one leading her to Jakob Gunderson.

Her gaze fell to the bouquet of roses.

She inhaled the sweet scent . . . and remembered how Mr. Gunderson had gazed upon her at the restaurant. And smiled.

No other paths were needed.

This courtship would end with a marriage. She was sure of it.

Chapter Six

Isaak cracked an egg into the bowl and dropped the shell into the bin beside the stove. In two more months, Ma would be home and take over the cooking and gardening again. While he was looking forward to having her here, he wasn't sure he wanted to give up cooking. Turned out he liked it. Plus, food didn't talk back or wander off or tell you it was going to do one thing and then do the exact opposite.

Unlike a brother.

He cracked another egg to make an even dozen in the bowl. After dropping that shell in the bin, he took up the whisk lying on the soapstone counter and started beating the eggs. He checked the clock. What was taking Jakob so long this morning?

As if in answer to his question, footsteps thudded down the stairs. "Breakfast ready?" Jakob's morning cheerfulness sounded somewhat forced.

Isaak poured the scrambled eggs into a heated cast-iron skillet. "It will be in a few minutes."

"Great." Based on the crunching noise that followed,

Jakob had helped himself to a bacon strip. "I need to wolf down breakfast if I'm going to make it over to Deal's Boardinghouse in time to pick up Miss de Fleur for church."

Miss de Fleur? Was that a French-sounding type of *nom de plume*, the same way Mac's mother had gone from being Mary Lester to Madame Lestraude?

Isaak turned over the eggs. "What are you doing after church?"

"I thought I'd take her out to eat, show her around town a little, and then . . . I don't know. We'll see." Another crunch and a whiff of bacon on the air.

Isaak held in a retort about how that would have been nice to know on Friday, before he purchased four lamb chops for today's lunch. He didn't want to start Sunday morning with an argument.

Pa often said, "Give Jakob some credit. He doesn't plan things the way you do, but he almost always lands on his feet." Isaak doubted Pa would give that same advice if he knew Jakob was shirking his duties at The Import Co. to squire a woman around town. Sure, he'd gone back to work after Isaak forced the issue yesterday, but Jakob had come home and refused to talk about the woman. Or about what he accomplished at the store, saying only that everything was on schedule.

On Jakob's schedule.

Isaak was certain it wasn't the one he'd written out last December, or any of the ones he'd altered in the months since then. Some of the changes were to be expected. Building a new business from the ground up was certain to involve adjustments. They didn't need additional, unnecessary ones because Jakob couldn't keep his focus.

Isaak's grip tightened on the wooden spoon. "Grab us some plates."

Some footsteps against the wood plank floor, a whoosh of air, and the scrape of crockery. "Here."

A blue plate appeared in Isaak's peripheral vision. He scooped fluffy yellow eggs on the plate.

"That's enough." Jakob pulled away his plate and held out the other one.

Isaak piled the rest of the eggs on his plate, then set the skillet in the sink. He turned to pick up the bacon, pleased to find that Jakob had left him a full four strips. Isaak added the bacon to his plate, then grabbed the teapot. "Bring the coffee to the table."

"Sure." Jakob held his plate with one hand and the coffee-pot with the other.

They sat down at the small kitchen table, said grace, and began eating.

Jakob ate quickly, eager to be on his way.

Isaak sipped his tea, added more sugar, and sipped again. He reached for the cream. Over the past year, he and Jakob had developed a breakfast routine. They would take turns reading the newspaper, occasionally commenting on something they found interesting or important, then head out to work or church. Any silence between them was comfortable.

Today, tension scraped through the silence.

Isaak didn't even reach for the newspaper because, although Jakob was clearly intent on eating as fast as possible, Isaak feared that one of their friendly tussles about who read which section first might turn ugly. Instead, he focused on making his tea perfect. By the time it was, Jakob was done eating.

He stood. "Thanks for breakfast. I'll see you at church." He carried his empty plate and coffee cup to the sink and hurried out the back door.

Isaak huffed. "Miss de *Fleur*. What a fraud."

Jakob opened the door and poked his head inside to say, "I heard that," before slamming the door behind him.

Somewhat chagrined at being caught speaking ill of a woman no matter how much she deserved it, Isaak crumbled the bacon over his eggs, took a bite, and reached for the Sunday edition of the *Daily Independent*. There, on the front page below the fold, was yet another article exposing a ring of females who had bilked a whole slew of men out of thousands of dollars by posing as European mail-order brides in need of money to travel. The interesting thing—what made it front-page news—was the erstwhile grooms. They were bankers and business owners, lawyers and landlords. In other words, men who weren't easily taken in under normal circumstances, yet they'd fallen for a mail-order bride scam all the same.

For European women. As in *French* women.

Isaak tossed the paper on the table. Ate his breakfast. Pushed the paper farther away. Drank his tea. Dragged the article back to the side of his plate and reread it.

Twice.

Zoe noted the number of people looking their way as Mr. Gunderson drew the little two-seater carriage to a stop next to a fringe-topped surrey that had been painted a shockingly bright shade of yellow. Was it traditional in western America to mingle outside the church before services commenced? At the New York church she attended, regardless of the weather, people arrived and immediately found an empty seat or, for the wealthier members, found their nameplate-designated pew.

The number of people standing outside the white-painted church neared a hundred. The building itself, while similar in size to the other churches she had seen in town, appeared to be able to house about that many. They should all be inside where it was warmer, away from the chilly March breeze, away from the tumultuous gray sky that Mr. Gunderson said looked as if it would rain but, in Montana, looks could be deceiving.

That made no sense.

In her experience, gray clouds always preceded rain.

Yet instead of looking at the sky, everyone was looking at her. Zoe twisted one gloved hand around the other, her stomach in knots.

Mr. Gunderson had warned yesterday that she would draw attention when they arrived for church together. As much because she was a new lady in town as because she was with him. Her silk crimson dress and matching bonnet were no more or less fancy than the clothes the other ladies wore, but her crimson paisley mantelet, with its chenille fringe and wooden beads looked foreign compared to their plain woolen ones.

She must look foreign to them, too.

"You do that a lot."

She turned to her right to see Mr. Gunderson standing there, smiling at her. "I did not realize you had climbed out of ze carriage."

"I could tell."

"What is it I do?"

His eyes fixed on hers with an expression of amusement. "When you're lost in your thoughts, you will"—he motioned to her mouth—"lick your bottom lip."

Zoe felt her cheeks warm. "Is zis an unflattering zing?"

"Unflattering?" He muttered something too softly for her to hear. And then he lifted her to the ground as if she were as light as a bird. He grinned. "Are you ready to meet everyone?"

She opened her mouth, then closed it, unsure if she should admit her worry. There were so many strangers, so many people staring at her, curious about her. And about her and Mr. Gunderson together. If that were not intimidating enough, the one person she wished to meet was nowhere to be seen. Had he stayed home to avoid her, as he had yesterday?

"What is it?" Mr. Gunderson asked softly.

"What if he dislikes me?"

"Who?"

"Your twin."

A look of utter dread crossed his face. He looked to the side, staring at nothing, and she knew he was thinking about his brother.

If they were close, as stated by his references and by Mrs. Luanne Bennett, why had his brother failed to greet Zoe at the train station yesterday? Or at The Import Company after lunch? Or joined them for a second meal at the Grand Hotel restaurant? Not once this morning had Mr. Gunderson spoken of his twin, unlike yesterday, when occasional mentions of *my brother Isaak* had peppered their conversation.

Something had occurred this morning before Mr. Gunderson arrived at the boardinghouse to claim her for church. Something unpleasant between the brothers.

If their relationship was strained because of her—

Mr. Gunderson abruptly smiled. "Isaak won't dislike you, although it might seem that way at first. He's been under more stress than usual because he's running for mayor and his employee, Emilia McCall, is away on her honeymoon, leaving him to manage The Resale Company without her help. He says I don't understand all the work he accomplishes in a day."

"*Do* you understand?"

He shrugged. "I couldn't live with his schedule and maintain my sanity. Life should be about more than just work. Life should be enjoyed, especially with"—he looked at her intently—"people who matter to you, because one day you may wake up and that person you love is gone."

Zoe's eyes blurred. She gave his gloved hand a gentle squeeze. "Zis I understand." She had experienced that loss twice in her life already.

His gaze fell to where their hands were joined. He looked at her. "Thank you."

She waited for him to explain his reason for thanking her, but when he stayed silent, she asked, "For what?"

"For many things." His look warmed her down to the tips of her toes. "For listening attentively when I talk. For being straightforward about why you left Paris and then New York. For being warm, sensitive, and kind. But mostly, Miss de Fleur, for answering my advertisement. You are a brave and adventurous woman to come out West all alone."

She tilted her head and smiled. The sheer joy she felt was too much to be contained. Papa had been the only other person who had ever told her she was brave. "Zank you, Mr. Gunderson, for not insisting upon a letter correspondence."

"It's nice to hear someone appreciates my spontaneity," he quipped.

"It is one of ze many zings about you I appreciate." Zoe knew her cheeks were pink, but this time she did not look away in awkwardness or embarrassment. She held his gaze.

Something about Jakob Gunderson made her feel bold.

She looped her arm around his left one. "I would like to meet your friends."

"And my brother?"

"Oh. He is here?"

"Isaak has never missed a Sunday service in his life."

"Zat is"—she paused to think of the right word— "exemplary."

He laughed. "Not the adjective I would use."

As they strolled toward the church, Zoe smiled in anticipation.

"Morning, Jakob!" someone called out.

People began to crowd around them.

Zoe eased closer to Mr. Gunderson, who shook hands with each member of the Watson family as he introduced her to the president of the Helena Public Schools board of trustees, his wife, and their five children. The oldest son looked to be near Zoe's age, early twenties, while the youngest was two and proud of his ability to stick his whole hand into his mouth and not gag.

One by one, people took turns welcoming her to Helena.

The Palmers were related to Mrs. Luanne Bennett of Denver. Miss Yancey Palmer hugged Zoe as if they were intimate friends. Mr. Geddes Palmer politely shook her hand and then smiled, patted Jakob's shoulder, and murmured, "Lucky dog," before walking away.

After the Palmers, Zoe lost track of the overwhelming number of names.

Between moments of being introduced, she glanced around in hopes of seeing Nico. Why had he missed breakfast? He needed to eat. He could be making a delivery for his new employer. Or perhaps he was hawking newspapers. When Mr. Gunderson had driven by the newspaper building, Nico was not among the handful of newsies filling their wagons. Perhaps he had found employment elsewhere.

The church bell rang.

The double doors opened. Two men, similar in size to Mr. Gunderson, stepped outside. Neither were smiling. While both wore black three-piece suits, the dark-haired, heavily bearded man looked as if he hadn't visited a barber in several years. The blond—

Her heart leaped.

It was him! It had to be. Alike but not identical.

The old-enough-to-be-her-father gentleman on Mr. Gunderson's right said, "Let me know if Tuesday doesn't work. We would be happy to reschedule."

"Tuesday is perfect, sir," answered Mr. Gunderson, drawing Zoe's attention. He smiled at the man's wife. "Aunt Lily, I sure do like your apple pies."

"Oh, Jakob, you know you just have to ask and I'll make you one. I can never say no to you." She looked at Zoe.

"Miss de Fleur, I'm looking forward to visiting with you more over supper."

Supper? Zoe felt her stomach drop. Oh no! She had missed part of the conversation.

She smiled at the woman. *And* hoped her initial expression had not conveyed her confusion. "I am looking forward to it, too."

The woman—Aunt Lily—stepped closer, and Zoe breathed in the familiar orange-blossom cologne, the same delicate and expensive perfume Mrs. Gilfoyle-Crane favored.

"Meeting so many new people at once can be overwhelming." The elegant woman's voice softened with motherly concern. "That's why I insisted to Jonas that we have you and Jakob over for a more relaxed time on Tuesday to get to know one another. Meals are easy moments to build friendships." She hugged Zoe. "Marilyn and David will be so pleased."

Marilyn and David? The names were familiar.

The dignified gentleman tipped his black top hat at Zoe and gave her a nod, small and polite. He then escorted his wife on to the church. This well-dressed, gracious couple should be a part of Mrs. Gilfoyle-Crane's social set, not residents of a frontier town. Who were they?

"The Forsythes," Mr. Gunderson whispered, even though he and Zoe were the only two remaining on the church lawn. "Your wondering is all over your face."

"Is zis unflattering?"

He chuckled. "Nothing about you is unflattering." Before Zoe had time to ponder his remark, he added, "Jonas Forsythe is one of four Montana territorial judges. And he's my godfather."

Judge Forsythe? She knew that name. Oh! He had written one of the letters of glowing reference for Mr. Gunderson. The words of his wife now made sense. Marilyn and David were Jakob Gunderson's mother and stepfather and were bosom friends with the Forsythes. Love for one another had proliferated every letter Mrs. Archer had read Zoe about Jakob and his friends and family.

If only she had taken notes . . .

All in Mr. Gunderson's file would stay in Mrs. Archer's possession until he married or canceled his service with her.

Zoe looked up at Mr. Gunderson. "I would like to share a meal with ze Forsythes."

"Is Tuesday all right?"

"I zink my schedule has an opening."

He let out a little laugh. "I hope so."

Zoe looped her arm around Mr. Gunderson's, then fell into step with him.

As they walked, she tilted her head and studied Mr. Gunderson's face. His gaze stayed fixed ahead. A growing scowl replaced his smile; unlike before, his pace seemed slower, the muscles under her palm tense. Something had soured his joy.

The most logical thing was—

She focused on the two men atop the church steps. Neither smiled. They exchanged words, their gazes on her, and then the dark-haired one disappeared inside the white-washed building.

"Zat is your brother, yes?" she said and wondered if she sounded as breathless to Mr. Gunderson as she sounded to herself. "Zere on ze church steps?"

He regarded her with a peculiar, steady gaze before looking to where his brother stood greeting church attendees. "That's him."

The church bell rang again.

A trio of redheaded boys raced around the building. They stopped abruptly at the bottom of the steps and lined up according to height.

"Ollie!" one yelled.

A fourth child—a girl with strawberry-blond braids to the

middle of her back—skipped around the building, dangling a rag doll in her left hand and wearing black stockings with a hole in one knee. She slid between the second and third boy. In a sedate fashion, the four marched up the steps and took turns shaking Mr. Isaak Gunderson's hand.

He then withdrew something from a waistcoat pocket, laid it in the girl's upturned palm, and curled her fingers around it.

She nodded.

He said something to the three boys.

This time they nodded.

". . . find you after the service," he was saying when Zoe and Mr. Jakob Gunderson reached the church steps.

"Mornin', Jakob," the tallest boy called out before ushering the other three children—presumably his siblings—into the church.

Mr. Isaak Gunderson said nothing.

His green eyes fixed on Zoe, and her breath caught. He looked at her exactly as Chef Henri always had. It took all her fortitude not to lower her gaze, as she had four years ago and every other time she had been in Chef Henri's presence. She held still. This man was not Chef Henri.

She lifted her chin and smiled. "*Bonjour*, Mr. Gunderson."

"Welcome to Helena, Miss de Fleur." He glanced over his shoulder into the church, then looked back and said, "The service is about to start."

"This is the moment"—Mr. Jakob Gunderson squeezed Zoe's hand, which lay on his arm—"when you should start calling me Jakob or things will get confusing. Trust me, if you say Mr. Gunderson, everyone in town will think you're talking about *him*."

Zoe looked from brother to brother. Two Mr. Gundersons. Jakob, with his happy eyes and easy grin, was the more attractive.

And charming. And likable.

Although Mr. Isaak Gunderson's dislike might not be aimed at *her*, he was glaring at his brother with bristling hostility, and Jakob's smile seemed forced. Twice in her life, she had awoken to discover a parent was gone: her mother, when she left to live in Italy, and then the day her father died. The Gunderson brothers needed to be reminded of the importance of family.

She must do something to help. But what?

Meals were easy moments in which to build friendships. Zoe had no kitchen to prepare a meal. Perhaps a good solution would be to ask Mr. Gunderson to join them for lunch. Surely the hotel restaurant could accommodate a third person added to their reservation.

"Jakob," she said, and instantly liked the way his name sounded on her tongue.

"Yes?"

"I zink we should invite your brother to share a meal with us."

The woman was everything Isaak feared she'd be: exotically beautiful, speaking with a fake French accent, and already bossing his brother around. He didn't see the poor relative but had no doubt one would turn up in a day or two.

And she'd made her first big mistake.

Isaak stared down at her from his superior height. "I think a shared meal is a wonderful idea. I'll cook."

The woman turned her chocolate-brown eyes on Jakob, who was too busy staring daggers at Isaak to notice.

Isaak smirked. Perhaps the vixen didn't have her claws in quite as deep as she thought. He raised his eyebrows and continued to meet his brother's glare.

"Zat will be lovely." There was a bit of uncertainty in her voice, which should have thrilled him.

It didn't. Isaak slanted his gaze to her, surprised and

annoyed at the prickle in his soul warning that he'd done something to upset her.

Oh, she was good. No wonder Jakob couldn't see past that pretty face and perfect figure.

"Church is about to start." Isaak stepped back to let them pass. "Meet me at home after service is over."

Miss de Fleur looked between him and Jakob before stepping across the threshold.

Jakob leaned close to whisper, "You can't invite a woman over to the house without a chaperone."

Isaak stiffened. As if he didn't already know that.

"I'll take care of it." He patted his brother's shoulder to move him along. Too bad Mrs. Hollenbeck wasn't back from her European tour. The conversation would have turned to travel, and then the de Fleur vixen would be caught in her own trap. Isaak doubted she knew anything about France except what could be gleaned from books.

Windsor Buchanan returned from wherever he had gone and closed his side of the double doors. "Thought you said she'd be ugly and at least fifty."

Isaak shut his door and turned to look at the pew where Jakob and Miss de Fleur stood chatting with Yancey Palmer. "I was wrong about that, but I'm not wrong on the whole." Sure, her appearance wasn't what he'd been expecting, but Miss de Fleur was too pretty, with her curling black hair that refused to stay pinned up so little ringlets framed her heart-shaped face and danced along the curve of her shapely neck. Had he not read the article about the intelligent men taken in by women claiming to be foreign brides, he might have fallen for her himself.

Windsor crossed his arms over his chest. "Whatever you need, I've got your back."

Isaak thanked him with a nod and surveyed the church attendees who were gradually taking their seats in search of anyone who had taken a European tour or had relatives in France. Only Edward Tandy fit the bill, and a third man around the dinner table with a lone woman was not appropriate.

If Isaak couldn't have Mrs. Hollenbeck as a chaperone, the next best person was his godmother, Lily Forsythe. Uncle Jonas was taking her to Paris for their tenth wedding anniversary, and she was a voracious reader. She'd know if something Miss de Fleur said about her supposed homeland was wrong. Isaak turned to his right and made his way down the aisle to the third row, where the Forsythes were sitting.

Murmuring his apologies, Isaak scooted past the Watson family. He reached the vacant seat next to his godmother just as Reverend Neven called for everyone to rise for the first hymn. Isaak took the hymnal from the pew back in front of him and opened to hymn number 323, "Blessed Assurance." He held it low so Aunt Lily could share it with him.

She chuckled. "Can you see the words from that great a distance?"

Isaak's lips twitched and the tension in his gut eased. "Shall I sit down so we're the same height?"

"That would help." The voice was Yancey Palmer's and came from behind him.

He craned his neck to look at her. "Sorry, Yance. I'll slouch during the sermon."

She grinned at him, and he was glad to see the humor reached her eyes. After Joseph Hendry died—and their engagement along with him—her parents had sent her to Denver for a long visit with her sister, Luanne. It had done her a world of good.

Isaak returned his attention to the hymnal for the duration of the song, but as they were sitting down, he leaned close to Aunt Lily and whispered, "Would you be available to come for lunch after church? I need a chaperone for Jakob's Miss de Fleur."

She placed a gloved hand at the side of her mouth. "I'm sorry, but we're promised to the Cannons this afternoon."

"I can come," Yancey spoke again. "And I'll bring Carline and Geddes, too. We'll have a merry time."

Isaak groaned.

Chapter Seven

"*Zat* is why your brother is upset with you?" Zoe whispered back in shock as she and Jakob stood in the foyer of his parents' home, still wearing their outer garments. She had been right to suspect a conflict between the brothers. "Oh, Jakob, do you not see how keeping your contract with ze Archer Matrimonial Company from your brother was most hurtful?"

"It wasn't Isaak's business to know." His expression grim, Jakob shrugged off his greatcoat. He laid it on the mirrored hall tree bench, atop the other coats and cloaks of those who had arrived before them. "Besides, Zoe, his feelings don't get hurt like a normal person's."

Zoe held back her retort. Everyone had feelings, even his brother.

She untied then removed her bonnet. "Are you ashamed of me? Is zat why you kept me a secret?"

"How could I be ashamed of you?" He hung her bonnet and his black hat on empty hooks and then continued to speak softly so no one in the drawing room would overhear them. "The only thing I knew about you was your name and that you'd arrived in Denver because you wanted to be my mail-order bride."

Zoe grimaced. Becoming his bride had never been a

consideration until Mrs. Archer revealed Nico's falsehood about someone wanting to hire a chef for the finest kitchen west of the Mississippi. She opened her mouth with the intention of finally telling Jakob about Nico, but this moment was about Jakob and his brother, not her and Nico.

Instead she said, "Zat was a misunderstanding."

"And I for one am quite thankful. What brought you to me matters little in light of the fact you are here." A smile lifted the corners of Jakob's lips. "We covered at least three months of correspondence with all the talking we did yesterday."

She nodded in response. Yesterday had been one of the best days of her life. Never before had she met someone with such an effortless ability to fill silences. Most of all, she appreciated the way he never pressured her for information she felt uncomfortable sharing.

She removed her gloves, then handed them to him before she unbuttoned the mantelet covering her crimson dress.

Jakob slid it from her shoulders. He added her belongings to the mirrored hall tree. "I'd planned to tell Isaak about you—or whoever answered my advertisement—when the time was right." He shrugged. "Things went faster with you than I expected. Don't look at me like that. I know . . . *yesterday* was the right time."

"Zen why did you not confess all?"

"It's a brother thing."

"What is a 'brother zing'?"

"If you had a sibling, you'd understand."

Zoe winced at the sting his words brought. Her life would be different had she had a sibling. Or a mother. Or if Papa were still alive.

Jakob rubbed the back of his neck. "Isaak and I are each other's best friend and worst enemy. We say and do things to each other that we'd never let someone else do. Does that make sense?"

How could something be both good and bad? Oh!

"You are salt," she said with a smile. "Too much ruins a dish. Ze right amount makes ze meal—*parfait*!

"Par-fay?"

"It means perfect in French."

"Isaak and I are both salt." He chuckled. "All right, I like that comparison. It makes us equals."

Zoe gripped his hands. "My heart breaks knowing you and your brother are at odds."

His hands moved to cradle hers. "You think *now* is my new right time to talk to him?"

She lifted her shoulder in a noncommittal shrug. It was not her place to force her opinions or views on anyone. But she wished harmony upon the twins. She could only hope in time they would repair the rift between them, preferably sooner than later.

His troubled gaze shifted to the drawing room, where the other guests were waiting. "Now isn't the right time anyway. I need to stay and help you socialize. When Yancey and Carline are together, they can be overwhelming, especially to people who are shy, like you are. Geddes will find something to distract himself from their loquacious exuberance."

Unsure of how to respond, Zoe stood there and waited. Clearly, he had to talk himself into a decision.

He released her hands, then gripped both lapels of his black suit coat. "The problem with discussing this with Isaak right now is that, when he's cooking, he doesn't want anyone talking to him." His shoulders slumped as he let out a long, loud exhale. "Seems to me the 'right time' would be when it's a good time for both people."

Zoe lifted her shoulder in another noncommittal shrug.

He groaned. "That's easy for you to say. You don't know Isaak like I do. Nothing I say will make a difference," he argued aloud, as if trying to convince himself. "Once Isaak believes he's right, he doesn't change his mind."

He fell silent.

After a long moment, and several paces around the foyer, he remarked, "If my parents were here, they would say, 'A kind word chases away wrath.'"

"It does."

He shook his head helplessly. "I really don't have a choice."

Zoe sighed.

"I need to go talk to Isaak anyway," he continued. "He ought to be warned that you're a highly trained chef—"

"Household cook," she corrected.

"—since he's so proud of his cooking," he finished with more conviction than anything else he'd said since their arrival at the house. He sighed wearily. "But first I'll apologize to him for keeping him in the dark about my contract with the Archer Matrimonial Company."

For a moment, she was struck dumb. Jakob Gunderson was *such* a good man to admit he had been in the wrong.

He stepped closer to her. "I probably ought to ask you this officially, instead of just depending on the contract you signed." He drew her hand to his chest, resting it palm down over his heart. "Zoe de Fleur, would you do me the honor of allowing me to court you for the next sixty days?"

"Fifty-nine," she corrected. "Ze contract began yesterday."

"Indeed it did."

She smiled. "Indeed you may."

Isaak was stirring potatoes on the cookstove when Jakob strolled into the kitchen and announced, "Zoe is worried that we're fighting."

This morning she was *Miss de Fleur* and now *Zoe*! Typical

of Jakob to remove respectful status boundaries after so short an acquaintance.

Isaak kept stirring, letting the rest of what his brother said sink in. "What did you say that made her think we were?"

Jakob leaned his hip against a cupboard. "She just sensed it. She wanted me to come in here and apologize to you for not saying anything about her before she arrived. I'm sorry I didn't."

Isaak stopped stirring. Clearly, the woman had figured out that, despite their current disagreement, both brothers would need to be persuaded into this crazy matrimonial plan.

Not going to happen.

Jakob crossed one ankle over the other. "I don't want to argue again. It seems it's all we've done for the past few days. I'm sorry I didn't tell you sooner about my contract with Mrs. Archer, but I'm not going to have you treat Zoe with disrespect because you don't agree with how she ended up in Helena."

Isaak didn't care about her being in Helena; it was her being in Jakob's life that was the problem. "Whatever possessed you to bring a woman all this way, one about whom you didn't even know the barest of facts?"

Jakob held Isaak's gaze for a moment before shrugging. "I guess that's a fair question. We were supposed to correspond by letter first. That's how it usually works. Mrs. Archer has never had a prospective bride show up uninvited, but after the interview, she realized Zoe was eminently suitable. Even you have to agree she is. She's smart. She's cultured. She's also tenderhearted and shyer than any girl we've ever met."

The change in Jakob's tone of voice on the last sentence said he expected Isaak to keep from questioning her too closely given her gentle disposition.

Ha! Her disposition was more coy than shy.

Isaak set the wooden spoon on the soapstone counter and

removed the potatoes from the heat. "She may not be who she says she is."

"I have sixty days to figure that out before she's contractually free to walk away from my courtship." Jakob shot a glance toward the kitchen door. "I like her. I like her a lot."

Isaak was afraid of that.

"Please be nice to her."

"Of course I'll be nice." But that didn't mean he wasn't going to ask some pointed questions.

Jakob let out a huff of relief, then looked at the cook-stove. "Need any help?"

Isaak shook his head. "As soon as I finish the potatoes, I'll warm the green beans and make gravy. The lamb chops are already cooked. I just need to cut them up and add them to the gravy."

"You're making gravy?" Jakob made it sound like the worst idea in the world.

"Of course. Mashed potatoes need gravy." And what else was Isaak supposed to do about only having four chops for six people?

Jakob rubbed the back of his neck, shifting awkwardly, as he always did when he knew he needed to 'fess up. "Um, this may not be the best time to tell you, but . . ." His gaze shifted again to the kitchen door.

"Say it." Isaak carried the kettle of potatoes over to the sink to drain.

"Zoe's a chef."

Of course she was! Just like she was French and the perfect wife for a man she'd never met as decided by a woman in Denver who made matches to make money—the more the better, at least for her.

Isaak inhaled through his nose and let out the air in a slow exhale to keep from stating his thoughts. "What do you mean, a 'chef'?"

"I mean exactly that. She's culinary trained. She's cooked

for those rich guys, Vanderbilt and Astor. Her father used to be the secretary of the Society of Culinary Philanthropy in New York City."

Isaak focused his attention on draining the potatoes to give him time to figure out what to say. He was proud of his cooking, something Jakob knew full well, so ignoring the woman's supposed skill wasn't an option. On the other hand, Isaak didn't want to appear to believe the obvious lie. A quick telegram to this society was all it would take to disprove her story—assuming the organization even existed.

"Why didn't you tell me that before I invited her to lunch?"

Jakob's hand appeared, holding the butter plate. "I didn't know myself until yesterday, and we didn't talk this morning about Zoe and me coming back here after church."

"Fair enough." Isaak took the butter and dumped all of it into the pot. He'd made a huge batch of potatoes, hoping people would fill up on them and not notice how little meat they were getting. "Grab the milk out of the icebox and then ask Yancey to come in here."

"You must be desperate if you're asking Yancey for cooking help."

Isaak mashed the potatoes, the extra quantity requiring greater force. He *was* desperate, at least about getting a telegram sent, something Yancey could help him with because her family owned both telegraph offices in town. As for the cooking, she'd improved once her mother forced her to stay in the kitchen and learn for an entire summer.

He added a large amount of salt to the pot. "There's nothing difficult about making gravy."

Jakob set the milk bottle on the countertop. "If you don't mind lumps." The usual note of teasing was absent from his voice. Was he worried that a hearty meal would scare off a woman claiming to be a chef?

Ridiculous. Miss de Fleur would probably eat sparingly in front of everyone for appearance's sake, but then she'd ask to take the leftovers back to the boardinghouse, where she'd shovel them down fast enough. Or share them with the relative who had yet to make an appearance.

Isaak added the milk and finished mashing. He tasted the potatoes. A little too much salt. He'd add less to the gravy, and once it and the potatoes were stirred together, the flavor would even out.

Jakob hadn't left the kitchen yet. "How are they?"

"They're fine." Isaak kept hold of the spoon to keep his brother from taking a bite. "Send Yancey in."

"Right." Jakob pivoted and sauntered out the door.

Isaak crossed to the stove to start the green beans. Doubt nipped at the edges of his confidence. A trained chef?

From her spot on the velvet-covered settee, Zoe glanced around the parlor that Mrs. Pawlikowski had decorated with damask wallpaper from baseboards right up to the cream-painted crown molding. One would think the burgundy rug and burgundy silk curtains next to the olive-green wallpaper would make the room seem like one was celebrating Christmas all year long. Instead, it looked exquisite. In her crimson gown, Zoe blended in perfectly.

She breathed in deeply. The house smelled wonderfully of bergamot and lemon oil . . . and of fresh-brewed coffee.

Miss Carline Pope sat at the upright piano, expertly playing a soft tune. Beethoven, Zoe guessed. She loved music, but she never listened to it enough to distinguish composers. *Maman* would know. There was not an instrument *Maman* could not play. Geddes Palmer sat in one of the Queen Anne chairs opposite Zoe reading a book.

Zoe smiled as she studied the pair. Someday she would have friends and family with whom she could sit in a room and not feel obligated to entertain the other.

Alone yet not alone. It sounded wonderful.

"Miss de Fleur?" came a gentle voice.

Miss Pope stopped playing. Mr. Palmer closed his book. Zoe followed their gazes to where Yancey Palmer stood on the drawing room's threshold.

Miss Palmer looked apologetic. "Please believe me when I say we tried our best."

Although confused by the vague statement, Zoe nodded.

"Follow me," ordered Miss Palmer. She turned around, raised her right arm, and waved in a circle. "To the dining room we go."

Mr. Palmer stood. "Ladies first."

Upon reaching the dining room, Miss Palmer led a pointed discussion with the Gunderson brothers over where everyone was to sit. Miss Pope and Mr. Palmer sat, only to be ordered to move by Isaak Gunderson, who claimed head of household status. Finally, Zoe and Jakob sat next to each other on one side of the rectangular table. Mr. Palmer and Miss Pope sat opposite them. Mr. Isaak Gunderson sat at the end of table between Mr. Palmer and Zoe. Miss Palmer sat on the other end between Miss Pope and Jakob, who asked the Lord's blessing on the meal.

"Amen," was said in unison.

Except by Zoe, who had not known she was supposed to join in.

When they had lived in France, she and Papa had taken their meals alone. The hierarchy among servants was strictly adhered to. After they settled in with Mrs. Gilfoyle-Crane, there had been more socializing, and only in English because doing so was, in Mrs. Gilfoyle-Crane's opinion, the best way to help Papa and Zoe become fluent. Meal prayers, if spoken, were always formal.

She liked the ease with which Jakob asked God to bless the food and their fellowship.

"Miss de Fleur?"

She turned left, toward the man who had whispered her name.

Mr. Isaak Gunderson offered her a bowl of coarsely mashed potatoes. He said nothing more as his intense gaze fixed on hers.

While his eyes were green and Jakob's blue, they both had stunning flecks of brown in the center. Why did Mr. Gunderson look at her so disapprovingly? Her skin next to her black hair must look pasty white compared to the soft bronze glow the Misses Palmer and Pope had, a lovely contrast to their blond hair. Zoe's crimson silk dress must seem pretentious next to the modest calico dresses the other ladies wore. She was nothing more than a blackbird amid these five popular—and astoundingly beautiful—canaries.

Zoe swallowed awkwardly, then accepted the bowl of potatoes. She added a scoop to her plate before passing the potatoes on to Jakob. Keeping her gaze lowered, she accepted the different bowls and platters Mr. Gunderson handed her. Soon the room filled with sounds of silverware clinking against china plates.

Miss Pope spoke first. "Jakob, how's work coming along at The Import Company?"

Before Jakob finished answering, Miss Palmer asked him a question. And then Miss Pope did again. Jakob had been right when he said the two ladies were overwhelming. They laughed and carried on as if everyone understood what they found amusing; they barraged him with questions, not once including Zoe in the conversation, although she minded not.

How nice to watch and listen.

She preferred to just watch and listen.

Mr. Palmer spoke to Mr. Gunderson, who nodded as he listened.

His handsome face was more square than rectangular, as Jakob's was. They both had the same strong jaw, the same heavy dark blond brows, the same ash-blond hair—no,

Mr. Gunderson's hair was a shade or two darker. Or perhaps Jakob's hair looked lighter because his skin was tanned from the greater amount of time he spent outdoors than his brother.

"Miss de Fleur," Mr. Gunderson said as he buttered a slice of bread, "tell everyone what you think of Helena so far." His pointed look contrasted with his added, "Please."

Chapter Eight

Zoe looked down at the fork in her hand and her food-filled plate, which she had yet to take a bite from because she had been enchanted with the effortless conversation among everyone else at the table. She raised her gaze to see Miss Pope, Miss Palmer, and Mr. Palmer, who all looked sincerely interested in her response.

She smiled softly, while keeping her gaze away from Mr. Isaak Gunderson. "It is all so much more zan I could have hoped to find. Zis morning I saw a woman in a cart being pulled by a bison."

Miss Pope nodded. "That was Mrs. Nanawity. She owns the icehouse. I can introduce you to her if you like."

Zoe hesitated. She was unsure if she wished to meet this Mrs. Nanawity. Thankfully, she was spared from answering. Miss Palmer leaned forward in her chair, smiling broadly. "What's your favorite thing so far?" Her amused eyes flickered to Jakob in a silent I-know-you-will-say-*him* look.

While Zoe liked Jakob, of all the things she had seen in Helena so far, what made her heart sing the most was—"I like how ze Montana sun awakes with a gentle crawl and yet sets with all ze power of a raging fire but none of ze destruction."

A *humph* slipped from between Mr. Gunderson's lips.

Zoe ignored him. "I watched last night and zis morning from ze balcony outside my room."

"Where are you staying?" Miss Pope asked between bites.

"Deal's Boardinghouse," Jakob answered. He gave Zoe a doting look before speaking to Miss Pope. "I wanted Zoe to stay in the one closest to The Import Company."

"And closest to you." Miss Pope sighed wistfully. "Oh, Jakob, that's so romantic."

Another *humph* came from Mr. Gunderson. Exemplifying the difference between himself and his brother were the smile lines on Jakob's face and the vertical crease Mr. Gunderson wore between his brows. Likely from scowling, as he was doing now.

Mr. Palmer's fork stopped halfway to his mouth. His brow furrowed, eyes narrowing. He looked at Mr. Gunderson. "Isn't Alfred Deal supporting Kendrick in the mayoral election?"

"Isaak is running for mayor," Miss Pope put in before Mr. Gunderson could answer. "We're all so proud of him. If you need a man to lead the masses, to charge into battle, to change a town for the better, Isaak is that guy."

"Hear, hear," Miss Palmer cheered.

Out of the corner of her eye, Zoe saw Jakob slide his left arm under the table, but not before she noticed the fist he had made. She scooped a bite of potatoes and gravy into her mouth . . . and managed to swallow the unsavory food. Meals at the boardinghouse were about as tasty.

"Deal *is* supporting Kendrick," Mr. Gunderson finally answered in that voice of his that was slightly deeper than his brother's, drawing Zoe's attention to him again. "So are Charles Cannon, J. P. Fisk, and most of the brothel owners in town. Including Lestraude." He said the latter with an inflection that must have meant something to everyone else in the dining room.

Zoe drew in a breath to inquire who Lestraude was, but

Mr. Gunderson turned her way, saw she was looking at him, and proceeded to stare. Zoe shifted uncomfortably in her chair. She moistened her bottom lip, but when his hard gaze lowered to her mouth, she pressed her lips closed, holding in her response, holding in her breath. With his jaw clenched, he looked as if he wished to be anywhere but sitting next to her.

Now that he was looking directly at her, she could see he was a more refined version of Jakob.

They are equally handsome. A bizarre flutter began in her heart and spread to her belly. Zoe ate her green beans in response. Never had overcooked, under- and over-seasoned food bothered her insides as this meal was doing.

"Salt," she whispered to Jakob.

He handed her both the salt and pepper shakers.

"Zank you." She peppered the potatoes and salted the beans.

"Right now, Isaak's campaign is unofficial," Miss Yancey Palmer said, because clearly silence was something she found dull. "He plans on making a formal declaration on May 4, during The Import Company's grand opening."

The men continued to eat while Miss Pope and Miss Palmer took turns explaining to Zoe what Mr. Gunderson's reasons were for running against the corrupt, according to them, mayor. Their conversation then turned to disagreements over what could help his campaign.

Paying no heed to their discourse, Zoe forced down the potatoes, lamb gravy, and green beans. The only way to keep from starving to death here in Helena would be to purchase her own home so she could do her own cooking. Or she could find employment until she married. Nico would say either option was too permanent and too soon. She needed first to open a bank account. The gold coins she had hidden away in her trunks needed to be safely secured in a bank.

". . . that's because *every* politician hosts a barbeque,"

Miss Palmer said in a loud voice. She slid her fork onto her empty plate. "We need to do something unexpected— something *different*—to set Isaak apart."

"Good point, Yancey." Mr. Gunderson was silent for a moment, just long enough for Zoe to finish chewing a piece of overcooked lamb, before he said in a cheerful voice, "Let's ask Miss de Fleur for her opinion."

Zoe swung her gaze to him. Why would he draw her into the discussion? She knew nothing of politics.

She settled on, "Zis is none of my business."

"She's right," Jakob said in a crisp voice. "It isn't."

"Surely she has an opinion," Mr. Gunderson prodded.

Jakob looked her way. "You don't have to answer him."

"I know." To his brother, she said, "On American politics, I have no opinion."

Mr. Gunderson's green eyes focused solely on her with unnerving intensity. He was studying her, looking for something. She was about to believe he had given up on his inquiry when he asked, "Do you have an opinion on the food?"

Zoe wet her lips. She could not think, not with him staring at her as if they were the only two souls in the dining room. He kept looking at her in clear expectation of a reply, but she was speechless. And warm. Strangely warm.

"Isaak, stop," Jakob ordered.

"I think we all are interested in her culinary-trained chef's opinion." Mr. Gunderson motioned to Zoe's dinner plate, to the remaining food she had yet to force herself to eat. "Go on, Miss de Fleur. Speak your mind."

Zoe looked about the table; everyone had stopped eating.

In her peripheral vision, she could see Jakob's left hand had balled into a fist again. What was she to say to his brother? She would not lie, but no man wished to hear criticism of his cooking. Of course, Mr. Gunderson could have intentionally sabotaged the meal.

"Why are you doing this?" Jakob asked his brother in

an almost malevolent growl. "You promised you'd be nice to her."

Mr. Gunderson smiled at Jakob. "How am I not being nice?" he said in a genial tone. "If she *is* a real chef, she will have an opinion about this meal." He rested his left arm on the table. "Well, Miss de Fleur? You are a chef, aren't you?"

"Household cook," she said weakly.

His brows rose. "You told Jakob you were a chef."

She looked to Jakob for help.

"A chef, a cook." He glared at his brother. "What does it matter? They're the same thing and you know it."

Mr. Gunderson nodded, as if that made sense to him, and yet he said, "*Are* they, Miss de Fleur?"

Zoe moistened her bottom lip. This meal was supposed to make friends. It felt more like an inquisition. "Zey are similar, but not ze same."

"Explain," he ordered.

The others at the table looked at her with curiosity. Except Jakob. He continued to glare angrily at his brother, who seemed unperturbed. Oh, how she wished she could flee the room and Isaak Gunderson's disconcerting presence.

Zoe lowered her gaze to where she could see nothing but her dinner plate. "Uh, men are chefs. Women can only be household cooks."

"Where did you live in France?" His tone sounded genuine and interested. "Your accent has a strange R-lessness."

She studied his intense gaze. "What do you mean?"

"You drop the R sound in words like people born and raised in New York do, like my godfather does. Instead of saying *pow-er* or *A-mer-i-can*, Uncle Jonas says *powah* and you say *A-meh-i-can*. No R sound. Just like your accent." He leaned closer. "Where did you say you hail from?"

"Isaak, stop!" Jakob tossed his napkin on the table. "Zoe isn't one of those mail-order bride schemers you've read

THE KITCHEN MARRIAGE 99

about in the papers. She doesn't deserve this." He stood and looked to their other guests. "Excuse us. I promised Zoe a tour of Helena."

Isaak stood out of politeness when Miss de Fleur rose and left the table.

Yancey popped up to chase after Jakob and Miss de Fleur. "Don't go. Please." She glared at Isaak, as if to say, *Apologize,* on her way out of the dining room.

But he'd done nothing wrong, and he wasn't sorry about asking a few questions. He pressed his lips together. He wasn't opening his mouth, because if he did, he'd yell that the woman was a fraud and *somebody* needed to ask questions until she admitted it or—more likely—disappeared one day, leaving a note with a fabricated emergency that took her back to Denver.

Carline's gaze flitted between him and the archway, as if she didn't know whether she should follow her best friend or remain where she was. She was still sitting at the table when Yancey returned with a blunt, "How could you be so rude?"

Isaak sat and placed his napkin in his lap. "Is asking questions considered ill-mannered now? How fortunate I am to have you to point that out to me."

"Don't get snippy with me." Yancey pointed her index finger at him. "You weren't asking questions; you were making accusations."

"I was acting in the best interests of my brother, and you aren't going to make me feel guilty about that." Isaak swirled his remaining potatoes and gravy together. "We know nothing about this woman except what she's told us, and I find even that suspect."

Yancey huffed, sat down, and stabbed her fork into her

green beans. "You're impossible when you get on your high horse."

Carline laid her napkin beside her empty plate. "I don't know, Yancey. Isaak has a bit of a point."

Yancey dropped her fork onto the side of the china plate with a clang.

Carline lifted one shoulder and leaned her head sideways at the same time, the gesture an act of contrition for disagreeing with her best friend.

Yancey looked to her brother. "What do you think, Geddes?"

"None of my business." He reached across the table and took another helping of mashed potatoes. "Carline, would you please pass the gravy?"

Jakob stormed back into the dining room. With a fire in his eyes that Isaak hadn't seen in years, Jakob leaned over Isaak's chair, one hand on the armrest, the other on the table. "How could you be so rude?"

Isaak wiped his lips with his napkin. "We can discuss that at a more appropriate time."

"Like you chose an appropriate time to interrogate Zoe?" Jakob shook his head. "I've never been ashamed to be called your brother until today." He pushed himself upright and stomped out of the dining room. The front door swooshed open and then slammed shut.

Isaak laid his napkin beside his plate. "I apologize for my brother's behavior. Would anyone like dessert?" He looked around the table for a response.

Carline's blue eyes couldn't get any wider.

Geddes was holding his fork aloft and swiveling his head between Isaak and the archway as though watching a tennis match.

Yancey covered her lips with a napkin, but hilarity pinched the corners of her eyes together. "You deserved that. You *know* you did."

Isaak scooted his chair away from the table and stood. If

he didn't leave the room, he was going to whack something, which was both a waste of effort and beneath the dignity of anyone claiming to be a gentleman. "I'll get the cake."

He picked up his and Miss de Fleur's empty dinner plates and carried them into the kitchen. After setting the plates in the sink, he hauled some deep breaths in and out of his lungs.

Yancey came through the door to the dining room carrying empty dinner plates she'd cleared from the table. She laid them in the sink. "I thought you might need help."

She didn't add, *with serving dessert*, to the end of her statement. Nor did she apologize for saying he deserved to be humiliated in front of guests in his own home.

"I'm fine." Isaak moved to the counter and lifted the glass dome covering the remainder of Aunt Lily's chocolate cake. Thank goodness she'd brought it over yesterday afternoon out of concern that "her boys" were running low on sweets. He sliced a hefty piece and laid it on the topmost dessert plate he'd stacked on the countertop near where he was working.

Yancey walked over to him and lifted the top cake plate from the stack, clearing it out of his way. "No, you aren't fine, but I won't say another word."

He gave her a look to convey his skepticism.

Yancey's grin deepened on the left side. "For now." She took another plate from the stack and held it closer to him so he didn't have as far to balance cake on the knife while transferring it. "You know how you're always teasing about marking a day in the calendar when Jakob does something to surprise you? Well, I'm marking today."

Because? he asked with raised eyebrows.

"This past year has changed you. I don't know if it was being put in charge of The Resale Company or your decision to run for mayor, but we've all noticed your benevolent arrogance."

His jaw sagged. "My *what*?"

"You heard me. We've put up with you bossing us around because we know you mean well. However, it was only a matter of time before someone stood up to you."

How was he supposed to respond to that? It was unanswerable. Isaak dropped his gaze to the cake to conceal his dumbfounded silence. He sliced a smaller piece and laid it on the plate she held. "Forks are over there." He pointed with the icing-covered knife.

"Clearly," she sassed.

On any other day, he would have chuckled at the way she'd called him out, but he wasn't in the mood.

She took the plates over to where the forks were piled, added one to each plate, and headed back to the dining room.

Isaak set down the cake knife and let out a breath. Did people really think he was arrogant—*benevolently* arrogant?

If Jakob had heard the phrase, it explained why he'd been so argumentative of late. This whole mail-order bride business was likely another attempt to show he was responsible enough to handle the commitment of a wife and family, the same way he'd insisted he could get The Import Co. built, stocked, and opened by the first of week of May.

Ma had been convinced, but not Pa, or he wouldn't have told Jakob how important it was that The Import Co. open on schedule. Of course, when Pa said "schedule," he meant as soon as was reasonably possible, but no later than whatever date Jakob advertised as the grand opening.

Which was the fourth of May, nine days after Ma and Pa were planning to be home.

Who could be enlisted to make Jakob see reason and end the courtship before Ma and Pa arrived? Mac was away on his honeymoon, and given how Miss de Fleur had turned Jakob's brain to mush in a matter of two days, waiting two weeks for the sheriff to return was out of the question. Hale had already said he didn't consider it his business if Jakob wanted to order up a bride like another parcel to be delivered to The Import Co., and Geddes said pretty much the same thing. Windsor Buchanan? His penchant for saying he had Isaak's back meant Jakob would attribute any criticism Windsor voiced of Miss de Fleur to Isaak. Quinn Valentine, the city marshal, might be of some help. He was dedicated to serving the community, but he was also likely to say he had no jurisdiction to investigate Miss de Fleur without proof of a crime.

Isaak was on his own.

Yancey returned to the kitchen, her expression serious. "Why don't you like Miss de Fleur?"

Isaak cut a third piece of cake and laid it on a plate. "I don't want to talk about it."

"But you will." She leaned her forearms on the kitchen counter. "You always do."

He didn't want to, but there was something uncanny about Yancey and her ability to make people talk. With him, she was direct, but he'd seen her worm information out of others by doing nothing more than sitting next to them and remaining silent.

Like she was doing now.

Waiting for him to talk about something he *did* want to talk about . . . just not with the girl he considered his baby sister.

Who was still staring at him.

Waiting.

And watching.

Isaak sighed in defeat. "You of all people should understand my wariness when it comes to mail-order bride schemes."

"Because of the way I was deceived by Finn Collins?" She pressed her lips into a flat line.

She wasn't to blame. None of them could have known that Finn would team up with Madame Lestraude to lure a woman into prostitution by pretending to court her through letters—even going so far as to use Yancey as a proxy bride in Emilia's place. When Joseph Hendry wrote the newspaper article a year ago, he'd exposed the scheme without naming Yancey, but people had shunned her for weeks afterward anyway. She was still sensitive about it.

"We were all deceived on some level," Isaak acknowledged, and some of the antagonism drained from her face. He held out the chocolate cake. "Peace offering?"

She eyed the plate. "Not with a slice that small."

Laughter shook some of the tightness from his chest. He held the knife at an angle over the cake, moving it to indicate a larger and larger piece. When her scowl turned to a smile, Isaak cut. "I wish you and Jakob would make a match of it."

Yancey reached for two forks, exchanging one of them for the cake plate he held out to her. "I've wished for that, too, but I haven't been able to make myself fall in love with him."

Isaak cut himself a large piece and put it on a plate. "I've never agreed with the idea that people fall in love. It makes it sound like love is something you trip over and land in without any effort. Real love takes time and tending to develop."

"But sometimes even that isn't enough."

He frowned. "What are you talking about?"

"Joseph Hendry. He was a good man and I could almost love him, but he was always going to be second-best. I . . . I was going to break our engagement the night he died." She sniffed. "I decided I'd rather have nothing than settle for . . ."

Someone other than Hale, Isaak silently filled in the rest of her sentence. He took a bite of cake while searching for a way to move the conversation to something less upsetting for her. "What do you require in a husband?"

"Are you asking me for a list?"

He nodded. "Anyone who's contemplating marriage should know what's important to them in a spouse."

"Are you telling me you have a list?" Yancey shook her

head as though clearing it. "Never mind. Of course you have a list. And a timetable, no doubt."

"Which isn't a bad thing." Isaak took another bite of cake. Schedules and lists kept him from wasting time and effort. In business matters, they kept others from spinning in circles when, with a little planning, they could accomplish a great deal.

Yancey tapped her fork on his plate to get his attention. "Then tell me this: Why did you propose to Emilia Collins? You can't tell me you planned that."

"True, it wasn't on my timetable, but it wasn't an impulsive decision."

Her tilted head and raised eyebrows said, *Go on. Tell me all about it.*

Isaak pushed away his plate, no longer starving. "Before I proposed to Emilia, I analyzed the situation. She needed protection which I could have provided. She's a wonderful person, and we could have built a solid marriage and grown to love each other over time."

Yancey cut a piece of cake with the side of her fork. "My parents said the same thing about Joseph, but there was no spark of romance between us."

"Not all women require that. My mother didn't. She wanted a man who would help her raise her child—well, what she thought was one child at the time."

"*Pfft.* A tale a mother tells her sons. I bet she left out all the romantic parts."

Doubtful. His mother wasn't one to shy away from what others might consider uncomfortable topics. Even if she had, it didn't change the facts. "Romance is a fine thing, but it's not the same as real love."

"Says the man who's never even taken a girl out on a surrey ride." Yancey lifted her chin in challenge.

A somewhat valid rebuttal, but—again—it didn't nullify sound logic.

"Romance is like dessert." Isaak pointed to his half-eaten cake as an example. "It's a wonderful addition to the meal, but if that's all you ever have, you'll soon make yourself sick. True love is the meal. It's heartier, more nourishing, and—yes—takes some planning to put together a good one."

Yancey chuckled. "A good point, but maybe not the best example coming from a man who's notorious for loving his sweets."

"Touché." He grinned. "Do you think it unromantic to have expectations and then discover someone who meets them? Because I can't think of anything *more* romantic."

Yancey shook her head. "You and I have different definitions of romance. I remember the exact moment I fell in love with Hale. My feet left the ground. I knew in the deepest place of my heart that he was my future. People have told me I was too young, but it's been ten years, and no other man has ever made me feel that way."

"I want to feel all those things, too. I'm not heartless, despite what some people might think. But all that emotion needs to be balanced with cold, hard facts. For example, what if the man who made your feet leave the ground was Ole Olafson?" Isaak named the town drunk.

Yancey laughed merrily. "You've made your point. I suppose what we disagree on is the balance between emotion and logic."

"I suppose."

She set down her fork. "Then who's to say which one of us is correct?"

Isaak lowered his eyebrows. She was building up to something, and he wasn't sure he was going to like it.

"And"—she looked him straight in the eye—"who's to say you get to decide that balance for anyone else?"

The question felt like another punch. "You mean my questioning of Miss de Fleur, I take it."

She nodded. "Jakob isn't some flibbertigibbet."

A matter of opinion.

Yancey scowled at him as though she could read his mind. "He's not, and Miss de Fleur may turn out to be a perfect match for him."

Not when she was only out for his money.

Yancey picked up her plate and held out a hand to take his. "I know you consider me too young to have any wisdom, but mark my words, Isaak David Gunderson. If you choose to exercise your benevolent arrogance by separating Jakob from a woman he's falling in love with, you'll live to regret it." She walked to the sink and placed their dishes inside it. "I'll leave you to your thoughts. Thank you for dinner."

Isaak nodded to acknowledge her gratitude. She left the kitchen, and he heard her rounding up Geddes and Carline, convincing them to leave their dirty dishes on the table and leave without saying good-bye.

Once the house was quiet, Isaak started cleaning the kitchen. Perhaps it was somewhat arrogant to assume he knew better than his brother, but Isaak was sure of one thing . . .

Zoe de Fleur did not belong with Jakob.

Chapter Nine

Deal's Boardinghouse
Monday morning
De Fleur-Gunderson Courtship Contract, Day 3

How could anyone say Isaak Gunderson was a nice man?

Zoe sipped her lukewarm tea. No matter how many times she replayed yesterday's lunch in her mind, she found no reasonable explanation for his animosity, other than the rancor that was native to his arrogant personality.

You drop the R sound in words like people born and raised in New York do.

How dare he question her accent!

She had gone to bed thinking about how angry she was with him. She woke thinking how angry she still was. The last time she felt this angry at anyone had been—

She grimaced, unable to think of a time. She abhorred being angry at anyone; harmony with others made life sweeter. Isaak Gunderson bore not a sweet bone in his body.

"Something wrong?" Nico asked.

She met his curious gaze. "I am angry."

"Really?" He squinted at her. "I can't tell. You'd make an excellent poker player because you always look so calm and expressionless. My cousin's ears turn red and his neck swells when he's angry. It's kind of creepy."

That did sound creepy.

Especially because he had never before mentioned having a cousin.

"Zoe," he said slowly, "have you ever actually been angry enough to know if you're *really* angry right now?"

Zoe stared at him in disbelief. There was no other explanation for the emotional upheaval she had felt since meeting Isaak Gunderson.

"I know how I am feeling," she insisted. "My stomach aches like a million butterflies struggling to escape a vat of boiling water."

"That makes no sense."

Exactly. Which made it fitting to describe how the man made her feel.

"Well, because you're too *angry* to eat"—Nico's gaze flickered to her breakfast plate—"do you mind?"

Zoe looked down at her still-full plate of hot cakes made from overmixed batter, bland sausages, and fried-to-a-burned-crisp potatoes. None of it was palatable.

And yet Nico's plate had been scraped clean.

She put down her teacup. After giving him her plate, which he cheerfully accepted, she removed the linen napkin from the lap of her amethyst walking suit and laid it where her plate had been.

"What are you going to do today?" he asked before shoveling in a mouthful of potatoes.

"First, I need to open a bank account. Zen I would like to visit Jakob at Ze Import Company before Miss Palmer and Miss Pope take me shopping." She paused to remember what she needed to buy. "I must purchase a bottle of wine for Mr. and Mrs. Forsythe. Zey invited Jakob and me to join zem for supper tomorrow night."

"There's a bank a block south from here."

"Zat would be convenient." And far away from Isaak Gunderson, whom she was going to avoid for as long as possible. No more thinking about him, either. "What was ze name of ze bank?"

Nico cut the sausage with the side of his fork. "I don't remember, but there's brass everywhere and crystal chandeliers, so I bet it's a good one."

Unable to watch him eat the unpalatable food, she glanced around the wood-paneled dining room. Of the two cloth-covered rectangular tables, she and Nico sat at the one closest to the warm hearth. Three genteel-looking men sat at the table nearest the door, which led to the parlor and front foyer, because Mr. Deal had encouraged them to sit there instead of at Zoe's table. They had looked her way before returning to their breakfast and newspapers.

Yesterday, after lunch, while Jakob had taken her on a tour of Helena, she had noticed the number of boardinghouses in town. None had a wraparound porch or a wraparound second-floor balcony like the Deals' lovely, white-painted home. What a blessing Jakob had given her by choosing this boardinghouse over all others. The balcony rocking chair near the railing that separated the men's balcony from the women's was the perfect place to watch the sun ascend in its golden glory, as she had both mornings since her arrival in Helena.

She also appreciated Mr. and Mrs. Deal's upmost propriety in providing separate entrances for male and female boarders to ascend to their rented rooms. Nothing about this boardinghouse was pretentious. No, it was more like a hearty bowl of chicken soup. Comfortable, warm, and stable.

Except for the food.

Which was as unpalatable as what Isaak Gunderson had cooked.

Zoe groaned inwardly.

No more wasting thoughts on him. No more! She looked around for something—anything—to distract her. The glassware looked similar to the crystal goblets Mrs. Pawlikowski owned. In fact, Mrs. Deal's porcelain china, glassware, and white tablecloths were as fine as the ones in the Grand Hotel.

"Look what I found!"

Zoe turned to Nico, who was holding a hair between his fingers. She held back a gag. "Was zat in your food?"

He nodded, then flicked it to the floor. "Not the worst I've ever found in something I was eating. Once there was—"

"You will speak—*and eat*—no more."

The corner of his mouth indented. "Are you sure? It—"

"Hush."

He laughed. "You should have seen the look on your face. I didn't think a person could turn green, but you did. Green skin next to a purple dress . . . not a good look, even on you, although I'm impressed with your show of emotion. Disgust you do well. Anger, I'm still not convinced."

Zoe grumbled, "You would feel ze same if you met him."

"Your new beau?"

"No! Jakob is wonderful. His brother—" Zoe gritted her teeth. "I wish to not speak of him."

Nico's face scrunched on the left side as he studied her. He then tossed his napkin onto the table. "I'm full anyway. I'm sure tomorrow's breakfast will be better. Come on. I'll walk you to the bank before I start my deliveries."

Zoe hesitated. A trip to the bakery around the corner would provide a little sustenance, but she needed more than bread to maintain good health. Tomorrow morning's breakfast plagued her.

"Gee, Zoe, you want to say something about the food, don't you?"

Zoe found herself nodding. Mortified at what she had

unwittingly admitted, she stopped nodding and looked at Nico. "It is none of my business," she said firmly.

"My employer says that sometimes the kindest thing we can do for someone is to be honest."

This was true. But the embarrassment from meal criticism would crush the kindhearted Mrs. Deal.

"We will leave now for ze bank."

"Of course," was what he said. What he did was stack their used dishes one on top of the other and stroll toward the entrance to the kitchen. "Hello," he called out. "Anyone in here?"

Zoe dashed after him. "Nico!" She entered the impeccably clean kitchen in time to see Mrs. Deal and her niece, Janet, exit the larder.

"Can I help you?" Mrs. Deal asked.

"Hi, I'm Zoe's brother, Nico. Yesterday in church, the preacher said that sometimes the kindest thing we can do for someone is to be honest with him." He gave the dirty dishes to Janet. "We found a hair in the food and wanted you to know."

Janet's mouth gaped.

Mrs. Deal's face whitened. "I . . . I . . ." Tears pooled in her eyes and she broke into sobs.

Zoe gave Nico a look warning him to stay silent. Then she wrapped her arm around Mrs. Deal's shaking shoulders. "Madame, I must apologize for"—the words *my brother* refused to pass her lips—"for Nico. He wished no ill will about ze hair. Zis happens to even ze best cooks."

Mrs. Deal looked up. "How do you know?"

"I have been cooking with my papa since I could walk." Zoe paused, searching for the right and gentle *and* truthful words. "When I was young, he loved me enough to point out my error and to chastise me until I remembered to cover my hair. Papa taught all his chefs zat attention to neatness was essential in all cookery."

"You're a chef?" Janet asked before exchanging glances with her aunt.

"I am a household cook," Zoe corrected. "Or I was, before I moved to ze territory."

The moment Nico straightened his shoulders, Zoe realized how much he had grown from the scrawny ten-year-old boy she had met four years ago on a street corner across from Central Park. "My sister doesn't like to brag," he said proudly, "but she's one of the best chefs in the country. Trained in Paris. Worked for the European aristocracy before coming to America. She's cooked for Queen Victoria, the American ambassador to France, and, most recently, Misters Vanderbilt and Astor, and the mayor of New York City."

Zoe nipped at her bottom lip to keep from chastising Nico in front of Mrs. Deal and her niece. Why had he lied? There was no reason! Never had she cooked for Queen Victoria or the ambassador to France, although the rest had at least attended one of Mrs. Gilfoyle-Crane's dinner parties when Papa was alive, as had the American vice president.

Nico's grin grew as Mrs. Deal and Janet exchanged glances. "My sister can make anything taste like manna from heaven. If people in this town knew how good a chef she is, they'd be throwing money at her feet. Once Zoe cooks for you, you'll see she's a gold mine waiting to be tapped."

Mrs. Deal and her niece exchanged looks again. Mrs. Deal's brows rose in a silent question Janet must have understood because she nodded.

Mrs. Deal turned to Zoe, all tears gone. "Would you give us lessons?"

"Of course she will," Nico answered. "She can start immediately."

Zoe swallowed to ease the sudden dryness in her throat.

She had other plans today. She needed to go to the bank, then she wanted to see Jakob before she went shopping with Misses Palmer and Pope. Nico knew this. She thought he was more considerate.

He and Mr. Isaak Gunderson would get along mightily.

Mrs. Deal squeezed Zoe's hand. "I can't believe you cooked for Queen Victoria." The hopefulness in her tone rivaled that in her eyes. "Please say you'll help us. Please. I'm at my wit's end at how to make this boardinghouse profitable."

"We both are," Janet put in.

Zoe gave a half-hearted nod. "I can go to ze bank tomorrow," she said weakly. "I can also wait until zis afternoon to see Jakob."

Janet's sigh was utterly melodic. "What I'd give to marry him."

Zoe ignored Nico's curled lip and Janet's sudden dreaminess. "I am to meet Misses Palmer and Pope at ten-thirty. Zis is not negotiable."

Mrs. Deal looked to the wall clock. "That gives us an hour and fifteen minutes. Is there anything we should do to prepare?"

Zoe eyed the chestnut braid hanging down Janet's back. "To begin with, hair should be neatly combed, bound, and covered. Arms, hands, and fingernails, before beginning any meal preparation, must be scrupulously washed with lye soap." She noted the heavily soiled aprons over their work dresses. "Kitchen aprons should be used in ze kitchen only, daily, and—"

"Excuse me," Mrs. Deal said with a smile. "Would you hold that thought while I go find a journal?"

As Mrs. Deal left the kitchen, Janet headed over to the sink. "I'll wash these dishes real quick and then find us some clean aprons."

Nico nudged Zoe's arm "Hey, um . . . Zoe, thanks for the breakfast," he said, walking backward to the kitchen door. "I'd like to stay, but I need to get on to work. See ya tomorrow."

"Wait!" She dashed to the door, grabbed his arm, and lowered her voice to keep Janet from hearing. "You must stop with ze lies."

"No more, I promise."

She released his arm. "Go to Ze Import Company after work. I wish to introduce you to Jakob."

"I can't wait." He gave her a cheeky grin and then disappeared into the dining room.

"You and your brother act nothing alike," Janet said from where she stood at the sink.

Zoe nodded politely.

It was the nicest response she could give at the moment.

Tuesday, March 20
De Fleur-Gunderson Courtship Contract, Day 11

"I am most displeased."

Isaak didn't have to finish rounding the corner a few blocks from Gibbon's Steak House to know who was speaking. The French accent told him. Besides enjoying a productive campaign discussion over lunch with Hale, Isaak had the good fortune to be in the right spot at the right time to catch her in her lies. He edged closer, using the brick wall of the floral shop to shield himself from Miss de Fleur's view.

". . . meet Jakob zis morning, and I expect you to arrive zis time. I will have lunch for us."

"Sorry, Sis. Got work to do."

Sis? As in *sister*? Isaak's chest tightened with satisfaction. He'd known the woman was keeping some poor relation hidden away, and here was proof.

". . . don't want to meet him." Based on the tenorlike pitch to the voice, Miss de Fleur's brother was a youth. "And you don't want me to meet him either."

"Nico!"

At the sound of footsteps coming closer, Isaak flattened himself against the wall—a ridiculous waste of effort for a man of his size but instinctual. A flash of brown clothing whizzed past. The boy—Nico—ran straight across the intersection. Isaak waited for the sound of footsteps to fade before peeking around the edge of the brick wall to see if Miss de Fleur was still there. A blue ruffle disappearing onto Eighth Street was his only view of her.

He waited for a moment before stepping out of the alley onto the sidewalk and walking to the intersection of Eighth and Warren Street. He turned his head left and right. Which one should he follow?

Going after Miss de Fleur accomplished nothing. She'd already proven herself a worthy adversary by turning Jakob into a complete dunderhead within a few days. Nico, on the other hand . . .

Now that was a possibility. Younger and sporting something of a chip on his shoulder, according to the belligerent tone in his voice, the boy might be enticed into spilling the sordid plot to entrap a rich husband.

Isaak rubbed his jaw. His other option, according to Yancey, was to turn around and forget all about it.

He turned left, lengthening his stride as he headed south along Warren Street until he spied the same brown fabric he'd seen flash by the alleyway opening on a dark-haired youth who, with an almost imperceptible swipe of his right hand, stole a fresh roll from the bread basket outside of O'Callahan's Bakery.

Quite the brother Miss de Fleur had.

Isaak continued to follow the boy down Warren Street for

ten minutes and into the red-light district. Nico walked straight into Madame Lestraude's *Maison de Joie*, a pseudo-hotel whose only residents were young women with names like . . .

Isaak's breath caught.

Everything in Madame Lestraude's business wore a fake French name: her hotel, her brothel girls, even her own pseudonym. And now she'd branched out into supplying fake French brides with names like Zoe de Fleur.

In the two years since laws were enacted to make prostitution illegal, brothel owners had begun diversifying their business practices to keep the money flowing. If he were a betting man, he'd lay odds Madame Lestraude and that matchmaker in Denver were in cahoots.

His blood heated. Who else had the madam and matchmaker targeted in Helena?

Whoever else they'd gotten their claws into, he'd figure out later and—when he was mayor—he'd shut Lestraude down so fast, she wouldn't know what hit her. Right now, he had a brother to convince, a business to run, a mayoral race to kick off, and a new storefront to make sure opened by May 4. Jakob said his mail-order contract allotted him sixty days to evaluate whether he and Miss de Fleur were a good match. She'd been in Helena for eleven days. That left forty-nine on the contract—days Isaak would use to unmask her as a fraudulent schemer.

The brothel door opened.

Nico darted down the steps and was on the last one when Madame Lestraude appeared in the doorway and yelled his name in a tone Isaak recognized: maternal vexation. She pointed at the door. Nico's shoulders slumped and he stomped back up the steps, closed the door, and gave what Isaak presumed was an apology for leaving the door open.

Lestraude straightened the youth's hat. As she spoke

to him, she slid a letter from the sleeve of her brown and burgundy dress.

Nico nodded, took the letter, then raced off in the direction of Main Street.

The madam watched him run away, a matronly smile on her face. She looked across the street in Isaak's direction. Her smile turned cynical when she locked gazes with him. *I knew your soul wasn't as lily-white as you pretend it to be,* she seemed to say, as though his presence in the red-light district meant he frequented its services.

Isaak glared back.

A flicker of unease crossed her painted features before she turned on her heel and reentered her den of wickedness.

Isaak spun around and headed north, back toward The Import Co. No wonder the Denver matchmaker could call Zoe de Fleur eminently suitable. No wonder Jakob, like other intelligent men who'd been taken in, fell for the woman. With Lestraude feeding the matchmaker information about Jakob, all Zoe de Fleur needed to do was play the role of the perfect bride for him.

Targeting Jakob was the only part of the plot Isaak couldn't figure out. True, he and Jakob were well-off, but they were by no means the wealthiest bachelors in Helena. It made more sense to target a Fisk boy, but—for whatever reason—Jakob was the women's chosen victim. Isaak was sure of it.

Now, he needed to convince his brother. Easier said than done.

As he neared The Import Co., raised masculine voices and the lack of pounding tested his resolve to stay out of Jakob's way. After Yancey's warning, Isaak had decided it was more important to let Jakob fail at opening the store than in marrying a fraud, although Isaak wasn't above making deliveries that took him close to The Import Co. to keep abreast of the progress.

He was ambling past, intent on glancing through the recently installed windows, when he heard Jakob shout, "They aren't straight!" followed a moment later by, "I don't care a fig about my brother or his precious schedule."

Isaak detoured to the open front door. Tin *fleur-de-lis* tiles littered the floor. Isaak stared at the mess, his blood heating and his determination to leave Jakob to his own devises crumbling like the plaster scraped from the ceiling along with the tiles. "What's going on here?" he asked, and every eye in the shop turned to him. "I thought these tiles were installed last week."

A few nods, a "Yes, sir," and several gazes dropping to the floor were all overshadowed by Jakob's, "They were crooked, so I tore them down this morning."

Isaak eyed the scattered tin, then his brother. "I hadn't noticed." He swung his gaze to the work-crew foreman. "O'Leary, how far will this set back the schedule?"

"It doesn't matter," Jakob answered. "It has to be done right."

"How far?" Isaak demanded, his focus never leaving the foreman.

Jakob stepped between Isaak and O'Leary, cutting off their line of sight. "Don't answer him. This is my crew and my job."

"Which you clearly aren't handling well."

Jakob's face suffused with red. He jabbed his index finger toward the open door. "Get out."

"No. Someone has to make sure this store opens on time."

"Pa trusted me to open it, not you. *Me*!"

"Not enough!"

Jakob's cheeks filled with blotchy pink. "What did Pa say?"

"It doesn't matte—"

"What did he say?" Each word was clipped and emphasized.

Isaak wasn't about to speak in front of the crew. "I'm sure you men have something you can do on one of the upper floors."

Never had Isaak seen those five men move so fast. They scampered up the stairs like mice chasing after moving cheese.

When he and Jakob were alone, Isaak took a deep breath, then answered. "I overheard him tell Ma he was worried you might lose focus." It was a private conversation, something Isaak shouldn't have heard and certainly shouldn't have repeated.

Jakob swallowed, his neck tendons visible above his shirt collar. "Is that why you're here instead of doing your own work?"

Now was not the time to mention that Miss de Fleur had a wayward brother, although it was tempting, given how Jakob's question was a thinly veiled accusation that Isaak was neglecting The Resale Co. "I had different business that brought me your way. I was intending to pass by, but then I heard . . ."

Words he should have ignored. Maybe he would have, were it not for the way Yancey had poked fun at his lists and schedules nine days ago.

Still, as the older brother and the future mayor of Helena, it was up to him to set an example of—

Benevolent arrogance.

Isaak winced as Yancey's description stabbed his inner ear. "I'll leave. As you said, I have my own work to do." He turned around.

"Yes. You've done enough damage," followed him out the door.

Chapter Ten

"*Poisson* is fish. F-I-S-H," Zoe spelled aloud while covering the shopping list—written in both French and English—on her lap with both hands.

"Fish is *poisson*. P-O-I-S-S-O-N. If we remove an *s* from *poisson*, the word becomes poison. Hm." Mrs. Forsythe turned away from the carriage's right-side window to look at Zoe, who was sitting to her left. "What's the word for poison in French?"

"*Poison*," Zoe answered without pause. "It is spelled P-O-I-S-O-N. *La méchante reine mit du poison sur la pomme qu'elle donna à Blanche-Neige.* Which means?"

Mrs. Forsythe's brow furrowed, her lips moving in silent speech. And then she smiled. "The wicked queen put poison on the apple she gave Snow White."

"Gave *to* Snow White."

"Oh, that's right. The word poison must have originated in French and the English adopted it, much like fiancé, chic, and . . ."

As Mrs. Forsythe shared additional words, Zoe's gaze fell

to the sheet of stationery resting in the lap of her sapphire silk day dress. The sheet contained a list of foods she needed to cook for Mrs. Forsythe's breakfast party. Who would have expected that the first meal Zoe and Jakob had shared with the Forsythes three weeks ago would turn into an every-Tuesday-and-Saturday occurrence? Or that the divine and gracious Mrs. Forsythe would be the one to recognize Zoe's inability to read and write English?

Their agreement to help each other improve fluency in the other's native language had birthed a treasured friend-ship. Like Zoe, Mrs. Forsythe preferred attention on others instead of on herself. To watch and listen. Jakob and Mr. Forsythe always carried the meal conversation. Zoe appreci-ated that the judge never seemed put out with his wife's gentle demeanor or lack of opinions.

The judge would never demand his wife speak her mind.

The judge would never demand his wife explain her thoughts.

Nor would Jakob.

He was a good man. And kind. He knew how to laugh and smile and make a girl feel at ease in taking time to enjoy the beauty of the world around them. Whenever Zoe visited him at The Import Company, he would stop work and talk with her. She had seen him do the same with others. Jakob truly cared about people.

She had felt such happiness when they were together that first week.

But now? She must bore him. What else would explain his absence? In the last seven days, she had spent more than a few minutes in conversation with Jakob only twice: Tues-day supper and Saturday lunch with the Forsythes. During those moments, Jakob had been distracted. After she recom-mended a breakfast feast to welcome home Mrs. Forsythe's friend, Mrs. Pauline Hollenbeck, when she returned from her six-month European tour, Mr. Forsythe had been the one to declare it "unusual" yet "a novel idea." Jakob had heartily agreed.

Yet Zoe wondered if he had even been paying attention to the discussion. Perhaps he was more like his brother than she thought.

You drop the R sound in words like people born and raised in New York do.

Ha! The man's ability to distinguish accents was as poor as his palate.

Zoe shifted on the carriage bench.

"What's wrong, dear?" Mrs. Forsythe said gently. "You suddenly seem troubled."

"A disturbing thought came to mind."

"Ah." She said nothing more as the carriage slowed to turn a corner, and Zoe knew the elegant woman had no intention of pressuring her into offering a confidence. She also knew Mrs. Forsythe was not concerned about the "disturbing thought" being about her. Lily Forsythe never assumed the worst of anyone.

Nor did Zoe.

Except with Isaak Gunderson.

That familiar ache she had experienced of late started again in her chest.

Weary of it, Zoe shifted on the carriage bench so she could face Mrs. Forsythe. "A disturbing thought plagues me. I wish to know how to never zink of zis zing again."

"How often does the thought come to mind?"

"Mornings are ze worst times . . . except for when I try to sleep. Zen I lie awake unable to zink of other zings. I replay zee moment in my mind, and it causes pain"—Zoe touched the spot right over her heart—"here."

A long beat of silence passed before Mrs. Forsythe said, "And you've now started having this disturbing thought during the day?"

Zoe nodded.

"Most likely it is fear, worry, or unresolved conflict." Mrs. Forsythe fell silent as she studied Zoe's face. She spoke in a gentle manner. "My dear child, *love* could just as well be the culprit."

"Love?" Zoe blurted out in revulsion.

Mrs. Forsythe chuckled softly. "I take it Jakob isn't involved."

"Not at all."

"Then I recommend you face whatever's causing you this pain. Confront it head-on. Win the battle."

The carriage rolled to a stop.

A trio of ladies passed by the carriage window. One lady wore a calico day dress like the one Zoe had seen at breakfast on the newest boarder at Deal's Boardinghouse.

"Another French word zat is the same in English is menu. M-E-N-U." She handed the breakfast menu to Mrs. Forsythe. "Zank you for taking me shopping with you. I enjoy zese precious moments together."

"I feel the same."

Zoe nodded. "I will see you Sunday."

Mrs. Forsythe folded the parchment in quarters, then slid it into her reticule, just as the carriage door opened. "The day isn't over yet. Before I return you to the boardinghouse, I need to see if the Minton china is still for sale."

"Ma'am," the hired driver said before taking her hand to assist her out of the carriage. He repeated the action for Zoe. The moment she stepped onto the sidewalk, her gaze caught on the words etched into the front window: THE RESALE COMPANY.

Zoe hesitated, having no inclination to face the cause of her pain.

Mrs. Forsythe wrapped her left arm around Zoe's right one. "This won't take long."

When Mrs. Forsythe walked forward, Zoe had no choice but to comply. Isaak Gunderson may not be at work. Jakob said his brother had many responsibilities, some of them requiring him to leave his employee to run the store.

She hoped now was one of those times.

The moment they strolled into the store, a petite brunette whom Zoe had yet to meet stopped petting the plump tabby cat resting on the service counter. Her curious gaze flickered for a moment on Zoe before she said, "Mrs. Forsythe, it's a joy to see you!"

"I heard you and Mac had returned. How was St. Louis?"

"Wonderful," the brunette said, then cringed. "And rainy. Mac lost three umbrellas. I didn't know he was so forgetful."

"A man on his honeymoon is more likely to be distracted than forgetful," Mrs. Forsythe remarked with a smile. "Emilia, let me introduce Miss Zoe de Fleur of Paris by way of New York City. Zoe, this is Emilia McCall. She's newly married to our county sheriff."

Zoe and Mrs. McCall exchanged pleasantries.

"What brings you to Helena?" asked Mrs. McCall.

Mrs. Forsythe answered for Zoe. "Jakob is courting her."

Mrs. McCall blinked repeatedly. "Jakob, as in Jakob Gunderson?"

Zoe nodded. "I am his bride by mail delivery."

"Not his bride yet," Mrs. Forsythe clarified. "They met through the Archer Matrimonial Company in Denver. Zoe is helping me improve my French. Jonas promised me a trip to Paris for our tenth anniversary this December."

"That's wonderful!" Mrs. McCall focused on Zoe. "I was a mail-order—"

"—walk you to the door."

Zoe tensed at the sound of Mr. Gunderson's deep voice. She looked toward his office, where he stood half-in, half-out. Twenty-two days of avoiding him ruined. Ruined! Unless she ran. To her misfortune, dashing out of the store was impossible with Mrs. Forsythe holding tight.

Mr. Gunderson strolled out of his office, his attention on

the talkative dark-haired woman in a gray-and-yellow-floral day dress. A mustached man holding a top hat and a wrapped package strolled behind them.

"I certainly will," Mr. Gunderson answered the woman.

And then he looked up.

If he was surprised to see Zoe, he was good at playacting, because nothing in his expression resembled the animosity she had last seen on his arrogant and, to her annoyance, handsome face.

Zoe raised her chin. She breathed slowly through her nose and let the air out just as slowly, hoping to calm her rapid heartbeat. If he could be so indifferent to her presence, she could reciprocate. And there was nothing to worry about. Manners dictated he would be kind and gracious because of the other women present, and because this was his place of business.

As the trio neared them, Mrs. McCall stepped to Zoe's side to clear the aisle. "Have a nice day," she said with a smile.

Instead of continuing past, they stopped. Or at least the unfamiliar woman did first; the two men, in good form, followed suit.

Her brown-eyed gaze settled on Zoe. "I don't believe we've met."

Mrs. Forsythe's right hand clenched her left wrist, thereby pinning Zoe's arm and keeping her from shaking anyone's hand. "May I present Miss Zoe de Fleur? Zoe, this is Mr. and Mrs. Kendrick. He is the *current* mayor of Helena."

Zoe dipped her chin in acknowledgment. "It is a pleasure to meet you."

"Oh, you're French!" exclaimed Mrs. Kendrick. "I've yet to meet someone truly from France." She looked at her husband. "Did you hear that accent? She's from France."

"I—"

"Zoe was born in Paris," Mrs. Forsythe interjected, cutting

off Mr. Kendrick's response to his wife. "Her father was a chef for the . . ."

As Mrs. Forsythe shared Papa's culinary accomplishments, Zoe nodded. She should say something. She ought to take part in the conversation, but even without glancing up at the man towering over them all, she knew he was looking at her. She could verily feel Mr. Gunderson's gaze. She shivered; the action caused her shoulders to shift and squirm.

Mrs. Forsythe stopped speaking and gave Zoe a strange look.

"Miss de Fleur," began Mrs. Kendrick, "would you care to join Harold and me for Easter lunch? We would love to hear—"

"She and Jakob are spending the day with us." Mrs. Forsythe's words held a crisp edge. "Jonas will be giving Zoe lessons on how to ride a horse. Our godson is courting her."

Mrs. Kendrick's surprised gaze shifted to Mr. Gunderson, who stood as still and silent as a statue, and then to Zoe, and then back to Mrs. Forsythe. "Oh, you mean *Jakob* is courting her."

"Jonas and I are quite pleased with Jakob's choice, as David and Marilyn will be once they meet Zoe," Mrs. Forsythe said with great feeling. "We couldn't adore her more if she were our own daughter."

An awkward silence stretched.

Zoe's pulse raced.

Mrs. Kendrick kept glancing between Mrs. Forsythe, Zoe, and Mr. Gunderson.

Eyes narrowed, Mr. Kendrick tapped his top hat against his thigh. He said nothing, but Zoe knew he was intently thinking. As his wife was. Why? There was nothing suspicious or odd or interesting about anything said.

Mrs. Forsythe drew Zoe back a step before saying, "We won't keep you."

The Kendricks nodded and continued to the door, Mr. Gunderson walking with them.

Zoe stared at the planked floorboards to keep from giving in to the desire to look Mr. Gunderson's way. Her heart continued to pound. Was he remorseful over his behavior? His bland expression had given nothing away, nor did he seem disapproving of her. Perhaps he realized how judgmental, unfair, and wrong his presumptions about her were.

Mrs. Forsythe released her grip on Zoe. "I can't believe their audacity," she said in a terse, low voice. "You'd think with Isaak running for mayor *against* Kendrick—" She broke off. "Jonas will want to hear about this. He distrusts Kendrick greatly."

A *humph* came from Mrs. McCall. "Mac warned Isaak that Kendrick or one of his supporters would try to bribe him to drop out of the race."

"Is Lestraude still backing Kendrick?"

"Yes."

"That can't please Mac."

"They've agreed not to discuss politics."

"How are things between the three of you?"

"As best as can be under the circumstances."

Zoe looked back and forth between the two women, expecting one of them to offer an explanation of who this Lestraude fellow was. Both stayed silent, which only added to Zoe's confusion. The Kendricks seemed a pleasant couple. Mr. Gunderson seemed at ease with them. How could they be political opponents? There was much about American politics she failed to—nor wished to—understand.

Mrs. McCall suddenly smiled. "What brings you two by?"

"Does Isaak still have that set of Minton tableware?" Mrs. Forsythe asked.

"Which ones are those?"

"White bone china with blue-printed, Chinese-inspired landscapes. Twelve place settings."

Mrs. McCall frowned. "I don't remember ever seeing anything like that." She glanced around the shop, which was strange, considering how her petite height limited her view. She looked to the front door, her eyes narrowing.

Zoe glanced over her shoulder. Mr. Gunderson stood outside under the portico talking to the Kendricks, his broad back to the store's entrance. Mrs. Kendrick's head turned in Zoe's direction. Zoe lifted the corners of her mouth in a polite smile. Mrs. Kendrick nodded, then returned her attention to the two men.

Mrs. McCall sighed, drawing Zoe's attention away from Mr. Gunderson. "Mrs. Forsythe, would you by chance remember when and where you saw those dishes last?"

"Last Friday," she said without pause. "That table that now holds clocks was set with four place settings, serving pieces, crystal goblets, and a silver candelabra. I first noticed the table arrangement the day after your wedding."

"No wonder I don't remember them. Isaak said he and Carline were adding new stock that weekend. Let me check the sales log." Mrs. McCall strolled to the counter, then pulled out a leather-bound book. After flipping through several pages, she said, "There's no record of a sale. Is there anything else you can tell me about the china?"

While the two women talked, Zoe glanced around the shop and up at the loft. Her breath caught. There on the second floor were several filled-to-the-ceiling bookcases.

"Zoe, dear, Emilia and I are going to check the storage room for the china. Would you like to stay here and look around, or come with us?"

Zoe continued to stare up at the loft. "Zere are books up zere."

"Isaak bought Edward Tandy's entire library," Mrs. McCall said. "Doubled our inventory, but I offer no complaint. Most of the books have been shelved."

"Any McGuffey Readers?" asked Mrs. Forsythe.

"We have at least one per level. They're a quarter each."

Mrs. Forsythe touched Zoe's arm. "McGuffey is spelled M-C-G-U-F-F-E-Y. If you're going up there, find us a second-level primer."

Mrs. McCall smiled at Zoe. "Look on the second bookshelf from the left, bottom shelf. Mr. Tandy's library begins on the far right."

"Zank you." After a glance to see Mr. Gunderson still outside with the Kendricks, Zoe hurried to the staircase. She raised the front of her skirts, then dashed upstairs. Two recipe books and Papa's Holy Bible were the only books she owned. While she would love to read anything written in her native tongue, she would settle for a children's primer to help her learn to read English.

The bookshelves ran along the building's west wall and curved onto the north wall, ending next to a closed door. Like the first floor, household goods sat on and below the tables, filling the loft.

Second case, bottom shelf.

Zoe knelt to read the book spines to be sure they were McGuffey Readers. She pulled out a second-level primer. For good measure—and because she could afford it—she added a first level and a third one, too. She stood and rested her reticule atop the pile of books on the nearest table before strolling to the far-right bookshelf. The door next to the bookshelf had intricate hand carving. She eyed the doorknob. It was likely another storage room.

"See something interesting?"

Chapter Eleven

Zoe flinched. She turned her head enough to see Mr. Gunderson leaning against the loft's iron railing, his arms folded across his broad chest. The tight fabric of his suit coat emphasized his muscular build. The man clearly did not spend his workday sitting behind a desk.

The tabby cat weaved around his legs, arched back and purring.

Mr. Gunderson's brows rose—a clear indication he knew she was studying him.

Cheeks warm, she turned back to the bookshelf. "I am looking for a book. Nothing more."

"But you *are* curious about what's behind that door."

"A little," she admitted in truth, "but it is none of my business."

"Have a gander. Door's not locked. I have nothing to hide."

At that, she turned to look at him again.

He was mocking her. She could feel it down to her bones. If Jakob were here, there would be no awkward silences. Jakob always knew what to say to make people feel comfortable. It was one of the traits she appreciated most in him.

Instead, she was stuck in the mire called Isaak Gunderson. As his gaze stayed fixed on hers, it took every bit of confidence—and bravado—she had to lift her chin and smile at him.

His eyes narrowed in a silent yet clear *I know you are hiding something and I will discover what it is.*

"Zank you for ze offer, but no." She breathed deeply, then focused on the bookshelf to distract her mind from his disturbing presence. The first book that caught her eye was *William Shakespeare* by Victor Hugo. She pulled it out. Her heart flipped. It was in French! But it was about Shakespeare. As much as Papa liked Hugo's writings, Zoe's own dislike for the English bard propelled her to put the book back.

If Mr. Tandy had one book in French, surely he had more.

She tipped her head back for a better look at the top shelf. Was that—? She eased onto her tiptoes, stretching her neck. It was! All twelve books of Jean de La Fontaine's classic work *Fables*.

Her heart pounding, Zoe glanced around for something to stand on. No ladder. No stool. She doubted the wooden crate could support her. The only option was the high-backed gold damask chair. Even if the bottom of her boots were clean, she could not stand on a chair. Doing so was gauche.

Leaving without those books was unacceptable.

She had no choice but to ask for help.

From Mr. Gunderson.

She pointed at the top shelf. "I would like to purchase ze books by Jean de La Fontaine. Ze red leather ones." She lowered her arm.

"It'll be ten dollars."

"Per book?"

"For the set."

The price was low. Almost an insult, actually. La Fontaine's works were a reading staple for every French schoolchild.

"I will take zem all."

"That's a lot of money to throw away on something you can't read." He pushed off the railing and strode over to her, looking none too pleased to be helping.

He was tall, as tall as Jakob, who was a foot taller than Zoe. She knew because Jakob had measured her after he refused to believe that she, in her stocking feet instead of her heeled boots, was exactly twelve inches shorter than his six foot, five inches. Mr. Gunderson seemed larger than his brother. No, not larger, because she had seen them side by side. More intimidating. More enveloping.

More the type who, once he decided to marry, would toss the woman he was courting over his shoulder and carry her to the nearest justice of the peace.

Miss Carline Pope would say that was so romantic.

That would *not* be romantic. It was inconsiderate, and something Jakob, thankfully, would never do. He was patient, kind, good, gentle—

Mr. Gunderson's throat cleared.

She looked up at him . . . and found herself struck mute. His eyes were as green as the valley north of town. The lovely flecks of brown in the center softened the green—like the barks of trees adding balance to a forest. Fitting because Mr. Gunderson was as unmoving and dependable as a tree.

Dependable?

"Ready?" he asked.

She nodded, her mind too confused to form words. She *liked* thinking of him as a man who could be relied on. Why? She disliked him as much as he disliked her.

With little effort, he reached the books, then handed them to her one at a time, building a stack that caused her arms to stretch downward. He laid the last one on the top.

Oof slipped from her lungs before she could stop it.

"Heavy?"

"A little, but I am stronger zan I look." The book stack

reached her chin and weighed down her arms. She hesitated and then, with what little courage she had, she looked up at him again. "Why are you like zis to me?"

His gaze darkened. "You know why."

"Tell me."

"I need to protect my brother from a woman who isn't what she claims."

Mr. Gunderson stood there and stared at Zoe as if he could see into her deepest secrets. He believed she was a liar, a schemer, and a fraud. He was a truly handsome man . . . who, sadly, had the bullish manners of a goat.

This man—this arrogant brother of her suitor—would not get the better of her. She would wear him down with kindness and love until he welcomed her into his family.

"You are wrong about me," Zoe said softly.

He grabbed the top book and flipped it open, turning the page to her. "Read. In English."

She looked to where he pointed. "'A lion of great parents born, passing a certain mead one morn, a pretty peasant maiden spied, and asked to have her for his bride.'"

"Continue."

Zoe resumed translating the lines. "'Ze sire with dread ze lion saw, and wished a milder son-in-law. He was embarrassed how to choose, 'twas hard to grant, and dangerous to refuse.' Why must I read zis to you?"

"You're good," he said in a flat voice. "Polished, demure, with just the amount of naïveté for a man to find alluring. It's only logical to believe you're working with someone. I know about the boy."

"Ze boy?"

"Nico."

Zoe tensed. He knew about Nico?

"According to Alfred and Martha Deal, Nico's your

brother," Mr. Gunderson continued. "You and I both know that's a lie."

"I never claimed he was my brother."

"Who is he?"

"Nico is a friend from New York. He traveled west with me." She intended to leave her answer at that, but Mr. Gunderson stood still, gaze suspicious, clearly expecting her to create an elaborate lie. She, though, was not Nico. "He calls me his sister because, like me, he has no other family. We are both orphans."

"Have you told Jakob about him?"

Zoe swallowed nervously. As long as Nico failed to visit The Import Company, she had no opportunity to introduce him to Jakob.

Mr. Gunderson released a wry chuckle. "I can tell from your silence you haven't." He closed the book and added it to the stack. "You can have the collection and every book on these shelves if you will leave Helena. I'll even buy you a ticket back to France."

"Is zis a bribe?"

He flinched. "What?"

"Like what Mayor Kendrick offers his political opponents so he can win."

"Who told you about him?"

"Zat is inconsequential. Zat you wish to bribe me is shameful. How can people speak so highly of your character? It is abominable." Emboldened by his gaping mouth, Zoe shoved the stack of books against him; one slipped and hit the floorboards. She scooped it up. "No man can purchase me," she said and slapped the book on the stack. "I will meet you downstairs to make payment. Unless you are too self-righteous to take my money."

Zoe strolled to the table, grabbed the three McGuffey Readers and her reticule, and descended the stairs with her

head held high. She was proud of not cowering before him.
Mostly because she knew he was watching her walk away.

Her lips curved. Oh, how wonderful it felt to best him!

Isaak followed the woman down the stairs, his arms
weighted down with her pile of books. Unease prickled
along his neck. She was buying English primers like someone who needed to learn a new language, had translated the
first few lines of the French book without pause, and hadn't
blinked at the ten-dollar charge for purchasing the set.

Which didn't make sense.

She should have struggled to understand the foreign
words, hesitated when he named the high price tag, and
stammered some excuse about how she didn't have enough
money with her but would be back later to collect them—
with Jakob, of course, who would plunk down the funds on
her behalf.

Then there was Aunt Lily's staunch patronage. She wasn't
one to be taken in by a pretty face or fine manners. She'd
spent the last several weeks with Miss de Fleur yet continued
to sing her praises.

And just now, the woman had acknowledged that Nico
wasn't her brother. Not with a blush or any other evidence
she was uncomfortable, but a straightforward explanation.

Not the actions of a woman acting a part.

If that weren't enough, Mrs. Deal—whom Isaak had
questioned extensively—had raved for a full twenty minutes
about what a wonderful cook and teacher Miss de Fleur was.
That and the return telegram from the culinary society in
New York City confirmed that the woman told the truth
about her father being a chef.

Evidence on top of evidence that perhaps—*perhaps*—
Miss de Fleur was telling the truth.

Isaak reached the bottom step. He waited to see if she

went to the counter to pay or to Aunt Lily to beg for money.
To his surprise and dismay, Miss de Fleur not only went
straight to the counter, she pulled money from the blue silk
purse that matched her form-fitting bodice. She laid bank
notes against the white-painted counter one by one until
eleven dollars lay side by side.

"Mr. Gunderson, you may keep ze extra quarter as my
gratitude for carrying my books down ze stairs." She gave
him a cheerful smile before returning her attention to
Emilia, who was gathering up the money.

No, not cheerful. Something more impudent, except
without defiance or rudeness.

And there was something familiar about her smile, something that weakened his resolve to see her as nothing but his
enemy.

*How can people speak so highly of your character? It is
abominable.*

She wasn't afraid of him or his inquiries, which only
made sense if she was telling the truth. He wanted to reject
the notion out of hand.

"—listening to me?" Isaak heard his Aunt Lily's voice the
same moment he felt pressure on his forearm.

He looked to his godmother. "I'm sorry. What were you
saying?" Amazing how normal his voice sounded when his
mind was vexed by a puzzle.

"I was wondering if you still had that Minton china. Mrs.
McCall looked in your ledger and saw no record of a sale,
but we couldn't find it in the storage room."

He set the books on the counter. "I have it in the back
with inventory going to The Import Company."

Aunt Lily frowned. "I hope that doesn't mean you've
raised the price."

Isaak brushed his hands together to rid them of dust. "I'm
sure we can work within your budget." There wasn't a more
frugal woman in Helena than Aunt Lily. She entertained

with great class without spending a fortune. Uncle Jonas said it was the reason he could contemplate the expense of running for a senatorial seat once Montana became a full-fledged state.

Isaak snuck a look at Miss de Fleur. Ten dollars was a large sum to spend on books in a foreign language, except if she was telling the truth, then they were written in her native tongue. Was paying ten dollars for a set of twelve books frugal or wasteful?

Miss de Fleur looked his way. Her lips curved again in that oddly familiar manner.

Isaak tugged at his shirt collar and turned his full attention on his godmother. "Would you like to come to the back room and look at the china?"

"I said as much, didn't I?" She looked to the other two women, who nodded their confirmation.

"I'm sorry. I—" He closed his lips over the rest of his apology. Admitting he was distracted by Miss de Fleur's smile was unwise. "I'll take care of Aunt Lily while you two finish up out here." He stepped back to allow his godmother to precede him.

Aunt Lily placed her hand on Isaak's arm as they walked toward the storage room. "I hope you'll still be coming on Saturday to discuss your campaign with Jonas. He's enjoyed planning how to beat that awful Harold Kendrick." She glanced around, as though looking for unseen listeners. "Losing the mayoral race to him—especially when Jonas knew Kendrick was bribing his way past a fair election—knocked more out of your godfather than he'll admit." She gave Isaak a significant look, one he interpreted to mean the information she'd shared was a secret between them.

"I understand."

She nodded. "I'll be forever grateful that Grover agreed to add a fourth territorial judgeship to Montana." Her right cheek indented with a conspiratorial grin. "Just as I've never seen Jonas as devastated by losing that mayoral race, I've never seen him as elated as when he recounted Kendrick's reaction when told the President of the United States was Jonas's personal friend from when they were law clerks together in Buffalo, New York."

It had been a rather stunning revelation to everyone in Helena, except Hale, who could also recount stories of personal interactions with President Cleveland.

"Now, about that china . . ."

For the next five minutes, Isaak assisted his godmother with her purchase. The instant she and Miss de Fleur left the store, he retreated to his office, where the same moment played over and over in his mind.

What was so familiar about that smile?

He sucked in a breath. Miss de Fleur's self-satisfied smile was just like the one Pa gave Ma on the rare occasions when he won an argument but was going to be gracious and not gloat.

Chapter Twelve

The Forsythe House
Friday, late afternoon
De Fleur-Gunderson Courtship Contract, Day 28

"What's your strategy for dealing with Kendrick?"

Isaak lifted the pencil off the journal page where he was jotting notes and looked across the desk between himself and his godfather. "Per Hale's advice, I planned to wait and see if Kendrick did anything underhanded first. If he does—and if I can prove it—I'll send proof to the papers."

"Hale is helping you with your campaign?" Uncle Jonas leaned forward and rested his forearms on the pinewood desk. Behind him was a wall of shelves from floor to ceiling, most of them filled with either law books or biographies of men he admired. "I thought Hale wasn't interested in politics. At least that's what he kept telling me last year, when I was pushing him to run for mayor. Has he changed his mind?"

Isaak shook his head. "No, sir. However, he's as concerned about Kendrick being mayor for another four years as the rest of us are."

"That's good to hear." Uncle Jonas grinned. "We'll make a politician out of the boy yet."

Not if Hale didn't want it—although Isaak wasn't sure that was the case. Hale had offered his help as soon as Isaak declared he intended to run. The way Hale spoke, he'd be happy to *be* the mayor of Helena; he just didn't want the hassle of campaigning. To someone like Uncle Jonas, who thrived on meeting people and persuading them to his point of view, Hale's reluctance to put himself forward was a foreign concept. Uncle Jonas thought it was a weakness he could force out of Hale with enough pressure.

His godfather usually had uncanny insight into people, but he underestimated Hale. Any man who could hold out against Yancey Palmer's incessant pursuit had more resolve in his pinkie finger than most men had in their entire beings.

The scent of baking bread wafted through the upstairs library.

Uncle Jonas inhaled. "Miss de Fleur is helping your aunt prepare for Pauline Hollenbeck's welcome-home breakfast tomorrow."

Isaak's mouth watered at the yeasty smell. Next to sweets, he loved bread best. Based on the aroma alone, he could have saved himself the trouble of telegramming Mrs. Gilfoyle-Crane in New York City to verify Miss de Fleur's employment as a household cook. After overhearing Yancey tell Carline the name of Miss de Fleur's high-society employer, Isaak had wired a telegram the following morning. A return telegram—one using a wasteful amount of words—arrived yesterday confirming Miss de Fleur's employment and heaping praise on her skill as a chef.

One more truth in a growing list of them.

Isaak tapped his pencil against his journal. "I'm afraid I misjudged Miss de Fleur when she first arrived."

"In what way?" Uncle Jonas looked up from the notes he was writing.

"I thought she was one of those women who pretended to

be a mail-order bride to swindle money out of her gullible, would-be groom."

Uncle Jonas pursed his lips and nodded. "An assumption I shared, so I made a few inquiries to verify her story."

"As did I."

"A reasonable precaution. We both know Jakob is the type to leap first and look later." Uncle Jonas set his pen in its holder. A furrow deepened between his brows. "I'll admit I like Miss de Fleur a great deal—and Lily adores her—but even though I'm fairly certain she's telling the truth about herself, I'm not altogether convinced she's the best match for Jakob."

Relieved that his godfather had spoken his misgivings first, Isaak said, "Yancey cautioned me that trying to separate Jakob from the woman he was falling in love with would be unwise."

"Yancey's a smart girl." Uncle Jonas speared Isaak with a meaningful look. "And she's a born politician's wife."

Isaak's jaw sagged. "Are—are you suggesting . . . ?"

"Married men are apt to win more votes."

Isaak searched his godfather's face for some indication he was joking. No twinkle lit his gray eyes. No grin twitched the corners of his lips. "But she's like a sister."

"Only she *isn't* your sister." Uncle Jonas placed his elbows on the desk and intertwined his fingers. "Marriage is about more than romantic feelings. It's about building a life with someone who shares your goals and priorities."

The same thing Isaak had said to Yancey, or close enough to it. But *marry* Yancey?

"Fact of the matter is," Uncle Jonas continued while Isaak was still recovering, "Yancey and Hale are well-suited, although I doubt he'd consider it even if God appeared in a burning bush and ordered him to marry the girl." He shook his head. "Your father was almost as stubborn when it came to marrying your mother."

Isaak set his pencil inside his journal and closed it. "May I ask you a rather personal question?"

"Certainly."

Ever since hearing the story of how Uncle Jonas had proposed to his mother before she eventually chose his stepfather as her husband, Isaak had wondered something. "Did you ever regret my mother's rejection?"

"Of course I did." Uncle Jonas scowled, as if the question was an insult. "Your mother's a fine woman, and life in Montana was lonely at times. The Palmers and your parents did their best to include me, but evenings always ended with me going home alone." He smiled slowly. "When I met Lily, everything changed. She could give me a look and I'd swear I knew what she was thinking."

"Is that how you knew Aunt Lily was the woman you wanted to marry?"

Uncle Jonas leaned back against the brown leather of his wingback chair. "No, but it's a piece of it. My attraction to your mother stemmed from her willingness to enter into spirited debates with me, which was something I thought I wanted in a wife. Had we married, our home would have been full of arguments, some of which undoubtedly would have turned ugly."

Isaak had witnessed his godfather's and his mother's debating skills often enough to believe it. "Most of the time, Pa lets her argue every side of an issue without ever entering into it."

Uncle Jonas grinned. "Lily handles me in much the same way, and she always ends with, 'You're a good man. I'm sure you'll come to the right conclusion.' It's a show of respect. I married her because I fell in love with her. Since then, every decision I make is motivated by my desire to keep impressing Lily, keep her believing in my goodness, and keep that glow of respect for me in her eyes."

A much better defining moment than Yancey wanting to feel as if her feet left the ground.

"I can be a hard man sometimes." Uncle Jonas crossed his arms over his chest. "Being a judge requires it. Lily's softness—which is not to be confused with weakness, mind you—balances me."

Isaak needed softness in his life, too. And someone who'd encourage him to stop and stare at clouds or put activities on his schedule other than work, church, and civic duties. He opened his journal and jotted "softness" and "clouds" in the margin of a page to remind himself to add the attributes to his list of desirable traits in a wife.

Uncle Jonas rubbed his chin. "We've strayed far from the topic of Miss de Fleur and your brother. What makes you question their suitability?"

Isaak took a moment to formulate his reasons. He knew Jakob better than anyone, even their parents. As twins, they'd shared everything from the very beginning. Yes, sometimes they fought, but most of the time they were each other's strongest defenders and best friends. Jakob came up with ideas all the time. Some of them wild and impractical; some quite good. Regardless, he could talk people into trying them. If it was a good idea, Isaak was the one who figured out the various tasks needed to accomplish their objective and which of their friends would be best suited for each. He was also the one to keep everyone on schedule because Jakob always lost interest or got distracted by details, to the detriment of the overall project.

"My brother needs a wife who'll challenge his ideas, as I often do, and then take on the role of organizer. Miss de Fleur values harmony over confrontation." It took accusing her of being a fraud and offering her a bribe before she'd pushed back. Even then, it was with grace and that soft smile Isaak couldn't shake from his memory.

"I agree." Uncle Jonas reached for his pen. "She'd be a far better wife for someone like you."

Isaak inhaled so fast he coughed. "For me?"

"Yes, although Lily is convinced Miss de Fleur and Jakob will be wonderful together. I've only observed them at a few dinners, so I'm reserving judgment as to their suitability for the time being."

Uncle Jonas dropped his gaze to the notes he'd been taking during their meeting. "I have one last thing to say about Kendrick."

Isaak coughed twice more, then focused on his godfather. "Yes, sir?"

"The man is a scoundrel and a cheat. You'll be tempted to sink to his level." He lifted his head to spear Isaak with piercing gray eyes. "Don't. Let me handle Kendrick. I'll expose his shenanigans to the papers while you remain above the fray. Your reputation as an honorable man is what sets you apart and will win you votes."

"Yes, sir."

"Now, about hosting a barbeque to announce your candidacy . . ."

Zoe rested the second pan of golden-brown croissants atop the cookstove to cool. "Come look! Zese are as perfect as ze first batch."

Mrs. Forsythe left the sink and walked over, using her white apron to dry her hands. She stopped next to Zoe and breathed in deep. "Mmm, I love the smell of freshly baked bread."

Zoe stirred the still-warm glaze in the saucepan. "I will add ze glaze while you go meet your friend at ze train depot."

Mrs. Forsythe rested her palm on Zoe's cheek. "You are so, so precious to me." She sighed, then lowered her hand. "Is there anything we may have forgotten for tomorrow?"

As Mrs. Forsythe untied the apron she wore over her calico day dress, Zoe dug into her own apron pocket for the menu they had decided upon for tomorrow's eight o'clock breakfast party. While she had disliked being volunteered by Nico into giving cooking lessons to Mrs. Deal, Zoe had enjoyed helping Mrs. Deal learn to cook better. Partially because Mrs. Deal and Janet, before she returned to Butte, were cheerful and willing learners. Volunteering to cook for Mrs. Forsythe's breakfast party would show the depth of Zoe's appreciation for the Forsythes.

Their love for the Gunderson-Pawlikowski family was as apparent as their love for her. The Forsythes were as close to a set of doting parents as Zoe could dream of having.

Feeling the warm sting of tears, she blinked rapidly and focused on the menu. "For ze first course," she said, "we will serve individual bowls of warm oatmeal with baked apples, topped with fresh cream. All ingredients are stocked in ze larder."

Mrs. Forsythe nodded. "Next one."

"Ze second course is scalloped fish and cucumbers." Zoe looked up from the menu. Both baked round dishes filled with layers of flaked fish, bread crumbs, and butter were also in the larder awaiting reheating. The cucumbers were marinating in vinegar. "All has been prepared. Do you remember seeing parsley in ze larder?"

"There isn't any."

Zoe looked back at the menu. "For ze third course, we will serve both sweetbreads and cauliflower with a cream sauce. All ingredients are in ze larder, but nothing can be prepared until ze morning." She followed Mrs. Forsythe's worried gaze to the counter on which sat a dozen jars of marmalade, olives, and pickles.

Mrs. Forsythe sighed. "I wonder if we should include a few relishes."

"Zere is no reason why we cannot serve zem." Zoe gave

a cursory glance to the menu. "Ze forth course will include fritters and delicate griddle cakes. Coffee zat was first served with ze fish will be refilled."

"Then it sounds like the only thing we need is fresh parsley."

Nodding in agreement, Zoe slid the menu back into her apron pocket.

Mrs. Forsythe chuckled, a sweet, melodic sound Zoe had noticed never failed to bring a smile to her husband's face. "I have been trying to figure out all week what it was I couldn't remember I needed. *Buy Parsley* was it. Jonas keeps telling me to make a list. After nine years of marriage, he ought to know me better."

Zoe held up the saucepan as she drizzled glaze from a spoon over the croissants. "Ze grocer is two blocks away. I will purchase some parsley."

"Oh, don't do that." Mrs. Forsythe removed the black netting covering the back of her ash-blond hair. "Marilyn grows herbs year-round in her greenhouse. Isaak can take you over there while I go to meet Pauline at the depot."

Zoe blinked, hoping she had misheard. She scooped another spoonful of glaze. "Mr. Gunderson?" she said, her heart beating faster at the mere mention of his name.

Mrs. Forsythe's gaze shifted to the pan of croissants.

Zoe looked down to see she had drizzled the last spoonful of glaze on only one croissant, soaking it. She dropped the spoon into the saucepan, then set it back on the cookstove.

Mrs. Forsythe gave Zoe a strange look as she said, "He and Jonas are in the library. Jonas surprised me by returning home early from his trip to Bozeman. He leaves again on Monday, so he sent Isaak a note asking him to reschedule their campaign-planning meeting to today."

Zoe glanced at the kitchen door in panic. *In the library* meant Mr. Gunderson was in the Forsythes' home. What was he doing here? He should be at home resting after a day of work, or be at The Import Company checking up on Jakob or—or—be anywhere but here. Where she was.

Mrs. Forsythe gripped Zoe's elbow. "What's wrong?"

"He dislikes me."

"Isaak?"

She nodded.

"Of course not," Mrs. Forsythe insisted. "Isaak is a nice young man."

"He zinks I am a schemer who wishes to rob his brother. He"—Zoe lowered her voice—"zinks I am a woman ze newspaper warns about."

Mrs. Forsythe's eyes widened. "Does Jakob know this?"

Zoe nodded.

Mrs. Forsythe shook her head in a disapproving manner. "Isaak's problem is he's jealous." She spoke with an impressive amount of assurance that she was right. "Jakob has always been the one girls flocked around and fawned over. Once Jakob marries, Isaak will be alone for the first time in his life."

"He has his mother and stepfather."

"Parents aren't the same as a sibling. I was devastated after my sisters married. They were in their twenties. I didn't marry until I was thirty-four." Mrs. Forsythe twisted her wedding ring. "The most caring thing I can do for Isaak is to intervene."

"Intervene?" Zoe wanted no part in this.

"Yes, dear. The best way to help Isaak is to find him a lady to court. Doing so will keep him out of Jakob's courting of you."

The idea was tempting. But what did Zoe know?

"The problem with this whole plan," Mrs. Forsythe mused, "is if there was a girl for Isaak here in Helena, he would've already found her. The man plans everything months and months in advance."

"Jakob has told me of ze calendar his brother keeps," Zoe

remarked, because she felt increasingly unsure about Mrs. Forsythe's impulsive idea. "His life is full with family, church, work, and running for mayor. Where is ze time for him to pursue a girl?"

Mrs. Forsythe sighed. "I know. I'd hoped he'd fall for Yancey or Carline or even Miss Snowe. Isaak Gunderson is the type of man who'll fall in love once he decides doing so fits in his schedule. There's no joy in that. Love is too wild, too unexpected, too grand an emotion to limit it to a timetable."

Or expect it to occur by Day 28 of a courtship contract.

Unlike during the first weeks of their courtship, work now consumed more of Jakob's time. Whenever Zoe inquired about his plans for the future—marriage, children—his answers had been vague. Sometimes she wished Jakob would be a little more decisive. And focused.

All courtships reached a point of stagnation, did they not?

Her heart felt no pull toward Jakob. Maybe Jakob's lost interest was the confirmation she needed to end the contract.

Zoe managed a small smile. "I wish you well, but zis is none of my—"

Before Zoe could say "business," Mrs. Forsythe grabbed her hand. "Come. You and Isaak need to clear the air."

Chapter Thirteen

"I do not zink—" Zoe bit off her argument as she hurried to keep in step with Mrs. Forsythe's determined pace to the front foyer and up the stairs.

They stopped at the second door on the right.

After a quick knock, Mrs. Forsythe opened the door. She pulled Zoe inside the library, breathed in deep, and smiled as if she had just sniffed the bouquet of roses. "Jonas, have you and our godson finished with your campaign planning?"

Mr. Forsythe, who was standing next to a wall of books, slid the one he held back onto the shelf. "We haven't, but what do you need done?"

Zoe did her best not to look at Mr. Gunderson standing next to the library's window. She had seen his scowl when they entered the room. She felt his gaze upon her. She must look unladylike to him, dressed in her serviceable gray work dress and her hair hidden by a white kerchief. And yet her heart fluttered, truly fluttered. Why? He usually made her sick with nerves.

Mrs. Forsythe squeezed Zoe's hand. "We need parsley."

"Parsley?" Mr. Forsythe echoed.

"Yes, darling. We need parsley from Marilyn's green-house."

"I'll ring over there," Mr. Gunderson said in a genial tone. "Mrs. Wiley is cleaning today. She can bring you some."

"Thank you, dear, but no." Mrs. Forsythe was smiling; Zoe could hear it in her tone. "Zoe needs to go herself to select the amount we need. You will escort her to the house so she isn't molested, as Miss Rigney was on her way home from school last week. It will be dark soon."

"In three hours," he clarified. "The greenhouse is only a couple of blocks away. There's no need for *me* to accompany Miss de Fleur. Marshal Valentine arrested the perpetrator."

"The *accused* perpetrator," Mrs. Forsythe corrected him. "Until the man is proven guilty in a court of law, I am *not* putting my daughter's virtue at risk."

"Miss de Fleur isn't your daughter."

"Isaak David Gunderson, do not take that tone with me." Her grip tightened on Zoe's hand. "As far as I'm concerned, she is."

Silence descended.

Zoe twisted the bottom edge of her apron. Whatever looks they were giving each other, she had no desire to see. Her life was more pleasant without Isaak Gunderson in it.

It was Judge Forsythe who finally spoke. "Isaak, do what Lily asks. We can continue this discussion tomorrow, after you've finished with work." He paused. "And *if* we're fortunate, there will be remainders from my wife's breakfast feast for us to enjoy."

"Oh, Jonas, I've repeatedly said you are welcome at the party."

"Yes, dear, I know."

Silence descended again.

Zoe tipped up her chin enough for her to see both men still stood where they had been when she entered the library.

Mr. Gunderson made no response to the judge's order.

Zoe said nothing either, but she suspected Mr. Gunderson, for the first time ever, appreciated her silence.

"Now that we've got that settled . . ." Mrs. Forsythe released Zoe's hand. "You'll love Marilyn's greenhouse. She designed it herself." To her husband, she said, "I'm leaving to meet Pauline at the depot."

"I'll go with you."

"There's no need."

"I know." He strolled toward his wife, the corner of his mouth indenting. "But a man would be a fool not to indulge in a private carriage ride with a beautiful woman. Heed my words, Isaak." He wrapped his wife's arm around his and escorted her out of the library, but not before Zoe noticed Mrs. Forsythe's blush.

Mr. Gunderson cleared his throat. "I have a Widows and Orphans Committee meeting to go to. Let's make this quick."

Zoe nipped on her bottom lip. This was her fault. She should never have confessed what she had about Mr. Gunderson's dislike to Mrs. Forsythe, or complied with her insistence about going to the greenhouse for the parsley.

"Well?" he prodded in that I-dislike-you-more-than-the-plague voice of his.

Zoe opened her mouth to apologize for putting him in this awkward situation. She wished to be kind to him, but—oh, how he unnerved her! So she pursed her lips tight. She should draw comfort in knowing Mr. Gunderson was no more pleased to be accompanying her than she was at this moment.

And yet tears pooled in her eyes.

Without waiting for Mr. Gunderson, Zoe hurried out of the library, removed her apron as she descended the stairs, hung the apron on the hall tree, and then ran out the front door and across the lawn. She reached the first intersection—and rid herself of tears—before he caught up to her.

He slapped his black hat atop his head. "I can't protect you if you run off."

"You should return to work," she said, suddenly warm at

how close he was standing. His arm could easily wrap around her waist and draw her against him, holding her close, never letting her go. Mortified at the thought, she blurted out, "I need no assistance."

"Your self-reliance is admirable."

As much as she wished to be immune to his biting honesty, his words stung.

"I prefer you leave me alone," she whispered.

Mr. Gunderson did not respond.

They stood there silent, waiting for a surrey to roll past.

Zoe looked anywhere but at him, hoping for a sudden outbreak of hives. Or a megrim. Or a plausible head cold. As fate would have it, nothing happened. She felt as healthy as ever.

The street cleared, and Zoe released a grateful breath.

Mr. Gunderson held on to her elbow and escorted her across the street without first asking if she needed assistance. He dropped his hold. They continued down the street.

She said nothing.

He said nothing, that perpetual scowl on his face.

Or perhaps perpetual was too harsh a word.

He looked happy to see some people. Just never her. Or his brother. She had yet to see him pleased with Jakob. That could be from concern and worry over Jakob's handling of the building of the store.

There—two houses away—was his three-story home. She again did not wait for him. She hurried up the street, turned onto the house's side path, and entered the white-picket gate leading to the back property.

She gasped at the heartbreaking sight of the neglected garden.

Jakob said his mother's beloved garden and greenhouse were the first two places everyone looked when wanting to find her. April was past the ideal time to cultivate the garden for spring planting. Why had this not been done?

Mrs. Pawlikowski would wish to come home and see her garden loved and cared for.

Not this!

Ashamed of the brothers' disregard, Zoe moved past the pitiful garden bed to the grand wood-and-glass building. She opened both double doors and stepped inside, just over the threshold, expecting to find the same neglect.

"Oh," she breathed in awe.

Both paths on either side of the center table had been swept yet held an occasional dropping from the little brown birds resting in the feeders hanging over them. None of the raised beds contained weeds. Dozens of sprouts and tomato plants grew from clay pots. The greenhouse smelled heavenly of lavender, rosemary, and roses from the three times as many aroma plants than budding ones, all looking lovingly tended to. Against the farthest wall a trio of citrus trees bore abundant fruit.

What she loved most were the birds.

"Zey are happy to live in zis heaven," she said as she sensed Mr. Gunderson quietly drawing up behind her.

"Are you talking to me?"

"Of course. Who else would I be talking to?" When he failed to answer, she asked, "What kind of birds are ze?"

"Finches." Then he was silent again for a long moment. "How can you tell they're happy?"

"Close your eyes and listen to zem sing," she said, and she did exactly that. "Zey sing with wondrous joy and with hope and loveliness." Curious to see if he had done what she asked, she looked over her shoulder. He stood there, right behind her, his eyes closed. Like his brother, he had thick lashes, darker and—

His eyes opened, and he looked sheepish at having been caught listening to the birds. "They . . . uh." He cleared his throat. "They chirp because that's what birds do."

"Oh, Mr. Gunderson, you are most—"

His hand rested in the middle of Zoe's lower back, sending a tingle up her spine, and it took all her fortitude not to move and give him any cause to believe his touch affected her so. Yet her heart beat so loudly she swore he had to hear it.

"Don't just stand there," he grumbled, along with a nudge, yet his hand stayed on her back, as if the action was natural to him.

Something tightened within her.

Zoe jolted into motion. She strolled down the right aisle to put needed space between them, peering at the various plants as she walked. He should not affect her so. He was the brother of the man courting her. He was the brother of the man who never made her feel uncomfortable in his presence.

She found the raised bed filled with fragrant herbs. Smiling, she ran the tips of her fingers along the tops, some recently trimmed. "Someone has been enjoying zese."

Mr. Gunderson drew up next to her, again closer than necessary. "Our housekeeper has access to the greenhouse," he said with none of the earlier gruffness. He offered a wicker basket.

Zoe took it. "Zank you."

"Fill it with as much as you want for . . ." His words trailed off as he stared at her.

As she stared at him.

It was the oddest, warmest, strangely familiar thing, standing there looking up at him and waiting for him to speak. Missing Jakob had caused her to feel this way. That was all the tingle was. That explained it.

Twins, yes. But not identical.

One could not be substituted for the other.

She lowered her gaze to Mr. Gunderson's tweed waistcoat, to the top button, the one that was directly eye level with her. "I apologize," she said in sincere penitence, "for keeping you from your meeting and for not being appreciative of your escort." She winced. "It has been two days since I have seen Jakob. I wish for his presence. And you are not him."

"I know."

It was not his words but his tone that drew her attention.

Zoe looked up at him, confused by the sadness she heard in his voice. Nothing about his vacant expression testified to him being sad. Or lonely. Or wishful for something more.

Yet his response had sounded . . . woeful.

Perhaps Mrs. Forsythe had been correct in her belief that he was jealous of Jakob. It was possible. People loved being around Jakob. Zoe had yet to see a crowd cocooning Mr. Gunderson like those that would seek out Jakob. Did Mr. Gunderson wish he had his brother's celebrity? What Zoe knew for certain was that Isaak Gunderson was unhappy. How she knew, she could not fathom. Nor could she fathom why that realization about him made her chest tighten or want to comfort him.

"I am sorry zat you feel a—" Zoe bit back her words before she embarrassed him by admitting she knew he felt alone. She gave him a weak smile. "I am sorry zat you were *forced* to escort me here. You should not have to be with me, should you not wish it."

He nodded in acceptance of her apology. Yet she knew *he knew* that was not what she had originally intended to say.

His gaze shifted to the herbs. "We couldn't have you molested."

Zoe studied his profile, unsure if he was jesting.

Mr. Gunderson stood there, saying nothing.

She glanced around the raised bed, searching for sheers to trim the herbs.

A pair appeared before her, held by Mr. Gunderson.

"Zank you." She took them from him, careful not to touch his hand. As deftly as she could, she trimmed the needed amount of parsley and added it to the basket Mr. Gunderson held with one hand while he checked his pocket watch with the other.

"That's all?" he asked, sliding the timepiece back into his waistcoat pocket.

"It is enough."

His troubled gaze shifted to the handful of stalks in the basket.

"Is something amiss?" she asked.

"You have a wealth of fresh herbs at your fingertips, and yet *enough* is all you choose to take. I don't know what to make of you."

Zoe stayed silent, unsure what to make of him. She wished to believe his words were a compliment, but for that to be the cause, his perception of her would have had to change. Isaak Gunderson, she had been told, rarely changed his mind because rarely was his opinion wrong. He was, though. Wrong about her.

She was not the schemer, liar, and fraud he believed she was.

That little pain above her heart returned.

She looked down at the herb garden.

One day, she would learn how to be unaffected by his words and touch. One day, she would have no care what he felt about her. One day, he would look her way and she would not sense his presence, because she had learned to be indifferent to him as she was to . . . to . . . to Yancey's brother, Geddes. Never did Zoe wonder anything about Mr. Geddes Palmer. Never did she hear sadness in his tone or see loneliness in his eyes or care what he thought of her.

Zoe laid the sheers next to the raised bed. "Papa taught me to live with *enough*. I am content with life."

"Are you?" she thought she heard Mr. Gunderson whisper.

Regardless if he had or not, she had to share the words

bubbling from her heart. "My life is good. What more should I want?"

"That, Miss de Fleur, is a question for another day." Perspiration beaded under the brim of his hat, his face glistening. Not surprising considering the temperature in the greenhouse. "We should go. I have a committee meeting."

"You are a kind and generous man for serving on ze Widows and Orphans Committee," she said as she followed him to the double doors. "Is it always zis warm in here?"

"It is."

"Your mother must enjoy zis in ze winter."

"She does. So do her chickens. I'll escort you to the boardinghouse."

"Zere is no need. I am staying ze night in ze Forsythes' guest room."

He stopped at the entrance, his scowl returning. "Why?"

"Mrs. Forsythe said it was unsafe for me to travel alone at five in ze morning. I must begin cooking before dawn."

"Jakob didn't offer to escort you?"

"I did not wish to impose," she explained. "He has been working late. He needs his slumber."

"He needs—" His words broke off. "Last chance, Miss de Fleur. Is there anything else you need for tomorrow's breakfast feast?"

She looked over her shoulder. Among the citrus trees at the southern end of the greenhouse stood a lemon tree. In gratitude for the Forsythes inviting her to stay in their home tonight—to convey the depth of love she bore for the couple who were as doting on her as Papa had been—she could make lemon *pots de crème* for them to enjoy after she returned to the boardinghouse.

She could make them *if* she had some fresh fruit. Because he was offering . . .

She touched Mr. Gunderson's arm. "May I have four lemons?"

His brows rose. "What are you going to cook?"

"Something wonderful."

"A dessert?"

Zoe nodded. "*Pots de crème*. It is a French custard zat can be flavored with coffee or a favorite liqueur, but I prefer lemon topped with fresh whipped cream best. I will make enough for you to enjoy, too, if you like."

After a quick "I would," he strode back into the greenhouse.

Zoe felt her lips curve into a smile. For all Isaak Gunderson's gruffness, he could be helpful and endearing when he wished to be.

Or he merely had a weakness for sweets.

Chapter Fourteen

Monday afternoon, April 9
De Fleur-Gunderson Courtship Contract, Day 31

"Which one *I* like doesn't matter," Jakob responded in a tone sharper than Zoe had ever heard him use before. "I want *your* opinion." He tapped wallpaper samples against The Import Company's eastern wall. "Which one of these do *you* like best?"

Zoe glanced back and forth between the samples Jakob held . . . and did her best to ignore the workmen standing on the stairs overhearing her and Jakob's conversation. "Zey are both lovely." She tried a new tactic to avoid answering because asking which wallpaper Jakob liked had failed to distract him from badgering her for an opinion. "But I zink you should ask your brother which he prefers."

"I don't care what Isaak prefers. I care what you prefer." There it was again—that why-won't-you-comply-to-what-I-ask edge to his voice. Jakob's blue eyes focused on her in expectation of a response. No, in expectation of a decision. A decision *he* should make.

Zoe clasped her gloved hands together and maintained a polite expression to cover her growing annoyance with him.

His desire for her to choose from the wallpaper samples—
like with the ceiling tiles and paint—in no way obligated her
to give it, especially when his brother should be helping him
decide. That Jakob continued to ask her opinion vexed her.
Literally and figuratively speaking, this was the Gunderson
brothers' business, not hers. Save for wallpaper, the store
was ready to be stocked with cabinets and merchandise. If
Jakob wished not to make decorating decisions, he should
have left the choices to his brother.

Isaak Gunderson could be counted on to make an immediate decision. The man had proven to her how quick he was
to rush to judgment about her being a schemer, a liar, and a
fraud. Oh, but he had also been so kind and gracious in
giving her lemons from his mother's greenhouse. Perhaps he
now realized how he had misjudged her.

But if that were so, why had he avoided her yesterday at
church? Why not sit next to her and Jakob? Why not join
them for lunch with the Forsythes? She had prepared extra
lemon *pots de crème* for Mr. Gunderson to enjoy. She wished
to know what he thought of her cooking. She wished
to know why he felt so alone. He had a family who loved him.
He had friends.

In truth, she had no knowledge of his friendships. Having
no confidantes could be why he felt alone.

"Zoe?" Jakob's voice drew her from her musings.

She looked his way. "Yes?"

"I don't know why you're making this difficult. Just tell
me which sample you like best."

Was this what Jakob would be like if she married him? In-
sistent that she make the decisions he was too unsure to make
on his own? Critical of her when she refused to comply with
his wishes? Too focused on his own life to be aware of her
obligations?

True, he had been appreciative earlier, when she arrived
unexpectedly with lunch. True, he had cleaned up the remains.

True, he had seemed sincerely apologetic about not being able to accompany her this afternoon to Mrs. Hollenbeck's home for tea.

What time was it? She looked to the grandfather clock Jakob had moved over from The Resale Company after she recommended bringing in a clock to help him better keep track of time while he worked.

"I need to leave," she said, "or I will be late."

"Mrs. Hollenbeck won't mind." Jakob waved the wall-paper samples. "Which one?"

"Ask your brother!" Zoe flinched at her harsh tone. No matter how vexed she was with him, she should not have been short. The poor man was upset about work, about dead-lines, about his parents returning in a few weeks.

Shamed at her outburst, she began an apology. "Jakob, I should not have—"

Something between a snort and a chuckle came from one of the workmen.

Jakob's eyes narrowed into a targeted glare, first at the workmen and then at her. "I don't need anyone's help making a decision."

Zoe gave a sad shake of her head. "If zat was possible, you would not have asked for my opinion. It is not a sign of weakness to ask for your brother's assistance. He cares about you."

Hurt flittered across his expression. "Give Mrs. Hollen-beck my apologies, will you?"

Zoe nodded.

He turned his back to her and focused on the samples.

"Which one costs more?" she asked softly.

He raised the cream one with the gold-foil stripes.

"Does cost matter?"

"We're under budget."

"Do either have to be ordered?"

"Charlie Cannon has both in stock, but only enough of

the expensive one to cover two walls. I'd have to order more, which would put us behind schedule again." He paused for a long moment. "If I purchase the more expensive one, Cannon will spread the word that we're sparing no expense on this storefront."

"Zat would not be good."

"You're right, it wouldn't—" He swung around to face her, his eyes widening, the samples slipping out of his hands. "That's *exactly* what we want." He dashed to his notebook sitting atop a stool, grabbed the pencil he had stuck behind an ear, and began to write.

Zoe waited a few moments for him to say more. When he did not, she strolled to the door. After one final look in Jakob's direction, she stepped outside and headed down the sidewalk in the direction of Mrs. Hollenbeck's house. Zoe stopped at the first intersection, waited for a lull in traffic, then crossed the street and turned north.

She still had the train ticket to return to Denver if the courtship floundered. If? It was already floundering. The kindest thing might be to end it now, instead of debating whether she should end it.

She wanted love. She wanted marriage, a home, and a family. She had hoped she would find that with Jakob, but with each passing day she felt less sure she wanted a future with him. She liked Jakob. She did.

But nothing in her heart spoke of love.

What was the proper etiquette in America for ending a contracted courtship? Should she be the one to speak first?

Zoe stopped at the next intersection. Closing her eyes, she allowed the afternoon sun to warm her face.

Tomorrow night, if Jakob failed to join her for dinner with Lily Forsythe, she would seek Mrs. Forsythe's wisdom about ending the courtship. If only Mr. Forsythe were here, Zoe would ask him, too. Both a maternal and a paternal perspective would be helpful. Of course, if she ended the contract, then what? While she had the train ticket back to Denver, she was under no obligation to return to the Archer Matrimonial Company and consider other suitors. She could create a life for herself here in Helena. Staying would be awkward at first, but she had the Forsythes, who had taken her under their wing. In time, she and Jakob could become friends, like he was with Yancey and Carline.

But Isaak Gunderson lived in Helena. If she stayed, avoiding him forever would be impossible.

Why did he dislike her so? She was likable.

While she would miss the Forsythes, returning to Denver was the wiser course of action. Because of Isaak Gunderson.

"Miss de Fleur?"

Zoe tensed. The sound of her name spoken by the very man she was thinking about increased the swish of her pulse. Unable to think of a logical reason to pretend she had not heard Mr. Gunderson speak her name—or to explain the breathless unease she felt in his presence—she reluctantly opened her eyes. He stood next to her, holding a crate of vegetables and looking none too pleased to see her.

In a voice that sounded as nonplussed as she intended, she said, "Good afternoon, Mr. Gunderson."

He dipped his head in acknowledgment. "Afternoon."

A wagon rolled past . . . and then two buggies and a youth pushing a wheelbarrow while they stood side by side in cumbrous silence, waiting to cross.

"Good day." She lifted the front of her red plaid dress and stepped into the street. To her surprise, he followed. Zoe stopped on the sidewalk and, in her annoyance that he viewed her as an obligation, swiveled to face him. "Zis is considerate of you to walk with me, Mr. Gunderson, but I have no need of an escort."

His face reddened. "I wasn't walking with you, Miss de Fleur. We merely crossed the street at the same time."

"Oh." Zoe moistened her bottom lip. "Mrs. Hollenbeck invited me for afternoon tea. And Jakob, too, but he cannot leave work."

"She invited you to tea *today*?"

"Yes."

"Now?"

"At four," she told him. "Is zere a problem?"

With a grim slant to his mouth, Mr. Gunderson shook his head, then started forward . . . in the same direction Zoe needed to walk.

She hurried to match his pace. "Did she invite you to tea, too?"

"No." He drew in a breath deep enough to expand the wide chest beneath his black coat and matching waistcoat. "She has a dried ham to add to the food the Widows and Orphans Committee is providing to the Sundin family."

"I zink it is admirable, ze way you and your brother have worked together to provide for Timmy and his mother."

"Jakob often finds people in distress. I then take it to the committee to determine the next step. A problem at The Resale Company prevented me from delivering the food sooner." And then he said no more . . . which was Mr. Gunderson's not-so-subtle way of warning Zoe not to engage in conversation with him.

And so she stayed silent as they walked to the next intersection, passing numerous grand homes along the road. They walked another block in silence.

Zoe released a weary breath.

"What was that sigh about?" he asked.

She should have no care what he thought about her, but she had to ask. She had to know why he thought she was unlikable. "Why do you care so little for me?"

* * *

Isaak stopped walking before he tripped over his feet. "I care."

Disbelief flashed in her beautiful brown eyes. "False compassion—zat is what zis is. Pretense." She said it with such assurance that his mouth gaped for a long moment in dumbfounded silence.

"Pretense? How in the world do you come by that?"

"If you truly cared, you would have been at ze train depot with Jakob to welcome me to Helena. If you truly cared, you would have supported Jakob's courtship." She poked his arm. "If you *truly* cared, you would treat me as if you are happy about ze prospect of my joining your perfect family and of me becoming your brother's bride."

Stunned at both the number of words that had left her mouth and how blatantly wrong she was with each one of them, Isaak offered no reply. He'd been busy the day she arrived and was justifiably suspicious of a mail-order bride. She was right about one thing, though. He *wasn't* happy about her joining his family as Jakob's bride.

"Indeed, Mr. Gunderson, you care nothing for me." Her indignation was at odds with her usual gentle manner. "You need not say ze words for me to know you still wish me to leave Helena and never return."

She was right. Being around her made him uncomfortable, which was better left unsaid at the moment. And because he couldn't justify it with a logical explanation.

Isaak started forward. He didn't want to add making her late for tea with Mrs. Hollenbeck to the list of his offenses.

Miss de Fleur fell into step next to him. "Zere is no reason to deny your feelings."

"I'm not denying anything." Her litany of complaints made sense from her perspective. So did his, but the middle of the street wasn't the place for this discussion. "Watch where you step."

She bumped into him in her quick avoidance of a manure

pile. "You reject my overtures because you still zink I am a fraud."

When they reached the opposite side of the street, she stopped and rested her hands on her hips. "Be honest with me, Mr. Gunderson. Is it because I am French instead of American? Or because I answered an advertisement to be a bride delivered by ze mail?"

It was a natural opening into one of the things about her that plagued him. "Tell me why you left New York."

She looked away, but not before he saw embarrassment—or was it guilt?—in her dark eyes. She drew in a breath. "I was relieved of my position as household cook for a New York society hostess."

"Why?" Miss de Fleur's brief explanation didn't match the glowing telegram he'd received.

"My employer said it was for my own good. She wanted me to open a restaurant."

Isaak conveyed his confusion with a look.

"Papa and I met Mrs. Gilfoyle-Crane four and a half years ago when she came to London for ze wedding of her daughter to ze nobleman who had hired Papa to cater ze reception. Mrs. Gilfoyle-Crane offered Papa double his usual pay if he would move to Manhattan and become her private chef. He agreed. Last year, after he passed away, I was promoted to household cook."

Isaak lifted his brows. "You really can't be called a chef because you're a woman?"

"Yes," she said matter-of-factly. "Zis past Christmas, Mrs. Gilfoyle-Crane had a dream in which I owned a restaurant. She began working tirelessly to help me bring her dream to life, so how could I tell her no?"

"Did you—*do* you—want to own a restaurant?"

"No." She spoke so softly he barely heard her response. She started walking up the Hollenbeck carriageway.

He followed. "You went along with what she wanted for

your life even though it wasn't something you wanted? I can't believe you would have opened a restaurant, spent all that money and time, just to please this woman."

She shrugged. "I did not wish to be ungrateful for her kindness. She paid for Papa and me to come to America. She opened her home to us. She hired a tutor to help us speak English."

The magnitude of her response sank in. Even if she discovered she and Jakob were unsuitable, she would marry him out of gratitude for bringing her to Helena and providing her housing, food, and friends.

Isaak didn't want to believe it. "Why come out West to find a husband?"

"I want a home and a family," she said without pause. "I want a husband who will laugh with me but mostly just sit in lovely, companionable silence. Together. Faithfully together." Her voice grew raspy. "I want until death does us part."

His heart kicked inside his chest. He wanted the same thing.

Isaak tromped up the carriageway to Mrs. Hollenbeck's house. "You could have found that there. In New York. Or anywhere. You didn't need to come to Helena. You didn't have to agree to be a mail-order bride. You didn't have to sign that"—he caught himself in time to substitute a more suitable word for her ears—"*foolish* contract with the matrimonial company."

She walked beside him, silent until they reached Mrs. Hollenbeck's porch steps. "Not foolish. Ze contract is prudent for all."

Isaak clamped his lips over a contradiction.

"When Papa asked if we should move to America, I happily agreed. It was another exciting adventure, but no longer do I have Papa to journey to ze unknown with. I am weary of being alone, Mr. Gunderson. I ache—" She looked away and whispered, "I ache for something more."

He paused on the fourth step. "Does Jakob know this?"

"He knows of my desire to marry."

"But not that you feel alone?"

Her gaze turned to his, and he read the answer in her eyes. She had shared her heart, her deepest desire, with him. Not Jakob.

Isaak's heart pounded. People confided in Jakob. Went to him for solace because he could cheer up a lemon. People came to Isaak for decisions—which travel trunk to buy, what gift to give a bridal couple. They didn't tell him they felt alone or what they ached for. It was a gift. One he didn't deserve after the way he'd treated her.

He turned away from her and continued up the stairs to Mrs. Hollenbeck's house.

Miss de Fleur climbed alongside him. "I am sorry zat I burdened you with my feelings. I should be sharing zis with Jakob."

If she intended to marry him, yes, she should. But saying as much was the exact opposite of what Isaak knew she should do. "That's not why I walked away."

"Zen why did you?"

Because he kept picturing the two of them sitting together in lovely, companionable silence. "I need to get this box to the Sundins before dinner tonight."

"I will take you to ze bank in ze morning and show you what is in my account."

Isaak stopped on the top step and stared at her. How her mind jumped from feelings to finances made no logical sense to him. "Why?"

"So you will believe my reason to marry is not for financial security." Her tone held equal amounts of innocent sincerity and how-is-this-not-obvious-to-you?

"I know that's not your reason." Although he was taking that on faith. He'd not verified her accounts.

She looked hopeful. "You no longer believe I am a

schemer, yes?" Before he could answer, she said, "You seem unhappy with zat realization."

He was . . . because he now thought of her as an honorable woman. Shame heated his chest as he recalled their previous encounters. He'd been rude, accusatory, and distant. Arrogant.

He ducked his head, staring into the vegetables as if they could absolve him. Pa had taught him that a man admits fault while looking the person he's wronged in the eye. So Isaak raised his chin and gazed into her deep brown eyes. "Miss de Fleur, every complaint you have against me is justifiable. I had my reasons. They no longer apply." Except for thinking she and Jakob didn't belong together. "Please allow me to apologize for my treatment of you."

She gasped. "Zis is a new beginning for us. No more dislike. No more distrust. We shall become friends, Mr. Gunderson, you and I." She held out her hand to him in a show of amity, her face glowing with delight.

He glanced at the box he held, preventing him from shaking her hand. "Sorry."

Undaunted, she laid her hand over one of his. "Zis is nice, yes?"

"Yes." And some other emotion he couldn't quite place.

Chapter Fifteen

The next morning

"Ze sky is sunshiny here and yet grimy over ze mountains," Zoe remarked in awe at the gray-and-white clouds in the distance. Without looking away from the window, she sipped the warm coffee Mrs. Deal said had too much cream in it to still count as coffee. "Nico, have you ever seen such a beautiful storm?"

"Stop being so happy," he grumbled in response.

Zoe turned to face him. Instead of looking at her, he aimlessly pushed his food around on his plate. Even the usually friendly male boarders seemed morose. None had smiled in her direction or offered anything more than a polite "Mornin', Miss de Fleur" and "Mornin', Nico."

"I am happy, but . . ."

Nico finally looked up. "But what?"

She wanted to say her spirit was as conflicted as the sky—part joyful, part turbulent. But a boardinghouse dining room was no place for an intimate confession.

Zoe rested her china teacup on its matching saucer. "Mr. Gunderson and I became friends yesterday."

"I thought you already were friends."

"With his brother, Jakob, yes"—she sighed—"but with Mr. Gunderson, no. Until yesterday. Our spirits are now in harmony."

Nico's brows furrowed. "Which one is courting you?"

"Jakob. His brother is Mr. Gunderson. Zat is how people keep zem separated," she explained. "Zey are twins."

"Oh, I get it. You're now bosom friends with your suitor's twin brother." Nico tapped his fork against his plate. "That's not strange at all."

She frowned. "What is zat supposed to mean?"

"Nothing," he insisted. He resumed pushing the food around on his plate. "I'm happy for you."

He was *not* truly happy for her; that was clear. Once he met Jakob, Nico would see what a good man he was.

Or she could end the courtship contract today. She could walk away and not look back, as her mother had. The other option was for her to hope for renewed interest, as Papa had with *Maman*. Zoe nipped at her bottom lip. Could she live with walking away? Probably. She disliked how sad Papa's longing for *Maman* kept him from finding a new love.

Zoe refused to miss out on love. She could live with the regret of not giving Jakob a second chance. She could not live with not honoring her promise to give Jakob sixty days to court her.

For the remainder of the contract, she would give a whole-hearted effort to this courtship. She would be understanding, patient, and supportive. She would show Jakob what a wonderful family he could have with her and Nico, too.

"You must meet him," she announced.

Nico stared at her, his eyes narrowed with suspicion. "Your new friend, the brother?"

"Not him. Jakob. It is past time you two met."

"You're right." Nico looked to the window. "Maybe the meeting should wait until the rain passes, though. I owe you another chance to beat me at chess. I'll spot you two pawns and a knight. I'm sure you'll win this time."

As tired as she was of losing chess matches to Nico, she felt no inclination to accept his offer. Nor had she lived in Helena long enough to judge the rain potential of the clouds. It could be minutes before a droplet fell. It could also be hours. The storm may not be heading to Helena at all.

Nico, for too long, had avoided meeting Jakob.

Zoe looked at the gray sky beyond the window . . . and then back at Nico. "Finish your breakfast," she ordered, and then she stood. "I must go upstairs to claim my umbrella. When I return, I will take you to meet Jakob."

Nico muttered, "Sure."

With a jubilance in her heart, Zoe hurried upstairs to her room. Once Jakob and Nico were friends, she would take him to meet Isaak Gunderson, who would realize what an upstanding citizen Nico was and would offer him employment as the delivery boy for The Resale Company. Mr. Gunderson would then train Nico to manage a business, to speak with honesty, and to make the community a better place by helping deliver food to needy widows and orphans. Jakob could teach Nico how to be charming and adventurous. Maybe one day, Nico could become mayor. Or governor of the entire territory. *If* there was a governor. Constable? Senator? Did territories have senators? Oh, she knew so little of American politics.

What mattered was that Nico's life would change for the better with the Gundersons in it.

As hers had.

Now that she had made things right with Isaak Gunderson, she needed Jakob and Nico to get along so all four of them could move closer to being a happy family. Zoe claimed her umbrella and smiled. For Nico's sake as well as her own, she would make this courtship a success. She had come West to marry the man of her dreams.

And marry him she would.

Eight minutes later . . .
The Import Company

"What do you mean, Jakob is gone?" Zoe said to Jakob's expert carpenter, Mr. Lucian Snowe, who stayed focused on the piece of crown molding he was measuring in the construction area on the building's ground floor. She tapped the tip of her umbrella on the sawdust-covered floor, her wariness growing. "Jakob always begins his workday speaking to ze crew. He should be here."

"Isaak sent a message saying he needed Jakob over at The Resale Company." Mr. Snowe drew a line onto the molding stretched across two sawhorses. He stuck the pencil behind his ear, then met her gaze. "If you hurry on over there, you'll probably catch him."

"How long ago did Jakob leave?"

"Five minutes, tops."

Which was how much of a head start Nico had had on her. She should never have gone upstairs for her umbrella. She also should never have expected Nico to wait for her, not after the many other times he had promised to go with her to meet Jakob yet never had.

"Oh, Miss de Fleur, my wife asked me to invite you and the Gundersons over for a coffee-and-cake social next Monday evening. Would around seven work?"

"Zat would be nice. Zank you." Zoe started to leave and then stopped at the first twinge of suspicion. She looked back at Mr. Snowe. "Did a young man with walnut-colored hair, blue eyes, about my height leave with Jakob?"

Mr. Snowe shook his head.

"Might you have seen who gave Jakob ze message from his brother?"

"Timmy, the lad who cleans up around here."

Zoe glanced around. Another five men worked. No little boy anywhere, but that could mean Jakob finally had convinced the boy to resume attending school. "Mr. Snowe, might you also have seen who gave Timmy ze message?"

"Now, that I don't know."

If she were a betting woman, she would place a wager on Nico. Since arriving in Helena, he had been resistant to Jakob courting her. Refusing to meet Jakob was one thing. Intentionally sabotaging their relationship by tricking Jakob into leaving this morning before she could arrive to talk to him . . . why?

She looked out a front window at the gray, cloudy sky.

Thunder rolled in the distance.

"I suggest you wait here," Mr. Snowe said with fatherly concern. "Storm's coming. The roof will keep you from getting drenched. Trust me; Jakob's bound to come back."

"Zank you, but—"

"You're gonna chase after him," he cut in and then chuckled. "My daughter's been doing that for years with no success, so I wish you all the luck catching Jakob. I'll let my wife know you'll be at the coffee-and-cake social." Mr. Snowe grabbed the hand saw and went to work cutting the molding.

Zoe hurried out of the building and down the boardwalk in the direction of The Resale Company. She crossed the street and headed north. The store came into view. Zoe waited for a lull in the traffic before she crossed the street. Then she strolled past the shop's paint-chipped front door, which was propped open. The moment Zoe stepped inside the shop, Emilia McCall stopped dusting a table of lamps.

"Well, good morning, Miss de Fleur. It's wonderful to see you again."

"And you." Zoe glanced in the direction of Mr. Gunderson's office. "I was told Jakob is here. His brother needed his help."

"That's strange. I haven't see Jakob since yesterday." Mrs. McCall hooked the feather duster onto the white apron she wore over her serviceable gray dress. "Maybe Isaak knows something. I'll walk you back there."

"Zank you, Mrs. McCall."

"As much as I love hearing 'Mrs. McCall,'" she said over her shoulder as she walked, "please call me Emilia. I doubt there's much difference in our ages."

"Zen you must call me Zoe."

"It's such a lovely name." Emilia veered around a stack of leather trunks. "My parents named me Emilia after my mother's second cousin, who was more a sister to her than a distant relative." She stopped near the partially open door to Mr. Gunderson's office, then looked at Zoe, her brows raised in a silent *how did you come by your name*?

"*Maman* liked how Zoe sounded."

Emilia seemed accepting of that answer, which was good, for it was the truth as far as Zoe knew. Once she had asked Papa why she was named Zoe. *Your mother liked how it sounded* had been his exact and only response.

"I hope you don't mind"—Emilia withdrew a notebook from the pocket on the right side of her apron—"but I did a little research on your name after we first met. Several notable women in history have had the name Zoe, including . . . Let me find where I wrote the information." She turned the pages. "Here we go. 'Two empresses in the Byzantine Empire, and St. Zoe, a Roman noblewoman martyred for her faith during Emperor Diocletian's persecution of the Christian church.'" She looked up. "Wouldn't it be nice to think your mother named you after one of those ladies?"

Zoe's throat tightened. She looked away from Emilia, blinking repeatedly to stop the tears from forming. To have named her after someone notable would have meant *Maman* cared. If *Maman* had cared about Zoe—if she had loved her—she would have stayed with Zoe and Papa instead of chasing her heart's desire.

"I lost my mother, too." The tenderness of Emilia's words drew Zoe's attention.

"How did you . . . ?"

"Know?" Emilia smiled gently. As her eyes welled with tears, she cradled her hand around Zoe's. "People whose mothers are alive don't tear up"—she blinked, then fanned her face with her notebook—"like we both have. Grief is sneaky. It hits us when we least expect it."

Zoe blinked away her tears. She liked the stability emanating from Emilia. Yancey and Carline exuded fun, but their golden beauty, spontaneity, and vivaciousness drew too much attention, too much focus. Like pastries, Yancey and Carline were enjoyed best in small doses. Plus, both still had their mothers to talk to. As much as Zoe would like Mrs. Forsythe to be her mother, how could she be a genuine substitute?

Zoe squeezed Emilia's hand. "Zank you for understanding."

Emilia gave Zoe a tentative smile. "We mail-order brides ought to stick together." Without releasing Zoe's hand, Emilia peered into Mr. Gunderson's office. "Well now, isn't this strange?" she murmured. She walked to the storage room, pulling Zoe with her. "Isaak?"

No answer.

Emilia released Zoe. "Stay there for a moment. I bet Mr. Jones arrived and they're outside negotiating a price on the plow." She walked to the double doors at the end of the hall. A brick kept the right door propped open. She stepped outside and, as she released her hold on the door, the door banged against the brick.

Zoe glanced inside the storage room, packed to the ceiling with household goods, yet all was neat, organized, and divided into sections. Two crates, almost reaching Zoe's shoulder in height and width, sat in the far corner with the red-stenciled words THE IMPORT CO. on the sides.

The door reopened.

Emilia stepped back inside. "I'm sorry. I have no idea where Isaak disappeared to. When he returns, I'll let him know you were looking for him."

"For Jakob," Zoe corrected, and ignored the sudden fluttering in her belly. "I am looking for—"

The black candlestick telephone on Mr. Gunderson's desk rang.

Emilia hurried into the office to answer it. "The Resale Company. How can I help you?" Pause. "He stepped out for a moment." Pause. "Jakob's not here either." Pause. Her gaze shifted to Zoe.

Something odd flickered in Emilia's caramel-colored eyes and then it disappeared, replaced with genuine pleasure.

Zoe looked to the door, feeing a sudden inclination to flee.

"What if I send someone else over?" Emilia paused, again listening to whoever was on the other end of the line. "Yes, ma'am, I'll be sure to tell Mac how blessed he is to have married me. You have a good day, too." She rehooked the earpiece, then turned to Zoe. "Would you mind doing me a favor?"

The Pawlikowski house

A month ago, Zoe stood in this very spot at the bottom of the steps, listening to Jakob boast about the locally quarried blue granite that framed his parents' three-story home. While the raised first floor, wraparound porch, and magnificent tower added a whimsical beauty to the house, what appealed to her most were the front steps. Painted red, the twelve steps matched the porch columns, railings, gingerbread trim, and the house numbers on the wooden shingle hanging from the porch awning. Four, perhaps, five people could sit across each stair tread.

A month ago, she had daydreamed about sitting on this porch with Jakob and their children, his brother, and his brother's wife and children for a family photograph. Mr. and Mrs. Pawlikowski would be in the middle, surrounded by their legacy. Love, so much love, would be captured in the photograph. For years, they would repeat this pose on these steps, well into the next century, when Zoe would be in the middle with her husband, surrounded by *their* legacy.

A month ago, she had hope.

Now she was determined to make her daydream a reality.

Smiling, she strolled up the steps to the double front doors and knocked.

The right door opened.

A bony woman with gray-tinged auburn hair cut close to her scalp stood there, curiosity in her blue-green eyes. "Can I help you?"

"Mrs. McCall sent me to provide ze assistance you requested."

The woman's amused gaze fell to Zoe's sapphire silk day dress. "You seem to be a woman of good breeding. I appreciate your willingness, but I need muscle, not beauty."

Zoe hesitated, unsure of how to respond, so she said the only thing that came to mind. "I am Zoe de Fleur."

The woman gasped. "Oh! You're Jakob's girl! Come in, come in." She pulled Zoe inside, tossed her umbrella onto the hall tree, and then shut the door. She leaned close and sniffed. "Jakob was right—lilacs at first bloom. His brother said you smelled like a bridal bouquet. I told Mr. Gunderson he needed to learn to be more romantic if he ever wanted to win a girl's affections, but he insisted he wasn't trying to be romantic, that the description fit."

Warmness spread under Zoe's skin. A bridal bouquet was far more romantic in her opinion than lilacs in bloom. The latter, to be fair, was the exact name of the perfumed glycerin soap she used—Colgate & Co.'s Lilacs in Bloom.

The housekeeper studied Zoe. "Goodness, you're so pretty. I took this job hoping to ingratiate myself so much into Jakob's life that he realized he couldn't live without me. My plan was to marry him this summer, but now that you're here . . ." She sighed. "You're fortunate I'm not fifteen years younger. I'm sure I could lure him away from you."

"I zink you are joking with me, but if you are not"—Zoe smiled and gave the housekeeper's arm a consoling pat— "zen I am sorry I ruined your plan to marry Jakob."

Merriment danced in the housekeeper's eyes. "You're here, so I might as well put you to work. Come along with me."

Zoe removed her bonnet, hung it on the hall tree, and followed the good-humored housekeeper down the hall.

"I'm Mrs. Wiley, by the way," she said over her shoulder. "You may call me Sarah, if you like. I've been working for the twins since mid-February. Twice a week cleaning." She opened the door and allowed Zoe to enter the kitchen first. "Mr. Gunderson gave me a list of what he wanted cleaned and the most efficient schedule to have it all accomplished by the time the Pawlikowskis return home."

As Mrs. Wiley continued on and on about what was on Mr. Gunderson's list, Zoe glanced about the kitchen, which was larger than the front parlor. Burgundy silk curtains lay across the corner table, next to the ironing board. On the back wall, between two tall windows, was a steel sink as wide as a drinking trough. Black soapstone framed the sink, leaving room on either side for dishes to sit. That same soapstone covered a counter in the center of the room.

And Mrs. Pawlikowski had two—two!—cookstoves.

Best of all, the greater size of the kitchen allowed people to enjoy each other's company while preparing a meal. And the two-person table under a window provided the perfect spot for one to look outside to the greenhouse, the what-should-be-lush garden, the carriage house, and the fenced yard for several horses, a cow, and chickens. If the Pawlikowskis no longer needed space for their animals, they could build two more homes on their property. Not that either would need a kitchen, considering the size of this one.

"She must enjoy cooking," Zoe said when Mrs. Wiley paused to take a breath.

"Who must?"

"Mrs. Pawlikowski. Jakob's mother."

"She prefers to call it *experimenting*."

Zoe looked out the kitchen's window. "Zank you for caring for Mrs. Pawlikowski's greenhouse. Zis is kind of you."

"Oh, that's all Mr. Gunderson's doing."

Other than Mr. Gunderson's godparents and a small circle of friends, *everyone* Zoe had met in town referred to him as Mr. Gunderson and Jakob as Jakob. Why that bothered her, she was not sure.

She returned her attention to Mrs. Wiley. "Why is ze garden untended still?"

"Fret not! Jakob will take care of it before his parents return." Mrs. Wiley patted Zoe's arm. "It's a good thing you learned about his minimal gardening skills before he proposed marriage, isn't it?"

Zoe laughed. "I see what you are about, Mrs. Wiley. You wish him to lose my favor so he will be free to marry you."

"Am I succeeding?"

Zoe let her answer be a smile. At that moment, she noticed a jar on the kitchen table.

Mrs. Wiley's gaze shifted to where Zoe was looking. "Those are Mr. Gunderson's."

Zoe frowned as she walked toward the table, her attention on the glass jar half-filled with strange kernels. "What are zey?"

"You've never seen candied corn before?"

She had made candied carrots, beets, fruit, lemon peel, ginger, and even horseradish, but never had she seen or heard of candied corn. "Are zey edible?"

Mrs. Wiley picked up the jar and removed the lid. "Here, try one. He won't mind."

Zoe chose one of the tricolored kernels. Instead of the crunch she was expecting, it was soft. How could such a sweet fondant have so little flavor? She tasted vanilla, butter, and honey, but the waxy texture was unappealing at best. This faux candy should be melted and turned into a crème. With a little cayenne and cocoa power—

No! This candy should be tossed to swine.

There was no polite way to spit it out, so she swallowed. "Zey are edible, but eatable?" She shook her head. "Zat is *not* candy."

Mrs. Wiley laughed. "Don't let Mr. Gunderson hear you. He has a serious sweet tooth."

"He eats candied corn because he knows not better. I could make him a treat zat would banish all desire for zis—" Zoe grimaced. "*Ick.* I have no words to describe it."

"The twins mentioned you're a chef."

Household cook, to be exact. Weary of explaining the difference, she looked at the curtains. "How may I help?"

Mrs. Wiley grabbed the hem of her calico skirt and tucked the edge into the waistband, exposing her white bloomers. "Pick up one end of the curtains here and I'll do the other. We can lay them over the divan. I'll climb the ladder; you certainly won't be able to manage it in that fancy gown." She picked up one end of the stacked curtains.

"Once we're in the parlor, you can hand me one curtain at a time."

While Mrs. Wiley walked backward down the hall, Zoe carried the other end of the stacked curtains, taking care not to let them wrinkle. They were midway in redraping the last parlor window when the rain began.

After hanging the curtain, Mrs. Wiley climbed down the ladder. She drew up to the window where Zoe stood watching the rain pound against the street, mud puddles everywhere. "I'll wager we have a good hour or two before this lets up. How about we—Miss de Fleur, is something bothering you? You seem distracted."

Zoe stared absently at the rain-splattered window. "Zis morning Mr. Snowe mentioned how his daughter had once favored Jakob."

"Miss Snowe is one of dozens who once favored him." Mrs. Wiley bumped her shoulder against Zoe's. "Or still do."

"Including you?"

"If I were fifteen years younger . . ." The besotted sigh that came from Mrs. Wiley seemed more fitting coming from Carline or Yancey. Zoe had uttered a few of those sighs herself after first meeting Jakob. Clearly, he had his choice of ladies who would happily allow him to court them.

Desperate for an answer to the question that had plagued her for weeks, Zoe turned to face Mrs. Wiley. "Why did Jakob write for a bride by mail delivery when zere are many eminently suitable women here in Helena?"

"I've wondered that myself." Her knowing gaze settled on Zoe. "For all Jakob's virtues—and that man has many virtues—he's impatient and can miss what's right in front of him. If the idea pops into his mind to put out an advertisement for a bride, he's going to do it. Why not? As he often says, *It'll be fun*."

Zoe nodded, having heard him say that. "Jakob knows how to make a girl smile and forget her worries."

Mrs. Wiley chuckled. "That he does. I doubt his brother has ever done a spontaneous thing in his life without Jakob leading him on. Compared to Jakob, Mr. Gunderson is quite the bore. You should see the cleaning schedule he gave me. He plans *everything*." The emphasis Mrs. Wiley put on *everything* made Mr. Gunderson's diligence seem a grave character flaw.

"Mr. Gunderson can be counted on to do what he says he will do," Zoe said in his defense, "to be faithful, to never leave because something new has caught his interest. Some women would find zat dependability as appealing as Jakob's *joie de vivre*."

A wrinkle deepened between Mrs. Wiley's brows. "I'm not even going to try to repeat what you just said."

Zoe chuckled. "It means a cheerful enjoyment of life. Jakob has happy eyes because he has a happy spirit. He will bring laughter into ze life of ze girl he marries." She turned to look out the window, her smile fading as understanding dawned. The more Jakob separated from Isaak, the emptier Isaak felt. "Mr. Gunderson needs to find a girl with happy eyes and a happy spirit who will bring *joie de vivre* into his life, as Jakob has done for him all zese years."

"She'll have to storm into his life like a cyclone because Isaak Gunderson would *never* go looking for a female version of his brother. There's not a soul in Helena who tries his patience more, and that's by his own admission." Mrs. Wiley stepped closer to Zoe and lowered her voice, even though they were the only two in the house. "I think young unmarried ladies intimidate him."

Zoe opened her mouth . . . yet no words came out.

Isaak Gunderson carried too much confidence to be intimidated by anyone, least of all a young unmarried lady. If anything, he was too busy to realize he was lonely. What he needed was a steady, gentle rain—not a cyclone—to remind him to work a little less and have fun a little more.

"He's never courted anyone," Mrs. Wiley remarked.

Zoe snapped to attention. His brother was the first person to court her.

"Never?" she asked even though this was none of her business. No one's romantic pursuits—or, more precisely, lack thereof—fascinated her as much as Isaak Gunderson's did. "How do you know zis?"

Mrs. Wiley paused for a long moment. "I've only lived in Helena for six years, but I can't remember seeing him with any girl besides Yancey Palmer or Carline Pope . . . or Emilia McCall before she married. He's always at work or helping at church with the Widows and Orphans Committee. Every widow in town knows to go to him for help. There isn't a more generous man or a more dutiful son than Isaak Gunderson."

"You said he was a bore."

"That he is. He's a good man, even if he's not as exciting to be around as Jakob is."

Zoe nodded in agreement. She glanced over her shoulder at the clock sitting on the piano Carline Pope had lovingly played a month ago. Not quite an hour had passed since Zoe arrived to help. Yet the rain still looked strong and steady.

Zoe smiled at Mrs. Wiley. "Is zere anything else I can help clean?"

"Do you *want* to clean?"

Zoe grimaced. "I *always* prefer someone else do ze cleaning, but I enjoy helping someone in need. And I like you." She motioned to the window. "Plus, I cannot leave. Ze rain holds me hostage."

"As it does me," Mrs. Wiley said grimly. "The rain *and* Isaak Gunderson's cleaning list." She looked from the window to Zoe, and the corners of her mouth slowly indented. "Miss de Fleur, please take no offense when I say I don't believe you can cook a better sweet than candied corn."

"You *like* zat wretched treat?"

"If I say yes, will you feel compelled to prove my opinion wrong?"

Zoe realized where this was headed. "You are hoping I am competitive enough to rise to ze bait."

"Seeing we have Mrs. Pawlikowski's grand kitchen all to ourselves," Mrs. Wiley said smugly, "I'm hoping you are mercilessly competitive."

"I feel strangely compelled to prove you wrong about my cooking skills." Zoe followed Mrs. Wiley back to the kitchen. What could she make based on memory alone? It needed to be simple. With limited ingredients. As they entered the kitchen, Zoe glanced at the icebox, then at the closet door she suspected led to the larder. The best sweet to fit the requirements would be—

"I shall make *praline de café*," she announced.

Mrs. Wiley walked to the wall-mounted coffee grinder. "What is a praw-leen do—I have no idea what you just said."

"All zat matters is zey are a million times more eatable zan candied corn." Zoe gave the housekeeper her most mischievous grin. "Every flavor of praline is as alluring to men as a siren's song. I shall make ones flavored with coffee. Zey were Papa's favorite candy."

Mrs. Wiley seemed sufficiently impressed. "Be forewarned: I fully intend on telling Jakob I made these."

Zoe laughed. Mrs. Wiley could tell Jakob anything she wished because Zoe intended on taking Jakob a jar of pralines, along with a personal invitation to join her for supper tonight with Lily Forsythe. He would say yes. She was a jarful of candy sure of it.

Chapter Sixteen

Later that evening
The Pawlikowski House

Isaak opened the front door. "Jakob? Are you home?"

Silence.

The scent of coffee and something sweet filled the air. Isaak's stomach rumbled in response. He'd gone straight from The Resale Co. to church to talk to the Ladies' Aid Society and missed dinner.

Isaak shut the door. Where was that heavenly smell coming from?

He headed straight to the kitchen. A small plate sat in the middle of the table; propped up in front of his candied corn was a note card. Isaak walked closer. Four caramel-colored blobs lay on a plate. He lifted one to his mouth.

Wow!

Sweet, crunchy, nutty, chewy. He ran out of adjectives while munching the savory treat. A note in Mrs. Wiley's scratchy penmanship rested next to the candy. He opened it and read:

*Zoe made these pralines for you. I told her that you
didn't care for coffee, but she insisted you would like
coffee served this way. She preferred to use almonds.
We could only find pecans. I finished everything on
your list.*

*P.S. She says your candied corn isn't eatable. I
wouldn't let her throw them away.*

He smiled and reached for another praline, unable to remember the last time someone had done something just for
him. He was self-sufficient, confident in his likes and dislikes, and busy being the man others relied on. All good
things, but they left him lonely.

Not an adjective he'd applied to himself until Pastor
Neven's sermon on Sunday describing how God created loneliness in Adam's breast by making him name the animals—
each of them with a mate—before bringing Eve to him.

Isaak had seen himself in the story. He enjoyed a great relationship with his parents. He and his twin shared a special
bond . . . most of the time. He had meaningful work to do.
And yet he was alone.

He scooped up the last two pralines, then crossed to the
stove. With one hand, he stoked the fire, lifted the cast-iron
pot onto the stove, and retrieved the covered bowl from the
icebox while polishing off the candy. He might have to pay
Miss de Fleur to make him a batch once a month.

Jakob breezed in half an hour later, just as Isaak was
sitting down to his stew, bread, and Earl Grey tea with lots
of sugar and a splash of cream. "Hope you ate," Isaak said,
"because I didn't save any for you."

"I had dinner." Jakob peered at the stew, a smile tugging
one side of his mouth higher than the other. "And I must say,
I ate better than you."

Isaak shoveled a bite of stew into his mouth so he
wouldn't say, *But you didn't get pralines*, out loud.

"By the way"—Jakob opened the bread box and took out a biscuit—"Jefferson Brady came by The Import Company today. He wants the big office, so I added two dollars to the monthly payment and sent him over to Hale to sign the lease."

"That's great, Jake. I was hoping to have all those offices leased by the time Pa got back. You're way ahead of schedule there."

Instead of appearing pleased at the compliment, Jakob stared at the biscuit in his hand. "Why was I about to eat this?"

"Instinct, I imagine." Isaak spooned stew into his mouth.

Jakob tossed the biscuit back into the bread box, then strolled to the table and sat down next to Isaak. He swiped his finger in the crumbs on the praline plate and licked it. "Did Zoe leave you some pralines?"

"Leave me?" came out in a tone of voice more suited to a ten-year-old.

"She brought a jarful down to The Import Company for me." Jakob held his hands six inches apart to indicate the height of the jar.

Jealousy stabbed Isaak in the heart. So she hadn't made the treat especially for him.

"You're in a cheery mood." Isaak bit into his biscuit with more force than necessary, making his teeth clank together.

"I had a great time at Aunt Lily's tonight."

Isaak didn't want to hear about it. Tuesdays were Jakob's night for dinner with Miss de Fleur at the Forsythes'.

Jakob circled his index finger around the praline plate. "Yancey and Carline joined us for dinner and helped us figure out what to serve at the welcome-home dinner."

Isaak held his spoon inches from his mouth while trying to untangle his brother's sentence and why he was jealous again—this time because Yancey and Carline were invited to share dinner at Aunt Lily's with Jakob and Miss de Fleur.

Isaak set his still-full spoonful of stew back in the bowl. "What welcome-home dinner?"

"For Ma and Pa." Jakob stretched his arms wide and yawned. "I'm bushed."

Isaak picked up his teacup to give his hands something to do. "Come on, Jake. Give me the whole story."

Jakob yawned again. "Sorry. It's been a long couple of weeks."

Did that mean he was on schedule? The question lodged in Isaak's throat. He'd committed to staying out of what was happening at The Import Co.

Jakob rubbed his left shoulder with his right hand. "Yancey showed up at the store in time to claim the last praline. She'd never tasted Zoe's cooking, although she'd heard plenty about Mrs. Hollenbeck's welcome-home breakfast last Saturday."

Who hadn't? It was the talk of the town.

"Yancey suggested Zoe cater a dinner party for when Ma and Pa get back, only this one large enough to include us and our friends." Jakob held up his hand. "Before you say anything about how I'm behind and don't have time to add another thing to my schedule, I've already planned how it will work."

Jakob planned something ahead of time? Isaak was tempted to make some smart-aleck remark about marking the occasion in his calendar. Instead, he sipped his tea and listened while Jakob glowed with enthusiasm as he explained how tasting pralines at The Import Co. had set in motion a grand dinner on the Friday night eight days after their parents were scheduled to return to Helena. The guest list included twenty-five people and would be held at Mrs. Hollenbeck's, if she agreed, because her house was the only one with a dining room large enough to accommodate that many people.

Isaak listened while sipping his extra-sweet tea, which did nothing to abate the sour taste in his mouth.

Jakob was as committed as ever to his courtship of Miss de Fleur.

Wednesday, April 18
De Fleur-Gunderson Courtship Contract, Day 40

Isaak sat in his office staring at a Spiegel catalog. He was supposed to be studying prices of new items so he didn't overpay for secondhand ones. He was supposed to stop thinking about Miss Zoe de Fleur and his improper attraction to her, too.

Neither of which was happening.

Isaak slapped the catalog closed with a huff. He needed advice, but he'd run through the list of possible people and disqualified every one of them. Right or wrong, his pride couldn't take admitting his preoccupation with the lady to anyone else. His heart leaped every time he saw a woman with black hair, whether it was curly or not. He looked for Miss de Fleur every time he delivered merchandise for the store or food to widows and orphans. And every time he returned home, he hoped to find a bowl of nuts or some other treat he could pretend she'd made special for him.

Meow.

"Hello, Harry." Isaak reached down and picked up the tabby cat Jakob had rescued when they were eleven years old. Jakob had lost interest after a few weeks of playing with the stray, so Harry had become Isaak's.

"You were the first time I realized it was up to me to follow through on Jakob's initial ideas." Isaak stroked the cat's head. "Not that I've minded much. We're a good team most of the time."

As they were with the Sundin family. On an impulse,

Jakob had hired Timmy to work at The Import Co. Once Isaak heard about it, he'd added the boy and his mother to the list of widows and orphans who received food boxes. Which made him think of walking to Mrs. Hollenbeck's house with Miss de Fleur.

Why did every thought either start or end with her?

Isaak held the cat aloft so they were eye to eye. "What do you think of Miss de Fleur?"

Harry blinked his yellow eyes.

"I agree. She *is* a lovely person, which is my problem." Isaak lowered the cat into his lap and reached into the bottom drawer of his desk. He pulled out a piece of paper. "See this?" He laid the paper on top of the Spiegel catalog. "It's my list of qualities I require in a wife."

Harry wriggled free to jump onto the desk and paw at the paper.

Isaak picked up the cat and held him away from the list. "I'll read it to you. Item number one: godly character."

There was a check mark beside it because Miss de Fleur had demonstrated grace and mercy every time she didn't return Isaak's accusations with ones of her own. The day she bought the books, she could have run straight to Aunt Lily, telling her about Isaak's bribe offer. But no, Miss de Fleur had remained silent. She even paid full price for the books when she could have bested him again by offering a ridiculously low price. Adding the two bits extra was her only comeuppance, and it was given with a smile.

"Item number two: balances me."

It was also checked. Like Uncle Jonas, Isaak was hard around the edges with a softer middle than most people knew. Like Aunt Lily, Miss de Fleur was soft around the edges with an inner strength.

Balance.

"Item number three: shares some of my interests." Isaak pulled Harry's claws from his tweed vest to prevent snags.

"Pay attention, because this one is important. See? No check mark. We both like to cook, but that's not enough for a strong relational foundation. The problem is, I don't know Miss de Fleur very well. I've been avoiding her, for obvious reasons."

Harry blinked his wisdom.

"You're right. The problem isn't my lack of knowledge, it's what happens if I get to know her better and she *does* share more interests with me." He looked at the list. "I take that back. My biggest problem is that I never should have taken this list out in the first place. I was trying to prove that my infatuation was unfounded."

Harry purred.

Isaak stroked all the way to the tabby's tail. "I believe I need to add one more item."

Meow.

"Yes, I should have thought of it long ago, but I never imagined this situation." After setting Harry on the floor, Isaak picked up a pencil and added a new item at the top of his list: **NOT JAKOB'S GIRL**.

Seeing the words failed to relieve Isaak's exasperation at his weakness.

Harry weaved his way around Isaak's ankles. "You're right again. Sitting here is doing no good at all."

Neither was talking to a cat. Isaak needed advice from someone other than himself. If only Pa were here. Or Ma.

Knock, knock, knock.

"Come in."

Mac opened the door, sidestepping to let Harry race past him.

Isaak checked the clock. Before Mac and Emilia married, they'd developed a habit of sharing their lunch hour together. "You're here early."

Mac closed the door and locked it. "I'm here to talk to you."

Isaak tucked his disobliging list inside the catalog. "Have a seat."

Mac hung his Stetson on the peg. "Remember that leveling foot I showed you last year after Finn died?"

"Yes."

He crossed the room and sat in one of the chairs on the opposite side of the desk. "Could you look through your father's ledgers and make a list of anything requiring one?"

"Why? Has something new come up about Finn's death?"

"What I'm about to tell you must remain between us. You can't tell Jakob, Hale, the Forsythes, or even your parents when they return home."

Isaak nodded his agreement to the terms.

Mac licked his lips. "Finn and my mother weren't selling women into prostitution. They were smuggling young girls out."

"What! I mean, yes. That makes sense." At least about Finn Collins. But rescuing girls with Madame Lestraude? That didn't make *any* sense. Isaak shifted in his chair. "What a relief to know your best friend wasn't deceiving you all these years."

Mac nodded. "Emilia has known since last June. She's been encouraging me to earn my mother's trust, so she'd tell me the story herself."

"Which I'm guessing was right before the wedding."

Another nod. "I showed my mother this a few minutes ago." Mac pulled the leveling screw from his coat pocket. "She gasped. It wasn't much, and she attempted to cover it with a cough, but she knows more than she's telling me."

Isaak harrumphed. Of course she knew more. A brothel owner who catered to the rich and powerful probably kept more secrets than a graveyard. "Do you need me to check my father's ledgers now, or can it wait until after the grand opening?"

"After is fine." Mac stood. "But then as soon as possible."

"Of course, but before you go . . ." Isaak opened the catalog. "I need your advice about something that also must remain between us."

Mac sat down again.

Isaak pulled the list he'd hidden from between the pages. "These are the qualities I require in a wife." He turned the paper around so Mac could see the bold print letters at the top.

Mac's eyes widened, then snapped to meet Isaak's gaze. "Oh, man."

Madame Lestraude stormed into his office, her burgundy silk skirt rustling like leaves in a windstorm. "You killed Finn Collins."

"I did not."

She gripped the back of the chair opposite his desk. "Don't play a game of semantics with me. You may not have shot the bullet, but you're responsible."

The rancher's death plagued his conscience enough; he didn't need Madame Lestraude fanning the flames. "Whatever gave you such an odd notion?"

Her brown eyes constricted. "A certain metal object my son showed me earlier today. One found in Finn's barn last year."

Heat snaked up his spine.

"As soon as I saw it and heard it was a leveling foot, I realized it belonged to that printing press you're so proud of."

He closed the file on his desk to give himself somewhere else to look other than in her too-intelligent eyes. That press was churning out page after page of near-perfect counterfeit money, so of course he was proud of it. He'd purchased it for pennies on the dollar because it required extensive repairs. Dunfree was supposed to find someone far from Helena for that job, but Collins was the only man in the territory who could fix the thing "What did you tell your son?"

"Nothing."

He looked up at her, a mistake because any doubts she might have had were eradicated by whatever she saw in his face.

She came around the chair, placed her hands on his desk, and leaned down close enough he could smell the rosewater on her skin. "I have tortured myself thinking I was responsible for getting that good man killed."

So had he.

She pushed off his desk and straightened her shoulders. With a deep breath and slow exhalation, she transformed herself into the passionless madam who cared for no one. "You and I have coexisted in this town for twelve years because our interests have never conflicted until now. Edgar Dunfree deserved what he got, and I was no fan of Joseph Hendry."

He flinched, unable to maintain the same disguise of disinterest. But then, she'd had more practice. "How did you know about Hendry?"

"I didn't until now, but I knew he wasn't killed for meddling in the red-light district. Was he getting too close to your precious counterfeiting?"

There was no point in denying it, but he wouldn't give her the satisfaction of confirming it either.

She stared down her nose at him. "We have reached an important point in our peaceful coexistence. Finn is gone. For us to feud over his death now is a waste of effort."

He nodded. He should have stood when she entered the room, a tactical error he wouldn't make again.

She took a step back. "We shall let Finn Collins rest in peace, but I swear to you on his grave, if you ever threaten my family or cause them harm, I will tear every one of your illicit businesses down with my bare hands."

Chapter Seventeen

Millionaire's Hill
Late afternoon, the next day
De Fleur-Gunderson Courtship Contract, Day 41

"Ma'am, I found these in the attic."

The sound of Miss Bloom's voice drew Zoe's attention away from the food crate she was filling in the shadow of Mrs. Hollenbeck's three-story mansion. Mrs. Hollenbeck's paid companion, with a jubilant smile that emphasized her deep dimples, stepped out onto the patio and gave the older woman three stacked baskets, each the size of a hatbox.

"Thank you, Miss Bloom." Mrs. Hollenbeck studied the stack. She took the largest basket, then handed the other two back to her assistant. "Choose the one you like best, then return the other from whence it came."

"I like neither," Miss Bloom said without losing her smile, "so to the attic they both go."

Mrs. Hollenbeck laughed. "My dear child, you will never win a gentleman's favor with that attitude."

"Then my surliness is working."

"Not if I can help it. I vowed to find you a husband by year's end, and I mean to fulfill my promise."

"I am most grateful for your concern over matters of my heart," Miss Bloom responded, even though her lack of gratitude for Mrs. Hollenbeck's matchmaking skills was clear to Zoe.

Ignoring their bantering, she added the final two onions to the food crate. Since arriving to aid in packing crates for a dozen church families, she had listened to Mrs. Hollenbeck extoll to her assistant the virtues of numerous Helena bachelors, including Geddes Palmer and Windsor Buchanan, the latter seeming to hold a tenderness in the rich widow's heart. Zoe had spoken on numerous occasions with both gentlemen—the former being friends with Jakob and the latter with Mr. Gunderson. Either would make a suitable husband, so she had no idea why Miss Bloom resisted being courted.

"—is why you will fill a basket. End of debate." Mrs. Hollenbeck strolled over to Zoe and the wooden patio table laden with food crates. "This one is yours."

Zoe reached for the basket.

"Don't take it, Miss de Fleur."

Heeding Miss Bloom's warning, Zoe lowered her hands. She looked at Mrs. Hollenbeck and the basket she held. Then she looked at Miss Bloom, whose perpetual smile had faded. Then Zoe looked back at Mrs. Hollenbeck, who wore an expression of mild disappointment at Zoe for not immediately accepting the basket.

"What is ze basket for?" Zoe asked with equal amounts of caution and curiosity.

"Lunch." Mrs. Hollenbeck moved the basket closer to Zoe, as if it were imperative that she take it. "Go on, dear. It won't bite."

"Am I to fill zis?"

"That is the plan."

Zoe looked to the table which had held food donations for the baskets. Nothing remained save for dusty burlap potato sacks. On her way home, she could stop at the grocer and bakery. The cost was little in light of helping a needy family.

The moment Zoe accepted the basket, Miss Bloom called out, "Miss de Fleur, you're going to regret not listening to me. Never feed a tiger. Oh, I hear the door knocker." At that, with her head held high, she sailed past the opened patio doors and into the mansion as if she owned it.

"One of these days, I shall relieve that girl of her employment with me." The flicker of amusement in Mrs. Hollenbeck's eyes belied her words.

Zoe smiled warmly. "I believe you like her . . ." She paused, trying to think of the right English word. "Cheek? Nerve? Oh, how do you translate *le toupet*?"

"Cheekiness?" Mrs. Hollenbeck offered. "Sass?"

"Yes! You like her sass."

"Like? No, I tolerate her sass because I don't wish to train another paid companion." In a softer voice, Mrs. Hollenbeck said, "You may be on to something, but let's keep that our secret." Her attention shifted to the crates of food. "All we need now are our delivery men." She grasped the pocket watch she wore on a pearl chain around her neck and clicked the cover open. "They should be arriving about now."

Zoe held up the basket. "For whom do I need to fill zis?"

"Oh, dear child, this isn't for a needy family. In two Sundays, on April 29, the Widows and Orphans Committee is hosting a lunch basket auction at our church. Unmarried ladies are to provide a lunch for men to bid on." At the sound of people talking, Mrs. Hollenbeck glanced toward the opened patio doors before refocusing on Zoe. "I've raved to everyone I know about the welcome-home breakfast feast you cooked for me. During past auctions, men have bid on baskets to secure the attentions of the lady who provided the basket. This year I intend to cause a bidding war for your food."

"A bidding war?"

"Indeed, Miss de Fleur. Jakob will obviously counter

every offer." She chuckled. "This will serve him right after all these years of running up bids."

Zoe hoped he would bid on her lunch basket. Yet a tiny part of her wished otherwise. After five days of focusing on nothing but Jakob's courtship, she was now doubting her decision to give him another chance because, after five days of renewed courtship, Jakob again had no time for anything save The Import Company.

Why did her heart fight against committing to him?

She sighed. Falling in love should never be this complicated.

She understood when he said he needed to give his full attention to stocking The Import Company because his parents were returning in a short seven days. Shelves needed to be arranged and stocked. Merchandise had to be priced. Decorations had to be hung. But did he have to work more than nine hours each day? Jakob had canceled Monday's picnic trip to watch the construction of the new Broadwater Hotel. He was late to Tuesday's coffee-and-cake social with the Snowe family, and he forgot about dinner with the Forsythes entirely, even though Mrs. Forsythe repeatedly reminded him that Judge Forsythe wanted to talk to Jakob after eight days of travel.

At least, Jakob's brother had been at the Snowes' social and the Forsythes' dinner to carry the conversation, so Zoe could contentedly watch and listen. Mr. Gunderson was kind enough to include her in the discussion and not demand she speak. He was considerate enough to change the topic of conversation when Miss Snowe's brother embarrassingly goaded Miss Snowe about thinking she could steal Jakob away from Zoe, who, according to Miss Snowe's brother, was "a more swell girl" than his sister was.

With all the lovely young women in Helena, with ones like Miss Snowe chasing after Jakob, it made no sense why he had placed an advertisement for a bride by mail delivery. A man besotted with a girl would wish to spend time with her. Zoe wanted to believe Jakob was besotted. Nothing testified to it. Could he be using this courtship to dissuade the attentions of marriage-minded females in town?

Zoe tensed. He could be using her to make someone else jealous. Yancey? Carline? Both ladies were close friends with Jakob. Almost every time Zoe had stopped by The Import Company in the morning to see Jakob, either one or both had been there.

Mrs. Hollenbeck rested her hand atop Zoe's arm, putting an end to her wayward thoughts. "May I ask what troubles you?"

I want to love Jakob, but my heart refuses. What do I do?

She yearned to say the words. She yearned to talk to someone about her heart's struggle, but everyone would say she needed to give the courtship time, at least follow it through to the end. Jakob was a good man. A hard worker. Someone worth waiting for. Mrs. Hollenbeck adored Jakob too much to understand Zoe's dilemma.

Truth was, maybe she did not *really* want to love Jakob. Maybe she wanted someone else, someone she could rely on to help her not feel so alone.

"Whatever it is, you can tell me," Mrs. Hollenbeck prodded.

Something about her expression comforted Zoe. Maybe the older woman would understand. "How does a woman know if she should—"

The arrival of a quartet of men prevented her from finishing her sentence. Miss Bloom stepped out onto the patio, followed by Misters Gunderson and Buchanan, Deputy Alderson, and Dr. Abernathy's son, who had recently returned to Helena after medical school. John? James? Oh, she could not remember.

"This is a first," Mrs. Hollenbeck whispered to Zoe.

"What is?" she whispered back.

"The first time I've been disappointed at someone's promptness." Mrs. Hollenbeck turned toward the men. "Gentlemen, we have a dozen crates. Once you each load three in your wagons, I will give you a list of where to deliver them."

"I already distributed the lists per your earlier instructions," Miss Bloom put in. "And I exchanged the Nolans with the Bumgardens because Deputy Alderson told me the Nolans moved out to Mr. Fisk's old cabin this morning. Switching makes the deliveries more efficient."

For the barest second, Mrs. Hollenbeck looked unsure of how to respond. "Thank you for the insight. Mr. Gunderson, you should have the Ziegler family."

"I do," Mr. Gunderson answered. His gaze flickered from Mrs. Hollenbeck to Zoe. Was it her imagination or did he look somewhat uncomfortable?

"I should leave," Zoe said, because her work here was done.

Mrs. Hollenbeck gripped Zoe's arm, stopping her from leaving, and said to Miss Bloom, "Escort Mr. Gunderson to the stable. The brown goat with the yellow ribbon around her neck goes to Mrs. Ziegler. I need you to accompany Mr. Gunderson and help manage the goat. She doesn't like wagons."

Miss Bloom smiled brightly at Mr. Gunderson. "We're partners! Isn't that—oh!" Her smile fell. She grimaced, then gave Mrs. Hollenbeck an apologetic look. "Miss de Fleur needs to go in my place. Deputy Alderson asked for my advice in planning his marriage proposal to Miss Rigney. Discussing this with him while making the deliveries would look less suspicious to his soon-to-be fiancée."

"Indeed it would," Mrs. Hollenbeck muttered.

Misters Gunderson, Buchanan, and Abernathy all looked at Deputy Alderson, who looked caught in a trap.

"It's going to be the best," Miss Bloom said in that dramatic way of hers, "the most romantic proposal any woman has every received. I'm so honored Deputy Alderson asked for my help."

He nodded, like a man with no choice but to comply.

Mrs. Hollenbeck gave Zoe's arm a little squeeze. "I know this is asking a lot for someone of your tenderhearted nature, but could you help Mr. Gunderson manage a feisty goat?"

Zoe's chin rose a half-inch in offense at Mrs. Hollenbeck's pronouncement. She could outwit a feisty goat just as easily as Miss Bloom could outwit her I-vowed-to-find-you-a-husband-by-year's-end employer. "Certainly, madame. It is but a goat."

Miss Bloom leaned close to Isaak, shielding her mouth with her hand. "Miss de Fleur is a charming girl but a bit too malleable. I don't know what your brother sees in her besides a pretty face, excellent cooking skills, a sweet spirit, and a willingness to help others."

Isaak pressed his lips together. Miss de Fleur was all that and more—including being concerned for widows and orphans. He could practically hear his pen scratching a check mark beside "shares some of my interests" on his list.

Had Zoe de Fleur arrived in Helena in any other manner than as his brother's mail-order bride, Isaak would revel in the way she made him feel. Over a long period of time—six months, at least—if her character still matched up with what it now appeared to be, they could have a romance that was a perfect balance of practicality and sentiment. But she *had* come as Jakob's bride, and Isaak would never betray his brother. When the time was right, Isaak would find another Zoe de Fleur who would fill his life with sweetness.

At least he hoped that was the lesson God was teaching him.

"The Widows and Orphans Committee needs your help." Mrs. Hollenbeck picked up a small basked and— were she any woman other than the most revered widow of his acquaintance—Isaak would describe the way she thrust a basket at Miss de Fleur as rude.

Miss de Fleur took it, but she seemed unhappy about it.

He took a step forward to discover why, but it wasn't his place to ease her burden. To protect her. Or to sit beside her for the next two hours delivering food as Mrs. Hollenbeck had decreed, although he would do so rather than be rude.

Fifteen minutes later, he had three food crates loaded into the back of the wagon and the goat tied to the wagon wheel to keep it from running off. Miss de Fleur placed her small basket onto the spring seat. She frowned at the wagon's side, then looked up at him.

"How do you climb into zis?"

"May I?" He moved his hands to Miss de Fleur's waist, close but not touching. "It'll be easier if I just lift you into the wagon. Then the goat. You can hold it while I climb in. Between the two of us, it won't go anywhere."

"Zat sounds like a good plan." She smiled at him with such trust in her eyes that his heart began to pick up speed.

His reaction when she'd caught him listening to the finches sing in the greenhouse was nothing compared to this moment. Against all logic, his determination to overcome his attraction to her was replaced by a fierce desire to kiss her until she admitted her life would be incomplete without him.

Isaak choked on air. He coughed into his hand until he could swallow. "Sorry, I—" His mind went blank, so he focused on putting her and the goat into the wagon. He'd helped a woman into a wagon before, but this felt entirely different. Private. Intimate. And—heaven help him— splendid. Doing his best not to think about how his hands had encircled her waist, he hurried around the wagon, climbed in, and set off down the road with the goat standing between them.

His attraction to Zoe was madness. Madness! It would pass. It had to. In the meantime, he just needed to keep himself from saying or doing anything stupid. He had to get the food and goat delivered then get Miss de Fleur back to her boardinghouse before he did something he would enjoy but definitely regret.

She sat on the spring seat, petting the goat's head as she spoke to it in French.

They traveled another block before Isaak gave in to his curiosity. "What are you telling it?"

Miss de Fleur gave him a tentative smile. "What it knows but is afraid to believe."

"Which is?"

"She is a good goat. She does not fear where ze wagon is taking her because she is going to her new home. She will have a family who loves her and who she can love."

Isaak shifted the reins to his left hand so he could pet the goat. "How do you know this goat so well?"

"She is a girl. I am a girl."

Girl was too simple a word to define Zoe de Fleur.

Isaak drew the wagon up to the first home on their route, a two-room house on the outskirts of Chinatown. He left Miss de Fleur to charm the goat while he gave the food crate to Miss Marie Ying and her younger brother. After accepting hugs from the Yings, Isaak climbed into the wagon and turned the wagon in the direction of the Zieglers' house

Miss de Fleur patted his arm. "I am glad we are friends, you and I."

Isaak called on every ounce of self-restraint and honor to

keep from confessing how her touch affected him. For a man to pursue another man's woman was treachery enough; for a man to betray his own brother in the same way was the deepest level of perfidy imaginable.

He gave her a steady look. "Everyone needs a friend." He motioned to the basket. "I take it Mrs. Hollenbeck wants you to contribute to the lunch basket auction."

She grimaced, her nose scrunching, something he'd never seen her do before. Something he never wished to see again because of how endearing she looked. "Mrs. Hollenbeck wishes for a bidding war—not for romance, but to raise money for ze Widows and Orphans Fund." She sighed. "Jakob will feel obligated to buy my basket. In no good conscience can I ask zis of him."

Isaak couldn't stop a burst of laughter. "It'd serve him right after all these years of running up bids."

"Zat is what Mrs. Hollenbeck said."

Which made him think of the way she'd thrust the basket at Miss de Fleur. "Instead of donating a lunch basket, you could make a monetary donation to the fund."

Her countenance brightened. "I did not know I could do zat. Yes! Zis is a wonderful solution. Zen Jakob will not have to be in a bidding war."

"You're more gracious to Jakob than he deserves." Isaak recounted the time Jakob had misjudged how angry his bidding was making a man intent on wooing the basket's owner, resulting in a round of fisticuffs before Sheriff McCall broke up the fight. "Your kindness in sparing Jakob retaliation is undeserved."

"If you were him, would you not wish for grace?"

Unsure of what to say, yet confident of what he *couldn't* say, Isaak turned the wagon onto the road leading to the Zieglers' ramshackle home. He listened to the rattle of the wagon's chains, the clomp of the horse's hooves, and the bleet of the goat to keep from thinking about things he shouldn't. Before he'd stopped the wagon and locked the brake, Mrs. Ziegler's two girls dashed from the house, only to stop and gasp when they saw the goat.

"Is that for us, Mr. Gunderson?" the older one said as their mother stepped outside.

He climbed down. "It sure is." After checking the rope around the goat's neck, he placed it on the ground, then led it to Mrs. Ziegler and gave her the leash. "The food is—"

Her gaze shifted to the wagon.

Isaak looked over his shoulder.

Miss de Fleur carried the food crate toward them. She placed it on the porch, spoke to the Ziegler girls about naming the goat, then shook Mrs. Ziegler's hand. "May zis be a blessing to you and yours."

"Thank you." Mrs. Ziegler's gaze shifted between him and Miss de Fleur. If she wondered why Isaak wasn't making the delivery on his own like usual, she kept it to herself.

Isaak said goodbye to Mrs. Ziegler then walked with Miss de Fleur back to the wagon. "You shouldn't have jumped out of the wagon. You could have twisted an ankle."

She laughed. "I am more clever zan you give me credit." Instead of stopping at the front of the wagon, she continued to the back. She turned her back to the wagon, placed her palms flat on the bottom board, then sprung in that fancy blue dress of hers onto the wagon box. She scrambled onto her feet. "*Voilà!*"

He folded his arms over the top boxboard. "You're pretty pleased with yourself."

She stepped around the food crate and over the bicycle, then leaned down and lowered her voice, as if imparting a secret. "You will be a gentleman and praise me for my ingenuity."

Isaak took his leisure in admiring the mischievous glint in her chocolate-brown eyes. The last time he'd been told to behave like a gentleman he was twelve years old and it had been a reprimand, not a pleasant bantering that made him desire to lean close to her mouth. Warmth filled his cheeks. "You can count on me to be a gentleman."

"And?"

And that needed to be the end of their repartee. With Yancey and Carline, he could tease because their flirtations weren't personal. Yancey loved Hale. Carline loved Geddes, or so Isaak suspected. Playful bantering with Zoe—

Miss de Fleur.

Using her first name was a line he could not cross, not even in the privacy of his thoughts.

With a shake of his head, he climbed into the wagon and slid onto the spring bench.

She sat backward on the seat. With the lift of her legs, she swirled around. "Mr. Gunderson, zat was no compliment."

Not a compliment? The woman couldn't be more wrong. Being on his best behavior around her was the highest compliment he could give her. He didn't want mere friendship. Or playful banter. He wanted friendship and banter, plus her secrets, her hopes, and her future—the things she was dreaming about with his brother. Wanting what he couldn't have was turning him inside out. He should never have made that list. He should never have compared it to her. He should have insisted he could make these deliveries on his own.

She fit perfectly into his life. Too perfectly.

"We should get on to the Wileys." Isaak loosened the brake and flicked the reins, starting the wagon forward. "Sarah has four children from her first marriage—Alexander, Dante, Olivia, and Thaddeus. Did Sarah tell you she came to Helena as Hector Wiley's mail-order bride? She wouldn't marry him until he adopted her children."

When Miss de Fleur didn't respond, he looked her way.

She was watching him with a curious, studious expression, as if he were a puzzle she needed—dare he think *wanted*—to solve. How was it possible she grew more beautiful each time he looked at her? His heart pounded, urging him to touch her cheek. To discover whether her heart was beating as wildly as his. To—

Isaak jerked his attention to the road.

She inched a little closer to his side of the bench. "You cannot allow yourself to have fun. I wonder why zat is." Isaak opened his mouth to answer, but she waved him away. "No, no. Keep your secret, Mr. Gunderson. Ze bicycle is for ze Wiley children, yes?"

"It was in a wagonload of secondhand goods I bought."

"Ze people of Helena are blessed to have you. I would vote for you for mayor if I could." She patted his arm. "You will win ze election. I know it."

"Thank you." He scooted farther away, her presence and touch too tempting for his peace of mind.

They sat in silence as Isaak turned the wagon onto the road to his parents' first home, Honeymoon Cottage, as Ma called it. His parents would adore Miss de Fleur.

"What do you do when you are unsure if you have made ze correct decision?"

"Pray. Talk to my parents." In the last year, he'd mostly sought counsel from—"Uncle Jonas is a wise man. You could talk to him or Aunt Lily. They love you like you're their daughter."

"If I talk to zem, zey may blame . . ." She sighed. "Ze fault is not one person's. I could not bear to have zem zink ill of him. But I feel sadness here"—she laid a hand over her heart—"and I know ze cause, but I fear I have not ze courage to do what I know I should."

Isaak tensed. This was about the courtship contract. It had to be. His heart pounded against his chest. "Is this about Jakob?"

She nodded. "I bore him. Next to Yancey and Carline, I am as bland as a flapjack. They know how to carry a conversation. They know how to make him laugh. I have not heard

his laughter in days, not since I gave him ze jar of pralines."
She sat still, not fidgeting, the blink of her eyes the only
movement. "Zere are nineteen days left on ze contract."

And eight days from now was the welcome-home dinner
for Ma and Pa that Jakob had talked her into catering—now
a mere day after they arrived home because, according to the
telegram Geddes delivered a few hours ago—Pa had sprained
his ankle and needed time to recoup before traveling.

Isaak waited for Miss de Fleur to say she planned to end the
contract before she was obligated to cook for the welcome-
home dinner.

She said nothing.

"And?" he prodded.

"My spirit is torn asunder. You are right to point out I am
cooking your parents' welcome-home dinner."

"I didn't mention the welcome-home dinner."

She frowned at him. "You did not?"

He shook his head.

"Well, I know it is what you were zinking. To end ze
courtship contract before ze sixty days are over would be
unkind to Jakob. He would feel crushed. I must carry zis
burden, for I cannot lay it on him." She patted Isaak's arm
again. "Zank you for being a good friend and giving me
advice about what I should do about your brother. I feel
better now."

At least one of them did.

Zoe could not be sure how long they sat in companionable
silence. It lasted until Mr. Gunderson stopped in front of a
one-story house. Unlike the other ramshackle houses they'd
visited, this one looked freshly whitewashed and had not a
missing shingle or broken board. And the flowers—from
what she could see—sprung along three sides of the house.

Mr. Gunderson jumped out of the wagon and made his way to the back to unload the bicycle. "Well?" he said, looking her way.

Zoe swiveled on the seat. She stepped to the edge of the wagon bed. In one gentle swoop, he placed her on the ground. She gripped the handlebars. He carried the food crate as she rolled the bicycle toward the house.

The door opened the moment they reached the porch.

"Mr. Gunderson!" exclaimed an auburn-haired girl, possibly six or seven years old. Her gaze shifted to Zoe. "Who are you?"

"Olivia Jane," scolded her mother. Mrs. Wiley leaned back inside the house. "Boys, Mr. Gunderson is here."

Within seconds, three redheaded boys surrounded Zoe and the bicycle.

"Is this for us?" asked the oldest.

"Sure is," answered Mr. Gunderson. He then looked at her. "Miss de Fleur, let me introduce you to Alexander, Dante, Olivia—whom you've already met—and Thaddeus Wiley. Children, this is Miss de Fleur, a friend of mine and Jakob's. Miss de Fleur is from France."

Each child shook her hand and muttered polite nice-to-meet-yous before their attention returned to the bicycle. Soon an argument commenced over who would get to learn to ride first.

Zoe touched Mr. Gunderson's arm, drawing his attention. "Would you like to show zem while I help Mrs. Wiley with ze food?"

A chorus of *please* rang out.

He shook his head. "Not today. I need to return Miss de Fleur to the boardinghouse."

All four children turned their pleading eyes on her and called out another chorus of *please*.

Zoe glanced back and forth from the children to Mr.

Gunderson. She was in no hurry. Her evening consisted of reading La Fontaine, but neither did she wish to impose on Mr. Gunderson's time. To him, she said, "Ze decision is yours."

Mrs. Wiley took the food crate from Mr. Gunderson. "I wouldn't mind a few minutes of Zoe's company. I've been meaning to ask her for the praline recipe."

Mr. Gunderson leaned close to Zoe. The movement was not enough to cross the lines of propriety, but it caused flutters in her stomach. "How can you, in good conscience, conscript me into this great torment?" he asked.

Zoe pinched her lips tight so she could keep from smiling. "Were you not a child once?"

"Once," he conceded.

"Zen zis will atone for all ze people zat you, during your childhood, inflicted great torment upon."

A faint smile played across Mr. Gunderson's face. "*Touché*, Miss de Fleur."

She patted his arm again. "You will survive." She cast a slant-eyed glance at the snickering children. "Do not hurt him too much. He must drive me home." Leaving Mr. Gunderson with the children and the bicycle, Zoe followed Mrs. Wiley into the house. "Zis is a lovely home."

"Thank you. It belongs to Mr. Gunderson's parents." She set the crate of food on the small dining table. "Would you like tea or coffee?"

"Whichever is easier."

"Then tea it is."

As Mrs. Wiley went to boil water on the cookstove, Zoe sat at the table, noticing the lavender tinge under the woman's eyes and the lack of neatness to her close-cropped auburn hair.

"Is zere anything I can do to help?"

Mrs. Wiley chuckled. "Entertain my children for a day."

Zoe sighed, wishing she could, but she had little experience with children. What the Wiley children needed was something to do, something adventurous while their mother worked. Papa used to say idle hands were the devil's playground.

Zoe glanced through the small house to the opened front door. Mr. Gunderson walked beside the oldest boy as he did a decent job of keeping the wobbly bicycle upright. The Wiley children clearly adored him. She smiled as he applauded Alexander. The lady who married Mr. Gunderson would be fortunate to have a husband so devoted to being a good father.

How was it he, like his brother, had yet to marry?

Any woman would be blessed to have Mr. Gunderson as a husband. He was kindhearted, generous, dependable, and knew how to manage children.

Zoe looked back at Mrs. Wiley, who had confessed to having two jobs besides housecleaning for the Gundersons. If Zoe remembered correctly from their conversation while making the pralines, with the twins' mother and stepfather returning next Thursday, Mrs. Wiley had a long list of Saturday chores.

Zoe gasped.

Mrs. Wiley sat the tea service tray on the table. "What is it?"

"Ze garden. I zink Jakob has forgotten his duty to cultivate it before his mother returns."

"You're right." Mrs. Wiley grimaced. "And Mrs. Pawlikowski loves that garden."

Zoe nodded. Her heart ached at the thought of his mother disappointed in Jakob because he had waited too long to complete his work. *She* was disappointed in Jakob enough for both of them. He should never have committed to courting her when he knew of his obligations to The Import Company. He should have put work and family above his quest to find a bride.

In addition to his obligations at the store, he had one to his mother.

Her mind was awhirl about the garden, idle hands, and how to give Mrs. Wiley a day away from her children.

Taking a moment to let an idea form, Zoe added milk to her tea.

"Sugar?" Mrs. Wiley offered the sugar spoon.

"No, zank you." Zoe stared at her teacup for a long moment. "Mrs. Wiley, I would like to hire your children zis Saturday."

Mrs. Wiley tipped her head in question. "You would?"

Without pause, Zoe detailed her plan to cook breakfast and lunch for the children in exchange for their help cultivating Mrs. Pawlikowski's garden. But Mrs. Wiley must keep it a secret from the Gundersons.

"You want this to be a surprise?"

Zoe nodded.

Mrs. Wiley sipped her tea. "You may have to bribe me to keep your secret."

Zoe smiled, knowing exactly where this was headed. "I will feed you, too."

"You strike a hard bargain. But I accept."

Chapter Eighteen

The Pawlikowski House
Saturday morning
De Fleur-Gunderson Courtship Contract, Day 43

"'There's nothing better than surface soil from an old pasture,'" Alexander Wiley read loudly, "'taken off about two-inches deep and thrown into a heap with one-sixth part well-decayed dung.'" He looked up. "I think this means we either need poop from an old cow or old poop from a cow that isn't necessarily old but could be."

Angling the brim of her straw hat to shield her eye from the midmorning sun, Zoe looked from Alexander to his snickering younger siblings—Dante, Olivia and her favorite doll, and Thaddeus—all four of them sitting on a wooden bench on the other side of the garden bed. Mrs. Gilfoyle-Crane's New York City mansion had comprised the entire lot, leaving no space for a garden, so Zoe had had to rely on making purchases from grocers and local farmers. While it had been over four years since Zoe had helped Papa cultivate a vegetable garden, she found suspect the amount of manure Alexander said they needed.

She reached into the apron over the faded calico dress

Mrs. Wiley had loaned her and withdrew Mrs. Pawlikowski's gardening gloves. "Are you sure we need zat much cow dung?" she asked Alexander before selecting a hoe from the pile of gardening tools.

"One-sixth." He turned the worn copy of *The Gardeners' Monthly* in Zoe's direction. He tapped the page with his index finger. "Says it right here, if you want to read it."

"I believe you." Or at least she chose to believe him.

Zoe eyed the six-hundred-square-foot garden Jakob should have cultivated in February. With Mr. and Mrs. Pawlikowski arriving in five days, the garden needed to be prepared quickly and efficiently to be ready for planting season. Putting Jakob out of her mind, she focused on the Wiley children, still sitting on the bench.

"Gather your tool of choice," she ordered the quartet. "Who wants to have fun today?"

"I do!" Olivia laid her doll on the bench, dashed forward, and grabbed a shovel with a handle taller than she was, even though she also had the choice of three smaller shovels.

The two older boys, Alexander and Dante, exchanged glances, then chose rakes.

The youngest, Thaddeus, stayed on the bench. "I'm starving."

Of course he was. At six, Thaddeus had eschewed most of the breakfast Zoe had prepared for the Wileys in lieu of the day-old biscuits Mr. Gunderson had baked. Mrs. Wiley had insisted her children would trade labor for food. Once they finished consuming their *omelettes aux pommes* and potato cakes stuffed with trout, the Wiley quartet's enthusiasm for helping cultivate the garden lacked much luster. The only thing so far that had elicited any response besides apathy was when Alexander said the word *poop*.

Zoe refocused on young Thaddeus Wiley. He sat on the end of the bench, swinging his legs and looking as if he wished to be anywhere but there. "Zere is a remaining trout inside for you to eat," she offered to appease him. "Would you like me to warm ze lemon-butter sauce?"

He shrugged.

She looked to his brothers.

They shrugged, too.

His sister dragged the shovel to where Zoe stood. In a soft voice, Olivia said, "Thaddy only listens to Mr. Gunderson."

Zoe looked at Alexander and Dante, who both nodded, and then at Thaddeus. "You may go find your mother."

Thaddeus dashed to the back door leading to the kitchen.

Zoe glanced up to the second-floor window of what she believed was the master bedroom. As she hoped, Mrs. Wiley was still cleaning the window.

Mrs. Wiley waved.

Zoe waved back, then focused on the three remaining children. "First, we must cull all ze weeds and ze grass. I will begin in ze center. You will start on ze outsides. After we have broken up ze soil, we will work in ze compost and manure. When we are finished, we will wash our hands and eat lamb's stew, and zen you can help me crush ze fruit for ze marmalades I must make."

"Uh, Miss de Fleur?"

She looked at Alexander. "Yes?"

"*The Gardeners' Monthly* said a garden needs old poop." As Dante and Olivia snickered again, Alexander tossed his rake back onto the pile of gardening tools. "I'll run over to Vaughn's Seed Store. Do you think one bag of their finest manure will be enough?"

"For a garden zis grand—" Zoe thought for a moment. "I wager Mr. Vaughn knows how much Mrs. Pawlikowski usually purchases." She looked to Alexander. "Better to take ze wheelbarrow."

"Yes, ma'am!" He slapped his brother's shoulder.

"I'll go, too," Dante blurted out. "Have fun, Ollie!"

Olivia waved vigorously. "Bye!"

Before Zoe could explain to Dante why the task only required Alexander's attention, the boys dashed around the greenhouse.

"Why did zey both leave?" she asked Olivia.

"They only listen to Mr. Gunderson."

Zoe studied the seven-year-old, who now chewed on the middle of one of her waist-length auburn braids. Surely all children were not as peculiar as these four.

The Resale Co.

"Thanks for the warning, Vaughn. I owe you." Isaak hung up the phone.

Zoe was supposed to be canning citrus marmalades this morning for the welcome-home dinner. Canning! Not cultivating Ma's garden. Why buy manure? There were bags on the east side of the greenhouse—bags he'd purchased in February, when, according to Ma's stated preference, Jakob should have cultivated the garden.

Instead, Miss de Fleur had sent Alex and Dante to Vaughn's. Unless the boys had lied and gone on their own.

An all-too-likely scenario.

Isaak pushed away from his desk, grabbed his hat, and strode out of his office. "Emilia, I need to go rescue—" What was Madame Lestraude doing in here? He stopped next to Emilia who held a paper-wrapped package to her chest. Did she know Mac had revealed the truth about Finn in Isaak's office three days ago?

Until he knew for certain, Isaak wasn't taking any chances. He offered the madam the same genial smile he gave to all his customers. "Good morning, Madame Lestraude. You're looking ever the proud mother-in-law."

The corner of her painted mouth indented. "That I am,

which is why I brought Emilia my gift instead of sending it with my new delivery boy. Good lad. Some things, though, can't be entrusted to others." Her gaze fell to Isaak's loosened tie and unbuttoned shirt collar. "You're looking ever the politician."

Isaak tipped his chin. Uncle Jonas had warned him that Lestraude offered exclusives to all the politicians and judges in Montana and the surrounding states and territories. If Isaak had the authority, he would shut down her *Maison de Joie*, and all the brothels in Helena, which was why she vehemently politicked on Mayor Kendrick's behalf.

"It would be worthwhile for you to pay me a visit sometime." She looked at him as if she were sincere. "I hear the Forsythes are besotted with that household cook your brother is courting."

"Chef," Isaak corrected.

"Ah yes," she said with a brisk wave of her bejeweled hand. "We can all agree, a beautiful French chef is always worth more than her weight in gold. I doubt the Forsythes, Doc Abernathy's Book of Wagers, or even Miss de Fleur herself realize how *valued* she is. I, on the other hand, have no need for a French chef."

Isaak tensed. Lestraude had never crossed The Resale Co.'s threshold before, and nothing would convince him it had anything to do with a package delivery or with complimenting Miss de Fleur. Lestraude was trying to convey something indirectly. But what?

He took a moment to consider his answer. "I'll be sure to let her know."

To his surprise, Lestraude volleyed no mocking retort.

He stepped around Emilia. "Ladies, if you'll excuse me, I need to run an errand." With that, he slapped his hat on his head and strolled to the propped-open front door.

Isaak had one foot outside when he heard Emilia say, "What was that all about?"

"It's best, dear, if you don't know. I'm looking for anything a fourteen-year-old boy would enjoy reading."

"Try Jules Verne. Second bookshelf from the left, middle shelf."

Isaak glanced over his shoulder at Lestraude. Without looking his way, she strolled over to the stairs leading to the loft bookshelves. Whatever the madam was up to was no concern of his . . . until he was duly elected mayor and he could shut down her repugnant business.

Only, what if running her brothel provided the perfect ruse for rescuing girls?

Isaak frowned. He'd need to think more on that later. Right now he had a more pressing problem to fix.

He headed west in the direction of the house, his chest pounding. He was the only one who could handle the three Wiley boys.

Oliva Wiley would adore Miss de Fleur. The boys—Isaak knew their capabilities.

While Miss de Fleur was smart and clever, those boys would use her gentleness against her. She was too gracious, too lenient, and too tenderhearted for her own good.

And beautiful, which wasn't relevant.

Although his molars ached from gritting his teeth yesterday while trying *not* to stare at her beauty.

Isaak picked up his pace. He and Jakob had left the house at seven-thirty that morning because Miss de Fleur was to begin making marmalades for the welcome-home dinner at eight when Sarah Wiley arrived—which she'd clearly done with her children in tow.

He darted across the street.

The Wiley children—Alex and Dante, at least—would run roughshod over Miss de Fleur. Their mother had to be behind this: Find a meek and malleable person to tend to her children so she wouldn't have to. Twice now, Sarah Wiley had manipulated Miss de Fleur.

That was why, with hat in hand, he was running up the street to his home at nine forty-five when he ought to be at The Resale Co.

As he slowed to a jog along the pebbled path by the house, the earthy smell of warm dirt greeted him. Isaak stopped at the picket fence.

And then he saw her.

Right palm turned up, Zoe knelt in the garden wearing a well-worn apron and a baggy calico dress, her straw bonnet shielding her face from view. Thad and Olivia knelt next to her, staring intently at whatever was in her gloved palm. She said something to them. They nodded and took turns touching whatever was in her hand.

She turned her head and saw him. Her smile stole the breath from his lungs.

He should have stayed at work.

"Mr. Gunderson!" Olivia exclaimed, to the piercing dismay of Zoe's right ear.

As Olivia and her brother dashed off to hug Mr. Gunderson's legs, Zoe gave her head a good shake to lessen the ringing. She slid the worm back into the dirt, then stood and looked at Mr. Gunderson. His jaw tightened. Oh, the action was minuscule, but she noticed how he now stood more stiffly, like when he was about his business. Not relaxed. Not at ease, even though Olivia and Thaddeus clung to his legs like husks around corn. Something worried him.

Zoe gasped, her heart pounding. "Did something happen to Jakob or the Forsythes? Or—" She drew in a slow, calming breath. "Is it Nico?" She had yet to see him since his last failure to meet Jakob.

Mr. Gunderson's head shook. "Vaughn called to say Alex

and Dante stopped by the store," he said in that direct, this-is-the-problem-at-hand voice of his.

"Zat is why you are here?" Zoe waited for further explanation. When none came, she said, "Zey went to ze seed shop for manure for your mother's garden."

Mr. Gunderson removed Olivia and Thaddeus from his legs. "Run inside and see if your mother needs help." Then he strolled to where Zoe stood in the middle of the fractionally cleared garden and, after gripping her gloved hand, led her along the greenhouse's south side to where a pile of manure bags and a pile of soil bags were stacked up against the brick wall. "Anything my mother's garden needs is here. Or in the shed. Or in the greenhouse."

"Yes, but—"

"Or three blocks away," he continued, "at The Import Company, working to ensure that all is ready in time for the grand opening." He released his hold on her hand. "This is Jakob's job, not yours."

Zoe responded to his brisk tone with a gentle, "If I were your mother—or even your brother—I would feel much love zat someone cared enough to cultivate ze garden for me because I had no time to do it myself."

"Jakob's had the time. He still has the time!"

"Zere is no need to yell."

His mouth opened, then closed, and then, in a moderate voice, said, "You're already doing enough for Jakob."

Zoe raised her chin. "I am doing no more for him zen I am doing for you."

He regarded her with a look that said, *I disagree with that statement, and as soon as I think of a suitable response to prove you're wrong, I will make it.*

Zoe merely smiled. She knew she was right . . . and knew he knew it, too.

He growled. "You're just like my father."

"Zen I know I will like him."

He blinked several times. "The point is, the next time Jakob or Sarah Wiley or *anyone* asks something of you, you will say no. You need to stop allowing people to obligate you into doing something you don't wish—or have the time—to do."

She looked at him in disbelief. "Isaak Gunderson, you have no right to tell me what I can or cannot do. I have everything under control."

Shock—or perhaps something in the lesser vein of surprise—at her outburst flickered in his eyes, and then it was gone. "You don't know how the Wiley children can be."

She touched his arm. "You worry for no reason." His brows rose, so she added, "I am providing food today in exchange for ze children's labor. I brought everything I need to cook both meals. If zey do not work, zey will not eat."

"You're cooking for them?"

"Papa said food can motivate a king to go to war."

"It can." His hand rested on the middle of her back, and he nudged her into walking. "What are you bribing them with?"

"Zis morning we had omelets, fried trout stuffed between potato cakes, and a lemon-butter sauce. Later we will enjoy lamb stew, fresh baked rolls, and—

He groaned. "Stop. Please, stop. I don't want to hear what I'm missing." As they neared the garden, he checked his pocket watch. "I need to get back to work."

"You want to." The words slipped out before she thought the better of them. But because they had been said, Zoe decided to go on. "Going back to work is a want, something you choose to do, not something you *need* to do."

He looked at her intently. "I *have* to go. Obligation, not want. Emilia is there alone."

"Zis is true." She sighed. "Zere is also a telephone in ze

house. You could call over zere and tell her to close ze shop. She may enjoy Saturday with her husband. Zey are newly-weds, yes?"

"But *I'm* not a newlywed, and I have a business to run."

"You are a dutiful manager."

He scowled. "What's that supposed to mean?"

Zoe stepped to the pile of gardening tools. She probably should have answered him immediately, but his arrival had put her in a cheeky mood, so she knelt and took her time examining the tools. She selected one and stood. With faux gravity, she said, "It means you must decide if you *want* to return to work where zere is no lamb stew, fresh rolls, and apple-raisin tarts with ze flakiest crust you will have ever tasted or if you *need* to."

One corner of his mouth lifted. "I'm fairly certain that's not what being a dutiful manager means."

As hard as she tried not to smile, she failed. Who knew she would have fun teasing him? "I am fairly certain zat what you will find at work will not be as enjoyable as what is here."

He glanced at the house and then back at her. "As much as I could agree with you, Miss de Fleur, there's the fact that I will find no children at work."

Zoe shrugged. "I see no children here."

"Oh, they'll be back. Trust me."

"How do you know?"

"Because you're here, and that's why my house is where they'll find the best food this side of the Mississippi."

"Zis is true." She stepped until she was right in front of him. Smiling—and ignoring the curious increase to her pulse—she offered him the hoe. "Take it."

"Why?"

"You need to work less and have fun a little more."

"Gardening?"

She nodded. "People call you Mr. Gunderson because zey

see you as a benevolent king reigning over his subjects. Zey follow your lead because zey know you care. And you believe zis is all you are. A man with responsibilities. You can be Mr. Gunderson all day, every day. Or you take a holiday from ze job and ze expectations and just be Isaak." She gave him a flirtatious grin. "I will feed you."

"Apple-raisin tarts?"

"I will make extra for you to enjoy tomorrow."

He gripped the hoe's wooden handle just above where she still held it. "I'll stay . . . but *only* because you don't realize yet how much you need me to help you wrangle the Wiley children."

"Zat sounds like an excuse to escape work." His mouth opened, and in case he was about to change his mind, she hastily said, "Nevertheless, it is also one I will accept." She released the hoe, swiveled around, and as she walked to the overgrown garden, snatched up a rake. She stopped in the garden's middle. Although her heart pounded fiercely, she glanced his way.

"Isaak?"

"Yes?"

"I zink I can *wrangle*, as you call it, rambunctious children *and* grown men just fine."

Chapter Nineteen

Wednesday afternoon, April 25
De Fleur-Gunderson Courtship Contract, Day 47

Isaak ran the entire eight blocks to The Import Co. He shouted, and the crowd gathered around the door parted like the waters of the Red Sea. He slowed to bypass them and cross into the store, shutting the door behind him. Splotches of white paint spilled down the walls, over wooden crates awaiting unboxing, and puddled on the floor. Isaak's nostrils stung at the fumes, making it difficult to catch his breath. "Jake? Where are you? Are you okay?"

"Iz?" Jakob's voice came from a distance. Footsteps thudded overhead, then down the stairs. He hustled into the retail space. "How did you hear?"

"O'Leary barged into The Resale Company, shouting that you'd been vandalized."

Jakob nodded. "He was here when I returned from lunch. He must have gone straight to you."

Isaak swung his hand to encompass the dripping mess. "Any idea who did this?"

"None, but I must have just missed whoever it was."

Jakob rubbed the back of his neck. "I was only gone for twenty minutes."

"Did you send someone to fetch Marshal Valentine?"

"No! I stood here wringing my hands, waiting for you to come tell me what to do."

Isaak bit back a retort. Watching the Wiley children bicker while they cultivated Ma's garden had been an eye-opener. The metaphorical slap had come when Miss de Fleur said the children were as snippy with each other as he and Jakob were.

Jakob rubbed his forehead with the heel of his hand. "Sorry. I'm not angry at you, it's just . . ."

When he didn't continue, Isaak stepped closer and put an arm around his brother's shoulder. "It's just what?"

"You'll say it's irresponsible."

Isaak dropped his arm. Was he really so overbearing, demanding work without relief? Memories of gardening with Miss de Fleur and the Wiley children rushed back. After taking the afternoon off, he'd felt refreshed in body and spirit. There was something to be said for balancing work with relaxation . . . and apple-raisin tarts. "Whatever it is, Jake, I promise I'm not going to pull my big-brother act on you."

Jakob raised his head, his blue eyes searching for any hidden message. "You mean that, don't you?"

Isaak tamped down irritation at having his veracity questioned. "Would I have said it otherwise?"

After another searching glance, Jakob took a deep breath. "I'm supposed to be going to dinner and then *Romeo and Juliet* with Zoe, Yancey, Carline, Geddes, and Windsor tonight. I don't think I can make it now and stay on schedule."

Shocked by Windsor Buchanan's anticipated attendance at the theater—to see *Romeo and Juliet*, no less—and Jakob's worry over keeping to a schedule, Isaak chose to respond to the latter. "I can take over here. I just need to—"

"No," Jakob interrupted. "I need to take care of this."

"What about the play?"

"Can you take Zoe instead of me?"

Yes! No! I shouldn't. "If you're sure . . ."

Jakob's eyes glinted with a speck of humor. "Would I have said it otherwise?"

Isaak chuckled at the repetition of his own question. Common sense pricked his conscience, prompting him to say, "I don't mind taking care of this." Not true, though it needed to be.

"No, but thanks for the offer, Iz. The Import Company is my responsibility."

The words, *I'm proud of you for doing the mature thing*, sat on Isaak's tongue, but to utter them would sound patronizing. Nor was it wise to throw stones at his brother when his own adherence to strict schedules and timelines was shifting.

A commotion outside drew their attention. Through the window, Isaak saw Marshal Valentine push through the crowd still gathered around as though they would be invited to view the vandalism the same way they would the store during the grand-opening celebration set for next weekend.

Jakob met them at the door. As he and the city marshal talked, Isaak slipped out the back. His brother had this well in hand. The best thing he could do was leave.

Besides, he was going to the theater with Zoe tonight. He needed to go home to make sure his dress shirt was ironed.

Deal's Boardinghouse

Despite the fact that she stood next to the warm cookstove, in a green-and-black silk gown more suited for an opera house than a kitchen, Zoe licked the last bit of soup from the spoon. The sweetness of the tomatoes flowed effortlessly with the beef stock.

Thank the good Lord above for Mrs. Deal's friendship with her neighbor, Mrs. Hess, who had more canned goods in her larder than Zoe had ever seen in one. Thank the good Lord above also for Mrs. Hess's willingness to trade.

"Zis is perfect tomato soup." Even from tomatoes canned last year. Zoe gave the tasting spoon back to Mrs. Deal. "Mr. Deal will be pleased you have mastered his favorite dish."

Mrs. Deal's brown eyes grew teary. "I thought I was a culinary failure. The lessons you've given me have done wonders, enabling me to reduce food expenses by half."

Zoe acknowledged the compliment with a simple nod of her head. It saddened her to know a well-to-do French family, even without a household cook, could live on what Mrs. Deal had been discarding because of improper storage, overpurchasing that led to spoilage, and ignorance of how to use seasonal purchases in multiple recipes. Good cooking was less about costly produce and meats and more about knowing how to compound a good and palatable dish from a limited larder.

Not that the dear woman had any canning skills.

That, though, was something Mrs. Hess could teach Mrs. Deal, and would now that Mrs. Deal, admirably, had found the courage to admit to her friend that she needed help.

Zoe turned to the rectangular pan resting atop the cookstove. "Let us taste ze biscuits." She waited patiently for Mrs. Deal to find two forks. The biscuits looked as perfectly baked as the spongy sweetbread Mrs. Deal had served during lunch.

Mrs. Deal cut into a corner biscuit. "For years I've told Mr. Deal that my cooking is the reason we have so many vacancies. Today is the first day ever that the men's side is full of boarders." She handed Zoe a forked piece of biscuit. "Word has spread about the meal you prepared for Lily Forsythe and about the lessons you've given me. The prices you could charge—"

"I have no wish to find employment," Zoe cut in.

"Then what do you want to do?"

"I want to be a wife and a mother."

Mrs. Deal smiled sweetly. "Jakob Gunderson is a blessed man."

Zoe nodded, wishing she felt more joy over Mrs. Deal's words. *Wait out the contract, and I recommend you don't share this with my wife* had been Judge Forsythe's advice Monday when she had stopped by his office after praying about Isaak's advice to seek parental wisdom. If Jakob had noticed Zoe had been keeping her distance, he had yet to say anything. All she had to do was make it through tonight, the welcome-home dinner the day after tomorrow, and the next thirteen days without him falling in love with her.

And then they could end the contract as friends.

Because things would be harmonious between her and Jakob and because Isaak was now her friend, she had no reason to leave Helena. She had friends. She had family in the Forsythes. For the first time since her childhood, she had a home.

Tomorrow she would find Nico and accept his offer to look for a house to purchase.

"Oh, dear," Mrs. Deal muttered. "I did something wrong. What is it you see that I don't?"

Realizing Mrs. Deal had assumed the worst from Zoe's silence, she quickly tasted the biscuit. The moment the flaky layers touched her tongue, she uttered an elongated, "Mmm." She returned the fork to Mrs. Deal. "You did nothing wrong. Good flour makes a better bread."

"You've said that repeatedly but haven't explained how I tell if the flour is good." While her words were clipped, Zoe knew they were not intended as a slight. In the last seven weeks of getting to know Mrs. Deal, Zoe had discovered how direct the woman was. And how benevolent and open to instruction.

"Place some flour in your hand, zen press your palms

together." Zoe mimicked the action. "Good flour will adhere and show ze imprint of ze lines of ze skin. Good flour tint is also cream white. Poor flour may be blown away with ease and appears dull, as though mixed with ashes."

"So it'll look dingy?" Mrs. Deal supplied.

"Dingy?"

"Dull. Like when water has sediment in it."

"Dingy," Zoe repeated. She liked the sound of it. "Zat is a good description."

The kitchen door opened. Mr. Deal stepped inside. "Mr. Gunderson is here."

"You mean Jakob."

Mr. Deal shook his head. "Isaak Gunderson is here. Is there a problem?"

There had to be one, or Jakob would be here to take her to the theater.

Mrs. Deal touched Zoe's arm. "If you ever feel things aren't working out with Jakob, Mr. Deal and I have friends all over this part of the territory who would pay richly to employ a ravishing French chef. Go on, dearie." Mrs. Deal motioned her forward. "I won't hug you and risk messing up your beautiful gown."

Zoe strolled to the kitchen door.

"I know I'm not your father," Mr. Deal said, "but if you need one, I'm here for—" His voice choked. "You're worth more than gold to me." He smiled a little as he opened the kitchen door for her.

"Zank you." Zoe stepped into the dining hall, where fourteen men sat at the two tables awaiting dinner. All stood. They smiled, as she had come to learn, in hopes of garnering her attention. She always strove to be polite in her response. This time she ignored them in light of how delighted she felt about Isaak's escort instead of Jakob's. Isaak made her laugh. He enjoyed silence, although not as much as she did.

Best of all, he knew how to manage Yancey and Carline and their constant chatter.

With a friend by her side, the evening would be bearable after all.

Isaak stood by the door, as handsome as ever in his black Sunday suit. Her ebony silk-and-lace cape lay draped over his arm, instead of over the chair where she had left it before going into the kitchen. He seemed as pleased to see her as she felt upon seeing him.

"Your carriage awaits," he said with a slight bow as she neared.

She stopped in front of him. "Where is your brother?"

"At work."

"Oh?"

"Someone vandalized the store. It'll take all night for him to repair to stay on schedule. He asked me to give you his regards."

"I am"—*partially*—"sorry he will miss ze play, but I am also happy to see you." She rested her palm against his exquisite green damask waistcoat and felt him tense, so she drew back. "Zis is nice you had something to match. Did Jakob tell you ze color of my gown?"

"Coincidental" was all he said.

Zoe studied Isaak's face as he reached around her to rest her cape across her shoulders, covering her green-and-black evening gown, the last dress Papa had purchased for her before they left Paris for America. When she had resisted the purchase, he had argued she would need it someday.

It had been worn twice, counting tonight.

Isaak's gaze settled on hers. At the curve of his lips, a strange, breathless, swirling feeling warmed her more than the cape about her shoulders.

"Zank you," she said and started to tie the cape's ribbon.

"Here, let me." As he knotted the ribbon at the base of her neck, she caught a whiff of his bergamot cologne.

It suited him. Why had she never noticed his cologne before? Perhaps this was his first time wearing it. Because of Carline? Or perhaps he favored Yancey. Both ladies were joining them for supper and the play. Those times Zoe had seen him talk to either lady, no time stood out as unusual. Or romantic.

But in one night, everything could change.

Not with Isaak, her heart whispered.

Jakob was fickle; Isaak was dependable. If he was going to fall in love with Carline or Yancey, he would have already done so. He had not, because he knew he needed someone who would make him sniff flowers and admire sunsets. He needed gentleness. He needed tender strength to tell him when he was wrong.

With one hand, he opened the door. With the other, he touched the middle of her back and nudged. "Move along," he whispered, his minty breath warm against her cheek. "We're already late."

Zoe froze. His hand flinched; the movement was small, yet she felt the tingle it caused rise up her spine.

"Zat is because *you* arrived late," she said in her defense.

"That's because I struggled over whether I should convince Jakob to trade places with me. I could have done his work for him."

"Why did you not?"

When he failed to answer, she turned her head enough to see him. The moment their gazes met, her breath caught. Her whole being sparked to life with joy and with hope . . . and with a mind as full of clear understanding as was in her heart.

The person he needed in his life was her.

He needed her.

And she needed him.

Stunned, Zoe dashed to the Forsythe carriage, blinking away her sudden tears. She was never supposed to fall in love with Isaak Gunderson. She was supposed to love Jakob and his happy eyes.

Not Isaak.

Never was it supposed to be Isaak.

He was her friend. He was only supposed to be her friend.

Without a word, he helped her into the carriage. "The Palmer house," he called out to the driver before climbing in.

Zoe scooted to the far-left side of the bench. She faced forward, not turning her head to look up at him, not wishing to risk him seeing the emotions in her eyes. Isaak sat in the far corner of the backward-facing bench. Diagonally opposite.

The carriage lurched forward.

He turned from the window to look at her. "You seem distraught. Is something wrong?"

"I am unsure."

"Do you want me to go trade places with Jakob?"

She wanted to say yes. Her heart needed time to rest from the sudden tumult of realizing she was in love with him. But to say yes would be a lie. She abhorred lies.

"I wish for you to stay."

"Zoe, I . . ."

"Yes?" She waited for him to finish his thought. She needed to know what he was thinking and feeling because she needed him to be alive and imperfect. To be real. To be hers.

"I'd like to stay, too." He paused. "It's not like tonight will last forever."

"It never does."

Isaak said nothing more, and Zoe turned her attention on the window, hoping they would reach the Palmer residence quickly. Yancey and Carline, like Jakob, could be counted on to add joviality and distraction to a gathering.

Chapter Twenty

Ming's Opera House

Zoe stopped in awe on the threshold, gasping just inside Mr. and Mrs. Forsythe's box, where two additional chairs had been added to accommodate their group of six. Brass railing. Red leather seats. Elaborate draperies framed and hid the stage. At this level, they would have a perfect view of the sets and performers, and even of the Helena Orchestra in the pit below. Surely the spectacle of it all would atone for tonight's pedestrian play.

Perhaps this English version would be better than the French translation she had seen with Papa. If not, based on the warm and lush sounds of the orchestra tuning their instruments, at least the music would be enjoyable.

Isaak's hand rested on the middle of her back, as it had at the boardinghouse. There was nothing inappropriate or possessive in his action. He was merely being polite, she knew. But upon every touch, the tingles returned to race up her spine. And then her neck and face warmed.

Was she blushing? She hoped not.

"Miss de Fleur, your propensity to block entrances is a problem," he said before nudging her farther into the box.

Zoe stepped to the left, annoyed as much by his criticism and bossiness as his exotic cologne. Mostly, she was content to wait for everyone else to choose seats first. Including him. Her plan was to sit on the other side of the box from Isaak Gunderson, so she would not be distracted by his presence.

Isaak, to her surprise, did not seek out a chair. Instead, he moved to her side, maintaining a polite distance behind her left shoulder. "Ladies, take the front row," he ordered their group. "The gentlemen will sit behind."

Carline and Yancey thanked him as they slid past. Yancey, in her exquisite violet gown, settled in the front middle chair and Carline, in a rose-pink gown, took the right one, leaving the one on the left for Zoe. They rested their fans in their laps and immediately started talking. Mr. Geddes Palmer sat behind his sister. Mr. Windsor Buchanan sat in the chair behind Carline, leaving the two far left seats for Zoe and Isaak.

He motioned toward the empty front seat. "You're next."

She looked to where Carline and Yancey were huddled close.

Tonight is a night for falling in love, Yancey had proclaimed the moment the carriage had arrived at the opera house. Why had she said that? Carline, not Yancey, was the one to make rash pronouncements. For someone as outgoing and talkative as Yancey Palmer was, she was also impressively circumspect.

Yancey could have noticed something in how Zoe had looked at Isaak in the carriage. Equally possible was that Yancey and Carline had plans they had failed to share with Zoe. To match Isaak and Carline?

Zoe studied Carline's flaxen hair, pinned in a simple bun. Everything about the beautiful woman was understated. Even her pink silk gown was modest and unadorned. Carline would be a benefit to Isaak and his election campaign.

Having lived all her life in Helena, Carline was well-suited to be the wife of Helena's next mayor.

Thinking of her marrying Isaak caused an ache in Zoe's chest.

Mr. Gunderson the mayor needed a wife like Carline, but Isaak the man needed a wife like Zoe.

"It's warm in here," grumbled Mr. Buchanan. He stood. The bladesmith removed his suitcoat, draped it over the back of his chair, rolled up his sleeves, and—

Zoe felt her eyes widen. Goodness, the man's forearms bulged with muscles and scars. And he wore two knives sheathed on the back of his hips. At the opera! Not that he needed anything to make him more intimidating. Or physically impressive.

Carline should focus her flirtations on him.

A strange noise came from Isaak.

Zoe looked over her shoulder. "What was zat?" she whispered.

"What was what?" he whispered back.

"I heard you grunt."

"I saw you ogling Windsor."

"What does zis 'ogling' mean?"

"Looking at him."

"Why would my looking at your friend cause you to grunt?"

"You were drooling."

Zoe touched her lips. "Zere is no drool. Stop scowling at me."

"I will once you stop casting amorous glances at Windsor."

"Amorous?" She coughed a breath. "It is impolite to grunt when ladies can hear." And because his eyes narrowed in response to her chastisement of his poor manners, she added, "Nor is it your business at whom I cast amorous glances."

"So you admit you were," he said with the startling smoothness of a man confident of the rightness of his opinion.

Her cheeks warmed. "Mr. Gunderson, I admit zat if I wish to admire someone, I will, but I was not admiring Mr. Buchanan. I was zinking Carline should flirt with him."

"Carline likes Geddes."

"She does?" Zoe whirled around to see that Mr. Buchanan had settled back down on his chair and was speaking to Mr. Palmer. Neither seemed happy to be there. Neither seemed romantically drawn to Carline. Although both men would make exceptional suitors for her.

Far better than Isaak.

A throat cleared.

Zoe peeked over her shoulder again to see Isaak watching her with an expression of pained tolerance. "I was zinking," she admitted.

"I could tell." His head cocked a little to the left, and he blinked, as if suddenly realizing something. "You think more and talk less than any woman I know."

She parted her lips, intent on defending her penchant for silent thinking, but as he continued to look at her as if she were an oddity, she closed her mouth and returned her gaze to the four other people in the box.

Zoe moistened her lips. "I suppose I should sit."

"What an innovative idea," Isaak whispered, his voice near her ear. His hand rested again on her lower back, and with a familiar gentle nudge—

"It is warm in here, is it not?" Zoe blurted out. Realizing how true her words were, she untied the black ribbon at the neckline of her lace cape.

"Let me help." Isaak removed it from her shoulders.

"Zank you." Zoe turned to take her cape from him. A mistake, because he stood closer to her, almost as if she was in his embrace.

His throat cleared. "We should sit."

"Sit?"

He motioned toward the empty chairs. "Before they notice and wonder why we aren't. Sitting," he said abruptly. "With them."

"Of course." She snatched her cape from his hold, then found solace—and comfort—on the chair next to Yancey, who immediately studied Zoe, then Isaak.

Her blue eyes narrowed. "All right, Isaak, what mean thing did you say to Zoe this time?"

"He said nothing," Zoe blurted out in his defense.

Yancey coughed a breath. "Hell hath no fury like Isaak Gunderson's icy stares."

"Drop it, Yancey," was all he said. More like grumbled.

"Someone is in a foul mood," Yancey quipped, and then turned around to face her brother. "Geddes, would you trade with me?"

"You *want* to sit by Isaak?"

"Of course not." She grimaced at the brass railing. "Unfortunately, I don't think I can sit this close without—" She covered her mouth and cringed.

Zoe turned her head enough to watch the play of emotions on Mr. Palmer's face. Confused and annoyed, to be sure. Yet the considerate man complied with his sister's request. Why was Geddes Palmer still a bachelor? Not that his reason was any of Zoe's business. But he was a kind man, a good listener, and not one to demand his own way. Much like Papa had been.

Carline likes Geddes.

Zoe smiled in remembrance of Isaak's words.

Yancey sat in the chair between Isaak and Mr. Buchanan. She smoothed the lap of her dress. "Perfect. And we"—she leaned forward and touched Carline's shoulder—"can still talk."

Carline shifted in her chair. "But my neck already hurts

turning around to hear you." She smiled at Mr. Buchanan, who sat directly behind her. "Windy, trade with me."

He stayed silent for a long moment before saying, "No."

"Must you always be so cantankerous?"

"I must."

Carline's loud gasp sucked the air out of the box. "I don't know why I keep trying to be nice to you."

"You may stop any—"

"Windsor," Yancey warned. "What is with you men tonight? Can't any of you be pleasant?"

Zoe jerked her attention back to the stage and ignored the lecture Yancey was giving to the men about manners. The only drama Zoe wished to be enchanted by was that from the orchestra. The lead oboe seemed exceptionally skilled. Was that a piccolo? She adored piccolos. She loved the high tone, the unique sound, and the utter happiness a piccolo provided in symphonic solos. If she played an instrument, she would play a piccolo. And a flute. They were too similar for her to choose one over the other.

"I'll trade seats." Isaak brushed against Zoe's arm as he slid between her chair and Mr. Palmer's. He leaned against the balcony railing, waiting for Carline to move.

Curious, Zoe turned her head enough to see Carline.

"I—uh . . ." The ever-confident Carline appeared unsure. "Of course. Thank you." She hurried to the seat behind Zoe. She touched Zoe's shoulder and Yancey's knee. "Wasn't that considerate of Isaak to afford us the closeness to talk?"

Zoe tensed. Talk? During the performance? Talking would hinder her from being able to hear the musicians. Talking occurred at intermission and after the performance. Not during. Never during.

Mr. Palmer, from what she could see, seemed enraptured with studying the playbill.

Isaak muttered something too softly for Zoe to hear.

"I agree." Mr. Buchanan leaned forward in his back-row,

right-side seat. He patted Mr. Palmer's shoulder. "Trade seats with me."

"Why?"

"She's *your* sister."

"Which is exactly why I prefer to stay in *this* seat."

"You owe me for distracting Miss Snowe," Mr. Buchanan countered.

Mr. Palmer groaned. Yet he stood. "This makes us even."

Zoe watched as the men switched seats, putting Mr. Buchanan directly in front of Yancey.

Before Zoe could silently celebrate the end of the chair exchanges, Yancey groaned loudly. "Oh, for goodness' sake, how am I supposed to see with this"—she motioned to the back of his head—"hairy mountain range in front of me?"

Isaak turned around in his front-row, right-side seat and scowled at Yancey. "This is why I said ladies sit in front."

"Why are you so snippy tonight?" she retorted. "This, Isaak, is why I don't enjoy social events with you"—she poked Mr. Buchanan's back—"or you."

That was all it took for Mr. Buchanan to turn around in his seat.

As he responded to Yancey, Zoe focused her attention on the black stage curtains. Occasionally, they would puff out, likely from someone bumping them. She noted that the gaslights on the walls matched those in the foyer and how the house attendants wore elegant coats, the same red as the leather seats and with brass buttons that matched the balcony railing. The opera house was styled after the circular plan used in European theaters and brimmed to capacity. A thousand people? Fifteen hundred?

Perhaps Mr. Buchanan would know the exact number of seats.

She looked to him to ask, but he was still turned around in his seat and engrossed in a glare showdown with Yancey.

Isaak gazed at Zoe, and all she could think of was the

rapid beating of her heart. Could he love her? She wanted to believe that was what she saw in his beautiful eyes. She loved him.

If he gave her any sign—any clue—he felt the same, she would happily run away with him.

Isaak shifted slightly in his chair. And then he looked away.

Zoe's chest tightened. What did his action mean? He reciprocated her feelings? Maybe it meant nothing at all. Maybe she wished for something not there. Her chest hurt. Love hurt.

The orchestra fell silent. A hush descended.

"Tell him to trade with me," came in a whispered voice.

From Yancey or Carline? Zoe was unsure and more than a bit annoyed. As much from their behaviors as from having to attend a play she had no desire to see because she disliked William Shakespeare. Mostly because she was in love with a man who seemed not to return her feelings.

"Geddes," someone whispered.

Zoe jumped to her feet, clenching her cape with her left hand. She turned around and pointed at Carline, and then at her own vacated chair in the front row. As Carline moved to Zoe's seat, Zoe motioned for Yancey to move to the left, to Carline's now-empty seat. Once Yancey obeyed, Zoe patted Mr. Buchanan's shoulder. He peered up at her. She flicked her gaze to the center chair in the back row, silently conveying her wish for him to move to Yancey's now-empty seat. He moved. After he settled into his new seat, Zoe focused on Isaak and Mr. Palmer in the first and second row, respectfully. Both leaned against the wall.

"Stay," she ordered.

Mr. Palmer nodded.

Isaak's gaze lingered on her face. Nothing in his expression indicated his thoughts or feelings. But then the corners of his mouth curved. Once his smile reached his eyes, she knew he was impressed with her actions.

A familiar warmth inched up her spine and spread through her body, causing her pulse to skip a beat. Fearful the others in the box would see what she felt for him in her eyes, Zoe claimed the seat between Carline Pope and Isaak. She straightened her shoulders, rested her cape and then her hands in her lap, and tried fruitlessly to look at the stage.

"Here we go," Yancey said in breathless anticipation.

Carline squealed in delight.

Sounds from the orchestra permeated the opera house. The gaslights on the stage brightened, and the curtains opened.

Isaak sat in the dark paying no attention to the performance on the stage. The conflict raging inside him surpassed the enmity between the Montagues and Capulets. The air inside the theater thickened. He inhaled but couldn't satisfy his need for oxygen.

He loved Zoe. Had loved her for weeks now, although he'd kept fighting it as a mere attraction because nothing about their relationship fit the way he'd always planned to court the woman of his choosing.

He almost laughed aloud at his arrogance, deciding beforehand when and how he would allow love into his life. His certainty that a reasonable person didn't trip and fall into love. His pity for Yancey because she'd set her sights on Hale when, with a little effort, she'd find any number of men who were suitable husbands. Then Zoe de Fleur arrived with both a shout and a whisper. Isaak understood Yancey's tenacity now. He knew in the deepest place of his soul that he belonged—would always belong—to Zoe de Fleur. God must be laughing in His heaven. *Pride goeth before a fall*.

Isaak stole a glance at her. She was enraptured by the

play, her lips parted and her chest rising and falling with rapid breaths. No artist's brush could ever capture what he saw. She was beautiful, yes, and so much more. Her gentle spirit urged him to soften his opinions. She'd talked him into slowing down to hear birds sing and to dig in the dirt. Her touch brought out the best in everything, from food to children.

He clawed his fingers into his knees, remembering how she'd confided in him that she ached for something more. He ached, too, in every joint and sinew holding his body in place.

I wish for you to stay.

Those six little words wreaked more havoc in his heart than when she'd called him Isaak last Saturday in the garden. He'd refrained from responding by calling her Zoe because it was a line he shouldn't cross, and yet he *had* crossed it less than an hour ago in the carriage.

Where was the line between love and duty? Between what he owed to himself and what he owed to honor? Because chasing after his brother's woman betrayed every code of decency.

Loving Zoe changed everything and nothing for him. If circumstances were different, he would pursue her until she fell in love with him, but what was the point? The only way they could be together was to run away—to turn his back on his family, the Widows and Orphans Fund, and his promise to make Helena a better place when he became mayor. But then what? A new job in a new town would be easy, but no woman should trust her heart to a man who gave up on his commitments.

Even if Zoe could, she valued family and harmony. Loving him in return would go against her gentle nature. She would never—*never*—make herself the cause of an irreconcilable rift between him and Jakob.

Isaak gripped his hands to keep from reaching over and wrapping an arm around her. To say without words how much he loved her. How much he wanted to protect her with his life.

He didn't know what he was supposed to do, and before, he'd always known the right and honorable course of action. *Always*.

Not now.

If only Jakob hadn't entered into that stupid contract. As usual, in thinking only of himself, his twin was making a mess for everyone around him while he skated off undamaged. Because, out of all the things Isaak didn't know, there was one he did.

His heart would vacate his chest if Zoe left Helena.

Chapter Twenty-One

By the time Lady Capulet and the Nurse beseeched Juliet to consider Paris's suit, Zoe accepted the strange and shocking truth: This dark, bawdy, and tragic play was *not* the one she had seen in Paris. Romeo and Juliet married in secret, without—not with—their families' blessings. Their families were enemies! Juliet's cousin Tybalt killed Romeo's cousin Mercutio, and then Romeo killed Tybalt. What was all this killing about? And friar Laurence? Like the Nurse, he was absent from the play she had seen. What possessed a friar to convince Juliet to "borrow death"?

Somewhere between Juliet's parents demanding she marry Paris and the friar delivering Juliet's eulogy, Zoe's tears began. They did not stop when the curtains darkened the stage.

Or when the orchestra fell silent.

Or when the applause died a death befitting poor Mercutio.

Zoe fought to collect herself as she stared at the tear-soaked handkerchief she clutched. Someone rubbed her shoulder in slow, circular motions. Carline, most likely, because she was sitting to Zoe's left.

"That was so romantic," Carline said in a dreamy voice.

Zoe stared at Carline. How could she view the play as romantic?

"You must have slept through the ending," Isaak said matter-of-factly. "The play is a tragedy, not a love story."

"You say that only because the hero and heroine died," Yancey argued.

"That's one reason," he replied. "The lords Capulet and Montague should have learned their lesson by play's end. Instead, they continued the feud, the same thing that led to Romeo and Juliet's deaths."

Carline stopped massaging Zoe's back. "I still think it's a love story."

"Me, too," Yancey put in.

A cough of breath came from Mr. Palmer.

Zoe turned around.

His gaze shifted back and forth between his sister and Carline. "You two do know you'll never convince Isaak to change his mind when he believes he's right?"

Carline and Yancey turned to Mr. Buchanan in hopeful support.

He held up his hands. "I'll always have Isaak's back."

"Zoe, what about you?" Carline asked.

Zoe dried her eyes with the handkerchief. What Romeo and Juliet felt for the other was infatuation, not love. Real love needed more than three days to develop. Real love was gracious and kind, while Romeo's "love" was envious, boastful, and dishonoring. Real love was patient. Infatuation led to hasty decisions. Marrying a man the day after meeting him epitomized haste. Marrying a person in secret epitomized selfishness. There had been enough quarreling tonight. Zoe would not add to it by pointing out the error of Carline's views. So instead, she offered a polite, "It was a nice performance."

"Surely you know what you liked," Carline argued in a

tone that implied Zoe should grow a backbone and stand up for what she thought.

Zoe stared at the handkerchief's black monogram: Isaak's. She had enjoyed the play far more than she expected to. Shakespeare's work should not be gutted of its potentially offensive elements, which she realized had been done to the performance she and Papa had seen in Paris. Amid the tragedy and moral ambiguity of the play, a warning could be found, which was why she stared at her lap and said nothing.

"Let's give Miss de Fleur a moment to collect herself," she heard Isaak say. "Geddes, take the ladies downstairs. We'll be down shortly."

"I'll have the carriage brought around," came from Mr. Buchanan.

Isaak uttered, "Thank you," and then another, "Thank you."

How long Zoe sat there, she knew not. The voices of those in attendance lightened as the hall emptied until the only other sounds she heard were muffled voices and the closing of music cases and an occasional door.

"Here."

She looked up. Isaak now sat in Carline's chair. Two white folded handkerchiefs lay in his outstretched palm.

"They're from Windsor and Geddes," he explained.

She took the top handkerchief, then laid the tear-soaked one atop the second one. She glanced around the box. Of course everyone had left. People always did what Isaak Gunderson asked them to do.

He folded the dry handkerchief over the wet one. He laid it on the chair Yancey had vacated. "If you need a shoulder, I have one you can borrow," he said, but she could tell by his lighthearted tone that the offer was nothing more than an attempt to be polite.

Zoe dried her wet cheeks. "I am not usually so . . . emotional."

"That's good to know."

She focused on the brass railing, unable to bear his scrutiny. She had never been easily moved to tears. Oh, she felt things. Sometimes she ached with loss, with heartbreak, with pride, joy, pity, loneliness, and even anticipation. When the tears came, she rarely succeeded in containing them. What she felt as the Montague and Capulet tragedy unfolded hurt terribly.

Grudges ruined families.

The welcome-home dinner was in two days.

Two days until she had to run away from Helena and the foolish de Fleur-Gunderson courtship contract.

Two days to hide her growing feelings from everyone she knew, especially Isaak. And Jakob. He could never know. The betrayal would crush him.

Zoe dried the last of her tears. "You need not feel obligated to sit with me," she said without looking Isaak's way. "I would prefer a moment alone."

"You need to talk."

Zoe shook her head. What was in her heart needed to stay *her* secret. As casually as she could, she stepped to the balcony wall to put needed distance between herself and Isaak. The lights in the opera house had dimmed. She gripped the railing, the brass cold against her skin.

"Please," Isaak said softly. "*I* need you to talk to me."

The entreaty in his tone drew her attention to him. Isaak Gunderson might not love her, but he certainly cared. For that, he deserved as much truth as her heart could bear sharing.

"I am fearful," she whispered.

"Of what?" Isaak sounded almost shy. This was not the Isaak Gunderson she knew—so confident, so in control of everything in his world. Nothing frightened him.

Though . . . maybe something did.

Zoe turned around. He was leaning forward, his elbows on his knees. And her chest tightened. "Of becoming my mother. *Maman* left Papa when I was nine to live in Italy with ze man she decided was the true mate to her soul. Every night, for years, Papa read First Corinthians before leading me in an evening prayer. He promised zat God would return *Maman* to us."

"She never returned."

Even though his words were a statement, Zoe responded with a small shake of her head. "Papa also promised one day I would find someone I would wish to spend ze rest of my life loving, as he loved *Maman* until his death."

"Have you found that someone?" Isaak asked in a painfully hoarse voice.

You, she wished to say.

And if she did, where would that lead them? She would never pit brother against brother. To the victor would go no spoils.

Better to leave now, before love had time to grow to full bloom.

"Would you . . . ?" He stared absently at the balcony, his lips moving as if searching for words. "Could you ever love a man who failed to live up to his commitments?"

"My heart would not be safe with"—*Jakob*—"such a man." Zoe released a weary breath. "I would never marry a man as fickle with his commitments as my *Maman* was with hers."

Isaak's hands were clenched so tightly, the whites of his knuckles showed. "You couldn't give him a second chance?"

"No. Zis play has confirmed zat Jakob and I are unsuited." The lack of feeling in her tone impressed—and saddened—her. "Once ze welcome-home dinner is over, I will discuss with him ze reasons why we should agree to end ze contract before ze agreed-upon sixty days." And then in a softer voice, she added, "It is as you said—ze contract was foolish of us."

"Once the contract is ended, will you return to Denver?" Isaak turned his head to meet her gaze.

She nodded. "Better to leave now before anyone's feelings grow too deep to be contained. I will have no one's heart crushed because of me. Jakob will understand. I hope you understood, too." She hated how heartbroken her voice sounded. The words hurt to say, hurt to feel.

Isaak was looking at her most intently, studying her, likely measuring her words and tone to determine if all she had shared had been the truth.

"We should go," he said abruptly.

Zoe nodded. She stepped forward and reached for her cape, but he swiped it away. His right hand captured her left one. She tried to pull away, but he held firm.

"For once in your life, oblige me."

"Zere is no need to hold my—"

And then, just like that, they stood there. Looking at each other. His lovely green eyes had darkened, and when his gaze lowered to her lips, Zoe's breath quickened and her legs quivered. It was a strange sensation, one she had never felt before. But Papa had warned her about it . . . and what would likely follow. A kiss.

She would let Isaak kiss her.

Oh, she would still leave Helena with a broken heart . . . and with the glorious memory of her first kiss.

She waited in anticipation.

He turned away. "The lights are off in the stairwell," he explained, leading her forward out of the box and toward the balcony stairs. "Stay close."

With her free hand, Zoe lifted the front of her skirts to keep from tripping as they descended the steps. "Isaak, please. I am capable of—" At his growl, she fell silent. While the lights were indeed out in the stairwell, those in the foyer provided ample viewing.

There, at the bottom of the stairs, stood Jakob.

With unhappy eyes.

The accusation in Jakob's eyes sent Isaak's temper flaring. Zoe tugged to free her hand, but Isaak stopped it by gripping her fingers and holding tight. He wasn't risking her well-being on account of Jakob. There'd been enough of that already.

When they'd descended the stairs, Isaak was surprised to see Windsor standing a few feet behind Jakob. "I thought you and Geddes took the carriage."

Windsor shook his head, his beard brushing against his chest. "I sent Geddes with the girls. I thought you might need some help." His gaze flickered toward Jakob.

Isaak led Zoe past Jakob and placed her hand on Windsor's arm. "Please see her back to Deal's Boardinghouse." In case Jakob planned to object, Isaak added, "I'm sorry the play upset you, Miss de Fleur. I hope you feel better in the morning."

She glanced back and forth between him and Jakob, her indecision evident. Windsor wrapped her arm around his and escorted her outside before she could utter a word.

Isaak turned around to face his brother. "Let's go home before we make a public spectacle."

Jakob fisted his hands. "Like you didn't already do that."

Clinging to his resolve to act like a gentleman by a solitary thread, Isaak looped his arm through Jakob's, pulling him toward the opera house doors.

Jakob yanked free. "I'm not a child who needs to be told what to do."

"Could have fooled me." The moment the words left his lips, Isaak wished he could take them back. Not because they weren't true, but because they would provoke Jakob.

Sure enough, his cheeks filled with splotches of red. "Am I about to hear another you're-so-irresponsible lecture? Because I'm tired of them."

"Then grow up," Isaak growled. "Think about the consequences of your actions before you embroil others in your messes."

"I just spent all day cleaning up a mess without embroiling you or anyone else, so don't pull that same trick out of your hat."

"That's not what I meant, and you know it. A little paint is nothing compared to the damage you've done by bringing Zoe to Helena."

Jakob reeled back for a punch, but Isaak was ready. He caught Jakob's fist with his open palm inches from his chin. They pitted their muscles against each other in a farcical arm-wrestling match.

Isaak exerted every ounce of strength to force Jakob's arm lower while leaning close to whisper, "Stop it, Jake. We're making a spectacle of ourselves."

"I think you already did that by cozying up to my girl in a theater box and holding her hand." Jakob stopped pushing against Isaak's fist.

Isaak lurched forward. Gasps from the theatergoers who remained in the lobby and were being treated to a second show of family rivalry snapped his last thread of patience. Isaak righted himself, his nostrils flaring when he saw the smirk on his brother's face. He tugged his coat back into place, grabbed Jakob by the arm—this time denying him the opportunity to pull free—and dragged him outside into the cool evening air.

The instant they were beyond the cluster of people waiting for carriages, Isaak let go. He strode across the street, his pace too fast for anyone but Jakob to keep up. When they were alone on Fourteenth Street, Isaak said, "You don't get to play the injured suitor when you're the one who asked me to escort Zoe tonight."

"Escort, not steal her away from me."

Thinking fast to cover how close the accusation came to the mark, Isaak stopped walking, forcing his brother to do the same. "Steal her away? You've all but ignored her since she came to town."

"Because the great Isaak Gunderson decreed that I had to follow his almighty schedule."

"Hogwash." Isaak slapped the back of his right hand into the palm of his left. "The schedule I made included plenty of time for you to go to dinner or attend the theater or do the thousand and one other things you'd rather be doing than work. You easily could have kept it and, using one-tenth of the famous Jakob Gunderson charm, made Zoe fall in love with you." Because, if she had, Isaak never—*never*—would have let himself picture a life with her. "But instead, you allowed yourself to be sidetracked by crooked ceiling tiles, the insignificant difference between one beige wallpaper and another, and whatever nonsense delayed the windows going in on time."

"You know what?" Jakob stuck his hands in the air as if he was surrendering. "I'm done trying to please you. I'm done trying to *be* you."

Isaak flinched. "Who has ever asked you to be me?"

"You!" Jakob stabbed a finger at Isaak's chest. "Every time you've given me one of your lectures or schedules or helpful hints on how I can do things better. I've had teachers, people at church, Uncle Jonas and Aunt Lily, and even Ma and Pa tell me what a fine example of a gentleman you are. It's their subtle way of saying that I should be just like you. I always come in second behind Isaak David Gunderson."

"Spoken as though I haven't heard similar praise about Jakob Matthew Gunderson. You have no idea how many times I've heard what a charmer you are, or how you light up a room just by walking into it. People think the moon and the stars hang on your wishes. It's how you get them to jump in the river with you before anyone has considered that there's a waterfall just around the bend. Amazing how you always get out of the boat just before it crashes. Everyone else is battered and bloody, but you walk away unscathed. You with your it'll-be-fun motto. Well, brother, you need to come up with a new adage to live by because no one is having fun right now."

"Meaning Zoe, I presume."

"How do you think she feels, having been brought to a strange city and forced to fend for herself?"

Jakob sneered and ran his eyes from Isaak's top hat to shined shoes. "Seems like she's made plenty of friends, and Aunt Lily has practically adopted her."

"Precisely my point." Isaak pivoted on his heel and marched toward their house. He waited for Jakob to catch up before continuing. "How do you think Aunt Lily is going to feel when Zoe leaves town?"

"What makes you think she's leaving town?"

Isaak snapped his lips together before he betrayed Zoe's confidence. Thinking fast, he rephrased her intention. "Do you think she's staying in Helena when your sixty days are up?"

"What makes you think I'm not going to propose?"

"Your inattention, combined with the fact that you haven't even told our parents about her yet. If you were seriously considering marriage, you would have sent a letter to one of the hotels on their itinerary. But no! Tomorrow, you're going to meet them at the train depot and say what? 'Welcome home. Meet Zoe. She's my mail-order bride, but don't get too attached because I'm returning her.'"

"Fine! I'll marry her."

Isaak stumbled to a stop, staring at his brother's retreating back. What had he done? This wasn't where he'd meant the conversation to go. "But you don't love her."

Jakob called out, "Since when have you ever thought love a necessary ingredient for a successful marriage?"

Blast Jakob and his sharp ears.

Waiting until his brother was way too far away to hear anything, Isaak whispered, "Since I met Zoe and fell in love."

Chapter Twenty-Two

As Zoe stepped on to the boardwalk in front of the board-inghouse, she felt awful. She had had naught but bits and snatches of sleep in the last night, the look on Jakob's face haunting her. She had tried on four dresses this morning before settling on this yellow-and-white-striped day dress, the only one she owned that did not accentuate the gloomy lavender circles under her eyes.

She should have had more than one coffee this morning, although Mrs. Deal said the way Zoe drank it, it had too much cream in it to still count as coffee.

With a sigh, Zoe headed west.

She would hide today . . . if it were not for the fact that she had another long day of cooking to be ready for tomor-row evening's welcome-home dinner.

But at least today she could avoid Mrs. Forsythe's curious looks and subtle questions about Jakob's courtship and when Zoe thought he would propose. Whereas Mrs. Forsythe was subtle, her husband was astute. One look at Zoe and the judge would see right into her heart.

If possible, she would leave on the first train on Saturday morning.

Leaving before anyone noticed she was gone depended on the train schedule.

Decision made, Zoe readjusted her grip on the basket of sweets she and Mrs. Deal had prepared to welcome Isaak and Jakob's parents home. The paper bags filled with *pistachios in surtout*, *nougat de Montélimar*, and *nougat de Provence* weighed down the basket. They need not have made the white and black nougats in addition to the sweetmeat, but the two nougats were part of the traditional thirteen desserts at a Provençal Christmas feast Zoe had helped Papa prepare every year since she reached her thirteenth year.

She would never cook Isaak a traditional French Christmas feast.

But she could leave him a taste of it.

Eyes blurring, she crossed the street, continued west, and ignored the ache in her heart.

Over rooftops, white plumes of smoke rose from newly stoked hearths. A chilly breeze likely reddened her cheeks on this, according to Mr. and Mrs. Deal, unseasonably cold April morning. Zoe disliked the cold, so it was good she was leaving. In two days.

For Denver.

For a new life.

For a time to forget about Isaak and what could have been were it not for his brother. Although were it not for his brother, she would never have met Isaak. Or fallen in love with him.

"Oh, ze irony," she murmured.

She paused at the next intersection, partially to admire the risen sun, partially for a trio of wagons to roll past. Even if the feelings she bore for Isaak had the potential to be true and deep and abiding, she refused to allow them to come between brothers. She refused to come between Jakob and Isaak. She would never ruin a family. The most loving thing she could do was to leave Helena. Broken hearts could heal.

Papa's never did, but she was not her papa. She would work away her feelings for Isaak. In time. Because she was hopeful and determined, unlike Papa, who never tried to stop loving *Maman*.

"Zoe, wait!"

She looked over her shoulder. Nico?

He raced down the block, hand gripping his newsboy cap, his arms pumping up and down as he ran. Why was he coming to her now? If he truly cared about her, he would have spent time with her. If he truly cared about her and their relationship, he would have met Jakob weeks ago. If Nico truly cared, he would have become involved in Zoe's life instead of staying on the breakfast-at-Deals' fringes.

Instead, he had made promises he never fulfilled.

And he lied. Too easily. Too readily.

Zoe sighed. She had tolerated Nico's behavior because she considered him her friend. In time, they could have grown as close as siblings, but he had used her to help him escape New York. He had used her to provide him free meals. She wanted to believe he could change. She had lost hope.

A means to an end.

Knowing that was how he saw her crushed her heart.

Nico stopped next to Zoe and bent over, hands on his knees to catch his breath.

"How are you zis morning?" she asked.

"All to the merry, I say." He regarded her, his face scrunching. "I went to the boardinghouse to meet you for breakfast, but Mrs. Deal said you'd left. Where are you heading at this time of day?"

"I have work to do."

He stood straight. "You have a job?"

"Ze Gundersons hired me to cater his parents' welcome-home dinner."

"When is it?"

"Tomorrow night. Zey arrive zis morning."

"Lemme get this straight. Your suitor and his brother, who is now your friend, *hired* you to cook for them?" The moment she nodded, his eyes narrowed and his head tilted as he asked, "How much are they paying you?"

"Zat is none of your business."

Nico's eyes widened. "Someone's testy. Is it because the Gunderson fellow hasn't yet asked you to marry him?"

Yes. No. The answer depended on which Gunderson the question referred to.

She chose to ignore the question. "What is it you want?"

"My employer gave me the day off," Nico said with a smile. "We ought to go do something together. I saw a couple of houses for sale in East Helena in that new addition Charlie Cannon is building. We should go find us one. Or we could go back to the boardinghouse and play chess. I'll even spot you three pawns and a knight."

"I have work to do today." *And tomorrow . . . until I leave everyone I love.* "Enjoy your holiday."

At the burn of renewed tears, Zoe resumed her pace to the Pawlikowski house. She clenched the basket handle until the wood pressed into her palm.

The first task of the day was to bake—

"I'm sorry I haven't been around in a while," Nico said, matching her steps. "My employer has been working me hard." Pause. "How come you've never asked me who I work for? And don't say it's none of your business. We're family."

Family?

The Forsythes had become more like family to her than he was.

And yet she made the half-hearted effort to ask, "Who do you work for?"

"Remember that grand lady sitting next to you on the train to Helena?"

Zoe nodded. She had admired the woman's lovely broach.

"That's her," he said proudly. "Miss Mary Lester. She's a wealthy, independent woman, much like you."

"What is ze nature of her business?"

"She runs a hotel, but she also teaches the young ladies who work for her how to improve themselves and be a positive influence in their community. She even requires I spend one hour a day reading. She says reading daily is the first step in becoming a gentleman."

"Zis is admirable of her." Not once could Zoe remember him speaking kindly of school and education. Were it not for the fact she was leaving Helena on Saturday, she would want to meet this Miss Mary Lester who seemed to have helped Nico make a home here.

After a quick glance at him, Zoe crossed the next intersection. He seemed happy, truly happy, more than she could remember in the years since they met.

"You like working for Miss Lester, yes?"

"Sure do!"

"And you like living here . . . in Helena." She did not phrase it as a question, yet he responded with a nod.

The realization of what she must do weighed down her heart.

She stopped, glanced around to see no one was within listening distance, and then looked at Nico. "I am returning to Denver Saturday morning."

His eyes narrowed. "Why?"

"Zere is no future for me here."

"I'm here," he said quietly.

"You know how important a home is to me." She rested her palm against his cheek. "You have one here." She lowered her hand. "I like seeing you happy. Zis is why I have no regret bringing you on my adventure."

He looked away, staring blankly at a nearby building. The muscles in his face flinched, then twisted into a frown. "Are you going to marry that guy?"

She shook her head. "We are unsuited."

"Ah, Zoe, I'm sorry he broke your—" His mouth gaped and his eyes grew wide in sudden realization. "That bad egg broke your heart and you're *still* going to cook for him?"

"I made a promise, a commitment." Something she doubted Nico would understand. "No matter ze pain I feel"— she rested a hand over her heart—"in here, I must be true to my word."

He uttered a string of ungentlemanly words.

Zoe stepped back, startled at his outburst.

"This is just like New York!" he snapped. His lips pressed tightly together as he glared at her. "Those swells mistreated you and you kept going back for more."

Zoe swallowed uncomfortably.

Nico looked at her in disgust. "Remember the Nephew? You lost your job and he still demanded you cook for him. If I hadn't talked you into running away, you would've done it, even though you didn't want to. You have no backbone."

Zoe stood there. She had no words to say in her own defense.

"I warned you that Gunderson fellow was a bad egg." He slapped his cap atop his head. In that moment, the anger in his eyes faded. "This is why," he said in a softer voice, "you can't leave Helena on your own. You need a brother to protect you. You need *me*."

Zoe looked away. She was tired. She was tired of Jakob's courtship, tired of cooking, tired of hating herself for falling in love with Isaak, and utterly tired of being told she was weak and malleable or, as Mrs. Gilfoyle-Crane declared, unimposing. Being unimposing was the only way Zoe knew to please others, to keep the peace, to make people like her. If everyone demanded his own way, harmony would have no place to take root and grow.

Yet though she knew making things right with Nico meant inviting him to leave Helena with her, she felt unable to say the words.

"Miss Lester is nice and all," Nico said suddenly.

Zoe focused on him, more aptly on his shockingly *wet* eyes.

"But you're"—his voice cracked—"you're my only family. I can't lose you. You're my sister and you'll always be my sister." He sniffed, then lifted his chin and spoke firmly. "We came to Helena together. We'll leave together."

To be accurate, they had arrived on the same train on the same day at the same time. Only one of them knew the other was there.

She gave him a weak smile. "I must go to work."

He responded with a terse nod. "Zoe?"

"Yes?"

If he noticed the sadness in her tone, he chose not to remark on it. "If you didn't have to cook for that dinner party, would you leave now?"

She released a weary sigh. "Yes."

"You're your own person. Why don't you just leave?"

"Zis is not like New York," she said roughly. "I cannot simply pack my bags and run away and no one will miss me. Zey are counting on me. Zey need my help."

"I suppose," he muttered. His hard blue eyes focused on a passing wagon. "The best thing that could happen is for that dinner party to be canceled."

Zoe sighed again. The Gundersons would never cancel the welcome-home dinner save a death in the family. Murder certainly was *not* something Nico would ever do. He had a good heart, however misplaced.

She gave him one of the paper bags filled with nougat.

"Deliver zis to the kind Miss Lester and zank her for me for all she has done for you."

A slow smile curved his lips. "My mum used to say flowers were always worth the rain." He took the bag and then enveloped Zoe in an awkward hug, pressing the basket she held into her ribs. "You're my sister, and I'll do what I must to take care of this for you." After a quick, "See you later," he dashed back down the street.

Later that morning

Isaak gripped his lapels and stared at the plume of gray smoke edging north toward the train depot. Jakob stood beside him, but he might as well have been a mile away.

Had he proposed to Zoe? He'd not said anything about it this morning when they broke their silence to discuss the logistics of getting Ma and Pa home from the train station.

Isaak dropped his chin as the front of the train appeared in the distance. When his parents disembarked, would it be to the news that Jakob was engaged? He'd not had much time between last night's rash pronouncement and now, but he'd left the house without eating breakfast . . . and without saying where he was going.

Isaak shifted his weight from one foot to the other. He looked over his shoulder to where Mr. and Mrs. Palmer, Aunt Lily and Uncle Jonas, and Mrs. Hollenbeck stood, as eager as he was for Ma and Pa's return.

The chug-chug of the train's engine grew louder, accompanied by the hiss of brakes. Passengers poked their heads out of the windows while the loose crowd on the platform congealed into a line as close to the railroad tracks as the wooden boardwalk allowed.

Jakob's posture stiffened an instant before he lifted his right hand, waving it back and forth in greeting. Isaak squinted against the cloud of steam until he saw his mother's favorite blue hat and then her face. Pa leaned out the window, wind blowing his hair into his eyes while he kept swiping it away with one hand and waving with the other.

The train braked, the squeal painful to Isaak's ear.

He kept waving and leaned close to Jakob's ear. "Remember, when they—"

"I don't need another lecture."

Isaak jerked upright as though he'd been slapped, even though Jakob's tone of voice lacked force. "I'm not lecturing. I'm confirming our plan to load luggage in the wagon that you'll drive back to the house while I bring Ma and Pa home in the surrey."

Jakob turned, his blue eyes icy. "I don't need a reminder, either."

Was this how it was going to be from now on? Every attempt at conversation rejected out of hand? "So glad we agreed to be cheerful today."

Jakob huffed but said nothing.

The train came to a complete stop. Ma and Pa ducked back inside the train and began to gather their belongings before disembarking.

Jakob stopped waving and walked to the stair portico to assist their parents' descent.

Isaak followed, frustrated that his brother would leave him standing alone when they'd agreed on presenting a united front after their near brawl last night. Sidelong glances and hands cupped beside mouths to cover whispers magnified his chagrin. He smiled and touched the brim of his black felt bowler, gratified when mortification pinked cheeks or hurried steps. The feud between him and Jakob wasn't something to be gawked at or exclaimed over as though they were the players on the stage.

Isaak stopped on the opposite side of the portico, his muscles tense. As soon as Ma appeared, his face broke into a huge smile. He bent his knees, and the instant her arms went around his neck, he wrapped his around her waist and lifted her off her feet. "Welcome home, Ma. It's good to see you."

He set her on the boardwalk, and she cupped his cheek with her palm. "It's good to see you, too." New lines creased the skin beside her blue eyes and a few gray strands of hair were intermingled with the blond ones, yet she seemed invigorated.

"You look remarkable. Travel agrees with you."

She laughed and patted his cheek. "You look like you're carrying the weight of the world, as usual." She turned and enveloped Jakob in a hug, trading places with Pa.

Isaak hugged his father tight. "I've missed you."

"I've missed you, too, son." The embrace was too short, but long enough for the sting inside Isaak's soul to melt under his father's love. Pa stepped back a pace, gripped Isaak's biceps, and looked him in the eye.

Isaak's throat swelled. Like his mother, Pa appeared older. The wrinkles around his brown eyes were deeper and his silvery hair was touched with more white. It wasn't much of a change, but enough to remind Isaak that his father wasn't always going to be around to settle disputes and mend hurts. "We have lots to discuss, but let's get you home and off that ankle. How is it?"

"Tender, but not so bad I can't walk on it a little."

"The cavalry has come out to greet you and Ma, so Jakob and I thought you should wait inside the depot where you can sit and chat while we load up your trunks."

Pa nodded. "Sounds like a plan." He reached inside his vest and withdrew the claim tickets. "I hope you saved a little extra room in the wagon." He gave Isaak a conspiratorial grin. "Your mother spotted a set of lamps on our way out of Denver."

Isaak chuckled. He looked over to where Jakob was

ushering their mother toward the depot. Had he told her about Zoe? If he didn't say something soon, someone in the crowd of friends surrounding Ma was sure to bring up Jakob's mail-order bride—a scenario Isaak had mentioned a few hours ago. But Jakob had refused to say how he intended to introduce Zoe before leaving the house.

". . . a good thing we sent the items for the stores ahead of us on last week's train."

Isaak returned his attention to his father. "The crates arrived undamaged. I wanted to wait until you got home to tell us exactly which pieces you wanted in which store, but Jakob opened them all while I was busy with something else."

"I'm sure it will be fine."

Isaak held the door open so his father could precede him inside the depot. Ma was already seated, Mrs. Hollenbeck on her right side, Aunt Lily on her left, with Mrs. Palmer standing and gesturing with her hands as she described her eldest daughter's wedding. Pa chose to sit a few feet away so Mr. Palmer and Uncle Jonas could bookend him in similar fashion. The conversation jumped straight into Pa's opinion on steam-operated streetcars as opposed to horse-drawn ones. Mr. Palmer was firmly in the camp of steam-powered, while Uncle Jonas favored horse-drawn—although Isaak had heard his godfather argue the opposite with Mr. Hess, the blacksmith, because Uncle Jonas didn't care either way. He just loved a spirited debate.

Isaak glanced into the telegram office and waved at Yancey. She smiled but didn't wave back, her hand busy taking notes while Mrs. Watson spoke.

A burst of feminine laughter drew his attention back to where his parents were sitting.

Jakob leaned to touch Ma's arm. "If you'll excuse us, Isaak and I will go load your trunks. I'll see you at home."

She patted his hand. "Thank you."

Isaak followed his brother to where two burly men

hoisted trunks, crates, hatboxes, and toiletry cases. Isaak and Jakob silently waited their turn, stepping forward as each customer claimed their baggage and moved on.

Either in agreement that they shouldn't get into another fight in front of a crowd or out of orneriness, Jakob didn't speak until they were loading the wagon. "Ma said the lamps she bought are for The Resale Company, so I'll drop those off on my way home."

"Put them in—"

"I know where to put them," he said with that same flat calm as the last time he'd interrupted.

Isaak set a wooden trunk in the wagon bed. "Is this how it's going to be between us now?"

"Until you stop commanding me with every sentence, yes."

"I'm not commanding."

Jakob's look said, *That's a matter of opinion.* "'Remember to do this, put that there.' Sounds like commands to me."

They went back for two more large trunks. Jakob hefted his trunk into the wagon box.

Isaak offloaded the trunk in his hands. "Where is this coming from?"

Jakob walked back to where the rest of the baggage was piled on the platform. He picked up a hatbox and tucked it under his left arm, then picked up two more.

Isaak followed, picking up a fourth hatbox, a toiletry case, and a small trunk he didn't recognize but the porter insisted belonged to them.

Jakob laid the hatboxes on the front seat where they wouldn't get crushed. "Per Uncle Jonas's advice, I refuse to either obey you or fight with you."

"You talked to Uncle Jonas?"

"Yes, Isaak. I do take advice from other people besides you." Jakob looked down for a moment, huffed, and straightened. His face was impassive and calm again. "Uncle Jonas came to The Import Company this morning. He was furious about our altercation at the opera house. He said the next time we decided to kill each other, we'd better do it in private. I told him I didn't know how to handle you. That's when he suggested I call you out every time you ordered me around."

"He didn't say anything to me." Although Isaak wasn't upset about it because spending the morning talking to Uncle Jonas left Jakob no time to propose to Zoe.

Jakob took the hatbox from Isaak and set it beside the other three. "Not every conversation or decision has to be run through you for approval."

Isaak set the toiletry case and small trunk in the wagon box. "That's not what I meant."

"Isn't it?" Jakob turned away and walked back for two tapestry bags.

Isaak didn't join him. He was no longer needed. He returned to the depot and stood just inside the door, watching his parents as they spoke with friends who, despite being apart for a year, were as close as ever.

Did he have any friends like that?

Hale was more like a big brother. Calm, rational, brilliant, and organized in his own haphazard way, he was someone Isaak trusted to dispense sound wisdom, but they weren't really friends. Mac was becoming more of a friend, but he was a newlywed who would—God willing—soon be a father. Windsor and Isaak competed back and forth in friendly one-upmanship, but the friendship was only three years old.

None of them were—or ever would be—Jakob.

Oh, for the days of catching frogs and watching clouds.

Pa gave him a searching look. Isaak shook his head to say he was fine, but after a few more minutes of conversing, Pa limped over to stand beside him. "Something's wrong, and I'd like to know what it is."

"Jakob and I are fighting again."

Pa chuckled. "I figured that out just by looking at you as we pulled in. What's wrong this time?"

"He thinks I order him to do things."

"You've always ordered him to do things. Why is he opposed to it now?"

Isaak took a step sideways to look in his father's face. "You're serious."

"About you always ordering Jakob around? Of course I am. I don't know why that stuns you." Pa put a hand on Isaak's shoulder. "Son, you order me around sometimes. It's as natural to you as breathing."

"Yancey says I'm benevolently arrogant."

Pa chuckled again. "That might be the best description of you I've ever heard."

Isaak's chest stung afresh. "I wish you hadn't left us to open this store without you."

"It was on purpose." Pa squeezed Isaak's shoulder. "Sometimes the best thing parents can do is get out of the way and let their children figure things out on their own. You and Jakob are good boys. Good men, I should say."

Not of late.

"Your mother and I knew we were taking a risk, leaving you with the responsibility of opening the new store, but we had faith we'd raised you well enough to do so without killing each other."

Isaak looked at his feet, summoning the courage to confess how close they'd come, when a shriek from inside the telegraph office snapped his head up.

An instant later, Yancey ran into the depot, her face white. "The Resale Company is on fire."

Chapter Twenty-Three

The Pawlikowski House

Leaving the stewed greens to simmer, Zoe scanned the menu she and the twins had agreed upon for the welcome-home dinner tomorrow night. With the last of the comfits and sweetmeats prepared, her next task was to make the brioche dough and puff paste for the morning's baking. She slid the menu into her apron pocket, then opened the right cookstove to check on the braised ham for the Pawlikowkis' return-home meal today, which neither twin thought necessary until she suggested it.

She breathed in the smell of garlic, thyme, carrots, wine, and brandy. Perfect! She closed the oven door.

A quick touch notified her that the baguettes had finally cooled. She stacked them in a basket, covered it with a napkin, and then carried the bread basket and a crystal butter dish into the dining room.

Zoe stopped and frowned. Why was the table set for five? She had asked Mrs. Wiley to set it for four—Mr. and Mrs. Pawlikowski and their sons. Perhaps Mrs. Forsythe had decided to join them. But why only her? Judge Forsythe would want to enjoy the meal, too.

After setting the butter and bread on the table, Zoe added a sixth place setting. Then she returned to the kitchen to start on the brioche dough.

You have no backbone.

Nico's words swirled around in her mind as she mixed salt and sugar into the bowl of flour.

Zoe poured the yeast mixture into the center of the flour mixture. She added eggs and stirred.

You have no backbone.

Zoe growled under her breath. She *had* a backbone. That was why she was leaving.

The telephone in the parlor rang.

On the fifth ring, it stopped. Presuming Mrs. Wiley had answered it, Zoe dumped the dough onto the floured counter. She kneaded in pieces of butter.

For her plan to work, she would have to leave without saying good-bye to anyone. With the side of her left hand, she pressed on her chest in a vain attempt to ease the aching. She wanted love now. She wanted a home now. She wanted family.

Most of all, she wanted Isaak.

"It can never be," she said because she needed to hear the words, to feel them killing any hope she may have otherwise. She had to leave Helena before her heart crossed the threshold into unrelenting love. She had to learn to forget him.

The kitchen door slammed open.

Mrs. Wiley looked horrified. "The Resale Company is on fire!"

Zoe could barely believe what she saw. Like knights storming a breach, firemen clambered up and down scaling ladders; two men leaned over the eaves pounding against the roof with their axes. On the ground level, a stately fireman bawled through a tin trumpet, telling the men where to direct the water hoses and where to chop vent holes. Zoe stepped over hoses, maneuvered past a horse-drawn water truck, and weaved through the hundreds of people whose gazes never wavered from the building, black smoke billowing from the second-floor windows.

Where were Isaak and Jakob? The depot?

Zoe grabbed the arm of the nearest person. "Do you know ze hour?"

The man checked his pocket watch. "Eleven-twelve."

The Pawlikowskis had been due to arrive on the ten-thirty train. Isaak and Jakob could still be there, loading luggage.

"Zank you," she said to the man, then hurried on, weaving through the crowd in hopes of finding someone she knew. Her gaze caught on a blonde standing next to a petite brunette.

Carline and Emilia! It had to be. Isaak left them to manage the store while he spent the day welcoming his parents home.

With "excuse me" after "excuse me," Zoe made her way to her friends. She touched Carline's arm.

"Zoe!" Carline enveloped Zoe in a tight hug.

Zoe pulled back. "Where are Isaak and Jakob?"

Carline's troubled gaze shifted to Emilia.

"I don't know where Isaak is," she answered, her voice strained. "But Jakob is"—she turned to The Resale Company—"in there."

"He went in after the cat," Carline explained before Zoe could ask why he would do such a foolish thing. Her heart managed to pound even harder.

Zoe looked to the front of the shop, where a fireman stood holding a hose nozzle and directing it to the awning over the door. She looked up to the roof. Flames flickered from the section between where the two firemen were cutting holes.

Suddenly, a cry arose.

Jakob stepped outside, fairly covered in ashes, dust, and smoke. He cradled the tabby in his arms. A fireman followed, patting Jakob's back.

"Get back! Get back!" yelled the tin-trumpeted man who Zoe presumed was the fire chief. He waved at the crowd. "Back farther! I can't guarantee this roof won't crash in!"

Jakob spoke to the fireman with him as they moved farther into the street. Someone called his name. He looked around. His gaze settled on Zoe, and he grinned.

She dashed forward and into Jakob's arms. "Oh, Jakob, I was so worried."

He drew back. "You were?"

She stared at him. Of course she was. For goodness' sake, she did not have to be in love with him to be concerned about his welfare. He had dashed into a burning building to save the cat. A cat!

"You could have died," she said, even though her throat felt it could not get any tighter. "My heart could not bear zat."

The fireman patted Jakob's shoulder. "My father's by the ambulance. He's fairly proud of his doctoring skills, so don't leave without seeing him first. You breathed in a lot of smoke."

Jakob nodded. "Thanks, Frank."

Zoe released a long, slow breath, hoping it would lessen the tension inside. "Ze fire is horrible, but at least you are safe. And ze cat is safe, too."

"I'm sorry I've been distant of late."

"You had to work."

"I thought you—Forget it! That was the past." He slid the tabby cat into her arms. And then he knelt. "Zoe de Fleur, will you consent to be my wife?"

* * *

Isaak pulled the horses to a stop, tossed the reins to his father, and jumped out of the surrey. He didn't care about the fire, not when Jakob was safe and kneeling in front of Zoe, not when the cat was in her arms, and not when Emilia and Carline were part of the crowd waiting with breathless anticipation for Zoe to answer Jakob's proposal. The only thing Isaak cared about was getting to Zoe before she said yes because she couldn't say no.

The scene blurred. Only Zoe was clear. She was wearing a white apron with green stains. She was beautiful and gracious and gentle and everything he'd ever wanted.

Part of Isaak's brain recognized that he'd stopped running and was standing before her, and that he had no idea how to tell her what was in his heart.

"Zoe, I . . ." He should get down on one knee. Everything about how he'd fallen in love with her was as far from tradition as it could get. At least one thing needed to be right. He kneeled, and the crowd gasped in unison. "From the moment I met you, my life went sideways. I think that's why I worked so hard to find fault. I wasn't ready—didn't even *want* to be ready—for love to upset my well-ordered world. I fought against you every way I knew how, but you slipped under my skin and into my soul. I've planned my future a hundred different ways, but now I know in the deepest place of my heart that you—and only you—are my future. Marry me?"

She stood there wearing an expression he couldn't read.

"Please say yes," he begged. "Please."

Firefighters sprayed water on the flames crawling up the sides of The Resale Co., but their gazes were locked on Isaak and Jakob kneeling side by side in front of Zoe.

Aunt Lily wept and clung to Uncle Jonas.

Ma and Pa stood still as statues, their arms wrapped around each other's waists.

Emilia had her hand over her mouth. Carline's mouth was wide open.

Mayor Kendrick was smiling as if he'd just won the election.

He probably had.

Isaak didn't care. He needed Zoe more than he needed to run the city of Helena.

She looked between him and Jakob.

Isaak knew her answer before she spoke, and it stopped his breath.

"No . . . to you both."

Minutes later

"Zoe, dear, please don't walk so fast."

She paused on the boardwalk long enough for Mrs. Forsythe to catch up to her. What Isaak and Jakob had done stemmed from pure selfishness. After a glance at Mrs. Forsythe, Zoe resumed walking. They had humiliated—*humiliated!*—her in front of her friends, in front of their parents, in front of dozens of people who would remember this moment for years. Years!

Two brothers proposing marriage to the same girl while their store burned. Not a good time. Not a good place.

Did they not care how foolish they looked? Or how foolish they made her look?

Now people would believe she had been flirting with both brothers.

They would view her as a strumpet.

Zoe let out a harsh laugh to release the painful pressure of anger growing within her. They had treated her as if she was nothing more than a bride-by-mail delivery. A prize to be won. If either of them truly cared about her, they would have considered her feelings. If they cared, they certainly would not have proposed to her in front of a crowd.

Was she *that* weak and malleable that they thought she would accept either proposal for fear of looking bad? She would rather look like a fool than agree to marry for the sake of appearances.

Never again would anyone say she had no backbone.

Zoe hurried across the intersection, then turned south toward the boardinghouse. She had known Jakob was hiding something. She had from the moment she saw him at the depot, but she had allowed herself to be swayed by his charm and happy eyes and she ignored her inner voice. She never had anticipated his secret to be as small and petty as feeling second-best to his brother.

And Isaak? From the day they met, she had recognized his arrogance. That should have been enough of a warning. If anyone was going to win a competition, it would be him. People listened to him. People followed him. People did what he said because he was Isaak Gunderson, a man who literally stood taller than them all. A king among men.

. . . you slipped under my skin and into my soul.

Pretty words, but how could he expect her to believe his profession of love while he was humiliating her in front of a crowd? If Isaak truly loved her—if he *knew* her—he would have known she was going to refuse his brother. If Isaak had truly listened to her words at the opera house, he would have understood her decision to end the contract with Jakob.

Isaak had heard nothing of her heart because his focus was on himself.

. . . you slipped under my skin and into my soul.

He loved her. Every word in his proposal professed his love. His desperation to stop her from agreeing to marry his brother professed his love.

And she had said no!

Good heavens, all she wanted was to say yes and marry him. But not like this. Not while there was no unity with his brother.

Her lungs grew tight and she fought to breathe.

Mrs. Forsythe grabbed Zoe's arm, stopping her. "Zoe! Weren't you listening to anything I said for the last two blocks?"

Zoe stood there, jaw clenched tight. She would not waste a single word defending why she had refused both twins, or why she had been ignoring Mrs. Forsythe's lecture.

Tears suddenly welled in Mrs. Forsythe's eyes. "I'm so sorry. They shouldn't have done that."

"Ze damage is done."

"But it can be fixed," she said with blatant optimism.

Zoe gave Mrs. Forsythe a look to convey the exact amount of hope she had for that to happen.

"I know things look dour." Mrs. Forsythe cradled her hands around Zoe's. "Give Isaak and Jakob a few days to make things right between them and with you. Instead of cooking in Marilyn's kitchen, you can use mine. I'll help as much as I can. I'll keep the boys away from you."

Zoe felt as if she had been slapped. "You wish me to stay and *cook* for them?"

For a moment, Mrs. Forsythe looked unsure of herself. "I do."

"Why do you zink I would help zem after"—Zoe jerked her hands free of Mrs. Forsythe's hold and pointed in the direction of the still-burning building—"after *zat*? Zey humiliated me."

"I know, and I'm ashamed of their behavior."

"Zen why do you ask me to stay? Because of your love for zem?"

Mrs. Forsythe's lips trembled. "Because of my love for you."

Zoe flinched.

"I can't lose you." Mrs. Forsythe's eyes showed bright with tears. "I can't. I'll say and do whatever it takes to convince you not to leave me. I need you to be my daughter, Zoe. Jonas needs you to be his daughter, too." A sharp whistle cut through the air. Mrs. Forsythe looked in the direction of the boardinghouse.

Zoe did, too.

Mr. and Mrs. Deal stood outside, a handful of male boarders on the second-floor balcony looking in the direction of the fire, all using their hats or hands to shield their eyes from the midday sun.

"You can come live with us," Mrs. Forsythe said softly. "Jonas and I have already discussed adopting you. Oh, don't say you're too old to be adopted. What matters is, we want you to be a part of our family forever."

Forever.

No word could be more bittersweet.

She could have the parents she dreamed of—a father *and* mother who loved her. If she stayed.

No. Not *if she stayed*. She could have had the family and home she yearned for if Isaak Gunderson had done the considerate thing and not proposed because he failed to trust her to refuse his brother. Because he failed to believe she could say no.

He had ruined everything.

Zoe stifled the cry that rose from her throat. She held her breath, reining in her broken heart. "I treasure you and Mr. Forsythe"—she looked away, unable to bear Mrs. Forsythe's hopeful expression—"but staying in Helena is not possible for me. Your godsons saw to zat. I am sorry." She placed a kiss on Mrs. Forsythe's cheek. "*Je t'aime*," she whispered, and then walked away.

As she neared the boardinghouse, Mr. Deal opened the front door. Neither he nor his wife said anything as she strode past them and up the stairs to her room.

* * *

Knock, knock, knock.

With strange detachment, Zoe turned her head far enough to look up at the doorknob but lacked the energy to rise from her seat. She rested her head against the door. "Who is it?"

"It's me, dear," came Mrs. Deal's voice. "I brought you some tea . . . and your brother. He's concerned. Said you were at the fire at The Resale Company."

Zoe sniffed, then, with the back of her hands, dried her eyes. She looked to the clock on the table beside her bed. Eight minutes of crying because, as angry as she still was with Isaak, if circumstances had been different, she would have said yes.

"I am pathetic," she murmured.

She scrambled to her feet and opened the door.

Mrs. Deal stood there holding a tea service. To her left stood Nico. Neither were smiling.

Zoe stepped back for them to enter.

Mrs. Deal took the service to the bedside table. Nico grabbed the wicker rocker and the chair from the secretary and dragged them to the bed. Once Mrs. Deal sat in the chair, Nico motioned to the rocker for Zoe to sit there. She closed the door. He sat on the edge of the bed.

With a sigh, Zoe sat in the rocker. "Milk, no sugar."

Mrs. Deal stopped pouring tea and looked to Zoe. "You always take your tea with sugar."

"Zat is how you serve it." Zoe took the teacup from her. "I saw no reason to make a fuss. But in ze last few moments, I have come to realize I can say *milk, no sugar* if zis is what I want. I have no obligation to drink tea with sugar so you will see me as a nice person. I have a backbone. I mean no offense when I say I prefer tea with milk, no sugar."

Mrs. Deal's mouth opened, then closed, as she looked

from Zoe to Nico . . . before saying to Zoe, "I appreciate your honesty."

Nico studied Zoe.

Uncomfortable with his perusal, Zoe looked away.

"Miss de Fleur, what's wrong?" Mrs. Deal spoke gently. "You look like the weight of the world is on your shoulders."

Zoe stared at the tawny liquid in her teacup. There had to be a way of saying, *I wish to be left alone in this pit of despair so I can bemoan my rejection of Isaak's romantic declaration of love,* and not crush Mrs. Deal's feelings.

"Zoe's been humiliated." Nico's teacup *ting*-ed against the saucer he held. "Her suitor asked her to marry him, but before she could answer, his brother ran over and asked her to marry him instead."

"I see." Mrs. Deal's tone was more grim than curious.

The silence was awkward, yet Zoe welcomed it. That a crowd of people had witnessed the most mortifying moment of her life was bad enough. Why relive it inside her mind?

She was about to say, *It has been a long day and I wish to be alone*, when Mrs. Deal looked at Zoe and asked, "Which one did you choose?"

"She turned them both down," Nico answered.

"Oh. Oh, my." Mrs. Deal sat her teacup and saucer back on the tray. "Isaak I understand. He's rather pious and snooty. If anyone deserves a comeuppance, it's him. But Jakob? Humph."

Nico's eyes widened. "You *like* him?"

"He reminds me of Mr. Deal"—she sighed—"twenty years ago."

Zoe stared stunned at the boardinghouse owner. Isaak, unlike his brother, was steadfast, organized, dependable, conscientious, and—Zoe clenched her jaw. She was still too angry with him to defend his better qualities to anyone.

"If I were you . . ." Mrs. Deal's slow, deliberate tone drew Zoe's attention. "Oh, I don't know if I should say this, but . . . considering how people in this town talk, if I were you, I would want to leave without anyone the wiser."

"If I could leave immediately, I would," Zoe admitted.

Nico handed Mrs. Deal his cup and saucer. "I'll go get train tickets."

"The train to Denver left the depot at eleven-fifteen." Mrs. Deal set Nico's teacup onto the tray. "Better check the stage instead. There should be one leaving in a couple of hours."

Zoe released a weary breath. "I cannot simply leave today. Zere are things to pack. I must close my account at ze bank and collect my knives and rolling pin from ze Pawlikowski house." She shook her head. "Ze earliest I can leave is tomorrow morning. Nico, you also need time to pack and tender your resignation to your employer. Doing so is most gentlemanly."

Mrs. Deal twisted her hands together. "I hate to be the bearer of bad news, but I know the Gunderson boys. They don't give up easily. Miss de Fleur, you and Nico are treasures to me. If you wish to go somewhere the Gundersons can't find you, Mr. Deal and I have friends in Idaho we can send you to who will help you and Nico find good, reliable work."

Perhaps she should not go to Denver. Her heart ached too much to consider another man's courting now. In time, once her heart healed, she would be open. The Archer Matrimonial Company simply had too many connections to Helena.

Zoe looked at Nico. He had said nothing since offering to buy the train tickets. They had played enough chess matches for her to know when he was analyzing moves ahead of hers. According to him, he found it challenging to see how many ways he could fit the various pieces of the whole together. She always hoped his silence meant he saw no way to beat her. That was never true. His silence meant something bothered him.

His silence meant something failed to fit.

"Nico, what is it?" she asked softly.

He met her gaze. Something—she almost believed she saw anger—flickered in his eyes. "Nothing." He grinned. "I was thinking of the things I need to do before I can leave."

"Are you sure zis is what you want to do?"

He nodded. "We're family. We leave together, we stay together." He smiled at Mrs. Deal. "You're swell for helping us."

Mrs. Deal touched her chest, her eyes growing watery. "Breaks my heart to see you go, but I understand that it's for the best."

Zoe swallowed to ease the tautness in her throat. If Nico had no misgivings, she would choose to have none. "Mrs. Deal, Nico and I would like to accept your offer to help us find a new home where no one can find us."

"Wonderful!" Mrs. Deal stood and collected the tea tray. "To make things easier for you, I'll send Mr. Deal to the Pawlikowskis to collect your things."

Nico stood. "Meet you at the depot in the morning?"

She nodded, then watched as Nico and Mrs. Deal left the room. Once the door closed, Zoe slid onto the bed. She stared up at the white-painted tin ceiling. In all her twenty-two years, she could never remember calling one place home.

Until now.

Chapter Twenty-Four

Later that afternoon

"There's nothing more can be done, Mr. Gunderson. I'm sorry."

Isaak nodded at Mr. Booker, the fire chief. "I'm grateful for all your work and that no one was hurt." At least not physically . . . and not by the fire.

The firemen had worked hard to save what they could, but when the roof caught, they shifted their efforts from The Resale Co. to the surrounding buildings. Four hours later, the store was a soot-stained stone shell with gaping holes providing an unimpeded view of charred rubble and shattered glass. Oddly, the stairs remained, only they led nowhere.

Isaak shook his head. Were he a poetic man, he'd say it was a perfect representation of his life. "Do you know how it started?"

Booker waggled his head, neither a nod to affirm nor a shake to deny but somewhere in-between. "We suspect someone set it deliberately, but the damage is so bad, we'll have to wait a week or two to sort through the debris before we can say for sure."

First the vandalism at The Import Co. and now arson.

Someone was intentionally sabotaging their businesses. To pressure Isaak into exiting the mayoral race? Or could it be a coincidence?

Isaak stuck out his hand. "Sir, thank you for all your work. You and your men deserve a raise."

Booker brightened, took off his leather glove, and shook hands. "Now that, young man, is the type of talk I like to hear from politicians."

"Again, thank you."

"My pleasure." Booker released his grip, then trudged toward his exhausted crew, who were coiling leather hoses back into the fire wagon.

Isaak swung his gaze left and right. Clusters of gawkers gathered on the south side of Helena Avenue, a few more at the point of Helena and Fourteenth Street. What was left of the store blocked any who might be on Joan Street.

He waved at the ones he could see, and they scurried off. He needed to be alone, a desire he'd expressed to the friends who'd stopped by to offer their condolences on losing the store.

No one had mentioned losing Zoe, either because they were too embarrassed or because they knew it was the deeper pain. No one except Nico, who—directly after Zoe had run off—had delivered hard punches to Jakob and Isaak's abdomens, along with a declaration that they were bad eggs for humiliating her.

Isaak spied his father driving the family wagon. After Zoe had stormed off, Pa had limped in between his sons, ordering Jakob to guard The Import Co. against more vandalism and Isaak to stay at The Resale Co.—the equivalent of being sent to their rooms until Pa was ready to dish out punishments.

Isaak stood straight. He'd take his scolding like a man.

Pa pulled the reins, bringing the wagon to a stop. He set

the brake. "Climb on up here. My ankle is throbbing, and I promised your mother I'd stay off it."

Isaak obeyed.

"I've spoken with Jakob and heard his side of the story. Now I'd like to hear yours."

Isaak didn't know where to start.

"Why don't you begin with your first impression of Miss de Fleur," Pa encouraged, as though he could read Isaak's mind.

"I thought she was a fraud."

"What changed your mind?"

Isaak spread his hands. "A hundred different things."

"Start with the first one."

He pictured her smile when she snapped the bank notes against the counter to pay for the primers and the set of La Fontaine books. "She gave me a dressing down that I richly deserved." And then the words flowed. For ten or twenty minutes—maybe more—Isaak recounted all the ways Zoe wriggled past his distrust until he'd recognized she was a ruby beyond price.

Pa nodded. "Between your story and Jakob's, I have to say I like this girl. She's exposed Jakob's feelings of inferiority and humbled your pride in less than two months, something your mother and I have been working on for years."

Isaak released the breath he'd been holding. "I'm glad you approve."

"Of *her*," Pa stressed. "Not of what you and Jakob did to the poor girl. I never thought I'd be more disappointed in the two of you than the day you stole money from the cash register because you wanted matching kites."

It was the day Isaak determined to never again fail his parents. "I'm sorry for being a disappointment both then and now."

"I expect you to also offer your apologies to Miss de Fleur and your brother."

"Yes, sir."

Pa nodded. "Jakob will be making his apologies, too."

"Good."

Pa's eyes narrowed. "Why do you say *good*?"

Isaak stared at his father. "Jakob should have known better than to write away for a mail-order bride. Did you even know about Zoe before Jakob decided to play the hero and pressure her into marriage?"

"Stop right there, because you"—Pa pointed his finger at Isaak's nose—"are the one most at fault."

Isaak's jaw sagged.

"Son, I can't imagine loving you more if you were my own flesh and blood, but it doesn't make me blind to your faults. You're so busy being a respected businessman, exemplary church member, and dutiful son, you've never considered that you take unholy pride in your righteousness."

The accusation left Isaak speechless.

"Have you ever considered," Pa continued, his voice softer but still convicting, "that God needed to humble you, so He used Jakob's impetuous nature as a tool?"

Isaak closed his eyes while wave after wave of shame crashed over him. If that had been God's plan, He couldn't have chosen a more effective means. Isaak pictured Zoe's face when she'd said no to his proposal. He was so afraid of her desire to please others, he'd used it against her by proposing publicly to force her to say yes to him. The very thing he was angry at Jakob for doing!

Oh, Lord. I'm sorry. I never saw it. I never . . . You know I didn't mean to . . .

Even his prayers were in shambles.

Pa put a hand on Isaak's shoulder. "You clearly love this woman. I've never heard a more eloquent proposal, so—"

"It doesn't matter." Isaak rubbed the back of his neck. "She's returning to Denver, and I can't leave my job or obligations here to chase after her." Which she wouldn't want, anyway. She'd already said she'd never trust a man who broke his commitments.

Pa chuckled. "Now you sound as daft as I was before deciding to court your mother."

Isaak swiveled his head to look at his father.

"When a man is determined not to love a woman he's already in love with, he uses excuses to shield his heart. I know, because I did the same thing. In my case it was fear." Pa smoothed his mustache. "In your case, it's more of your pride. You think this town, the Widows and Orphans Committee, and even I can't function without you."

The loving rebuke burned inside Isaak's chest. "More of my benevolent arrogance?"

Pa squeezed Isaak's shoulder. "Yes, but all men are afflicted with some measure of it. And all men are fools in love, so you're in good company."

Isaak bowed his head. *Lord, cleanse me of my pride. Teach me to walk humbly before You.*

"Let's go home, son. You need a bath and some food."

With a big slice of humble pie as the main course.

Ninety minutes later

Isaak removed his bowler and stepped inside Hale's law office. The double doors between the parlor and office were wide open.

Hale looked over the pile of work littering his desk. "Isaak. A pleasure to see you. Come in."

Isaak crossed into the cluttered room, amazed, as always, that Hale knew the subject matter of every stack and could locate whatever he needed without wasting time searching. Knowing that didn't keep Isaak from testing his friend once in a while by pointing to a mound and demanding the subject matter of each.

Today wasn't the time for games, however, so Isaak sat down in an empty wooden chair, ignoring the one next to him except to place his hat on top of the paper heap occupying it. "I've come to convince you to run for mayor."

Hale sat back and touched his finger to the bridge of his wire-rimmed glasses. "If this is about today's . . ." He spread his hands but didn't finish his sentence.

Isaak's lips twitched. "It comforts me that a skilled lawyer who forms arguments for a living and reads the dictionary for fun can't find a word to describe this morning's . . . whatever it was."

"Debacle?"

"Too benign."

"Fiasco?"

"Too insipid."

Hale grinned. "Whatever it was, it doesn't disqualify you from running for mayor. As I told you before, voters have short memories."

Isaak shook his head. "This isn't about the voters or anyone else. This is about me stepping away from something that's feeding my pride."

A long, considering look. "I see."

Had Isaak needed further proof of his besetting sin, those two little words would have provided it. "I need to withdraw, but Kendrick needs to be defeated. The only man who can do it is you."

Hale pursed his lips.

Isaak gave him a moment to come to the same conclusion. "You know I'm right."

"Says the man trying to overcome pride."

Isaak snorted. "Oh . . . you don't know how much I needed to laugh."

Hale looked at the corner of the room, took a deep breath, and returned his focus to Isaak. "I don't want this. I've never wanted this."

"Which is why you're the man for the job." Isaak let that settle. "At the risk of being put in my place again, I repeat, you know I'm right. No one else has the skill, the reputation, and the political backing of a territorial judge."

Hale glowered. "I hate nepotism. It would gall me to win an election because of my uncle's connections."

"Is that what's held you back? Because you do yourself a great disservice in thinking that." Isaak leaned forward and put his forearms on the slender line of space between the edge of Hale's desk and one of his stacks of paper. "You're an excellent lawyer, you have good ideas about what to do and how to go about it, and we've discussed the campaign multiple times. All that's needed is to switch the man running. Nothing else changes."

For another five minutes, Hale came up with excuses and Isaak rebutted them. Hale took longer and longer to formulate each argument. He stared over Isaak's shoulder for a full thirty seconds before releasing a sigh. "This isn't a good time."

When he didn't elaborate, Isaak prompted, "Why not?"

Hale tilted his head and stared Isaak in the eye. "You're really going to drop out."

It wasn't a question, it was acceptance . . . and an excellent change of topic. "And you're really going to run." Isaak picked up his hat and stood. "Be at the . . . Sorry. Would you be amenable to announcing your candidacy at the The Import Company's grand opening a week from tomorrow?"

Hale came around the desk to walk Isaak toward the door. "You're going through with that?"

Isaak nodded, his throat tightening. "With The Resale Company gone, I'll put my effort into making The Import Company a success." Because he needed to work and keep working until the void in his chest went away.

They reached the front door, and Hale opened it. "You're *sure* about this?"

"That you're the right man for the job? Absolutely." Isaak

fit his bowler on his head. As he crossed over the threshold and walked into the street, he called over his shoulder, "I can't wait to see Uncle Jonas's face when he hears you've agreed to run."

Hale responded by slamming his door closed.

Isaak's good humor lasted until The Import Co. came into view. This was going to be a much more difficult sell. He and Jakob had twenty-two years of sibling rivalry to overcome. They also had twenty-two years of practice at making up after fights. They ought to be good at it by now.

Isaak rehearsed his apology as he covered the remaining distance.

Jakob was standing by a window waiting. He opened the door and swung it wide. He'd also cleaned up since the fire. "I'm glad you came."

"Did you think I wouldn't?"

Jakob's expression froze.

"Sorry." Isaak took off his hat and held it with both hands. "Humility is going to be a learned skill. Let me try that again. I'm glad to see you, too." When Jakob cocked his eyebrow, Isaak chuckled and stepped into the store.

It smelled of milled pinewood, lemon oil, and fresh paint. Unlike The Resale Co., where an eclectic array of goods was displayed according to category, here they were placed with an eye toward showing each piece as it would be used. A mahogany dining room table set with china, crystal, candles, and linens, as though waiting for a Christmas feast. A sofa and two wingback chairs framed a coffee table holding a stack of three books and a pair of reading glasses. The accompanying sofa tables were set with matching Tiffany lamps. Behind them was a carved-wood grandfather clock, the pendulum swinging and the hands at the correct time. Farther back, a four-poster bed with slippers on the floor and a dressing gown laid over the quilted bedspread. Paintings were grouped on the walls so they didn't overwhelm but rather helped create the illusion that each designated space was its own room.

Isaak had helped uncrate a number of items, but he hadn't been around to help with the display. "This is incredible, Jake. I never imagined it would look this good." He sucked in a breath and turned. "I'm sorry. I didn't mean for that to sound like—"

"I know you meant it as a compliment." Jakob pointed at the living room display with an open palm. "I thought we could sit while we talked."

"Good idea." Isaak chose the wingback chair and waited long enough for Jakob to sit on the sofa before he said, "I'm at fault."

Jakob took a moment before settling back against the brown leather and crossing his legs. "All right. I'm listening."

Isaak began as he'd rehearsed. "I was born with an inflated sense of duty and responsibility. Because my diligence, organization, and planning have always resulted in success, I've viewed myself as superior to you."

"To everyone," Jakob corrected.

Isaak grimaced. "To everyone." He opened his mouth to continue, but Jakob held up a hand.

"Wait." The corner of his mouth indented. "I'd like to relish this moment a bit longer."

Isaak grinned. "Please, relish as long as you need. I deserve it."

The amusement faded in Jakob's eyes. "You don't deserve it. Not really."

"I do." Isaak tugged his shirt collar away from his neck. "Every time you got in trouble for doing something impetuous, I determined to plan more. Every time I was rewarded for doing the responsible thing, it stoked the fire of my pride. Your failures reinforced my belief that I was the better son, the better person, the better man." He paused for Jakob to nod his assent. "I'm sorry for that, Jake. Truly sorry."

"Thank you." Jakob uncrossed his legs and shifted on the sofa. "Truth is, I've made plenty of mistakes through the years. I do need to think through consequences a little more and stop thinking every suggestion you give is a criticism of my character." Jakob gripped the V-shaped opening of his vest. "You have to agree my idea to bring Zoe here wasn't all bad."

"I'll concede that point." Isaak scooted forward on the chair. "Do you love her?"

Jakob inhaled and held the breath before exhaling with a whoosh. "I'd like to love her, but it's not the same thing as actually being in love with her."

No. It wasn't. "I never wanted to love her, but I do."

A twinkle lit Jakob's eyes. "I caught that."

The band of tension around Isaak's ribs loosened an inch. If Jakob was already finding humor in his loss, they were going to be fine. Isaak rubbed the knuckles of his right hand and looked around The Import Co. stocked with items from all over the United States and the world. He knew—was *almost certain* he knew—why his brother had chosen to send for a mail-order bride, but he was *un*certain how to balance his God-given talent for recognizing it with respect for Jakob as a man who had the right to come to his own conclusions.

Pa said Zoe had exposed faults. Had she done the same for Jakob?

Isaak looked his brother in the eye. "What is it about her that you find most attractive?"

Jakob jerked backward. "What?"

"Please, just answer." Isaak gripped his hands together. "I'm curious."

The room was silent except for the ticking of the grandfather clock. Jakob's attention swirled around the room, as though he was searching for inspiration. His eyes settled, and Isaak looked to see the painting of Notre-Dame Cathedral beside the Seine River. "I loved that she didn't grow up here, that she didn't know me as Isaak Gunderson's irresponsible twin."

"So you threw yourself into work and pushed Zoe to the side."

Jakob scratched an earlobe. "Told myself I was doing the mature thing—the Isaak thing, so to speak."

"Is that why you proposed?"

Jakob shrugged. "I care for Zoe a great deal, and the thought of her with you stings."

Isaak swallowed against the tightness closing his throat. "I don't want to lose you, Jake. Not over Zoe."

Jakob was silent for long moment before he leaned forward, his expression sober. "What if I said you had to choose between her or me?"

Isaak's heart tilted sideways. What would he do? "I want to say I'd choose you, but"—he looked his twin in the eye—"I can't. Not if she'll have me."

Jakob grinned. "Good answer." He sat back again. "We sure made a mess of it. If I were her, I'd never speak to either of us again."

Isaak rested his elbows on his knees. "How do I win her back?"

"I don't know, Iz," said the man who persuaded people to jump into raging rivers using nothing but his charm.

A skill Isaak had underestimated until now.

Jakob touched his stomach. "But you might start with that young man who punched us both."

Ten minutes later

Isaak left The Import Co. intent on one more apology . . . the most humbling one yet.

The walk to the red-light district only took five minutes, but with the late afternoon sun providing no cover, he endured enough stares to last a lifetime. Last year, when Emilia and Yancey avoided people for fear of censorious glances after the article about Finn was published, Isaak told them to put on a brave face and look people in the eye. To make them back down.

Maybe he was right to offer them such wisdom, but it was equally likely he was wrong. He'd never walked that proverbial mile until now. Nevertheless, he followed his own advice. He kept his chin high and his shoulders straight. Yes, he was Isaak David Gunderson, and yes, he was walking straight to the *Maison de Joie*, Madame Lestraude's brothel.

He stopped at the door. Was he supposed to walk in or knock? When in doubt, err on the side of being a gentleman; he lifted his hand and knocked.

A massive Chinese man opened the door. He didn't speak. Or move. Or even blink. And he was looking *down* at Isaak.

Intimidation was a new sensation. Isaak usually inspired that emotion in others. Evidently, God was pulling out all the stops for this lesson. "I'm here to speak to Nico."

A feminine "Let him come in" moved the wall of muscles out of Isaak's way.

He stepped inside and stopped in his tracks. It looked like a regular home with a huge parlor and grand staircase leading to a second floor. Six women sat on sofas and chairs dressed in plain, high-collared dresses reading what looked like school primers.

Not how he'd ever imagined—or tried *not* to imagine—a brothel.

Madame Lestraude looked up from where she was bent over a pretty blonde's shoulder. "Ah, Mr. Gunderson. What a pleasure to see you here."

He should return her greeting, but his tongue refused to come down from the roof of his mouth. He dipped his head in a polite bow only because his neck muscles remembered on their own that they were supposed to greet women with that courtesy.

"You've caught us at our lessons, as you see, but we were just finishing. Ladies"—she clapped her hands—"if you would give us the room, please."

"Yes, ma'am," was spoken in unison. The women rose, gathered their books, and filed up the stairs. They greeted Isaak with polite nods and an occasional, "Sir," but didn't flirt or . . . or *anything*.

After the last woman left, he swung his gaze back to Madame Lestraude and was taken aback by the fury in her brown eyes. She glanced at his forehead. Heat flooding his face, he swiped off his hat. "I beg your pardon, ma'am."

"I see Mac never told you that I give my girls lessons. This group is new, so we're starting with basic reading, writing, and arithmetic."

Isaak didn't know what to think. It had stunned him when he learned the madam was rescuing girls from prostitution. It was almost as shocking to see her teaching lessons like a school marm. "I, uh, guess . . . I mean, I think that's . . . admirable?" His voice lifted of its own accord.

She laughed, though it lacked mirth. "Oh, Mr. Gunderson, you are a delight."

It was said like a compliment, but it wasn't. And yet it was. Which reminded him of how conflicted he was over Zoe and brought him back to his purpose. "I'm looking for Nico."

The fury she'd masked earlier flickered in her eyes again. "Why?"

"I need to ask him a question."

"What kind of question?" Her voice hardened.

Isaak looked at her more closely. She'd been beautiful once, but now she wore too many regrets for the term to fit. Her dyed blond hair appeared brittle, the skin at the corners of her eyes was crosshatched with thin wrinkles, and the lace around her high collar was unable to disguise the deep creases in her neck.

And she was afraid of something.

It pricked him the same way Zoe's discomfort had when he greeted her that first Sunday morning. He didn't brush past it this time. "I haven't brought law enforcement with me, if that's what you're thinking."

She didn't appear mollified. "That doesn't tell me why you need to speak with Nico."

Isaak gripped his hat brim tighter. "I need to ask him a question regarding Miss de Fleur."

Nico pushed through a door to Isaak's right. "What d'ya need to ask about my sister?" Belligerence filled his face and his question.

"Nico," Madame Lestraude bathed the two syllables with censure. "I told you to wait until I called for you."

"But he said this was about Zoe, not the—"

"Hush."

As if Isaak didn't already know illegal activity went on upstairs. "Madame Lestraude, might I have a word with Nico in private?"

"No."

He blinked at her rudeness.

Before he could think of a suitable response, Nico said, "It's all right, Miss Lester. I can handle Mr. Goon-der-son."

Isaak vacillated between astonishment and irritation at the names rolling off Nico's tongue.

Madame Lestraude remained rooted for another moment before speaking to Nico. "I'll be in my office. If you need anything"—she slid a meaningful glance at Isaak—"call me or Mr. Lui. Do you understand?"

Nico nodded.

Isaak checked to see where Mr. Lui had hidden himself, but the mountain of flesh had somehow slipped away unnoticed.

After squeezing the boy's shoulder, Madame Lestraude swished out of the room using the same door Nico had earlier.

Nico fisted his right hand and pounded it into his left palm as though he was imagining punching Isaak in the stomach again. "Why're you here?"

"Because I need to apologize for the way I've treated both you and your sister."

Nico's eyes narrowed to slits. "You think wearing a fancy suit is going to make me forgive you just like that? I'm not a jellyfish, Mr. Goon-der-son, and neither is my sister."

Isaak swallowed his first response. Jakob had said winning over this young man was going to be nigh impossible, but the only way to do it was by treating him with honest respect. Good advice Isaak intended to follow, no matter how difficult Nico made it. "I'm not wearing this suit to make you forgive me but because it's what a gentleman wears to pay important social calls."

"You saying I'm an important social call?" Nico made it sound like an insult.

"I am."

"Why?"

Isaak lowered his chin so Nico could look him straight in the eye. "As Miss de Fleur's only family member, I should have come to you to declare my intention of courting her before asking her to marry me."

Nico's eyes widened for an instant before sliding back into narrow suspicion.

"May I have your permission to court your sister?" Isaak held the young man's stare.

Seconds ticked by.

Nico didn't move.

Isaak barely breathed.

"What if I say no?"

Isaak's heart pounded. This was the crucible. Unlike with Jakob, if Nico said he wouldn't give Zoe up, there was no going around him. "Then I'll honor your wishes."

"You will?" Nico's voice pitched an octave higher, a reminder that he was a boy on the verge of manhood. He coughed and said in an exaggerated bass voice, "I mean, of course you will."

The temptation to laugh at his attempt to appear older and wiser than his years was tempered by the seriousness of the topic. Isaak gripped his hat so hard, he was certain the brim would have permanent imprints of his fingers.

Nico shifted his weight from his right foot to his left. Stared. Shifted his weight back. Stared some more. "If I say yes, you'll just take her from me."

Isaak inhaled. This was the crux of the matter for Nico. Zoe once said he called her his sister because he had no other family. To win Zoe, Isaak needed to expand his future to include not only a wife but an imp of a brother-in-law who thought nothing of lying, stealing, and living in a brothel with a madam as a surrogate mother.

Nico would also defend his sister to his last breath.

Isaak could deal with that.

"I give you my word as a"—he revised his usual promise— "as the gentleman I hope to become that, should I be fortunate enough to win your sister's heart, you will always be a member of our family."

After a flickering glance at the door to the hallway that

presumably led to Madame Lestraude's office, Nico said, "All right. You can court her."

Isaak took his first deep breath since seeing Jakob's proposal six hours earlier. "Thank you, Nico. I'll do my best to deserve the faith you're putting in me."

"You figured out how you're going to win her heart? Because you made her angry, and I mean an-gry."

Isaak cringed. "She has every right to be, which brings me to my second request."

"Go on."

"I need your help."

Nico stood taller. "You want me to help you court Zoe? You and me together?"

It wasn't exactly what Isaak was picturing, but he'd do whatever it took. "Sure. We'll court her together."

Nico beamed. "She likes surprises."

"And sunrises."

Nico looked impressed. "How'd you know that?"

"She mentioned it the first time she was in my home for dinner." Isaak winced, remembering his behavior that day. If he was lucky enough to win her love, he'd spend the rest of his life living up to the grace she'd extended to him that day . . . and the weeks that followed when, in his arrogance, he'd refused to believe his initial impression of her was wrong.

"We could tell her you're dying."

Isaak snapped his attention to Nico.

"Or that you'll hang yourself if she doesn't marry you."

The boy's line of suggestions needed to stop. Isaak searched for a gentle way to say it. "Your sister doesn't like lying."

Nico's expression soured. "It got her here, didn't it?"

"You lied to get her here?"

"She needed to get out of New York."

There was more to the story but pressing for details might make the boy change his mind about helping to woo Zoe, so Isaak remained silent.

Nico crossed his arms over his chest. "She can't read English too good, so I pointed at the advertisement for a mail-order bride and pretended it was for a cook instead. When she found out what I'd done, she asked that Archer lady about the man looking for a wife. She saw your brother's smiley eyes and decided to come here even though I told her it was a mistake."

Regardless of whether Zoe agreed to marry him, Isaak would never think of her coming to Helena as a mistake. She'd enriched his life, humbled his pride, and made him a better man. At least he hoped he'd be a better one from now on. "I'm glad she came, but I don't think lying to her now is our best plan."

Nico remained stony for a long moment before wilting. "Yeah. You're right."

Isaak waited for the boy to come up with another suggestion.

Silence.

Outside of lying, it appeared he didn't have any ideas. Isaak didn't offer any of his own, though, because it was important for Nico to take the lead.

He shifted his gaze between his feet and Isaak. "Way I see it, the problem is that Zoe doesn't get involved in what's not her business."

Isaak nodded. An idea struck. "What if we do things together that *aren't* her business, but we make sure she sees us together."

Nico nodded. "She'll get so curious, she'll have to come around to figure out what we're doing. I think this might work, but . . ." His expression grew serious.

"What is it?" Isaak curled his fingers into fists as he waited for another objection.

Nico's gaze flickered at the door to Madame Lestraude's office. "Miss Lester told me something, and I don't want to tell Zoe about it."

"Why not?"

"She's a girl," he said as though it explained everything. Nico shifted from balancing on his left foot to his right. "When I went to check on her after you'd humiliated her, Mrs. Deal said she knew a place where me and Zoe could disappear. It sounded funny, so I asked Miss Lester about it. She said the Deals sometimes sell women and children—even boys—into prostitution."

Isaak's jaw fell open. "Why hasn't she told her son?"

"She just found out about it." Nico's brow furrowed. "If I can get Mr. or Mrs. Deal to tell me the address of these friends in Idaho they're sending us to, do you think Sheriff McCall could arrest them?"

"No, but he could send the information to a sheriff in Idaho. Great idea!"

The boy beamed.

"But Nico . . . ?" Isaak waited until he had the boy's full attention. "While I understand wanting to keep Zoe from feeling betrayed by the Deals, sometimes we men assume"—*in benevolent arrogance*—"that we know what's best for the people we love."

"Yeah. So?"

Pa was right. All men, even those on the cusp of manhood, were filled with pride. A lesson Nico needed to learn over time as Isaak had. "If our plan to woo Zoe fails, promise me you'll tell her about the Deals. No lying to protect her."

Nico's posture relaxed. "Because people who love each other trust them with the truth."

Out of the mouth of babes . . . and young men.

"And we both"—Isaak pointed a finger at himself then at Nico—"love her very much."

Nico pivoted on his heel. "Let me tell Miss Lester I'm going with you." He opened the door and was almost through when he leaned back to add, "You and me courting Zoe together is good and all, but you might have to spend *some* time alone with her."

Isaak placed a hand over his heart. "I shall endeavor to make the sacrifice."

Chapter Twenty-Five

The next morning

Zoe grabbed the quilt from her bed and then slipped out onto the boardinghouse's wrap-around balcony, careful not to make any noise to wake her fellow boarders. When she had first settled into her room almost two months before, she and Janet Deal had been the only females. Now nine ladies stayed one and two to a room. Zoe would be surprised if *her* room was not let by the time her last piece of luggage was removed.

Someone had turned her favorite wicker rocker to face the direction of The Resale Company fire. She adjusted it to face east, then unfolded the quilt and draped it over the rocker. Once settled in, she wrapped the edges over her head and around her amethyst traveling suit, leaving only her face to endure the nippy morning breeze.

Zoe closed her eyes and waited for what was sure to come.

Crickets chirped.

Horses clomped on the dirt-hardened street.

A dog barked from somewhere in the distance.

Finally . . . what she had been listening for happened: a rooster crowed. She smiled. Other roosters joined in.

How they knew it was dawn never ceased to amaze her. The first rays of light had yet to grace the Earth. The under-bellies of the clouds had yet been lit to a glow.

Yet the roosters crowed.

Their hearts told them it was time.

. . . you slipped under my skin and into my soul.

Stop! No more reliving Isaak's proposal.

But if his brother had not proposed and The Resale Company not burned and the moment had been absent several hundred bystanders, she would have said yes.

She *might* have said yes.

She certainly would have taken a moment to relish the thought of saying yes and all the wonders that would come with it. A kiss.

Zoe pressed her eyes tighter. No sense dreaming about what she could have had with Isaak. This would be her last Montana sunrise. She would enjoy it to the fullest. She would enjoy it without regrets. Just as she had enjoyed watching last night's sunset after finishing letters of farewell to the people she was too cowardly to visit in person. Her own heartbreak hurt enough. She refused to live with the images of their tearstained faces as they looked upon her own tearstained face.

"I cry too much," she muttered before focusing on what she needed to do today before she and Nico could start a new life somewhere exciting.

Sunrise.

Breakfast with Nico.

Load belongings into Deal's wagon.

Bank.

See Jakob, despite the Deals' recommendation she avoid him. Ending the contract personally was the right thing to do.

Board train and—

Oh! Sensing the moment she had been waiting for, she opened her eyes. The blue-black of night eased up, a gentle escape from the approaching sun minutes from breaking dawn.

"Shhh."

After a second, louder "shhh," Zoe stood and looked over the balcony at the single-story home directly east of the boardinghouse. She leaned forward, squinted, blinked. Only one person in Helena wore a flattened beige derby and a brown corduroy coat. Nico! But why was he sitting on the top ridge of the slanted roof? Who was that sitting to the right of—

The man in the black suit and bowler looked over his shoulder up at the boardinghouse balcony.

Isaak?

Her chest tightened. What was he doing with Nico?

With the back of his hand, Isaak tapped Nico's shoulder and said something, all the while never looking away from Zoe.

Nico turned around. He smiled and waved . . . and then elbowed Isaak. He waved, too.

Zoe lifted her hand, but the quilt hindered her from waving back, so she smiled. At least she thought it was a smile. It may have been more of a toothy, what-are-you-doing-on-a-roof-at-this-time-of-the-morning gaping mouth.

She waited for an explanation, but both Isaak and Nico turned back to watch the sunrise.

Why?

She specifically remembered Jakob saying Isaak needed a good hour in silence and two cups of sweetened tea along with a hefty breakfast before he became tolerable. Nico, she knew, could put on a good and false show of morning joviality. Never had Isaak or Nico expressed interest in admiring the sun during any time of day. Not to her anyway.

Zoe worried her bottom lip. How did Isaak know where to find Nico? Unless Nico found him first. But why would Nico want to find Isaak?

Shadows inched west as the sun peeked over the horizon.

As Isaak and Nico sat watching.

As the rising sun cast a golden glow about them.

As Zoe leaned over the balcony and waited and waited for them to do something.

And then . . . both released a heavy breath, their broad shoulders rising and falling. Nico patted Isaak's back. They took turns climbing over the ridge, easing down to the eaves, and descending the ladder that rested against the house's west wall.

Unable to fathom what was going on, Zoe looked to where the sun had warmed the sky and turned the clouds into pink spun sugar. She growled softly. In her concern for why Nico and Isaak were together, she had missed what she had risen early to see. She dashed around the rocker and to the front balcony railing, looked down, and saw no one.

Where had they disappeared to?

Breakfast!

After ridding herself of her quilt cocoon, Zoe hurried into her room, ignoring her black traveling bonnet and the clothes on her bed that she had yet to pack, and scurried down the stairs to the dining room.

The *empty* dining room.

She walked to the parlor. Also empty.

She peeked inside the kitchen and found Mrs. Deal cooking.

Zoe returned to the front of the boardinghouse. Upon looking outside, she saw neither Nico nor Isaak or the ladder against the house next door. What were they about?

It is none of my business. That decided, Zoe returned upstairs to her room to pack.

* * *

One hour and fifty-three minutes later

As Zoe gazed through the dining-room window, analyzing the view, she sipped her morning café au lait. She nibbled on a piece of buttered toast. Sipped coffee. Nibbled toast. Sipped. Nibbled.

Directly across the street, Nico and Isaak sat under the covered porch of the shoemaker's shop, the very place they had been when she sat down in her usual chair at the breakfast table, at her usual time of eight o'clock. Neither wore shoes. Between them was a chess set on a barrel. Not once had either looked in her direction.

Isaak's socked foot tapped the boardwalk under them as he studied the chessboard.

Nico moved a pawn. Or maybe a rook. From this distance the piece was difficult to discern.

Isaak's foot continued to tap.

Zoe let out a long breath. Her neck ached from how long she had been staring out the window. She focused on the breakfast in front of her, rested her teacup on its saucer, picked up a knife, heaped marmalade onto the last half of her toast, removed most of the marmalade from her toast, put down her knife, took a bite of bread, and chewed carefully. What Isaak and Nico were doing was none of her business. She had tasks to do before she could, in good conscience, leave Helena.

She had no care why Isaak and Nico were at the shoemaker's.

Or playing chess.

Or together at all.

Mrs. Deal entered the dining room carrying a coffeepot. She refilled cups at the other table. Someone said something that caused the men to laugh.

Zoe slanted her eyes toward the window.

"My dear, would you care for a refill?"

"No, zank you." She looked up to see Mrs. Deal's gaze flicker momentarily to the window, and then she smiled at Zoe.

"Mr. Deal has the wagon ready to load whenever you're ready."

"I am almost finished."

After a "Good, good," Mrs. Deal returned to the kitchen.

Zoe looked sideways.

Still there.

Isaak replaced one of Nico's pieces with one of his own.

Nico raised both arms. He pointed to the board and yelled something.

Isaak shrugged.

Zoe took another bite of marmalade and bread.

Whatever they were doing at the shoemaker's was not . . . not . . . *not* her business. Once finished with her meal, she would go to the bank and close out her account. And then she would make her peace with Jakob. Hearing her side of things, he would understand Isaak was not to blame for the failure of the courtship contract. She must do what she could to help repair the rift between the brothers and give them a more harmonious future.

You are my future whispered across her heart.

How could Isaak say that? How could a person know such a thing about the other?

She looked out the window.

The shoemaker exited his shop with two pairs of black boots. He handed Isaak one, then gave the other to Nico. They pulled on their boots.

Nico paid the man. Isaak did, too.

The shoemaker said something as he took turns shaking hands with them.

And then the new bosom friends walked away.

Zoe released the breath she held and ate the bite of bread.

They were gone, and she was delighted to be able to finally finish her breakfast in peace. After the Deals loaded her luggage in the wagon to deliver to the depot, she would go to the bank and then . . .

Zoe frowned at the teller, a balding gentleman with rosy cheeks and a boyish voice that belied the streaks of gray at his temple. "You are holding my money hostage. Why?"

The man looked left, then right, then leaned closer to the ornate brass separating them. He spoke quietly. "Until we've ascertained that none of the greenbacks in the vault are counterfeit, I can only give you the gross of your account in gold coins or a bank check."

Coins? Her luggage was already loaded into the wagons. There would be no way to stow away her gold without being seen. To carry a bag of gold across town would invite ruffians.

Zoe rested her gloved hand on the marble counter. "Other banks will honor ze check?"

He nodded.

She sighed. "Zen a check, please."

"Excellent choice. Have a seat while I have one filled out and signed." He took a step away from the counter and then looked back. "This may take longer than usual. If you don't want to wait, I can hold the check here for you."

"Zat would be helpful. Zank you." Zoe looped her reticule around her wrist. By the time she reached the double front doors, the right one opened.

Nico smiled at her. "Hey, Zoe."

She looked past him to Isaak. His eyes met hers, and she swore she could see right into his soul, feel his breathless longing. Or maybe it was hers. *Marry me.* Or maybe it was *Marry me!* Her heart beat too frantically for her to hear his thoughts—to hear *her* thoughts, not his. Indeed, she was no mind reader, despite her *grand-mère*'s Romany blood.

Zoe felt her cheeks grow warm. "I am sorry," she said to cover the awkward silence. "Did you say something?"

Nico backhanded Isaak's arm.

Isaak removed his hat and said, "Good day, Miss de Fleur."

They backed up and motioned for her to walk past.

She did. Before she could formulate a response, they walked inside the bank; the brass-covered door closed with a rattle.

Zoe looked at the door, then down the boardwalk to where Mr. Deal was standing beside the wagon, waiting to take her to The Import Company. He waved.

"Excuse me." A gentleman brushed past Zoe to enter the bank.

The door opened and closed before Zoe could catch a glimpse of Isaak or Nico.

With a growl under her breath, she strode to the wagon. Whatever they were about was none of her business.

"Zis truly is a beautiful shop," Zoe remarked, standing at The Import Company's entrance as she studied the grandeur of Jakob's creation. "Your parents must be proud."

Jakob nodded, his smile taking its own sweet time to grow. He gave her a mischievous sideways look. "My parents enjoyed yesterday's lunch. They were looking forward to tonight's dinner."

"Mrs. Wiley and Mrs. Forsythe can salvage dinner from what I had already prepared."

"Aunt Lily does work wonders with food." He gripped the lapels of his suit coat. "I know I don't deserve an answer, but I just have to know." He swallowed, his Adam's apple shifting. "Was it only Isaak for you from the moment you two met?"

"He was hard to love at first."

"It's not easy living in his shadow."

Zoe reached up and touched his cheek. "Jakob Gunderson, you are a *good* man. Just as good and kind and honorable as your brother is. Zere is a girl for you."

His eyes grew watery.

Zoe pretended interest in her reticule to give him a moment to collect himself . . . and for her to blink away her tears as well. Her heart hurt. Like someone had hacked a cleaver into her breastbone.

He cleared his throat. "Hey, um, how about a tour of the rest of the building?"

"Zat would be lovely, but Mr. Deal is waiting outside. I promised him I would be but fifteen minutes." She grimaced. "It has been twice"—she glanced at an ebony grandfather clock and corrected herself—"three times zat."

"Most of that time was spent listening to you apologize for ending our contract."

Zoe raised her brows. Jakob had talked and apologized far more than she had.

Jakob broke into that easy laughter of his that never ceased to make Zoe smile. "You're a good sport, Zoe de Fleur. Let me escort you out of here before I decide to charm you into staying in Helena." He opened the door.

Zoe stepped outside and stopped; Jakob bumped into her back.

"Sorry," he muttered, moving around to her side. "Is something wrong?"

She blinked. "I believe I saw—" She leaned to the right to get a better look at Dr. Abernathy's front window across the street, but all she saw through the clear glass was the dentist writing something in a book that rested on his counter. She could have sworn Nico and Isaak had been standing on either side of the man.

She looked at Jakob. "What is on your brother's schedule today?"

He shrugged. "I haven't seen him since last night. Best guess is he's organizing fire cleanup. Have you forgiven him?"

"Not particularly." Zoe looked back at the dentist.

He waved.

She did, too.

"Miss de Fleur?"

Zoe looked to where Mr. Deal stood next to the wagon. "Yes?"

"We should get moving. The train leaves the station in less than an hour, and I need to take you back to the bank."

Jakob placed a brotherly kiss on the back of her gloved hand. "I hope you find what you're seeking."

Zoe nodded and walked away before she gave in to her tears.

Northern Pacific Railway Depot

Zoe settled onto the two-person upholstered seat, impressed at how the gold baroque fabric matched that of the rolling shade. Mr. Deal had been more than generous to upgrade her ticket from second class to the plush Pullman Palace car. The ornate rococo style, with its gold accents, shell-like curves, and mahogany wood, made her feel like she was in a chateau.

She peeked around the shade and breathed a sigh of relief. Yancey had been too busy in the telegraph office to notice Zoe walking through the depot.

Saying good-bye to Jakob had been difficult enough.

The train whistle blew one final call for boarders.

The blue-uniformed railroad officer who had escorted Zoe to her seat stepped back into the car. His gaze moved past the two older ladies in the seat two rows ahead of Zoe. "Miss de Fleur?" he said, looking at her.

"Yes?"

"Excellent." He turned around, and after saying, "She's in here," he exited the car.

Nico dashed down the aisle, tapestry bag in one hand, rolled up sheet of paper in the other. "Sorry I'm late," he said breathlessly. "I had Mr. Deal write down the address for us to go to in Coeur d'Alene in case his niece is unable to meet us." He looked around and whistled. "Whoa, this is what I call first class."

"Sit down."

His gaze shifted from her seat to the one facing hers. "Does it matter where I sit?"

"I do not know," Zoe said with a sigh. "Never have I been in a car like zis. Ze railroad officer said zere is also a dining car and"—she pointed to the upper berth—"zat folds down and zese two facing seats fold over to make a bunk for sleeping."

"Humph. Seems like a lot of work just to have somewhere to lay down." Nico tossed his tapestry bag onto the seat across from her. He plopped down next to his bag. "Ready to start a new adventure?"

Zoe nodded. "Why were you late?"

"I had things to take care of."

"Oh?"

"Things," he answered, tapping the rolled paper on his thigh. "Important ones."

Zoe eased the shade back enough for her to see the boarding platform. Mr. Deal stood there. The remaining people milling about were unfamiliar to her.

The train jerked forward, momentum increasing with each turn of the wheels.

"You looking for someone?" Nico asked.

Zoe released the shade and the smidgeon of hope that Isaak would chase her down and beg her not to leave him because she was his *forever*. Life would be wonderful because they were together. Or so he would say, and so she would agree. *If* he had chased her down.

"Why do you zink I am looking for someone?"

Nico shrugged. "You seem lonely."

"I am happy you are with me."

"We're a good team, aren't we?"

"Zis is true."

He shrugged off his corduroy coat, then laid it and his flattened derby next to his tapestry bag, which he then opened to remove a leather-bound book. He looked up and saw her watching him. "It's from Miss Lester. She said the author, Jules Verne, is French."

"Papa used to read his stories to me when I was a little girl."

Nico said nothing for a long moment. "I did all of this for you because we're family. We'll always be family. Always. Sometimes a team is better with three. Or four. Or twelve." And then he opened his book and started reading aloud. "'Chapter one in which Phileas Fogg and Passepartout accept each other, the one as master, the other as man. Mr. Phileas Fogg lived, in 1872, at . . .'"

Zoe closed her eyes and listened.

When she lived at the Crane house, she had dreamed of her husband and the cottage where they would live with their children and a bird that talked. He would bring her fresh flowers every day when he returned home from work. She would love, feed, and cherish him. Not once had she imagined Nico in her idyllic dream. But here he was. And here she was. They would be happy.

Because they were together.

Carpe diem.

The tear slipped out of the corner of her eye, and the pad of a thumb gently brushed it away.

Zoe jolted and looked up.

Isaak stood there, gripping a traveling bag and a small paper sack. He reached inside his suit coat and withdrew a train ticket. "According to this"—his gaze flickered to the space next to her—"that's my seat."

His seat?

"Hey, Isaak."

"Hey, Nico."

"What took you so long? I've been stalling as best I could, but my sister is impatient."

Zoe stared speechless at them both.

"Sorry." Isaak set his traveling bag next to Nico's, then settled next to Zoe. "They put me in the dining car. There were pastries."

"Whoa. Could you eat as many as you wanted?"

"As many as they let me."

"That's less impressive." His eyes narrowed. "Did you really let free pastries delay you when the love of your life is waiting for you to sweep her off her feet?"

"I figured a little delay would make her miss me more. Did it work?"

Nico laughed. "Sure did."

Isaak tossed the paper sack onto Nico's lap. "Those are for you."

Nico gave Isaak the rolled-up paper. "Don't know if this'll help Sheriff McCall, but it's something."

"Sure is." Isaak tucked the paper inside his suit coat.

Zoe finally found her voice. "What is going on?"

Nico sent Isaak a meaningful look. "We'll tell you in a minute, but first, me and Isaak want to know if our plan worked."

"Worked?" Zoe repeated, still at a loss.

Isaak cradled her left hand in his right one. "Your brother and I have spent the day fishing."

"That was my idea," Nico put in.

"Fishing?" Zoe looked back and forth between the pair. Their smiles gave it away. "I am ze fish you were baiting."

They both nodded.

"But what makes you zink I wish to be caught?" she said with as much false indignation as she could muster.

Isaak looked at Nico.

"Excuse me, Zoe." He closed his book, grabbed his sack of pastries, and stood. "This is my cue to give you two some time alone." He eased past Isaak and moved up to the front of the car, sitting on the bench to the right of the car's only other passengers.

Isaak shifted to face Zoe. "After the way I mucked things up yesterday, I figured you'd never wanted to see me again. I used all my fine words in my proposal. I was out of ideas, so I found your brother."

She spoke softly. "You know Nico is not my real brother."

"He's as much your brother as Jakob is mine."

"You truly believe zat?"

"With all my heart." His gaze flickered to Nico. "He loves you."

"I know," Zoe whispered.

"Not as much as I love you." Isaak eased the glove off her hand, then placed a kiss on her upturned wrist.

Zoe's pulse quickened.

He threaded his fingers through hers. "Today has been torturous. Being that close to you yet unable to hold you in my arms. You'll never know how many times I imagined—" He cleared his throat. "I want to marry you, Zoe de Fleur. I started falling for you when you made me close my eyes and listen to Ma's finches."

"But for Jakob . . ."

Isaak sighed. "But for him . . ."

Zoe rested her head against the side of his arm. "Your brother and I agreed to end our courtship contract. I zink we are still friends."

"He and I are still friends, too. Did I mention my train ticket goes all the way to Portland?"

She shifted to face him. "Why are you going all ze way to Portland?"

"I have tickets for you and Nico to go to Portland, too." Isaak looked hesitant, tense, worried.

"Are you moving to Portland?"

"I will if you will," he said firmly. "I'm running away with you and Nico, if you'll let me."

"I have no wish to live in Portland." Zoe moistened her bottom lip. "Or Coeur d'Alene, no matter how lovely ze Deals say it is."

"There are things lovelier than Coeur d'Alene. Trust me." His gaze fell to her lips. He slowly met her gaze. "Where do you want to live?"

Zoe dipped her chin, hoping the brim of her bonnet would shield her teary eyes. Her pulse raced as the words formed in her mind, growing from her heart, spreading out from her soul. She could no longer hide from him.

She breathed deep and looked him straight in the eye. "I want to live wherever you are. I love you more zan you love sweets."

"Then how about we get married?"

"Married?"

"We can elope in Portland. Does that interest you?"

Her heart fluttered with thousands of yeses.

"What about Nico?" she whispered.

"He can tag along. We need a reliable witness."

"He *is* family."

"That he is. I love you," Isaak whispered, and then winked, "*almost* as much as I love sweets."

Zoe gasped. "You are most—"

"Wonderful?"

A host of adjectives rose to mind as a response, but Zoe chose to be harmonious and say, "Yes, you are most wonderful, indeed."

Epilogue

Saturday, May 5

He was admiring a set of silver candlesticks imported from Spain when Madame Lestraude strolled up, a primal smile on her rouged lips. She held out a folded piece of parchment sealed with burgundy wax imprinted with a solitary rose.

Furious at her bold approach, he took the letter. "I hope you're enjoying the grand opening."

"Immensely. Everyone is abuzz with the grandeur of the store and Mr. Gunderson's withdrawal from the mayoral race. I can only imagine your feelings on the matter."

"It came as something of a shock."

"Ah." The puff of air conveyed nothing. "As for me, the announcement was . . . enlightening. A pleasure to see you as always. I trust we will meet again very soon." With that, she bid him adieu and slipped back into the crush of people eager to touch, smell, and own pieces of the world outside Helena.

He snapped the wax seal while checking to see how many people noticed their exchange. No one was looking at him with shock or censure—why would they, when Big Jane,

Chicago Joe, and several other wealthy brothel owners were shopping and exchanging pleasantries in their midst?—but his chest remained tight. He glanced down and read:

C'est guerre!
ML

Why declare war? He'd done nothing to her family. Emilia McCall had escaped the fire with no damage save a bit of ash falling on her hair and shoulders.

He crumpled the parchment between his fingers. The madam and her enigmatic message would have to wait. He weaved his way closer to the door. His lungs needed air untainted by scented candles, quarreling perfumes, and hair pomade. As he stepped into the sunshine, he saw Madame Lestraude step into her carriage. Her driver closed the door and mounted the box.

Madame turned, her eyes on him as deliberate as her slow pull drawing down the shade.

Did she think he would come to her now? No, their next meeting would be the time and place of his choosing.

Only . . .

He craned his neck to look over his left shoulder and then his right. No one would think twice if he crossed the street to join husbands biding their time with cigars and conversation while their wives spent money on things they didn't need but could afford. From there, he could stroll to the shuttered bank as if he was returning to his office and duck into the carriage when no one was looking.

Fisk lifted a hand in greeting.

He waved back and stepped into the street, careful to avoid the dense piles of manure testifying to the success of today's grand opening.

He took his time chatting with Fisk, Cannon, Watson, and several other important men of Helena, relishing the way it kept Madame Lestraude waiting. Her carriage remained motionless except for an occasional horse's stamp of impatience. Anyone who had noticed her ascent was gone, and everyone else would think it empty.

He excused himself from the men after sparking a debate sure to consume their full attention. As he drew even with the door of her carriage, he stopped, pulled out his pocket watch, and pretended to check the time while skittering his gaze left and right to see if anyone was watching him.

No one.

He opened the carriage door and climbed inside. "I am not your lackey to command."

"Yet here you are." Madame Lestraude knocked on the wall of her carriage and it sprang to life. "Don't worry, we shall set you down somewhere close enough for you to walk back to the grand opening, but far enough away that no one will observe your descent."

"What if someone had seen me?"

"Then you should have taken even more care in your circuitous route." She inclined her head toward the curtains. "I find it quite useful to observe without being observed myself."

He picked up the cane he'd tossed inside before his hasty ascent to cover his embarrassment. "What is so important it couldn't wait until a more opportune time?"

"Ah." The syllable scraped across his nerve endings. "I shall enlighten you, because Helena has grown too large for one man to know all that goes on within it."

His pride pricked, as she'd meant it to. Once upon a time he had known everyone and everything that happened inside of Helena. Had campaigned on it, as a matter of fact. The city was too large now. He was no longer at the center of every social circle as he once had been.

"Alfred and Martha Deal, in addition to running a

second-rate boardinghouse, sell women who will not be missed into prostitution."

He jerked backward against the padded seat. *"How long have you known this?"*

"It doesn't matter. As long as people stay out of my business, I return the courtesy." She paused for a moment. *"Sometimes the Deals ride the trains, offering their card and a shoulder to cry on to naïve young women who, when their rosy dreams are shattered, want to disappear to wallow in self-pity. They approached Emilia on her way into town last year."*

"I assume they did the same for Miss de Fleur."

She nodded.

"Excuse my cynicism, but why do you care?"

"Were it just Miss de Fleur, I wouldn't. She made her bed, so she can lie in it."

Her callous answer didn't surprise him, but he was hard-pressed not to reach across the seat and throw her from her own carriage. *"So why the dramatic declaration of war?"*

"Because she dragged my Nico along with her."

"Your Nico?"

"He's a good boy. I'm thinking of adopting him when he gets back from his grand adventure."

He choked on a laugh. *"Replacing Mac?"*

"Nico loves me as the mother he's never known. Mac keeps telling me love can redeem any soul. Who knows, maybe it will." She pierced him with her brown eyes. *"Nico is family."*

"Fine, but I've not hurt the boy."

"Oh, but this was not our agreement. You were not to even threaten *my family."*

He gritted his teeth. He didn't see the connection and he didn't want to ask.

"Your fire at The Resale Company resulted in a breach of our . . . understanding. *This was not your intention, but the*

consequences will be meted out just the same." She cocked her head. "I'm curious. Did you set it yourself or hire an underling?"

He'd used one of his best employees, a man who had followed instructions to the letter before slipping out of town unnoticed. Unlike Edgar Dunfree who, against orders, used his own name to purchase the printing press, a sale recorded and preserved in a cloth-bound ledger now burned to cinders. If anyone else made the connection between a man who used to boast of their once-close working relationship, the leveling foot found in Collins's barn, and a printing press, there was no longer any proof.

"Are you afraid your Nico will be accused of arson given his . . . other activity?"

Her patronizing smile mocked his mimicry of her dramatic pauses. *"You refer to his vandalism at The Import Company, of course. I have chastised him and acknowledge that he played some part in the threat against him for which I blame you."*

"Speak plainly, woman. I tire of your games."

"Very well. In plain terms, you pitted Isaak and Jakob Gunderson against each other by using Miss de Fleur to fuel their long-standing rivalry as a means to force Isaak from the mayoral race. As a result, in the literal heat of the moment, they humiliated the girl with dual proposals. She turned to the Deals for a solution. Nico, although he loves me, is more attached to his sister. He planned to flee with her and would have met with her same fate. My disgust for children conscripted into prostitution is well-known to you. It is for this that I will destroy you."

"How could I have foreseen such a convoluted turn of events?"

"Ignorantia juris non excusat. I laid down the law, and now I will not excuse you."

He tapped the gold-plated top of his cane. *"You've gone*

to great lengths to keep your little rescuing ring hidden from the other brothel owners, and with good cause. How do you propose to destroy me when I have the means to destroy you, as I did Hendry, by stirring up hatred against you?"

Her countenance held no fear. "When one side has all the weapons, it is a slaughter. That is why, my dear Jonas, this is war."

DON'T MISS

New beginnings await in Helena, the Montana Territory's most exciting city—where faithful hearts stay strong and true as they pursue their passionate dreams.

TO CATCH A BRIDE
A Montana Brides eNovella

Available wherever eBooks are sold.

Enjoy the following excerpt from *To Catch a Bride*. . . .

Chapter One

Montana Territory
July 13, 1865

Marilyn Svenson sat still, clutching her reticule and maintaining a placid expression despite the indignation growing inside. She had no wish to speak ill of the dead, but why had the late President Lincoln appointed Judge Williston over the newly created Montana Territory when the man clearly wished to be anywhere but here?

In a calm, measured tone, she said, "Your Honor, I own a copy of the Homestead Act of 1862, if you would like to verify the law." Although it was back on her ranch and an hour's drive each way to retrieve. "It clearly states that a widow can file for head-of-household status."

"And I told you to remarry or go home." The heavily bearded man repeated his earlier advice without giving her the courtesy of looking her in the eye. Judge Williston had latched onto the first option she'd presented when he'd asked why she needed a meeting with him—that of remaining in Montana Territory and proving up her claim alone—as though it was her only option.

Outside of remarrying or going back to Minnesota, she had two other options: to purchase the homestead outright or to hire men tired of searching for gold to do the hard work required to prove up her claim. Her late husband, Gunder, had cultivated only two of the requisite five acres, and although she could harness the oxen well enough, breaking thick sod as well as digging out and hauling away large rocks on an additional three acres was beyond her physical strength.

She had plenty of gold stashed in cleverly disguised canning jars to pay for both land and labor, but she was vulnerable enough these days as a single woman in an area where males outnumbered females three hundred to one. Letting anyone know she had that much gold invited ruin.

Which was why she hadn't mentioned it to Judge Williston. She didn't know him or his reputation well enough to take such a risk. More to the point, it wasn't the judge's place to tell her what she could and couldn't do. The law said a widow had a right to take over a claim. What she did with it after that was *her* business, not a complete stranger's.

Marilyn opened her overstuffed reticule and retrieved her copy of the homestead claim Gunder had filed with Idaho territorial authorities two years ago. "Sir, all my records are in order." She unfolded the documents and held them out toward Judge Williston. "As you can see, this is an addendum noting the change from Idaho to Montana territorial jurisdiction last year."

The judge looked up, but his gaze focused on the papers in her hand. "Mrs. Svenson, all the record-keeping and legal understanding of the Homestead Act will not help you chop wood, plow acreage, or complete any of the other chores God built a man to accomplish. If you insist on remaining in Montana, your only option is to remarry"—his gaze flicked to her green-checkered calico dress as though it proved she was past mourning—"at which time your claim will be transferred to your new husband. As I said, either remarry or go home."

Marilyn breathed deep. She wasn't about to justify herself, her clothing choices, or her behavior to him, but she'd specifically worn this dress because of the sheer fabric. Etiquette required mourning colors because Gunder had passed only two months ago, but with the temperature being what it was, black wool was too impractical. Besides, this was the first dress Gunder had bought her after their wedding six years ago. Regardless of the temperature—and despite how snug it was—wearing it honored him more than black, gray, or lavender could.

Facts that were irrelevant to the matter at hand.

If Judge Williston wanted her to go home, he should help her claim head-of-household status to sell the land before she returned to Minnesota, a fact so obvious she questioned the judge's competence. Furthermore, returning home—and remarriage, for that matter—was an *option*, not a forgone conclusion.

She folded the papers back into fourths and stuffed them into her reticule. "I have no intention of losing my homestead because I have not been granted head-of-household status. It is my right to claim that status. I insist you tell me how to accomplish the change."

Judge Williston's expression hardened. "I shall do no such thing, madam. I'll not aid a woman on a fool's errand no more than I would have a hand in her death. Both apply in this situation."

Why did men always underestimate her intelligence and resolve? She knew full well that her best option was returning to Minnesota. In the two months since Gunder's death, she'd considered every possibility, but she wasn't going home without some compensation for all the hard work she and Gunder had put into their claim.

Marilyn stood. Out of courtesy, the judge should have arisen as well, but he didn't because they both knew she was a good three inches taller than he. "If you will not help me, sir, I shall find someone else who will."

His laughter filled the room. "Good luck, madam, because *I* am the only person who can grant you head-of-household rights."

She refused to believe that. If she chose to stay or sell, she'd figure out a way to get what she needed. "Good day, sir."

Marilyn strolled out of the office, into the bright summer sun, and—

She stopped in midstride. What looked like dozens of small blobs floated across her field of vision.

"You all right, Mrs. Svenson?"

Marilyn looked left. Young Simpson stepped away from the hitching post in front of the judge's temporary office. "I don't know. I see—" Before she could say *spots*, a wave of dizziness struck. Marilyn closed her eyes. Instantly she felt the lanky youth gripping her arm and waist.

"Please don't faint," he whispered. "I don't think I can hold you up, and Judge Williston will never let me be a deputy if I let a woman fall."

Marilyn breathed deep until the dizziness stopped and she could open her eyes without fear of spots clouding her vision. Young Simpson had grown a good three inches since she saw him last, but he was still six inches shorter than she and didn't look like he'd weigh more than a hundred pounds soaking wet.

"I walked outside too quickly," she reasoned aloud, "and my eyes couldn't adjust to the brightness."

"I bet you're getting a migraine. Ma has them often." He

released his hold on her yet didn't step back. "You need help walking to your wagon?"

"No, no, but thank you for the offer." Marilyn walked toward her buckboard at a slow pace. She kept her chin down, fanned her face with her reticule, and used her straw hat's wide brim to shield her eyes from the sun. Upon reaching the buckboard, she looked back at the judge's office.

Young Simpson stood where she had left him. She waved to let him know she was fine. He waved back and headed inside the ramshackle building.

She climbed into the seat, jerked on her riding gloves, and took up the reins with her right hand. After releasing the brake with her left hand, she clicked her tongue at Archimedes, and they headed north up the street toward The Repair and Resale Shop to drop off a wagon wheel needing a new rim.

Marilyn gritted her teeth in exasperation.

Judge Williston treated her like she didn't belong in Montana Territory, or like she and Gunder had been foolish to come. He didn't know how much thought they had put into everything, from when to leave Minnesota, what to bring, and where to settle.

They'd specifically chosen land halfway between the two major gold strikes in Bannack and Kootenai to be far enough away from the mining towns to ensure Marilyn's safety from the rough men. They'd made peace with the Chippewa Indians, trading beads, candles, and yards of silk their first summer in exchange for food while they planted their garden and built outbuildings to shelter their chickens and Jersey cow. Once eggs and milk were plentiful, they traded them for dried meat so Gunder could concentrate on building their cabin and they didn't have to deplete their small herd of sheep before breeding them for more stock.

It had worked perfectly. They'd made a significant amount of money by selling meat, eggs, milk, butter, cheese, and a plethora of fruits and vegetables to the men who'd come to dig gold out of the ground.

When gold was struck only a few miles away last year in Last Chance Gulch, Gunder and she were too well established to leave simply because a mining town sprang to life nearby, complete with all the typical squalid conditions. Gunder had simply exchanged his weeklong trips to deliver goods to the mining camps in Bannack or Kootenai for an hour-long trip into Helena.

Marilyn thought back on her conversation with Judge Williston. Had she mentioned that, during their first year in Montana, when Gunder made those weeklong trips, she'd chopped wood and guarded the livestock? Would it have made a difference in the judge's decision about helping her claim head-of-household status?

Probably not.

As the buckboard bounced along the rutted dirt road, several miners emerged from the dingy canvas tents lined up in a neat row. Prostitute Alley, as it had been unofficially named, was busy. She recognized several of the men who were handing palm-sized cloth bags to half-dressed women as those who had proposed marriage to her at Gunder's funeral.

Marilyn looked away, mostly to keep any man from inferring her attention welcomed his pursuit, but partially so none of the prostitutes would see her pity and interpret it to be condemnation. How many of those women had lost the protection of husbands, fathers, or brothers in the War Between the States? How many of them saw no other option but to sell themselves for a canvas tent and a crust of bread? Survival over morality.

"There but for the grace of God . . ." Marilyn kept her eyes on the road ahead. She wanted to help them but had no means, not when she needed every bit of ingenuity and gold to keep from ending up in Prostitute Alley herself. One day, though, perhaps she would be in a position to offer assistance.

She slowed the wagon, drawing it alongside The Repair and Resale Shop. The owner, David Pawlikowski, had been the only man at Gunder's funeral or in the two months since who *hadn't* used every opportunity to tell her how much better off she'd be if she married him to save her homestead.

She climbed out of the buckboard and waited for the spots to reappear. None did. Other than heavy perspiration, obviously from the summer temperature, she didn't feel nauseated or dizzy. No brimming migraine either.

Her earlier near-fainting spell had to have been the drastic change in light.

The moment Marilyn stepped over the shop's threshold, a handful of men surrounded her, shoving one another out of the way as they strove to shake her gloved hand and to remind her of their names, businesses, and wealth . . . or wealth to come any day now.

Clang. Clang. By the third clang, they fell silent.

Marilyn stepped to the side to see Mr. Pawlikowski standing behind his sales counter.

He laid a cowbell and the wooden spoon he'd used to bang it next to the register. "How about we give the lady a moment to shop?" His voice reminded her of the reverend back home in Minnesota. Was it the deep timbre? Or how he commanded respect through gentleness? Perhaps the shop owner had been a chaplain during the war. That could be why he seemed more like a reserved, dutiful man of the cloth.

Marilyn gave the men surrounding her an expectant look. With murmured apologies, they meandered back into the store. She strolled down the center aisle through an assortment of crates, barrels, and mining equipment, amazed that such a hodgepodge of goods were in such neat array. Her home, which was half the size of the store with a fraction of the items, was in a constant state of disorder now that Gunder was gone.

Once she returned home, she'd clean her messes and not let anything distract her.

Definitely this time.

When she reached the back of the store, Mr. Pawlikowski extended his hand across the L-shaped counter to shake hers. "Mrs. Svenson, it's lovely to see you this afternoon. How are you?"

From anyone else, she would know the question was nothing more than a toss-away phrase said in greeting. Not with Mr. Pawlikowski. If he asked how someone was doing, he truly wished to know. It took a special kind of person to care for others with such genuine consideration. Which explained why his shop was always busy, or at least was busy anytime she had visited. A person could find a listening ear from David Pawlikowski.

She admired that about him.

He was also taller than she, which was a rarity, although he was several inches shorter than Gunder had been. Except for Mr. Pawlikowski's height, he was the opposite of Gunder. Where her husband had been thickly muscled, wore his blond hair closely cropped, was clean-shaven, and symmetrically handsome, Mr. Pawlikowski was on the lanky side, wore his dark hair to his shoulders, had a mustache, and was more irregularly featured.

"Mrs. Svenson?" Mr. Pawlikowski said, looking vaguely amused.

Her checks warmed at having been caught studying him. "Yes?"

"How can I help you today?"

"I have a wheel rim that needs repair." She motioned to the front door. "Could you—?"

"Of course." He came out from behind his counter.

"George, I'll be outside with Mrs. Svenson. Make sure no one leaves with something they haven't paid for."

"You got it." The short, bearded man wasn't wearing a shopkeeper's apron. Was he an employee or just someone Mr. Pawlikowski trusted?

As she led Mr. Pawlikowski to the door, Marilyn glanced about the shop. If only she had time to peruse this cornucopia of goods. Her gaze caught on an unfamiliar gadget. She stopped at a bookshelf beside the door and picked up a brass circle with what looked to be tin windmill blades surrounding a scale in the center.

Mr. Pawlikowski stopped next to her.

"What's this?" She held it up for him to see.

"It's an anemometer. It measures wind speed."

"Interesting."

"I used to have a model much older than this one," Mr. Pawlikowski said, while she spun the blades and imagined the wind flow. "That anemometer had four cups attached to horizontal arms. The cups would catch the wind, moving the arms and spinning the center rod. The faster it spun, the faster the wind blew. It was quite fascinating to watch an unseen force at work. It's a quarter, if you're interested."

"Just a quarter?"

"If you insist, I'll accept two quarters for it."

Marilyn chuckled. Although tempted to buy the anemometer, she put it back on the shelf. Gunder would say she didn't need it. She didn't. But if the shop had multiple anemometers, she could place them around Helena and study the wind patterns. Oh! What would be even more fascinating was putting an anemometer inside something like a tornado. But how? There had to be a way. Maybe if—

The touch of a hand against her waist drew her attention.

Mr. Pawlikowski spread his other hand, palm up, in the direction of the door. "Shall we?"

Marilyn nodded. She stepped out onto the covered porch.

Again, a wave of dizziness assaulted her. She grabbed hold of a post supporting the small portico roof and waited for it to pass.

"Mrs. Svenson? Are you all right?"

The concern in Mr. Pawlikowski's voice warmed her more than the July heat. She took several deep breaths to compose herself. She wasn't an emotional woman, some would say unnaturally so. First embarrassment and now a sensation she couldn't identify. Odd.

The sound of multiple footsteps drew her attention back to the store. A host of men crowded behind the open door, faces of many more pressed against the glass-paned windows on either side of it.

Marilyn let go of the post now that her dizziness had passed. "The wheel is in the back of my wagon."

Mr. Pawlikowski followed her to the buckboard and examined the wheel rim. "How did you get this heavy thing in here?"

Was he underestimating her the way Judge Williston had? "I'm not made of sugar."

He chuckled. "That you aren't."

He would be a good husband. Surprised at that sudden realization, Marilyn gave words to the question that had been plaguing her for weeks. "Why have you never asked me to marry you?"

Mr. Pawlikowski blinked twice and coughed into his hand. After another moment, he said, "I'm not a marrying man."

She eyed the strands of gray in his hair and wondered his age. Late thirties? He could be in his early forties, but it was reasonable to presume he was about ten years older than she was. "How is it you never married? Did you wish to join the church?"

He didn't flinch or show a smidgen of awkwardness this time. "I had a wife. She died fifteen months ago." He said nothing more, which seemed unusual. Custom was to praise the lost loved one to avoid the appearance of speaking ill of the dead.

"I'm sorry," she said automatically, while doing mental calculations. He'd arrived in October, around the time the city was named. That was nine months ago. So he'd come West within about six months of his wife's death. "Were there any children?"

"No." The word was flat and unemotional, but something flashed in his eyes she found familiar. Loneliness.

There seemed little point in pretending she saw nothing. "I wish Gunder and I had been fortunate enough to have a child."

"Ah, yes," he remarked with an odd edge to his tone, "to carry on his name."

Marilyn nodded. And yet, if she were being honest, she would have said her reason was less about giving Gunder a namesake than about her desire to have a family. Gunder's death had left her wanting. Just as Mr. Pawlikowski's wife's death had left him wanting. As long as he saw himself as *not a marrying man*, his want would never end.

She gave him a weak smile. "I'm sorry you have no son to pass down your family name."

"I'm sorry you have no husband to give you a child to pass on his name." His smile seemed as sad as she felt. "You should remarry."

"Is that a proposal?" she teased.

His face paled. "Ah . . ."

Marilyn chuckled. "Thank you for that laugh. After my meeting with Judge Williston, I needed it." She touched his arm, her mood growing serious. "Thank you for your friendship with Gunder. He appreciated your patience with his accent."

His dark eyes grew watery. He cleared his throat. "I, um, I'm actually the middle of seven children, three girls and four boys."

She knew his change of topic was intentional, so she complied. "Are they all married?"

"Absolutely, and they've reproduced five or more times over. At least twelve are boys," he said with an overt amount of pride, "so I think it's relatively safe to presume Pawlikowskis will be around for generations yet to come, even without my help."

"Family is important."

As the words left her lips, she made her decision. She would go back to Minnesota. Someday she wanted to remarry, perhaps even be a mother, if God granted it, but there were no *marrying men*—as Mr. Pawlikowski termed them— here in Helena. In the meantime, she could be the spinster aunt who doted on her nieces and nephews. Although *doting* might be too strong a word. She'd be more interested in expanding their minds than their bellies by giving books instead of treats.

"If you decide you want to return to your family," he said, as if he could read her mind, "I'll buy whatever you wish to sell."

"Thank you, but first I need to figure out how a widow files for head-of-household status on a homestead claim, so I can legally sell it."

"Excuse me." A masculine voice came from the right of her. "I have no wish to interlope on a private conversation, but I can help you with that." An unfamiliar man bowed in almost a regal way. "Jonas Forsythe, at your service."

Marilyn turned away from the wagon to get a better view of the man who she guessed to be near her age. Tall, blond, studious in appearance, and wearing a three-piece suit with a gold fob dangling from his black brocade vest. He reminded her of Judge Williston—at least in attire.

Mr. Pawlikowski came closer to stand next to her. "Welcome to Helena. I'm David Pawlikowski, owner of The Repair and Resale Shop." He shook Mr. Forsythe's hand, then said, "May I have the honor of introducing you to Mrs. Gunder Svenson?"

Mr. Forsythe bowed to her again. "A pleasure, ma'am, although please allow me to express my sympathy for your loss. Your husband?"

Marilyn smiled to acknowledge his polite condolence. "Yes. Are you a legal expert?"

"I'm a recent graduate of Harvard Law School."

An impressive achievement. Which was why she couldn't help but ask, "Then why come to Montana Territory?"

The corners of Mr. Forsythe's mouth lifted a fraction of an inch. "My friends and family asked a very similar question when I shared my plans to come West. In short, I see the territories as the next great land of opportunity."

"As a miner?" asked Mr. Pawlikowski.

"A bit," Mr. Forsythe admitted. "I reckon I ought to get in on the gold rush while nuggets are so plentiful they can be picked out of creek beds."

Marilyn sighed. Someone needed to squash his Eastern naïveté.

The first snicker came from Mr. Pawlikowski.

Marilyn looked at him and then Mr. Forsythe, whose smile had grown broad. She glanced between the two of them twice more before she understood their humor. "Oh, goodness, for a moment there I believed you to be serious."

Both men laughed. There was a natural ease between the two men that she liked . . . and envied. How could two people instantly connect as friends?

Mr. Forsythe's broad grin melted into a polite smile. "Truth be told, Mrs. Svenson, my aspirations are more political in nature. I'd like to be a state senator or a state supreme court judge someday. The states back east are swollen with politicians. Out here, I can be one of the few men who are here for political reasons."

If he was as knowledgeable as he was friendly, she foresaw great things in his future.

Marilyn shifted her stance. "Seeing you're from back east, have you any experience helping a woman claim head-of-household status for a homestead? Being a male, you'll certainly have better luck securing help from Judge Williston. I advise you not to mention your business until after you're sitting in his office."

"My, my, Mrs. Svenson, you are direct." His words were punctuated with a smile.

"That she is," Mr. Pawlikowski confirmed, his voice just as pleasant.

Marilyn looked back and forth between the men, trying to decide if the two of them were sharing another joke. The expressions on their faces—and her knowledge of Mr. Pawlikowski—denied it. He wasn't a man to be demeaning to anyone.

She turned her attention to Mr. Forsythe "I know my directness doesn't endear me to men, but I wish it wouldn't stop them from helping me."

Silence greeted her pronouncement.

Mr. Pawlikowski cleared his throat.

It took an instant for Marilyn to understand the gentle rebuke in Mr. Pawlikowski's throat-clearing. She turned to the lawyer. "My apologies for telling you how to do your job." Although she *was* right.

Mr. Forsythe gripped both of his lapels. "Mrs. Svenson, how about we strike a bargain? If I procure your change of status within the next four months, you'll owe me three dollars. If not, I'll continue to help you until your status is changed, but you'll owe me nothing." He looked at Mr. Pawlikowski. "Would you act as witness?"

"I'd be honored."

Marilyn tapped the side of the wagon. Four months? If it

took him that long, she wouldn't be able to sell until the beginning of November. Not a good time to begin travel to Minnesota.

She turned to Mr. Pawlikowski. "Do you know when another wagon train trail master will come through Helena on his way back east?"

He thought for a moment. "Shannon could be here in August, depending on whether he decided to marry or not. Hawks will definitely be here in early September."

"Mr. Forsythe," Marilyn said, "would you be open to a negotiation of 'within the next two months' instead of four? I need to leave Montana while the weather is still good."

"Where are you heading?"

"I'm returning to family in Minnesota."

He paused, studying her face. "I'm agreeable."

Mr. Pawlikowski touched her arm. "I'm willing to give you a fair price on your land."

A lawyer to help her with her head-of-household status and a shop owner to free her of the burden of her land. In two—no more than three—months, she was on her way home.

Now it was her turn to smile at the town's newest arrival. "Mr. Forsythe, I believe you've retained your first client."

Chapter Two

While Mrs. Svenson and Mr. Forsythe chatted about legal matters, David stepped to the back of the buckboard to attend to the damaged wagon wheel. He had nothing to contribute to the conversation. Truth be told, he needed something to occupy his hands. And to keep from staring at Mrs. Svenson. One little question from her—a woman who was the exact opposite of his late wife in every way—dredged up every painful remembrance of Klaudia.

Why have you never asked me to marry you?

Mrs. Svenson's questions thereafter proved she had no specific interest in his answer. She was simply curious—a trait that defined her as much as Klaudia's madness had defined her by the end of her life.

A madness for which he was responsible . . . at least in part.

David hoisted the wagon wheel out of the buckboard and set it on the ground. If only mending a broken soul was as easy as mending a bent rim.

Bits and pieces of Klaudia's accusations flung at him over their ten years of marriage escaped the box he usually kept sealed inside his mind.

You are a terrible husband.

Why won't you give me what I want?
How can you call yourself a man?
I hate you!
This is all your fault.

And on the day she finally got what she wanted—a child in her belly—she'd leveled her most devastating blow: *It's not yours. I had to find a* real *man to do the job.*

David winced at the memory. Klaudia had filed for divorce on the grounds that he couldn't consummate their marriage. It was a false accusation, but that made no difference to her or the newspapers that reported it as fact. He fought the lie, fought to keep his marriage together, fought the humiliation until Klaudia ran off with her lover. Even then David stayed in Ohio, hoping she'd come to her senses and return home.

She did come back—four months later, with hollow cheeks, hollow eyes, and a hollow womb—but she never came to her senses. To the bitter end, she blamed him for every misfortune, whether real or imagined, her claims growing wilder and her physical outbursts more frequent, until David started the process of putting her in an asylum. He was only saved from such a drastic step when she took her own life.

At which point a rumor swirled through his tight-knit community that he had killed her. How could people who had known him all his life believe such a thing? The answer still eluded him.

Once the local police cleared him of all wrongdoing in his wife's death, David had loaded a Conestoga wagon with anything and everything he thought he could sell or rent and fled to Montana Territory to create a new life. Mostly to escape memories of his wife. But he couldn't escape one fact: Though he could perform his husbandly duty in the marriage bed, he hadn't been able to give his wife a child, and it had destroyed her.

He'd not make another woman so miserable.

The conversation between Mrs. Svenson and Forsythe drew to a close. The lawyer handed her his calling card. "I'll let you know the moment I have an office secured."

She slipped the card into her little purse. "Thank you. I'll look for you the next time I'm in town, which should be in a week or two."

Forsythe held out a second calling card to David. "Sir, I hope we meet again soon."

David took the card and tucked it into the front pocket of his white apron. "We don't have a church building yet, but if you're so inclined, a number of folks meet in my store at eleven o'clock every Sunday morning."

"I'd be delighted." Mr. Forsythe dipped his head in a polite bow and turned to make his way along the street, presumably to introduce himself to more business owners in Helena.

Mrs. Svenson stared after the lawyer's retreating back. "Mr. Forsythe seems like a nice man."

He was exactly the sort of man she should marry. David winced at the internal prick that thought gave him. "I agree. He—" She turned and let out a little gasp, cutting off his words. The moment she began tilting to her left, David reached out and grabbed her waist to steady her. "Is everything all right?"

She didn't nod. Or move. Or even breathe for what seemed like a full minute.

His heart banged against his ribs in a rapid tattoo, like that of a signal calling soldiers to quarters. It wasn't calling him to her. It couldn't.

Yet something tightened within him.

Desire, to be sure. Desire to hold her in his arms forever—a pointless feeling. He had work to do, a business to run, and a bride *not* to catch.

Just when he was about to ask if she needed the doctor,

she turned to face him, seemingly oblivious to his hands still on her waist. "I'm fine, but I need you to do me a favor." She opened her eyes wide. "Look into my eyes and tell me what you see."

"Excuse me?" His voice sounded brusque even to his own ears. David dropped his hold on her and stepped back, needing space.

She closed the distance between them. "Please, just look and describe what you see."

What he saw were eyes the deep blue of Lake Helena on the clearest day of summer, with flecks of brown near the pupils, as though God knew a man would need something to ground him so he didn't drown while looking into them.

"Well," she said in that forthright manner of hers, "what do you see?"

Everything I ever hoped for but never received. David shook his head to clear away the absurd notion. "Blue eyes. What else do you want me to say?"

She ran her tongue over her top lip while staring at him for a long moment. "Would you say my eyes are more deep set than normal?"

He looked back and forth between her left eye and right. "Not that I can tell."

She nodded for some reason. "How about my pupils? Would you say they're smaller than normal?"

He bent his head closer and squinted a bit. "Maybe."

She inhaled with a little gasp. "What about drooping eyelids or swollen veins in the corners of my eyes?"

Why on earth was she asking such questions? Partially because she was asking and mostly because he felt inclined, he took his time looking into one eye, then the other. She really was the loveliest woman he'd ever laid eyes on. Blond, with a narrow-bridged nose, high cheekbones, and a perfectly oval face, she was so tall her lips were mere inches from his.

Something he shouldn't be noticing.

But he *was* noticing. And now that he'd noticed, he couldn't *stop* noticing . . . and wondering if they were as soft as they looked.

She leaned forward a bit more and blinked repeatedly, a clear sign she was waiting for his answer.

He heaved a breath in and out of his tight lungs. "I don't see any drooping, but there are a few veins at the corners of your eyes."

Her face scrunched in an adorable manner as she seemed to be considering his observations. After a moment, she nodded and stepped back a few paces. "Thank you."

Now that she wasn't so near—and he could think more with his mind than with his body—he noticed the pallor of her skin. "Are you all right? You seem a little pale."

Mrs. Svenson started to laugh. There was a deep-throated quality to it, not the high-pitched cackle he found so annoying in some women. "I'm fine. I won't detain you any longer." She hurried to the front of her buckboard.

He followed and assisted her into the wagon. "Are you sure you're all right?"

"I'm fine," she repeated with a smile—although it didn't reach her eyes.

And yet David still couldn't breathe. She was far lovelier than a widow ought to be in a town of reprobates and heathens. For her safety, she needed to return to Minnesota. Or find a husband here.

She gathered the reins and released the brake. "Thank you for your assistance, Mr. Pawlikowski. I'll check back with you on the wheel next . . . um, soon." She snapped the reins and the buckboard started forward.

David pressed his lips together and rubbed the seam with his fingers, unsure if he should go after her or not. Mrs. Svenson was the most capable woman he'd ever met. And the most honest. If she said there was nothing wrong, she meant it. Besides, she was heading home. Being alone with her was the last temptation he needed.

He picked up the wagon wheel and headed back inside his shop.

Marilyn held Archimedes to the slowest possible pace to lessen the wagon's jostling while heading straight to Dr. Tolbert's medical tent.

Facts didn't lie. Her cycle, while never regular, hadn't visited since Gunder's death. Between the shock of losing him so unexpectedly and the additional work around the homestead, she hadn't noticed being overdue—hadn't even thought about it—until the third wave of dizziness hit outside The Repair and Resale Shop. She'd already been in the bright sunshine, so the cause couldn't be a change in light.

There was a distinct possibility she was pregnant.

However, Mr. Pawlikowski's observations of her eyes were unreliable at best. Nor was there any substantive research in any of the journals she owned to verify Dr. Jacques Guillemeau's theories about how a woman's eyes changed when she was with child. The one other time dizziness had overtaken her was during her first pregnancy, which had lasted a mere seven weeks. Drawing a correlation between then and now was, at best, inconclusive.

If she'd noticed her missed monthly, she would have conducted a wheat and barley experiment before riding into Helena. She'd thought it odd when she first read about how the Egyptians discovered that, by watering bags of seed with a woman's urine, they could determine not only whether the woman was pregnant but also the sex of the child. The wheat and barley experiment had accurately predicted all her pregnancies, although she'd never carried a child long enough to know if she'd now be the proud mother of three boys and two girls. Had she done the experiment and one of the bags sprouted, she never would have risked a miscarriage by riding from her ranch to town for an hour over bumpy roads.

She reined Archimedes to a stop outside the doctor's tent.

An inebriated miner stumbled through the canvas door flap and greeted her with a slurred, "How'r ya doin' there, Mrs. Lady," before wandering off in the direction of Prostitute Alley.

Interesting how some men, when intoxicated, turned jovial, and others turned mean. Was it possible to test for the reason why? People were unique. Even those who shared the same circumstances were different because of their individual desires or interests. She had twin uncles, and despite being raised in the same household, they were as dissimilar as apples and pickles.

Dr. Tolbert stuck his head outside the tent flap. "Well, hello, Mrs. Svenson." He stepped into the sunshine to help her down from the buckboard. "What can I do for you today?"

"I think I may be with child." Her heart lifted saying the words aloud, but hope was a dangerous thing.

The doctor's auburn eyebrows lifted. "Congratulations."

"Thank you," she responded as was expected. The doctor didn't know his felicitations were premature. She couldn't afford to accept them into her heart. "I'm not certain of it yet. I was hoping you could examine me."

"You won't be the first mother I've attended to." He motioned to the tent flap. "Please."

She ducked inside the tent. As she looked around, she waited for the sight of a bloody towel to make her nauseous.

Nothing.

She peeled off her gloves and tossed them on a nearby chair, then set her reticule on top of them. As she untied her bonnet, Dr. Tolbert grabbed the red towel and shoved it inside a large barrel.

He cleared the examination table of some bandaging. "I'll need you to disrobe to your undergarments and lie down. I'll wait outside until you're ready."

Once he left the tent, Marilyn unbuttoned her dress, let it drop to her ankles, then worked to loosen the petticoat. Down to her bloomers, she stepped out of the circle of fabric and crossed to the wooden table, positioning herself as instructed. "I'm ready!"

Dr. Tolbert reappeared. He stepped close to the table and placed his hands on her abdomen. "Yes, quite firm and a little rounded. How far along are you in this pregnancy?"

"I'll need to consult my calendar at home to be certain"— assuming she could find it, of course—"but I believe I know when I conceived. If I'm correct, I should be approximately eleven weeks."

Frowning, he pressed his fingers against her abdomen again. "Your uterus is almost rounded to your belly button. I'd say that puts you at closer to four months."

Four months? That wasn't possible.

"I'm certain I had a monthly cycle in April." She remembered because of how late it had been—thirty-six days—and how, when it arrived, it had dashed her hopes.

Dr. Tolbert stepped away from the table. "Some women have a bit of bleeding at the beginning of a pregnancy, which they mistake for a monthly. Most often it stops on its own, but sometimes it leads to a miscarriage."

Flutters of hope filled her breast. "Are you saying I might have suffered a near miscarriage but didn't?"

He nodded. "You seem to have a specific reason for asking."

"I've experienced five miscarriages, all before my twelfth week."

"I see." In those two simple words she heard sympathy and maybe a bit of understanding.

He couldn't understand. He couldn't truly know what it

felt like to lose five children before meeting them. To wonder if they would have looked like Gunder or her, if they would have his persistence or her curiosity, and if they would grow up to go their own way or stay close to home. Few things made her cry, but if she dwelt too long on how much she and Gunder had wanted children, the tears flowed.

"What forms of treatment have you tried?"

The doctor's question drew Marilyn out of her reflection. She ticked off the various—and useless—remedies on her fingers. "Lying supine with my hips elevated, an abdominal support belt, and bloodletting."

"I see." This time those two words held no sympathy, no understanding. They conveyed that he knew something and dreaded telling her.

"Doctor—" At his look, she bit back her question.

He held out his hand and assisted her to a sitting position. "I'll give you a moment to get dressed and *then* we'll talk."

Marilyn waited for him to exit the tent before easing herself off the table and getting dressed. She replayed what the doctor had said about mistaking a bit of bleeding for a monthly. Other than being later than normal, was her last monthly unusual in any other way? She closed her eyes to concentrate. No. At least not enough for her to recall now.

Tears prickled under her eyelids. A baby! And perhaps one she'd carried beyond the first three months. She opened her eyes and blinked until the sensation eased. "I'm ready," she called loud enough for Dr. Tolbert to hear.

He ducked back inside the tent, a frown just visible underneath his mustache. "Have you made any decisions about what to do with your homestead now that your husband has passed?"

"As soon as head-of-household status is legally changed into my name, I intend on selling it and returning to Minnesota. That's where Gunder and I have family."

Dr. Tolbert nodded. "I see. Although going back to Minnesota now is—"

"Out of the question," Marilyn finished his statement.

"Exactly. Too risky in a normal pregnancy, let alone for someone who has had five miscarriages. In fact"—he rubbed his hands together like he was washing them—"I don't think it's wise for you to ride back to your ranch."

Marilyn nodded. "I know." She knew what he was saying and what he'd left unsaid. She knew the dangers of traveling while pregnant. She knew the dangers of being alone on her ranch, an hour away from civilization. She knew she needed a doctor to deliver her child.

Most of all, she knew she couldn't manage this pregnancy alone.

If she managed not to miscarry again.

Dr. Tolbert picked up a journal with a pencil acting as a place mark and jotted something down. "I'll need to see you once a month and at any point if you sense anything unusual."

"Such as?"

He paused. His brow slowly furrowed. "I have something that may interest you. Stay here for a moment."

As he left the tent to retrieve his mysterious item, Marilyn ran through her options as well as their various merits and difficulties. Her goal had been to change head-of-household status, sell the homestead by October 1, and return to Minnesota with the aid of the first available trail master. Now, leaving Helena was impossible until March of next year at the earliest. She had to think of her baby's safety. And even then, she was limited to when someone could escort her across Dakota Territory.

Unless she had a miscarriage—or the Union Pacific built a railroad from St. Paul to Helena practically overnight—she faced nine months minimum of living in Helena.

Quite ironic, given the circumstances.

What was she supposed to do before she was able to sell the homestead? Without her there, squatters could take over in the two months before Mr. Forsythe could secure her head-of-household status, and once squatters were entrenched, it would be difficult to establish what improvements were hers and which were theirs. The legal hassle and expense to dislodge squatters made some people walk away from their claims without a penny in recompense.

She needed Mr. Forsythe to work a miracle.

Unwittingly, she touched her belly where, it seemed, God was working another miracle. A fragile one she needed to protect lest it end as all the others had.

The option of hiring men to continue working the land, even just for two months, was foolish. It would have been risky even with her on hand to supervise. To leave them to their own devices was akin to throwing away gold.

Another option was remarriage. Then she could keep the homestead she and Gunder had built. She'd wed a stranger before—although her parents had met Gunder a few times before agreeing to the marriage—so she knew it was possible for affection to grow over time. Since Gunder's death, she'd received at least a hundred proposals.

In her estimation, only two men in Helena were husband material. One was her lawyer, the other a self-avowed "not a marrying man."

Neither were homesteaders.

Thus, neither were realistic options if—now that returning to Minnesota was impossible for almost another year—she wanted to keep the land. Both men were possibilities if she wanted to sell the homestead and settle down in Helena. Marilyn pondered that for a moment. Life in town? Not that Helena was much of a town yet. She could build a home here. Raise her child here. The thought didn't seem so unappealing . . . if she found a suitable man to marry.

Until she knew if Mr. Forsythe was truly the nice man he seemed—and he didn't have a wife or fiancée back east—she'd need to sell whatever she could and pray no squatters took over her land. She also needed to find someone trustworthy enough to tend to her livestock and retrieve her gold-filled canning jars. She knew only one person for the last job.

Too bad he wasn't a marrying man.

Connect with Us

Visit us online at
KensingtonBooks.com
to read more from your favorite authors, see books
by series, view reading group guides, and more.

for sneak peeks, chances to win books and prize packs,
and to share your thoughts with other readers.

facebook.com/kensingtonpublishing
twitter.com/kensingtonbooks

Tell us what you think!

To share your thoughts, submit a review,
or sign up for our eNewsletters, please visit:
KensingtonBooks.com/TellUs.